STAR WARS REBELS™

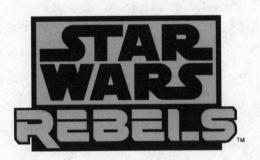

ALSO FROM JOE BOOKS

Star Wars: A New Hope Cinestory Comic
Spark of Rebellion: A Star Wars Rebels Cinestory Comic
Disney Big Hero 6 Cinestory Comic
Marvel Thor: Dueling with Giants
Marvel Guardians of the Galaxy: Castaways
Marvel Captain America: Sub Rosa
Marvel Sif: Even Dragons Have Their Endings
Marvel Warriors Three: Godhood's End
Marvel Guardians of the Galaxy: Space Riot
Marvel Iron Man: Mutually Assured Destruction
Marvel Spider-Man: Enemies Closer
Marvel Avengers: The Serpent Society

STAR WARS REBELS™

PATH OF THE JEDI

CINESTORY COMIC

JOE BOOKS LTD

Published simultaneously in the United States and Canada by
Joe Books Ltd, 489 College Street, Suite 203, Toronto, ON M6G 1A5.

www.joebooks.com

First Joe Books edition: November 2017

Print ISBN: 978-1-77275-504-6
ebook ISBN: 978-1-77275-854-2

Library and Archives Canada Cataloguing in Publication
information is available upon request.

Printed and bound in Canada
1 3 5 7 9 10 8 6 4 2

CONTENTS

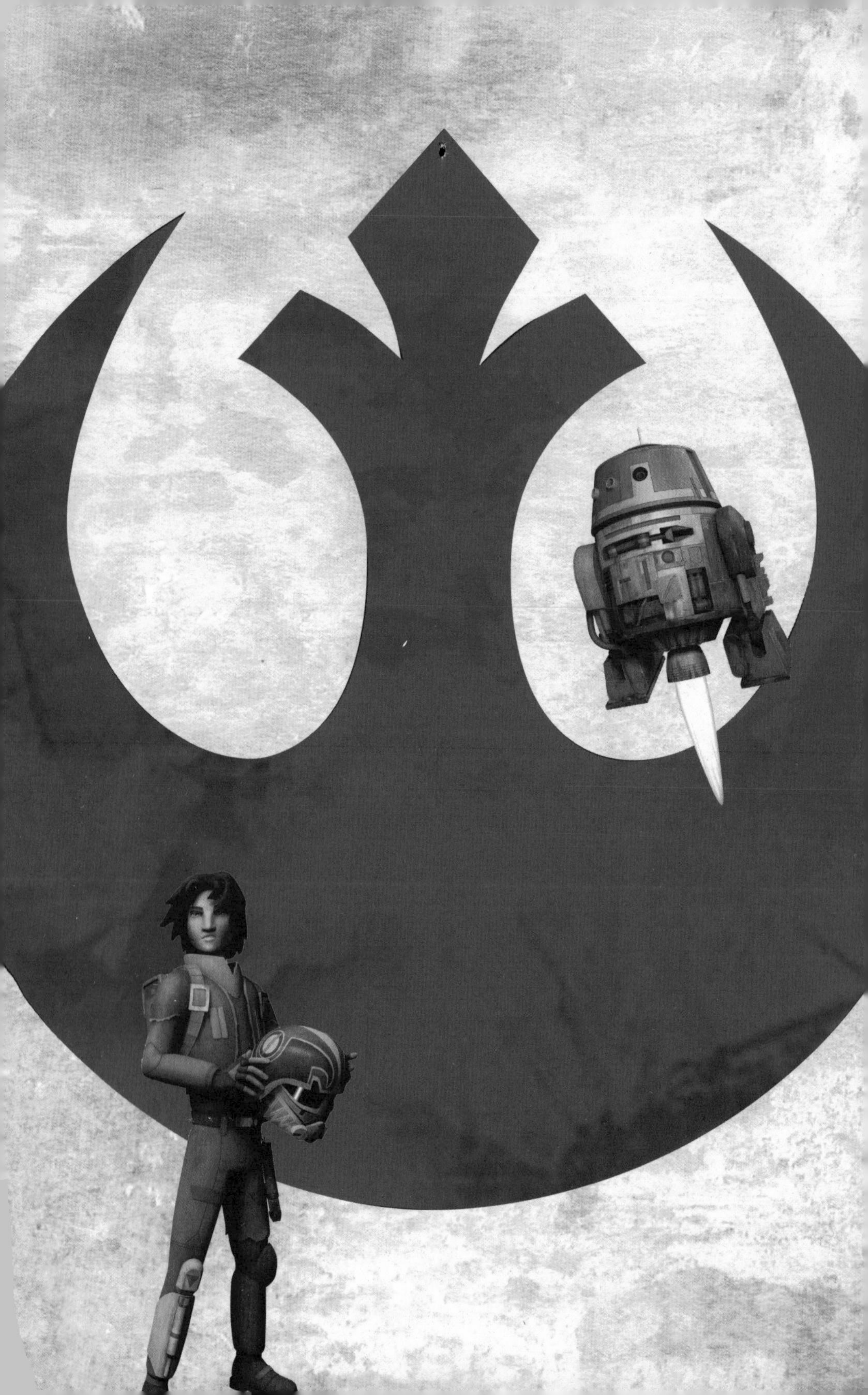

STAR WARS REBELS™

EMPIRE DAY

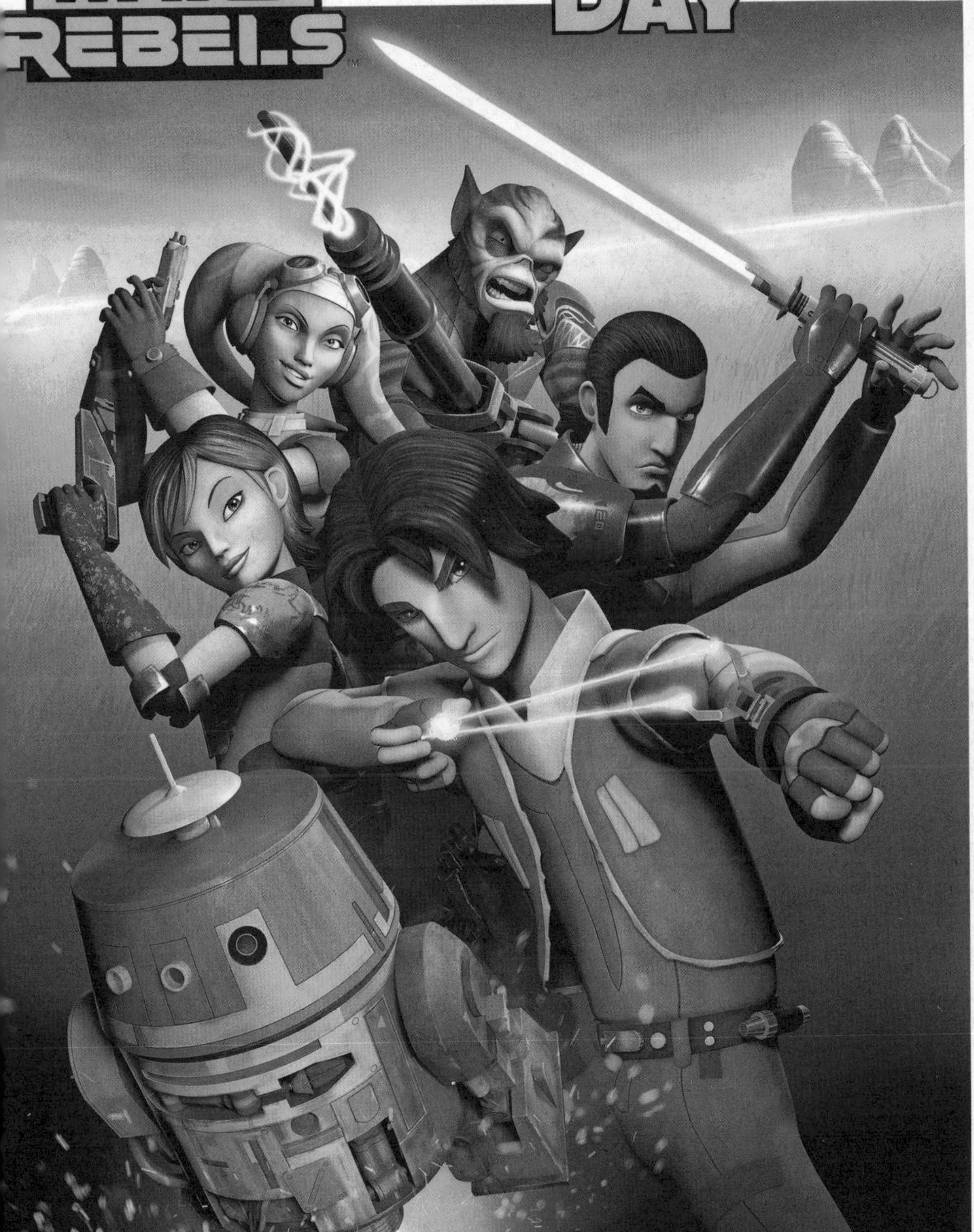

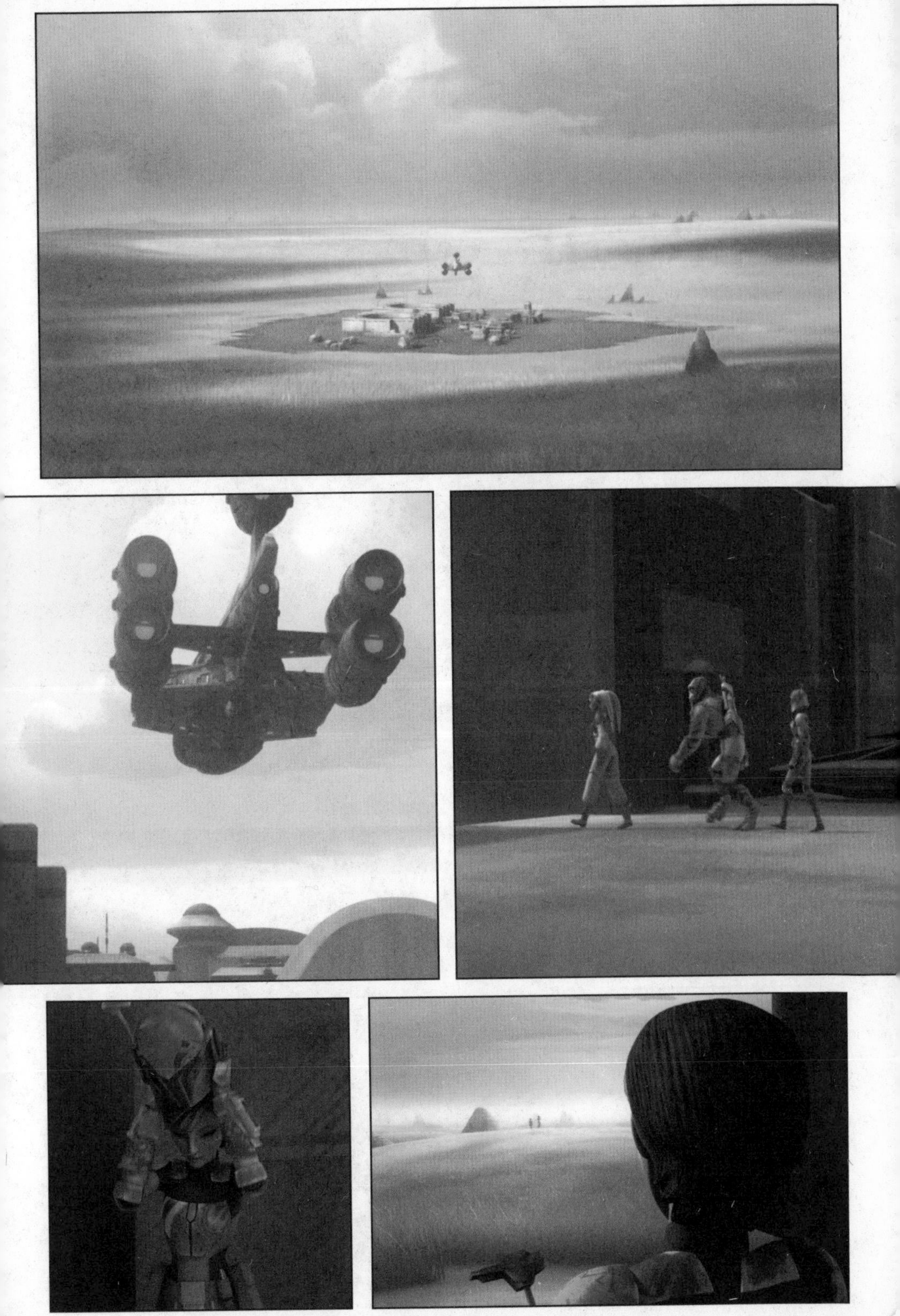

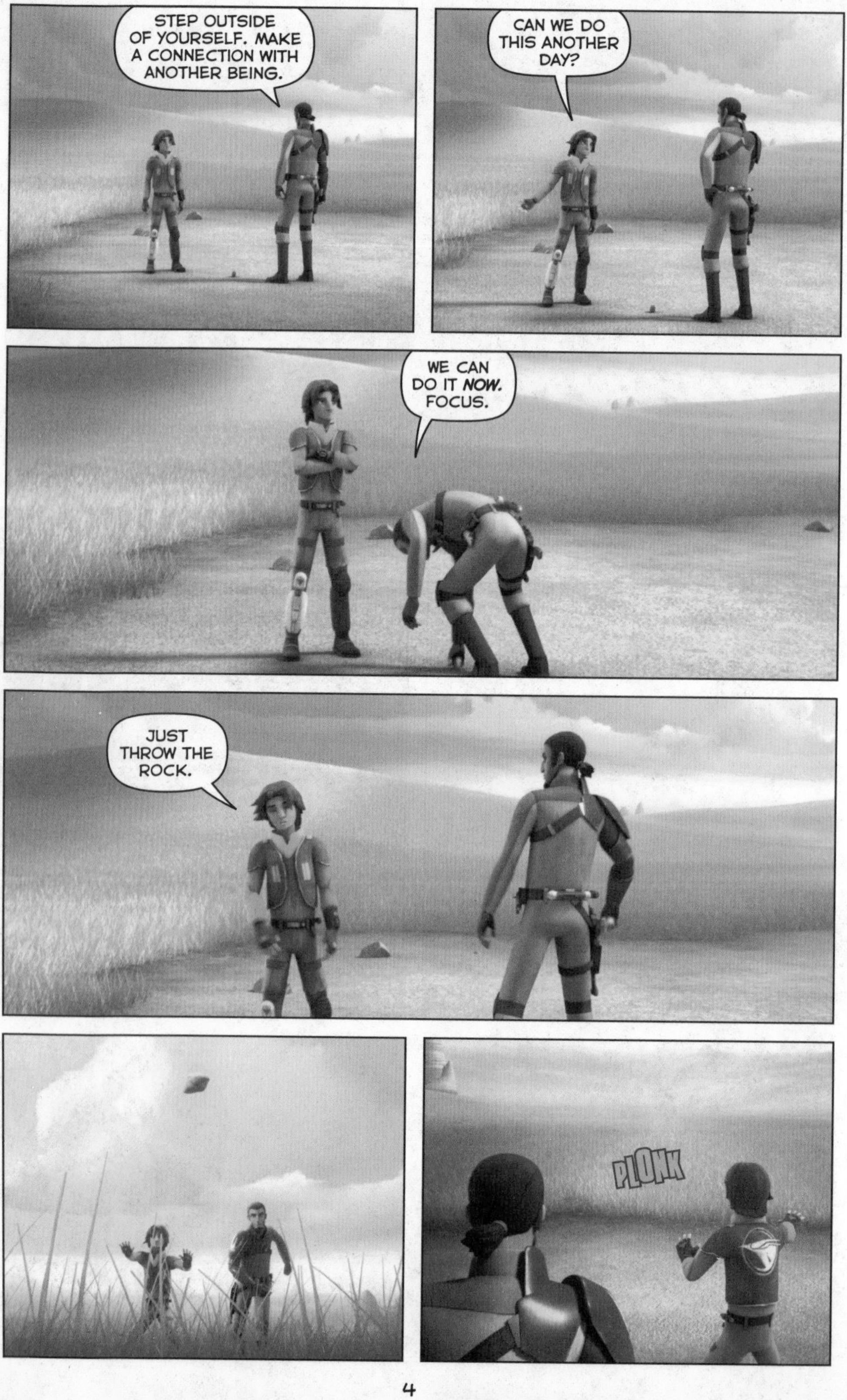
STEP OUTSIDE OF YOURSELF. MAKE A CONNECTION WITH ANOTHER BEING.
CAN WE DO THIS ANOTHER DAY?
WE CAN DO IT *NOW*. FOCUS.
JUST THROW THE ROCK.
PLONK

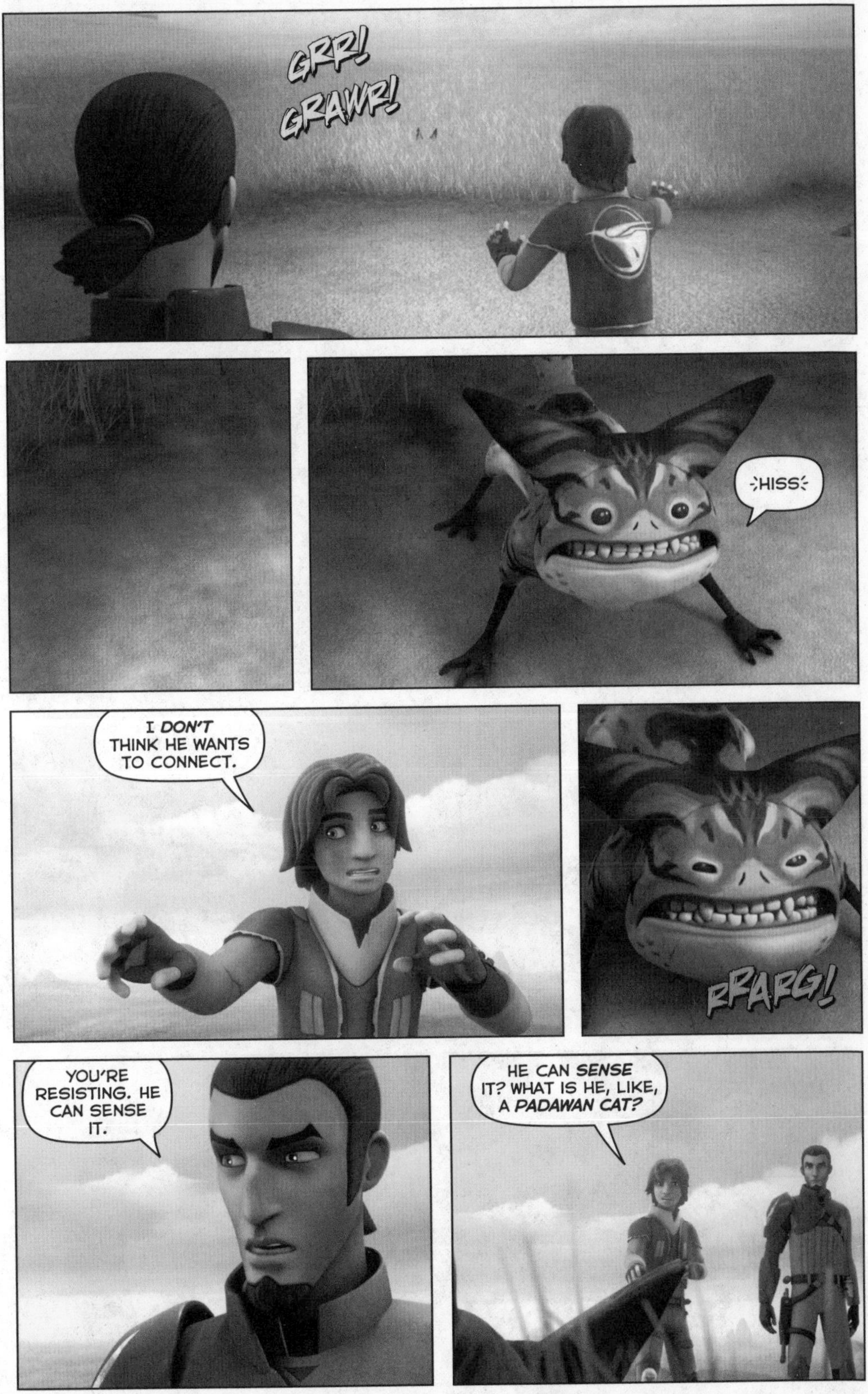
GRR!
GRAWR!
HISS
I DON'T THINK HE WANTS TO CONNECT.
RRARG!
YOU'RE RESISTING. HE CAN SENSE IT.
HE CAN SENSE IT? WHAT IS HE, LIKE, A PADAWAN CAT?

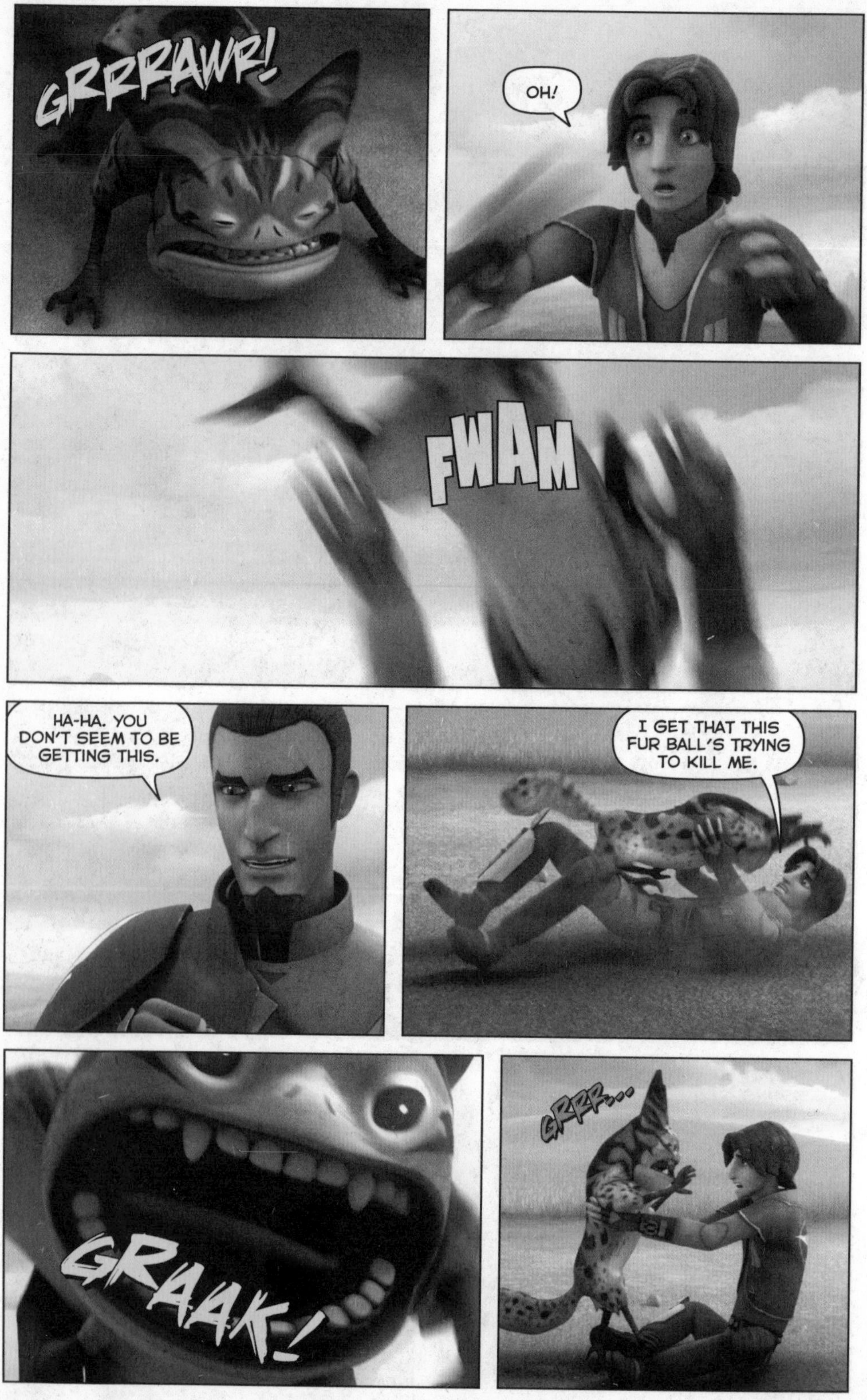
GRRRAWR!
OH!
FWAM
HA-HA. YOU DON'T SEEM TO BE GETTING THIS.
I GET THAT THIS FUR BALL'S TRYING TO KILL ME.
GRAAK!
GRRR...

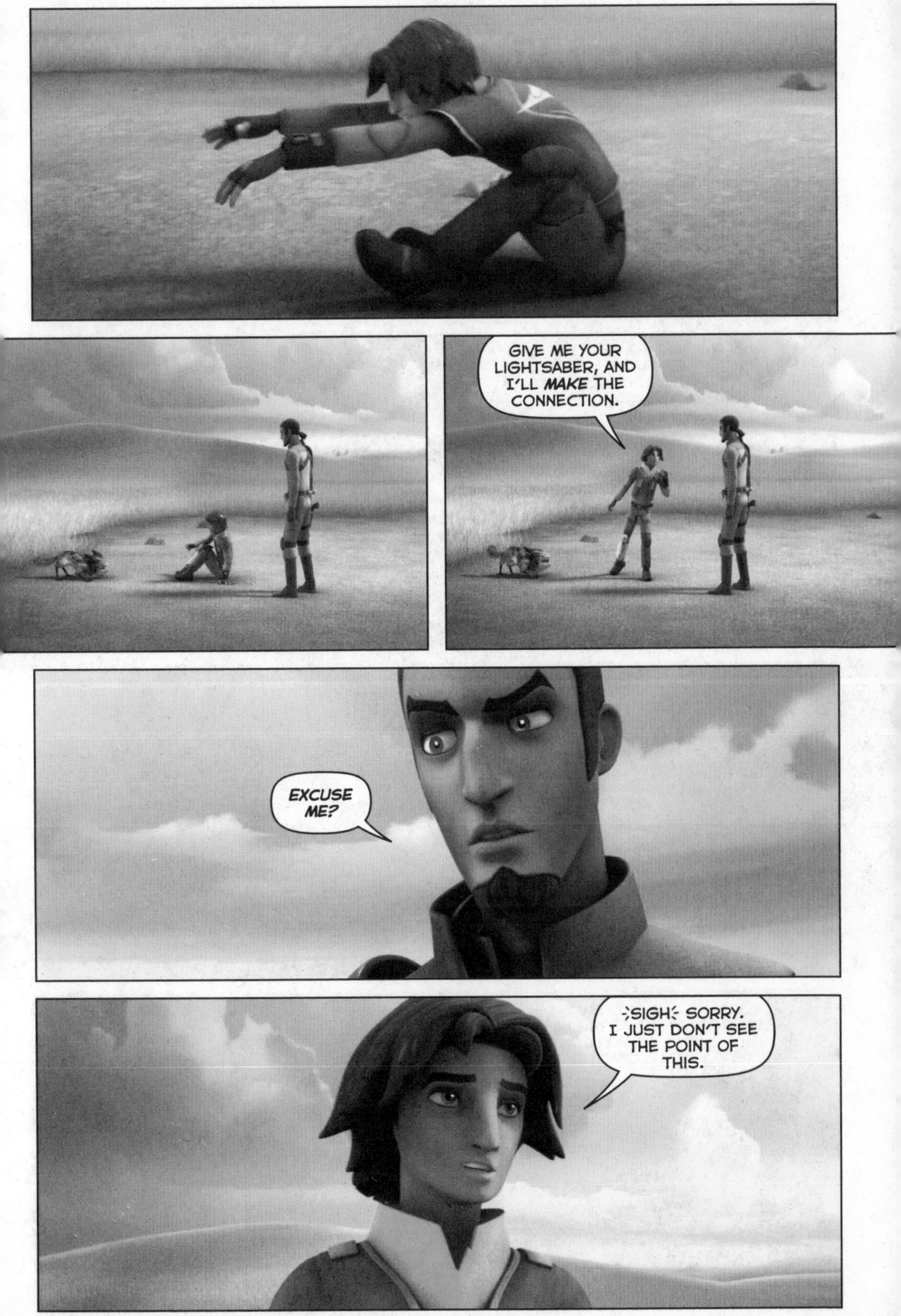
GIVE ME YOUR LIGHTSABER, AND I'LL *MAKE* THE CONNECTION.
EXCUSE ME?
SIGH SORRY. I JUST DON'T SEE THE POINT OF THIS.

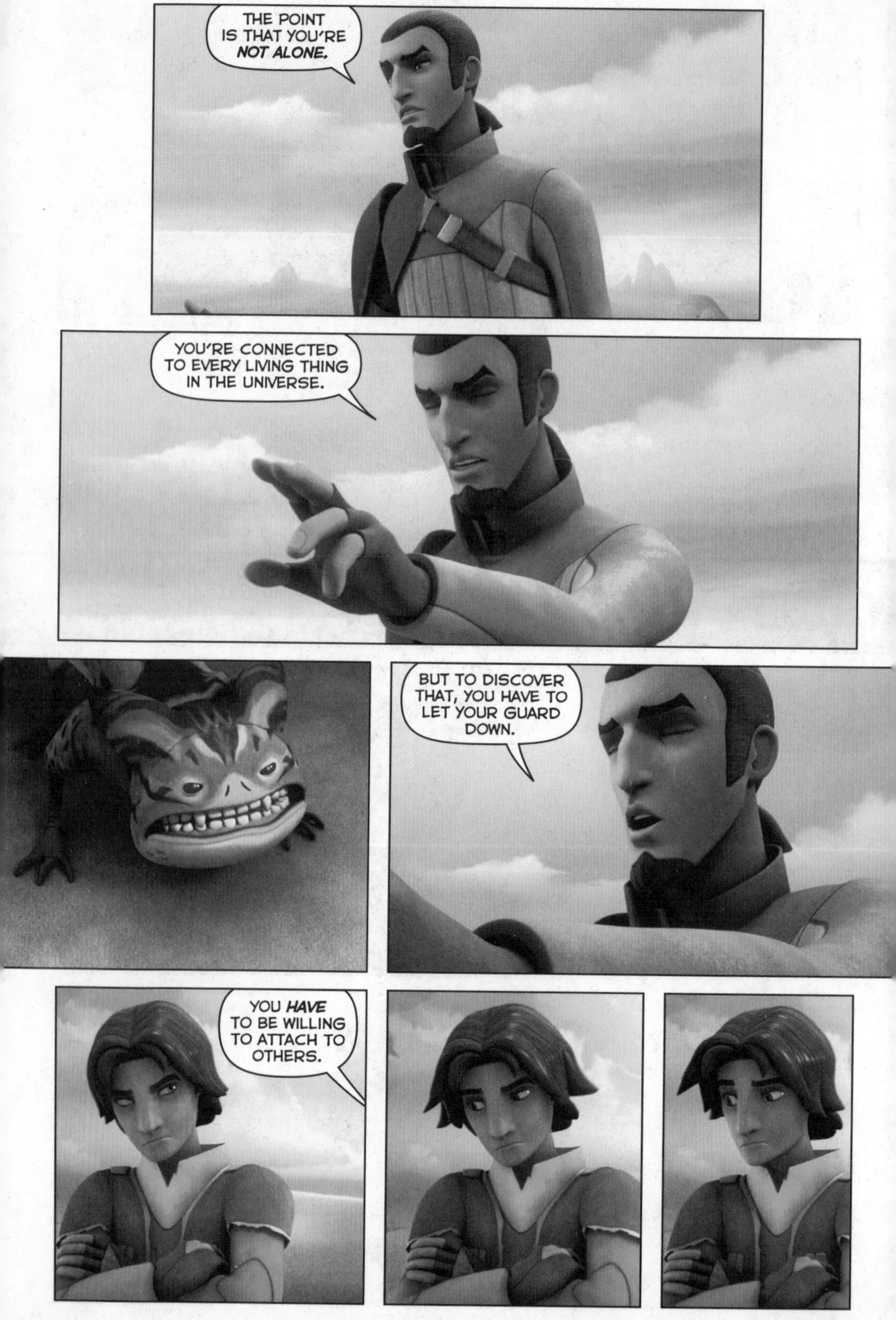
THE POINT IS THAT YOU'RE *NOT ALONE.*
YOU'RE CONNECTED TO EVERY LIVING THING IN THE UNIVERSE.
BUT TO DISCOVER THAT, YOU HAVE TO LET YOUR GUARD DOWN.
YOU *HAVE* TO BE WILLING TO ATTACH TO OTHERS.

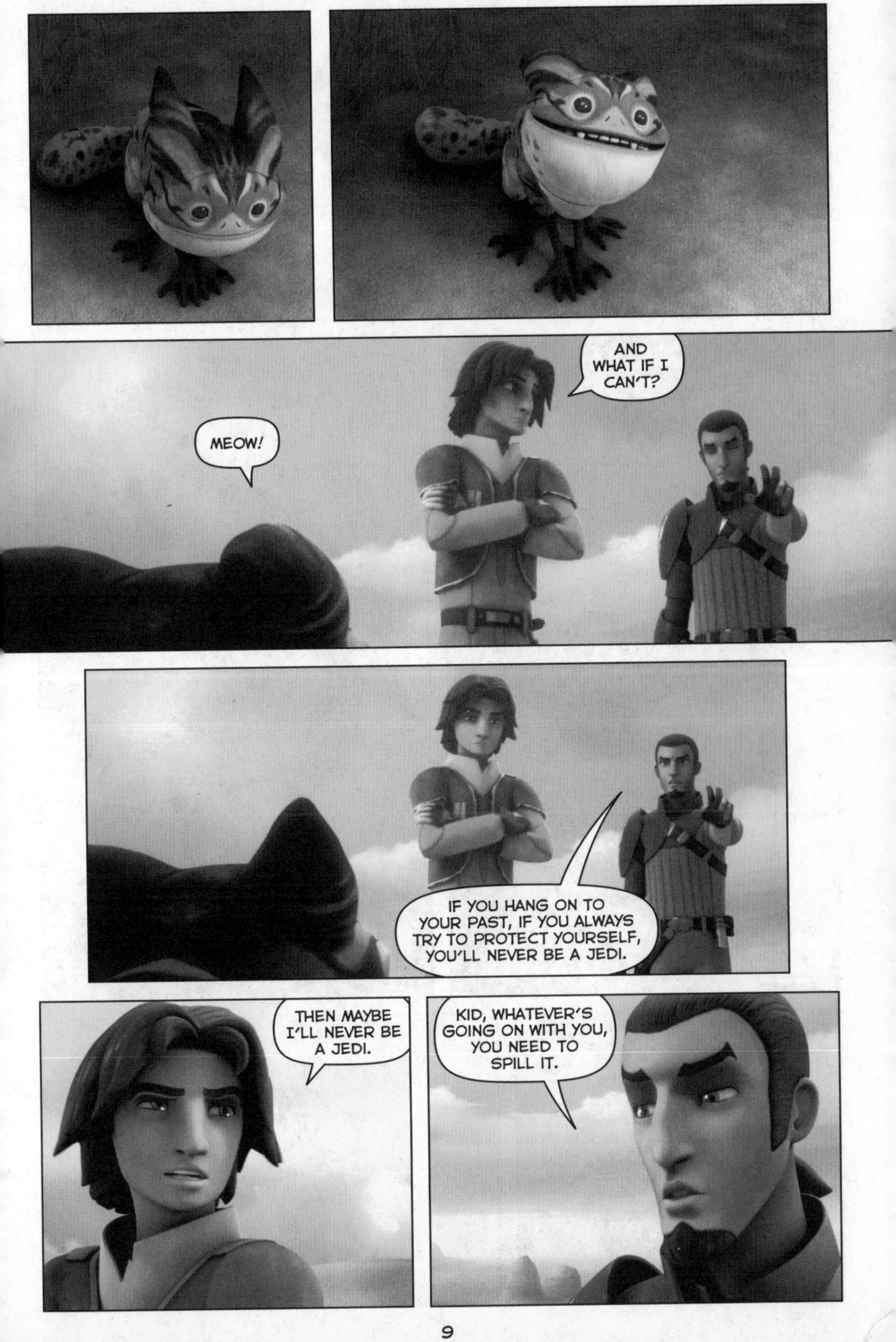

AND WHAT IF I CAN'T?
MEOW!
IF YOU HANG ON TO YOUR PAST, IF YOU ALWAYS TRY TO PROTECT YOURSELF, YOU'LL NEVER BE A JEDI.
THEN MAYBE I'LL NEVER BE A JEDI.
KID, WHATEVER'S GOING ON WITH YOU, YOU NEED TO SPILL IT.

:SIGH: I'M SORRY, KANAN, I DON'T MEAN TO WEAR YOU OUT. TODAY'S NOT A GOOD DAY. IT'S NEVER A GOOD DAY.

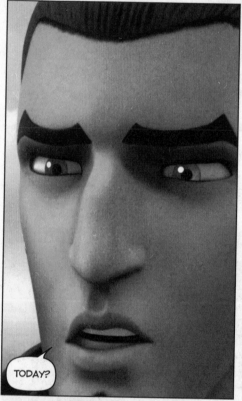

TODAY?

EMPIRE DAY.

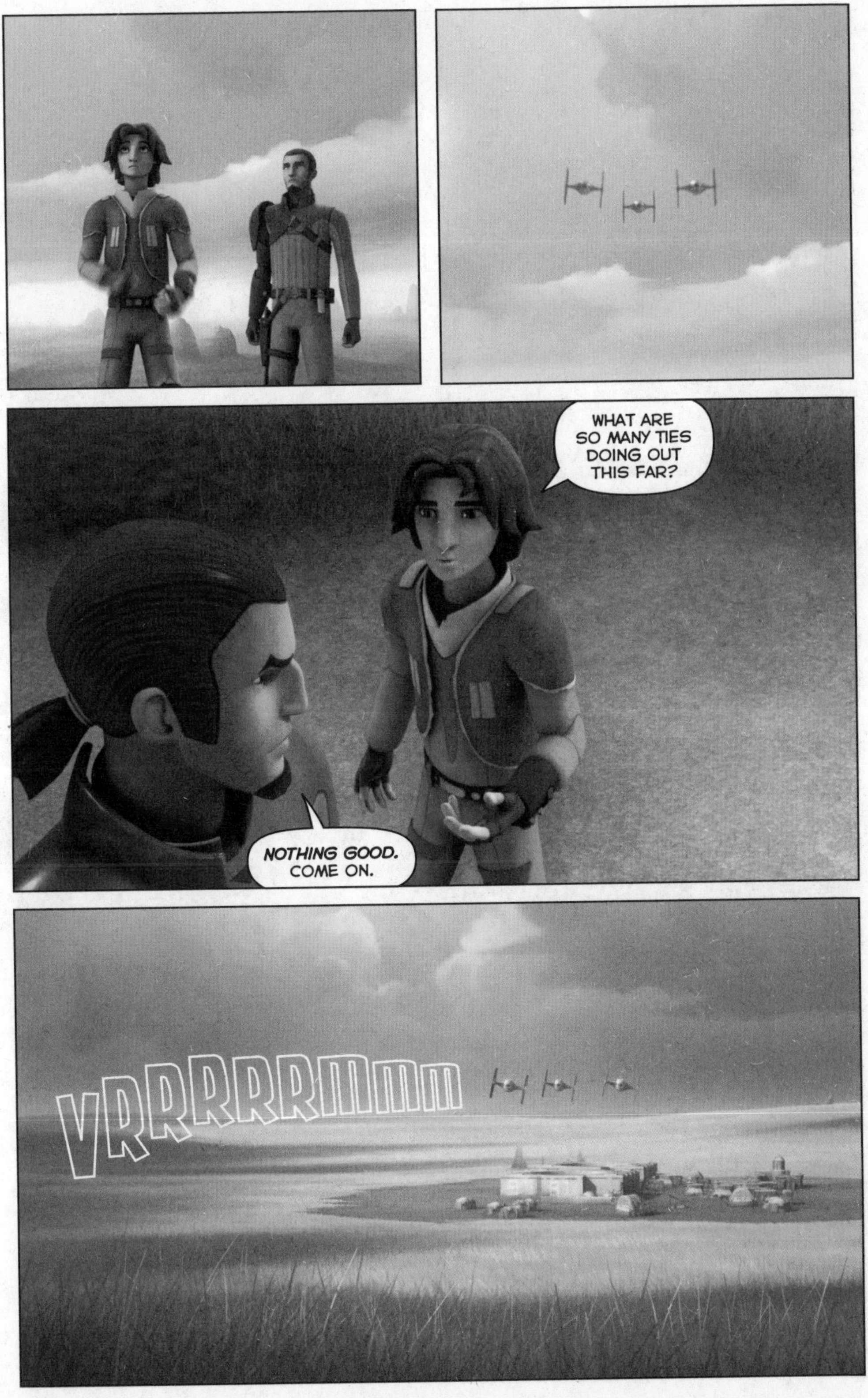
WHAT ARE SO MANY TIES DOING OUT THIS FAR?
NOTHING GOOD. COME ON.
VRRRRRMmmm

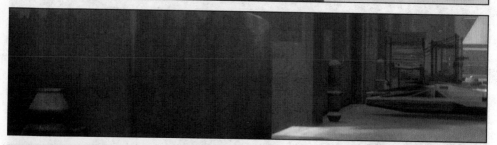

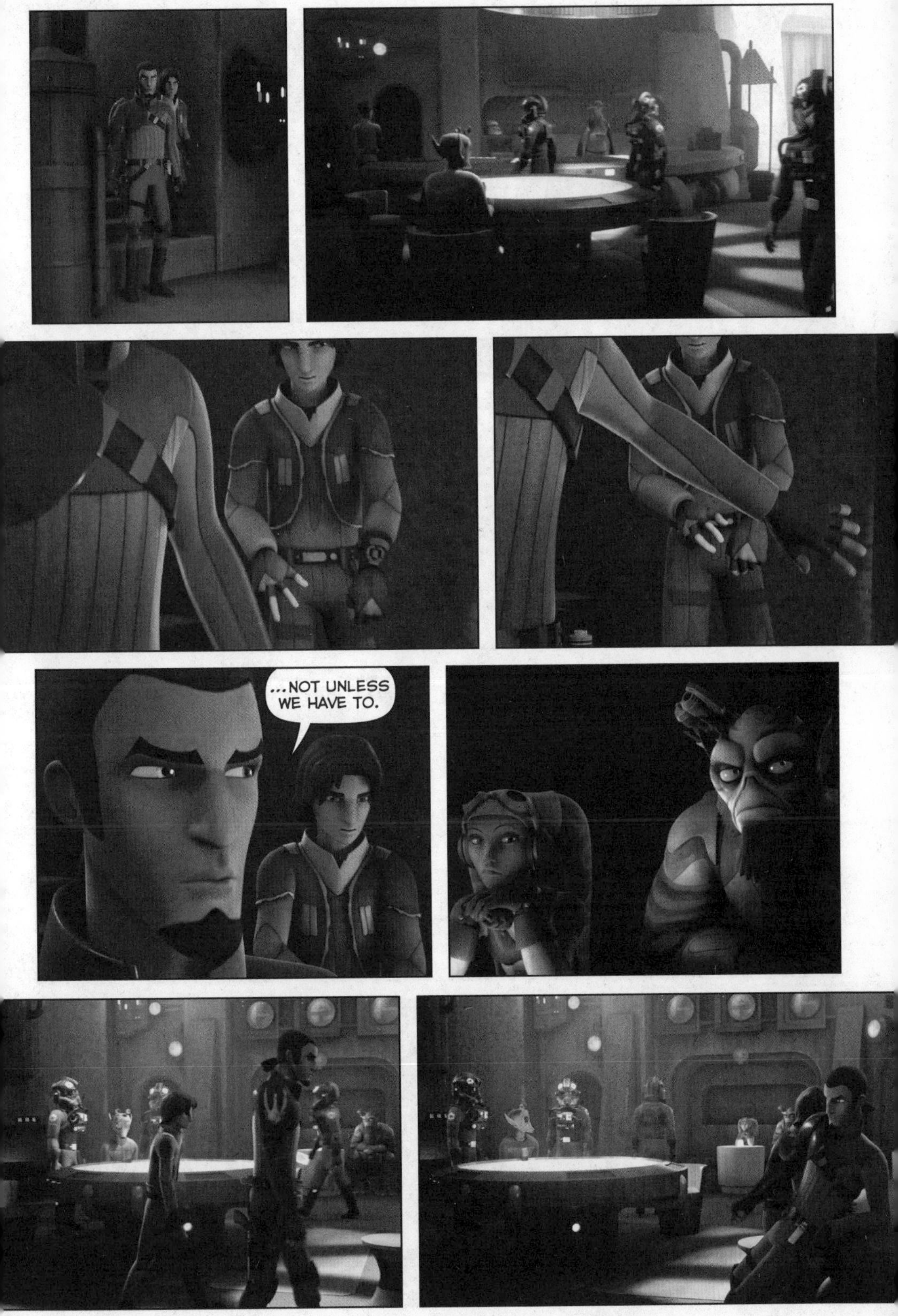
...NOT UNLESS WE HAVE TO.

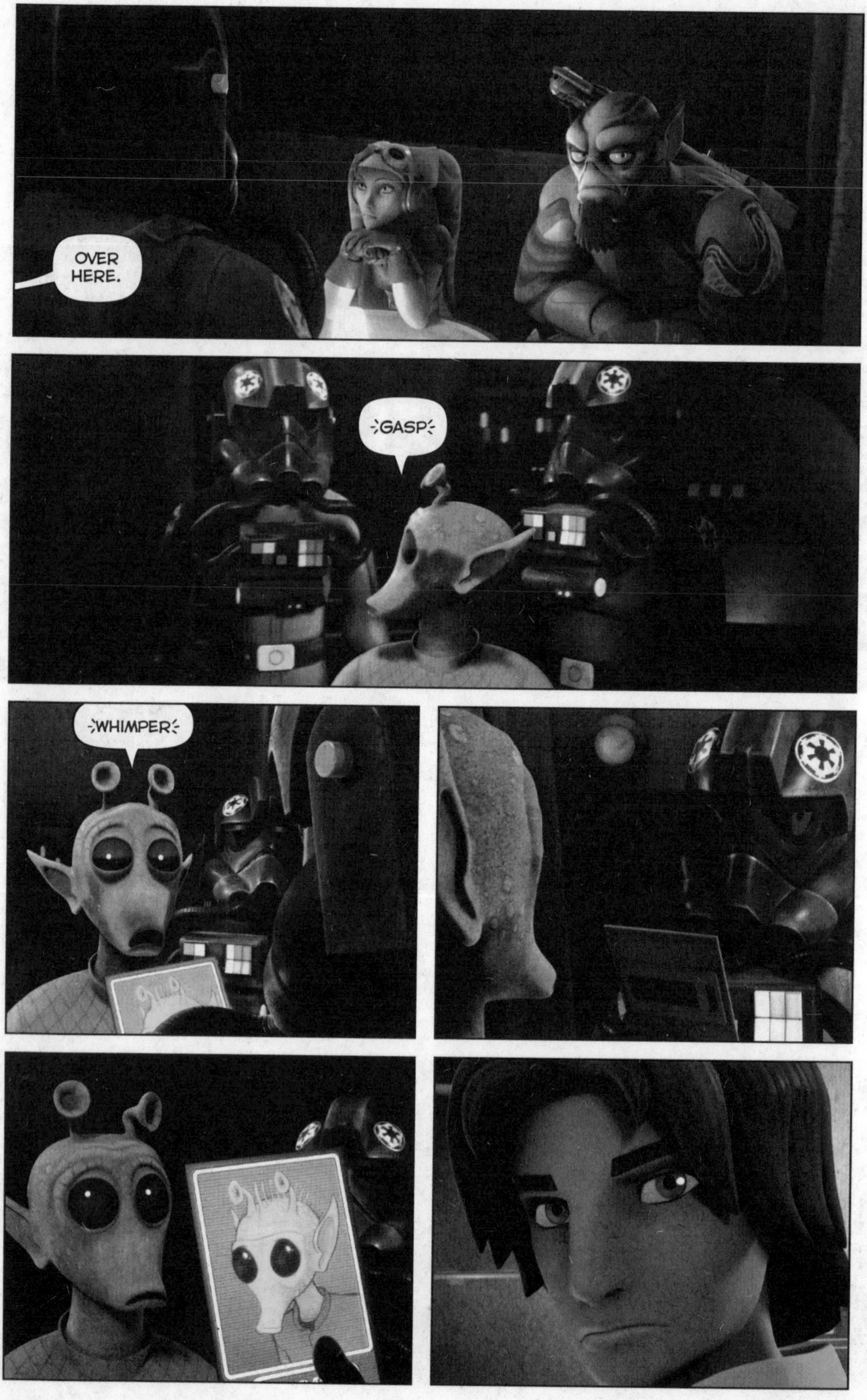
OVER HERE.
GASP
WHIMPER

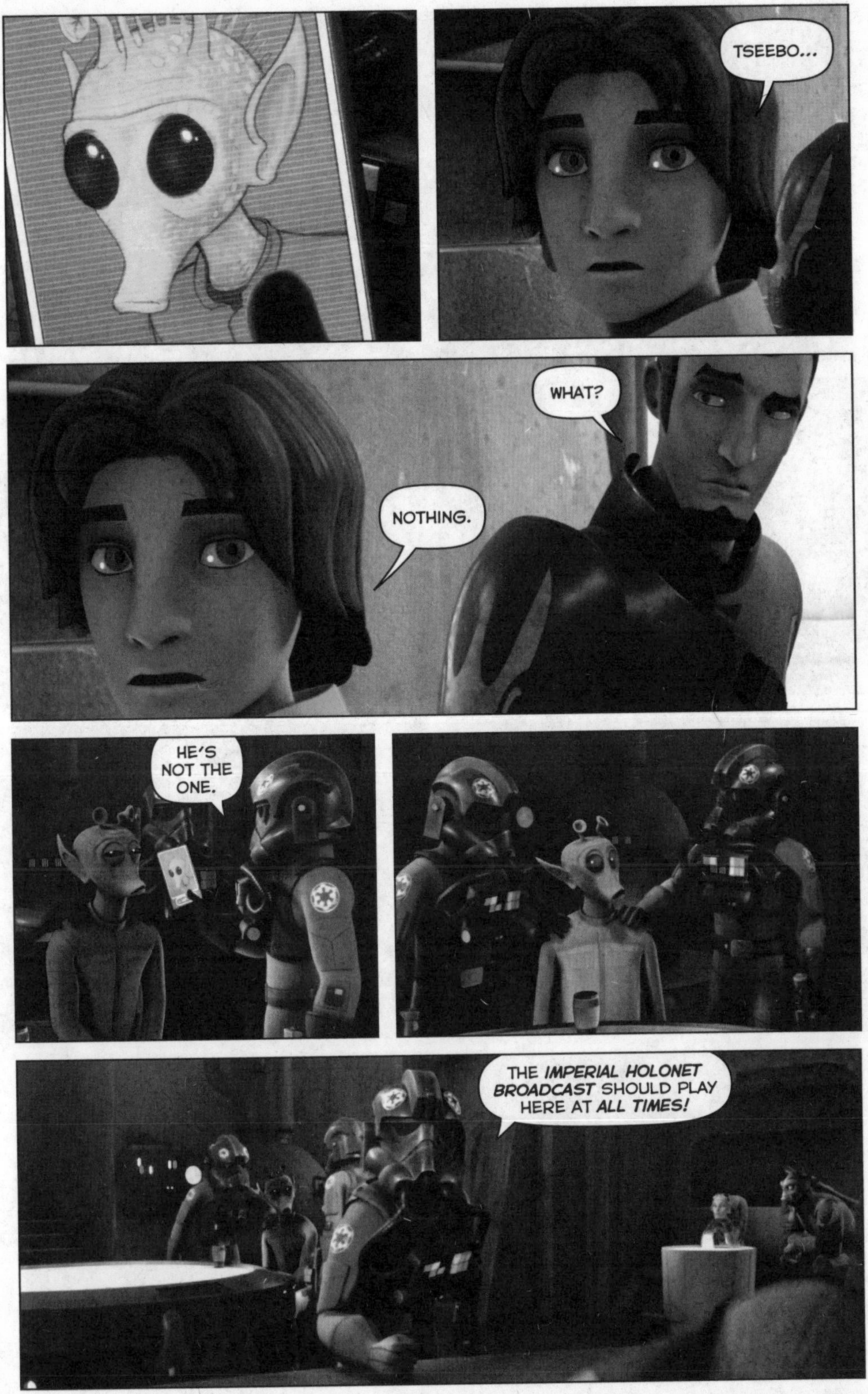
TSEEBO...
WHAT?
NOTHING.
HE'S NOT THE ONE.
THE *IMPERIAL HOLONET BROADCAST* SHOULD PLAY HERE AT *ALL TIMES!*

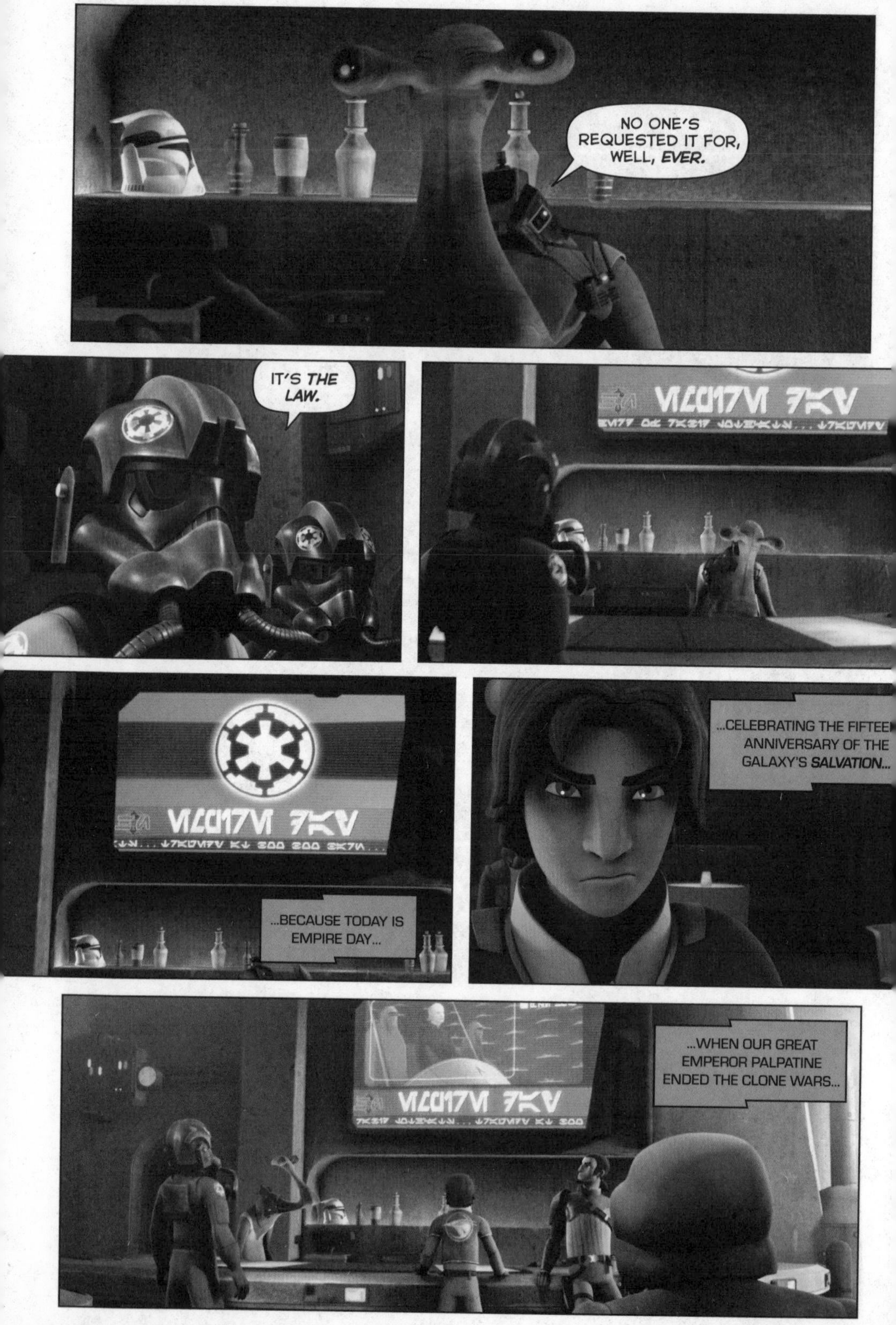
NO ONE'S REQUESTED IT FOR, WELL, *EVER.*
IT'S *THE LAW.*
...BECAUSE TODAY IS EMPIRE DAY...
...CELEBRATING THE FIFTEE ANNIVERSARY OF THE GALAXY'S *SALVATION...*
...WHEN OUR GREAT EMPEROR PALPATINE ENDED THE CLONE WARS...

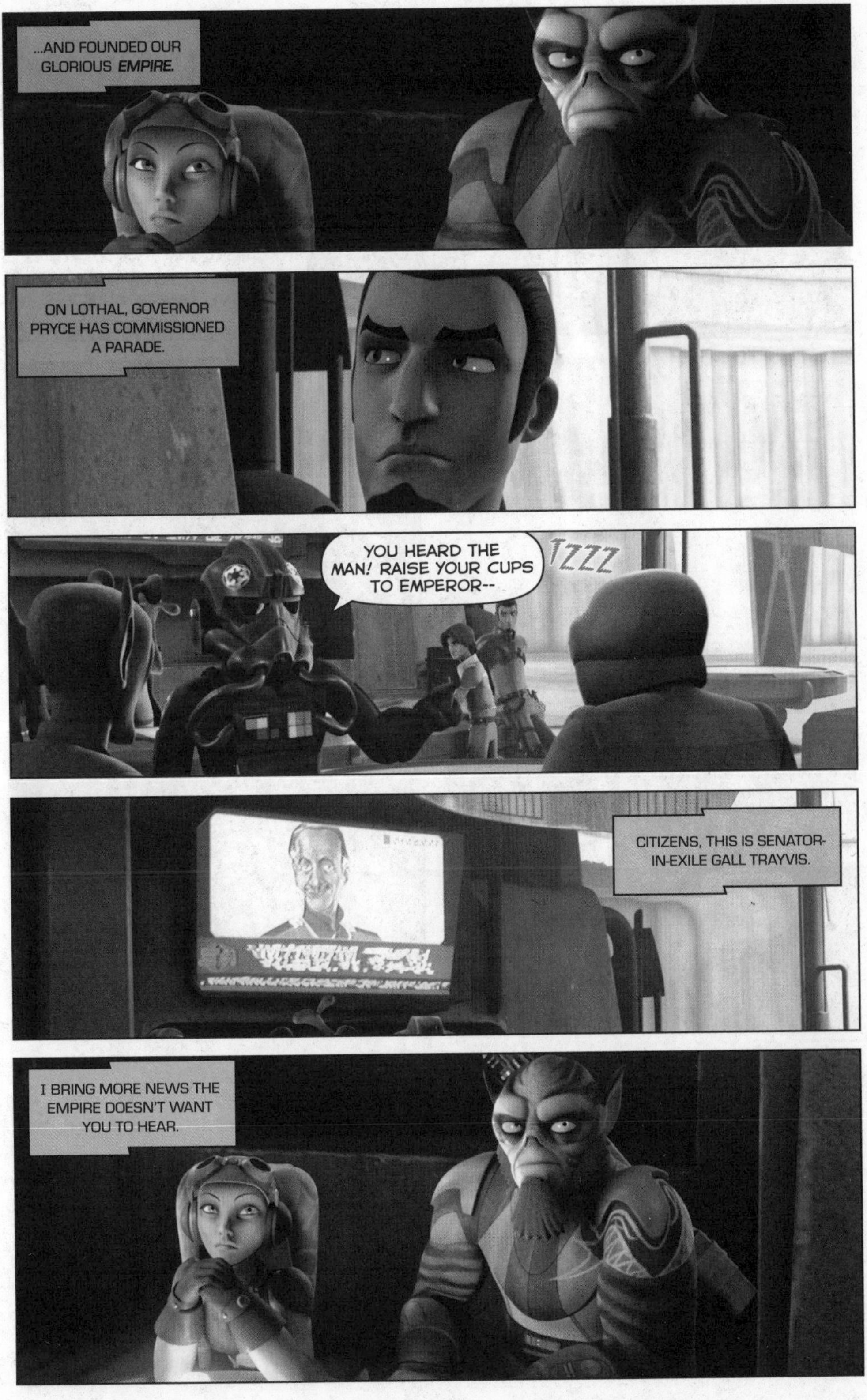
...AND FOUNDED OUR GLORIOUS EMPIRE.
ON LOTHAL, GOVERNOR PRYCE HAS COMMISSIONED A PARADE.
YOU HEARD THE MAN! RAISE YOUR CUPS TO EMPEROR--
TZZZ
CITIZENS, THIS IS SENATOR-IN-EXILE GALL TRAYVIS.
I BRING MORE NEWS THE EMPIRE DOESN'T WANT YOU TO HEAR.

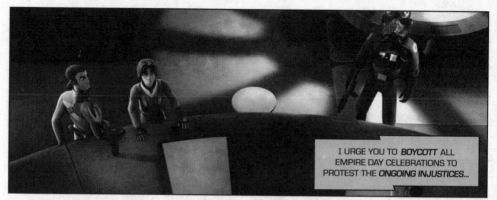

I URGE YOU TO *BOYCOTT* ALL EMPIRE DAY CELEBRATIONS TO PROTEST THE *ONGOING INJUSTICES...*

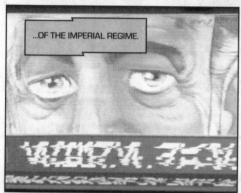

...OF THE IMPERIAL REGIME.

SHUT THIS OFF!

CAN'T. IT'S *THE LAW.*

WE'RE DONE HERE.

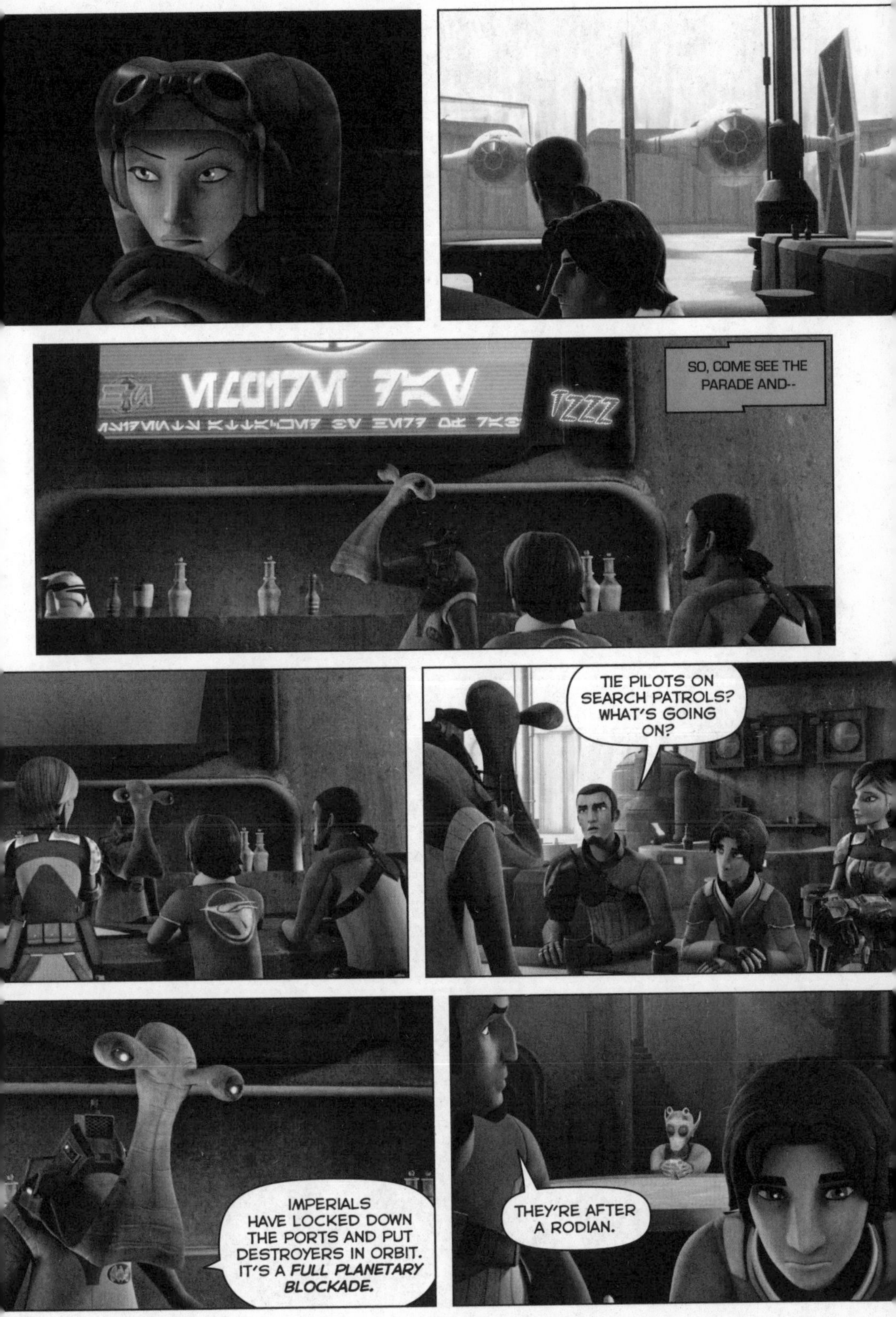
SO, COME SEE THE PARADE AND--
TIE PILOTS ON SEARCH PATROLS? WHAT'S GOING ON?
IMPERIALS HAVE LOCKED DOWN THE PORTS AND PUT DESTROYERS IN ORBIT. IT'S A *FULL PLANETARY BLOCKADE.*
THEY'RE AFTER A RODIAN.

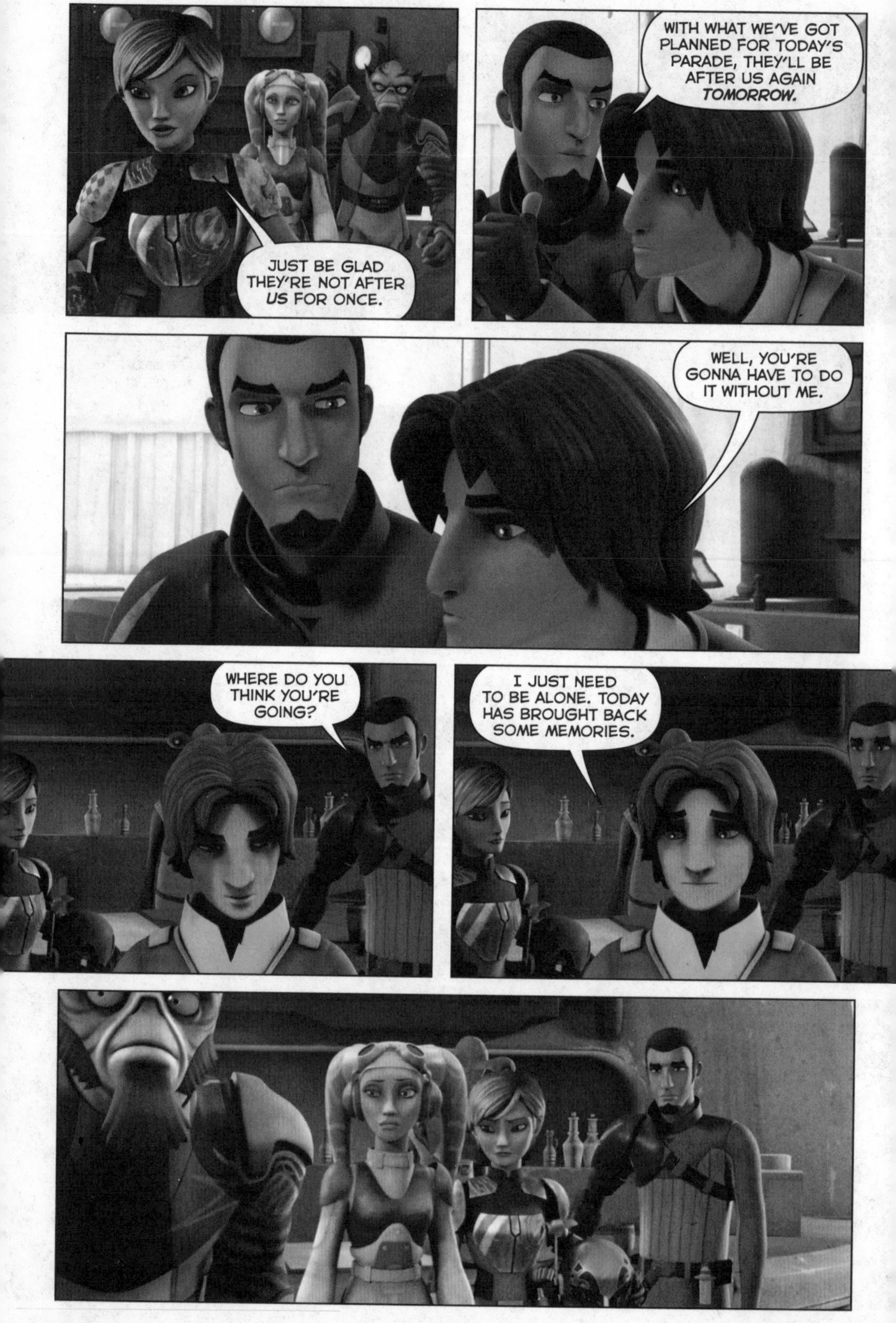

JUST BE GLAD THEY'RE NOT AFTER *US* FOR ONCE.
WITH WHAT WE'VE GOT PLANNED FOR TODAY'S PARADE, THEY'LL BE AFTER US AGAIN *TOMORROW.*
WELL, YOU'RE GONNA HAVE TO DO IT WITHOUT ME.
WHERE DO YOU THINK YOU'RE GOING?
I JUST NEED TO BE ALONE. TODAY HAS BROUGHT BACK SOME MEMORIES.

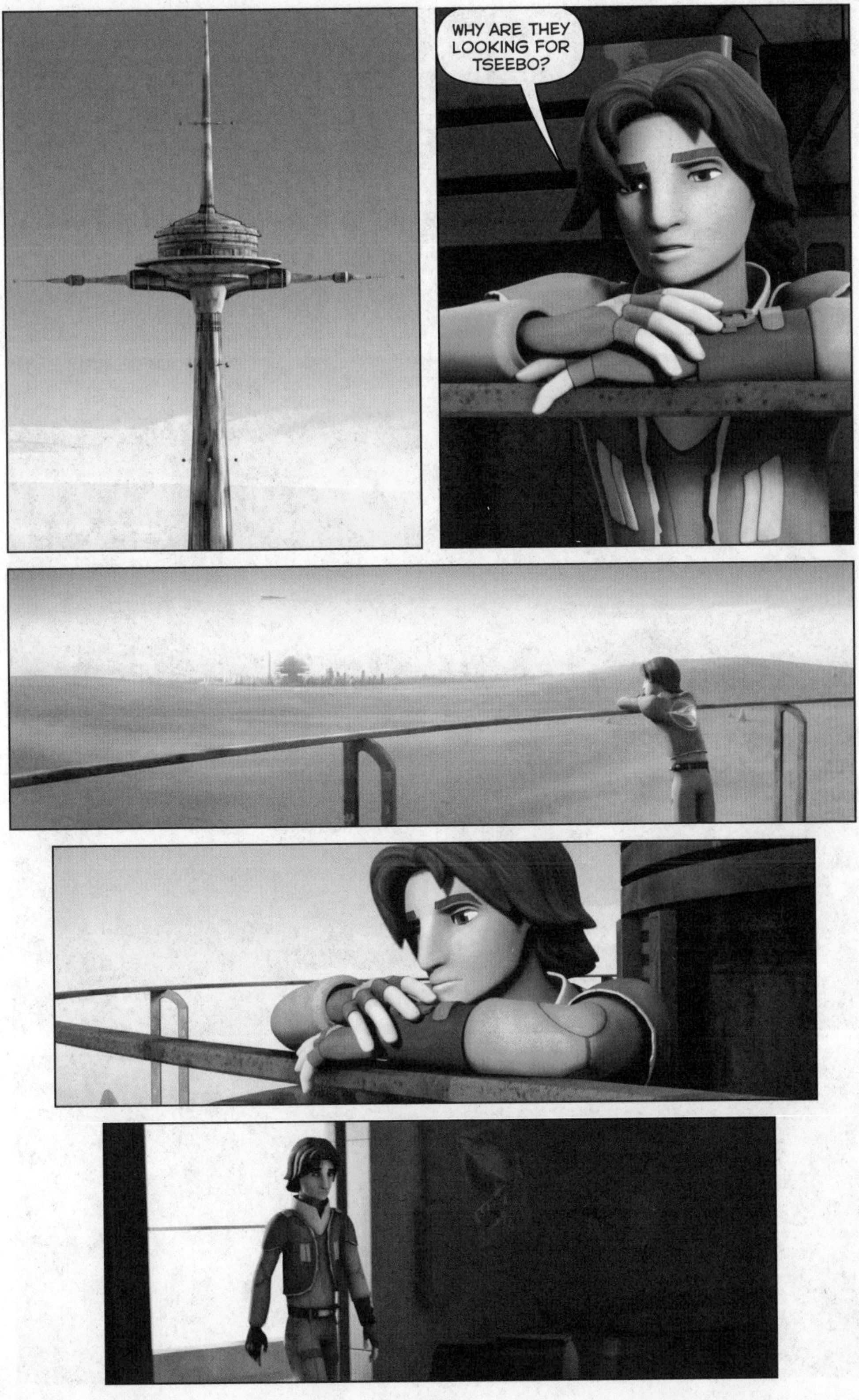
WHY ARE THEY LOOKING FOR TSEEBO?

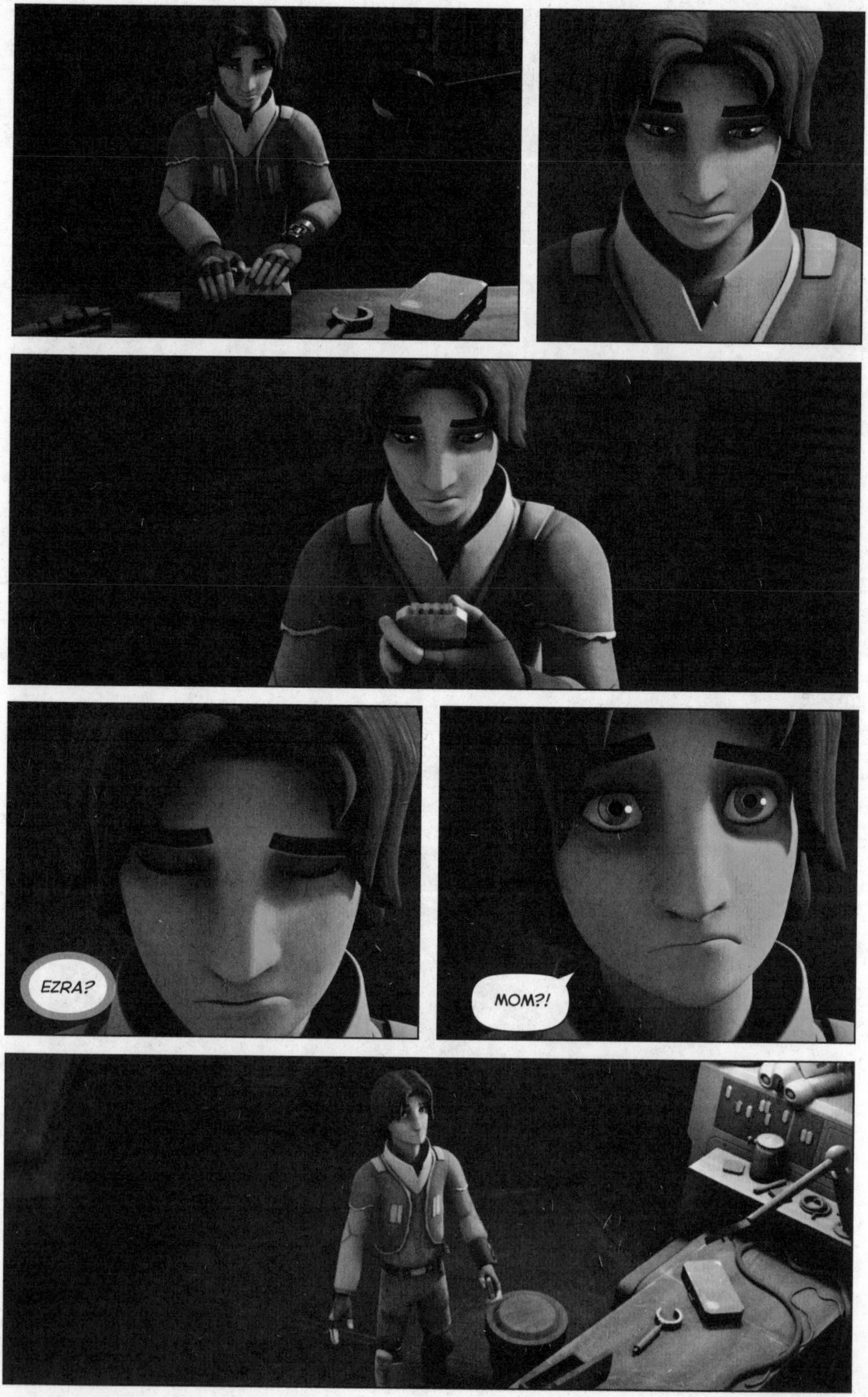
EZRA?
MOM?!

-SIGH-

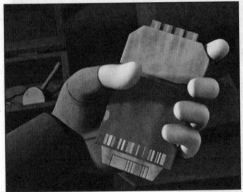

EZRA.

DAD.

EZRA, WE HAVE TO STAND UP FOR PEOPLE IN NEED, ESPECIALLY THOSE IN TROUBLE WITH THE EMPIRE.

TSEEBO. I KNOW WHERE HE IS.

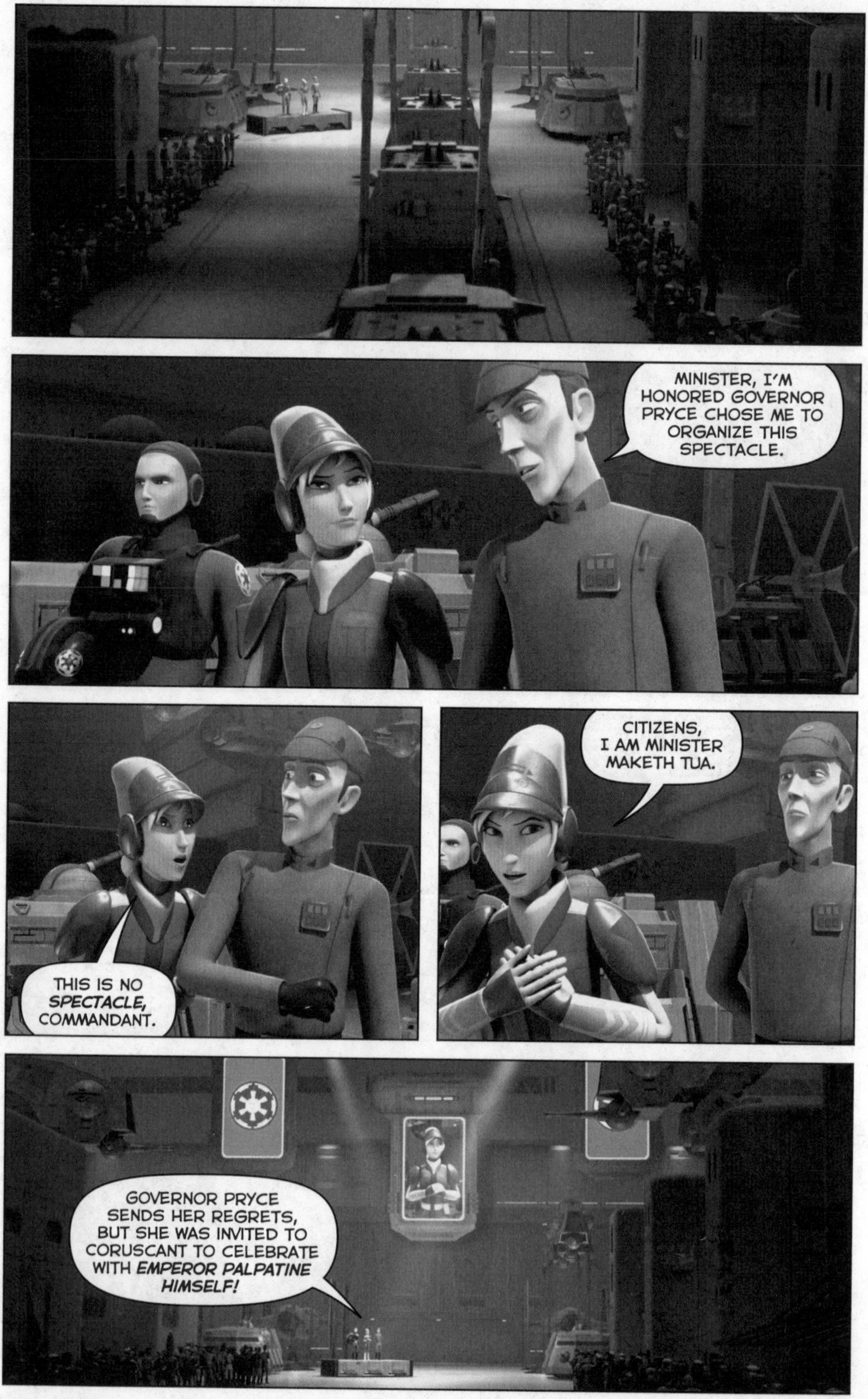
MINISTER, I'M HONORED GOVERNOR PRYCE CHOSE ME TO ORGANIZE THIS SPECTACLE.
THIS IS NO *SPECTACLE,* COMMANDANT.
CITIZENS, I AM MINISTER MAKETH TUA.
GOVERNOR PRYCE SENDS HER REGRETS, BUT SHE WAS INVITED TO CORUSCANT TO CELEBRATE WITH *EMPEROR PALPATINE HIMSELF!*

LET'S HEAR SOME **ENTHUSIASM!**

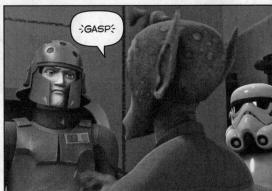

-GASP-

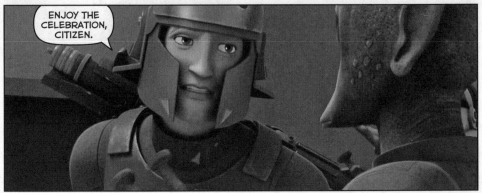

ENJOY THE CELEBRATION, CITIZEN.

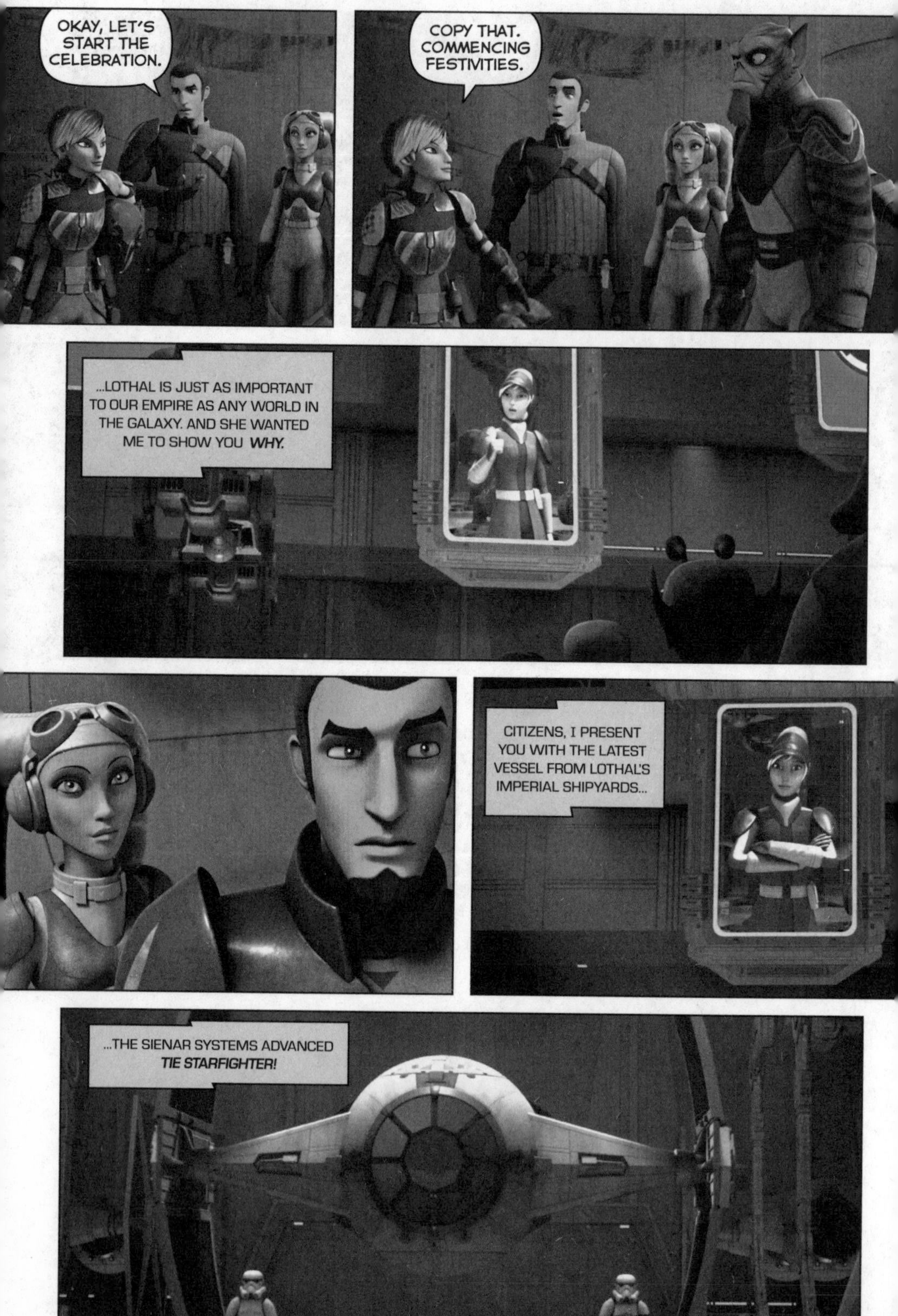
OKAY, LET'S START THE CELEBRATION.
COPY THAT. COMMENCING FESTIVITIES.
...LOTHAL IS JUST AS IMPORTANT TO OUR EMPIRE AS ANY WORLD IN THE GALAXY. AND SHE WANTED ME TO SHOW YOU WHY.
CITIZENS, I PRESENT YOU WITH THE LATEST VESSEL FROM LOTHAL'S IMPERIAL SHIPYARDS...
...THE SIENAR SYSTEMS ADVANCED TIE STARFIGHTER!

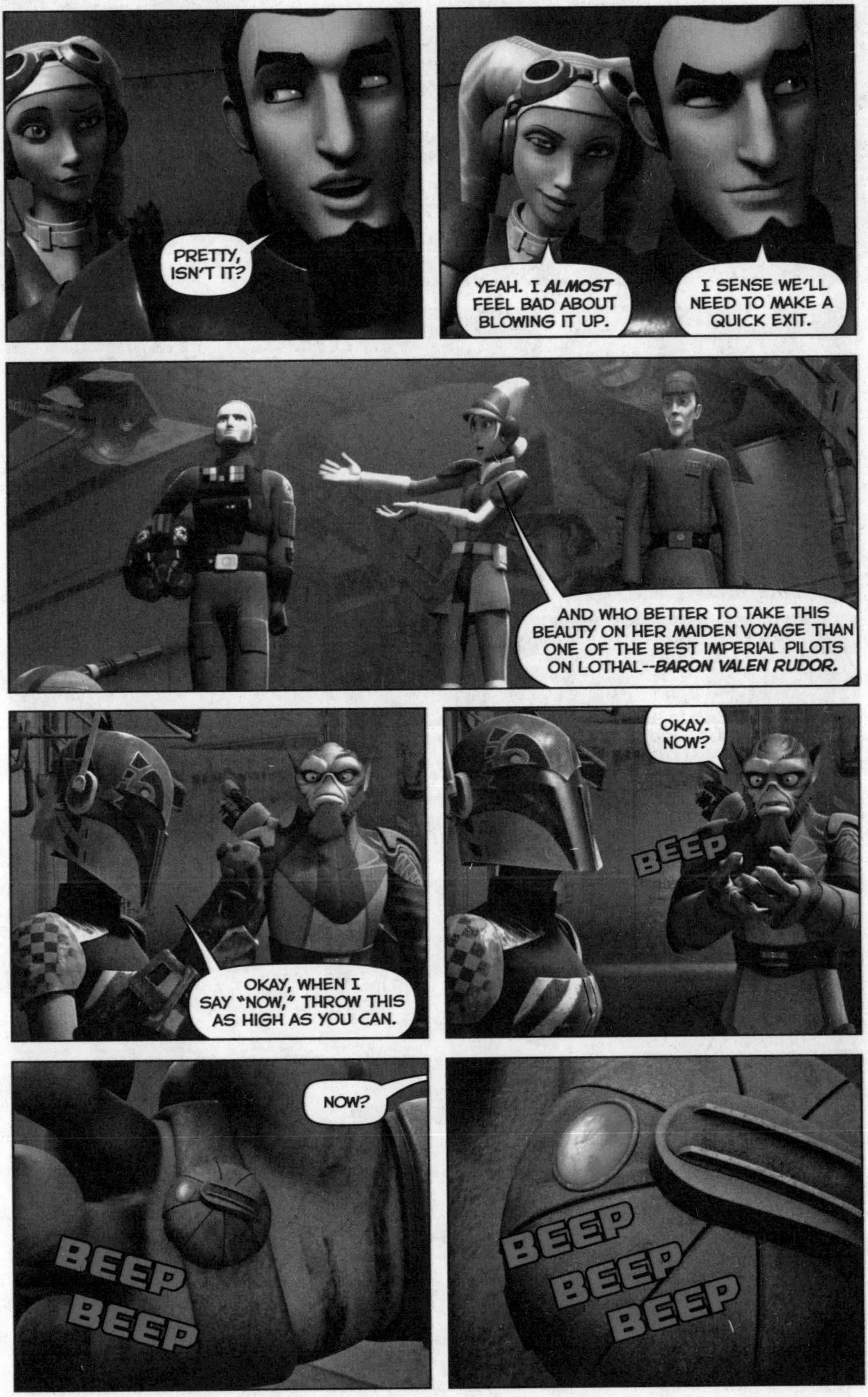
PRETTY, ISN'T IT?
YEAH. I *ALMOST* FEEL BAD ABOUT BLOWING IT UP.
I SENSE WE'LL NEED TO MAKE A QUICK EXIT.
AND WHO BETTER TO TAKE THIS BEAUTY ON HER MAIDEN VOYAGE THAN ONE OF THE BEST IMPERIAL PILOTS ON LOTHAL--*BARON VALEN RUDOR.*
OKAY, WHEN I SAY "NOW," THROW THIS AS HIGH AS YOU CAN.
OKAY. NOW?
BEEP
NOW?
BEEP
BEEP
BEEP
BEEP
BEEP

NOW?!

NOW.

HRRAGH!

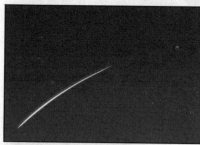

KABOOM

YAY!

WOO!

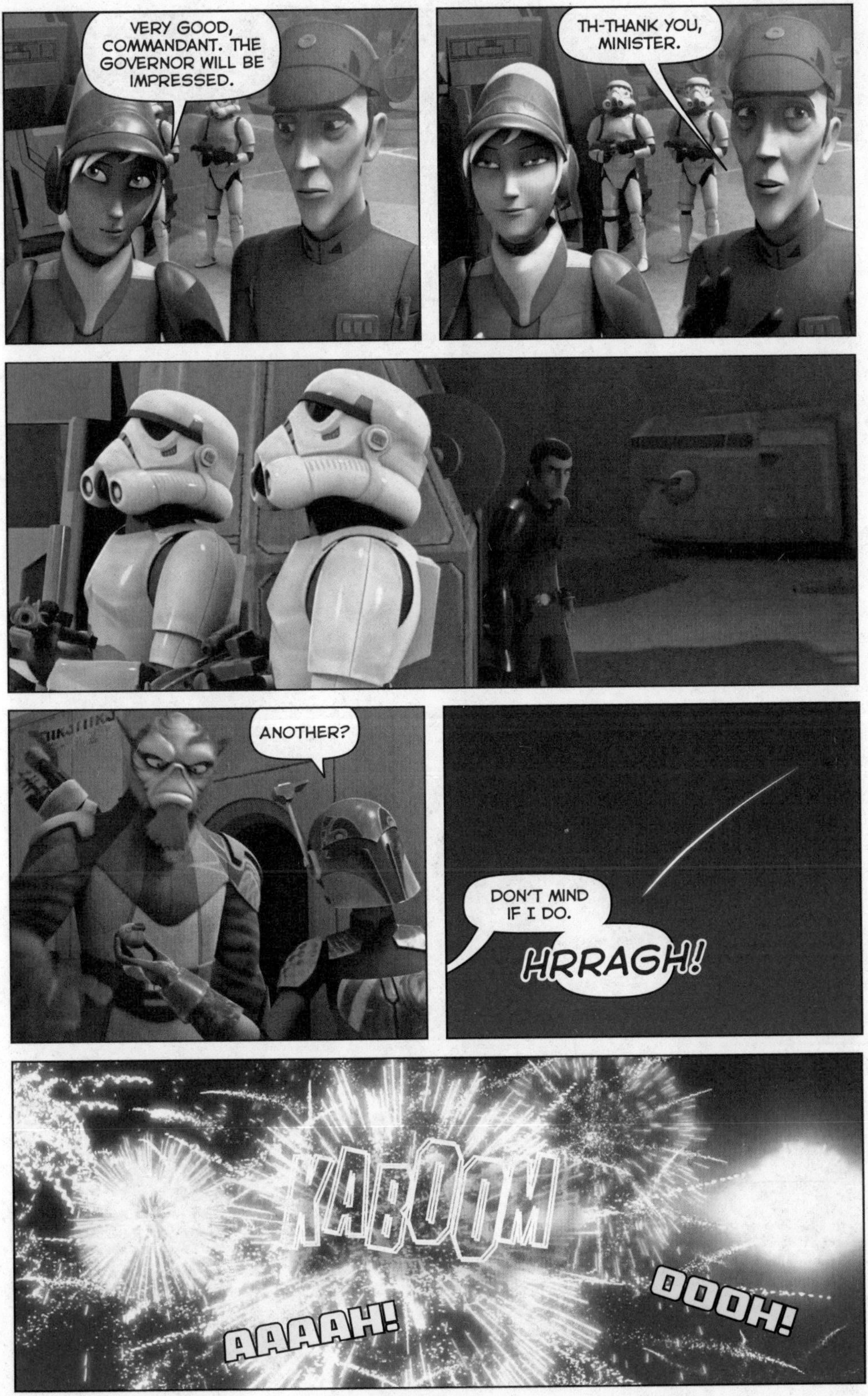
VERY GOOD, COMMANDANT. THE GOVERNOR WILL BE IMPRESSED.
TH-THANK YOU, MINISTER.
ANOTHER?
DON'T MIND IF I DO.
HRRAGH!
KABOOM
OOOH!
AAAAH!

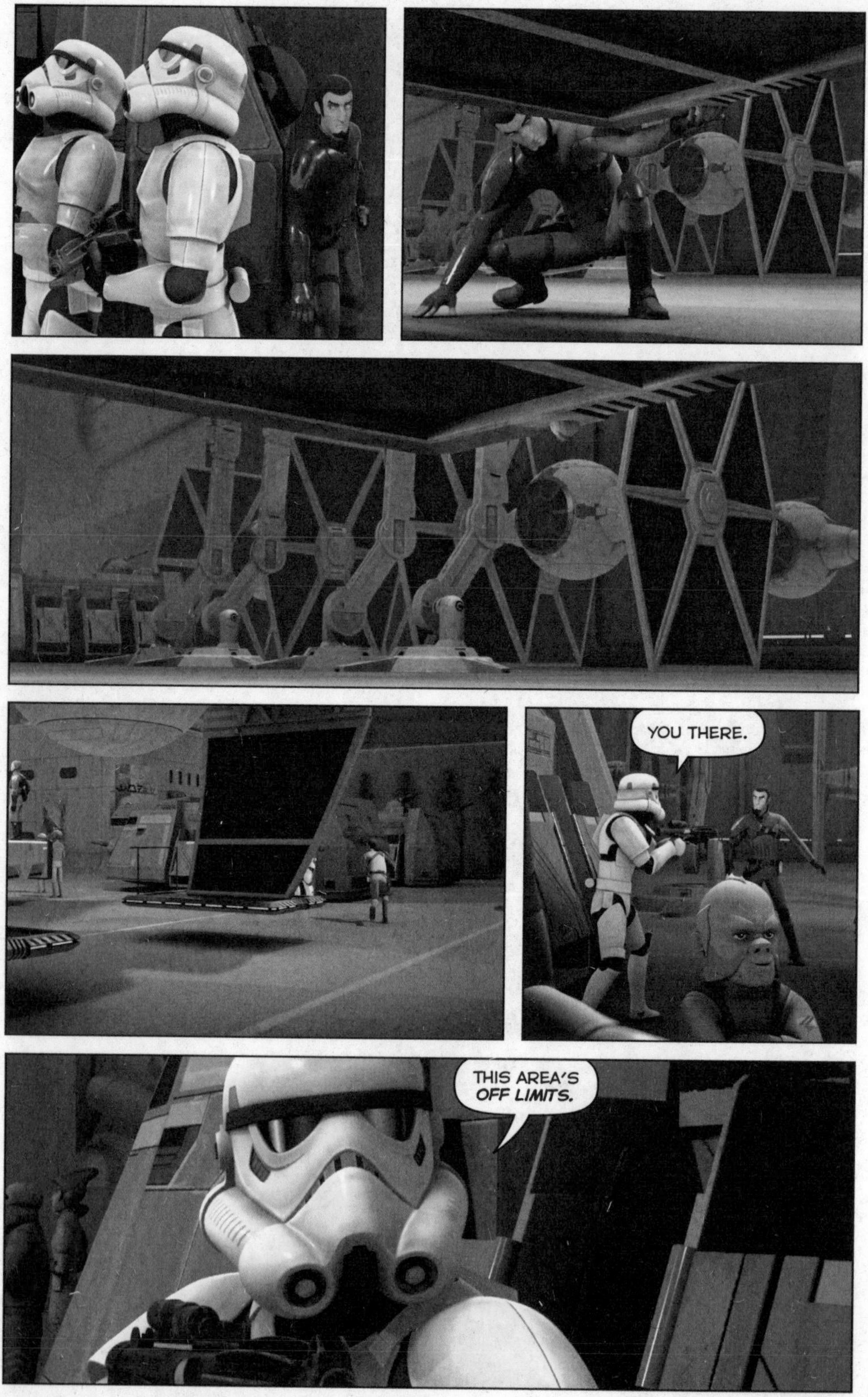
YOU THERE.
THIS AREA'S OFF LIMITS.

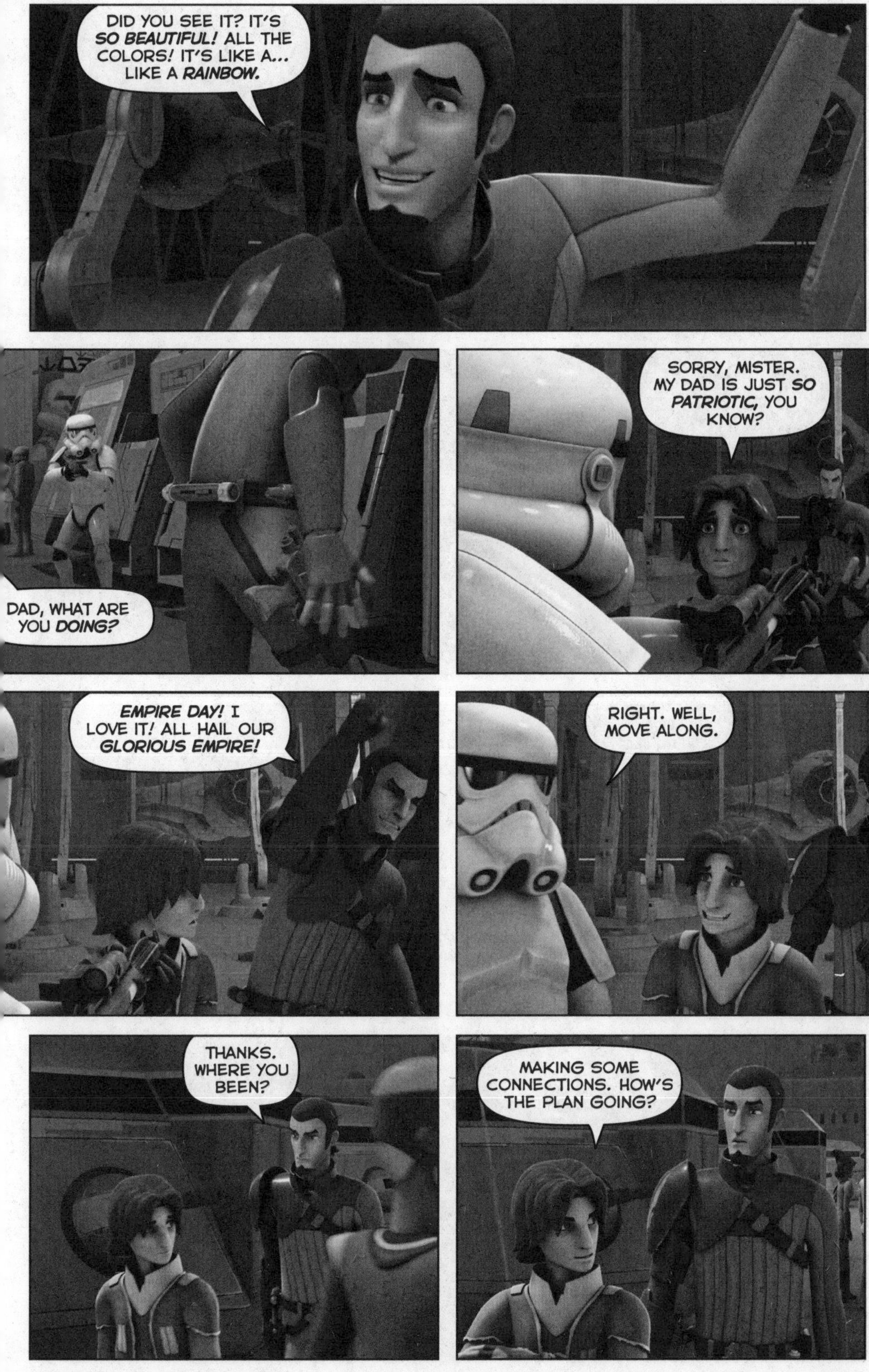
DID YOU SEE IT? IT'S SO BEAUTIFUL! ALL THE COLORS! IT'S LIKE A... LIKE A RAINBOW.
DAD, WHAT ARE YOU DOING?
SORRY, MISTER. MY DAD IS JUST SO PATRIOTIC, YOU KNOW?
EMPIRE DAY! I LOVE IT! ALL HAIL OUR GLORIOUS EMPIRE!
RIGHT. WELL, MOVE ALONG.
THANKS. WHERE YOU BEEN?
MAKING SOME CONNECTIONS. HOW'S THE PLAN GOING?

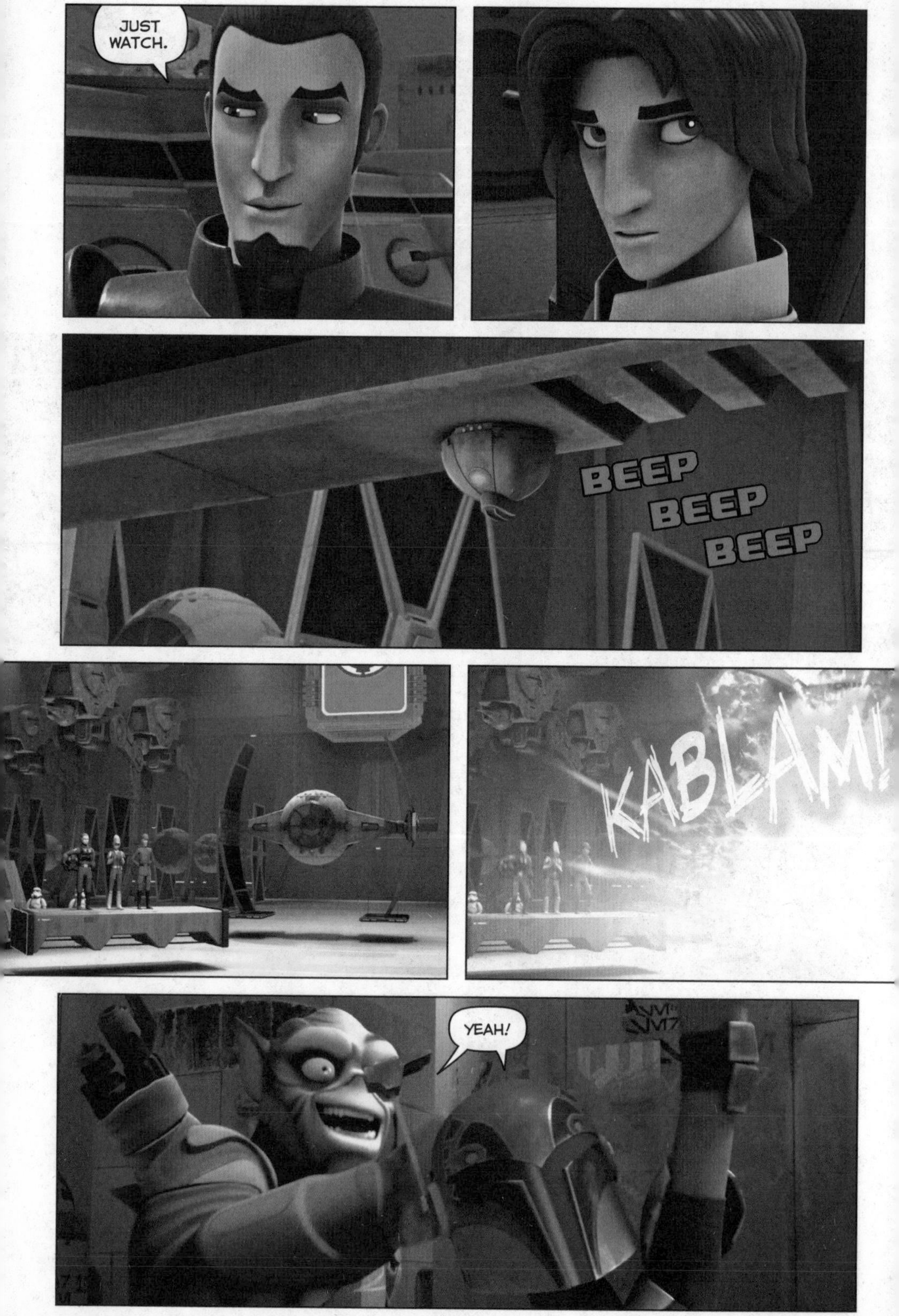
JUST WATCH.
BEEP
BEEP
BEEP
KABLAM!
YEAH!

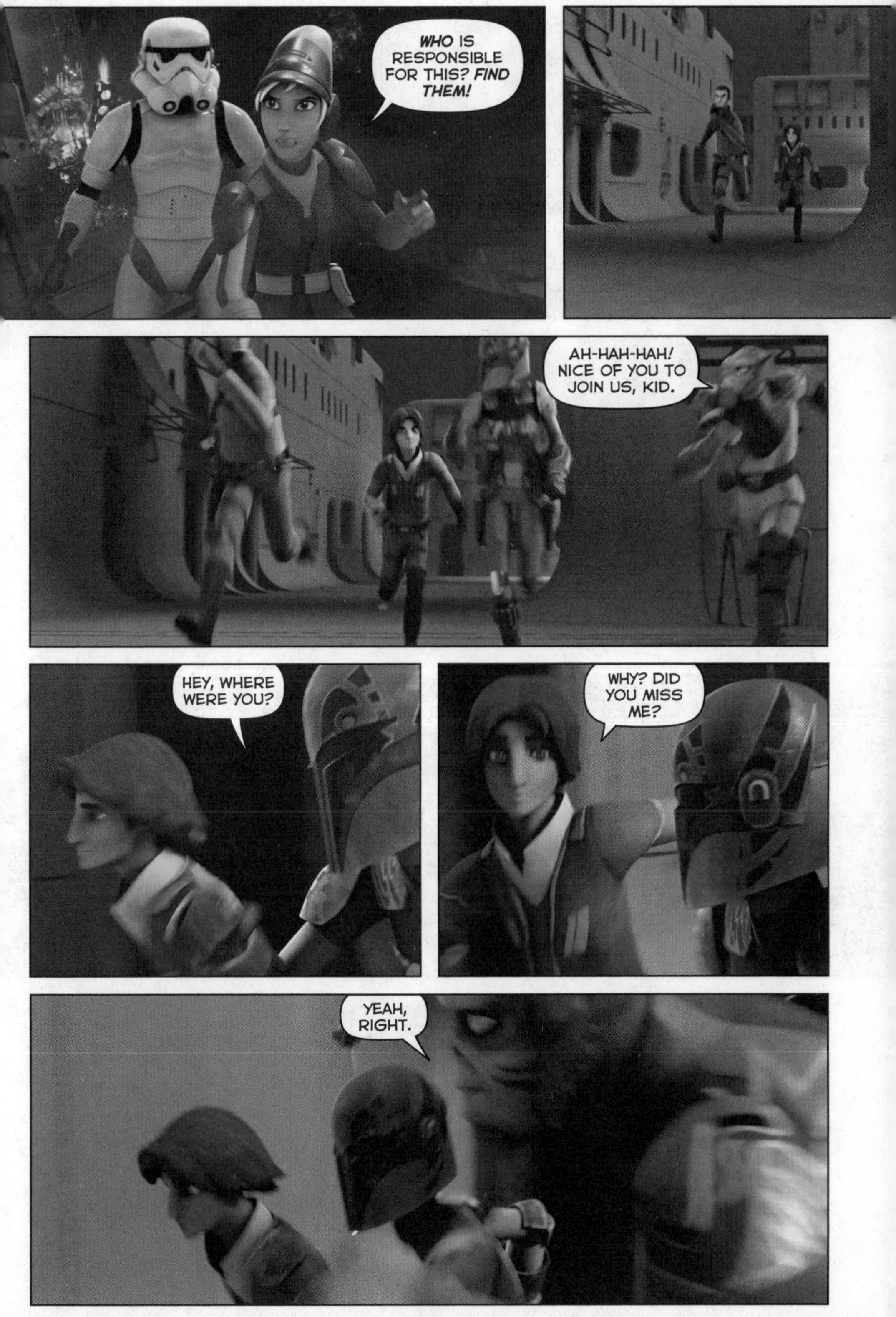
WHO IS RESPONSIBLE FOR THIS? FIND THEM!
AH-HAH-HAH! NICE OF YOU TO JOIN US, KID.
HEY, WHERE WERE YOU?
WHY? DID YOU MISS ME?
YEAH, RIGHT.

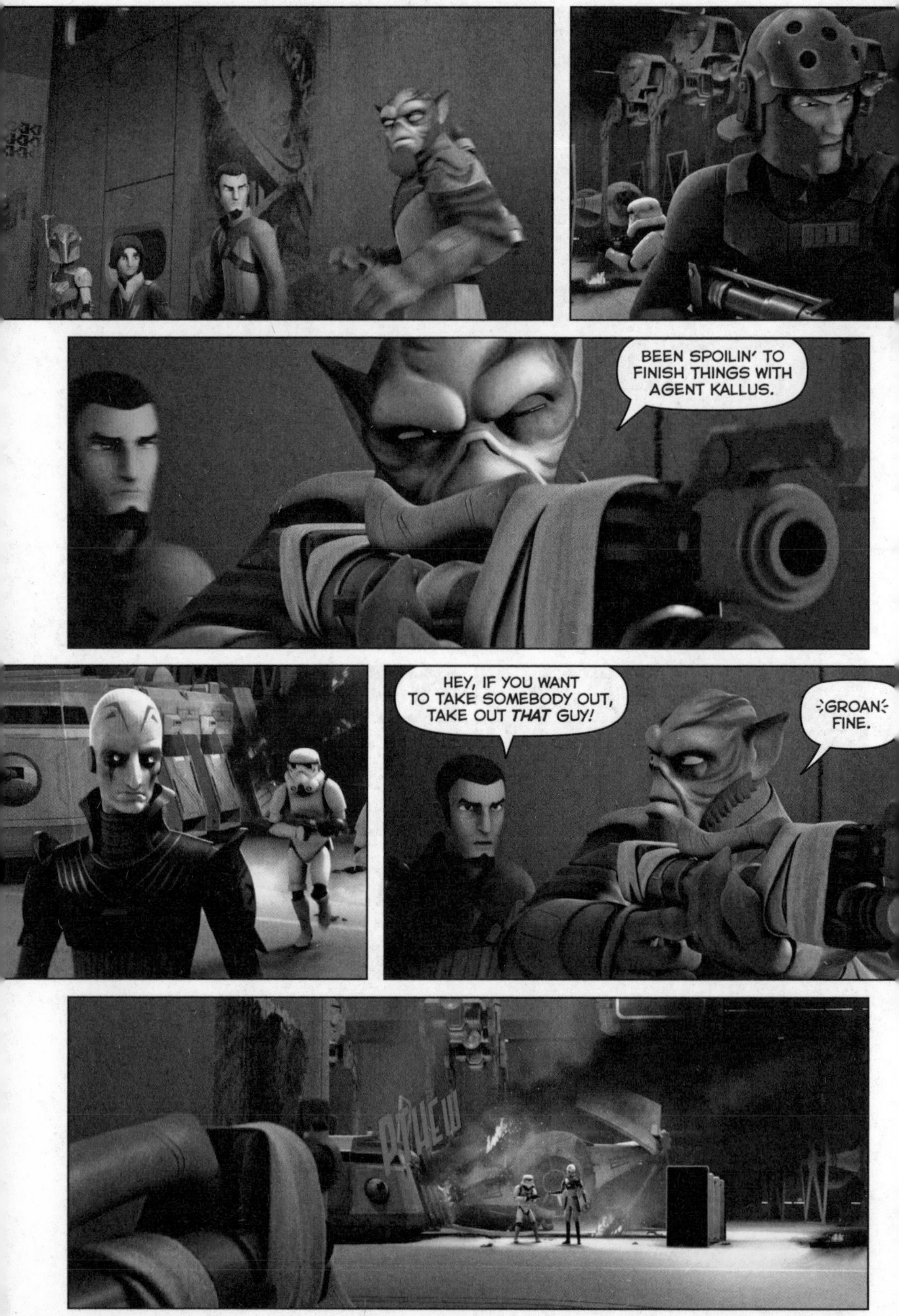
BEEN SPOILIN' TO FINISH THINGS WITH AGENT KALLUS.
HEY, IF YOU WANT TO TAKE SOMEBODY OUT, TAKE OUT *THAT* GUY!
GROAN
FINE.

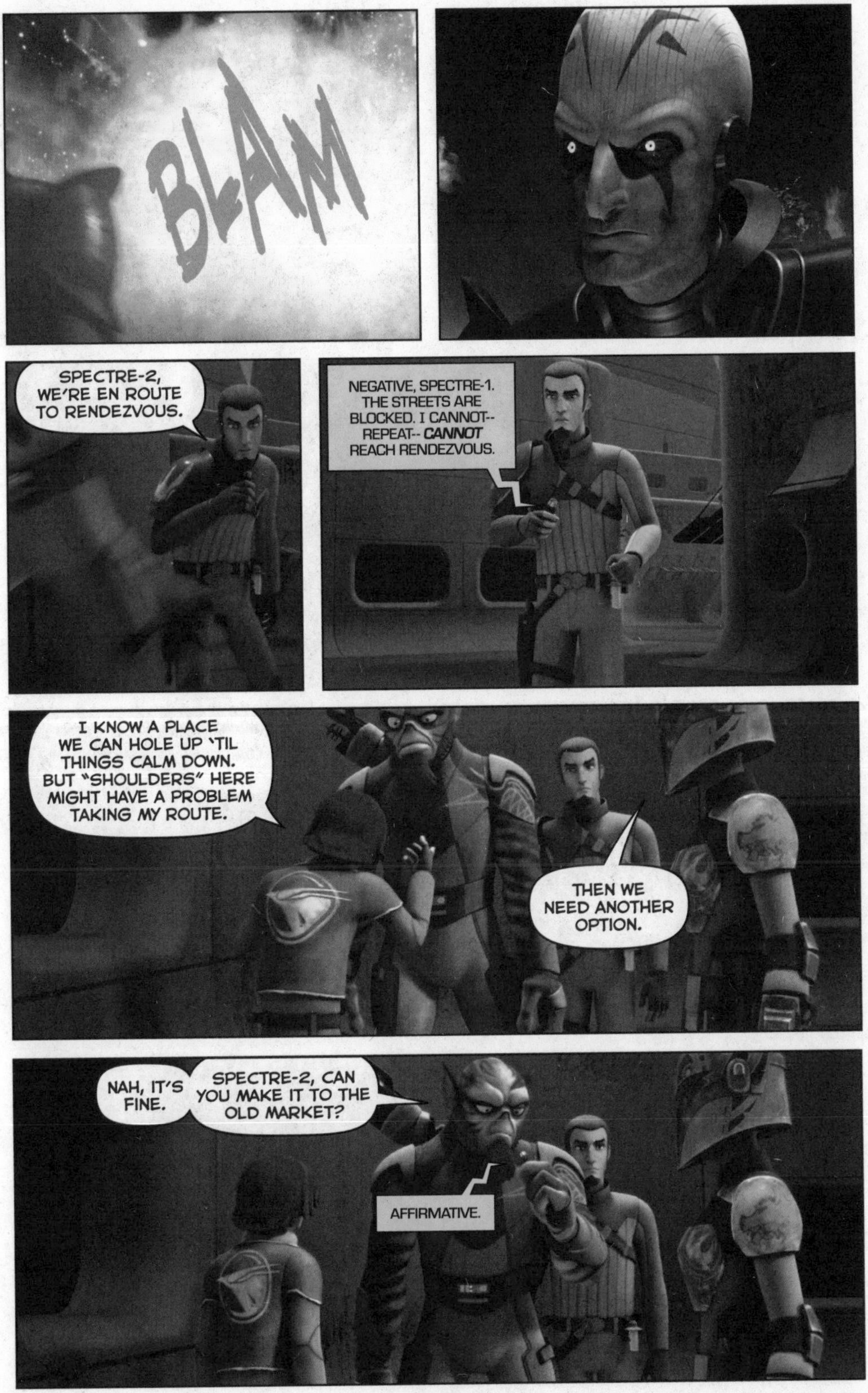
BLAM
SPECTRE-2, WE'RE EN ROUTE TO RENDEZVOUS.
NEGATIVE, SPECTRE-1. THE STREETS ARE BLOCKED. I CANNOT-- REPEAT-- *CANNOT* REACH RENDEZVOUS.
I KNOW A PLACE WE CAN HOLE UP 'TIL THINGS CALM DOWN. BUT "SHOULDERS" HERE MIGHT HAVE A PROBLEM TAKING MY ROUTE.
THEN WE NEED ANOTHER OPTION.
NAH, IT'S FINE.
SPECTRE-2, CAN YOU MAKE IT TO THE OLD MARKET?
AFFIRMATIVE.

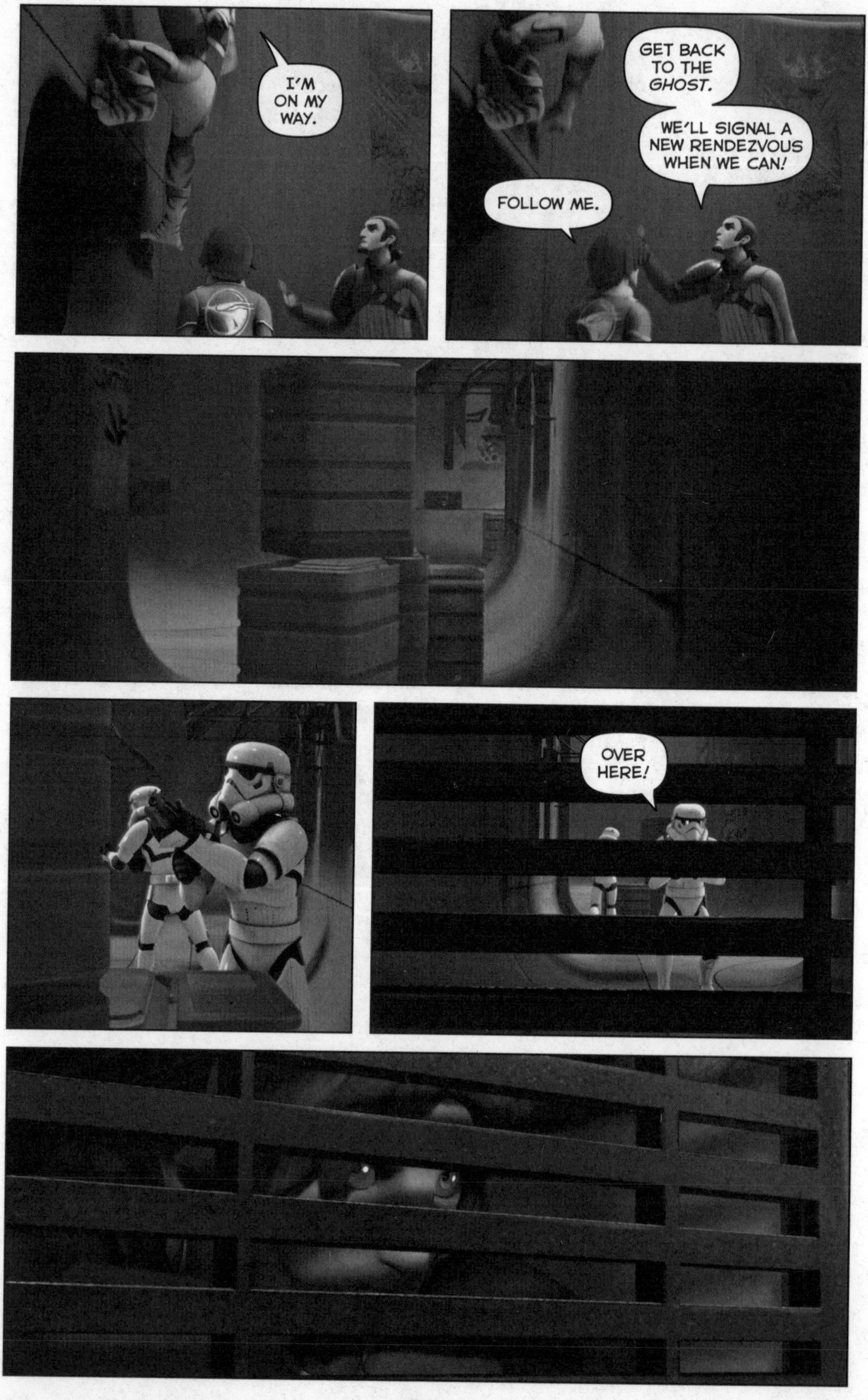
I'M ON MY WAY.
GET BACK TO THE *GHOST*.
WE'LL SIGNAL A NEW RENDEZVOUS WHEN WE CAN!
FOLLOW ME.
OVER HERE!

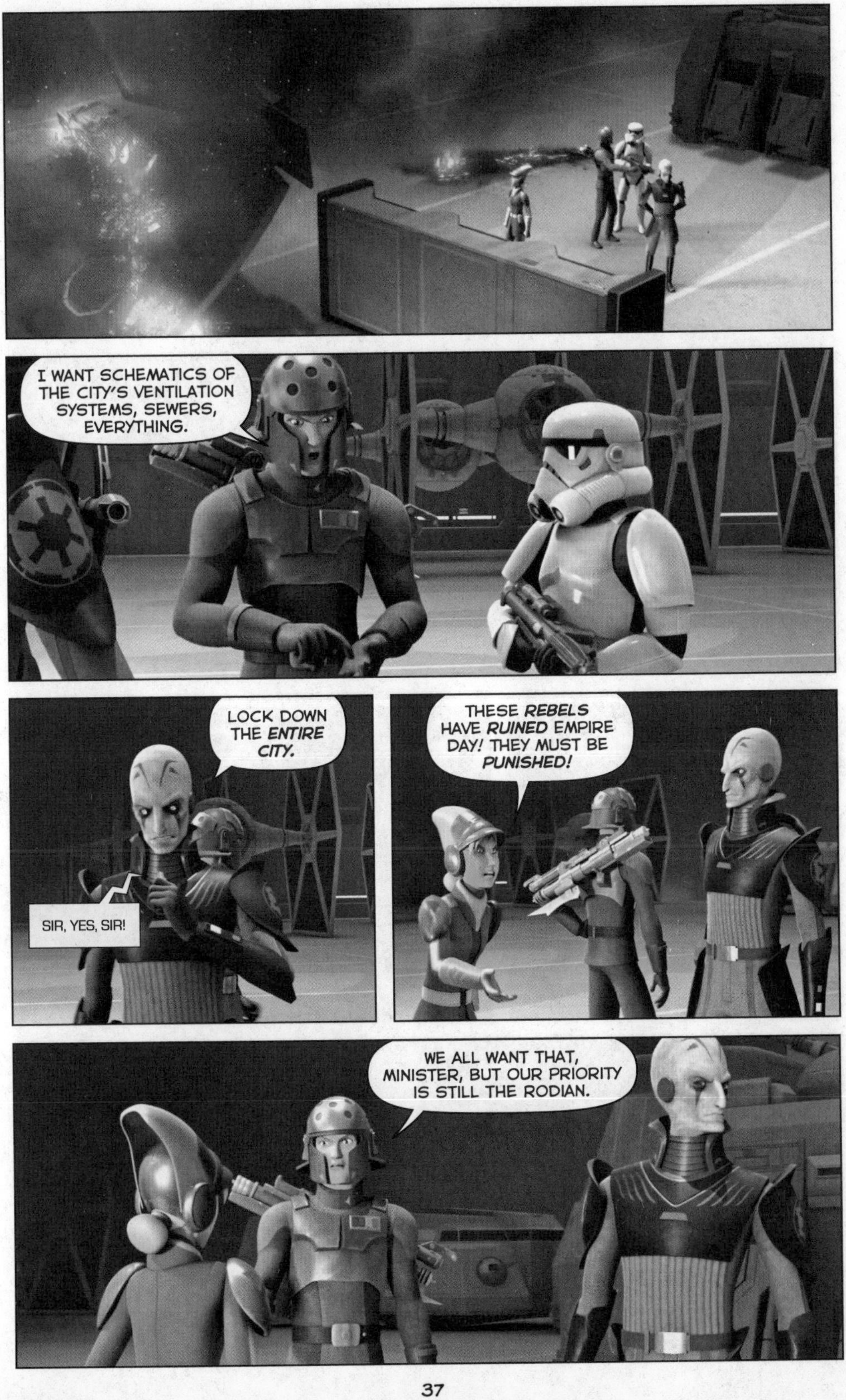

I WANT SCHEMATICS OF THE CITY'S VENTILATION SYSTEMS, SEWERS, EVERYTHING.
LOCK DOWN THE ENTIRE CITY.
SIR, YES, SIR!
THESE REBELS HAVE RUINED EMPIRE DAY! THEY MUST BE PUNISHED!
WE ALL WANT THAT, MINISTER, BUT OUR PRIORITY IS STILL THE RODIAN.

THAT'S AN IMPERIAL
WARNING DECLARING THIS
BUILDING OFF LIMITS. WHAT
IS THIS PLACE?

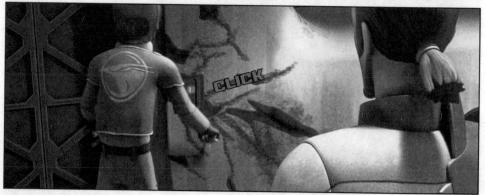

CLICK

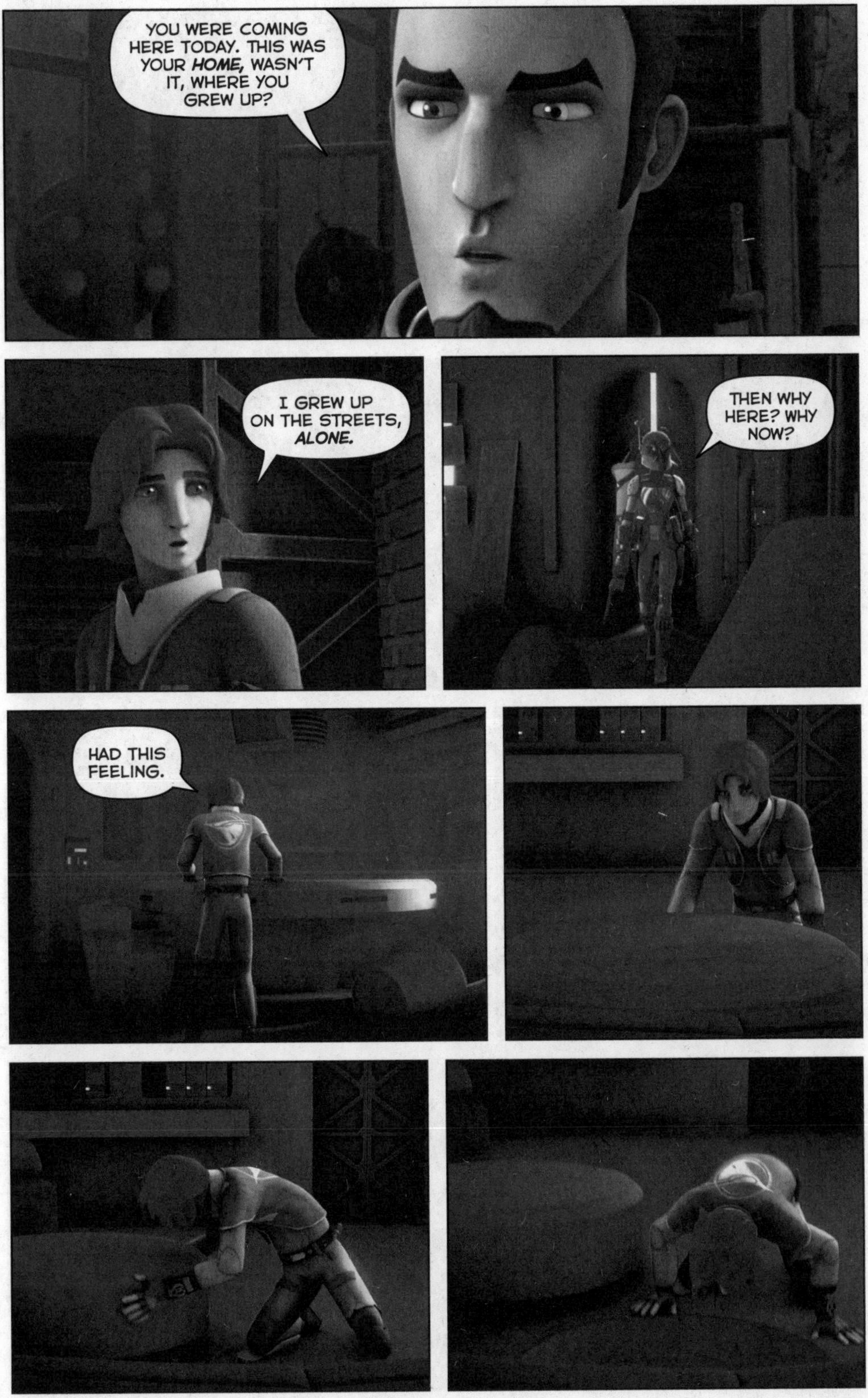
YOU WERE COMING HERE TODAY. THIS WAS YOUR *HOME,* WASN'T IT, WHERE YOU GREW UP?
I GREW UP ON THE STREETS, *ALONE.*
THEN WHY HERE? WHY NOW?
HAD THIS FEELING.

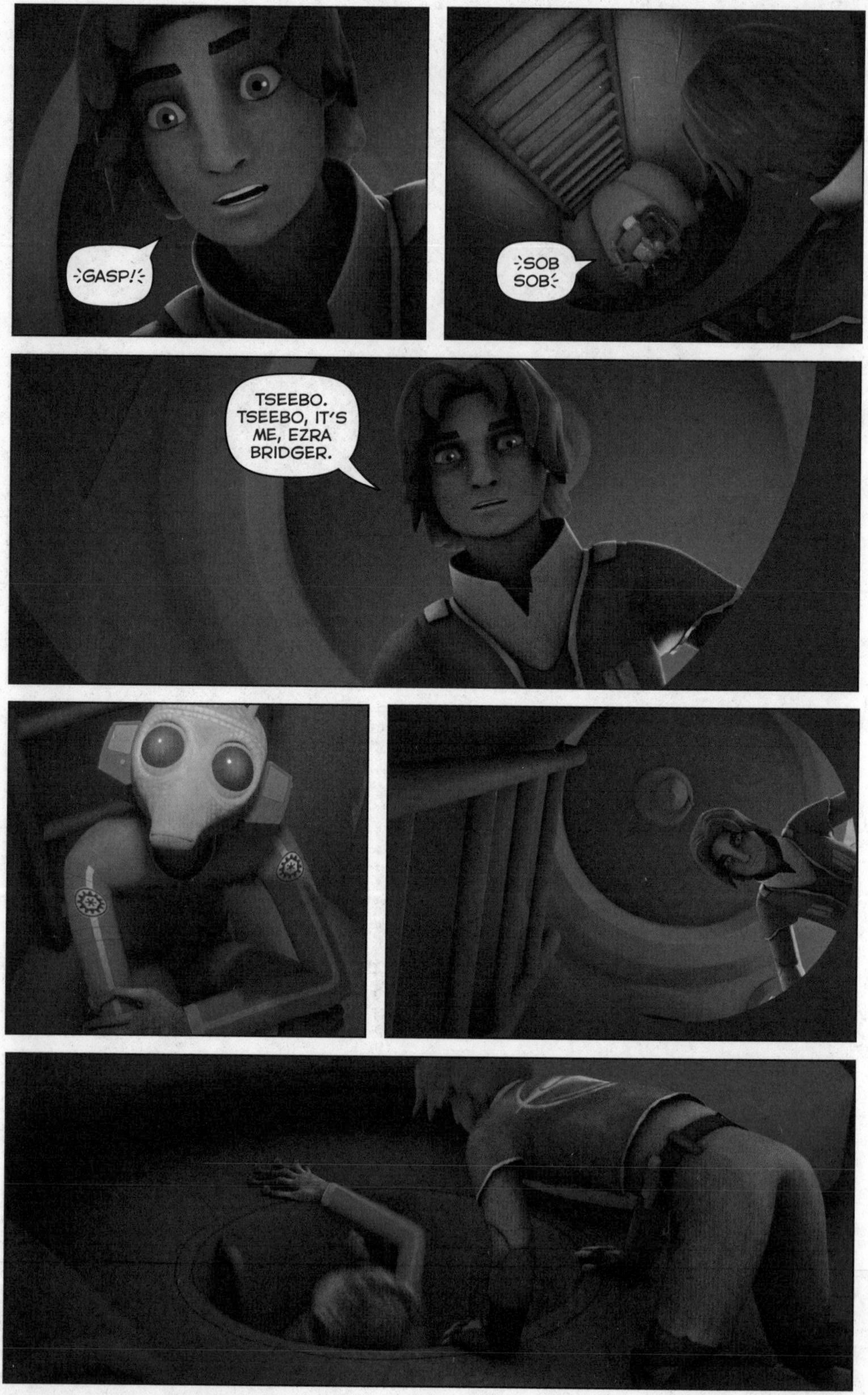
GASP!
SOB SOB
TSEEBO. TSEEBO, IT'S ME, EZRA BRIDGER.

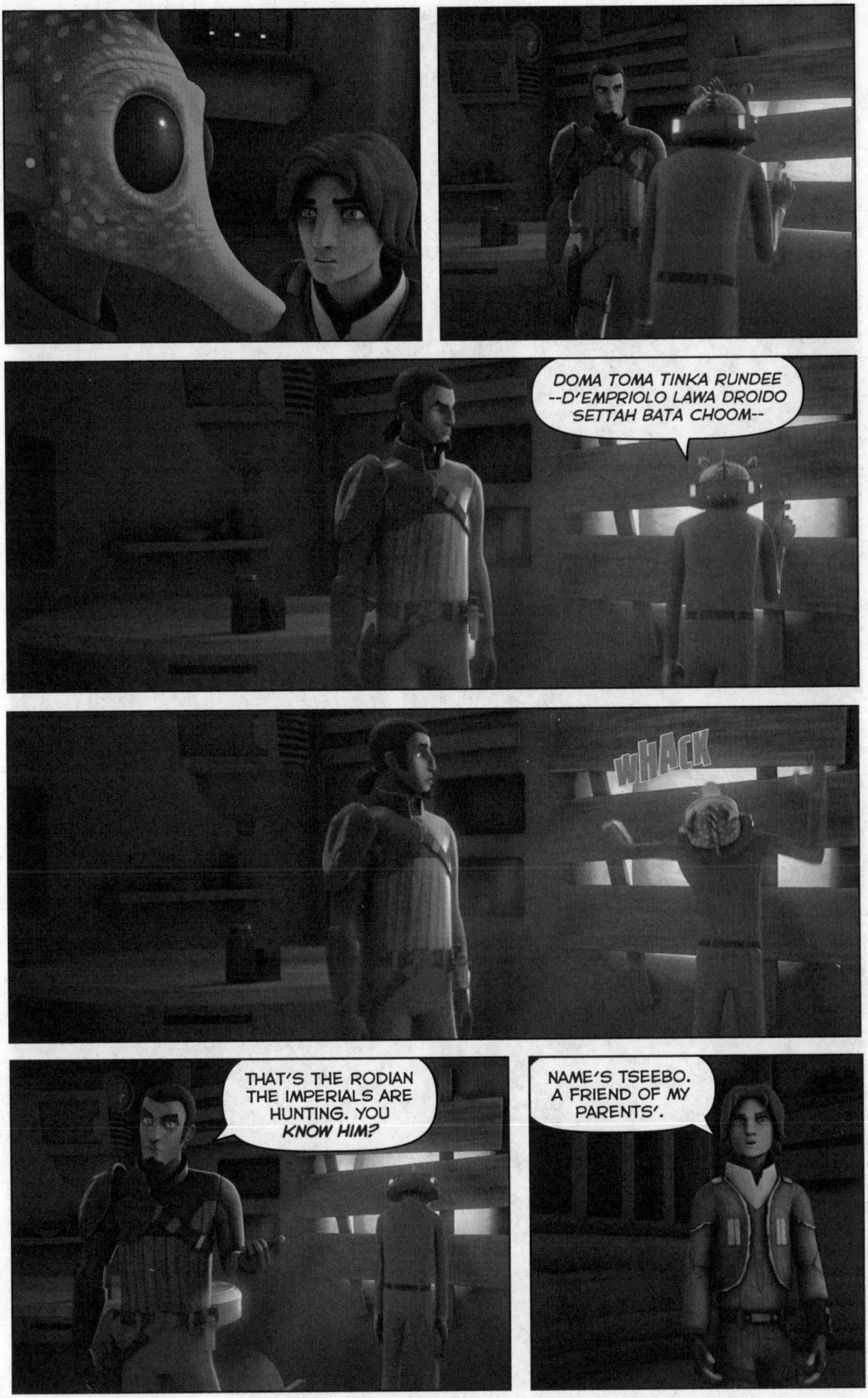
DOMA TOMA TINKA RUNDEE --D'EMPRIOLO LAWA DROIDO SETTAH BATA CHOOM--
WHACK
THAT'S THE RODIAN THE IMPERIALS ARE HUNTING. YOU *KNOW HIM?*
NAME'S TSEEBO. A FRIEND OF MY PARENTS'.

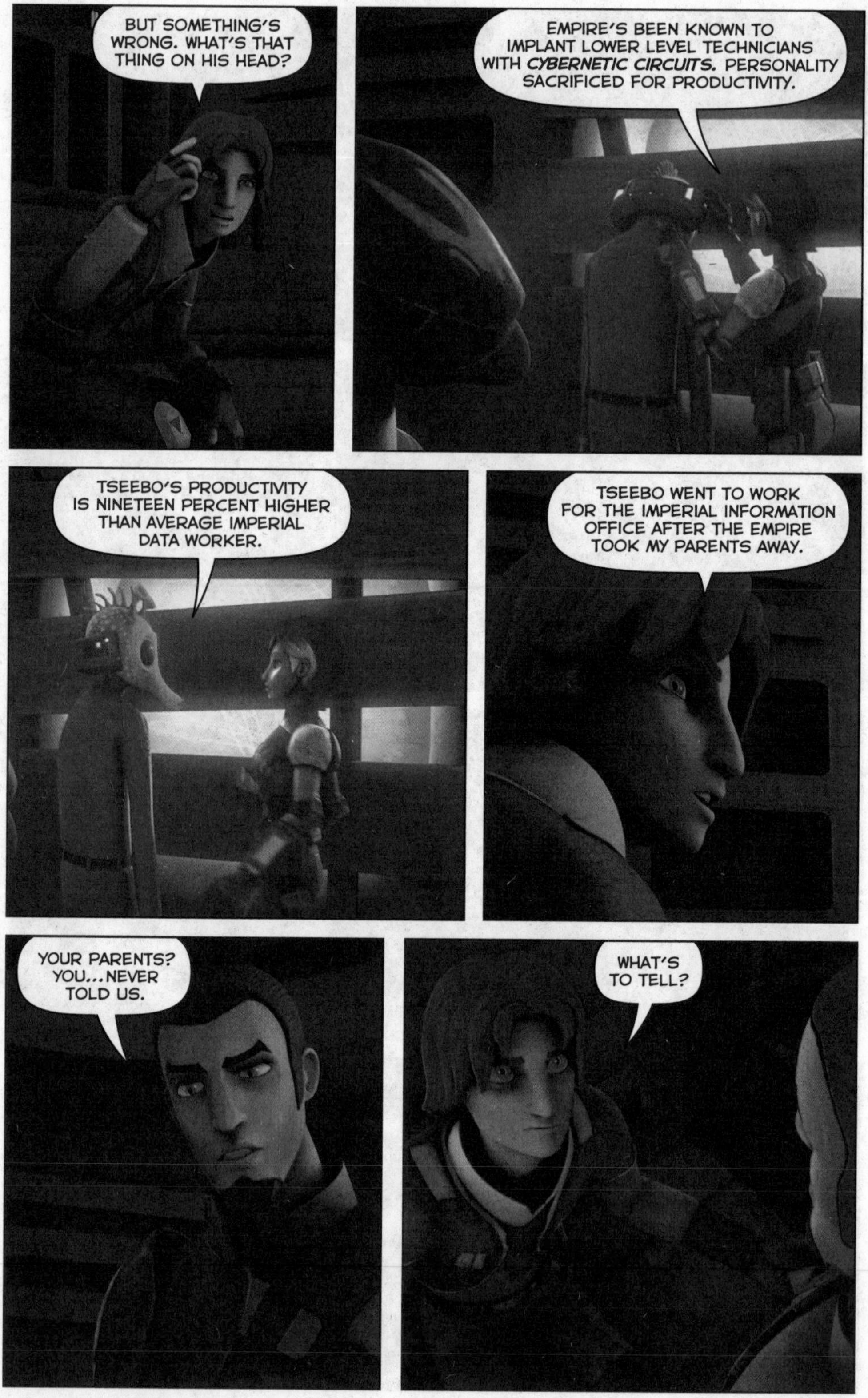
BUT SOMETHING'S WRONG. WHAT'S THAT THING ON HIS HEAD?
EMPIRE'S BEEN KNOWN TO IMPLANT LOWER LEVEL TECHNICIANS WITH *CYBERNETIC CIRCUITS.* PERSONALITY SACRIFICED FOR PRODUCTIVITY.
TSEEBO'S PRODUCTIVITY IS NINETEEN PERCENT HIGHER THAN AVERAGE IMPERIAL DATA WORKER.
TSEEBO WENT TO WORK FOR THE IMPERIAL INFORMATION OFFICE AFTER THE EMPIRE TOOK MY PARENTS AWAY.
YOUR PARENTS? YOU...NEVER TOLD US.
WHAT'S TO TELL?

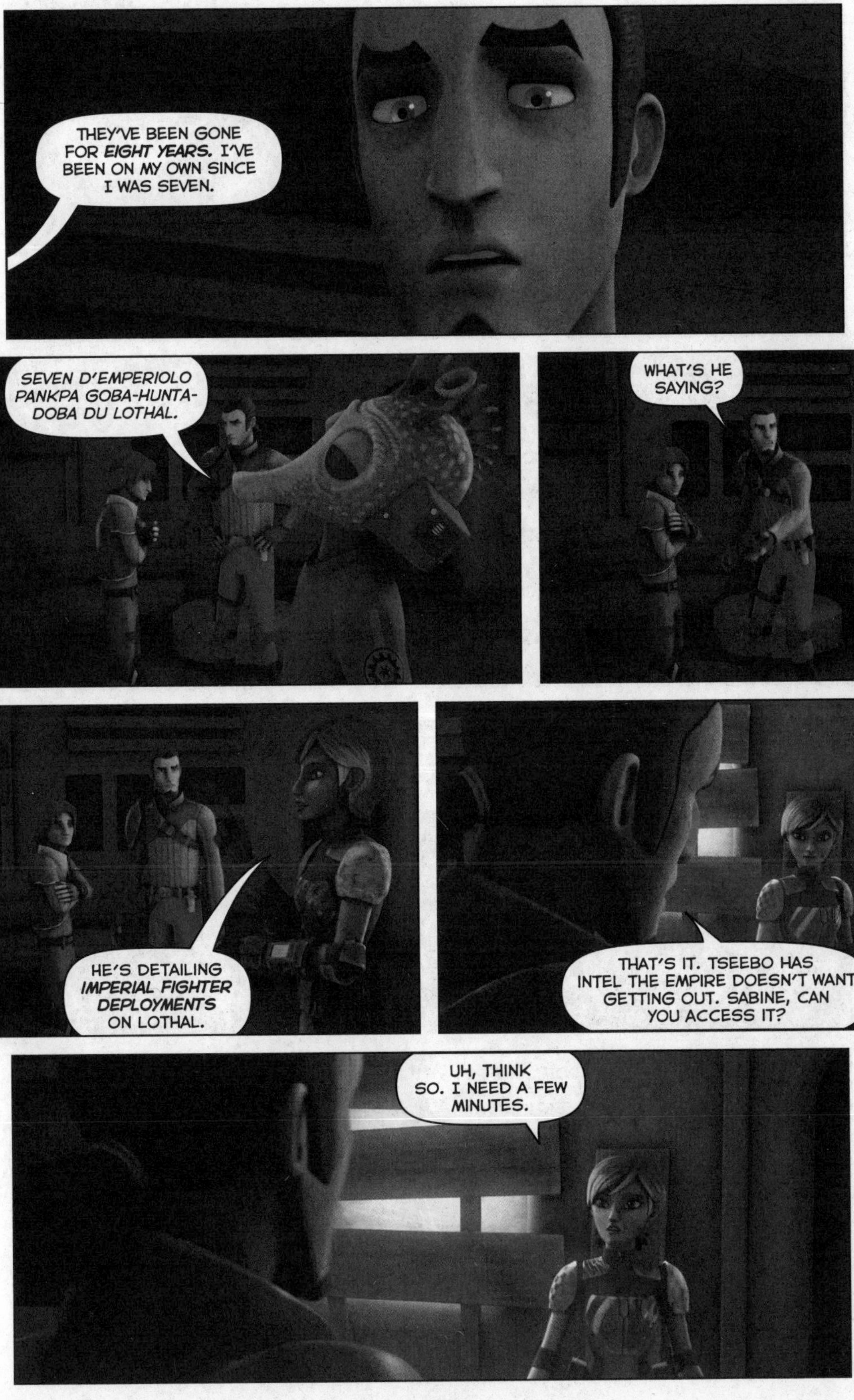
THEY'VE BEEN GONE FOR EIGHT YEARS. I'VE BEEN ON MY OWN SINCE I WAS SEVEN.
SEVEN D'EMPERIOLO PANKPA GOBA-HUNTA-DOBA DU LOTHAL.
WHAT'S HE SAYING?
HE'S DETAILING IMPERIAL FIGHTER DEPLOYMENTS ON LOTHAL.
THAT'S IT. TSEEBO HAS INTEL THE EMPIRE DOESN'T WANT GETTING OUT. SABINE, CAN YOU ACCESS IT?
UH, THINK SO. I NEED A FEW MINUTES.

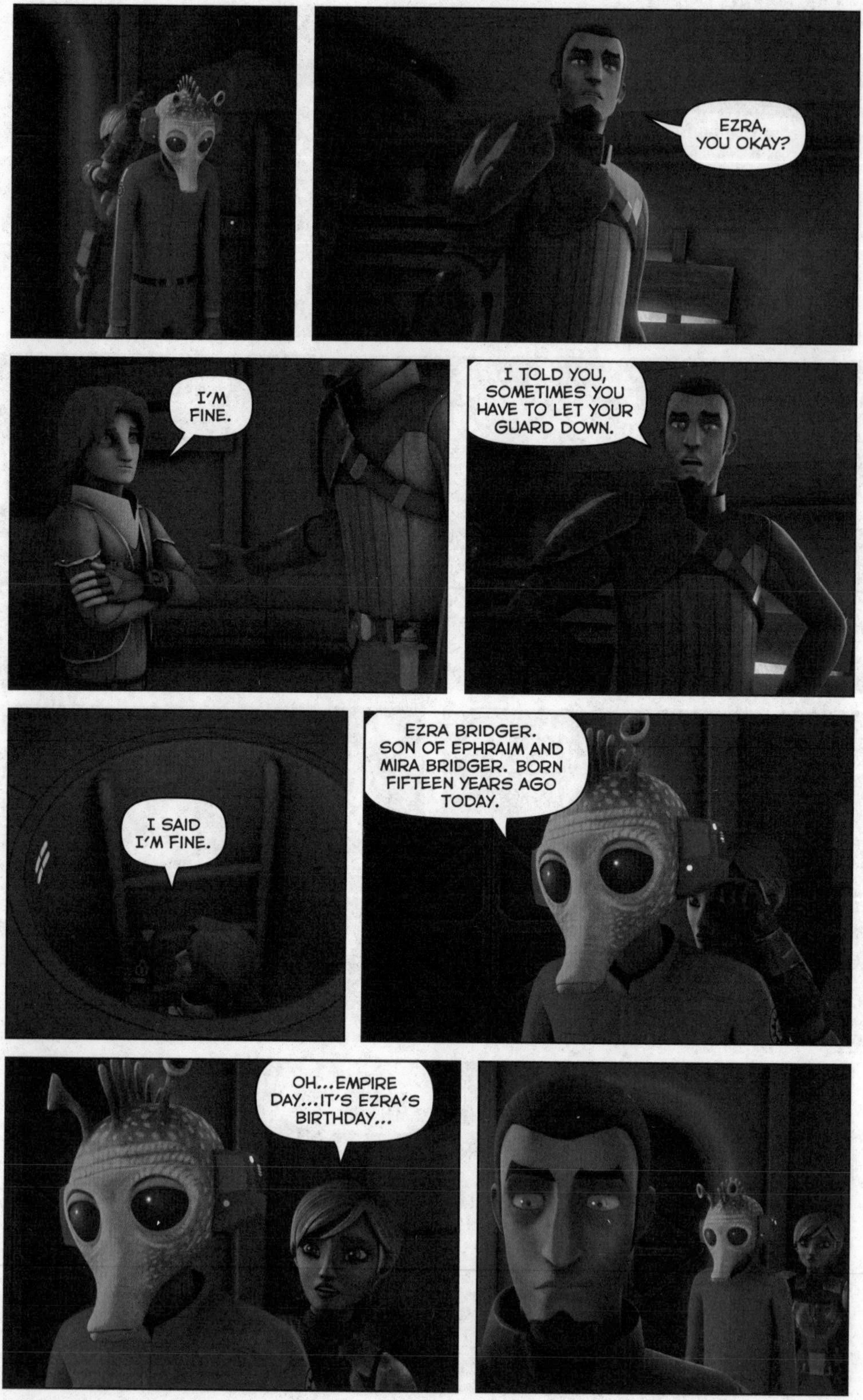
EZRA, YOU OKAY?
I'M FINE.
I TOLD YOU, SOMETIMES YOU HAVE TO LET YOUR GUARD DOWN.
I SAID I'M FINE.
EZRA BRIDGER. SON OF EPHRAIM AND MIRA BRIDGER. BORN FIFTEEN YEARS AGO TODAY.
OH...EMPIRE DAY...IT'S EZRA'S BIRTHDAY...

THE RISK YOU BRIDGERS TAKE. TSEEBO SAY YOU MUST THINK OF YOUR SON.

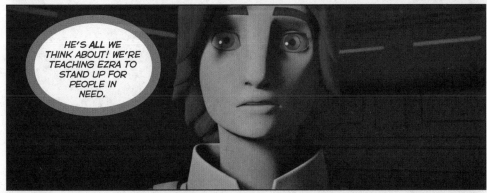

HE'S ALL WE THINK ABOUT! WE'RE TEACHING EZRA TO STAND UP FOR PEOPLE IN NEED.

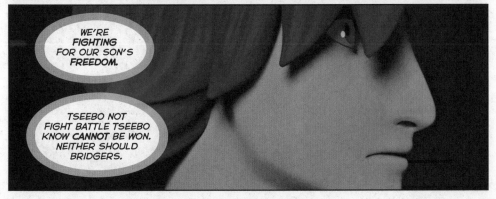

WE'RE **FIGHTING** FOR OUR SON'S **FREEDOM**.

TSEEBO NOT FIGHT BATTLE TSEEBO KNOW **CANNOT** BE WON. NEITHER SHOULD BRIDGERS.

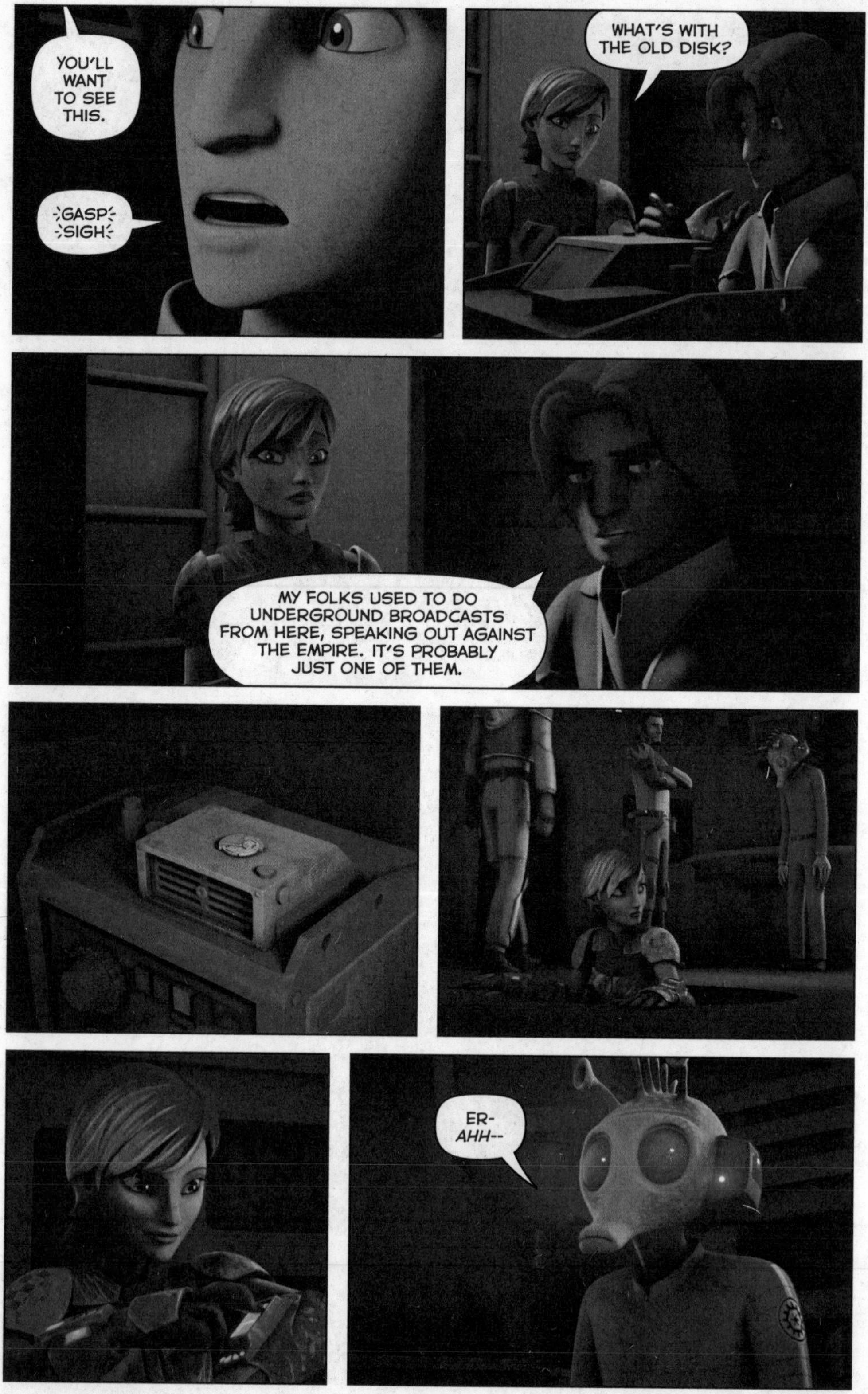
YOU'LL WANT TO SEE THIS.
:GASP: :SIGH:
WHAT'S WITH THE OLD DISK?
MY FOLKS USED TO DO UNDERGROUND BROADCASTS FROM HERE, SPEAKING OUT AGAINST THE EMPIRE. IT'S PROBABLY JUST ONE OF THEM.
ER- AHH--

WHAT ARE WE LOOKING AT?

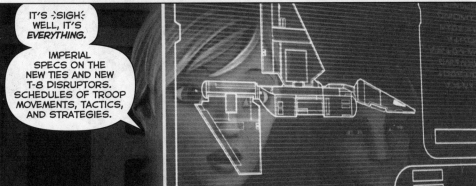

IT'S ⊰SIGH⊱ WELL, IT'S *EVERYTHING.*

IMPERIAL SPECS ON THE NEW TIES AND NEW T-8 DISRUPTORS. SCHEDULES OF TROOP MOVEMENTS, TACTICS, AND STRATEGIES.

HALF OF IT'S ENCRYPTED, BUT IT LOOKS LIKE THERE'S A FIVE-YEAR PLAN FOR LOTHAL AND EVERY OTHER WORLD IN THE OUTER RIM.

NO WONDER HIS BRAIN'S SHORTING OUT--ALL THAT DATA'D OVERLOAD ANYONE.

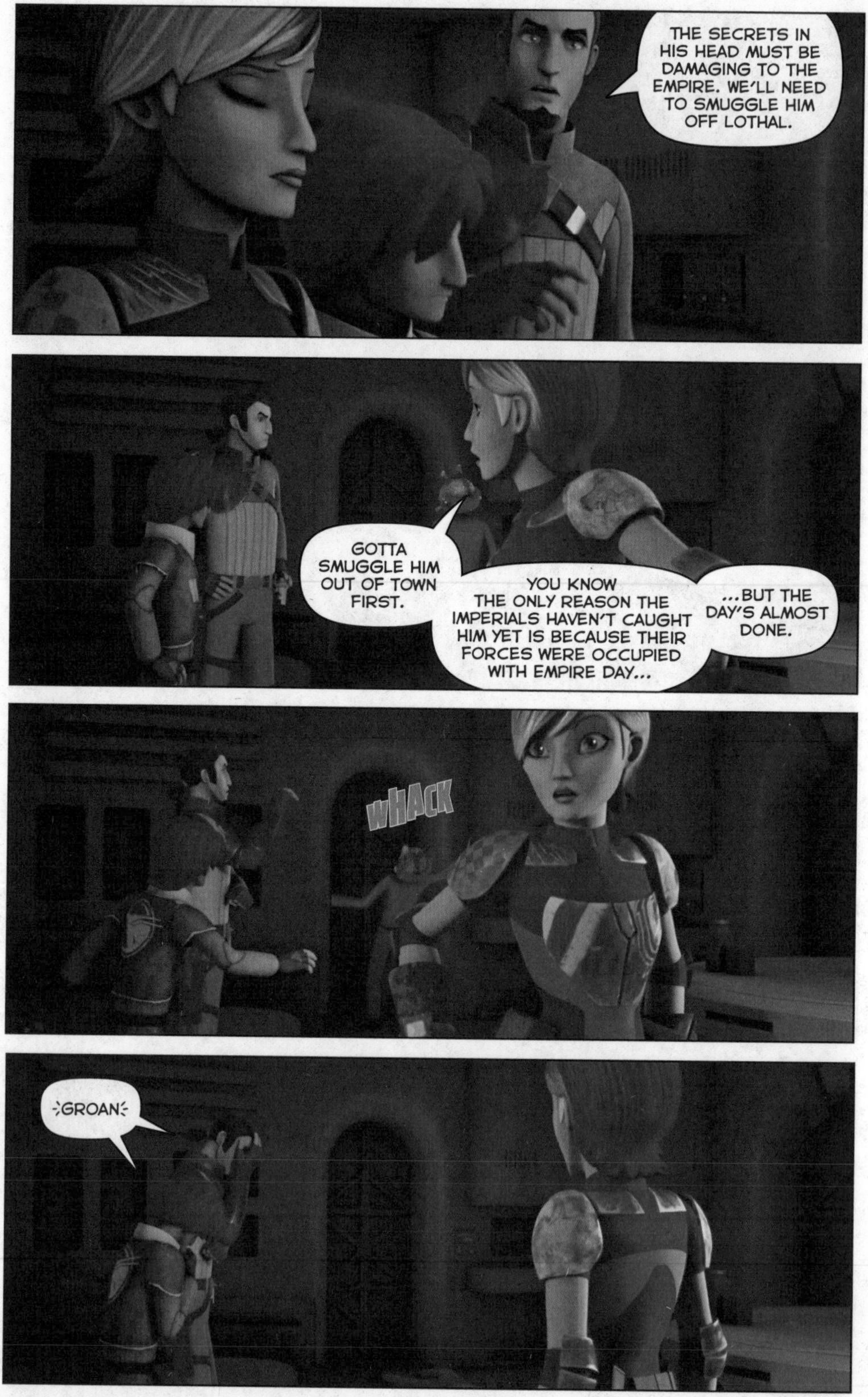
THE SECRETS IN HIS HEAD MUST BE DAMAGING TO THE EMPIRE. WE'LL NEED TO SMUGGLE HIM OFF LOTHAL.
GOTTA SMUGGLE HIM OUT OF TOWN FIRST.
YOU KNOW THE ONLY REASON THE IMPERIALS HAVEN'T CAUGHT HIM YET IS BECAUSE THEIR FORCES WERE OCCUPIED WITH EMPIRE DAY...
...BUT THE DAY'S ALMOST DONE.
WHACK
GROAN

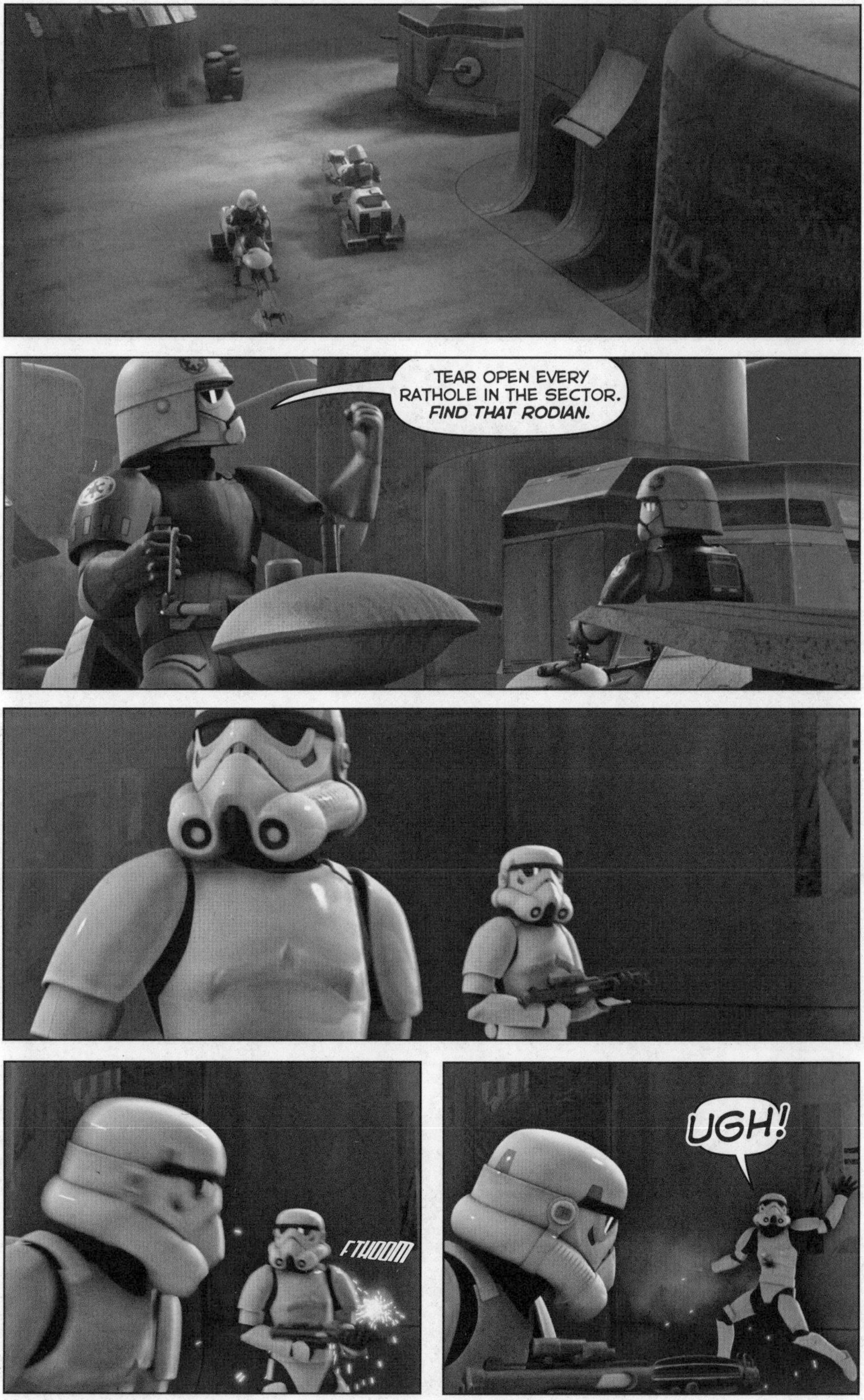
TEAR OPEN EVERY RATHOLE IN THE SECTOR. *FIND THAT RODIAN.*
FTHOOM
UGH!

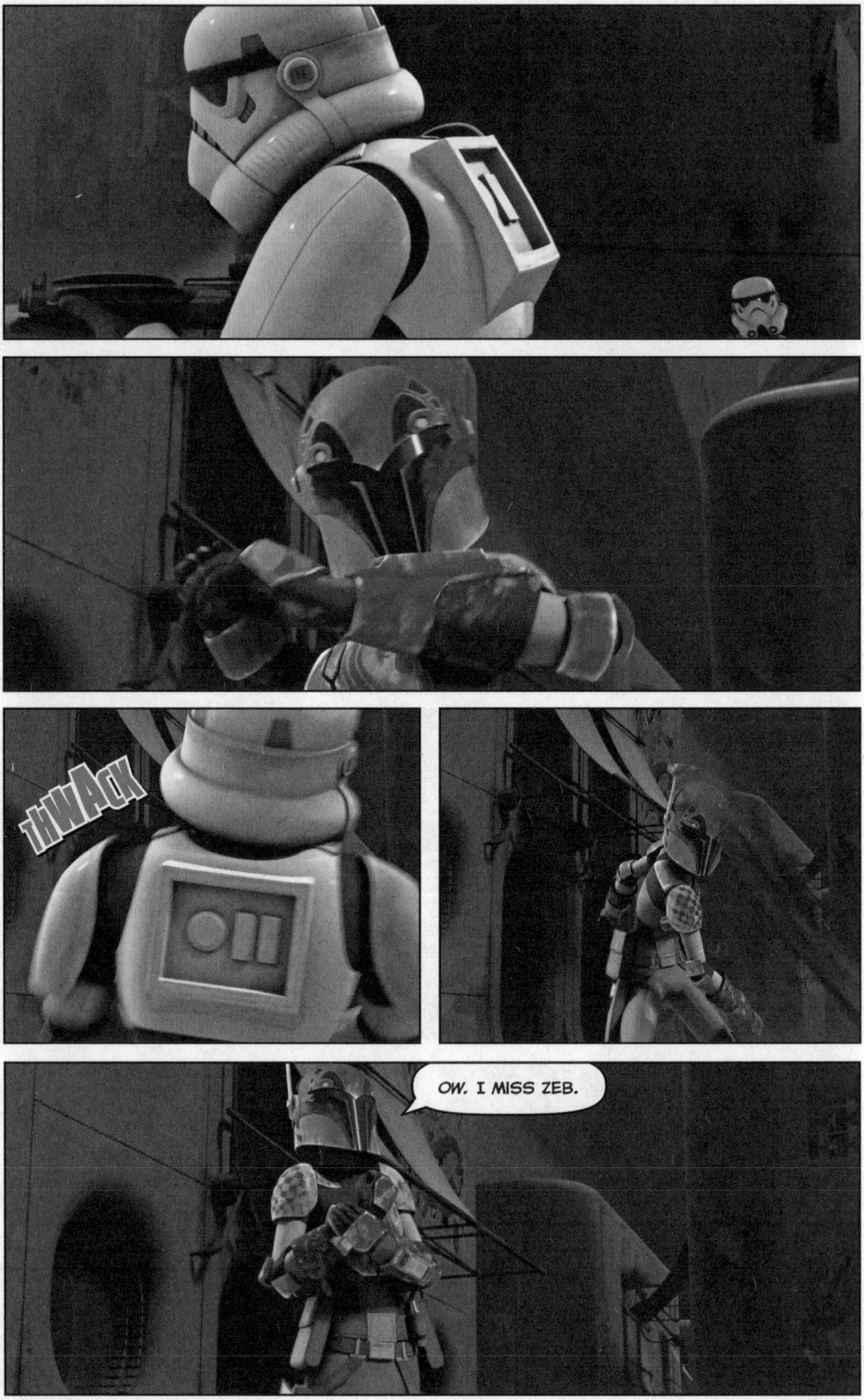
THWACK
OW. I MISS ZEB.

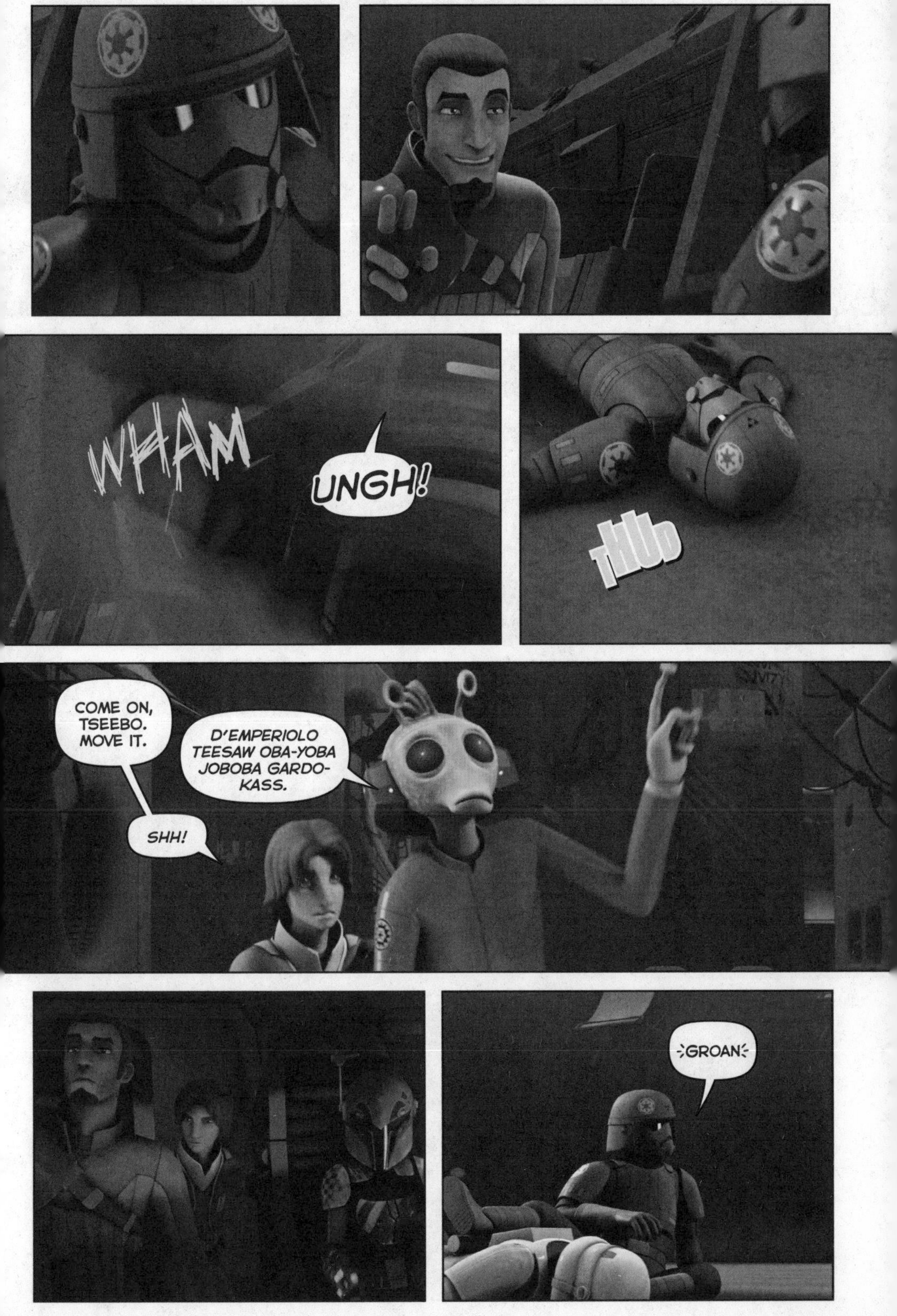
WHAM
UNGH!
THUD
COME ON, TSEEBO. MOVE IT.
D'EMPERIOLO TEESAW OBA-YOBA JOBOBA GARDO-KASS.
SHH!
GROAN

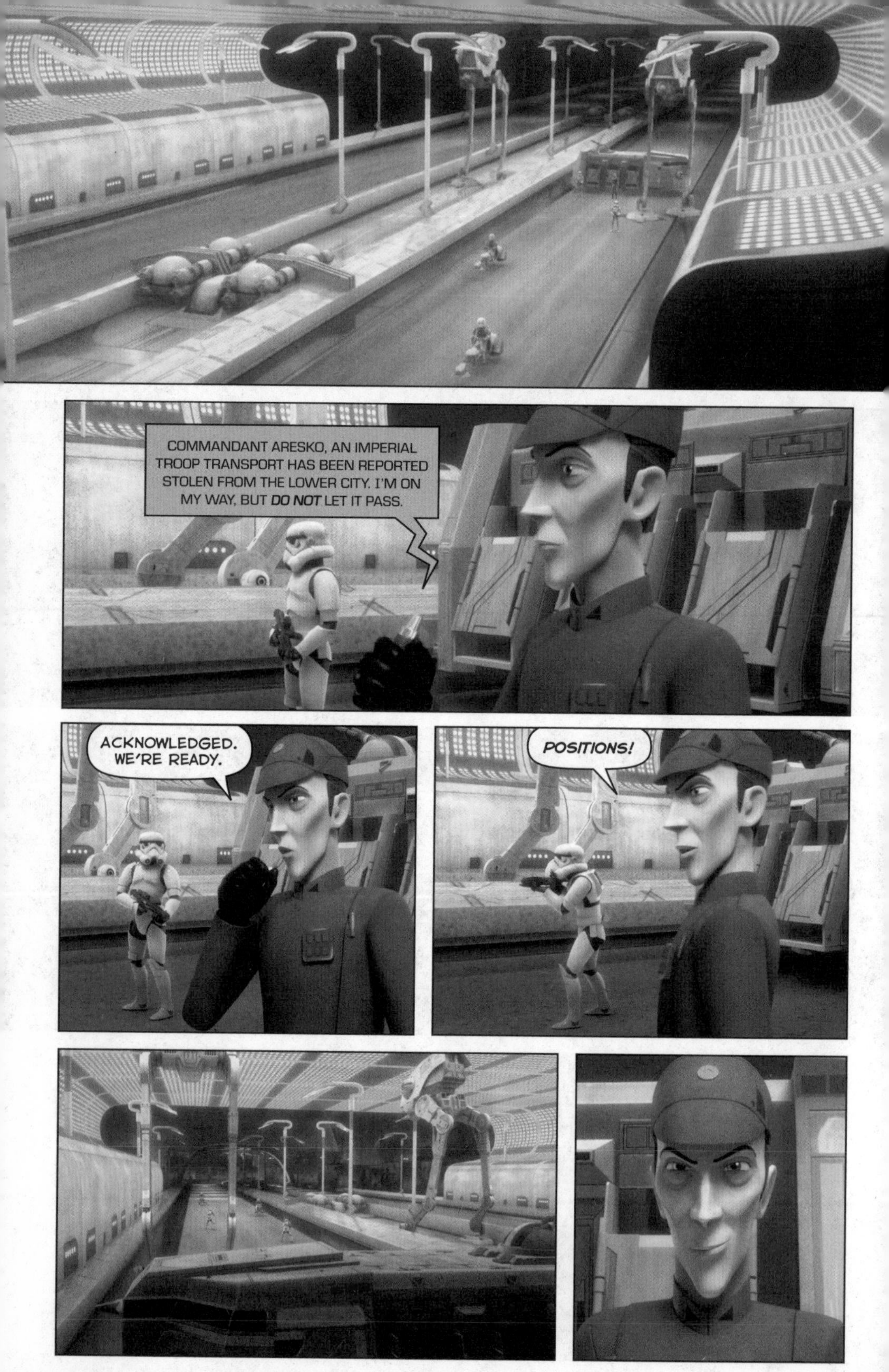
COMMANDANT ARESKO, AN IMPERIAL TROOP TRANSPORT HAS BEEN REPORTED STOLEN FROM THE LOWER CITY. I'M ON MY WAY, BUT DO NOT LET IT PASS.
ACKNOWLEDGED. WE'RE READY.
POSITIONS!

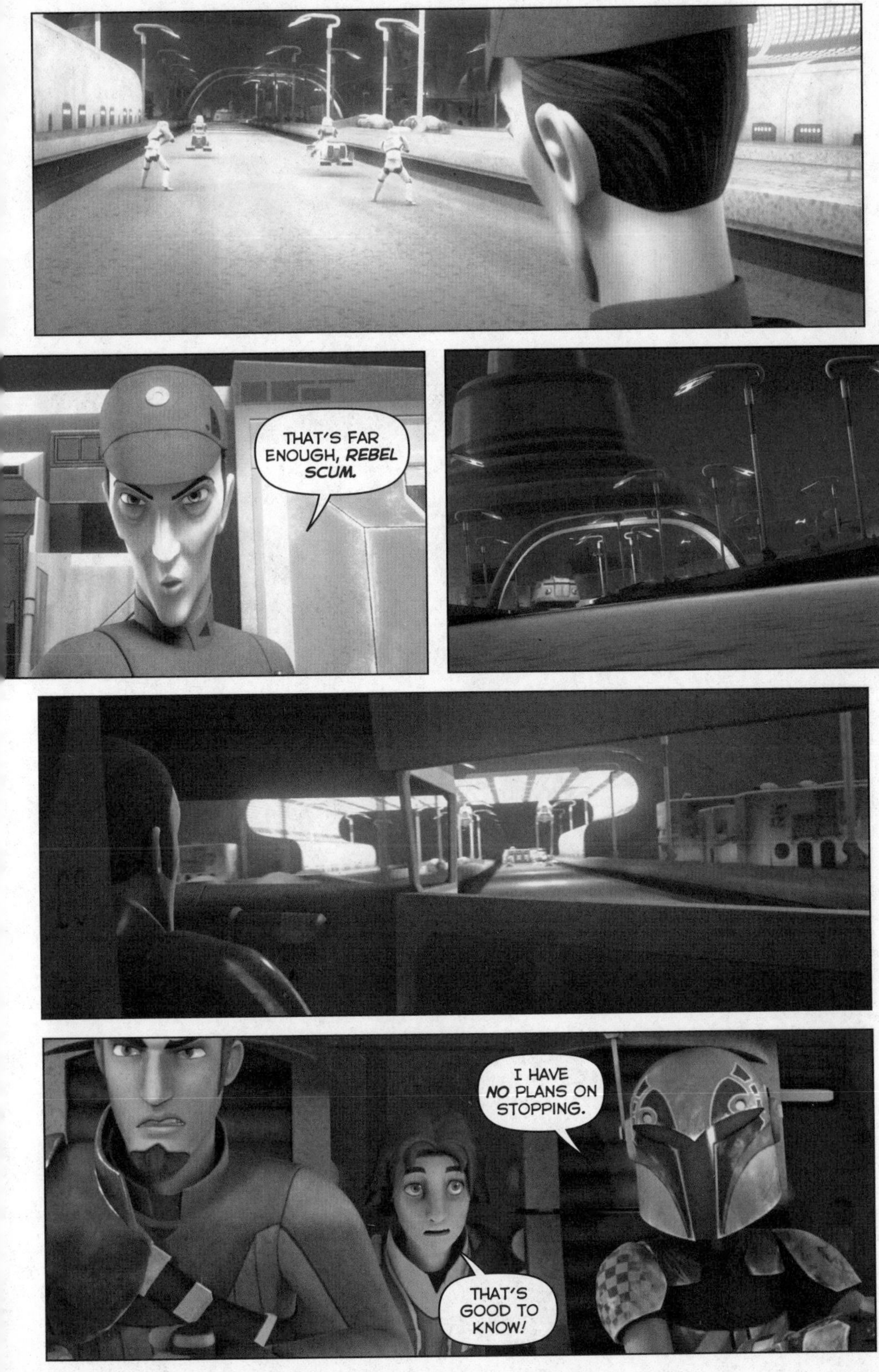
THAT'S FAR ENOUGH, *REBEL SCUM.*
I HAVE *NO* PLANS ON STOPPING.
THAT'S GOOD TO KNOW!

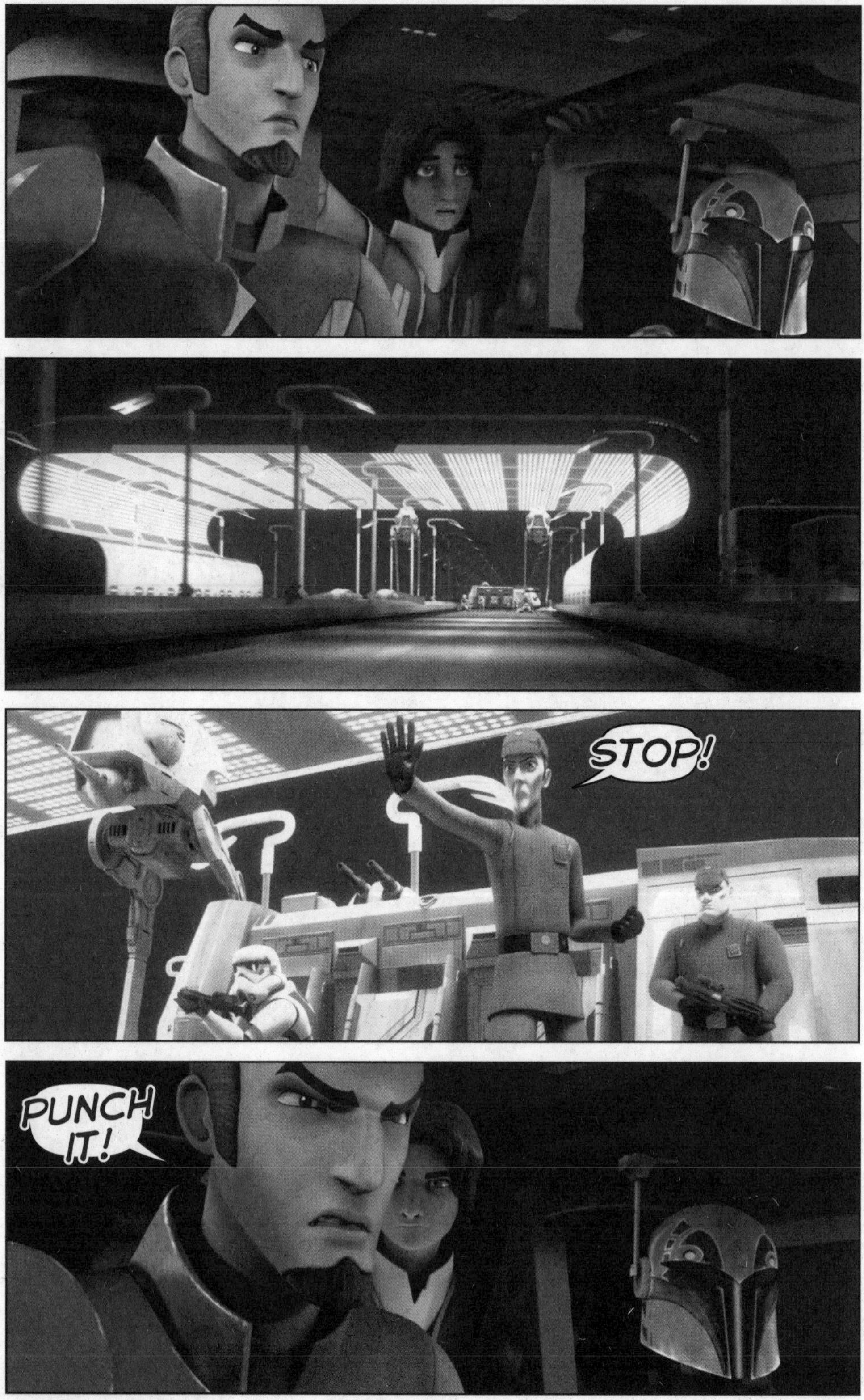
STOP!
PUNCH IT!

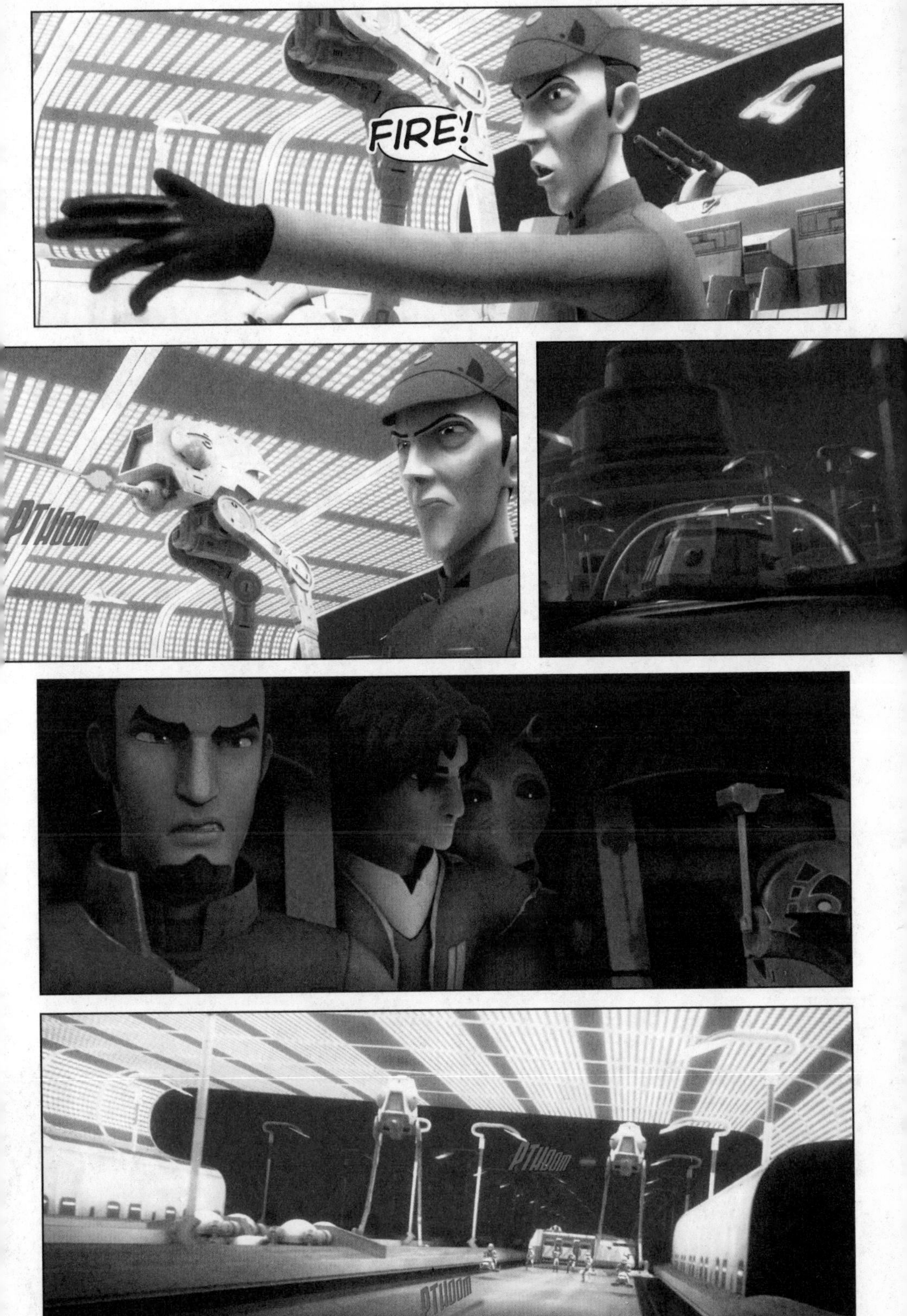
FIRE!
PTUOOM
PTUOOM
PTUOOM

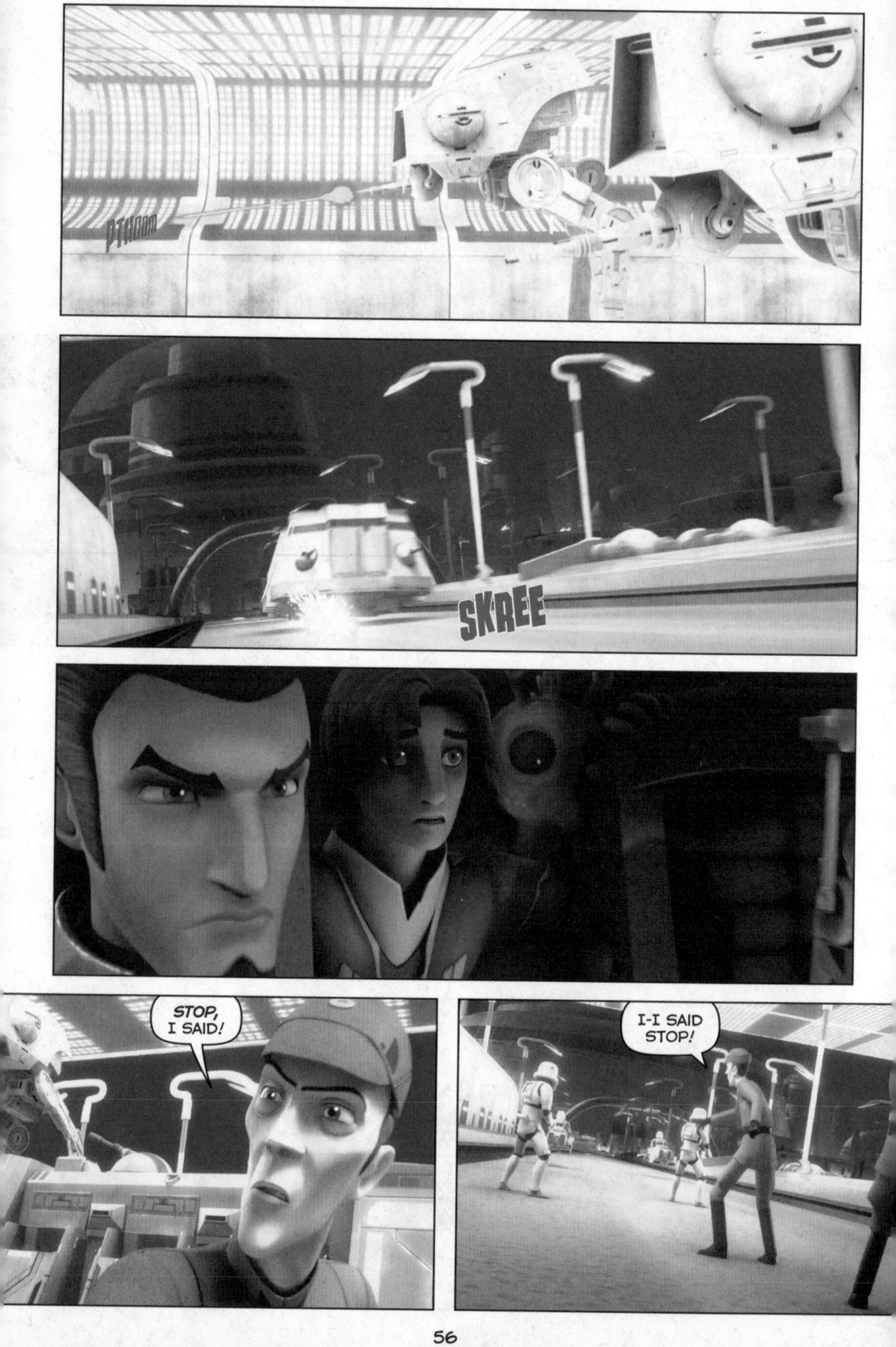
PTHOOM
SKREE
STOP, I SAID!
I-I SAID STOP!

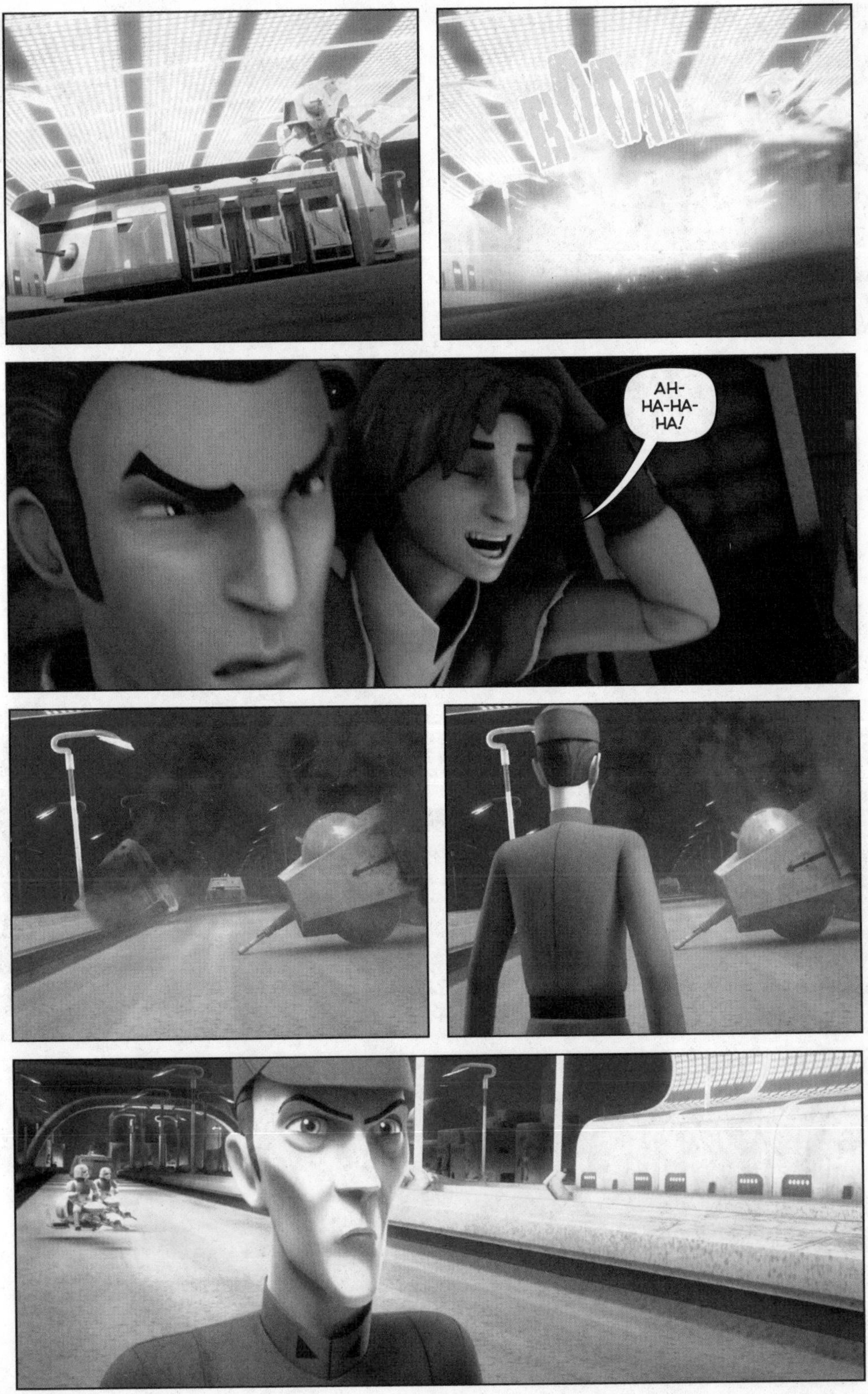
BOOM
AH-HA-HA-HA!

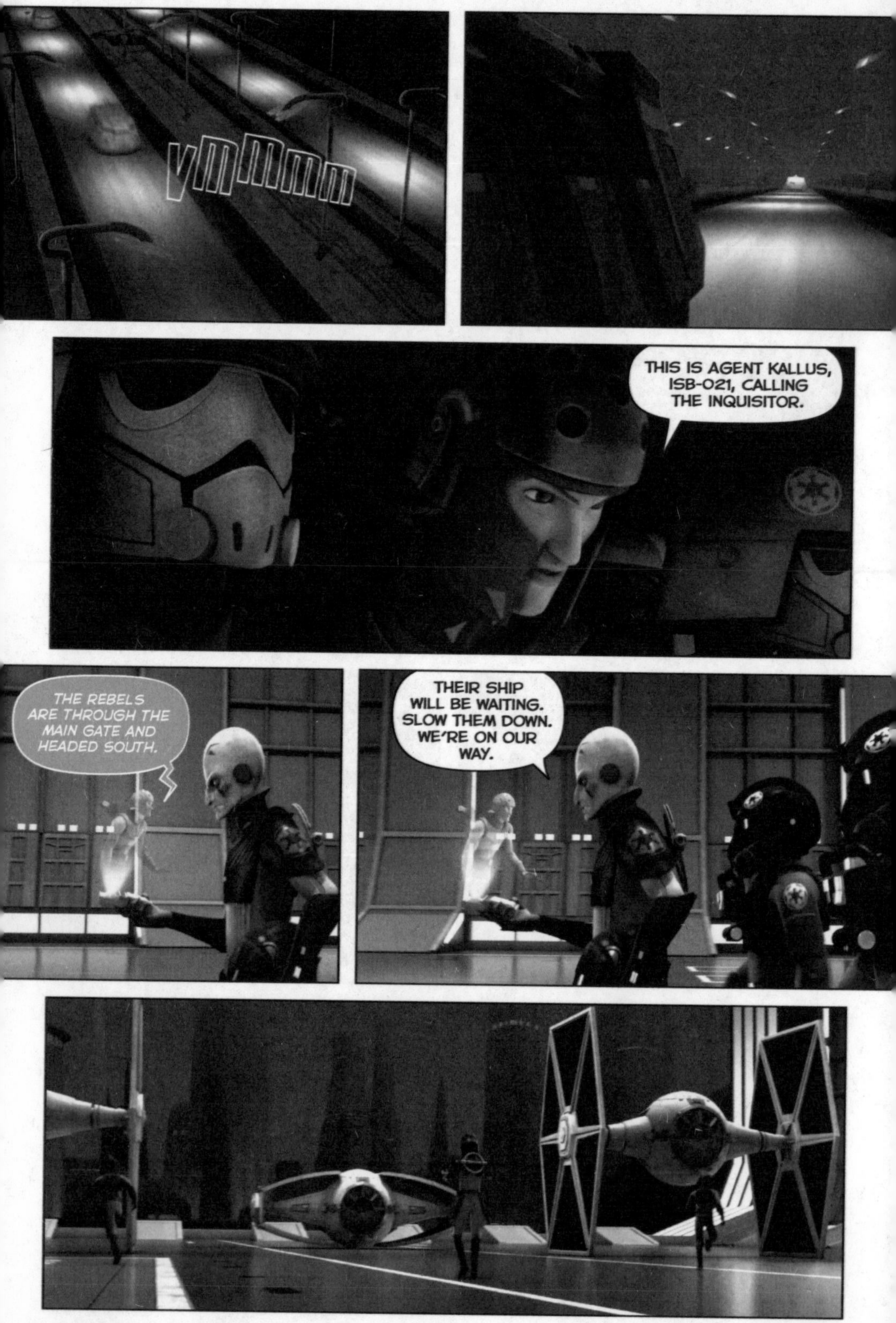
VMMMMM
THIS IS AGENT KALLUS, ISB-021, CALLING THE INQUISITOR.
THE REBELS ARE THROUGH THE MAIN GATE AND HEADED SOUTH.
THEIR SHIP WILL BE WAITING. SLOW THEM DOWN. WE'RE ON OUR WAY.

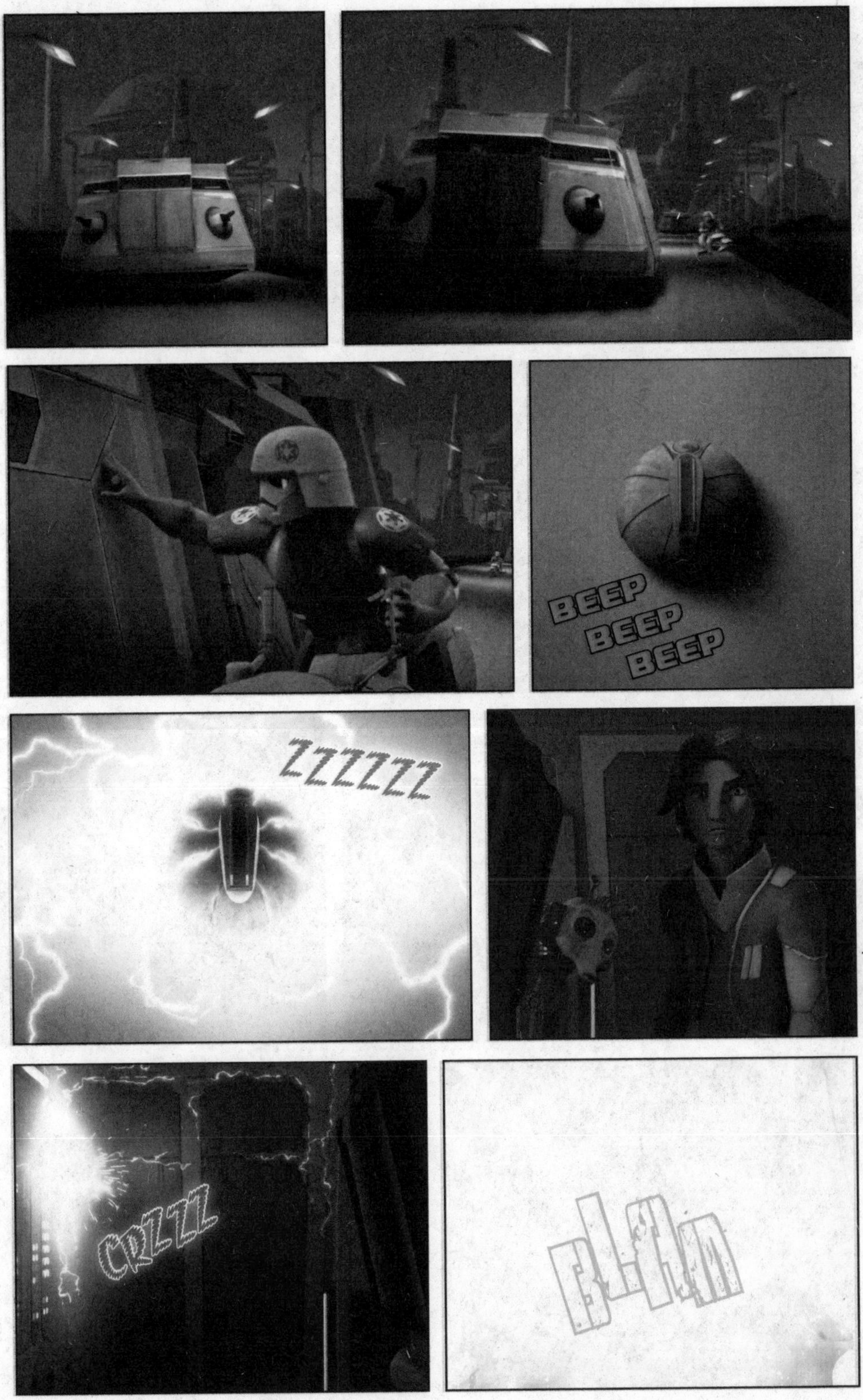
BEEP
BEEP
BEEP
ZZZZZZ
CRZZZ
BLAM

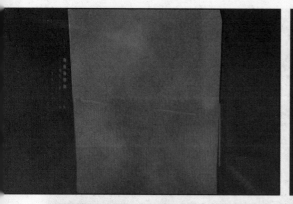

HYAH!

‹UNGH!›

THE RODIAN!

RRGH!

UGH--

WHAM

THUNK

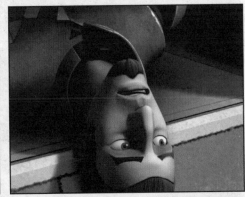

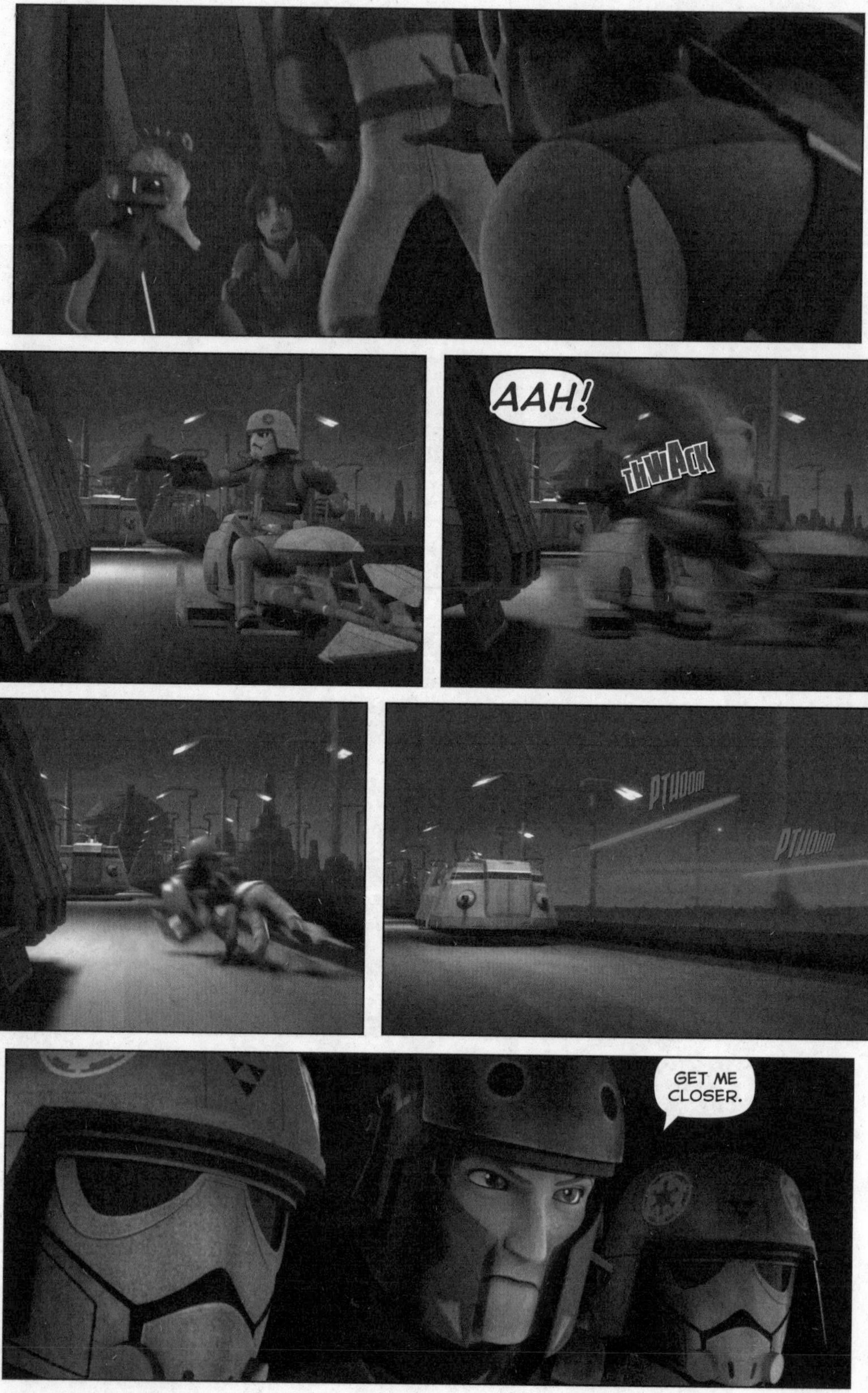
AAH!
THWACK
PTHOOM
PTHOOM
GET ME CLOSER.

BAM
BAM
WHUNK
OOF!

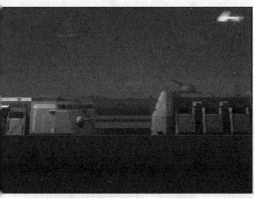

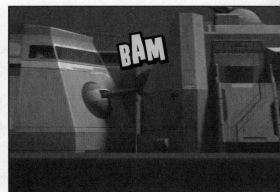

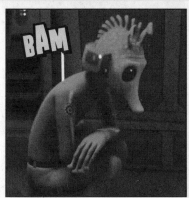

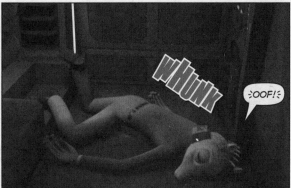

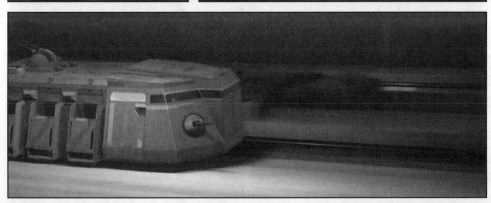

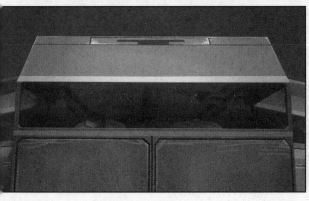

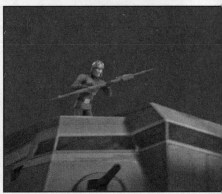

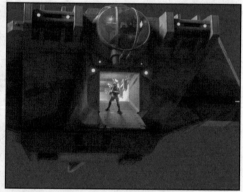

REMEMBER ME?

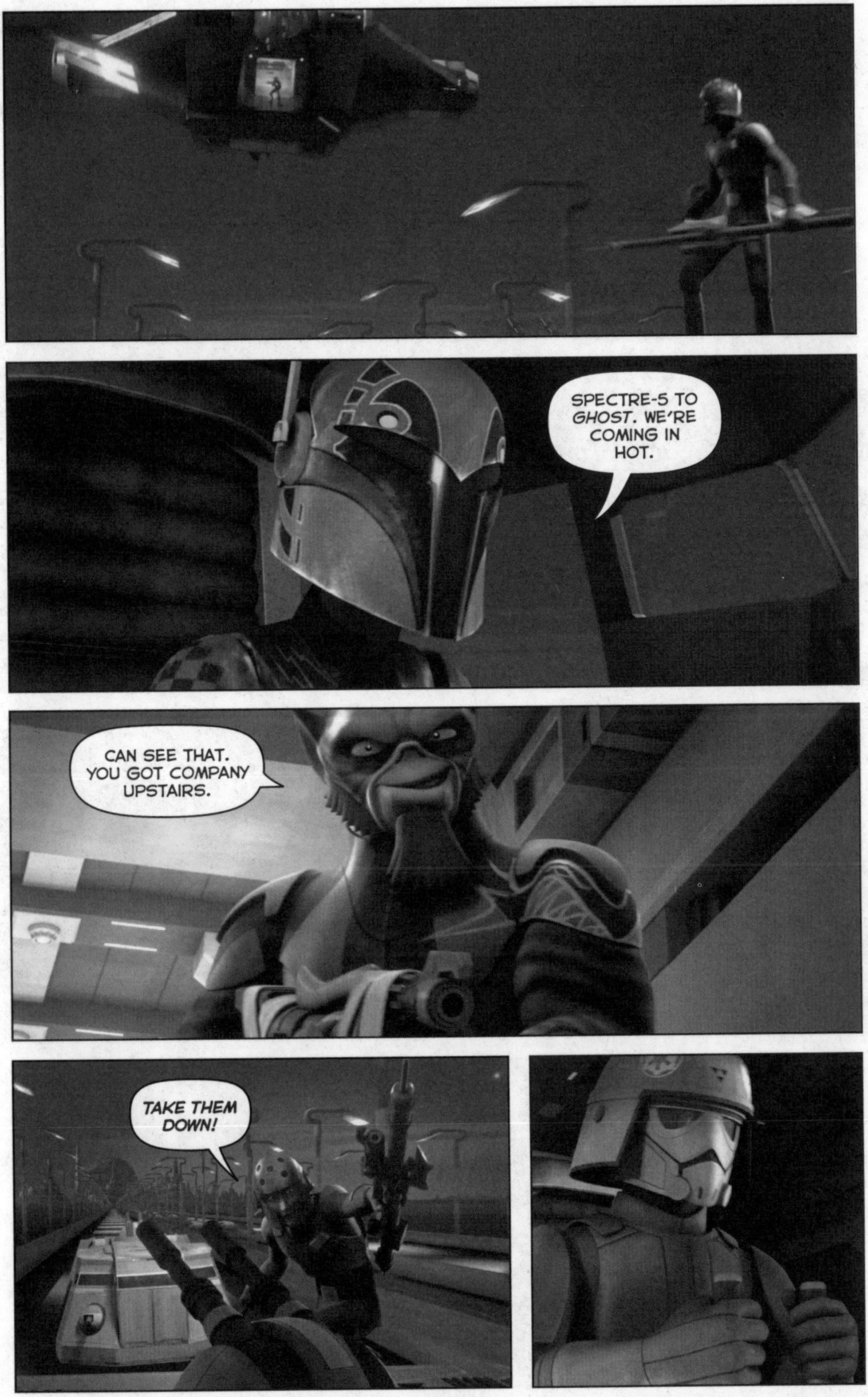
SPECTRE-5 TO GHOST. WE'RE COMING IN HOT.
CAN SEE THAT. YOU GOT COMPANY UPSTAIRS.
TAKE THEM DOWN!

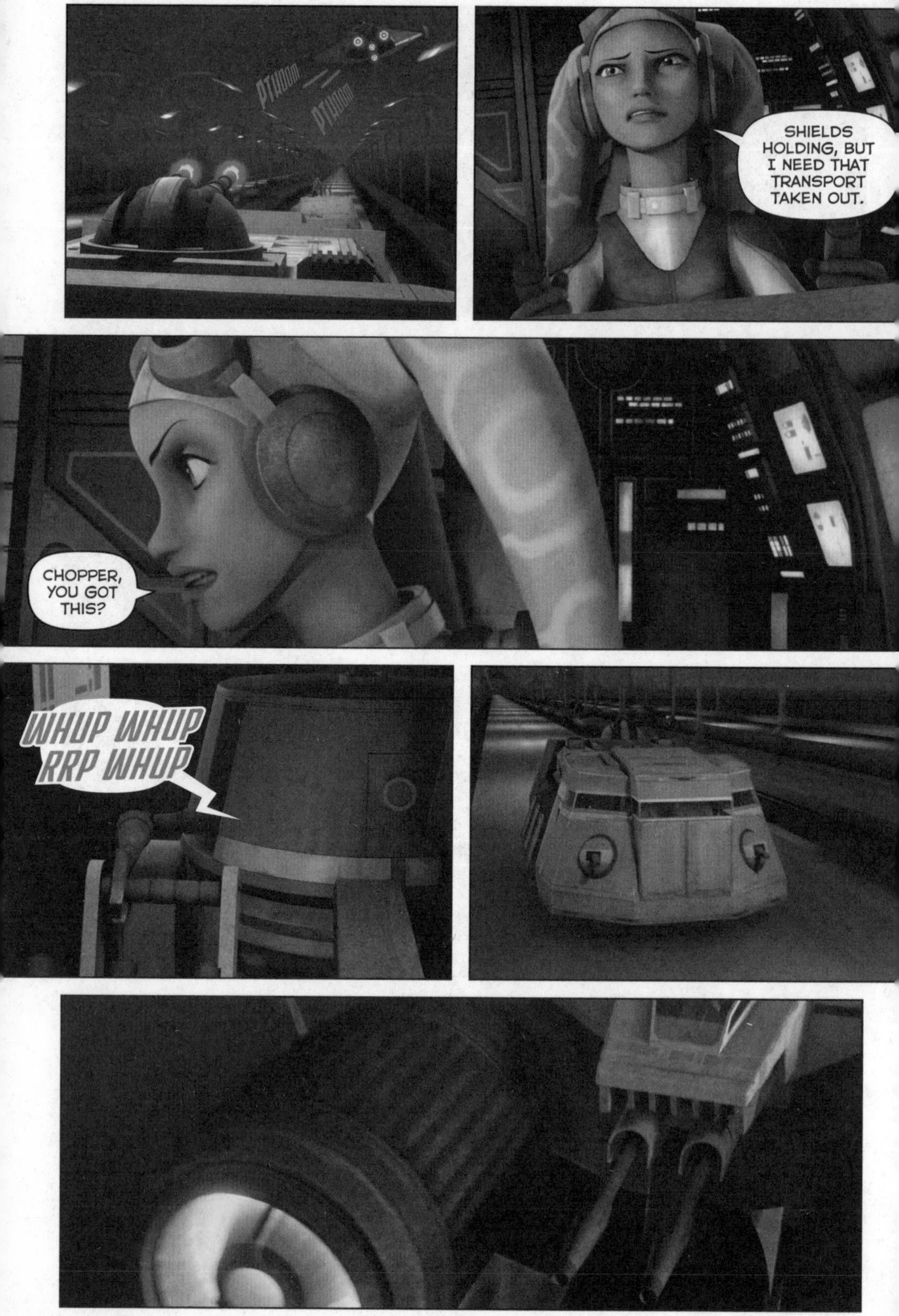
PTHOOM
PTHOOM
SHIELDS HOLDING, BUT I NEED THAT TRANSPORT TAKEN OUT.
CHOPPER, YOU GOT THIS?
WHUP WHUP RRP WHUP

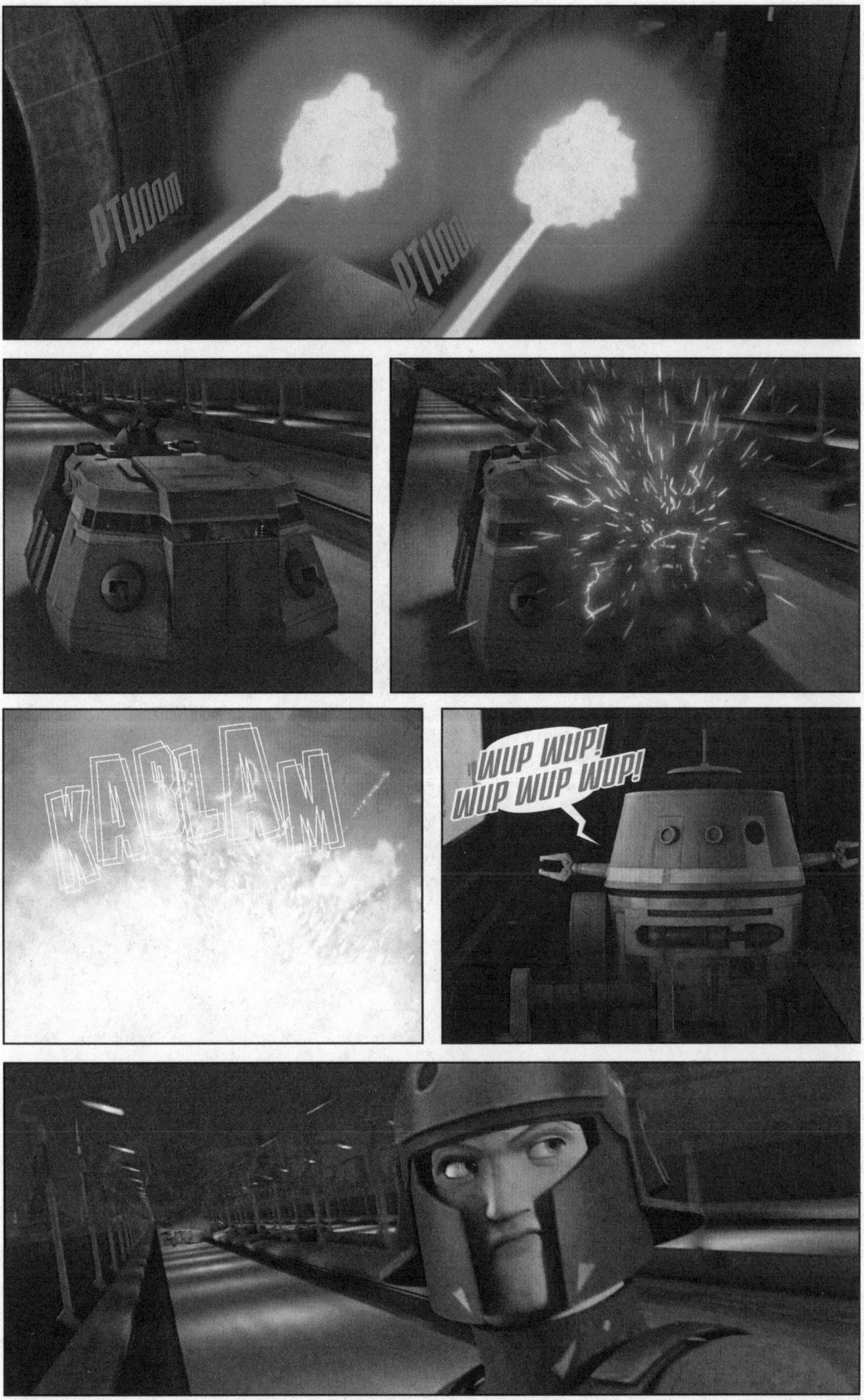
PTHOOM
PTHOOM
KABLAM
WUP WUP!
WUP WUP WUP!

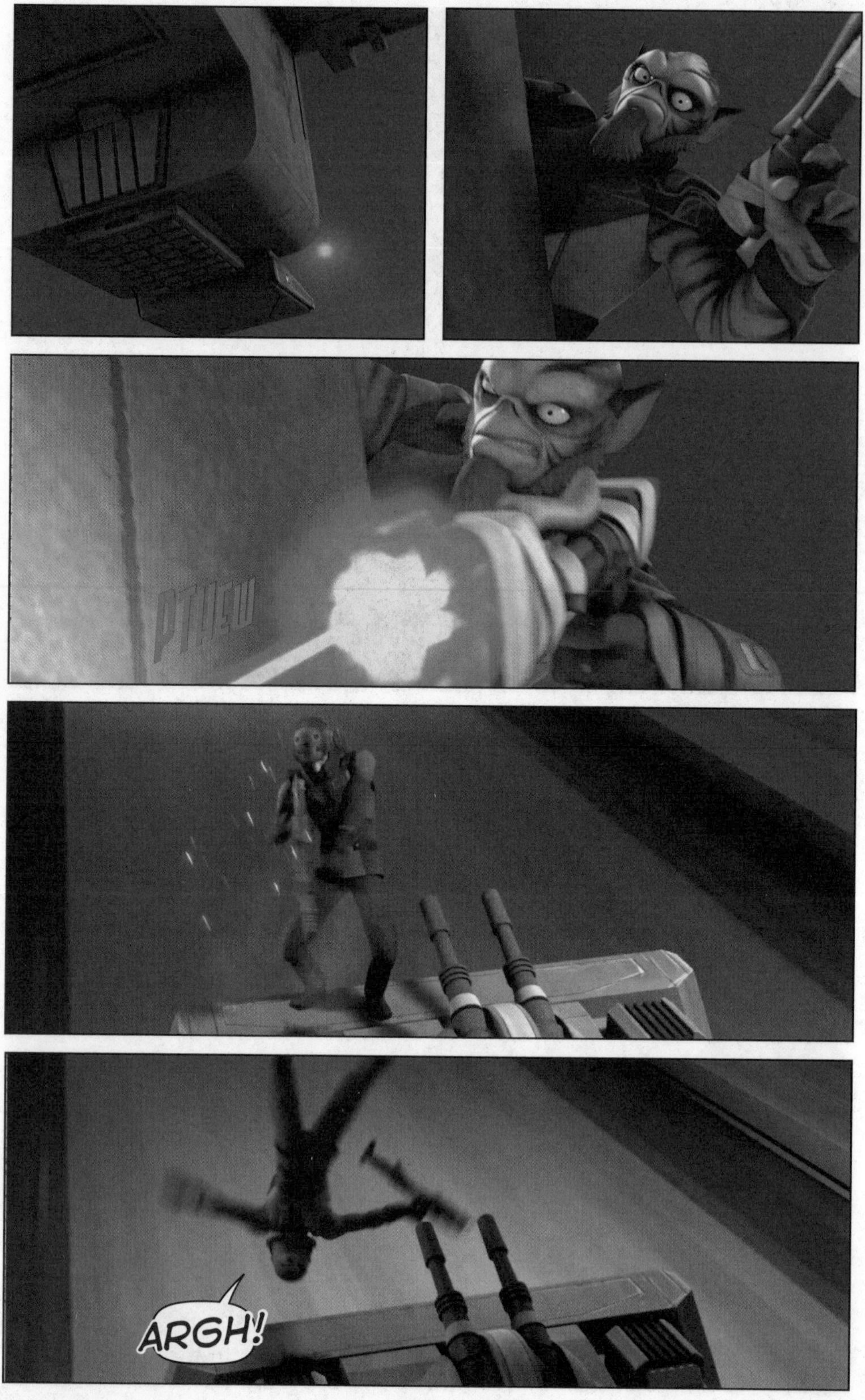
PTHEW
ARGH!

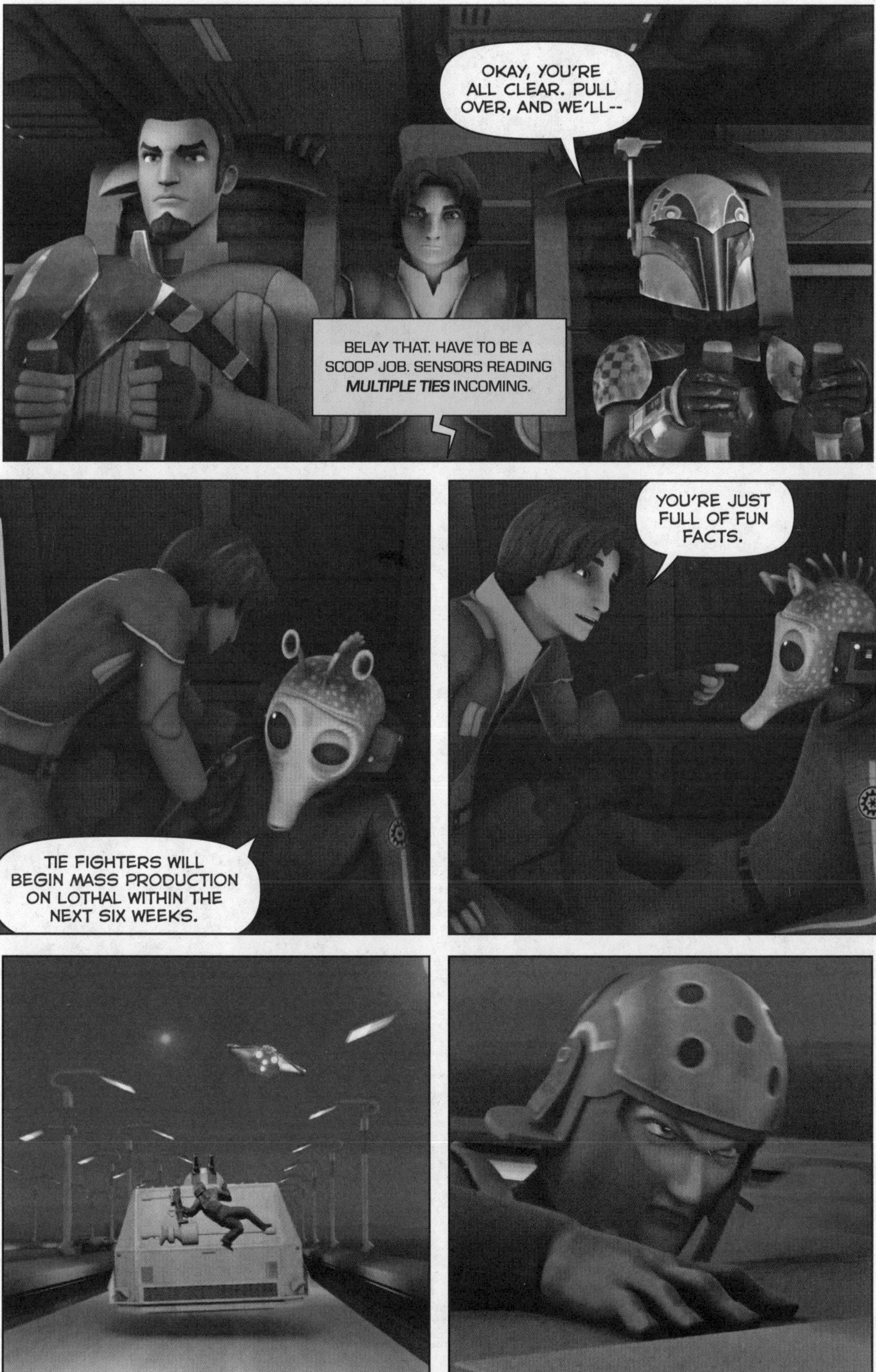
OKAY, YOU'RE ALL CLEAR. PULL OVER, AND WE'LL--
BELAY THAT. HAVE TO BE A SCOOP JOB. SENSORS READING MULTIPLE TIES INCOMING.
TIE FIGHTERS WILL BEGIN MASS PRODUCTION ON LOTHAL WITHIN THE NEXT SIX WEEKS.
YOU'RE JUST FULL OF FUN FACTS.

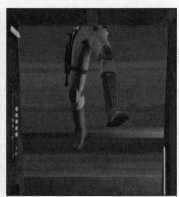

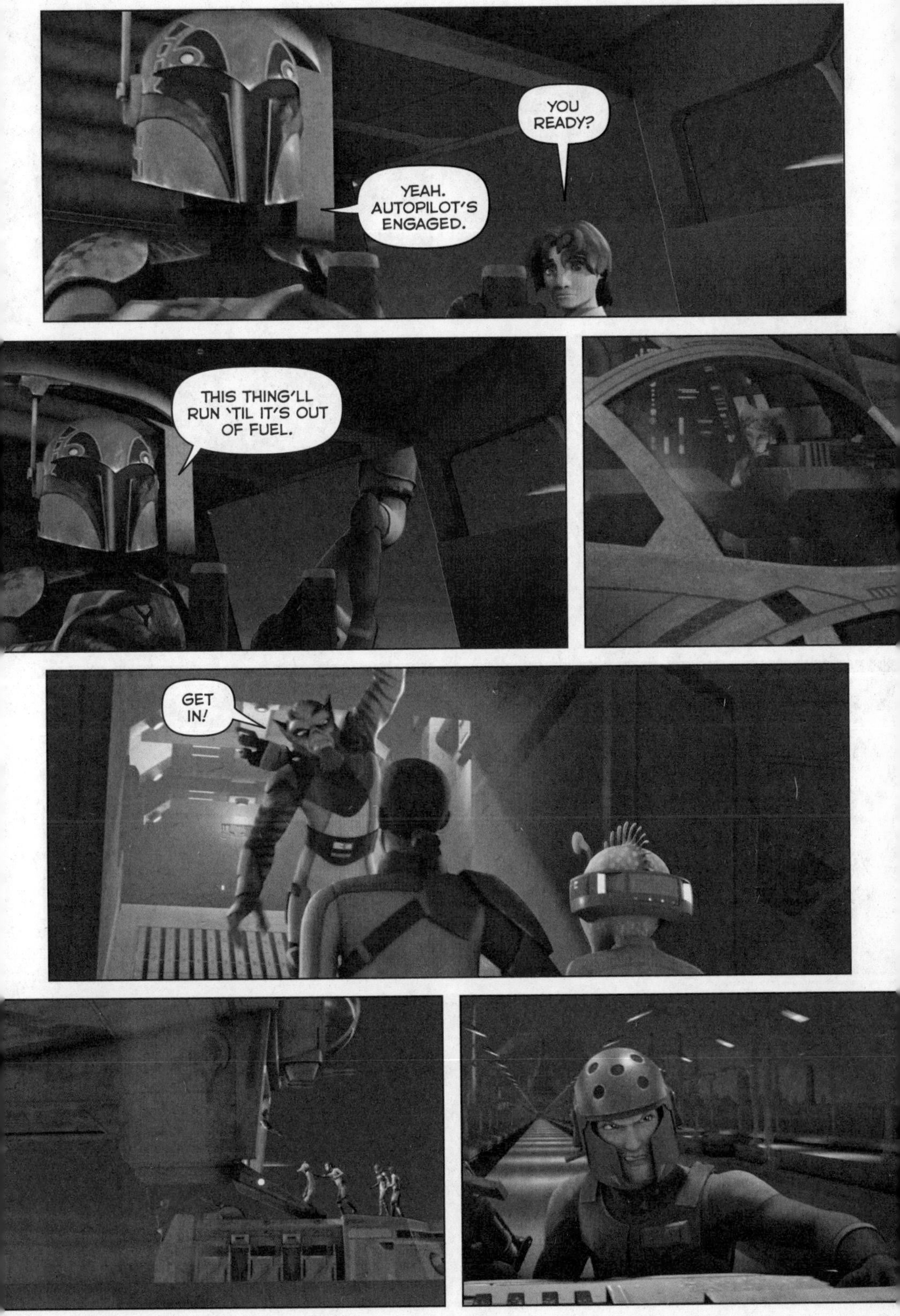
YOU READY?
YEAH. AUTOPILOT'S ENGAGED.
THIS THING'LL RUN 'TIL IT'S OUT OF FUEL.
GET IN!

GO! GO!

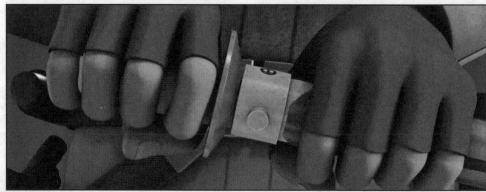

TSHEWWWWWWW!!!

PTHEW!!!

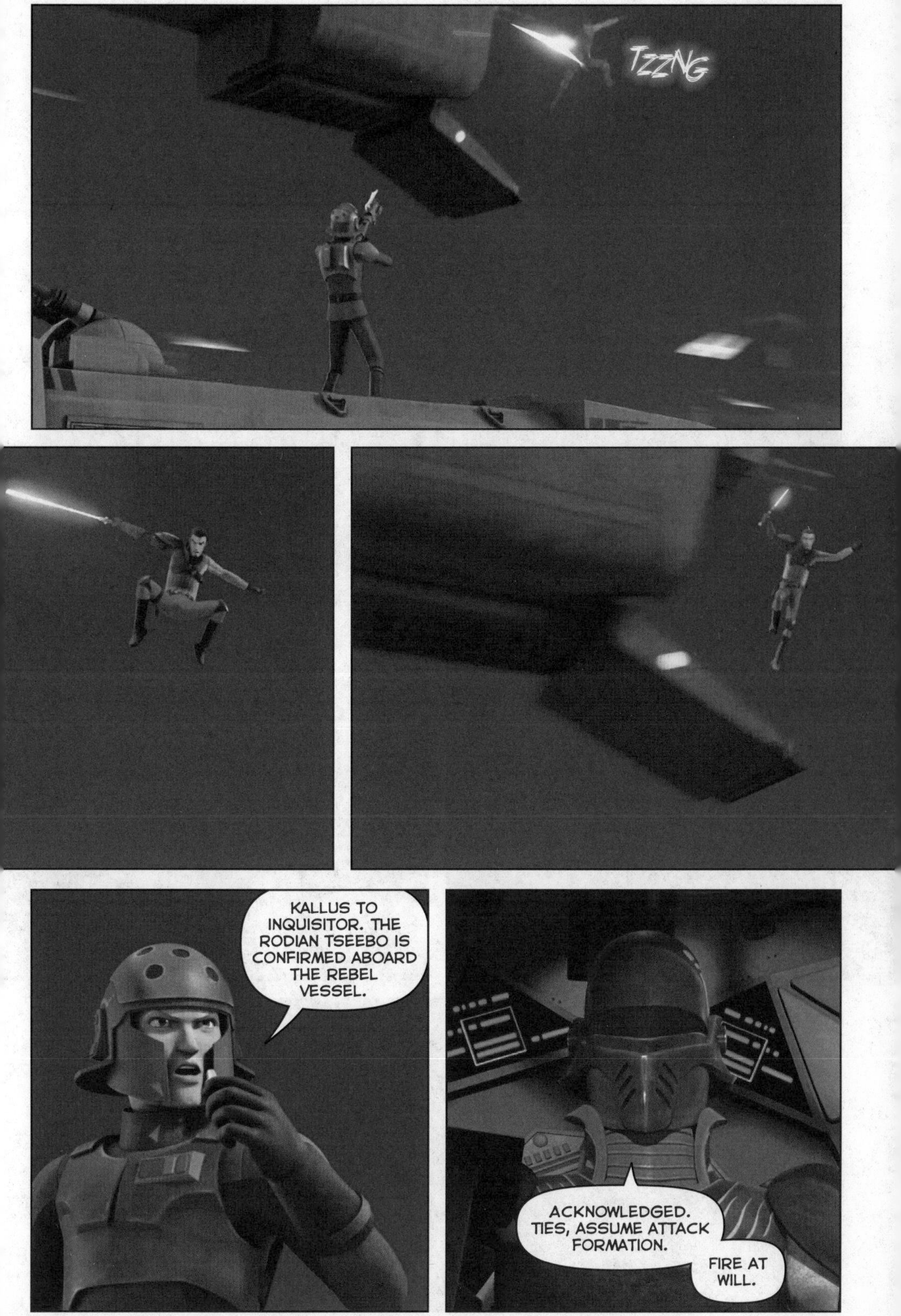
TZZNG
KALLUS TO INQUISITOR. THE RODIAN TSEEBO IS CONFIRMED ABOARD THE REBEL VESSEL.
ACKNOWLEDGED. TIES, ASSUME ATTACK FORMATION.
FIRE AT WILL.

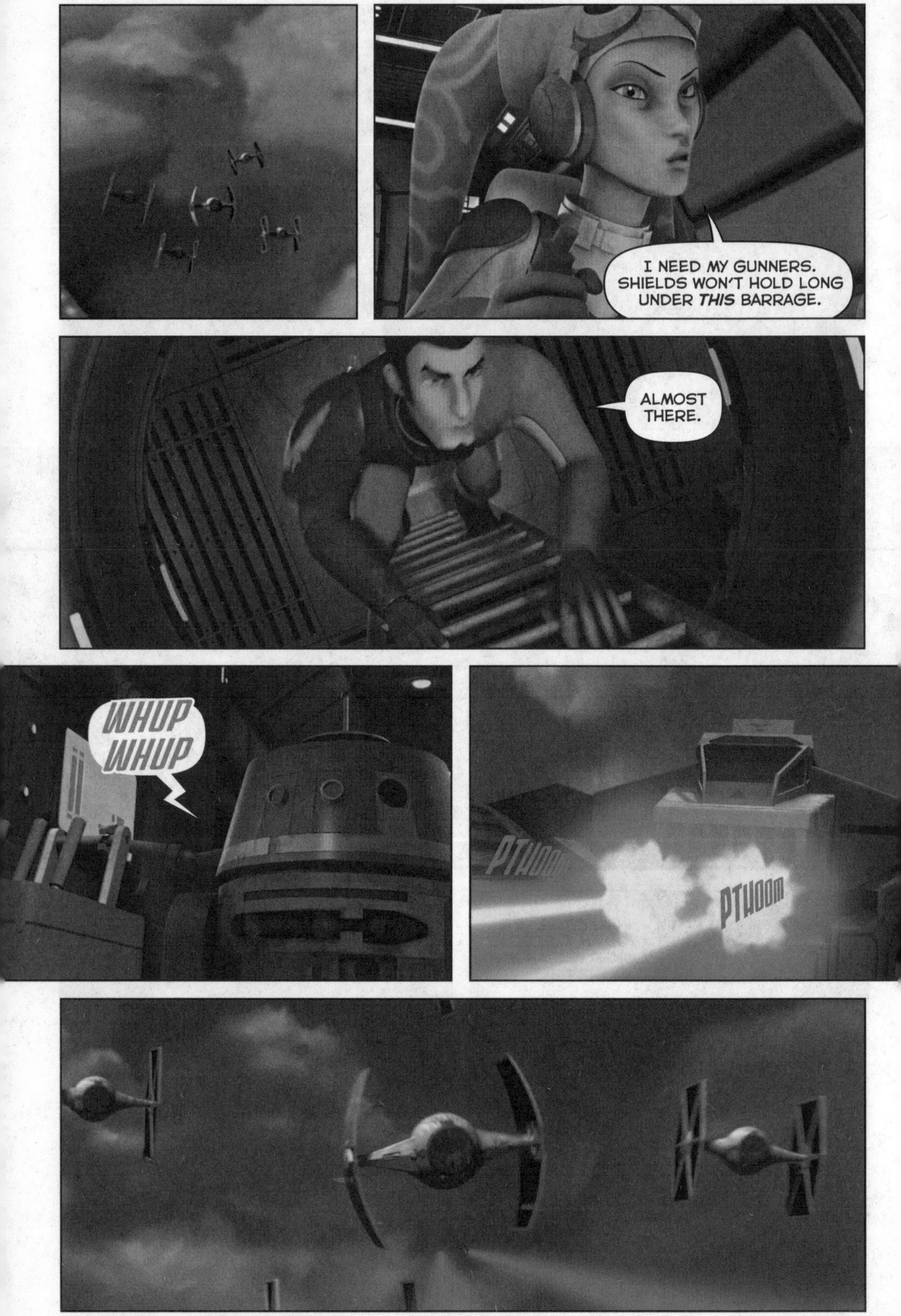
I NEED MY GUNNERS. SHIELDS WON'T HOLD LONG UNDER *THIS* BARRAGE.
ALMOST THERE.
WHUP WHUP
PTHOOM
PTHOOM

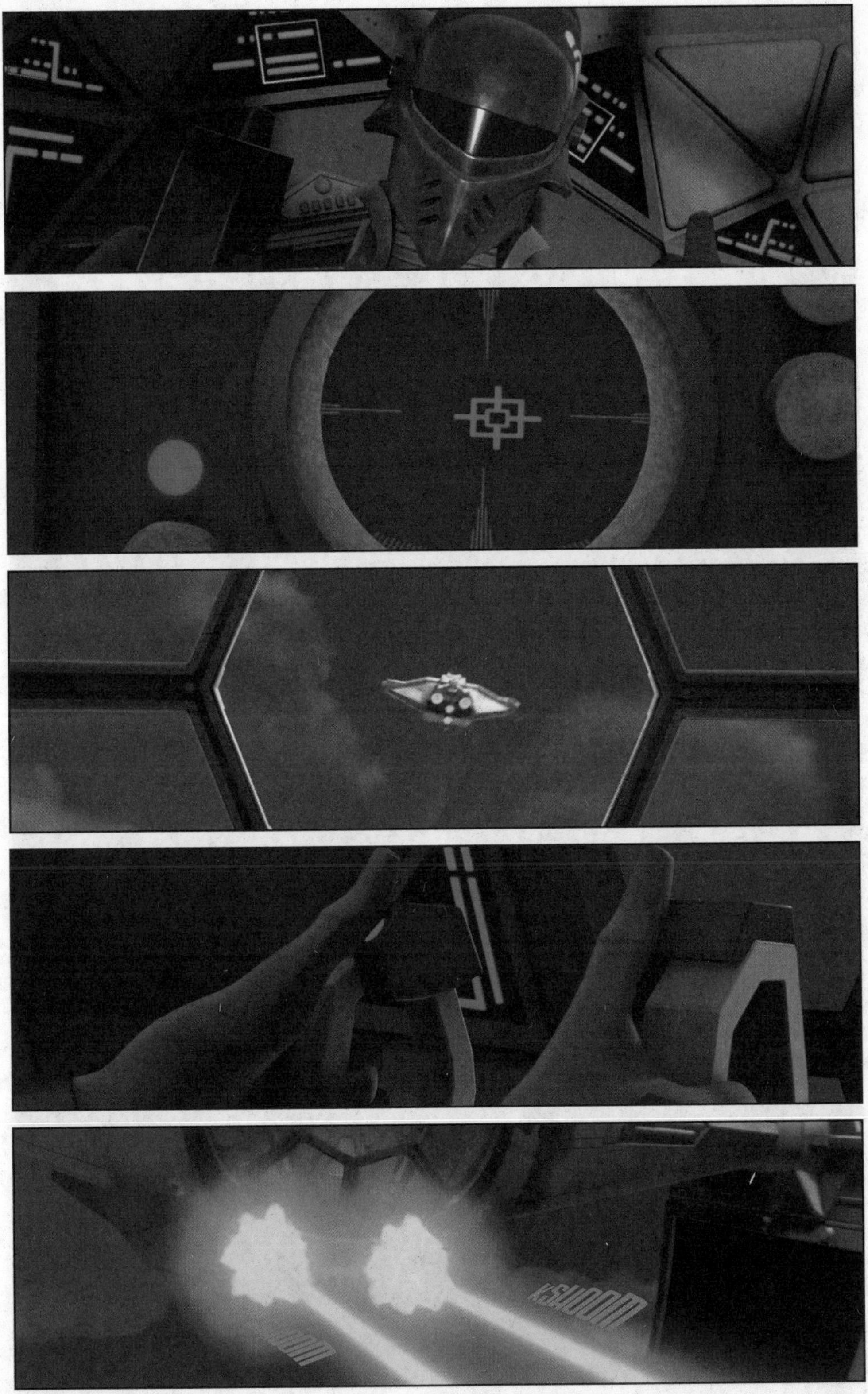
KSHOOM

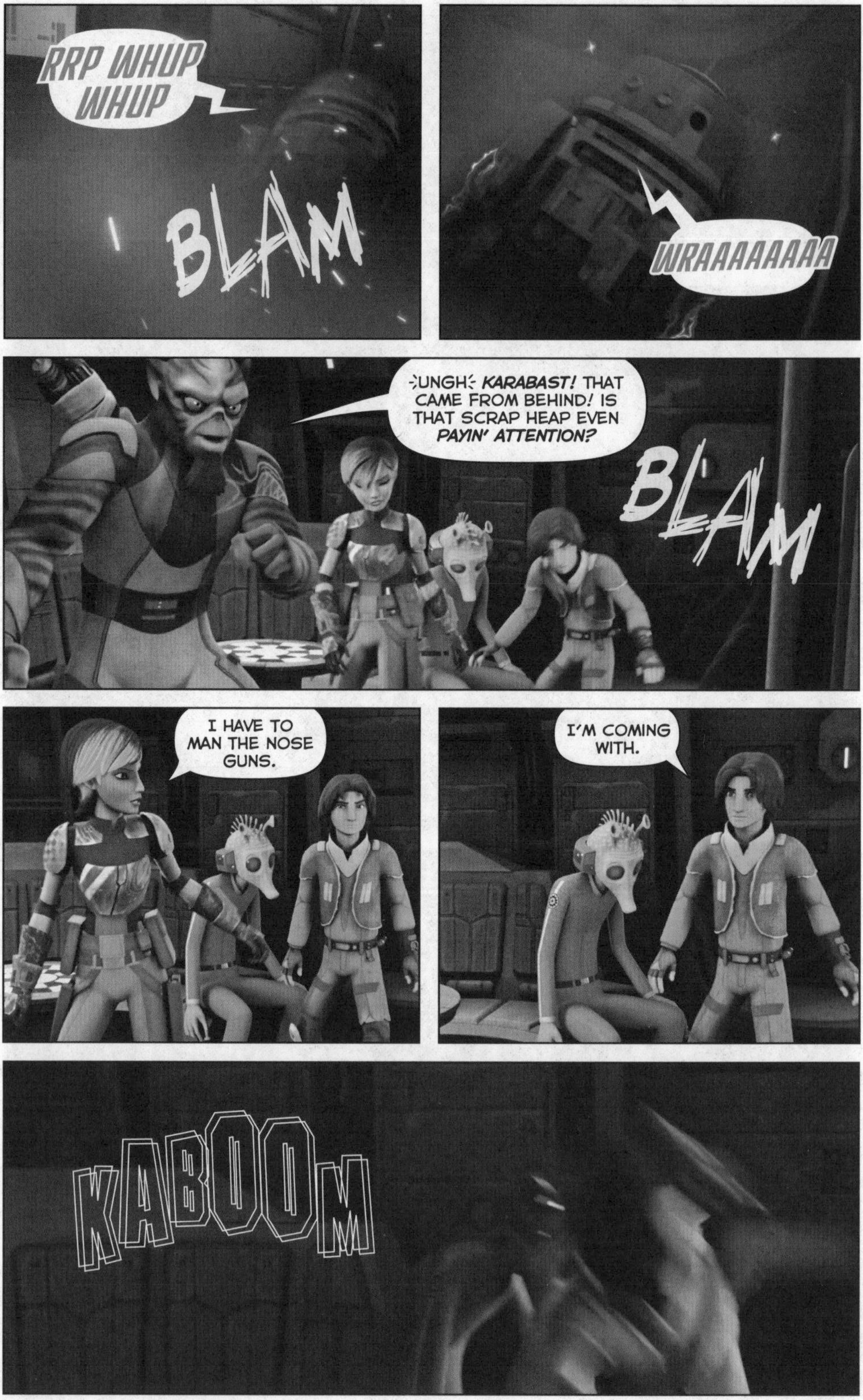
RRP WHUP WHUP
BLAM
WRAAAAAAAA
-UNGH- KARABAST! THAT CAME FROM BEHIND! IS THAT SCRAP HEAP EVEN PAYIN' ATTENTION?
BLAM
I HAVE TO MAN THE NOSE GUNS.
I'M COMING WITH.
KABOOM

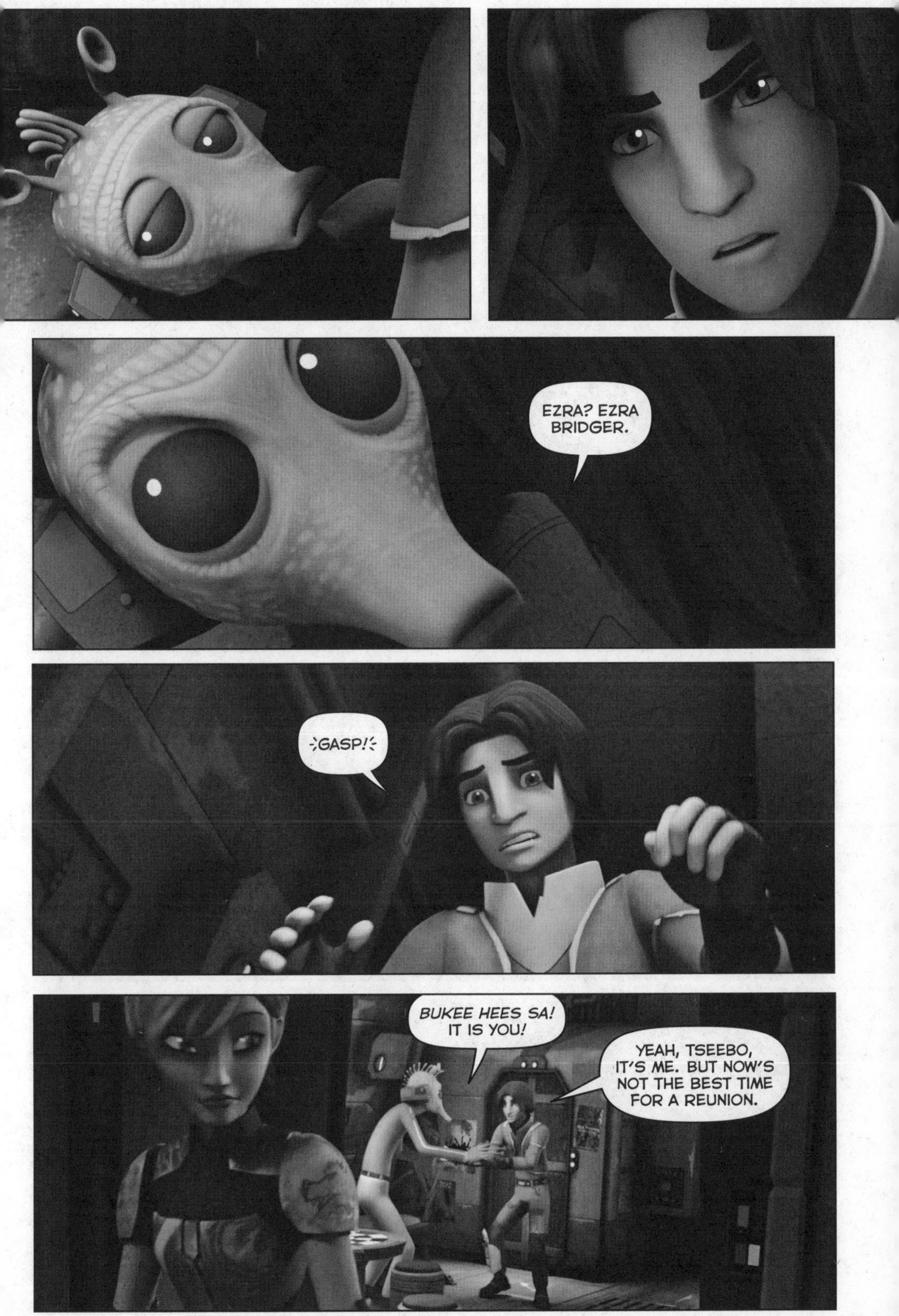
EZRA? EZRA BRIDGER.
-GASP!-
BUKEE HEES SA! IT IS YOU!
YEAH, TSEEBO, IT'S ME. BUT NOW'S NOT THE BEST TIME FOR A REUNION.

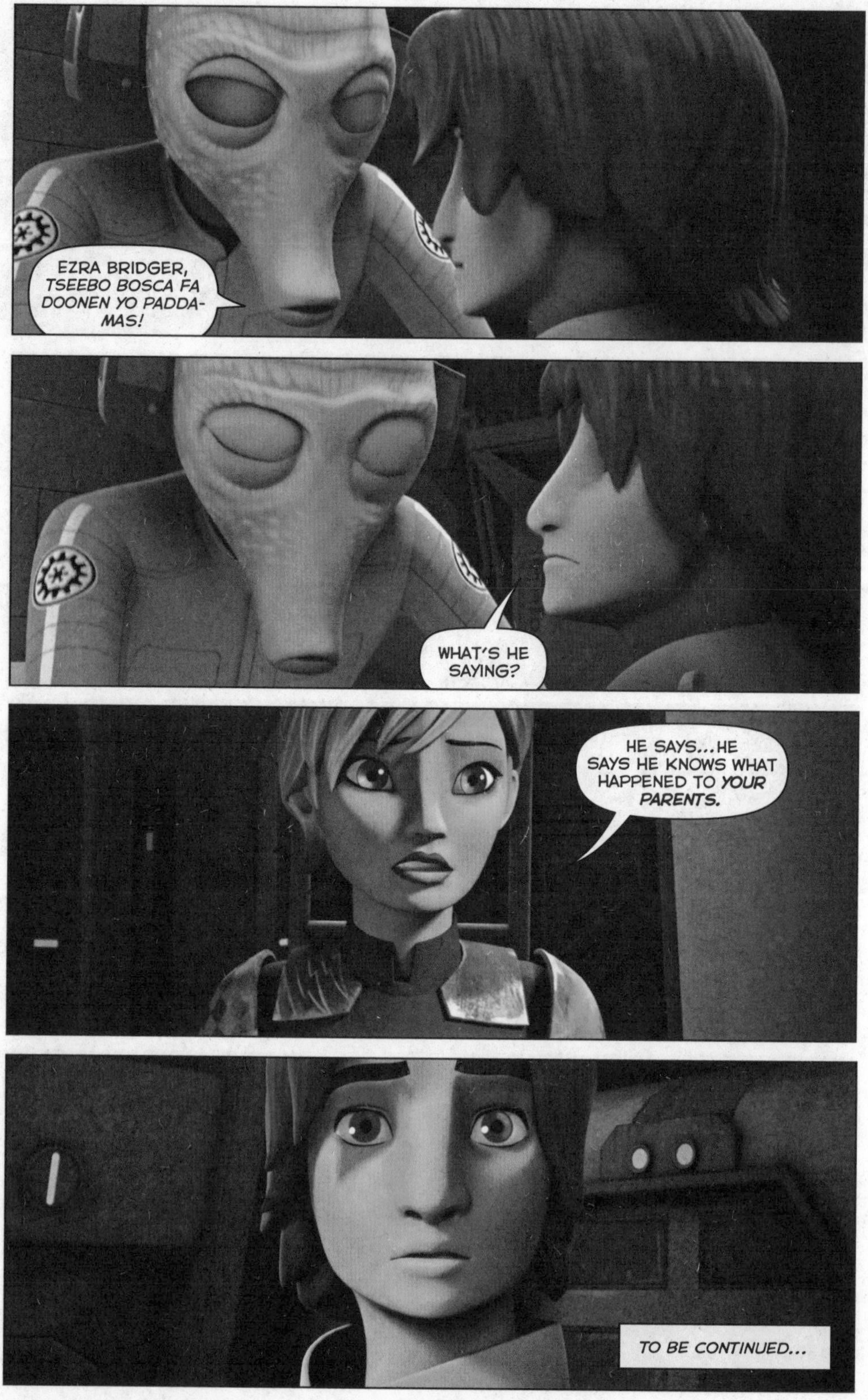
EZRA BRIDGER, TSEEBO BOSCA FA DOONEN YO PADDA-MAS!
WHAT'S HE SAYING?
HE SAYS...HE SAYS HE KNOWS WHAT HAPPENED TO *YOUR PARENTS.*
TO BE CONTINUED...

STAR WARS REBELS™

GATHERING FORCES

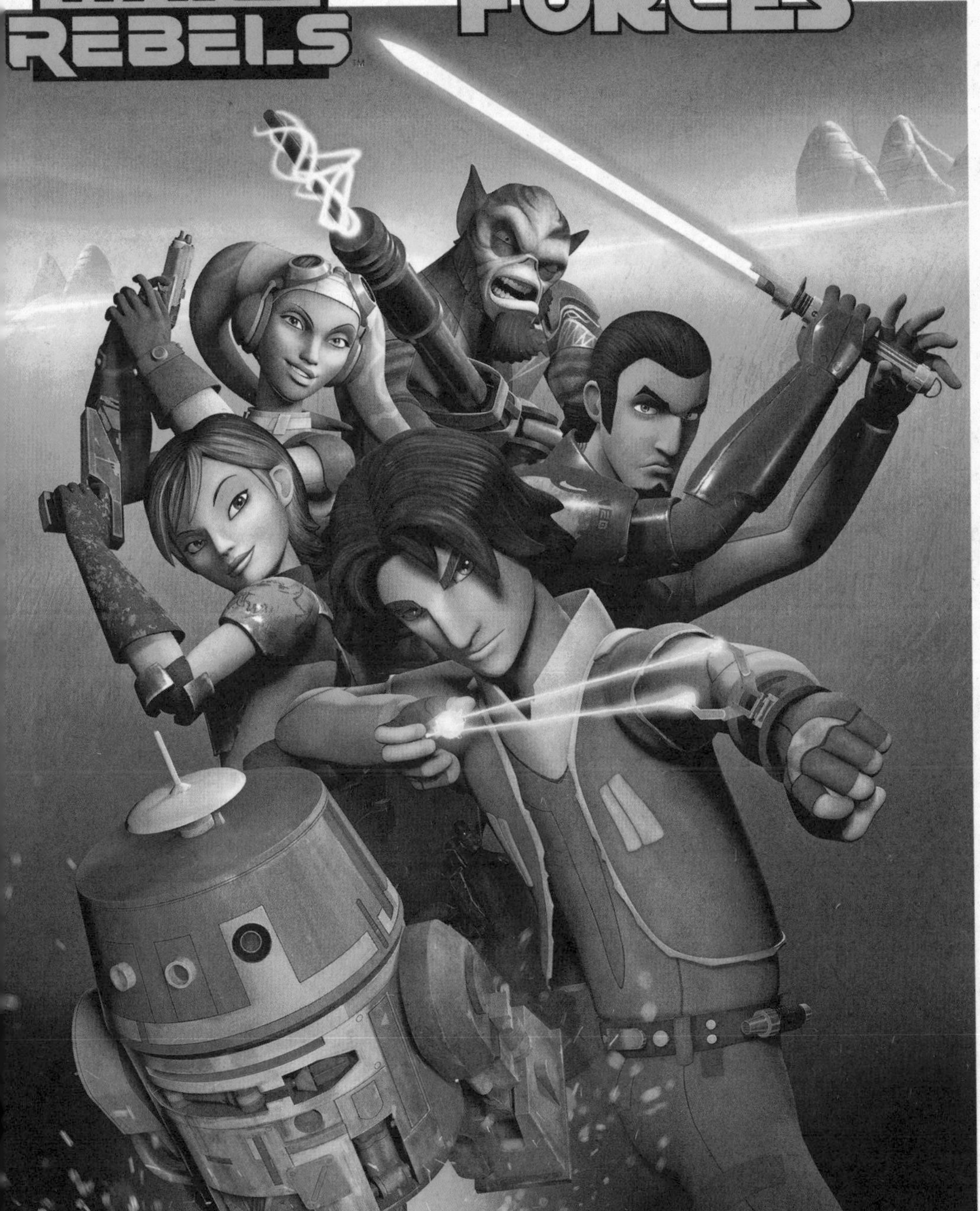

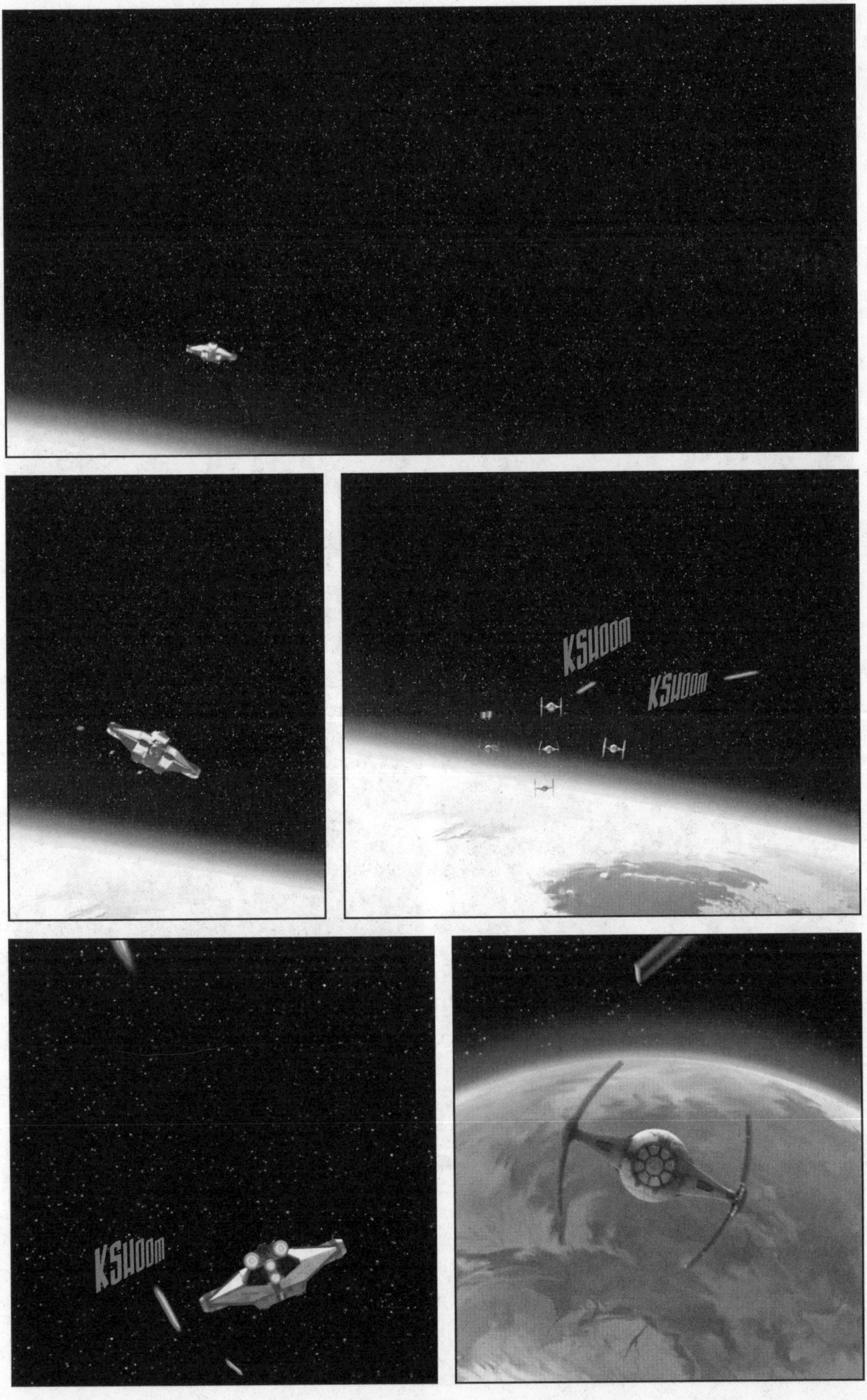
KSHOOM
KSHOOM
KSHOOM

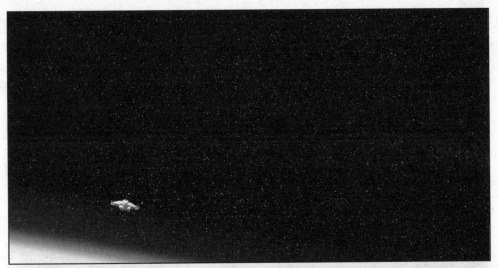

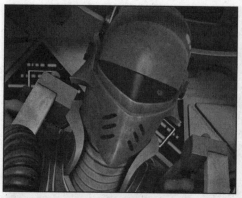

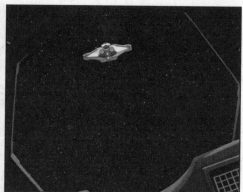

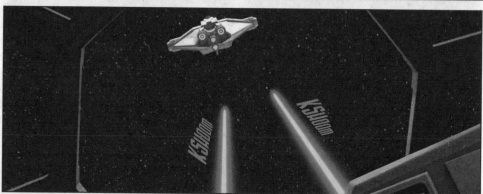

KSHOOM
KSHOOM
"CHOPPER, I'M ROLLING US STARBOARD. BE READY TO FIRE THOSE REAR GUNS!"
KSHOOM
KSHOOM
KSHOOM
KSHOOM
KARABAST! CHOPPER'S DOWN!

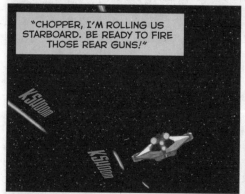

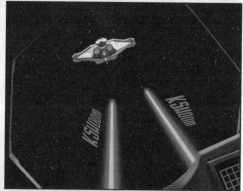

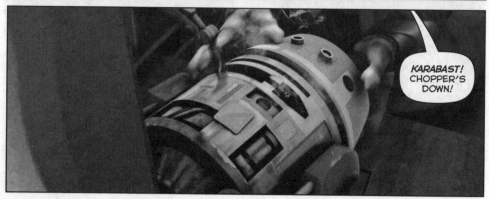

OW! OW!

PAT PAT

I'VE GOT YOU COVERED, HERA. ROLL AWAY!

KSHOOM

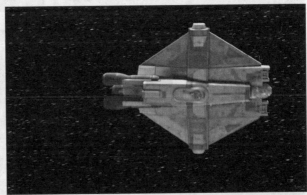

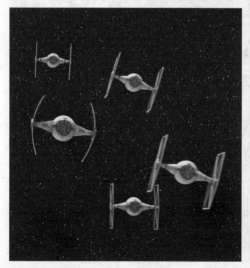

OPEN FIRE. THEIR SHIELDS WILL NOT HOLD INDEFINITELY.

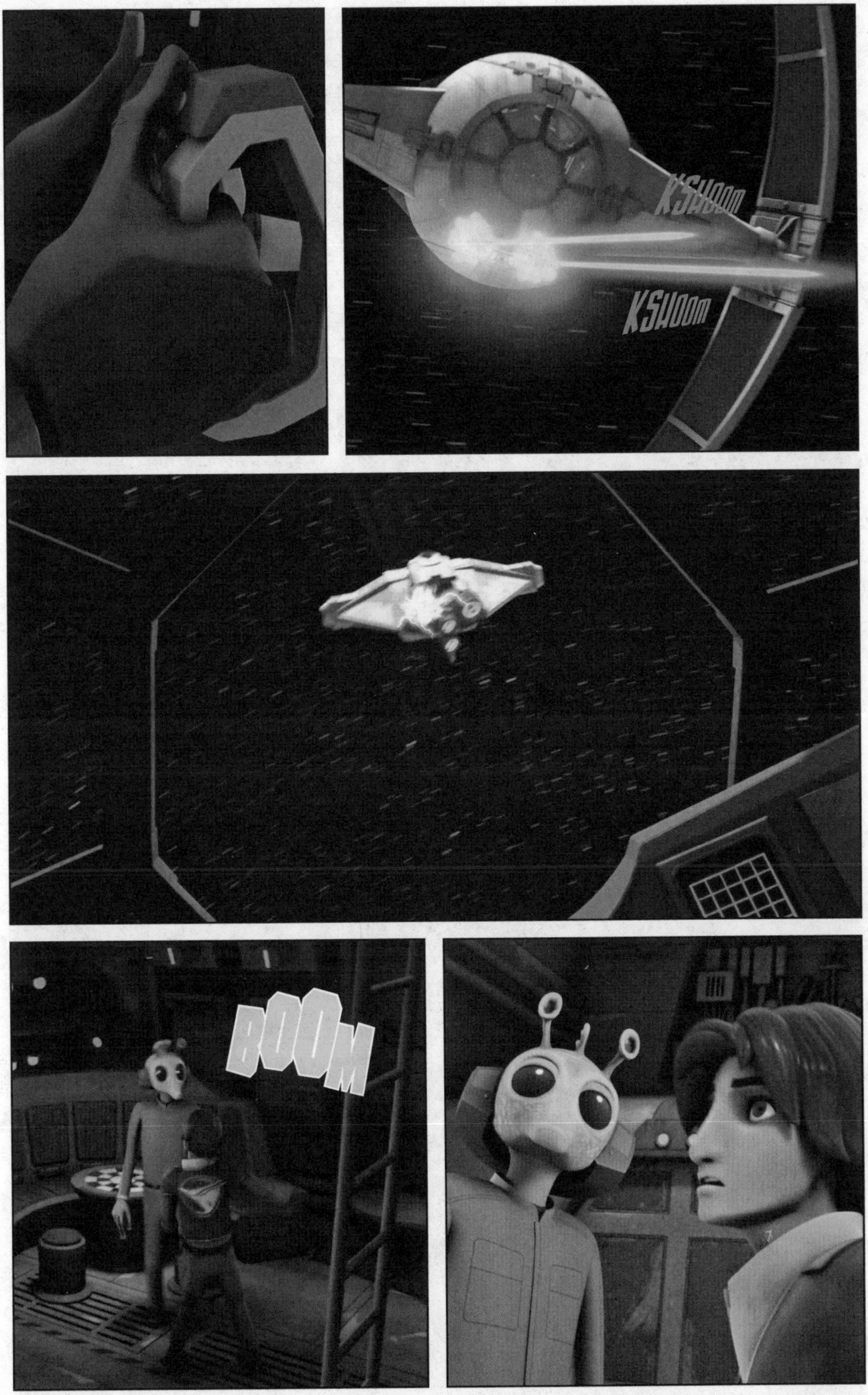
KSHOOM
KSHOOM
BOOM

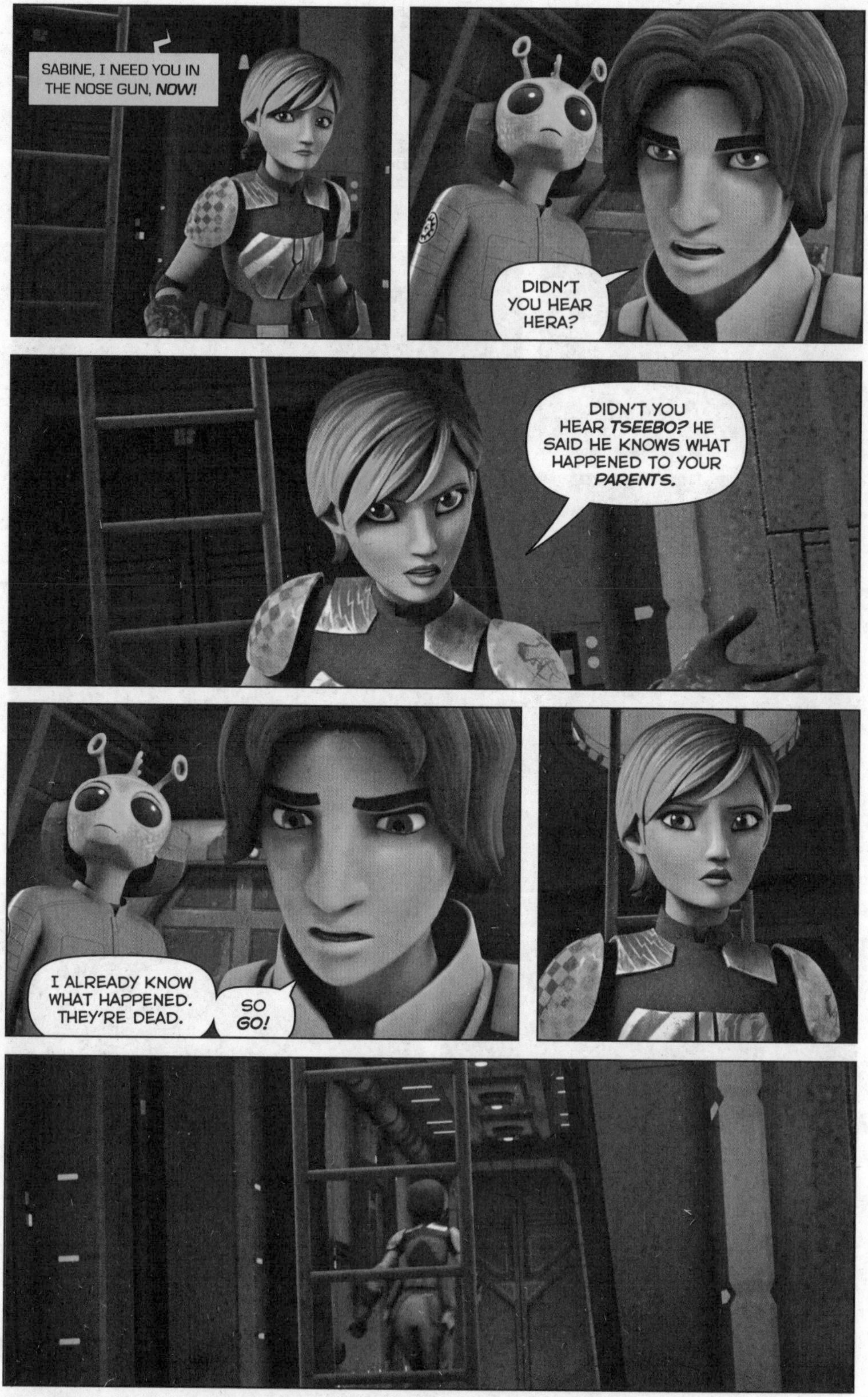
SABINE, I NEED YOU IN THE NOSE GUN, NOW!
DIDN'T YOU HEAR HERA?
DIDN'T YOU HEAR TSEEBO? HE SAID HE KNOWS WHAT HAPPENED TO YOUR PARENTS.
I ALREADY KNOW WHAT HAPPENED. THEY'RE DEAD.
SO GO!

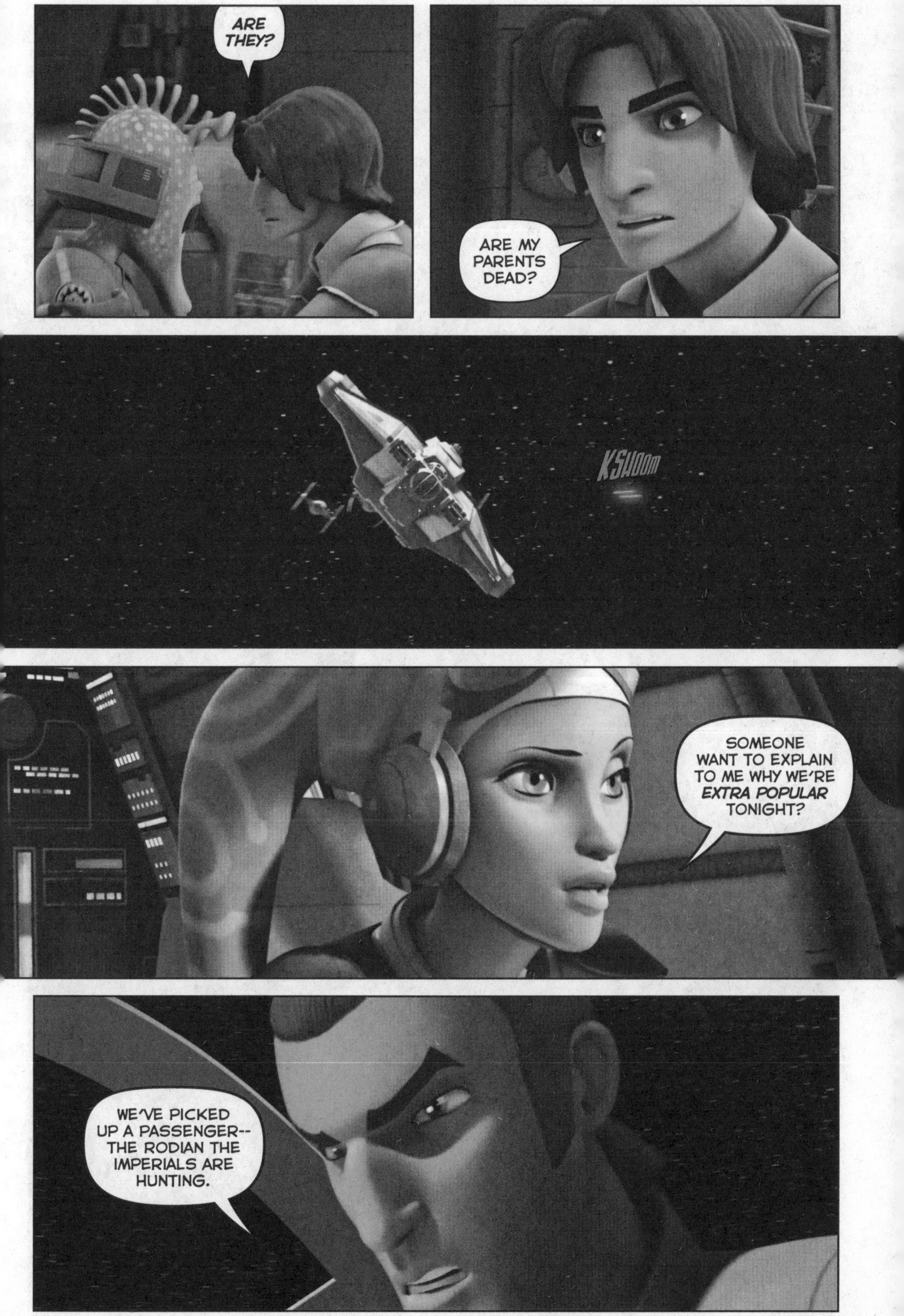
ARE THEY?
ARE MY PARENTS DEAD?
KSHOOM
SOMEONE WANT TO EXPLAIN TO ME WHY WE'RE *EXTRA POPULAR* TONIGHT?
WE'VE PICKED UP A PASSENGER-- THE RODIAN THE IMPERIALS ARE HUNTING.

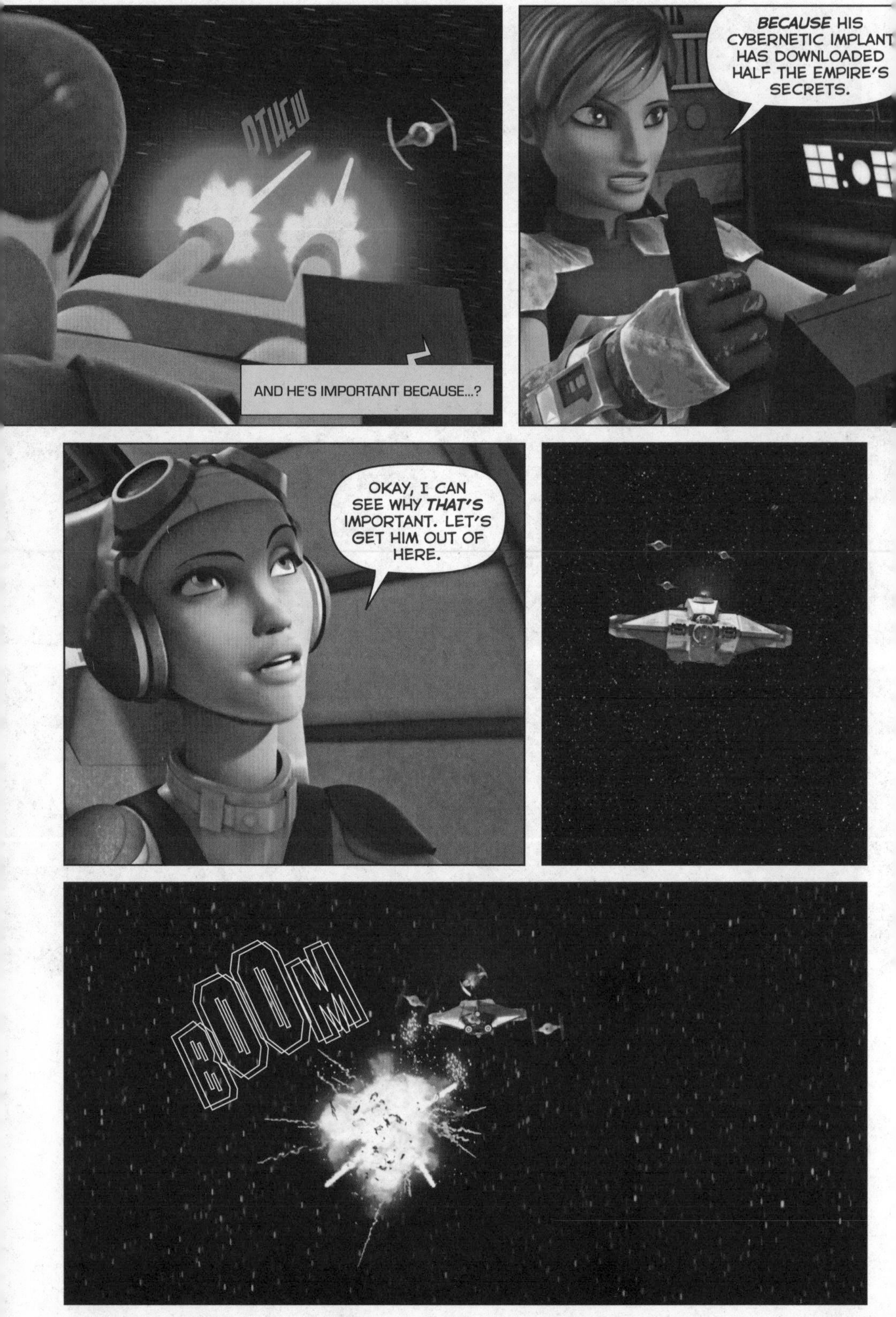
PTHEW
AND HE'S IMPORTANT BECAUSE...?
BECAUSE HIS CYBERNETIC IMPLANT HAS DOWNLOADED HALF THE EMPIRE'S SECRETS.
OKAY, I CAN SEE WHY *THAT'S* IMPORTANT. LET'S GET HIM OUT OF HERE.
BOOM

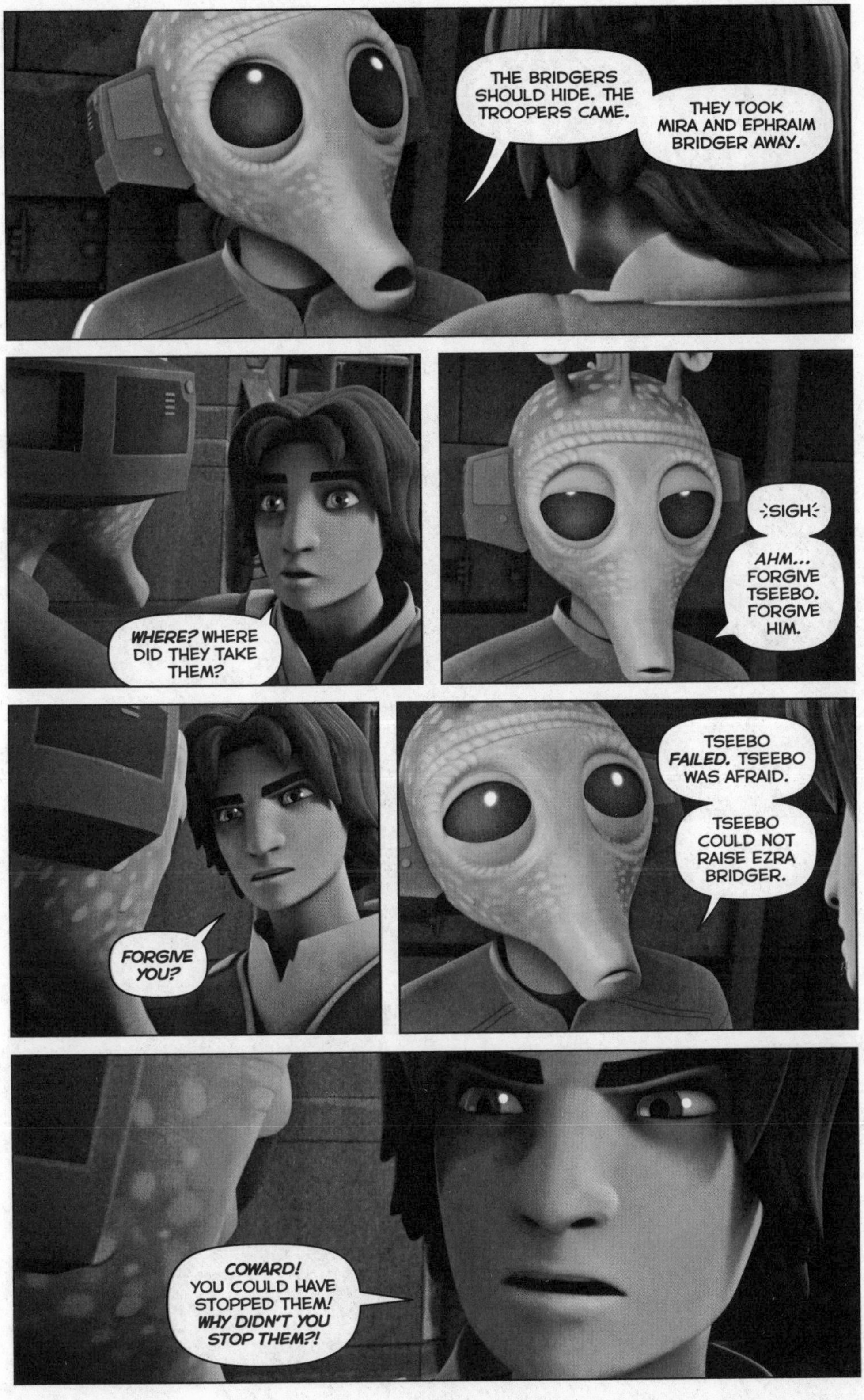
THE BRIDGERS SHOULD HIDE. THE TROOPERS CAME.
THEY TOOK MIRA AND EPHRAIM BRIDGER AWAY.
WHERE? WHERE DID THEY TAKE THEM?
SIGH
AHM... FORGIVE TSEEBO. FORGIVE HIM.
FORGIVE YOU?
TSEEBO *FAILED.* TSEEBO WAS AFRAID.
TSEEBO COULD NOT RAISE EZRA BRIDGER.
COWARD! YOU COULD HAVE STOPPED THEM! *WHY DIDN'T YOU STOP THEM?!*

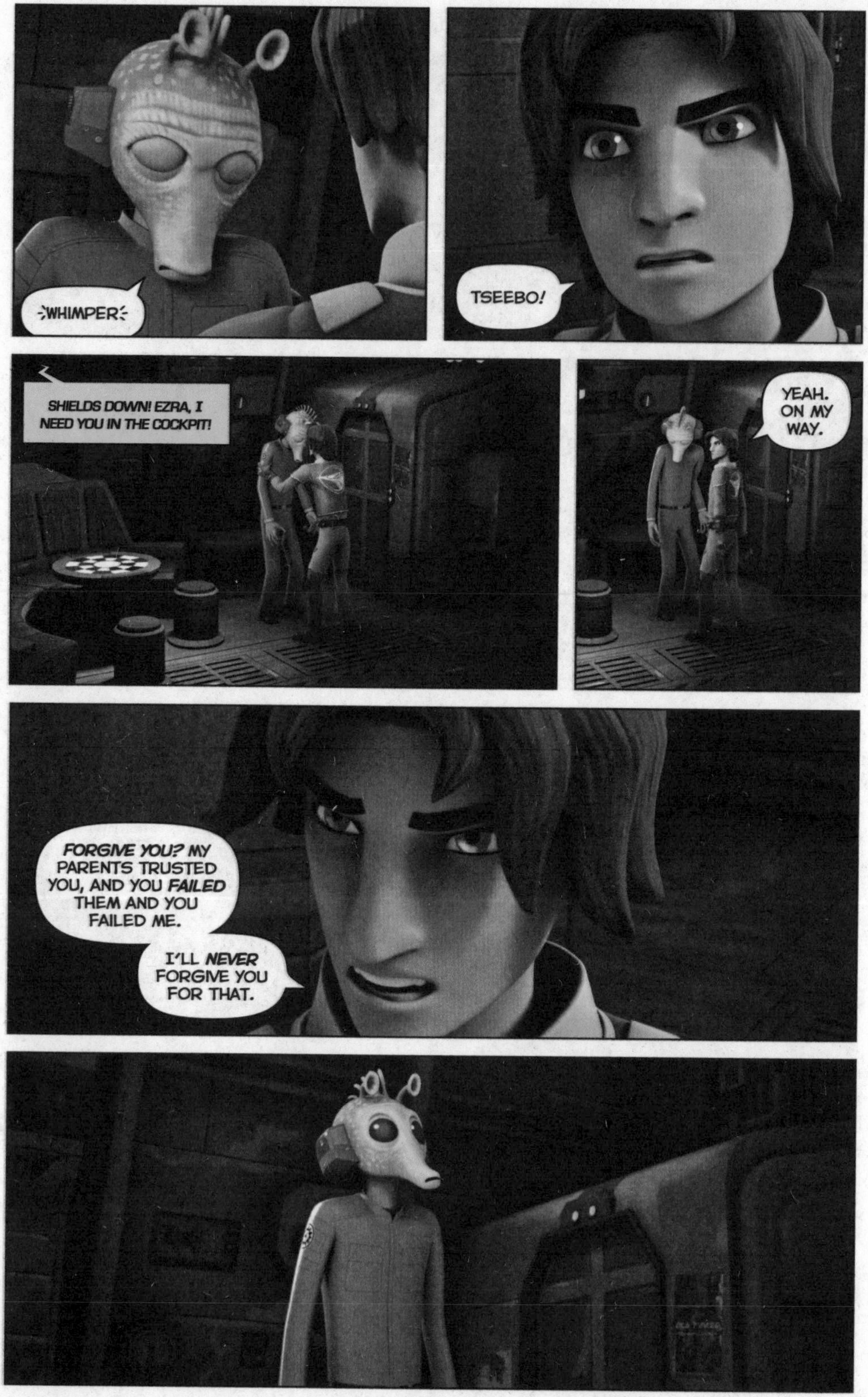

WHIMPER
TSEEBO!
SHIELDS DOWN! EZRA, I NEED YOU IN THE COCKPIT!
YEAH. ON MY WAY.
FORGIVE YOU? MY PARENTS TRUSTED YOU, AND YOU FAILED THEM AND YOU FAILED ME.
I'LL NEVER FORGIVE YOU FOR THAT.

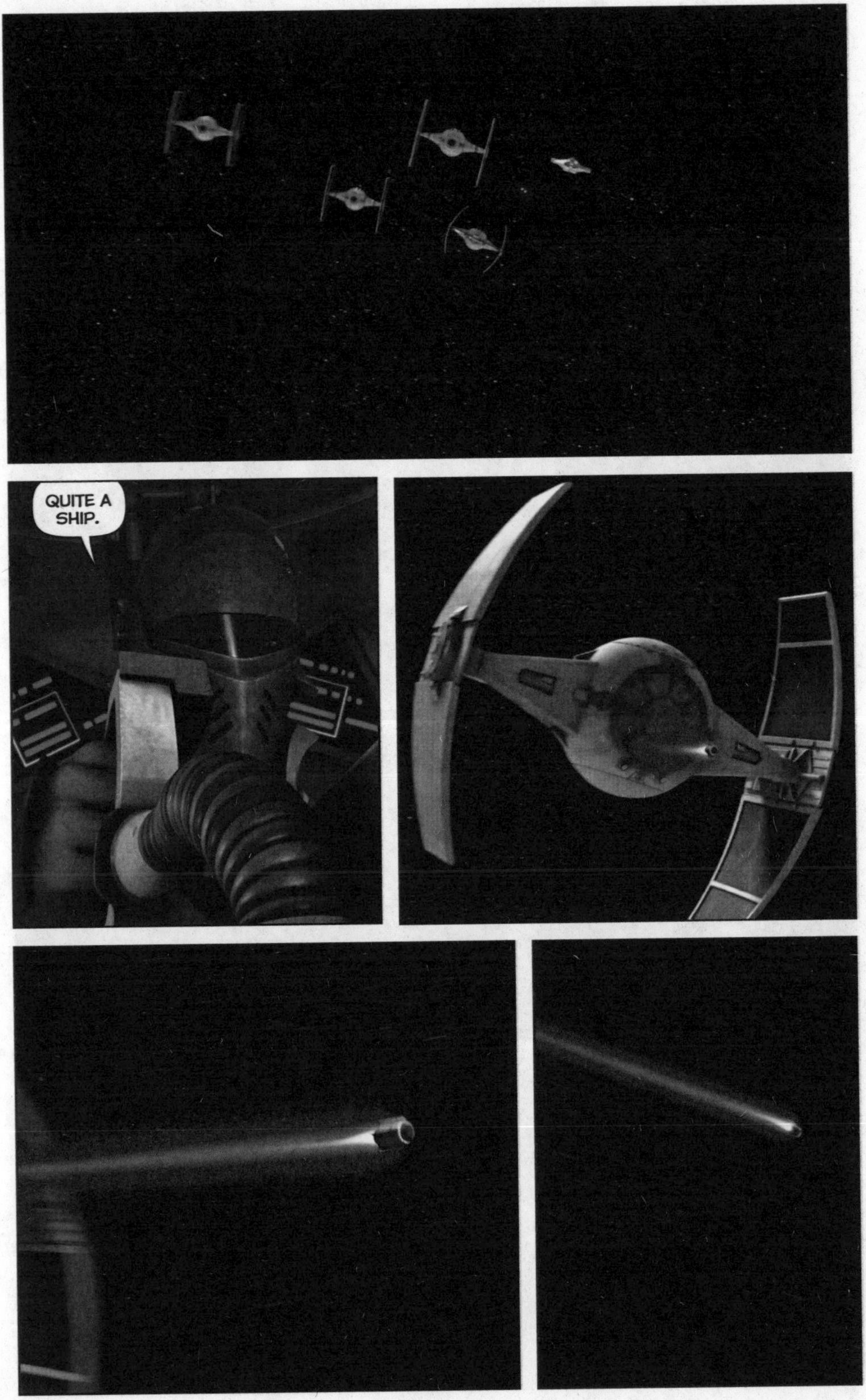
QUITE A
SHIP.

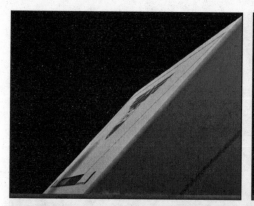

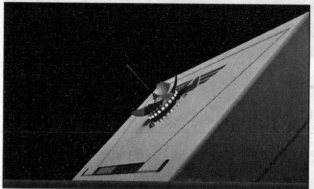

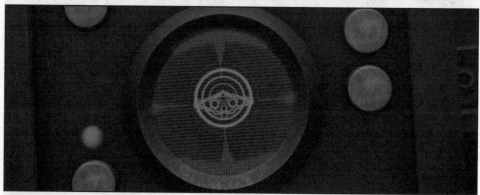

EZRA, NAV COMPUTER'S OFF LINE. WITH CHOPPER DOWN, I NEED YOU TO FIX IT.

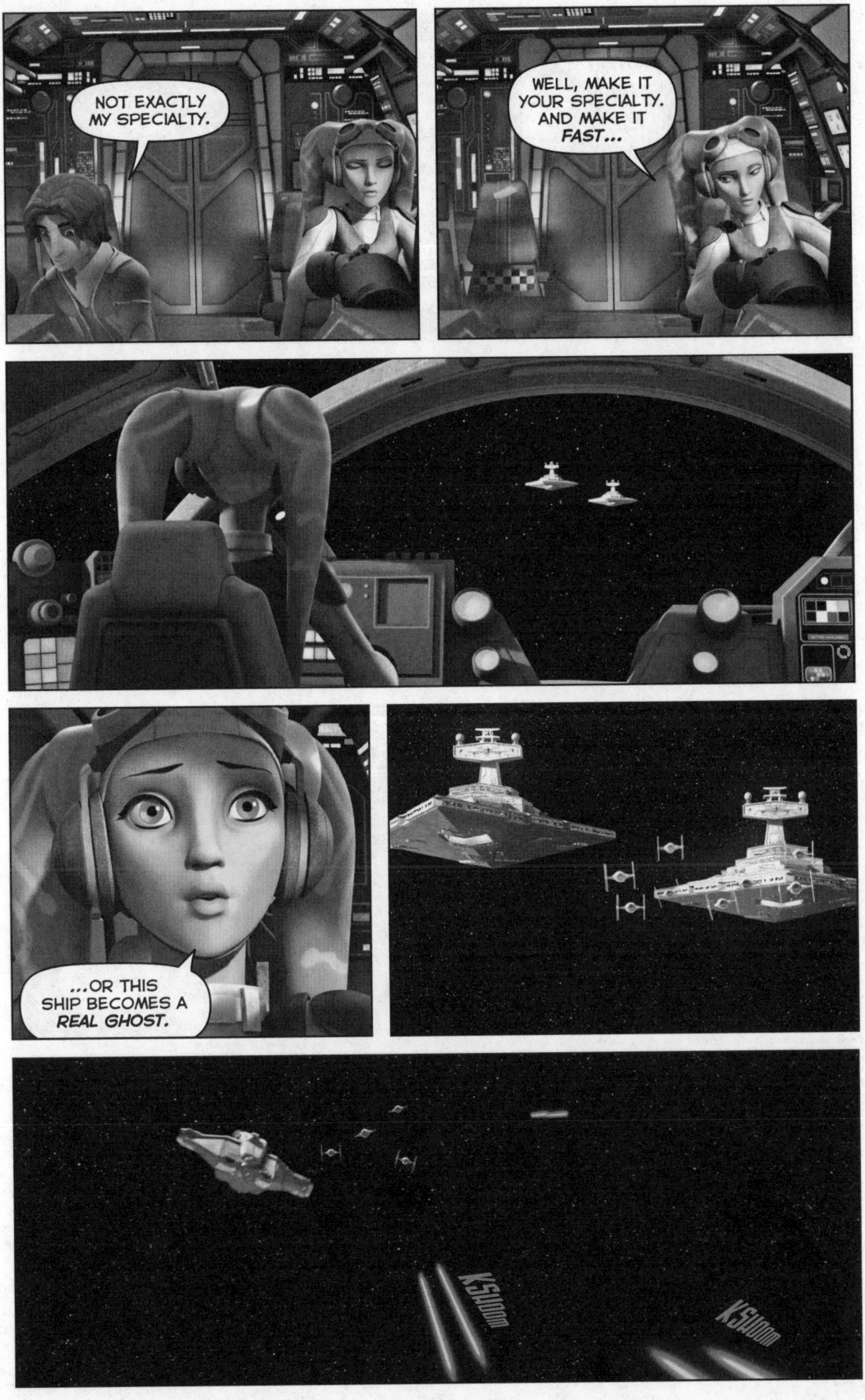
NOT EXACTLY MY SPECIALTY.
WELL, MAKE IT YOUR SPECIALTY. AND MAKE IT *FAST...*
...OR THIS SHIP BECOMES A REAL GHOST.
KSHOOM
KSHOOM

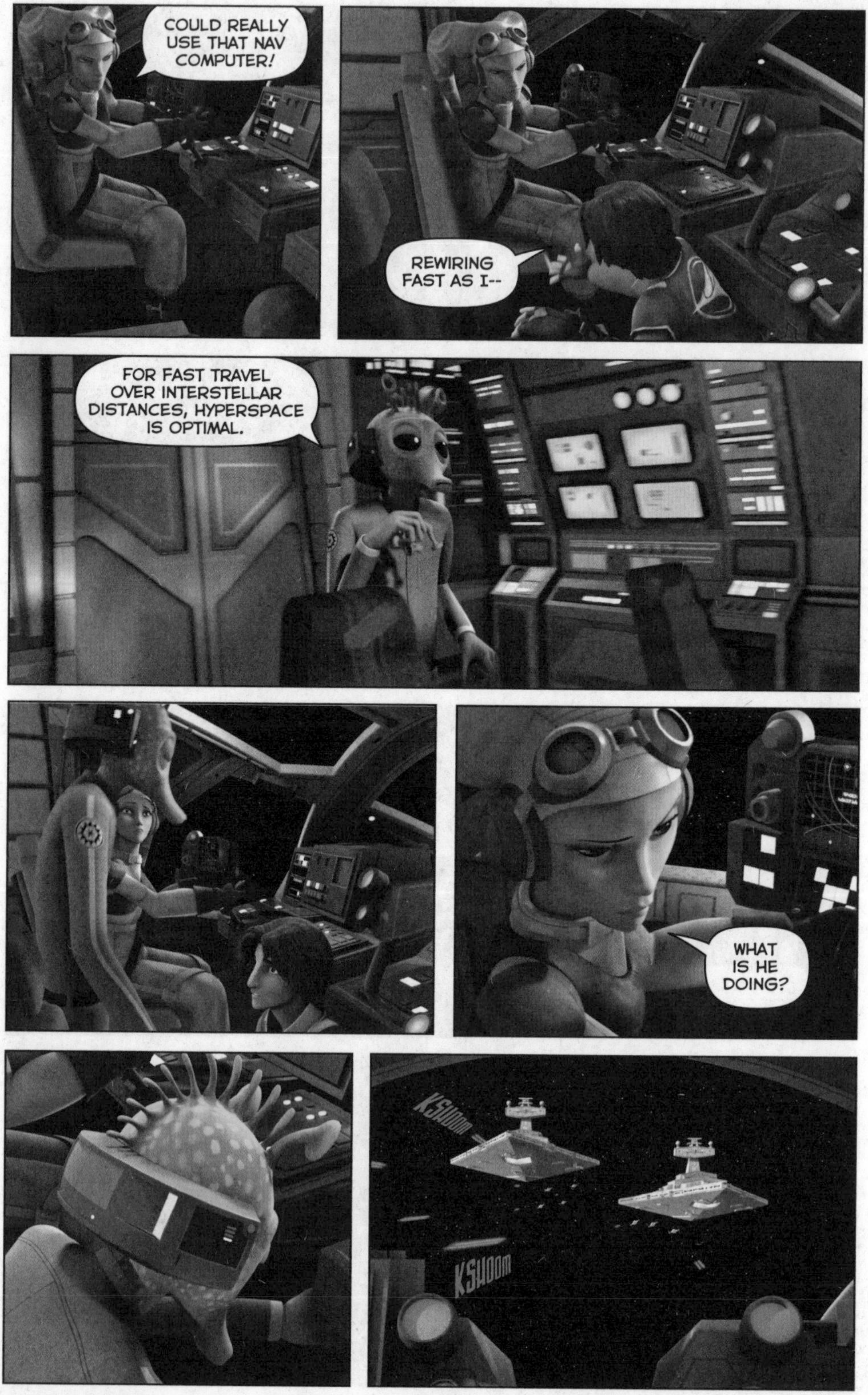
COULD REALLY USE THAT NAV COMPUTER!
REWIRING FAST AS I--
FOR FAST TRAVEL OVER INTERSTELLAR DISTANCES, HYPERSPACE IS OPTIMAL.
WHAT IS HE DOING?
KSHOOM
KSHOOM

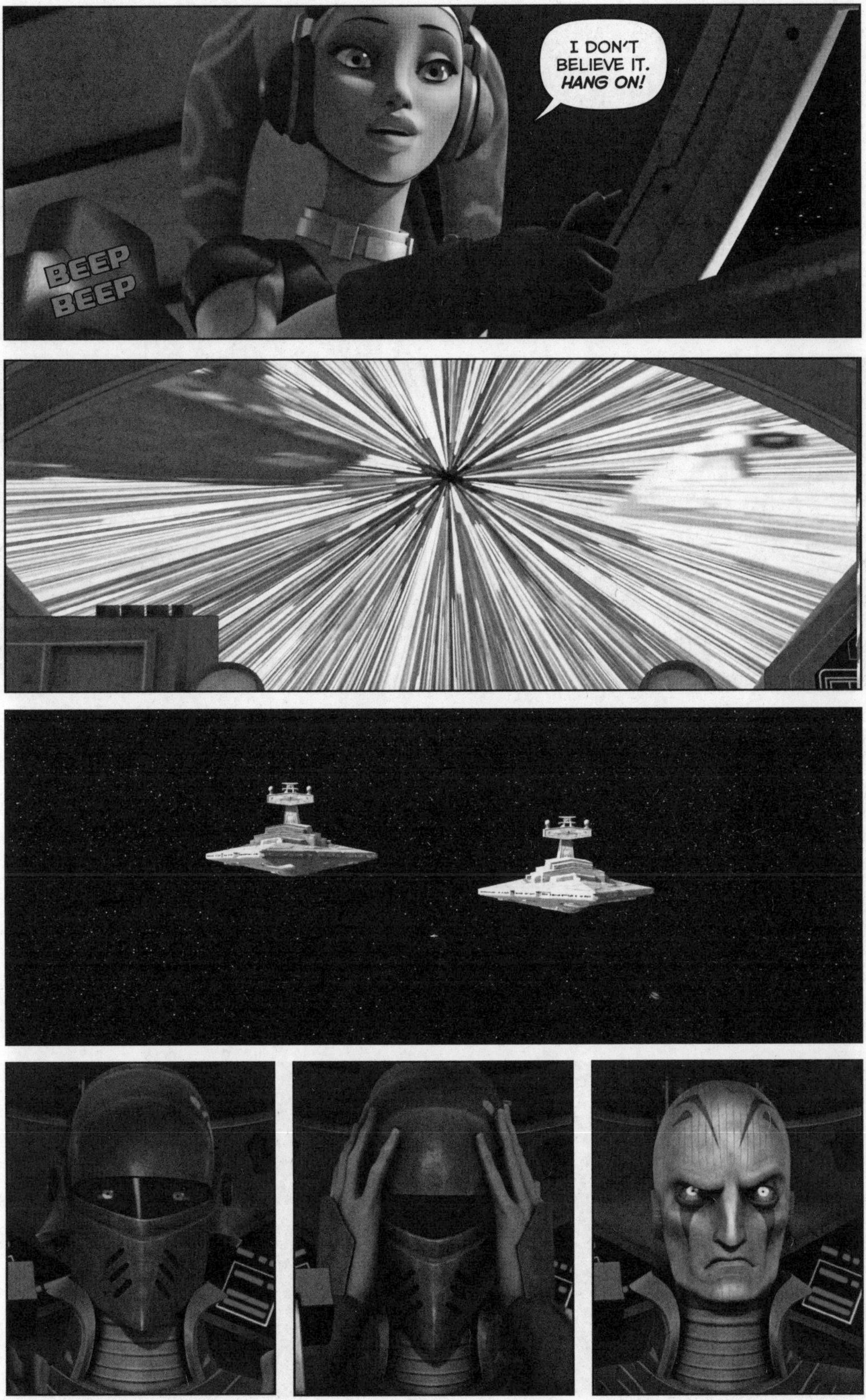
I DON'T BELIEVE IT. *HANG ON!*
BEEP BEEP

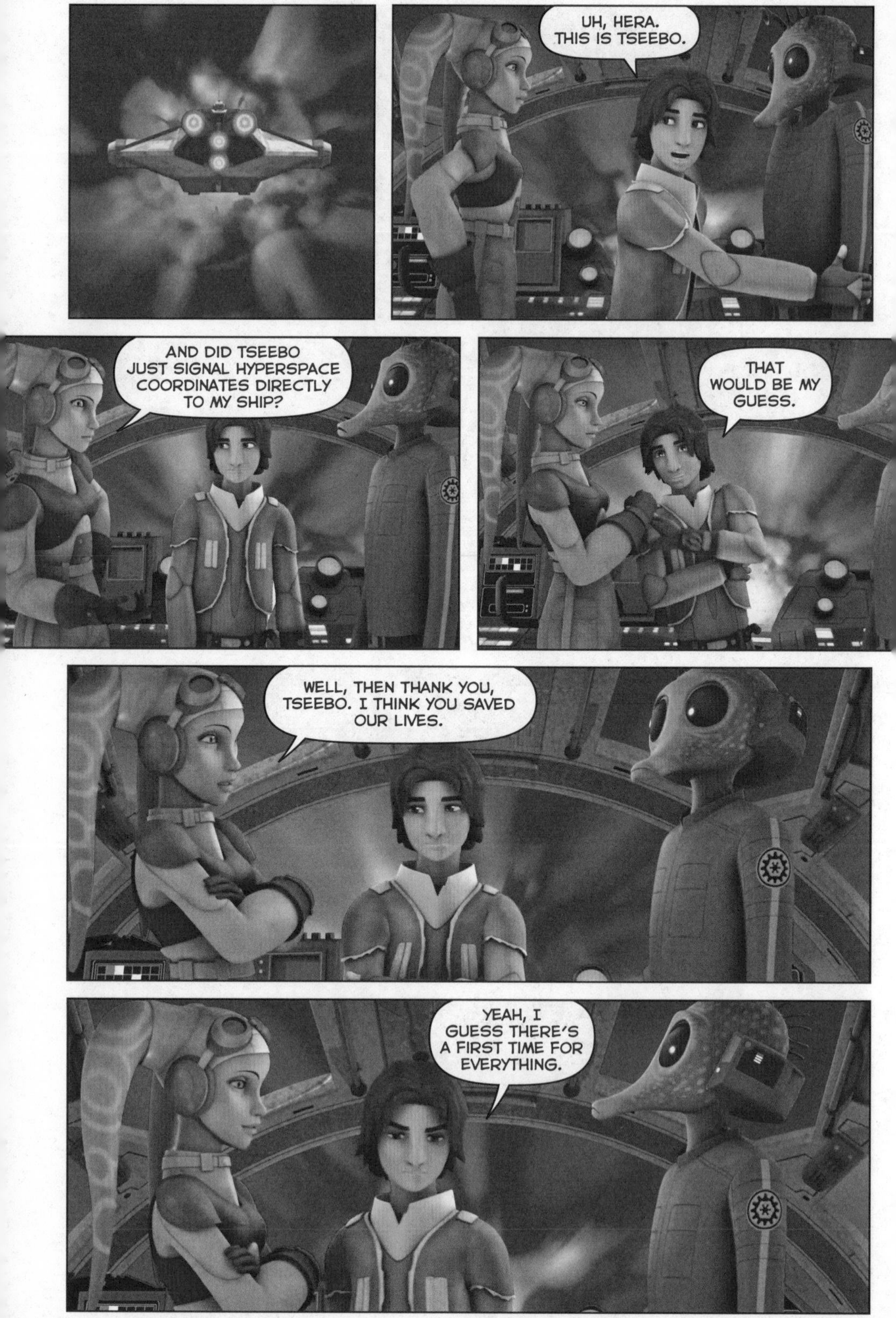
UH, HERA.
THIS IS TSEEBO.
AND DID TSEEBO JUST SIGNAL HYPERSPACE COORDINATES DIRECTLY TO MY SHIP?
THAT WOULD BE MY GUESS.
WELL, THEN THANK YOU, TSEEBO. I THINK YOU SAVED OUR LIVES.
YEAH, I GUESS THERE'S A FIRST TIME FOR EVERYTHING.

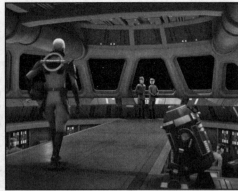

WE ARE RECEIVING A SIGNAL FROM THE TRACKER. THEY WILL *NOT* BE ABLE TO OUTRUN US FOR LONG.

I STILL SENSE THE JEDI AND HIS PADAWAN WITHIN MY GRASP.

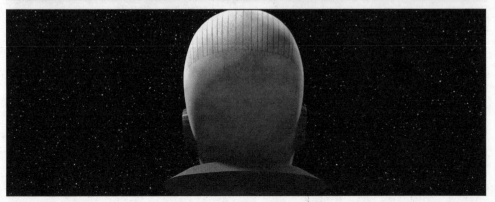

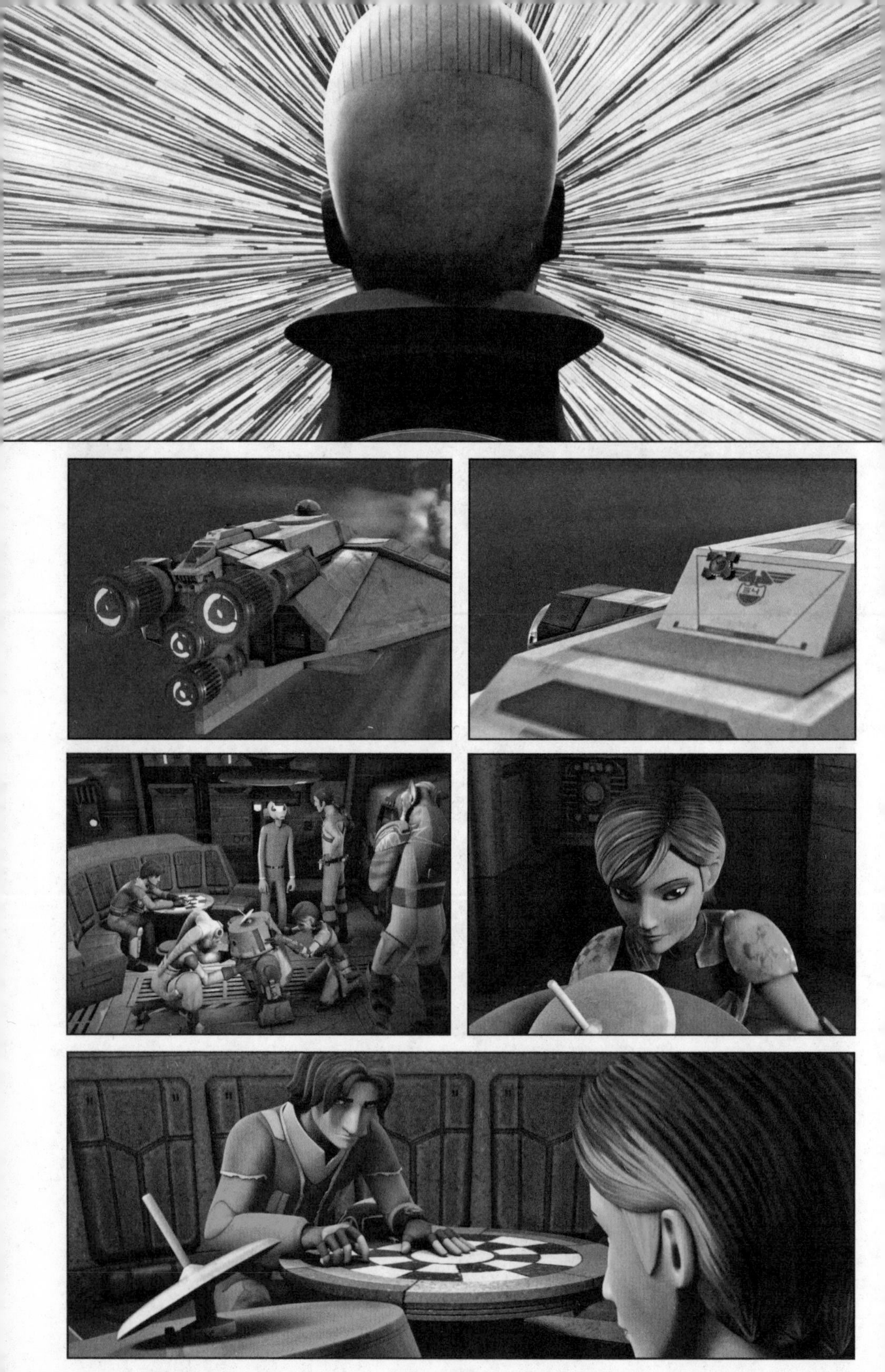

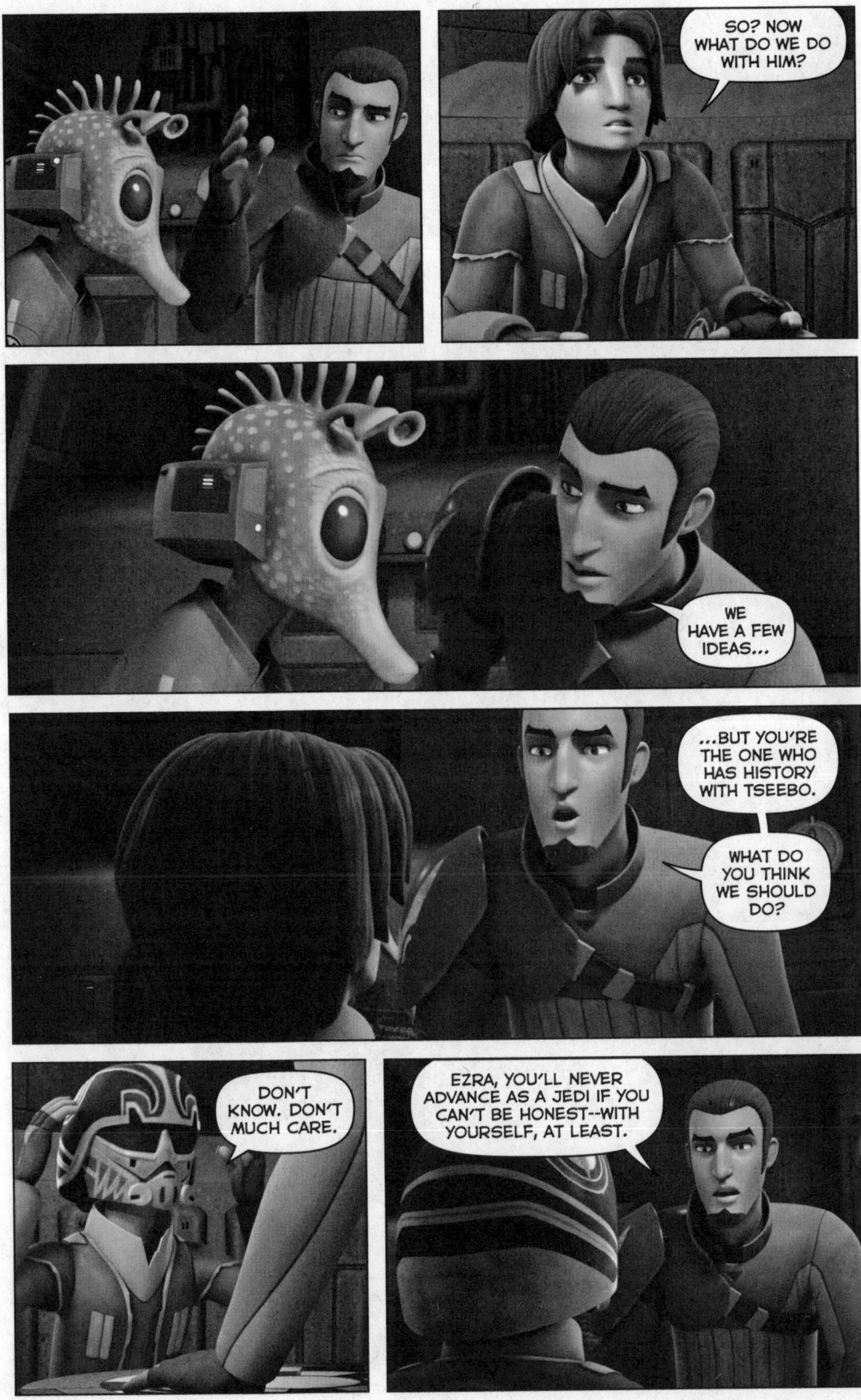
SO? NOW WHAT DO WE DO WITH HIM?
WE HAVE A FEW IDEAS...
...BUT YOU'RE THE ONE WHO HAS HISTORY WITH TSEEBO.
WHAT DO YOU THINK WE SHOULD DO?
DON'T KNOW. DON'T MUCH CARE.
EZRA, YOU'LL NEVER ADVANCE AS A JEDI IF YOU CAN'T BE HONEST--WITH YOURSELF, AT LEAST.

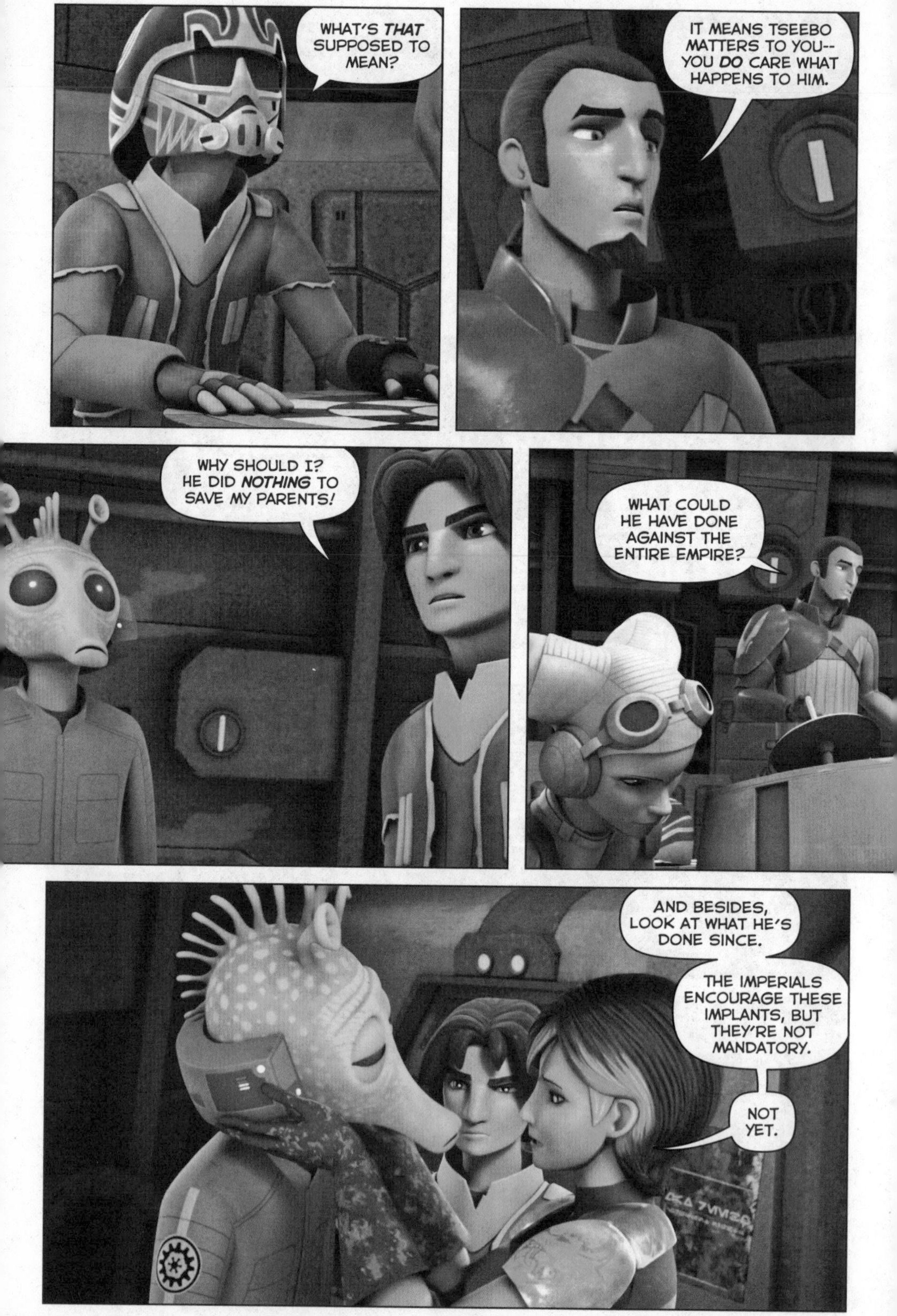
WHAT'S *THAT* SUPPOSED TO MEAN?
IT MEANS TSEEBO MATTERS TO YOU-- YOU *DO* CARE WHAT HAPPENS TO HIM.
WHY SHOULD I? HE DID *NOTHING* TO SAVE MY PARENTS!
WHAT COULD HE HAVE DONE AGAINST THE ENTIRE EMPIRE?
AND BESIDES, LOOK AT WHAT HE'S DONE SINCE.
THE IMPERIALS ENCOURAGE THESE IMPLANTS, BUT THEY'RE NOT MANDATORY.
NOT YET.

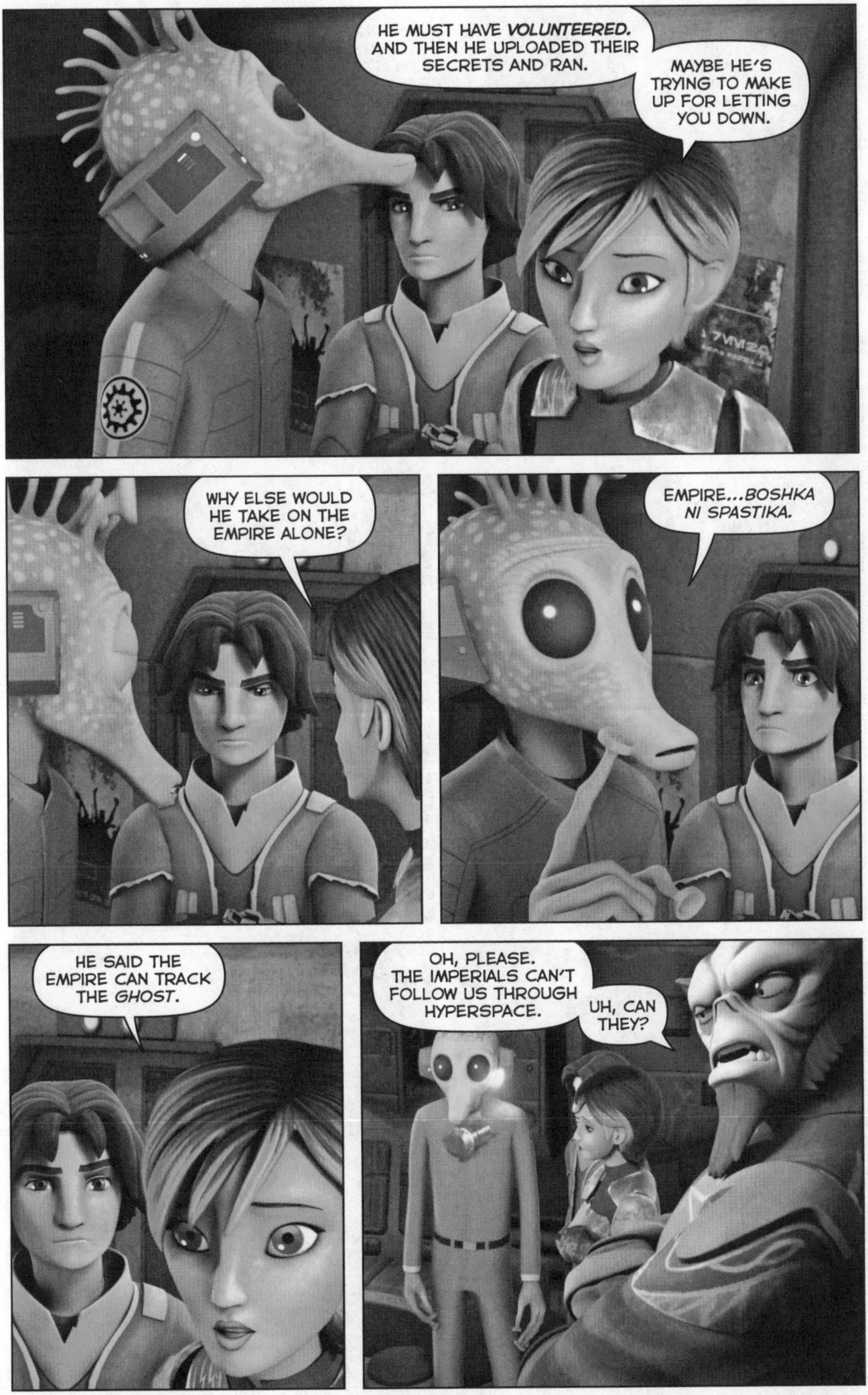
HE MUST HAVE *VOLUNTEERED.* AND THEN HE UPLOADED THEIR SECRETS AND RAN.
MAYBE HE'S TRYING TO MAKE UP FOR LETTING YOU DOWN.
WHY ELSE WOULD HE TAKE ON THE EMPIRE ALONE?
EMPIRE...*BOSHKA NI SPASTIKA.*
HE SAID THE EMPIRE CAN TRACK THE *GHOST*.
OH, PLEASE. THE IMPERIALS CAN'T FOLLOW US THROUGH HYPERSPACE.
UH, CAN THEY?

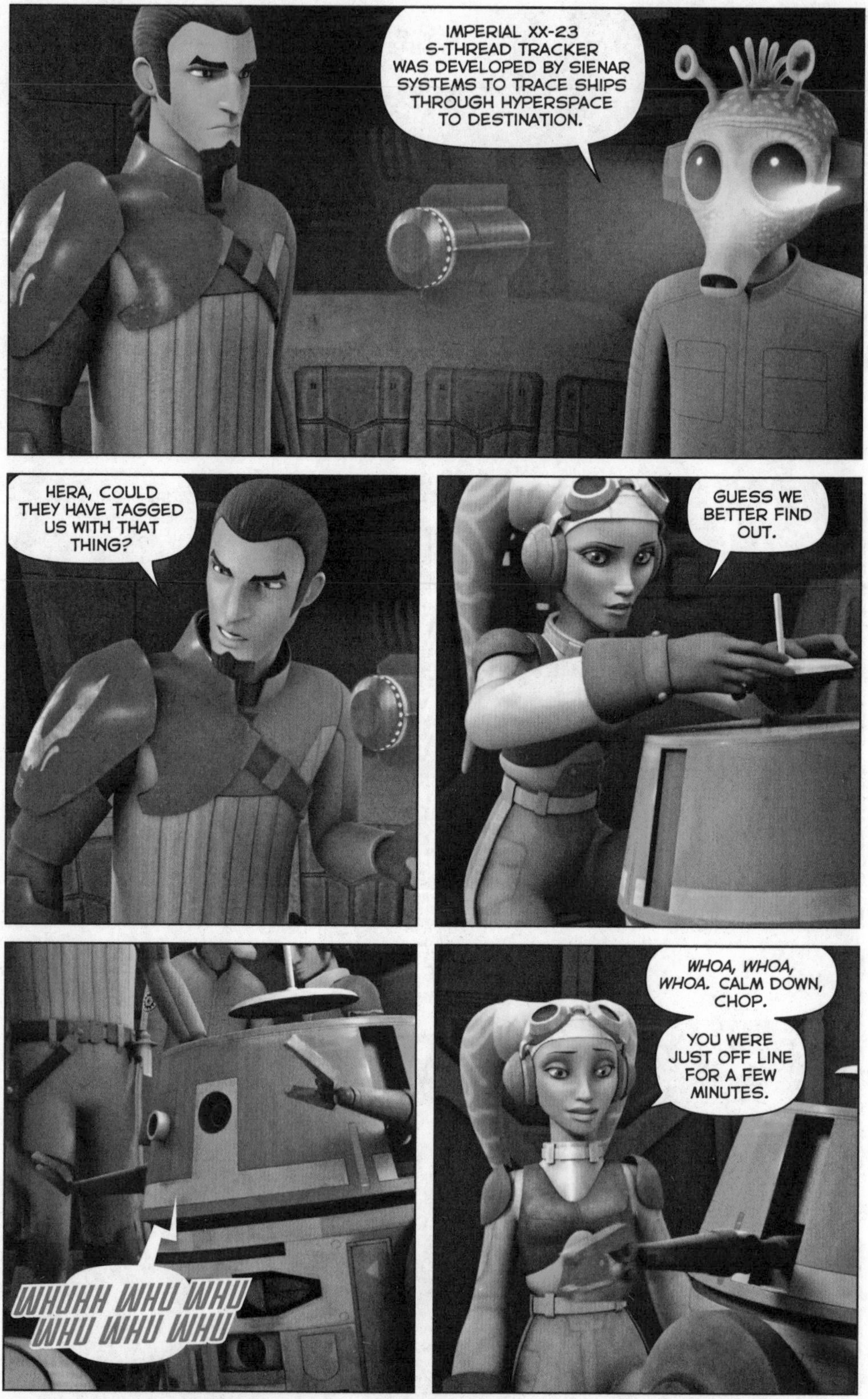
IMPERIAL XX-23 S-THREAD TRACKER WAS DEVELOPED BY SIENAR SYSTEMS TO TRACE SHIPS THROUGH HYPERSPACE TO DESTINATION.
HERA, COULD THEY HAVE TAGGED US WITH THAT THING?
GUESS WE BETTER FIND OUT.
WHUHH WHU WHU WHU WHU WHU
WHOA, WHOA, WHOA. CALM DOWN, CHOP.
YOU WERE JUST OFF LINE FOR A FEW MINUTES.

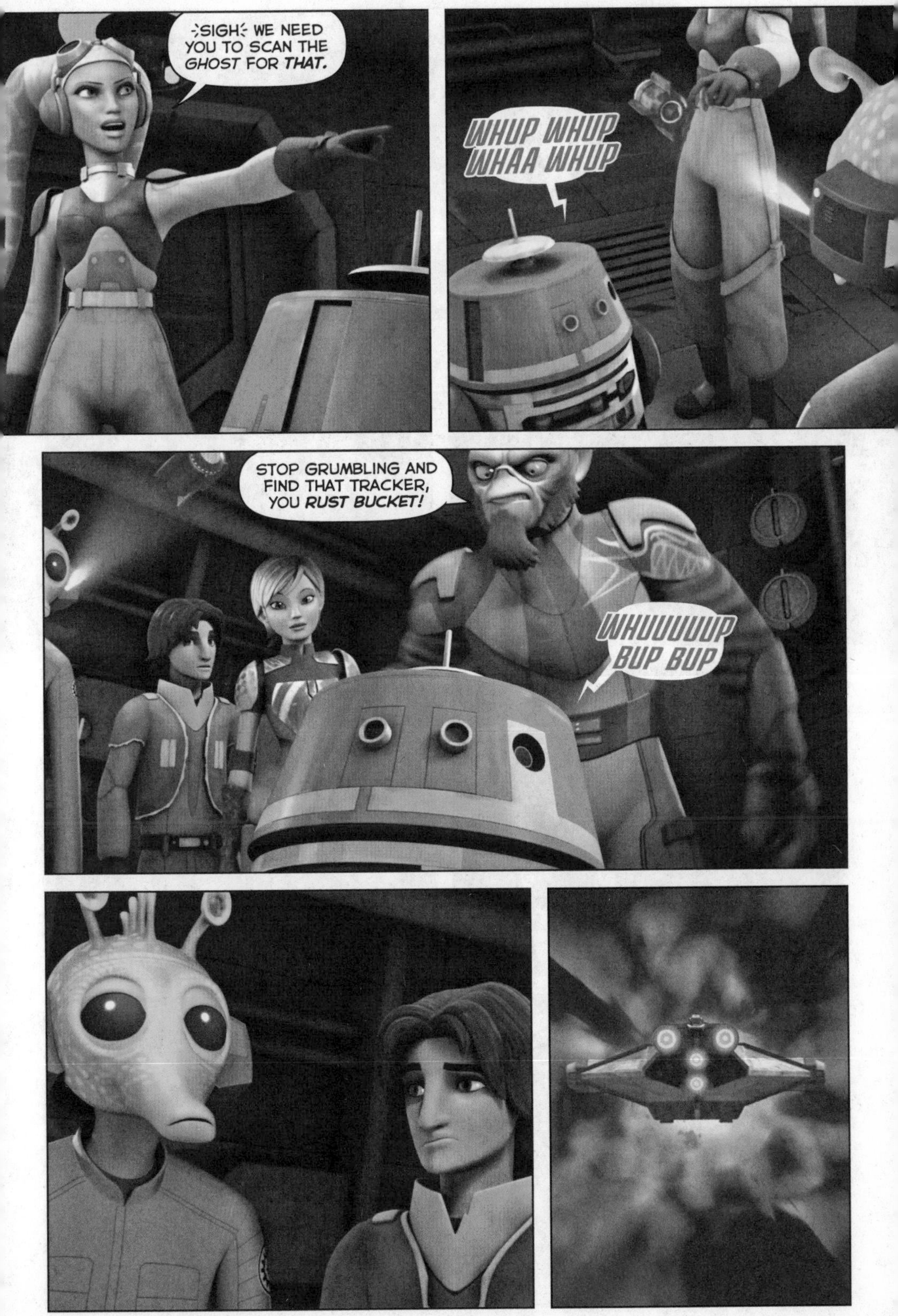
SIGH WE NEED YOU TO SCAN THE *GHOST* FOR ***THAT.***
WHUP WHUP WHAA WHUP
STOP GRUMBLING AND FIND THAT TRACKER, YOU ***RUST BUCKET!***
WHUUUUUP BUP BUP

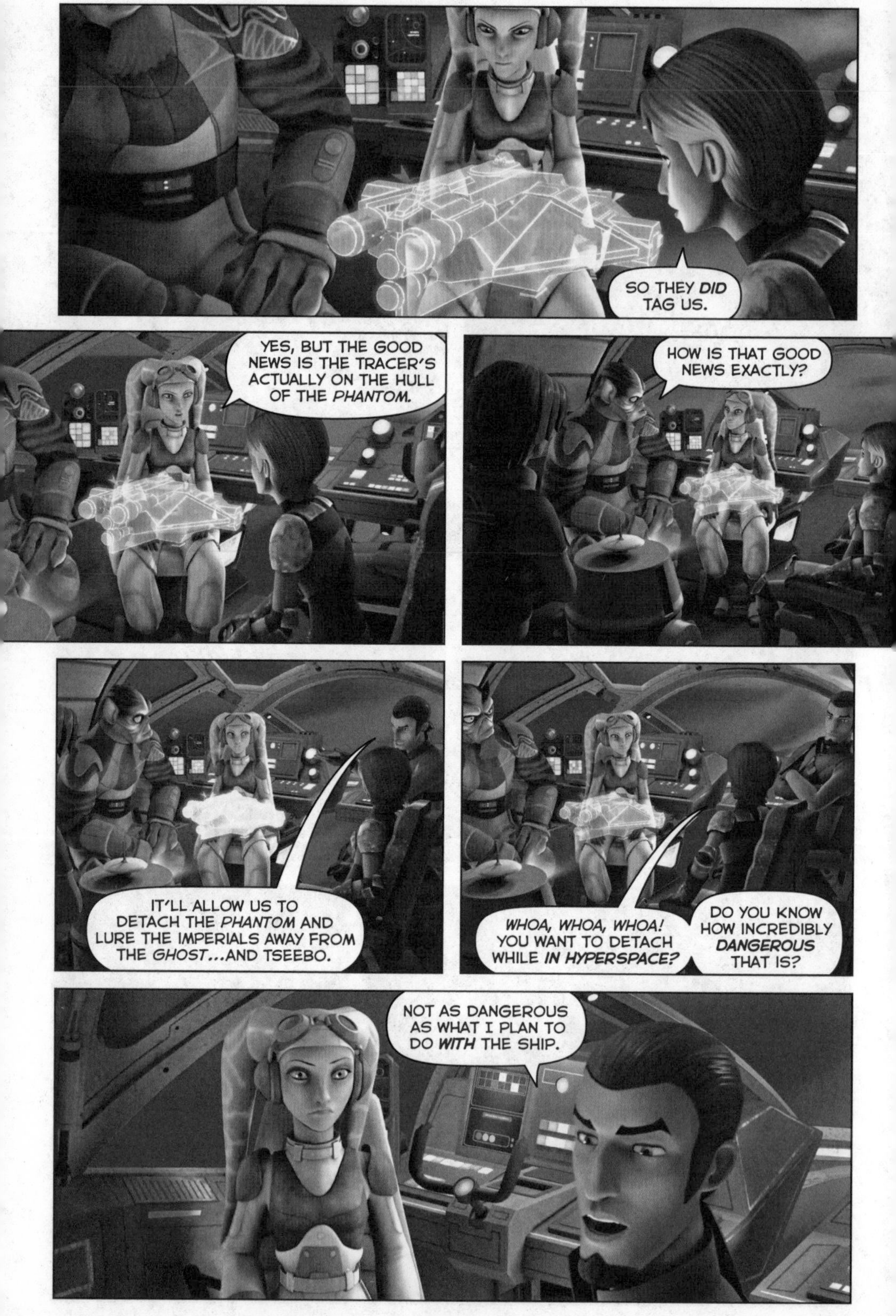
SO THEY *DID* TAG US.
YES, BUT THE GOOD NEWS IS THE TRACER'S ACTUALLY ON THE HULL OF THE *PHANTOM.*
HOW IS THAT GOOD NEWS EXACTLY?
IT'LL ALLOW US TO DETACH THE *PHANTOM* AND LURE THE IMPERIALS AWAY FROM THE *GHOST*...AND TSEEBO.
WHOA, WHOA, WHOA! YOU WANT TO DETACH WHILE *IN HYPERSPACE?*
DO YOU KNOW HOW INCREDIBLY *DANGEROUS* THAT IS?
NOT AS DANGEROUS AS WHAT I PLAN TO DO *WITH* THE SHIP.

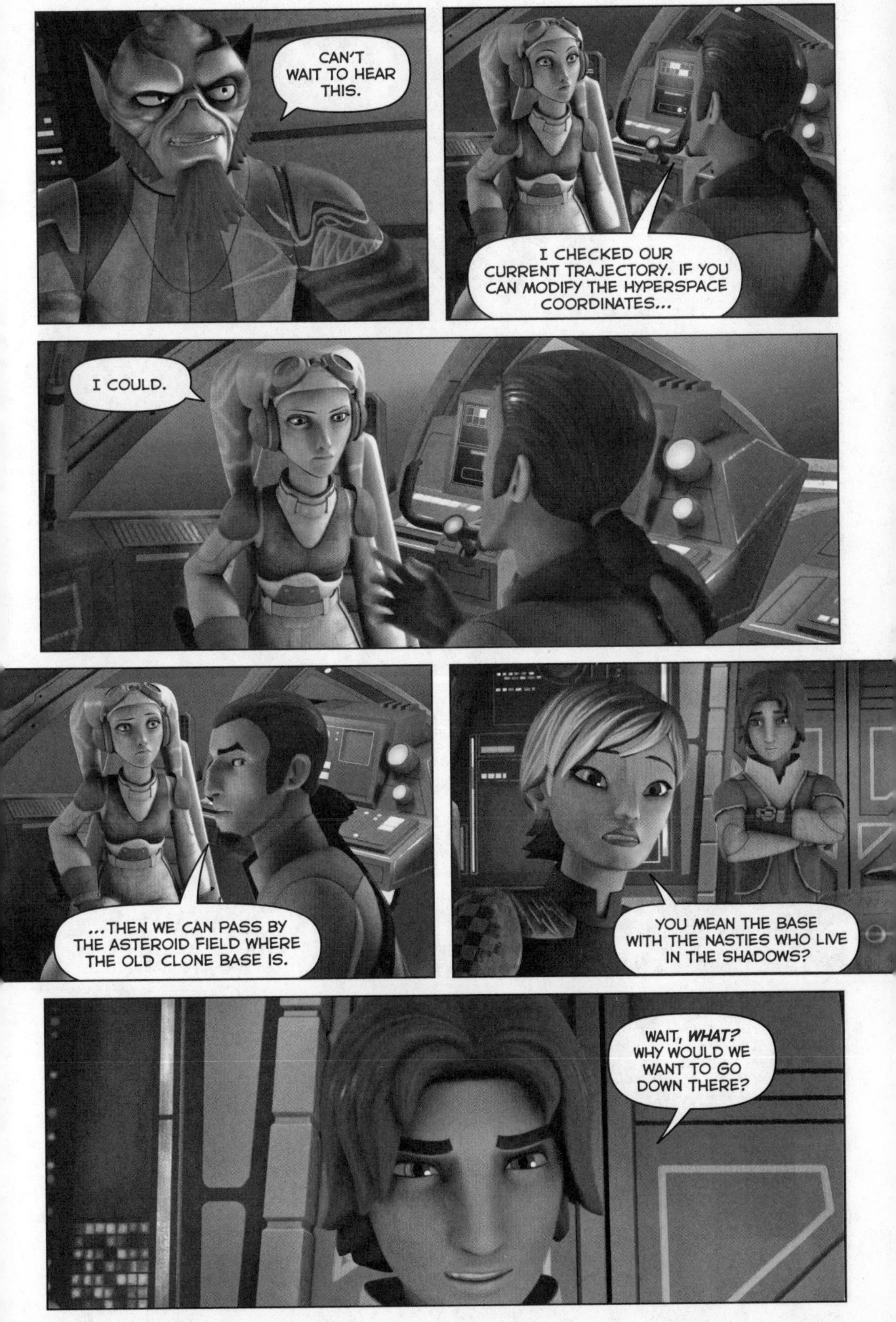
CAN'T WAIT TO HEAR THIS.
I CHECKED OUR CURRENT TRAJECTORY. IF YOU CAN MODIFY THE HYPERSPACE COORDINATES...
I COULD.
...THEN WE CAN PASS BY THE ASTEROID FIELD WHERE THE OLD CLONE BASE IS.
YOU MEAN THE BASE WITH THE NASTIES WHO LIVE IN THE SHADOWS?
WAIT, *WHAT?* WHY WOULD WE WANT TO GO DOWN THERE?

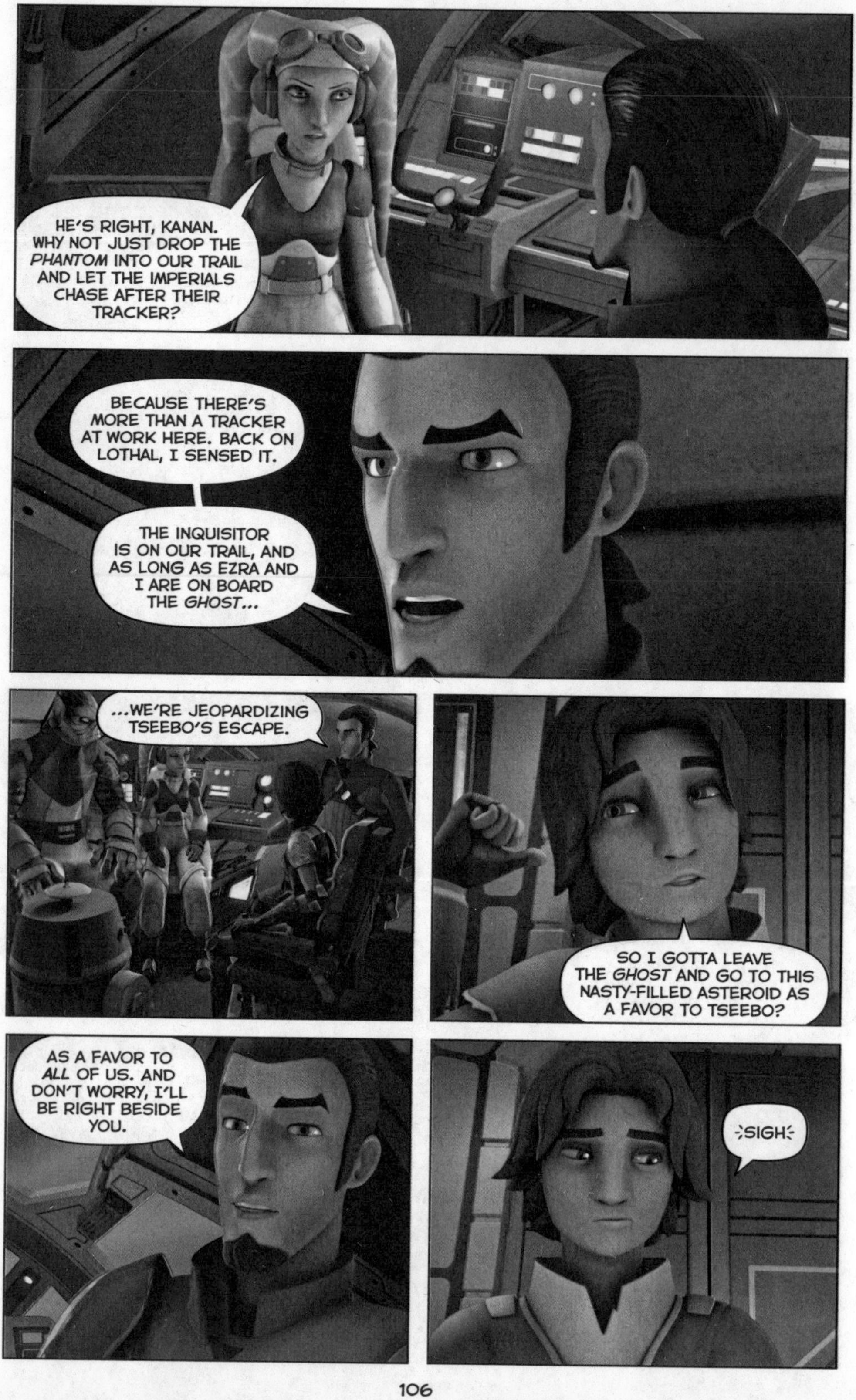
HE'S RIGHT, KANAN. WHY NOT JUST DROP THE *PHANTOM* INTO OUR TRAIL AND LET THE IMPERIALS CHASE AFTER THEIR TRACKER?
BECAUSE THERE'S MORE THAN A TRACKER AT WORK HERE. BACK ON LOTHAL, I SENSED IT.
THE INQUISITOR IS ON OUR TRAIL, AND AS LONG AS EZRA AND I ARE ON BOARD THE *GHOST*...
...WE'RE JEOPARDIZING TSEEBO'S ESCAPE.
SO I GOTTA LEAVE THE *GHOST* AND GO TO THIS NASTY-FILLED ASTEROID AS A FAVOR TO TSEEBO?
AS A FAVOR TO *ALL* OF US. AND DON'T WORRY, I'LL BE RIGHT BESIDE YOU.
SIGH

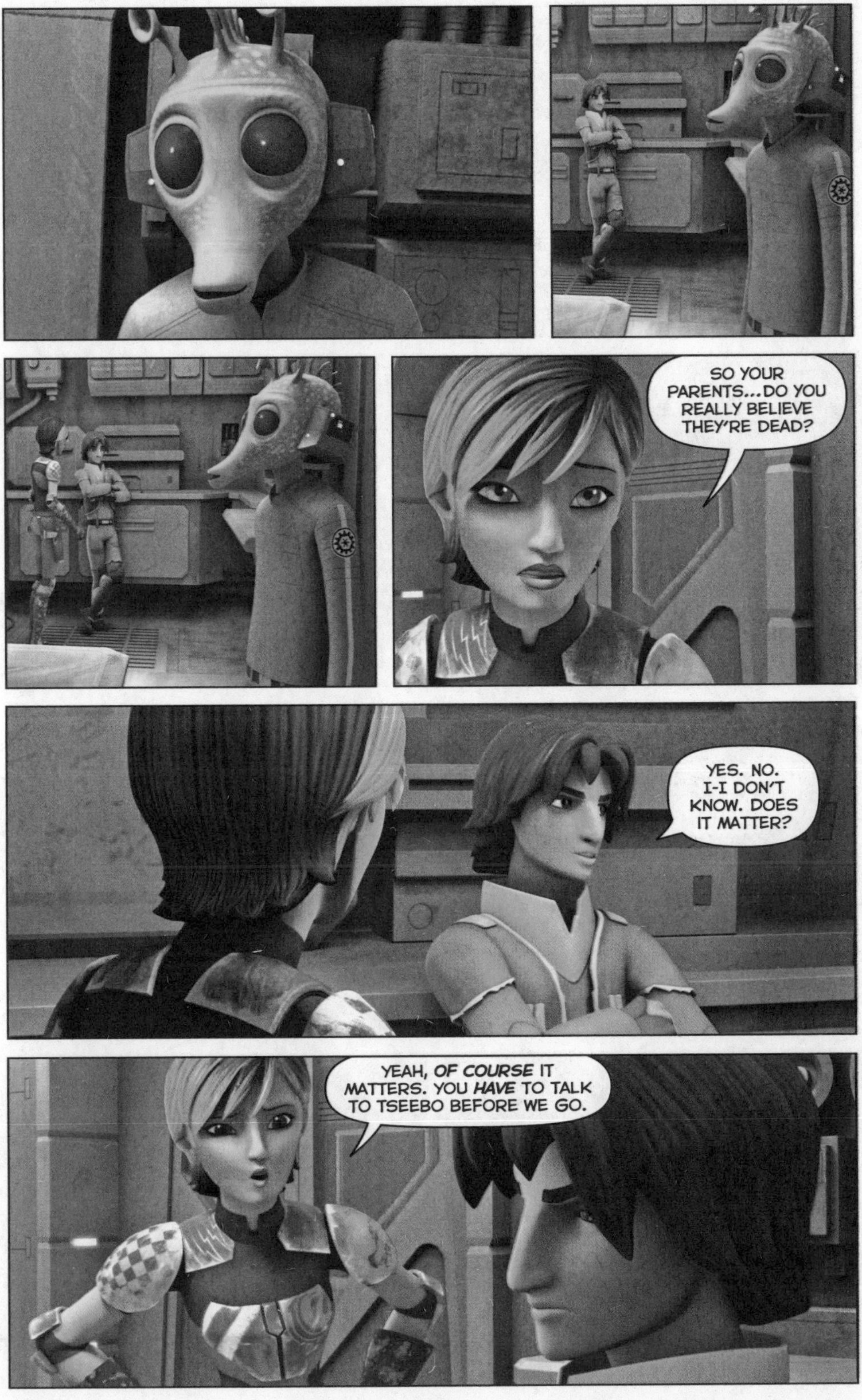
SO YOUR PARENTS...DO YOU REALLY BELIEVE THEY'RE DEAD?
YES. NO. I-I DON'T KNOW. DOES IT MATTER?
YEAH, *OF COURSE* IT MATTERS. YOU *HAVE* TO TALK TO TSEEBO BEFORE WE GO.

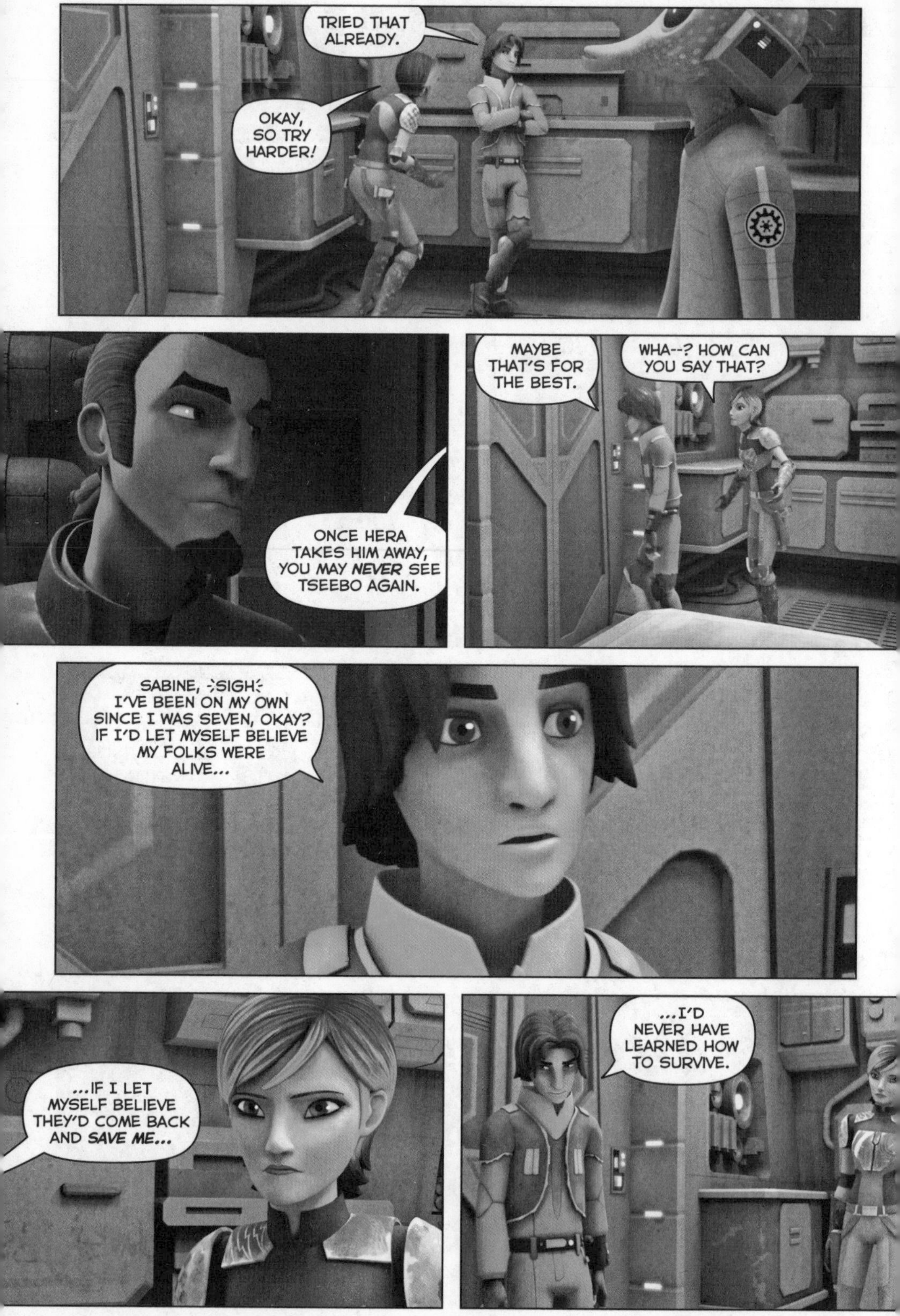

TRIED THAT ALREADY.
OKAY, SO TRY HARDER!
MAYBE THAT'S FOR THE BEST.
ONCE HERA TAKES HIM AWAY, YOU MAY NEVER SEE TSEEBO AGAIN.
WHA--? HOW CAN YOU SAY THAT?
SABINE, *SIGH* I'VE BEEN ON MY OWN SINCE I WAS SEVEN, OKAY? IF I'D LET MYSELF BELIEVE MY FOLKS WERE ALIVE...
...IF I LET MYSELF BELIEVE THEY'D COME BACK AND SAVE ME...
...I'D NEVER HAVE LEARNED HOW TO SURVIVE.

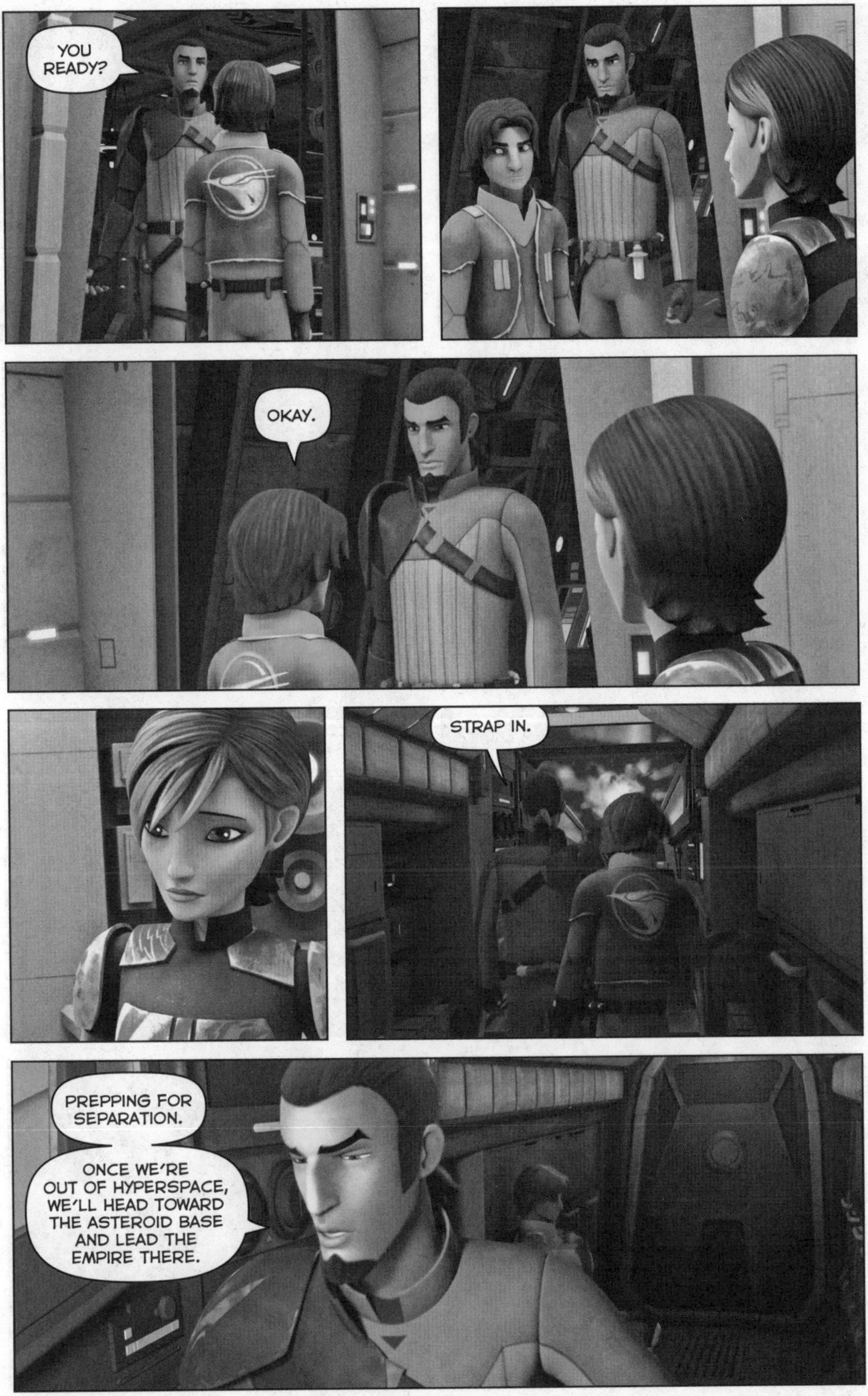
YOU READY?
OKAY.
STRAP IN.
PREPPING FOR SEPARATION.
ONCE WE'RE OUT OF HYPERSPACE, WE'LL HEAD TOWARD THE ASTEROID BASE AND LEAD THE EMPIRE THERE.

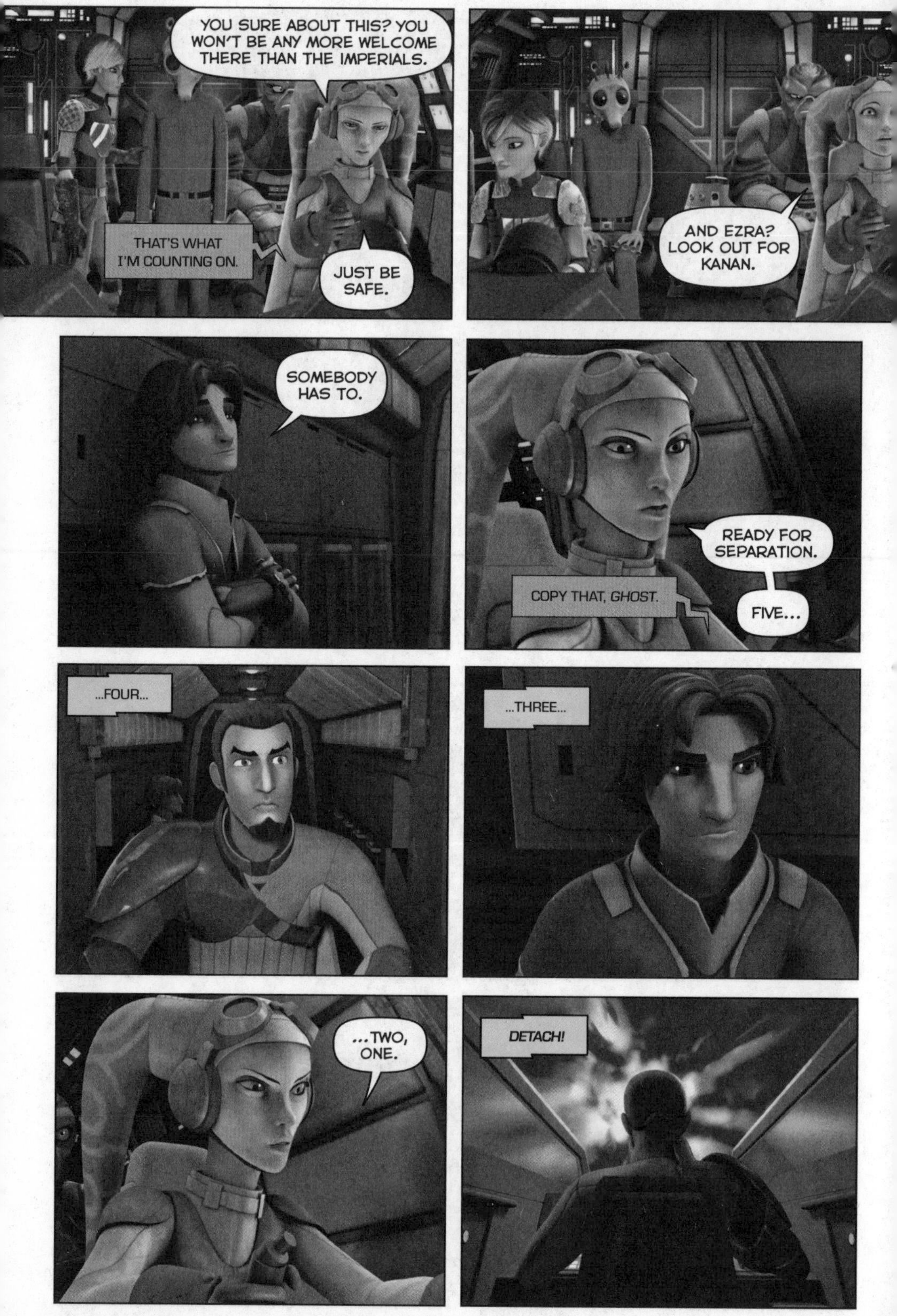
YOU SURE ABOUT THIS? YOU WON'T BE ANY MORE WELCOME THERE THAN THE IMPERIALS.
THAT'S WHAT I'M COUNTING ON.
JUST BE SAFE.
AND EZRA? LOOK OUT FOR KANAN.
SOMEBODY HAS TO.
READY FOR SEPARATION.
COPY THAT, *GHOST*.
FIVE...
...FOUR...
...THREE...
...TWO, ONE.
DETACH!

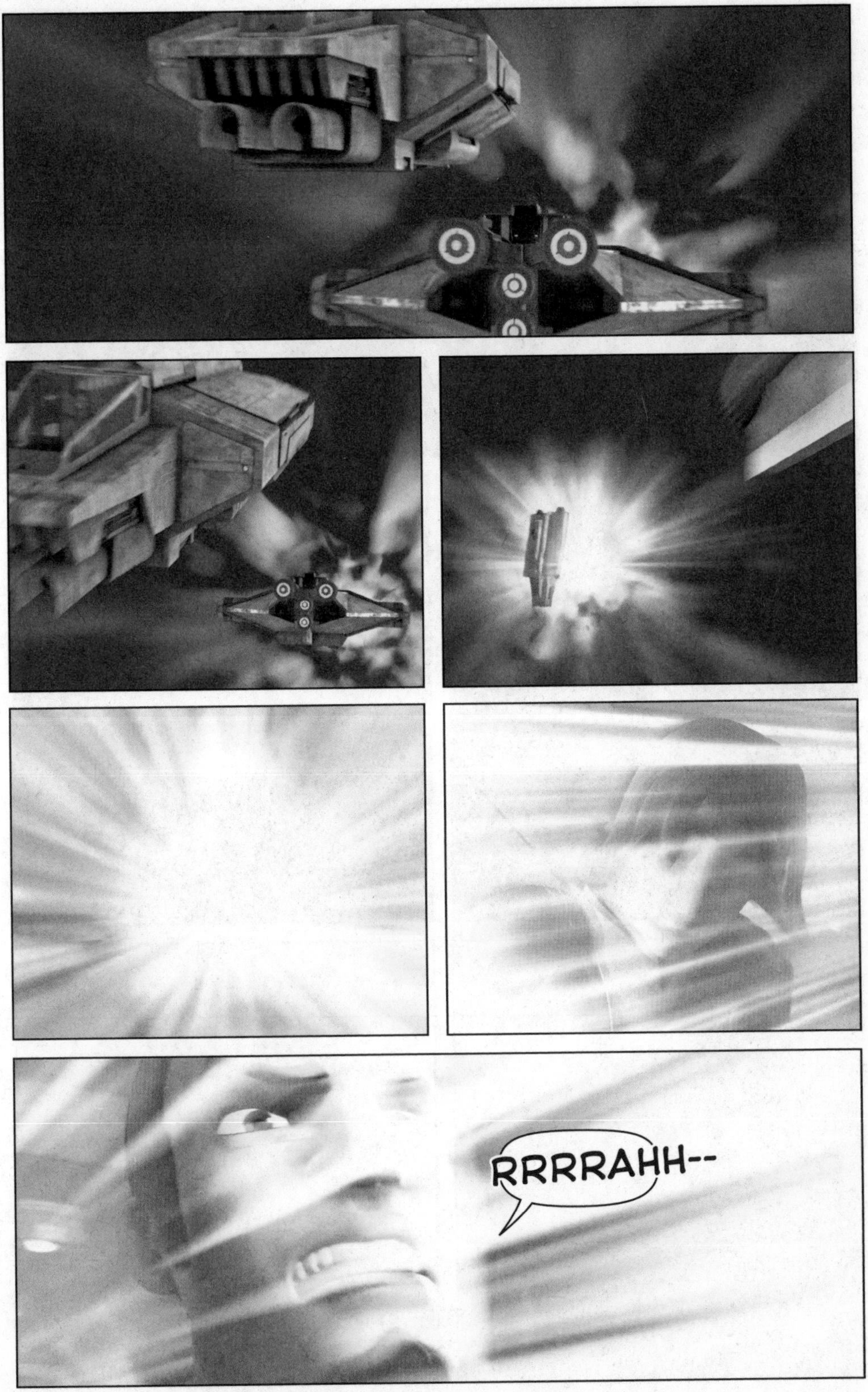
RRRRAHH--

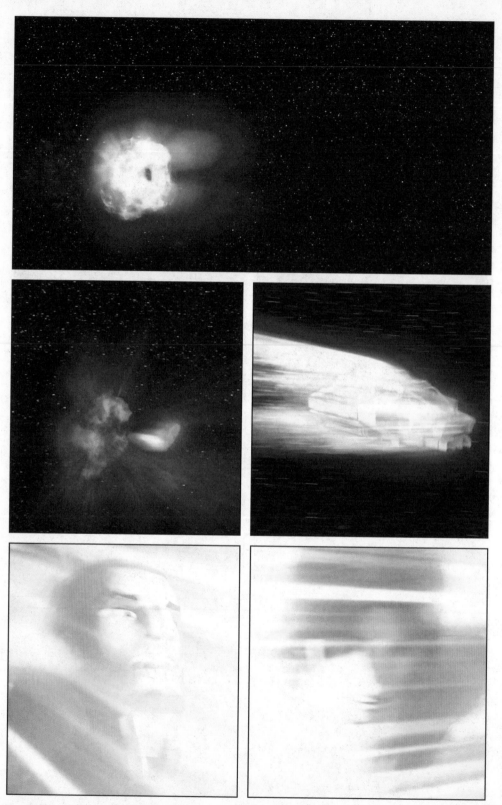

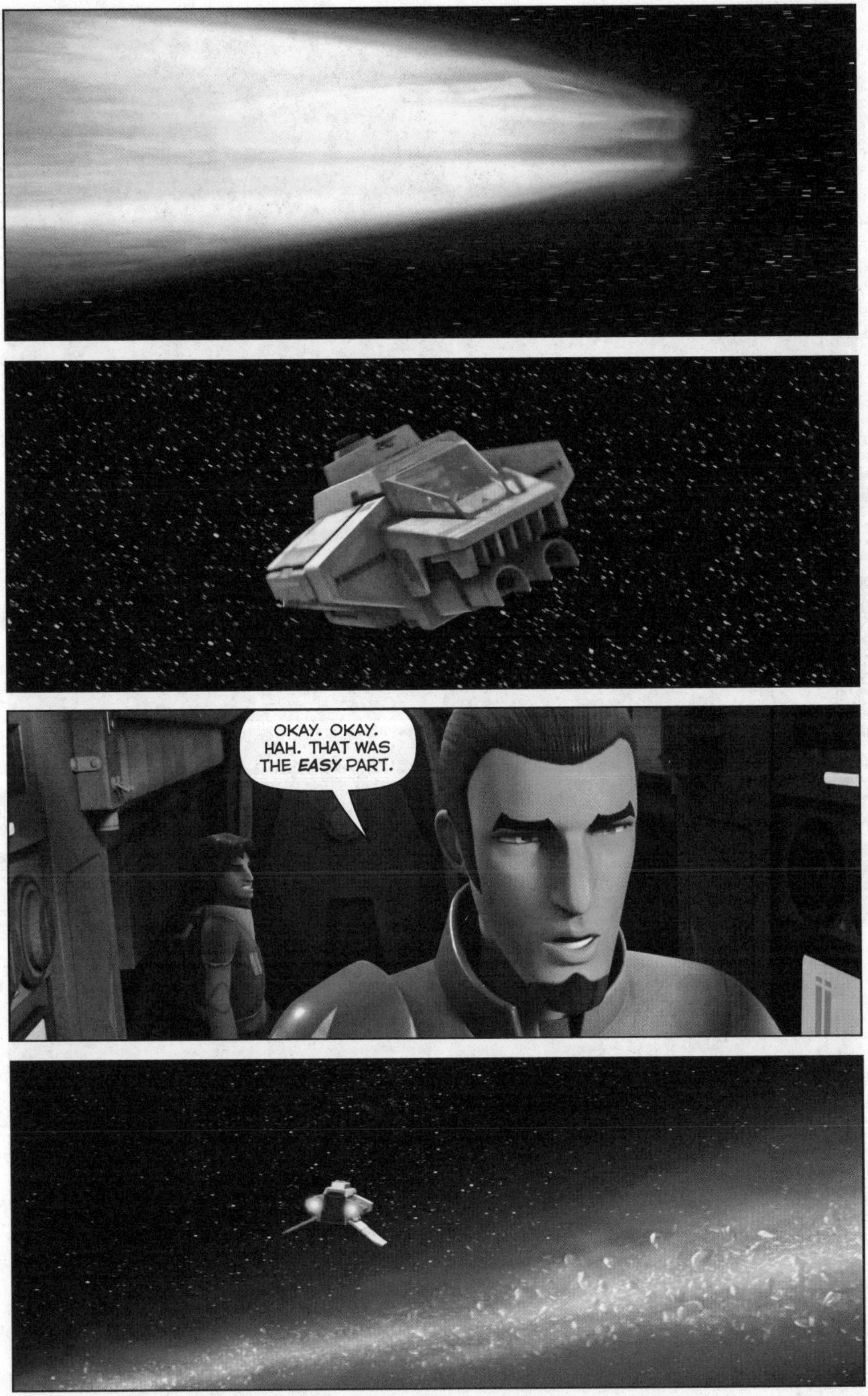
OKAY. OKAY. HAH. THAT WAS THE *EASY* PART.

I SENSE MOVEMENT IN THE FORCE.

Y-YES. THE TRACKER INDICATES THE REBEL SHIP HAS EMERGED FROM HYPERSPACE. SHOULD WE--

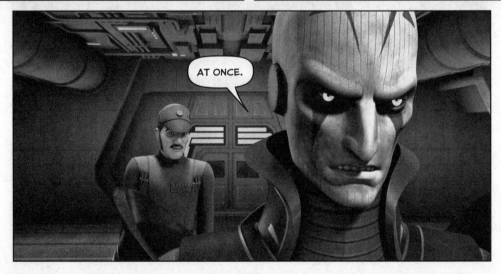

AT ONCE.

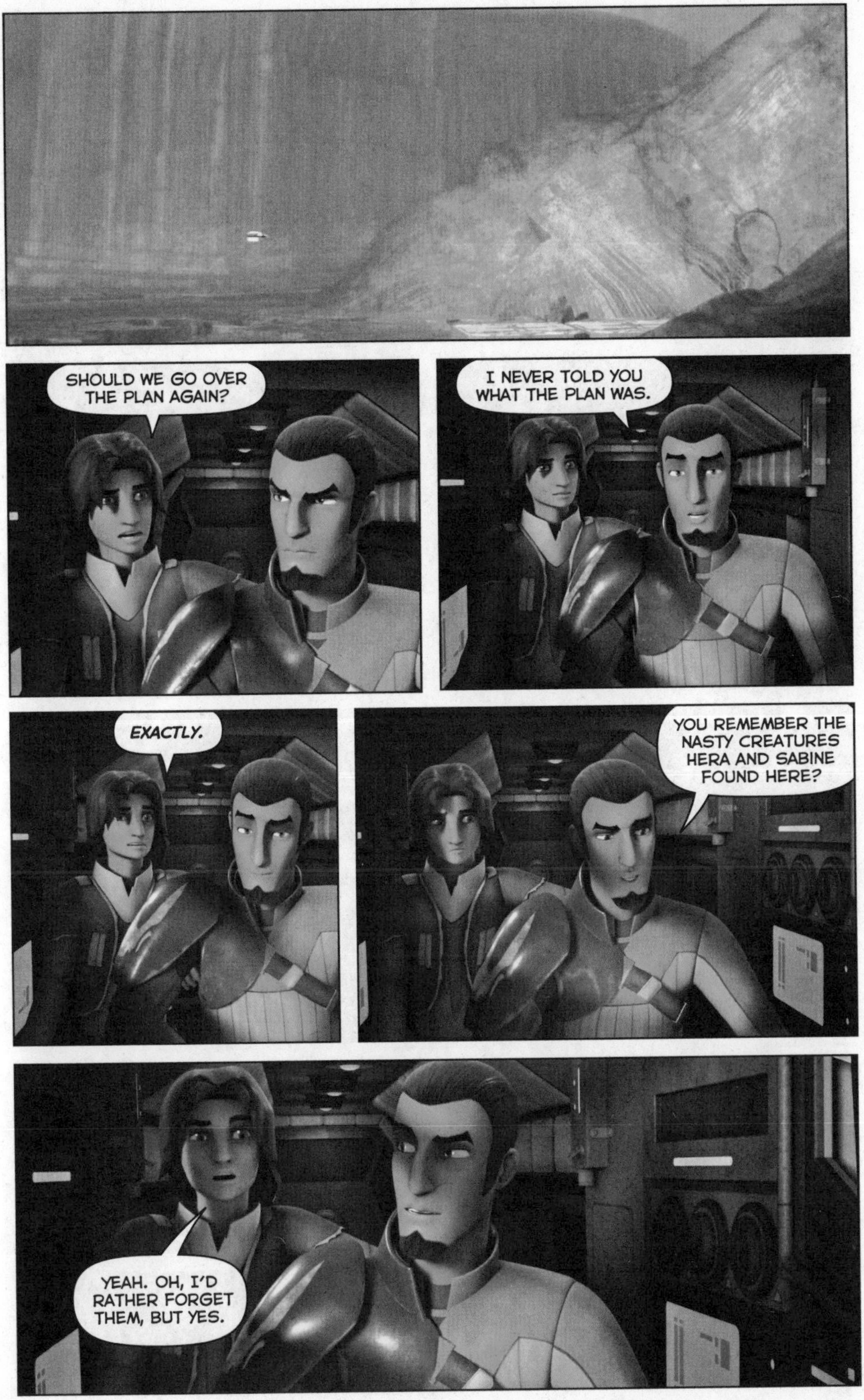
SHOULD WE GO OVER THE PLAN AGAIN?
I NEVER TOLD YOU WHAT THE PLAN WAS.
EXACTLY.
YOU REMEMBER THE NASTY CREATURES HERA AND SABINE FOUND HERE?
YEAH. OH, I'D RATHER FORGET THEM, BUT YES.

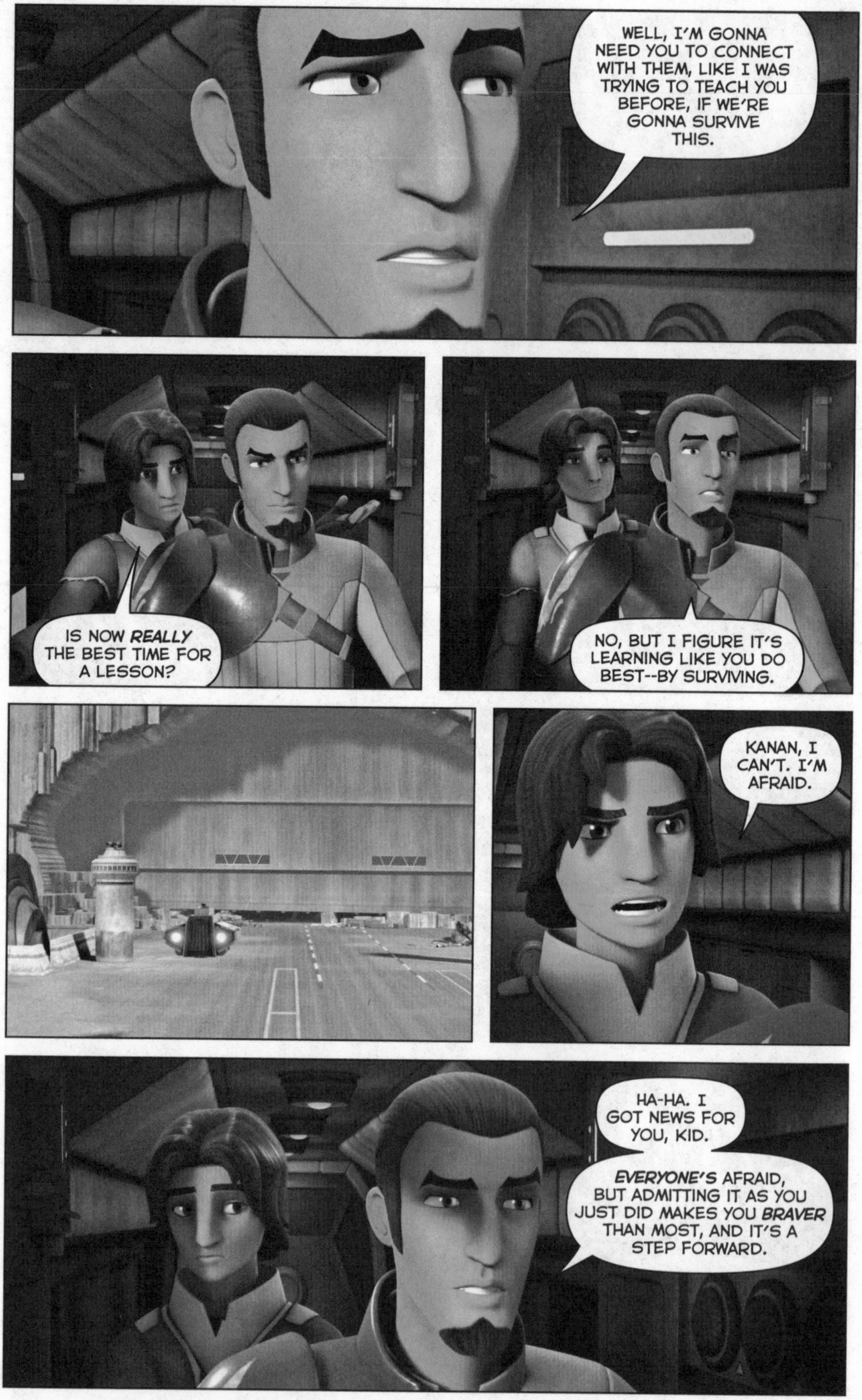
WELL, I'M GONNA NEED YOU TO CONNECT WITH THEM, LIKE I WAS TRYING TO TEACH YOU BEFORE, IF WE'RE GONNA SURVIVE THIS.
IS NOW *REALLY* THE BEST TIME FOR A LESSON?
NO, BUT I FIGURE IT'S LEARNING LIKE YOU DO BEST--BY SURVIVING.
KANAN, I CAN'T. I'M AFRAID.
HA-HA. I GOT NEWS FOR YOU, KID.
EVERYONE'S AFRAID, BUT ADMITTING IT AS YOU JUST DID MAKES YOU *BRAVER* THAN MOST, AND IT'S A STEP FORWARD.

YEAH, INTO THE JAWS OF A *NIGHTMARE.*

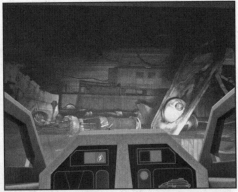

OKAY... OKAY...

I'LL GET THE TRACKING DEVICE OFF THE *PHANTOM.*

YOU...GO MAKE SOME NEW FRIENDS.

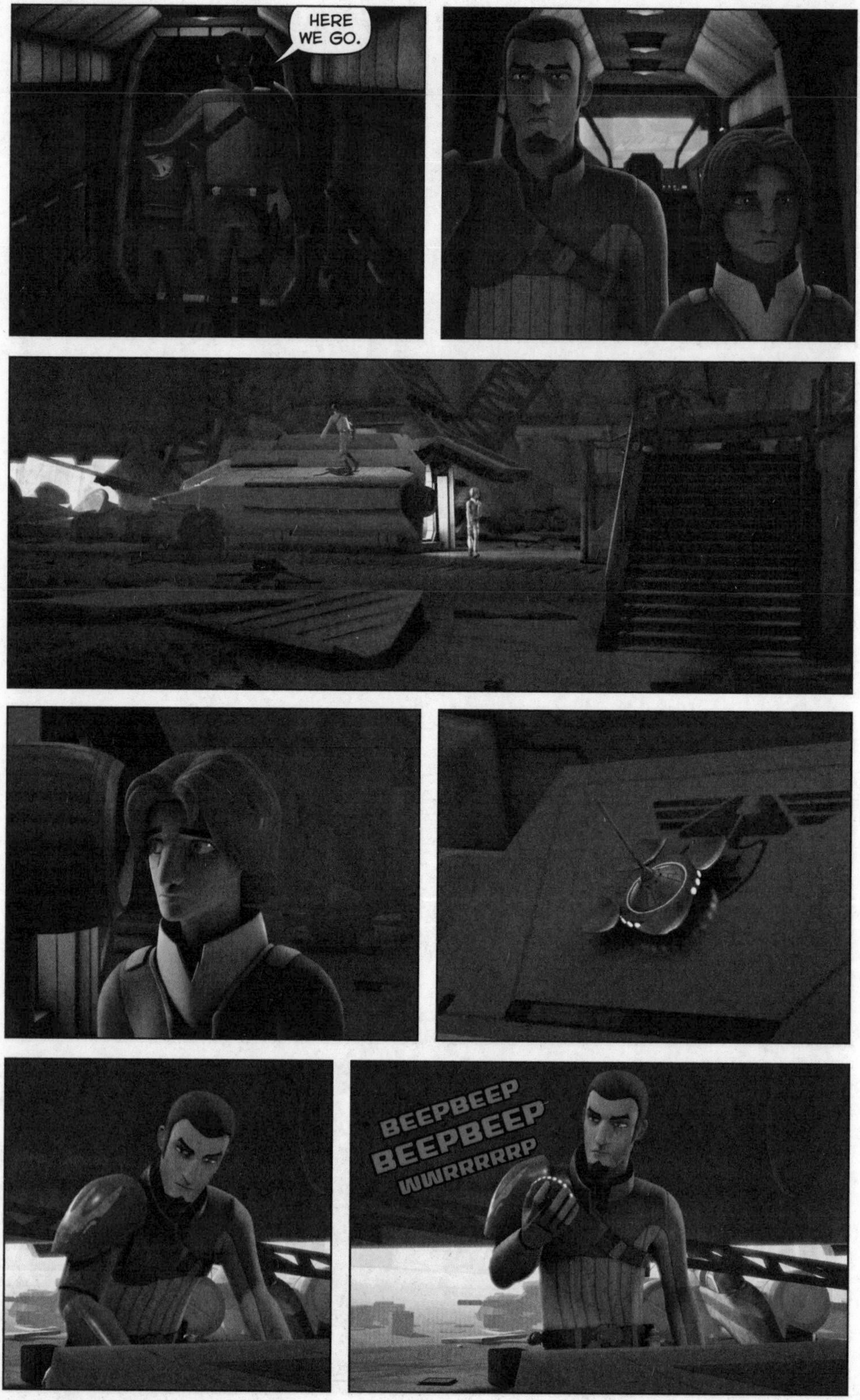
HERE WE GO.
BEEPBEEP
BEEPBEEP
WWRRRRRP

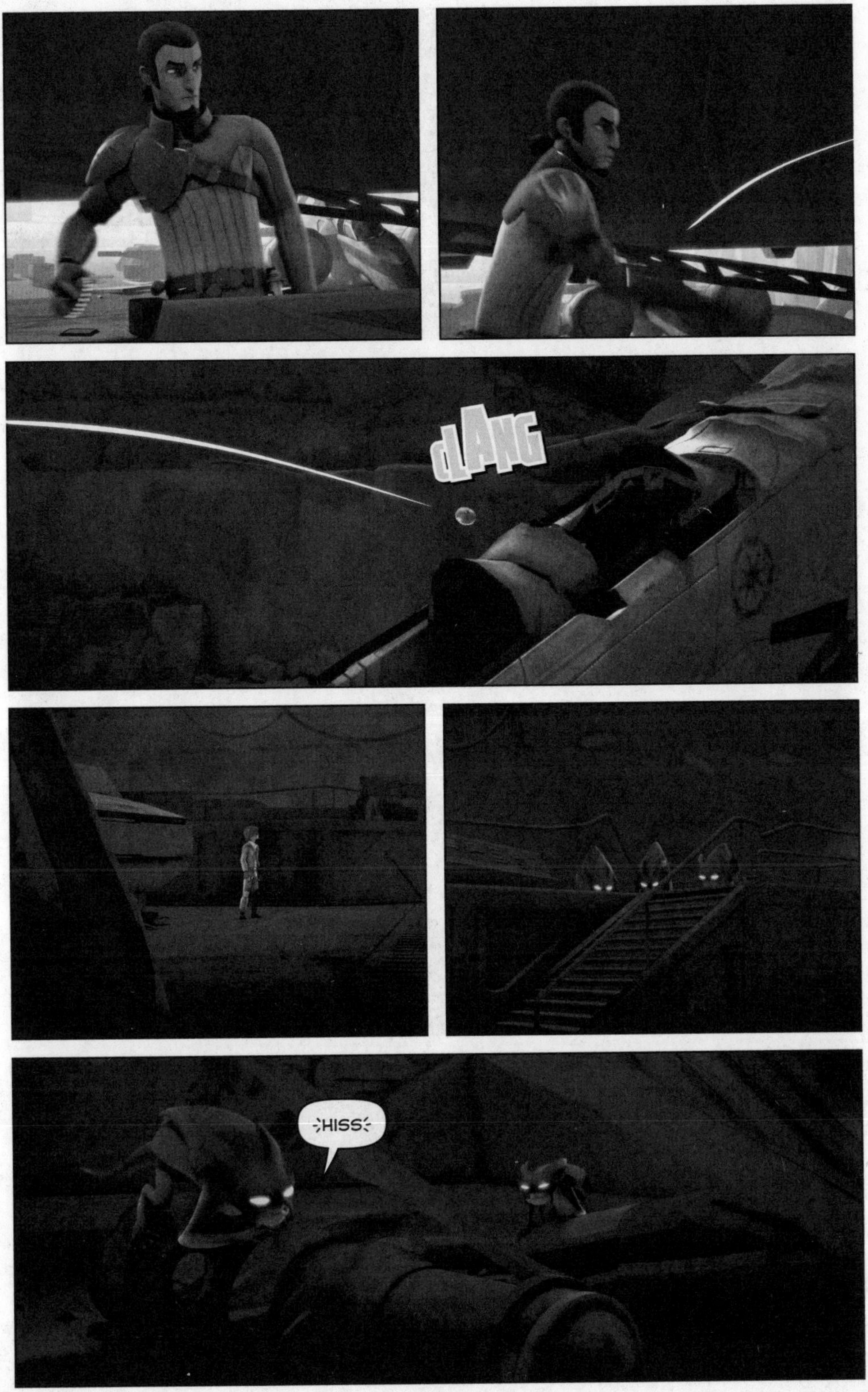
CLANG
HISS

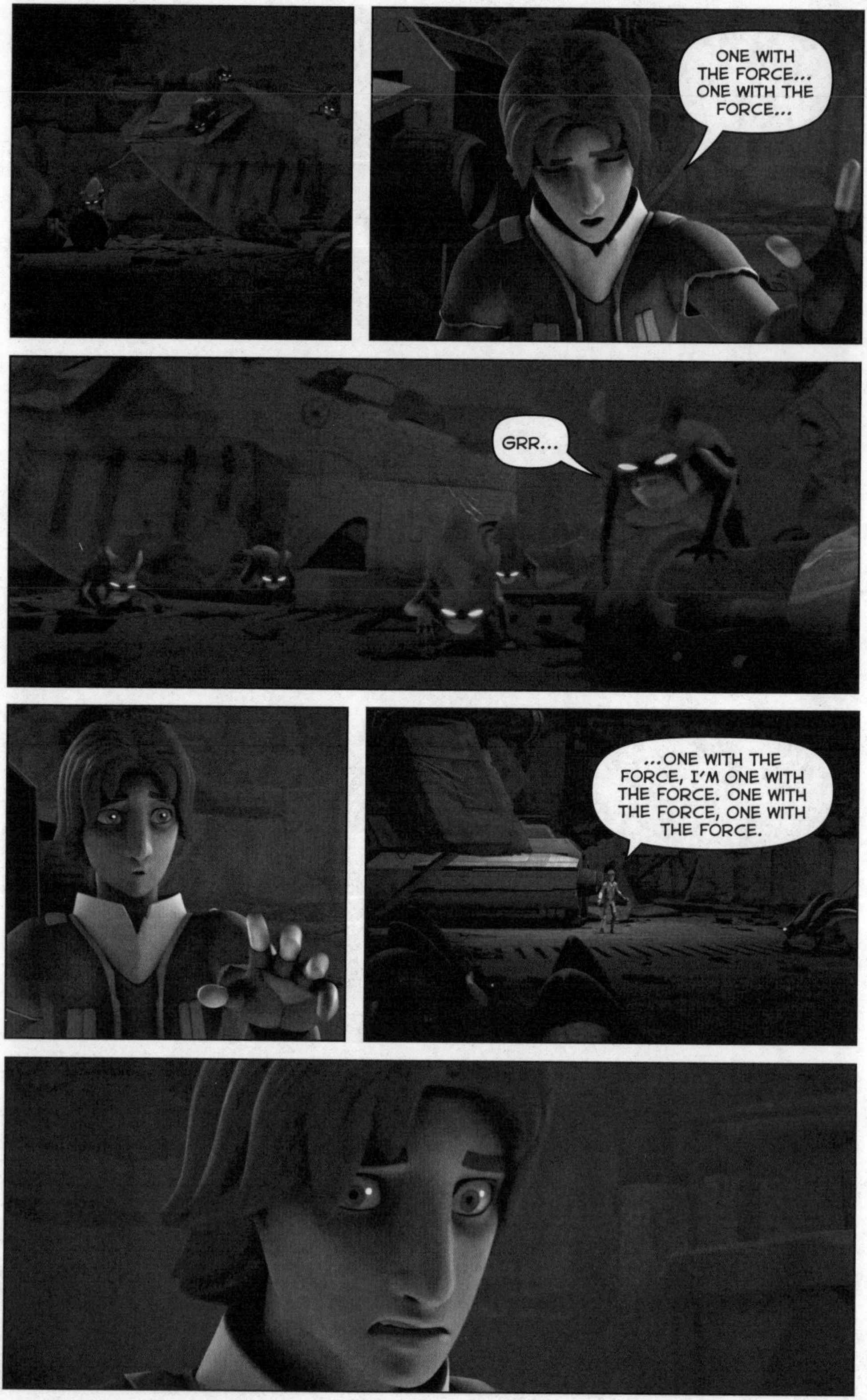
ONE WITH THE FORCE... ONE WITH THE FORCE...
GRR...
...ONE WITH THE FORCE, I'M ONE WITH THE FORCE. ONE WITH THE FORCE, ONE WITH THE FORCE.

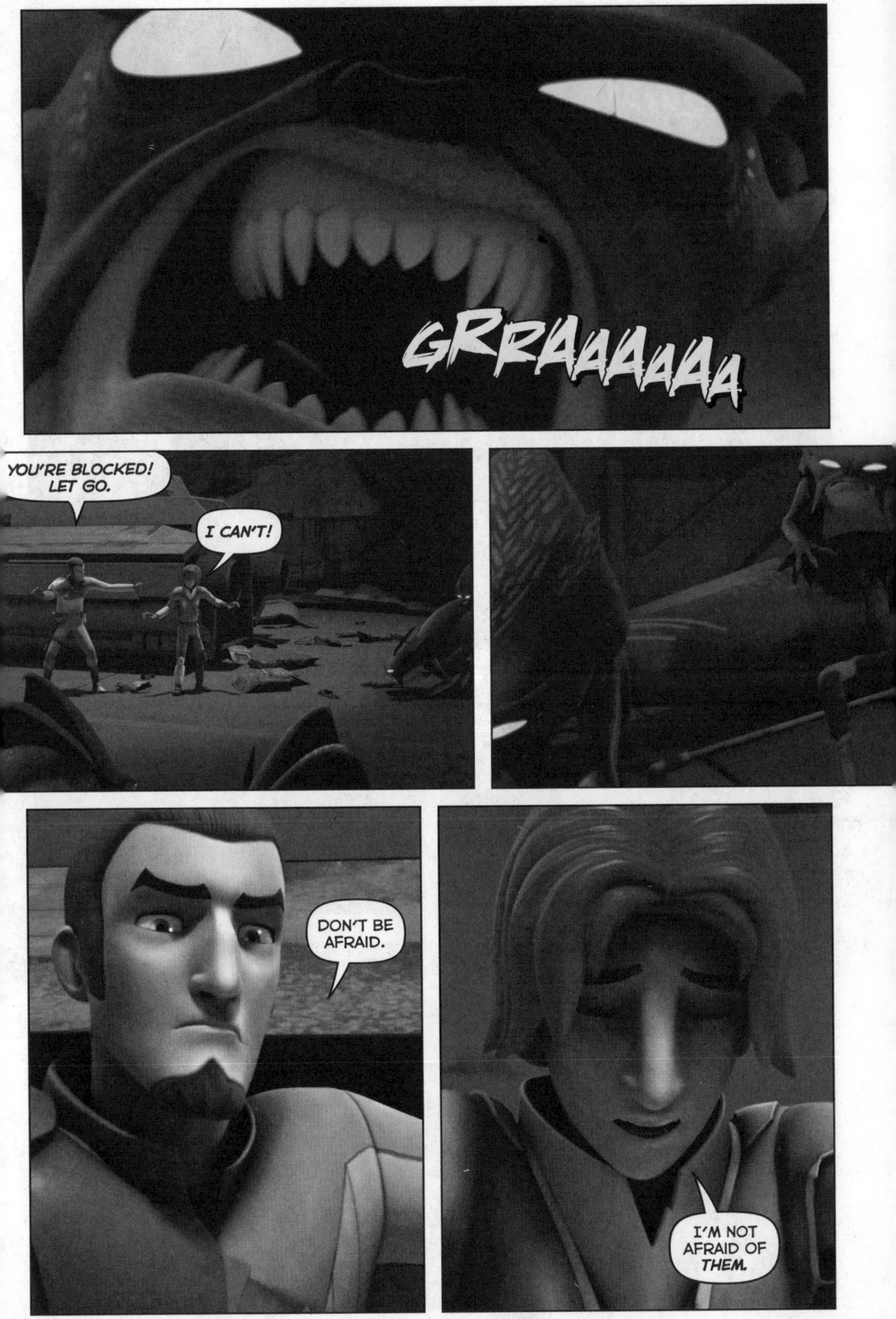
GRRAAAAAAA
YOU'RE BLOCKED! LET GO.
I CAN'T!
DON'T BE AFRAID.
I'M NOT AFRAID OF *THEM.*

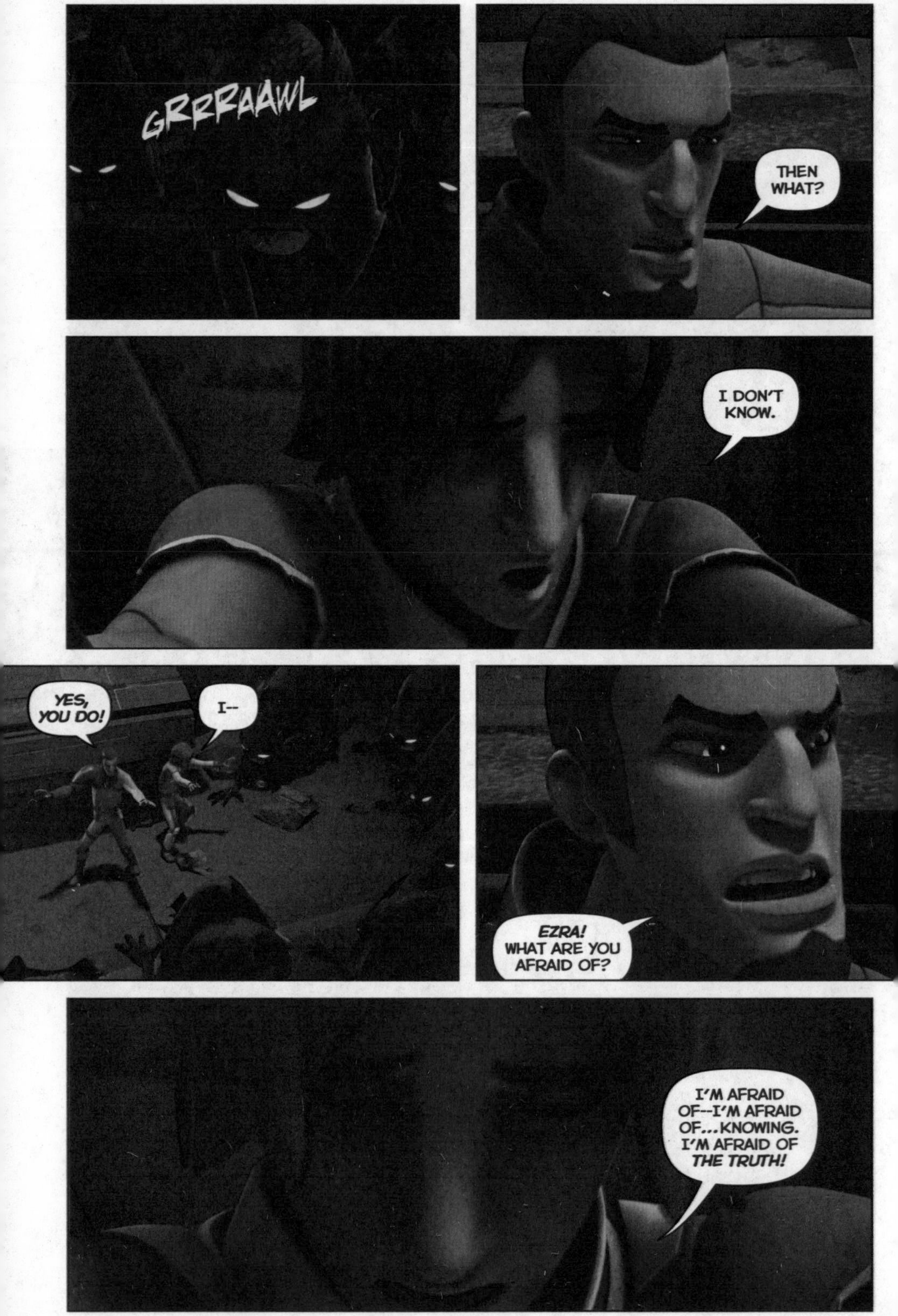
GRRRAAWL
THEN WHAT?
I DON'T KNOW.
YES, YOU DO!
I--
EZRA! WHAT ARE YOU AFRAID OF?
I'M AFRAID OF--I'M AFRAID OF...KNOWING. I'M AFRAID OF THE TRUTH!

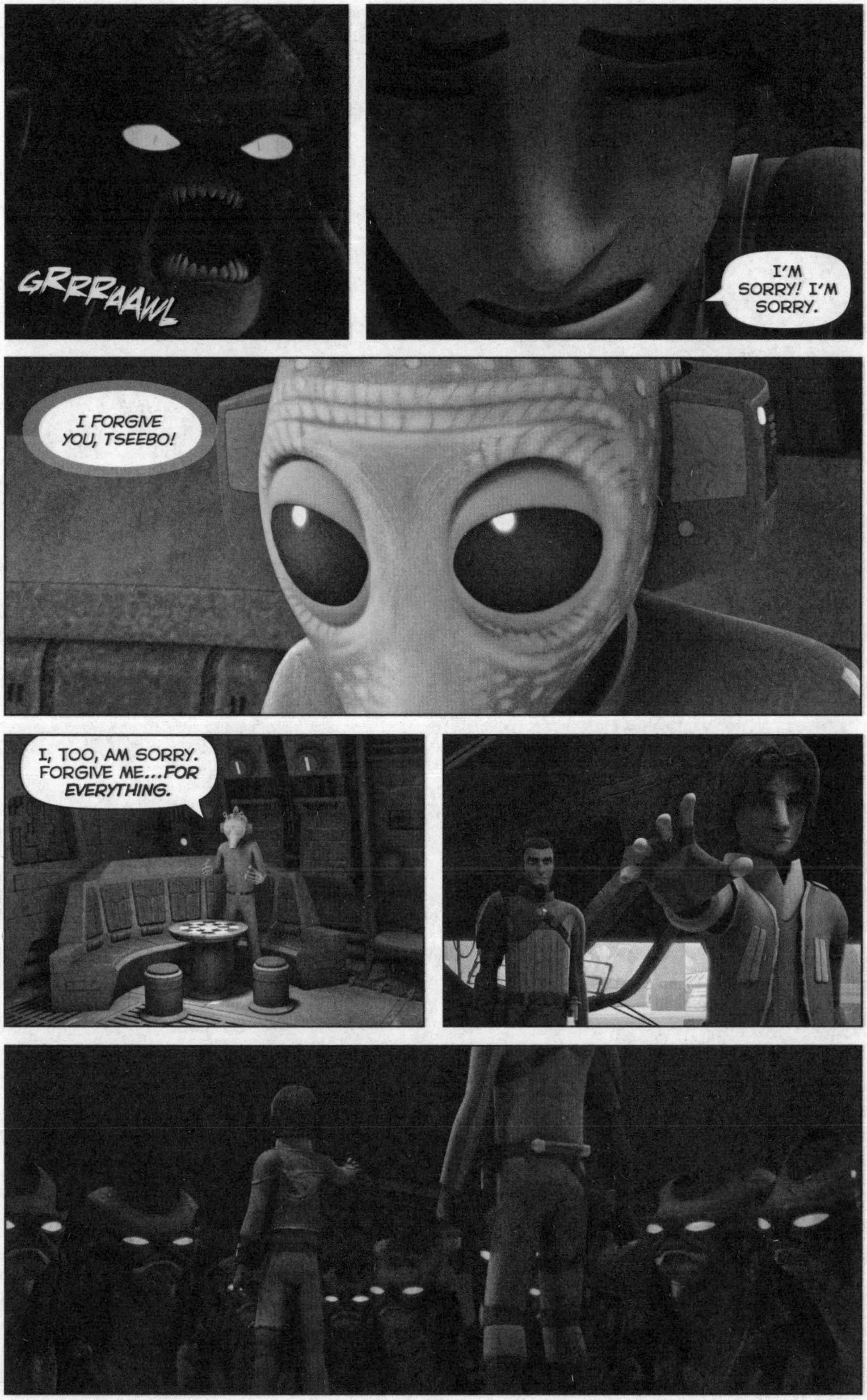
GRRRAAWL
I'M SORRY! I'M SORRY.
I FORGIVE YOU, TSEEBO!
I, TOO, AM SORRY. FORGIVE ME...FOR EVERYTHING.

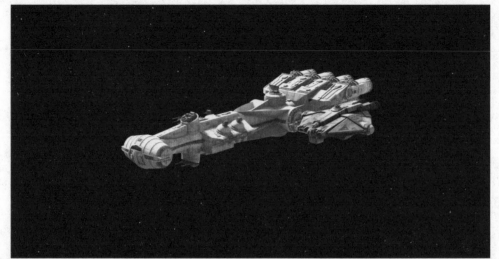

FULCRUM TO *GHOST*. DOCKING COMPLETE. HEADING TO THE AIRLOCK NOW.

ACKNOWLEDGED, FULCRUM. WE'RE READY AND WAITING.

I DON'T SUPPOSE ZEB AND I COULD GET TO MEET FULCRUM THIS TIME?

NOPE. THIS TIME YOU STAY IN THE COCKPIT.

THAT'S WHAT WE DID *LAST* TIME.

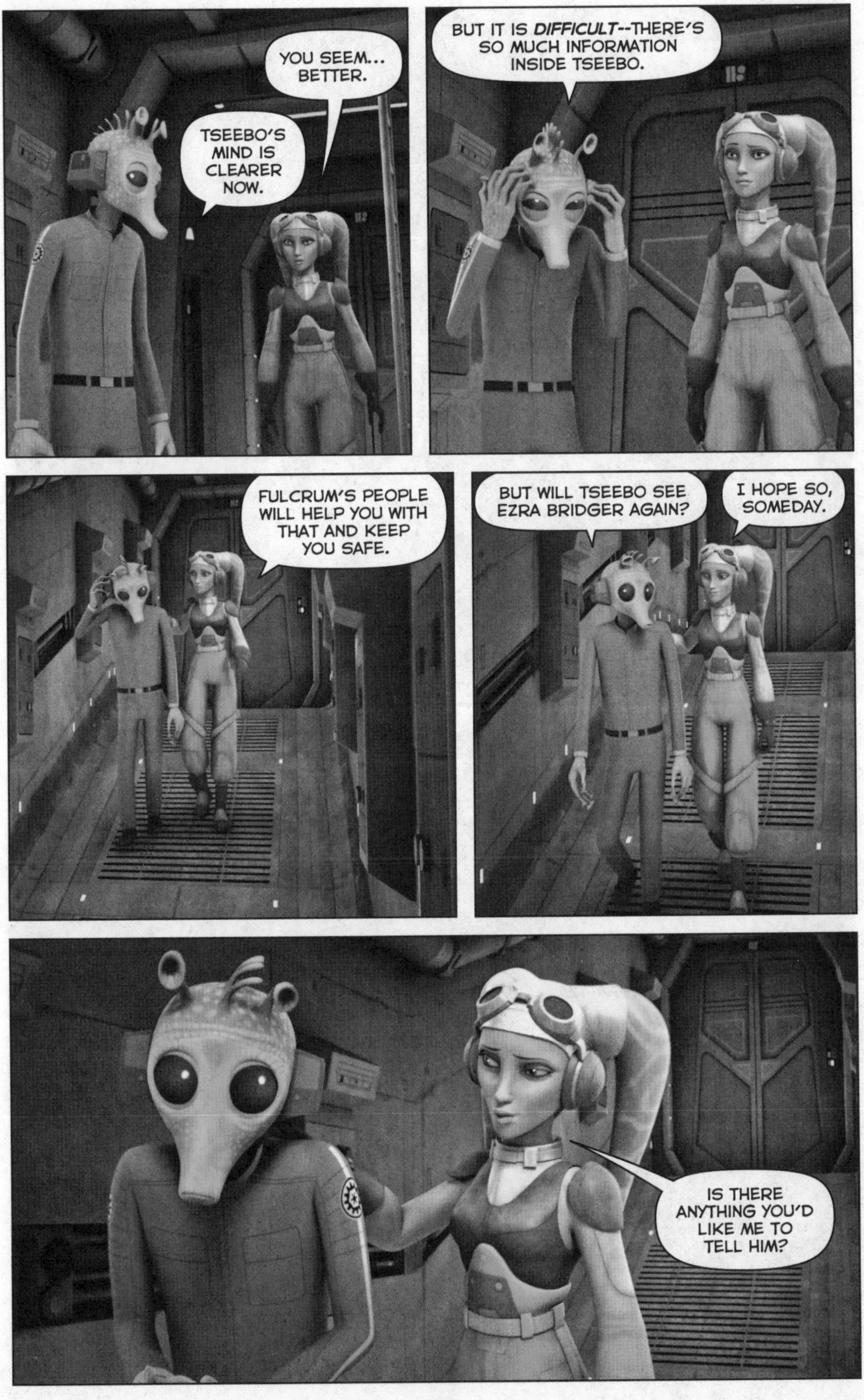
YOU SEEM... BETTER.
TSEEBO'S MIND IS CLEARER NOW.
BUT IT IS *DIFFICULT*--THERE'S SO MUCH INFORMATION INSIDE TSEEBO.
FULCRUM'S PEOPLE WILL HELP YOU WITH THAT AND KEEP YOU SAFE.
BUT WILL TSEEBO SEE EZRA BRIDGER AGAIN?
I HOPE SO, SOMEDAY.
IS THERE ANYTHING YOU'D LIKE ME TO TELL HIM?

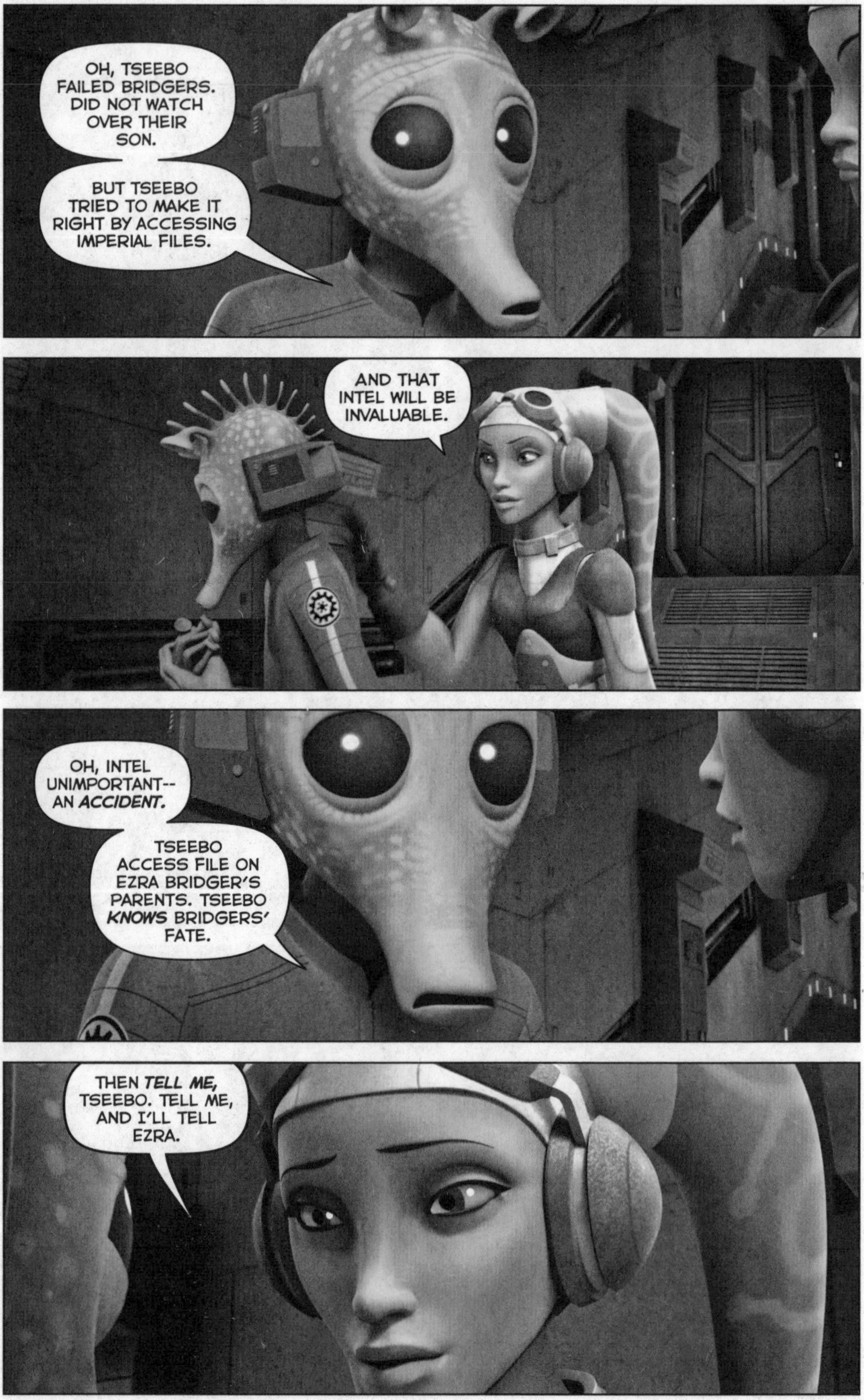
OH, TSEEBO FAILED BRIDGERS. DID NOT WATCH OVER THEIR SON.
BUT TSEEBO TRIED TO MAKE IT RIGHT BY ACCESSING IMPERIAL FILES.
AND THAT INTEL WILL BE INVALUABLE.
OH, INTEL UNIMPORTANT-- AN *ACCIDENT.*
TSEEBO ACCESS FILE ON EZRA BRIDGER'S PARENTS. TSEEBO *KNOWS* BRIDGERS' FATE.
THEN *TELL ME,* TSEEBO. TELL ME, AND I'LL TELL EZRA.

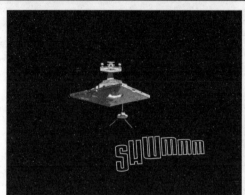

SHWmmm

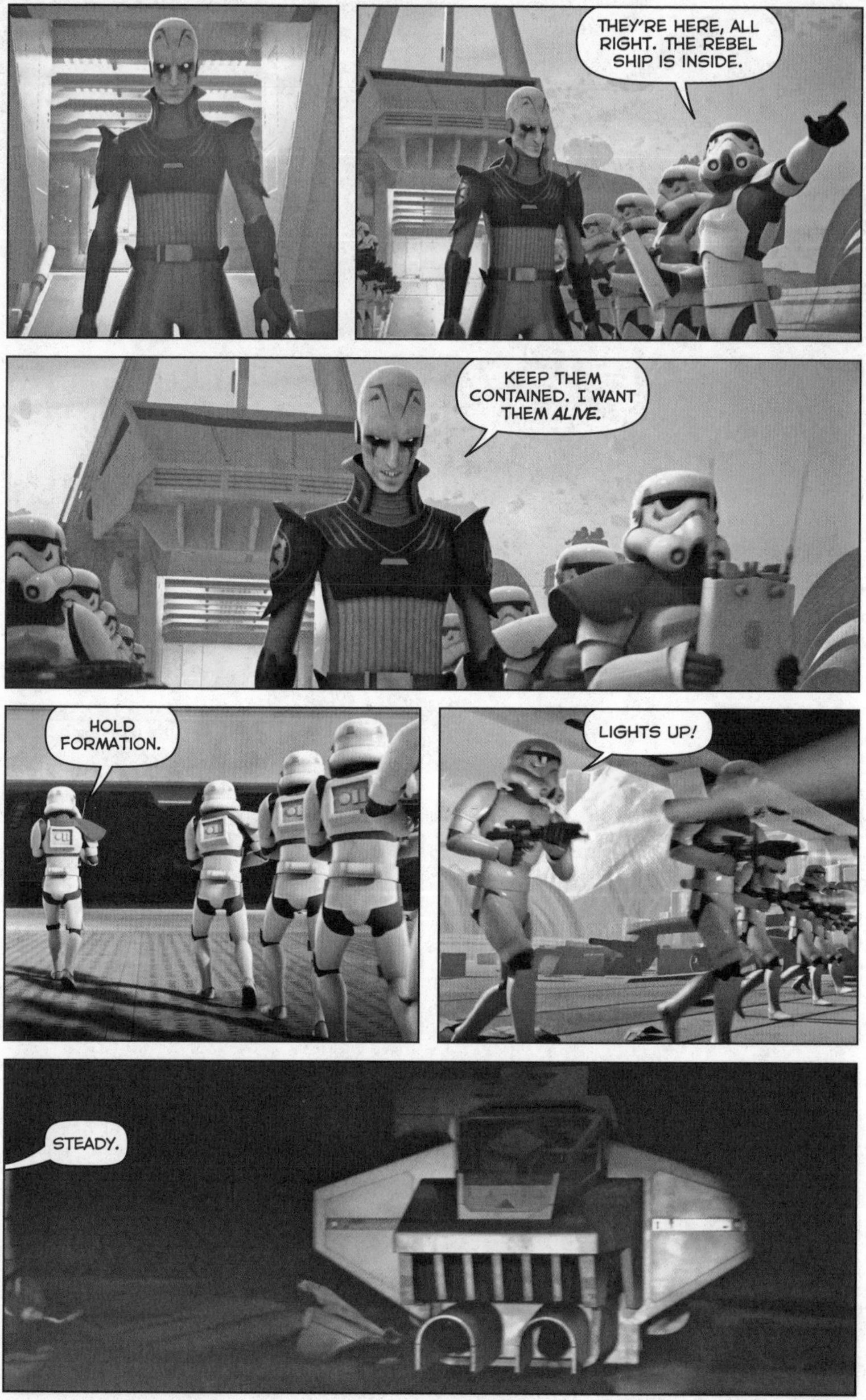
THEY'RE HERE, ALL RIGHT. THE REBEL SHIP IS INSIDE.
KEEP THEM CONTAINED. I WANT THEM *ALIVE.*
HOLD FORMATION.
LIGHTS UP!
STEADY.

SIR, THEY'RE OVER...HERE.

WAIT. I SENSE--

SIR! THEY'RE NOT ALONE.

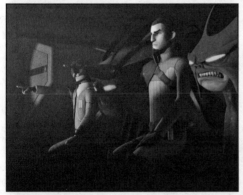

GRAAAAAA!

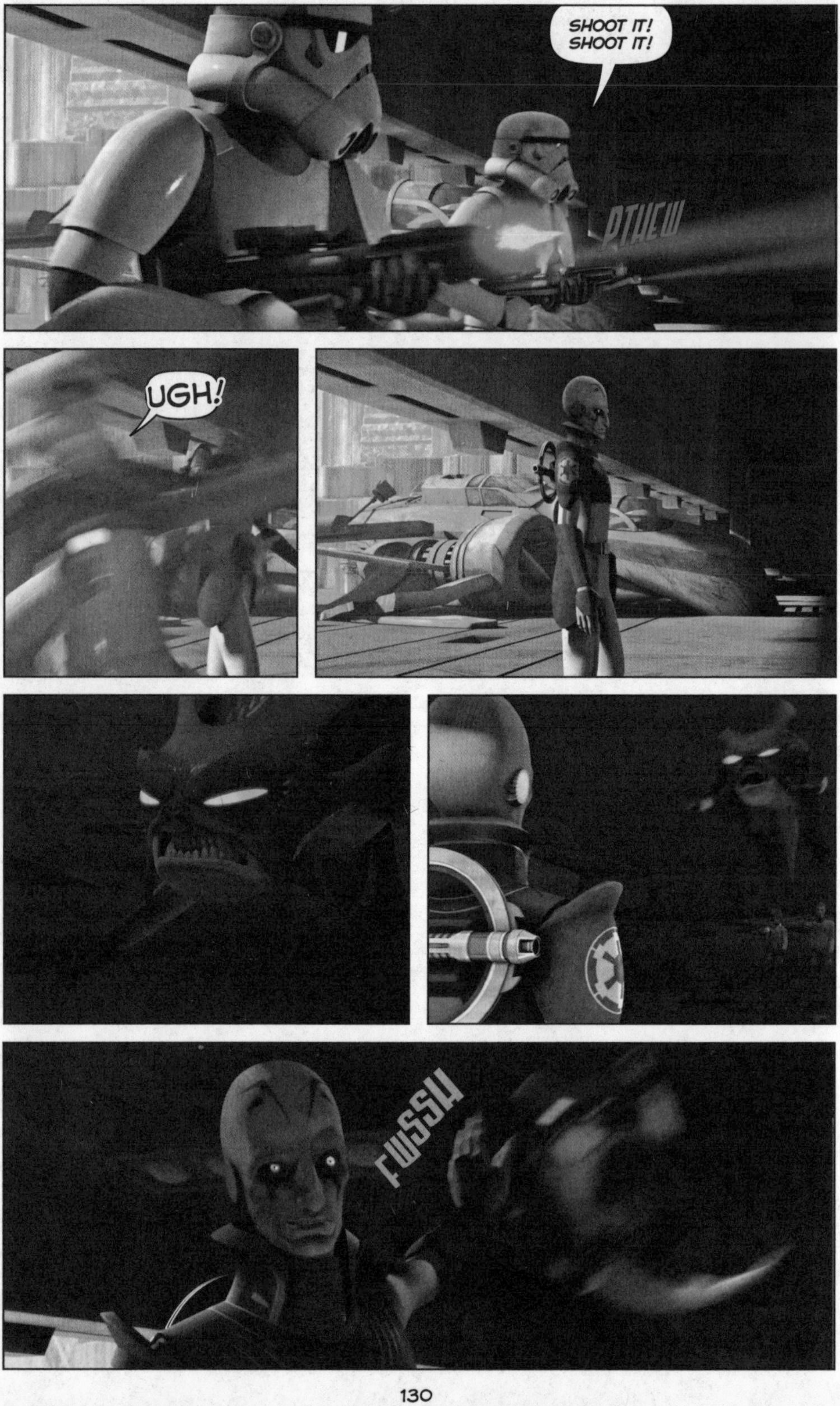
SHOOT IT! SHOOT IT!
PTHEW
UGH!
FWSSH

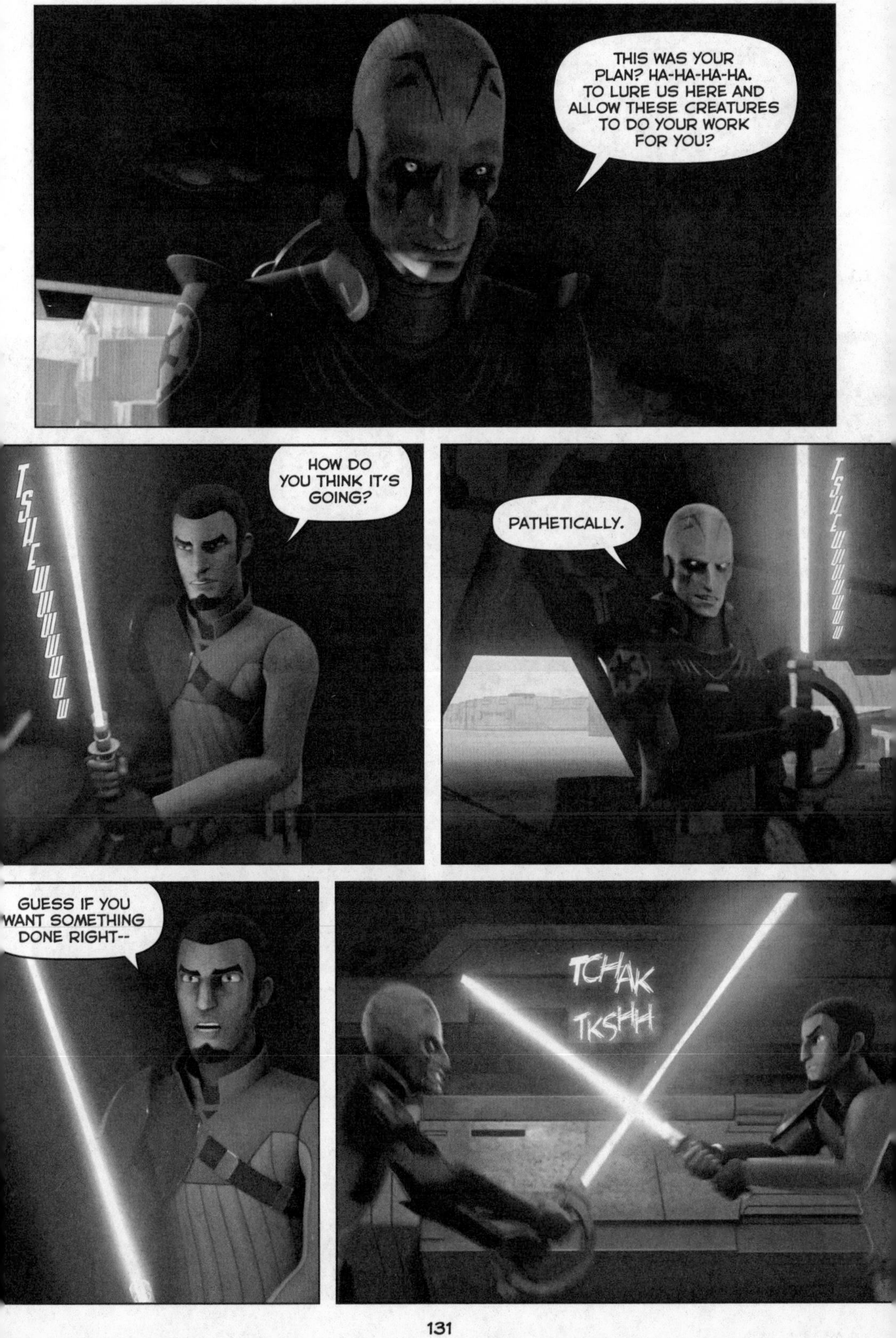
THIS WAS YOUR PLAN? HA-HA-HA-HA. TO LURE US HERE AND ALLOW THESE CREATURES TO DO YOUR WORK FOR YOU?
TSHEWWWWWWW
HOW DO YOU THINK IT'S GOING?
PATHETICALLY.
TSHEWWWWWWW
GUESS IF YOU WANT SOMETHING DONE RIGHT--
TCHAK
TKSHH

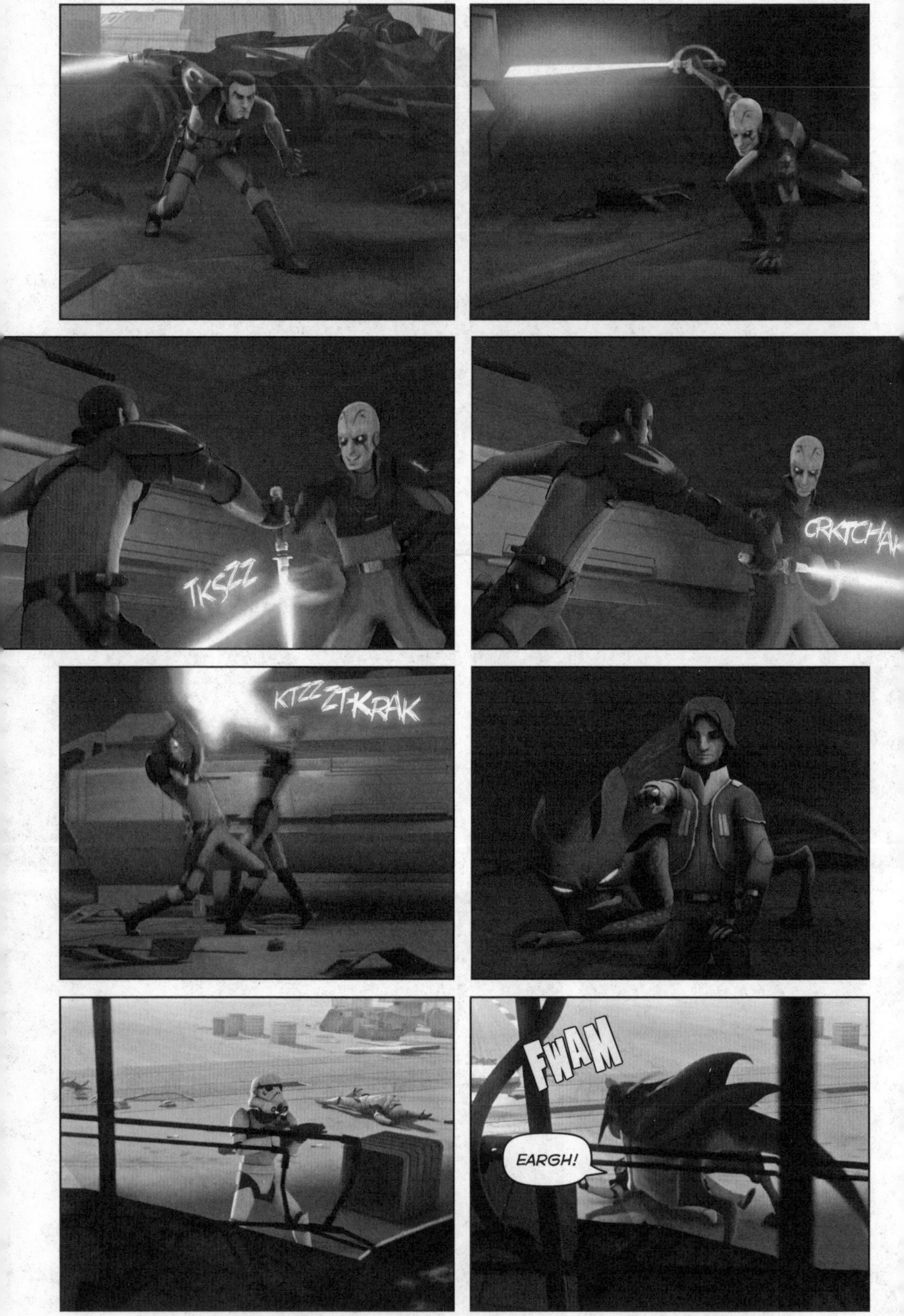
TKSZZ
CRKTCHA
KTZZ ZT-KRAK
FWAM
EARGH!

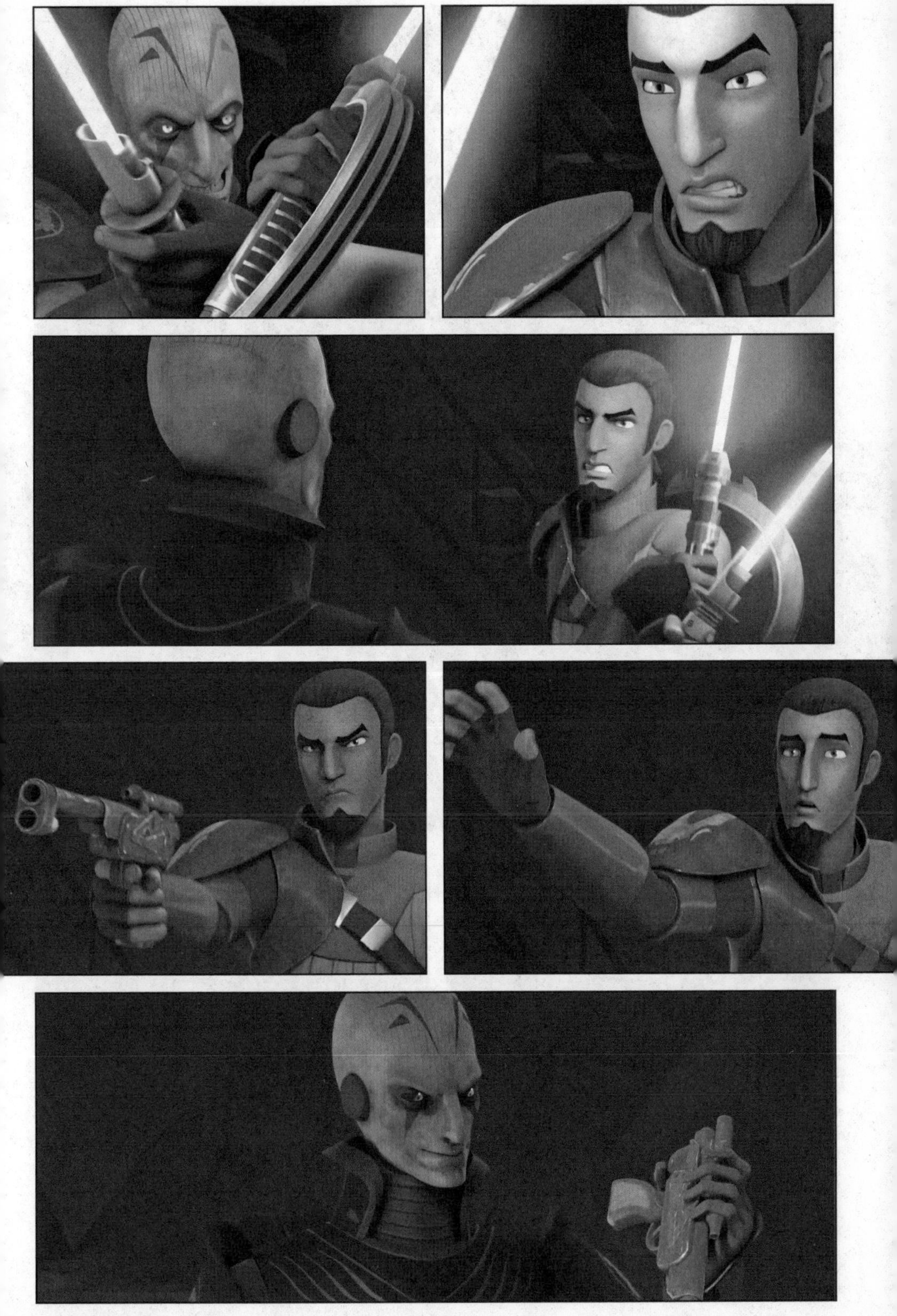

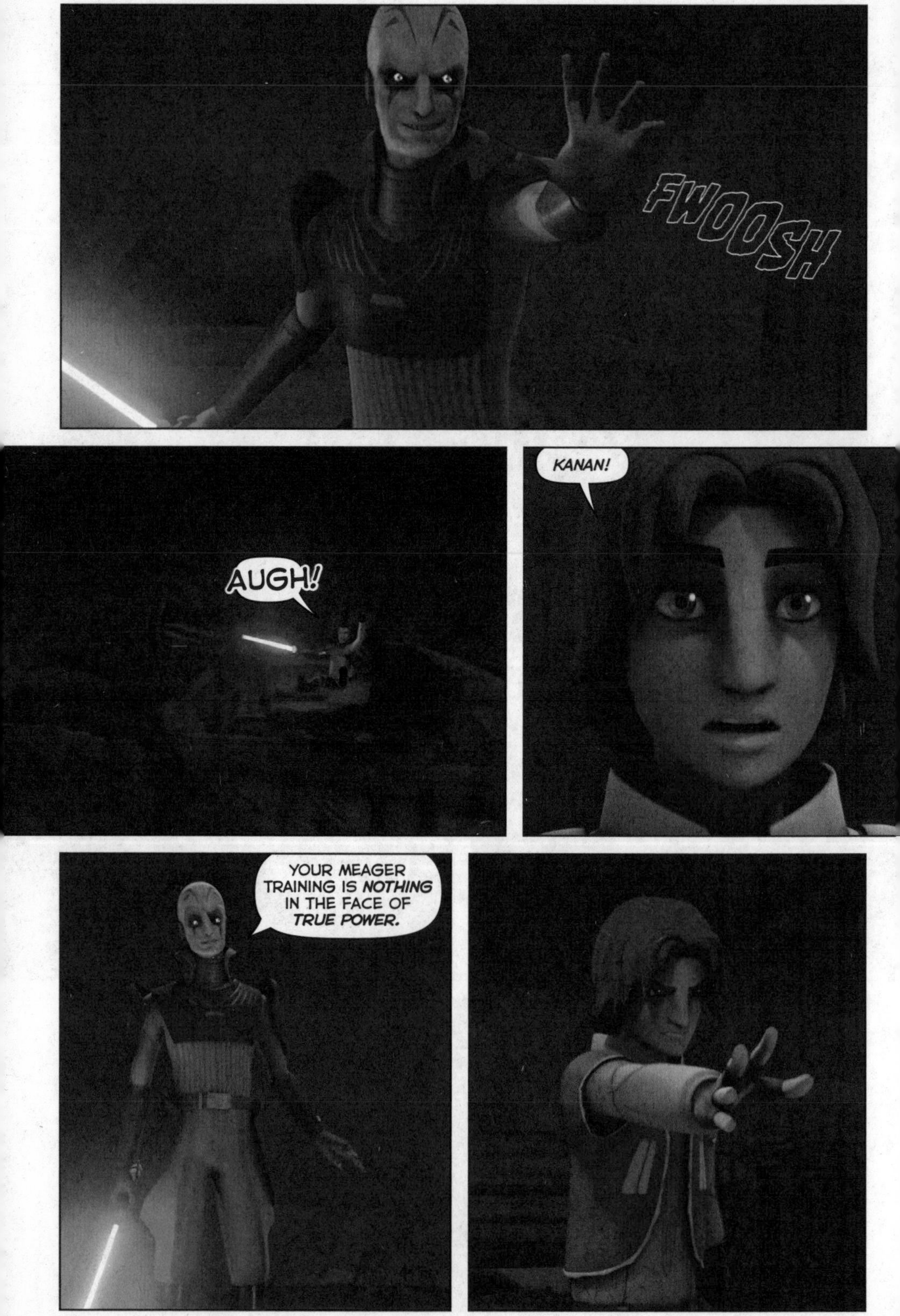
FWOOSH
AUGH!
KANAN!
YOUR MEAGER TRAINING IS *NOTHING* IN THE FACE OF *TRUE POWER.*

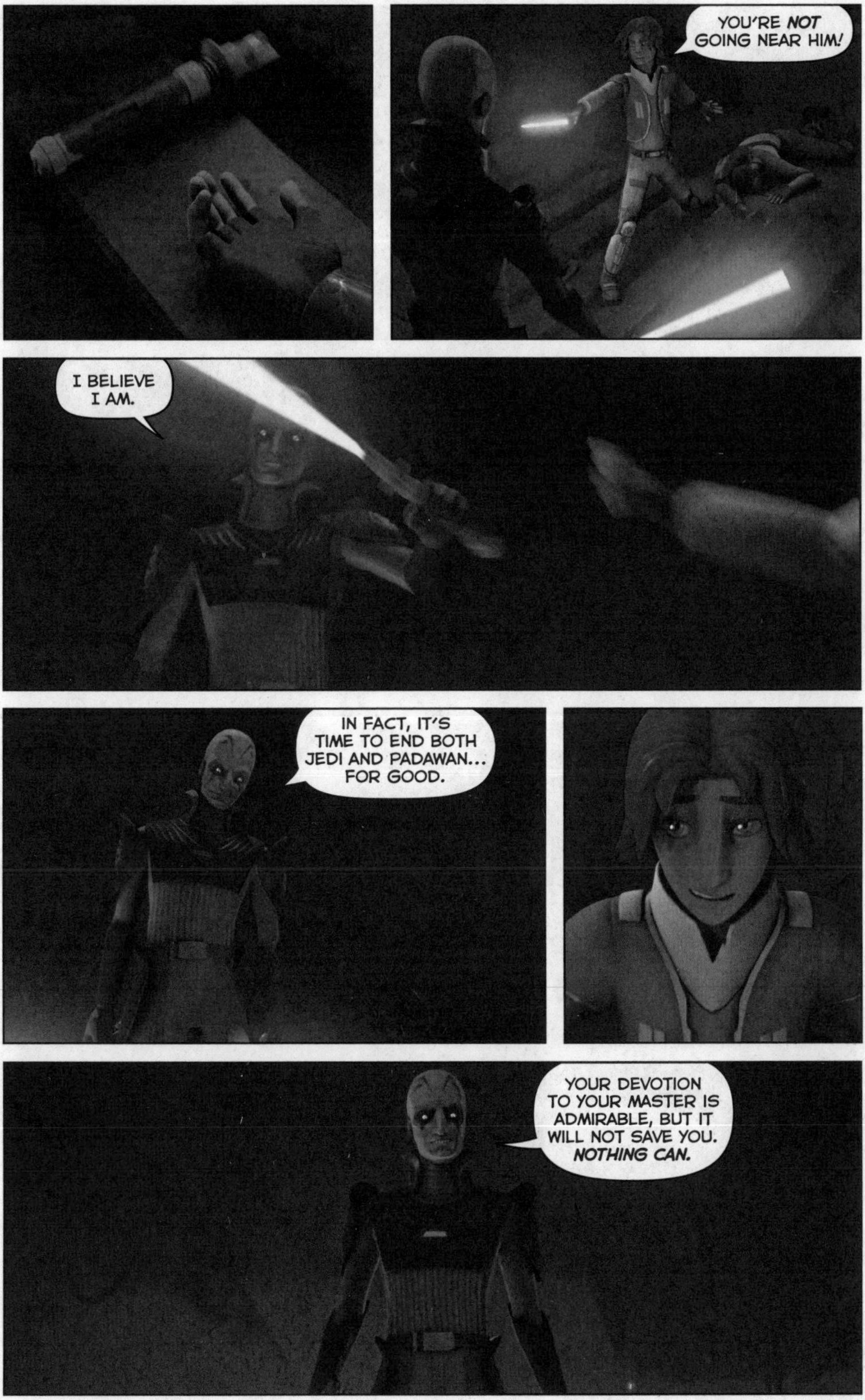
YOU'RE *NOT* GOING NEAR HIM!
I BELIEVE I AM.
IN FACT, IT'S TIME TO END BOTH JEDI AND PADAWAN... FOR GOOD.
YOUR DEVOTION TO YOUR MASTER IS ADMIRABLE, BUT IT WILL NOT SAVE YOU. ***NOTHING CAN.***

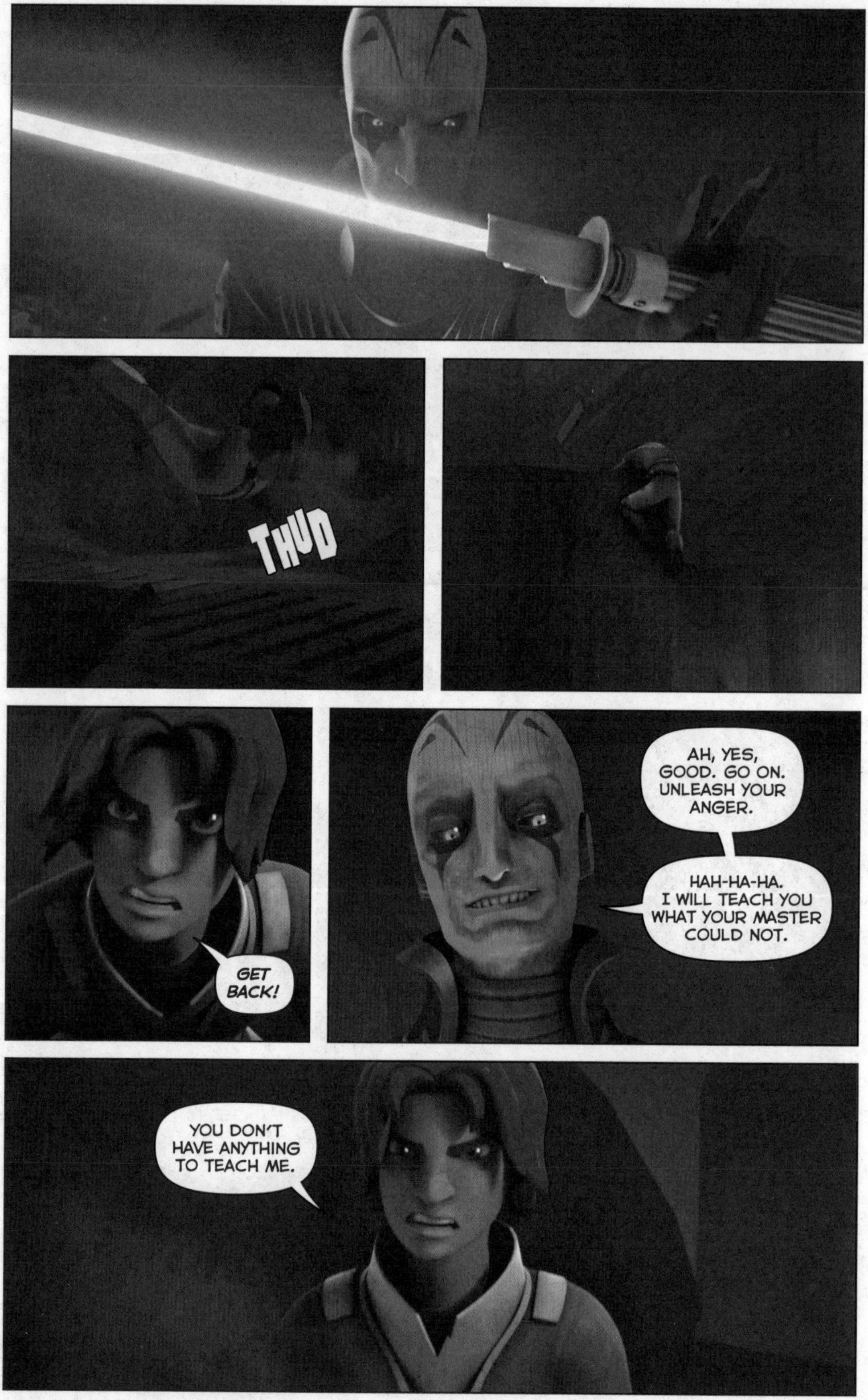
THUD
GET BACK!
AH, YES, GOOD. GO ON. UNLEASH YOUR ANGER.
HAH-HA-HA. I WILL TEACH YOU WHAT YOUR MASTER COULD NOT.
YOU DON'T HAVE ANYTHING TO TEACH ME.

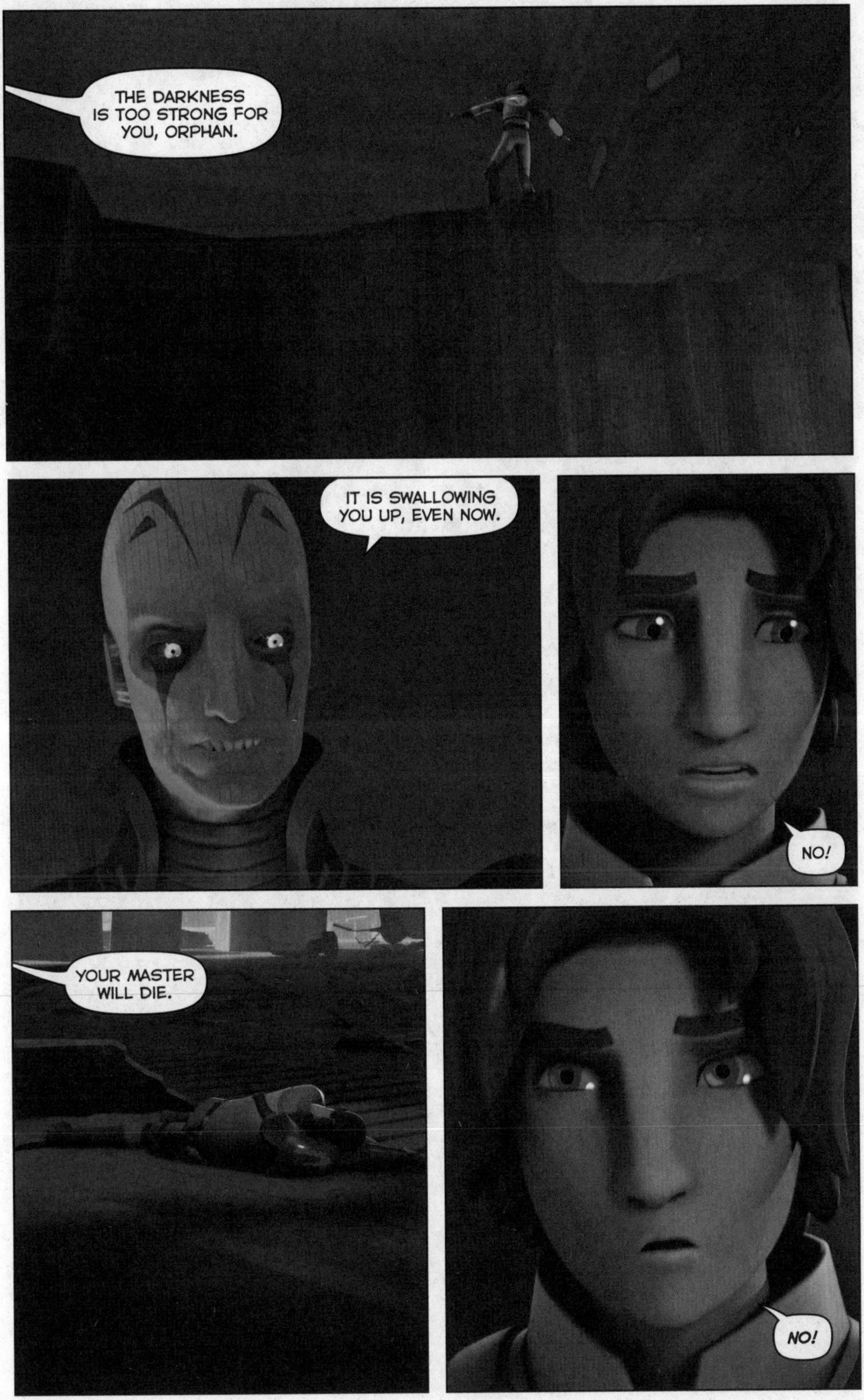
THE DARKNESS IS TOO STRONG FOR YOU, ORPHAN.
IT IS SWALLOWING YOU UP, EVEN NOW.
NO!
YOUR MASTER WILL DIE.
NO!

YOUR FRIENDS WILL DIE. AND EVERYTHING YOU'VE HOPED FOR WILL BE *LOST.* THIS IS THE WAY THE STORY ENDS.

NO!

HA-HA-HA.

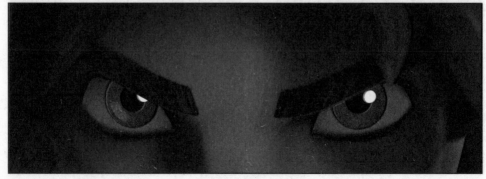

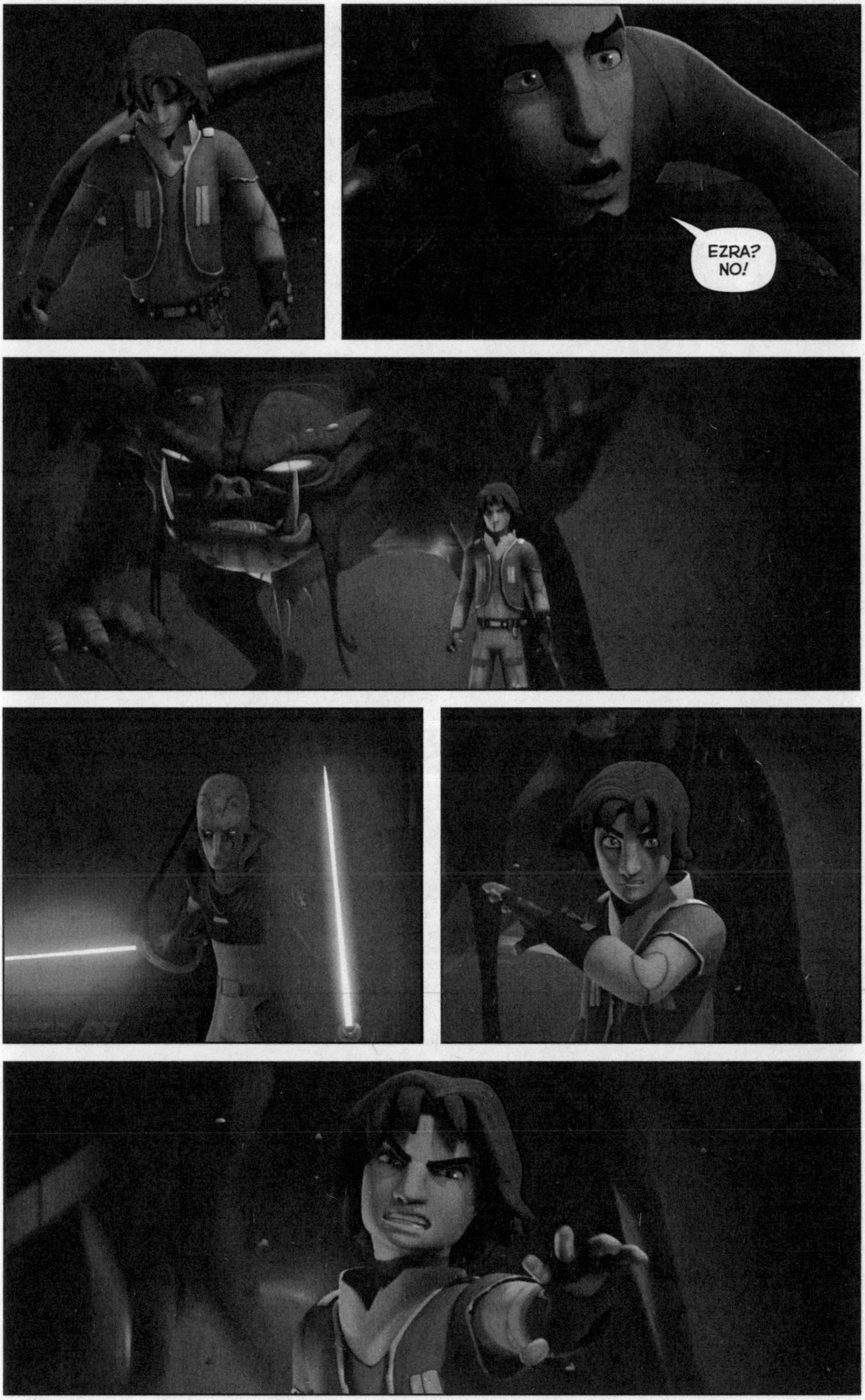
EZRA?
NO!

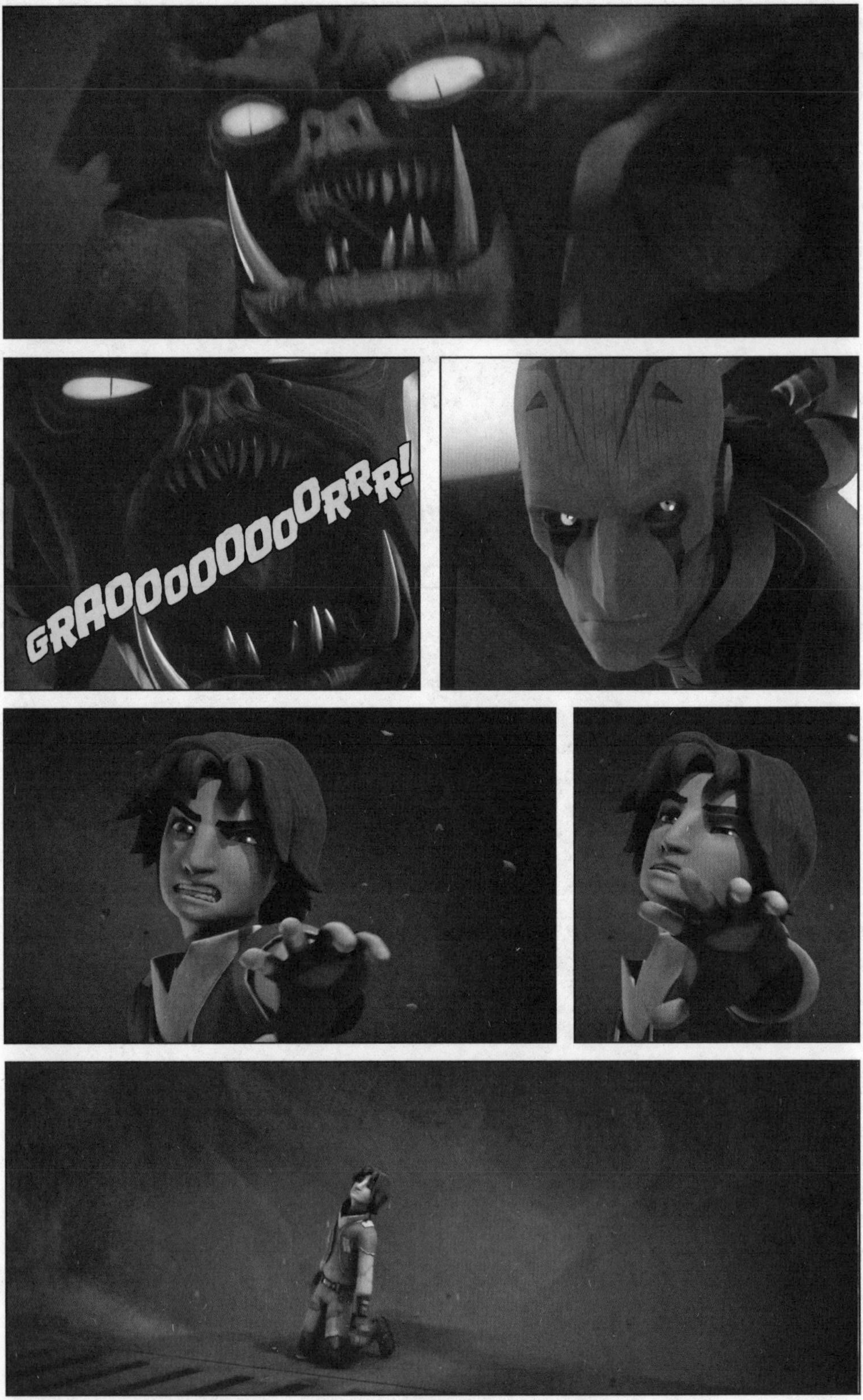
GRAOOOOOOOOORRRR!

EAAAAAAAA!

GRAAAR!

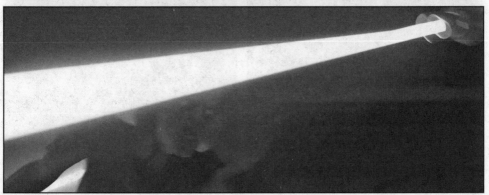

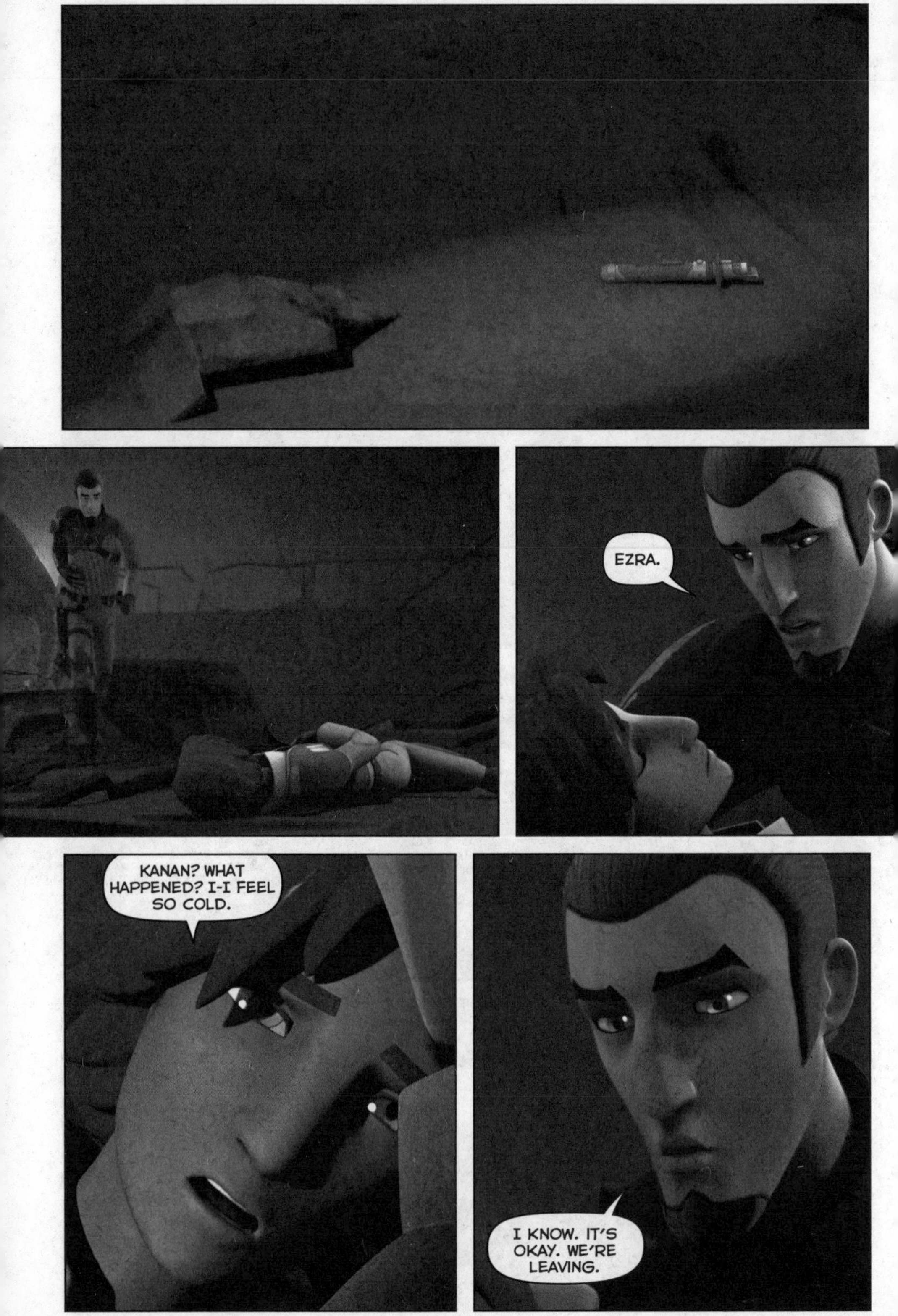
EZRA.
KANAN? WHAT HAPPENED? I-I FEEL SO COLD.
I KNOW. IT'S OKAY. WE'RE LEAVING.

RRRAHHH!

GRAAAOOOR!

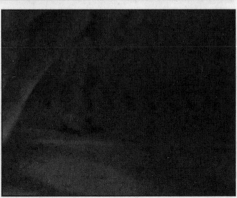

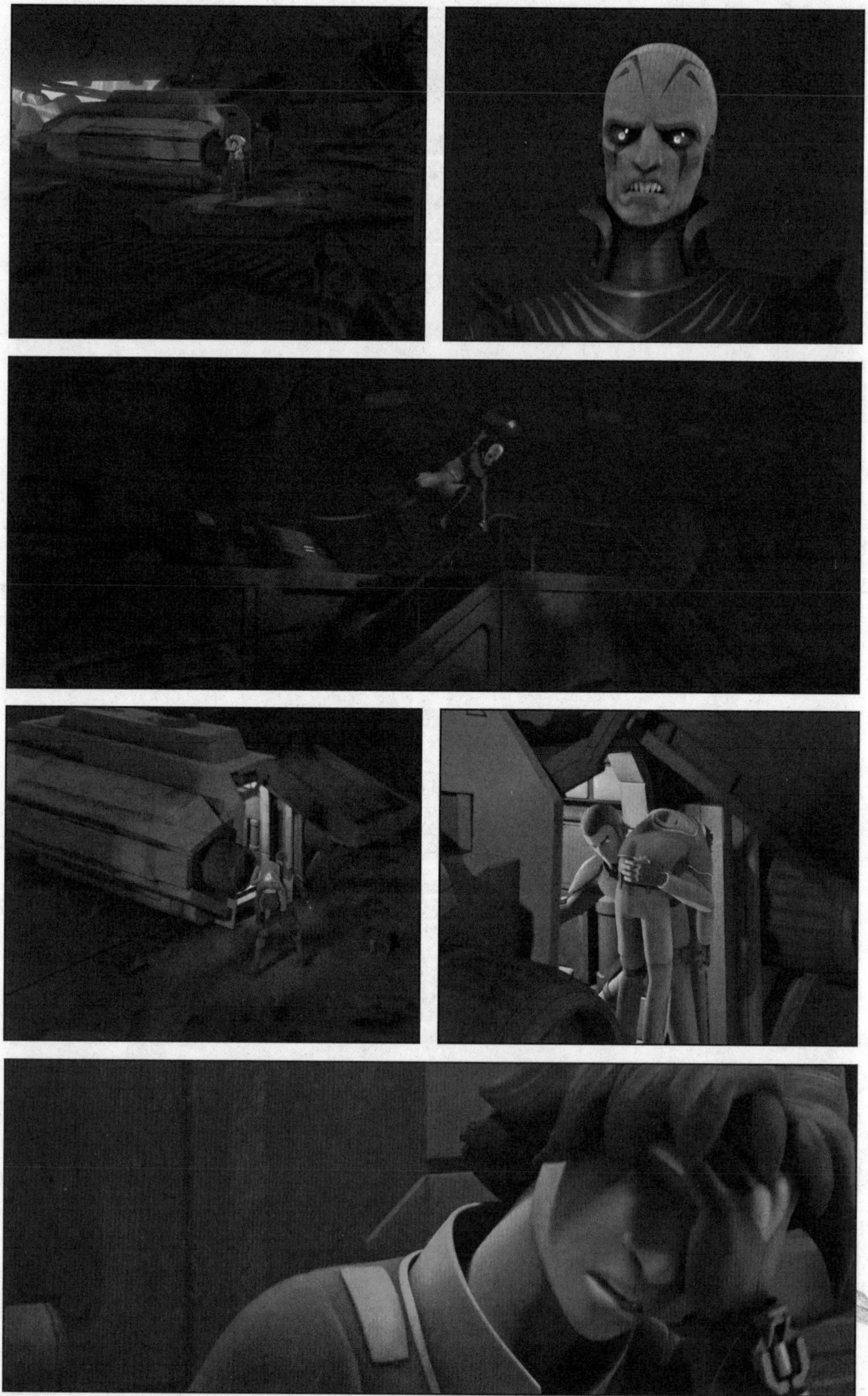

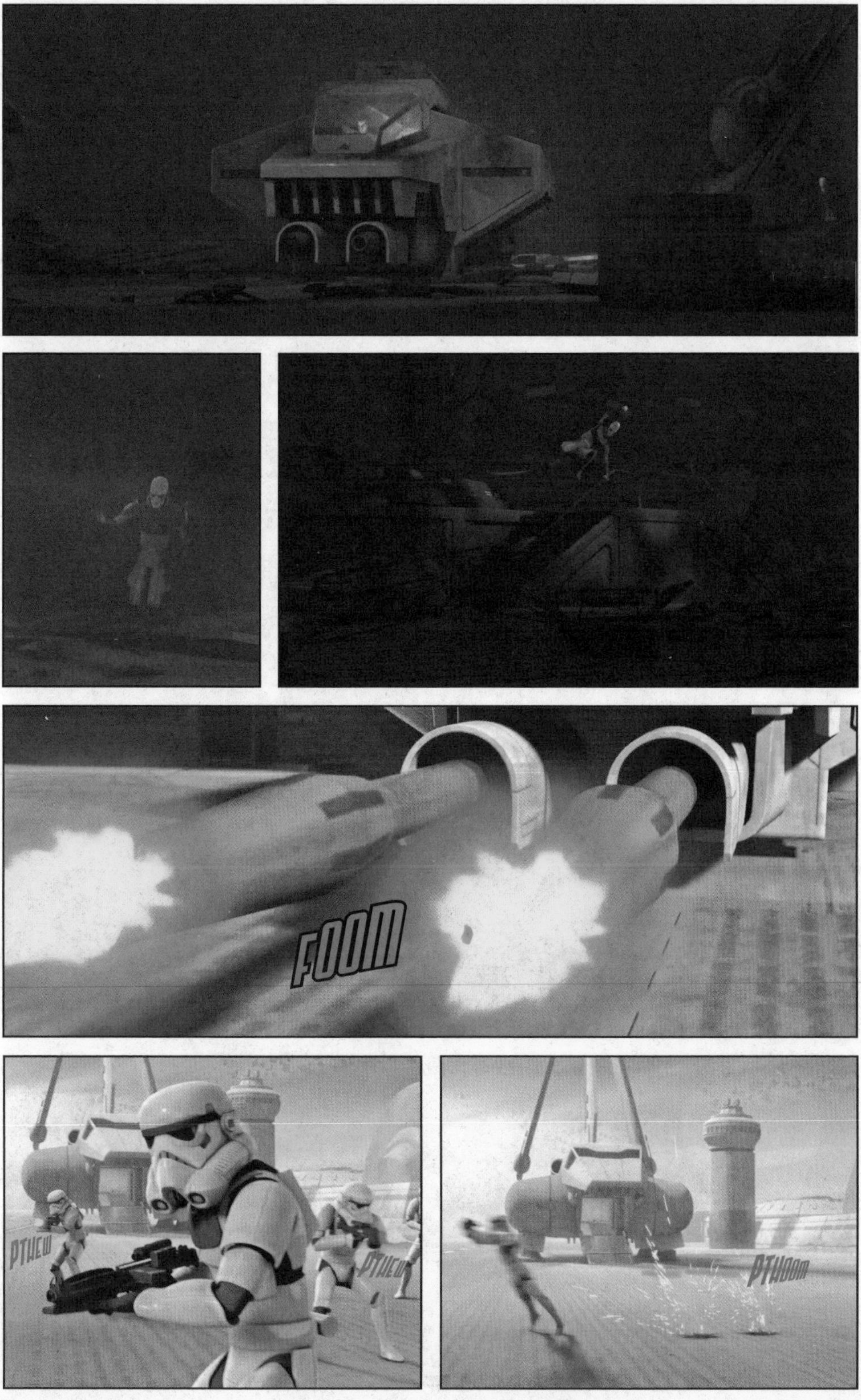
FOOM
PTHEW
PTHEW
PTHOOM

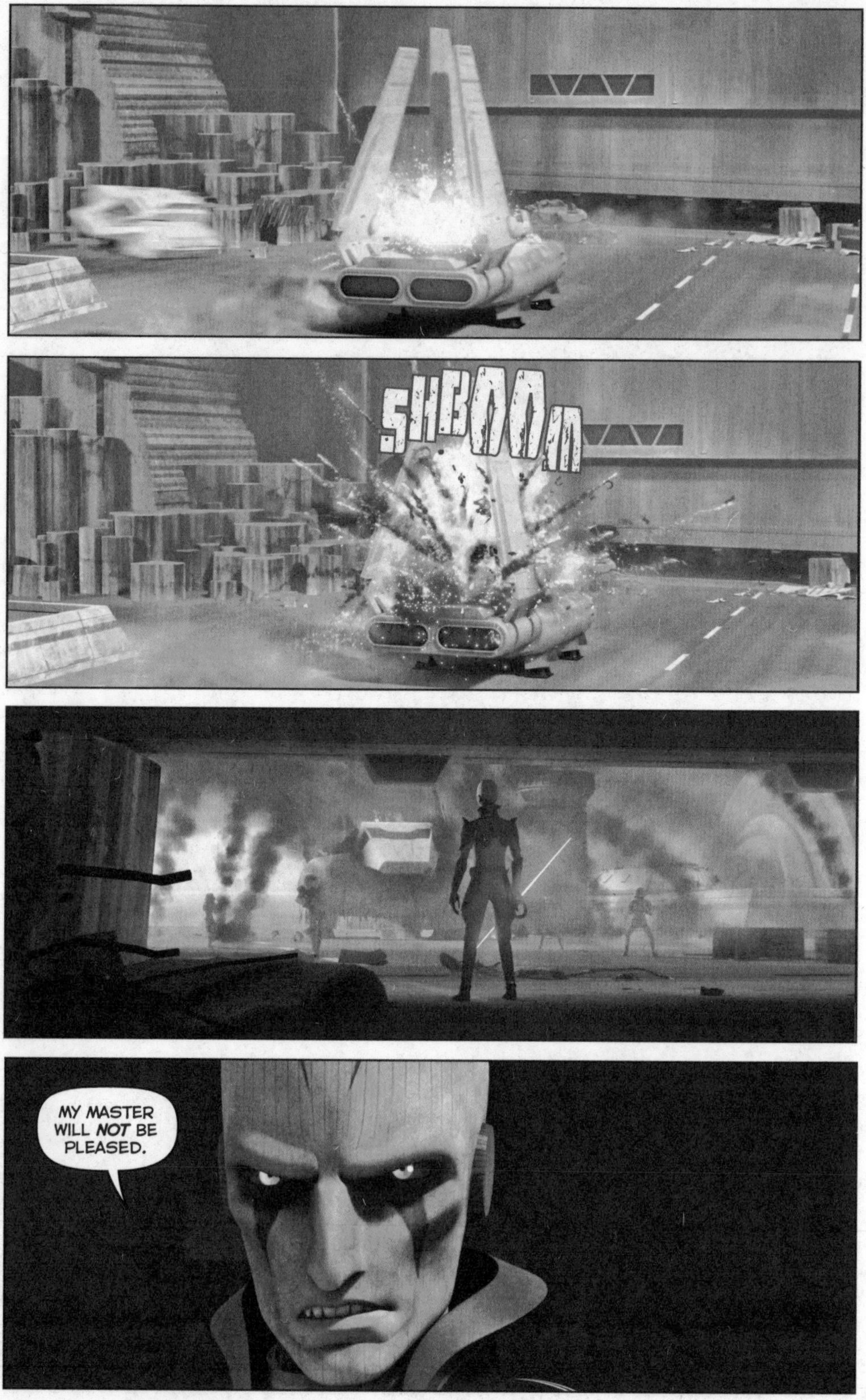
SHBOOM
MY MASTER WILL *NOT* BE PLEASED.

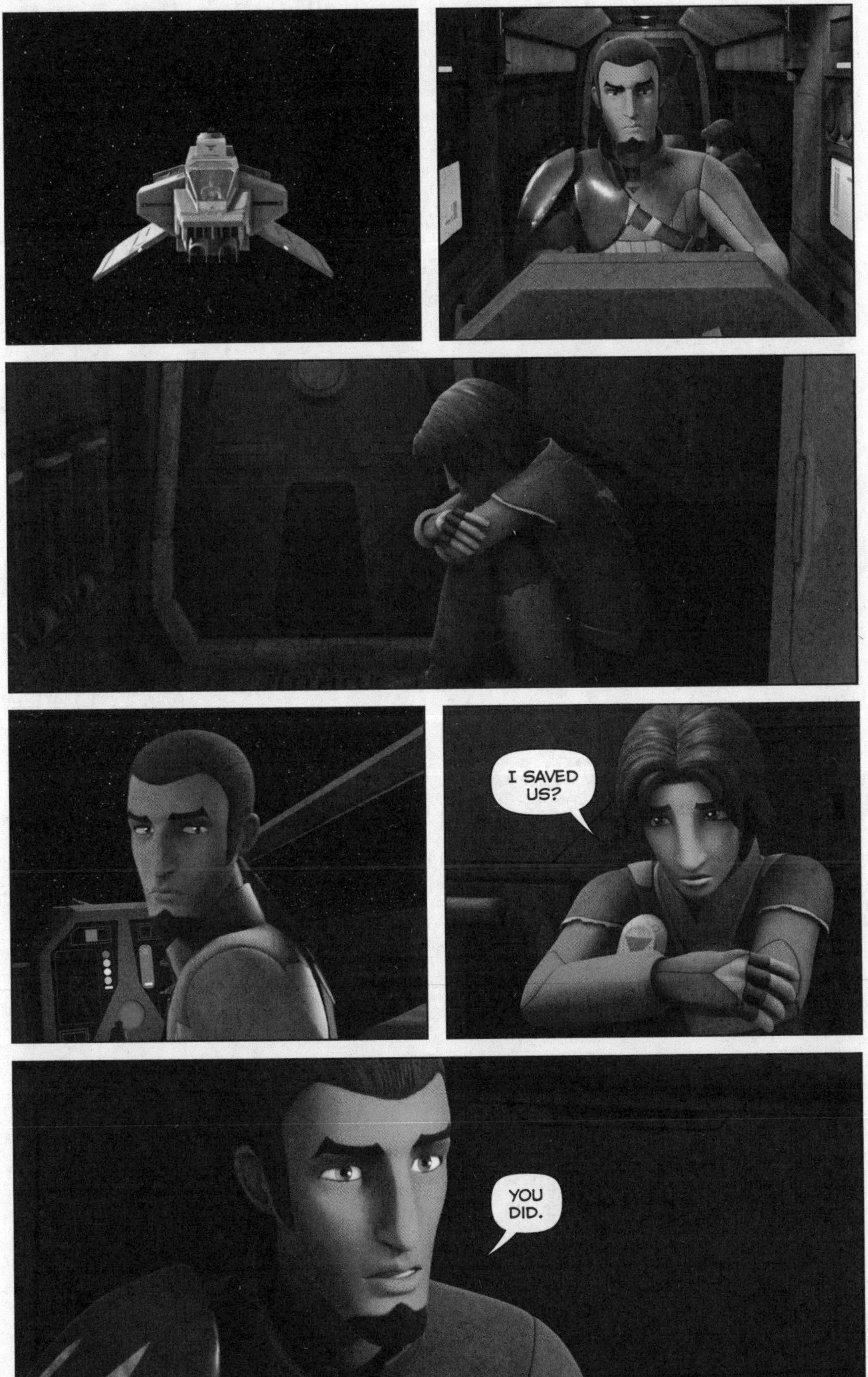
I SAVED US?
YOU DID.

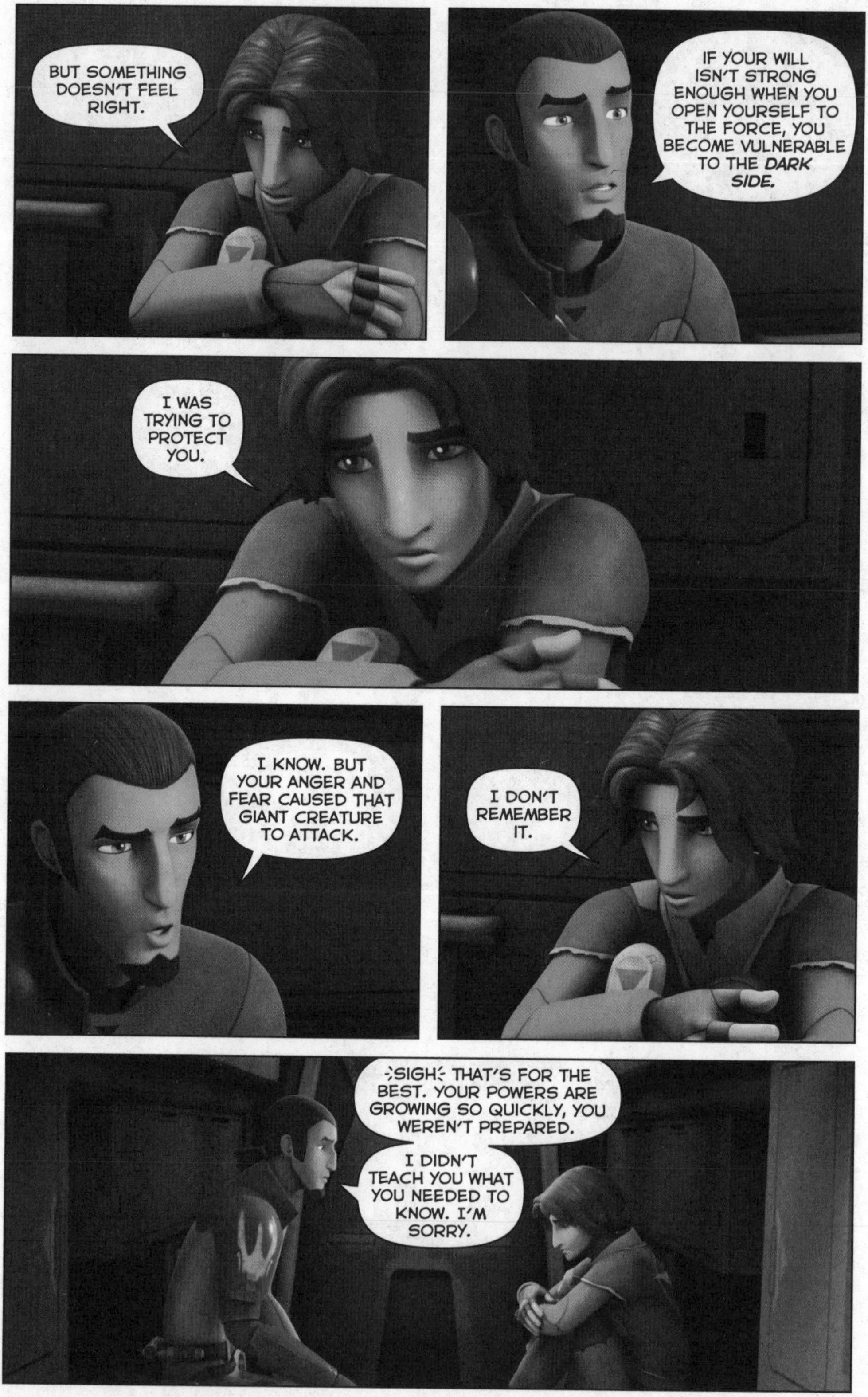
BUT SOMETHING DOESN'T FEEL RIGHT.
IF YOUR WILL ISN'T STRONG ENOUGH WHEN YOU OPEN YOURSELF TO THE FORCE, YOU BECOME VULNERABLE TO THE *DARK SIDE.*
I WAS TRYING TO PROTECT YOU.
I KNOW. BUT YOUR ANGER AND FEAR CAUSED THAT GIANT CREATURE TO ATTACK.
I DON'T REMEMBER IT.
-SIGH- THAT'S FOR THE BEST. YOUR POWERS ARE GROWING SO QUICKLY, YOU WEREN'T PREPARED.
I DIDN'T TEACH YOU WHAT YOU NEEDED TO KNOW. I'M SORRY.

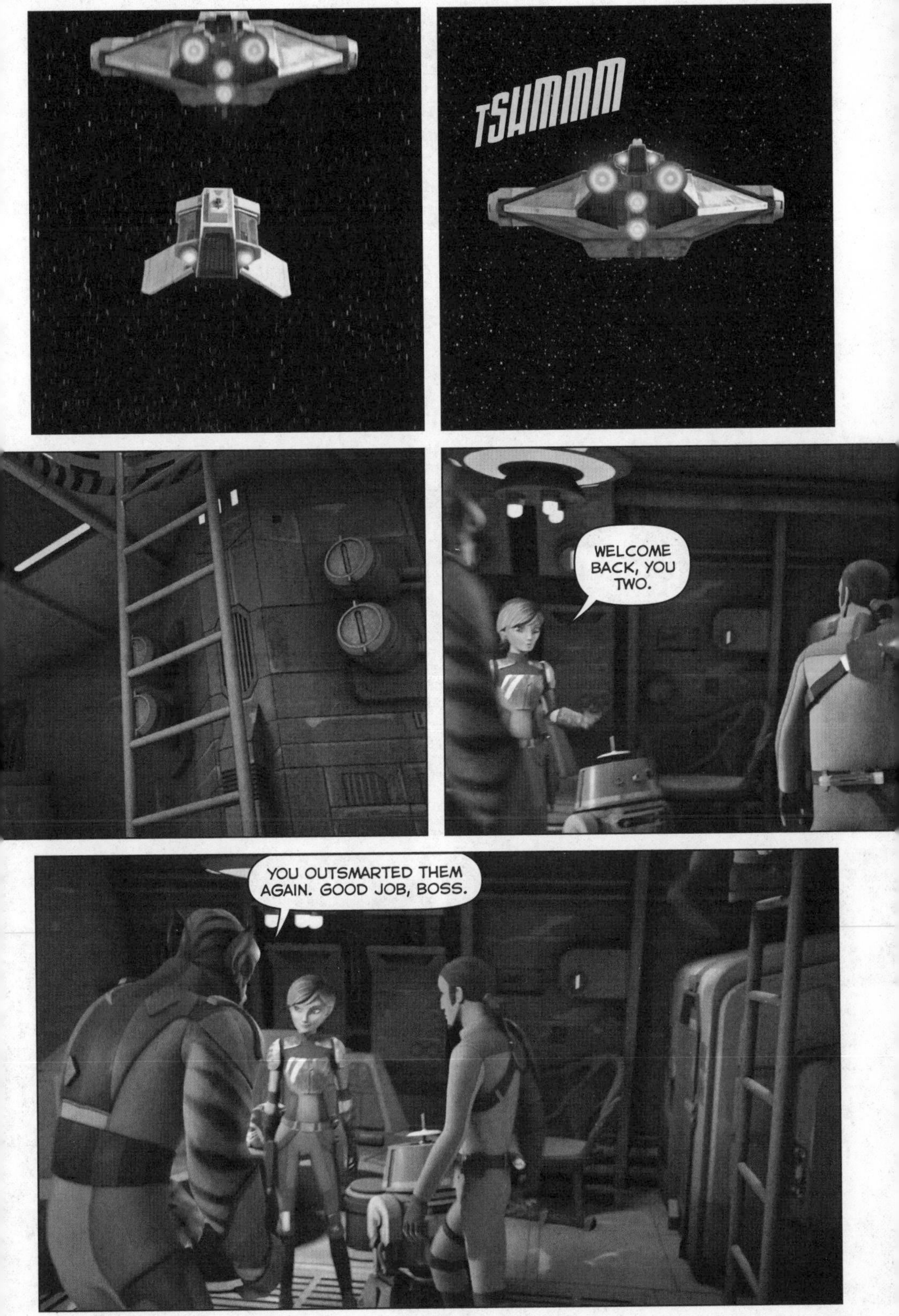
TSHUMMM
WELCOME BACK, YOU TWO.
YOU OUTSMARTED THEM AGAIN. GOOD JOB, BOSS.

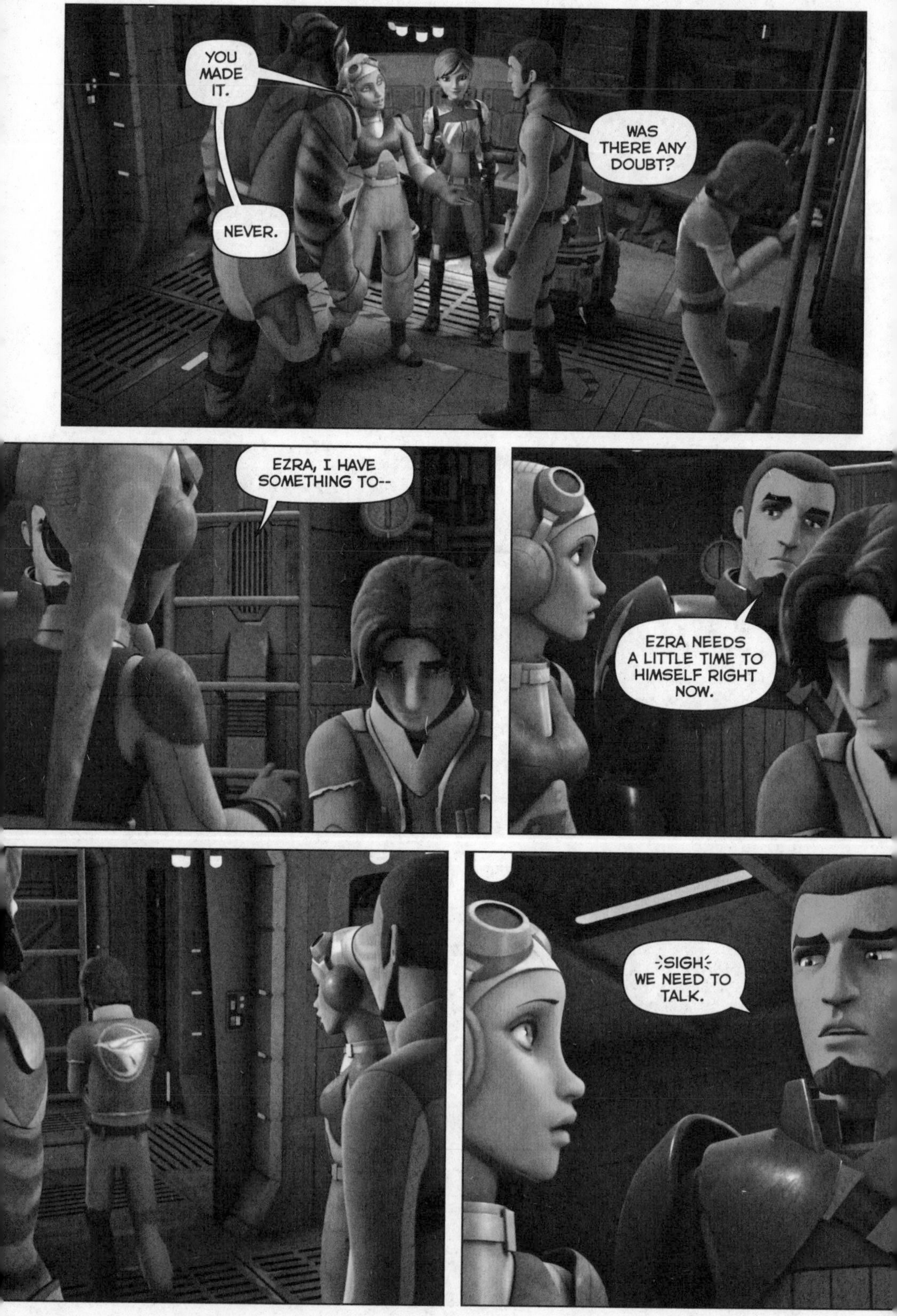
YOU MADE IT.
NEVER.
WAS THERE ANY DOUBT?
EZRA, I HAVE SOMETHING TO--
EZRA NEEDS A LITTLE TIME TO HIMSELF RIGHT NOW.
SIGH
WE NEED TO TALK.

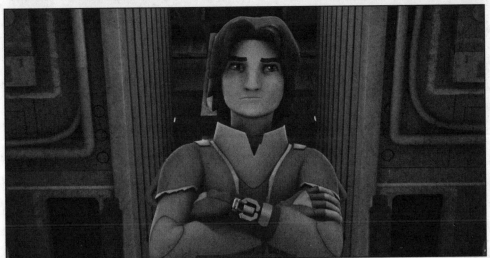

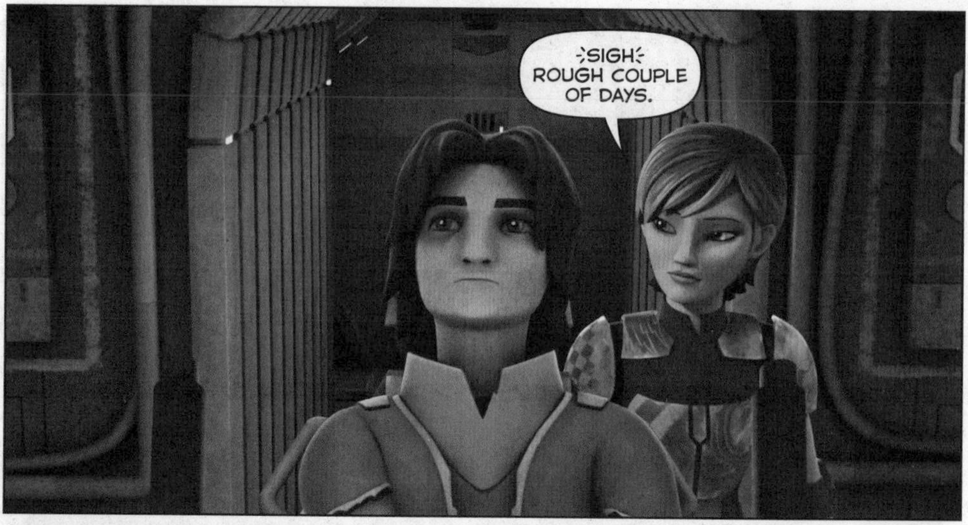

SIGH
ROUGH COUPLE OF DAYS.

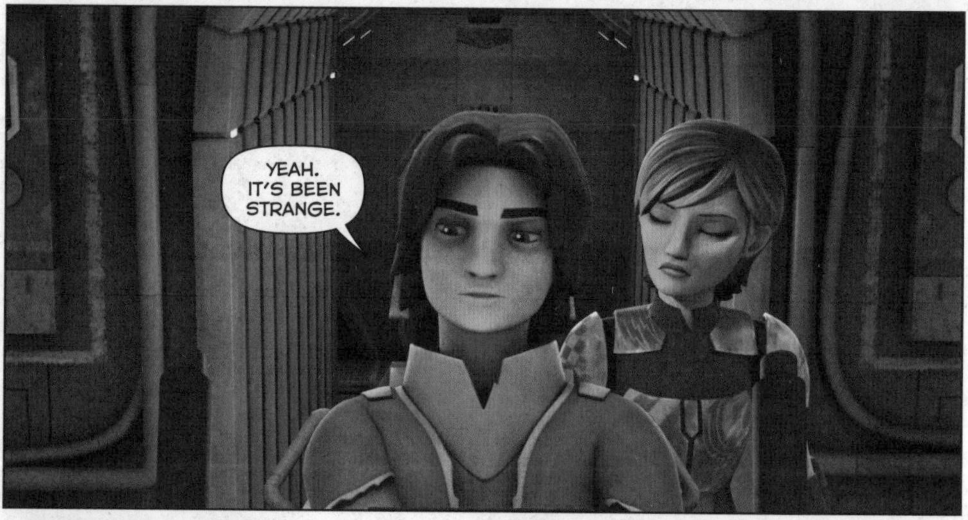

YEAH. IT'S BEEN STRANGE.

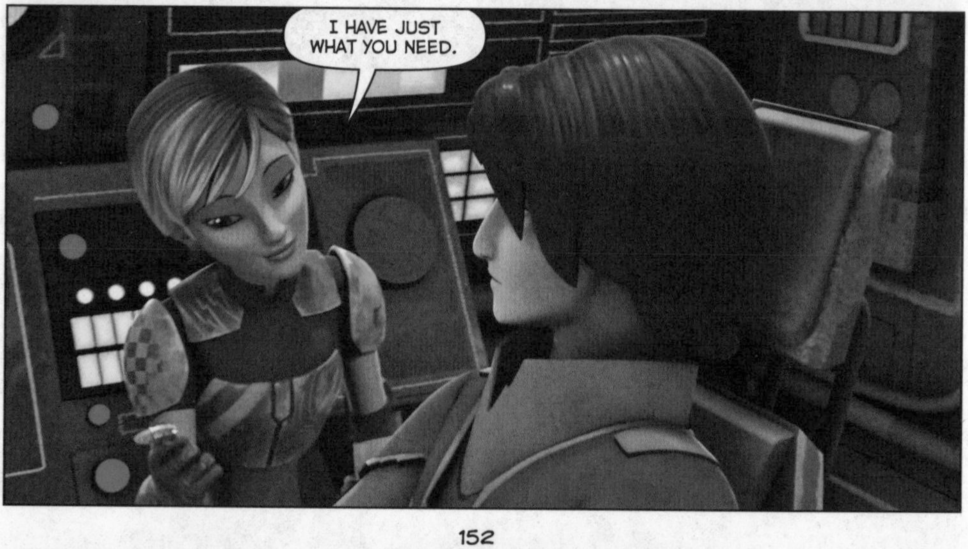

I HAVE JUST WHAT YOU NEED.

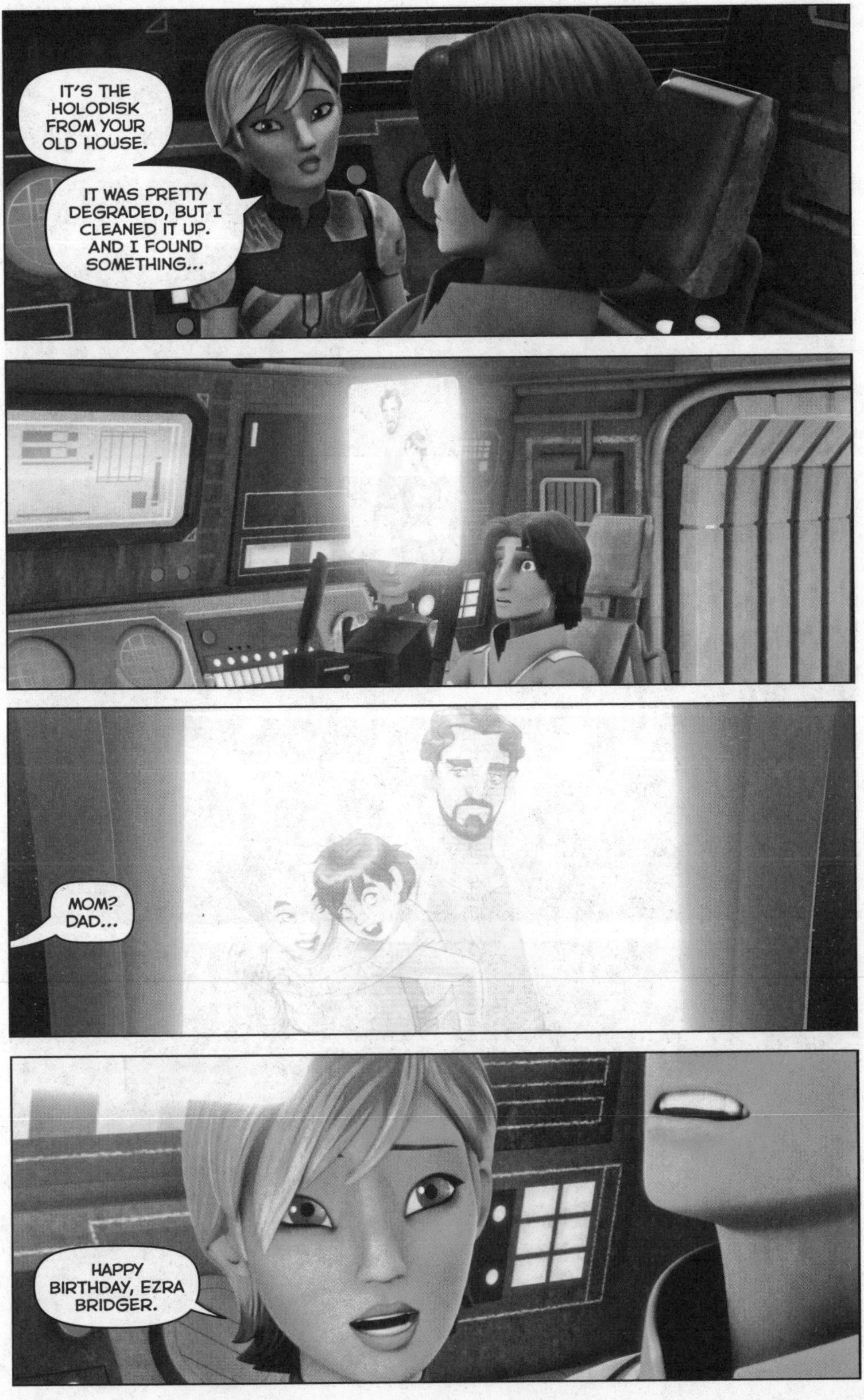
IT'S THE HOLODISK FROM YOUR OLD HOUSE.
IT WAS PRETTY DEGRADED, BUT I CLEANED IT UP. AND I FOUND SOMETHING...
MOM? DAD...
HAPPY BIRTHDAY, EZRA BRIDGER.

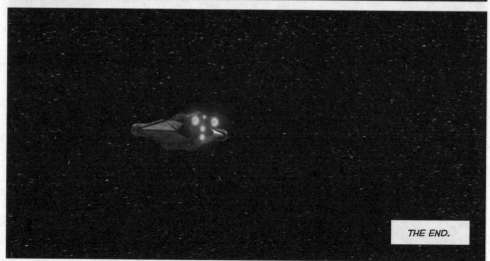

THE END.

STAR WARS REBELS™

PATH OF THE JEDI

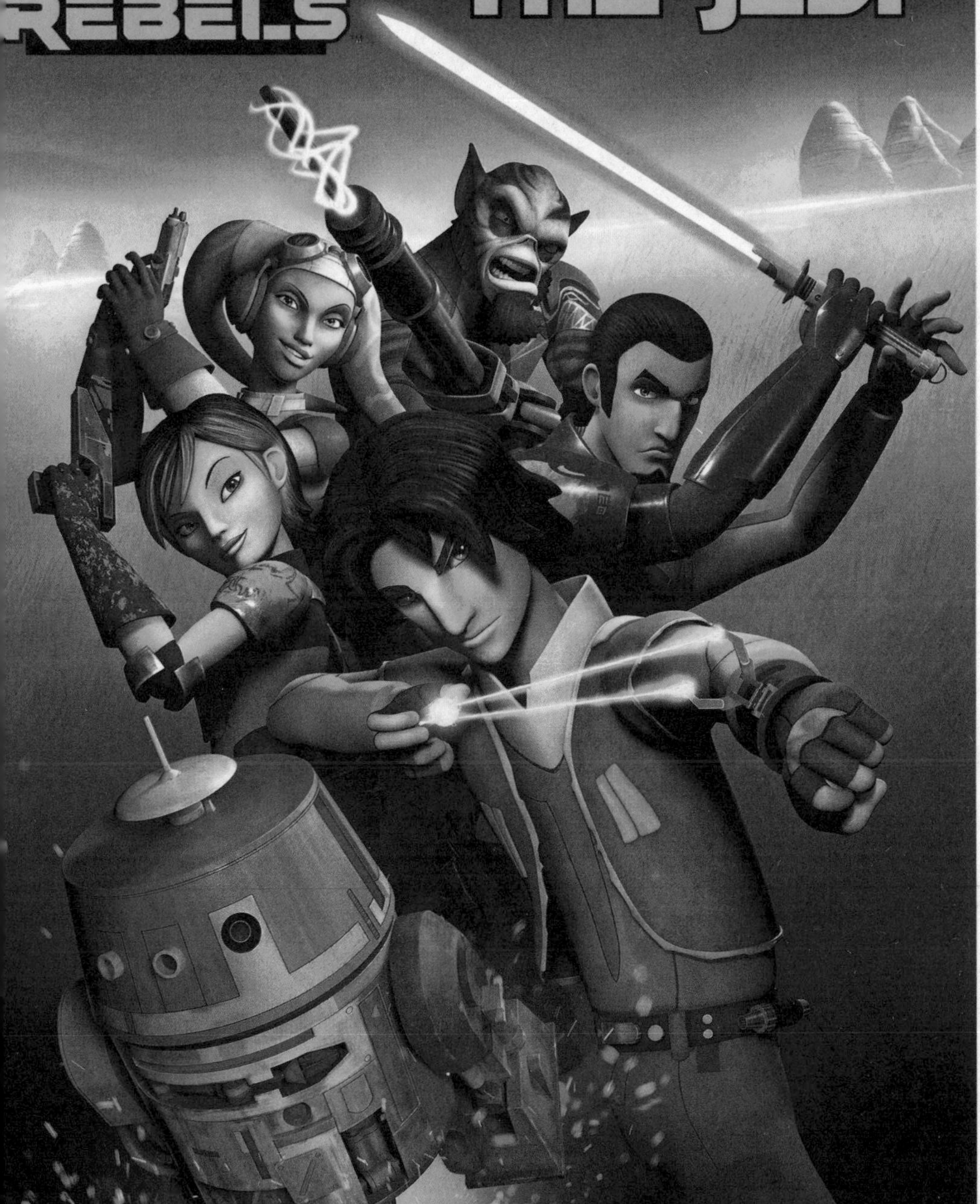

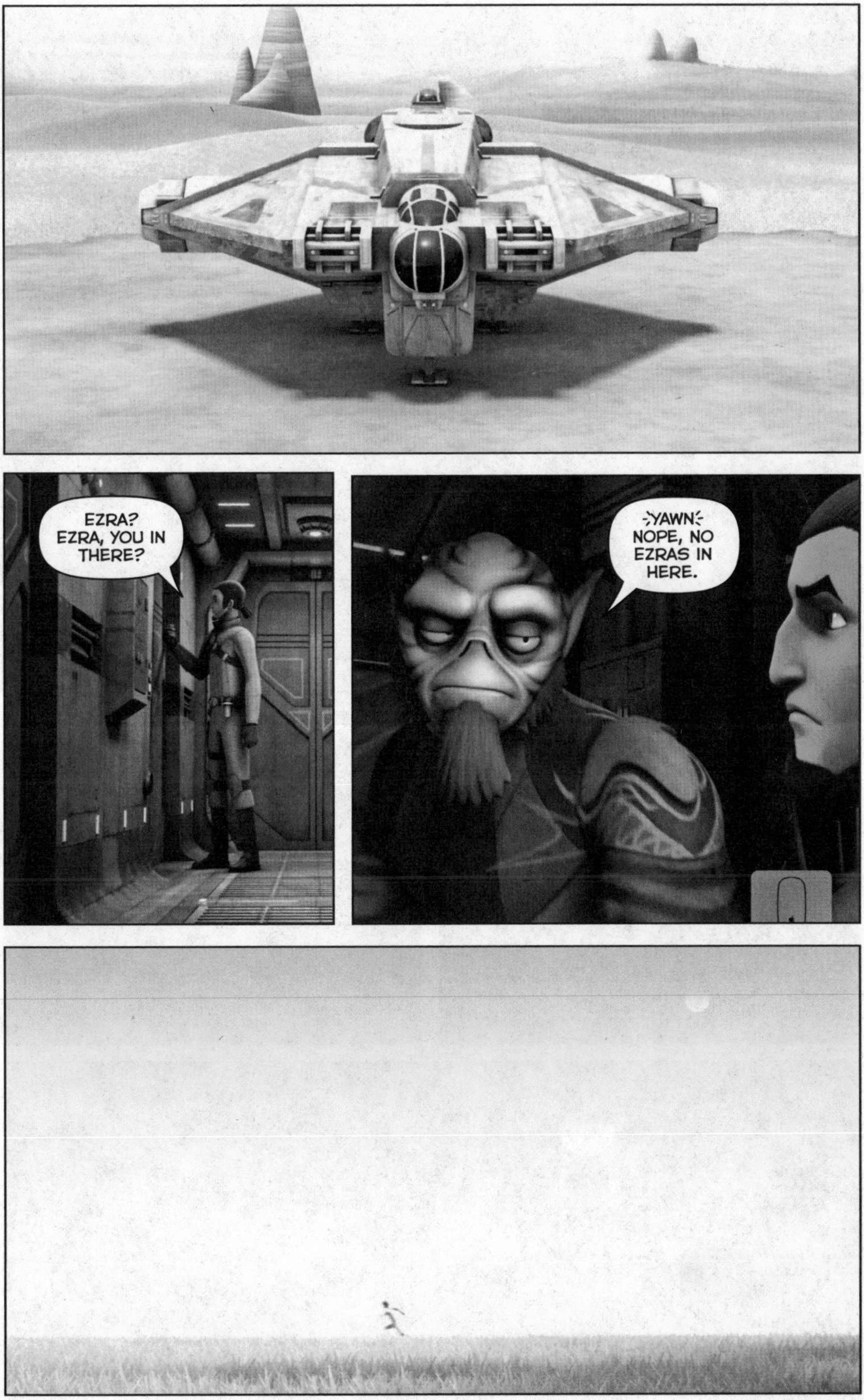
EZRA? EZRA, YOU IN THERE?
-YAWN- NOPE, NO EZRAS IN HERE.

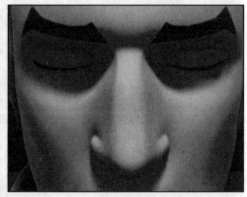

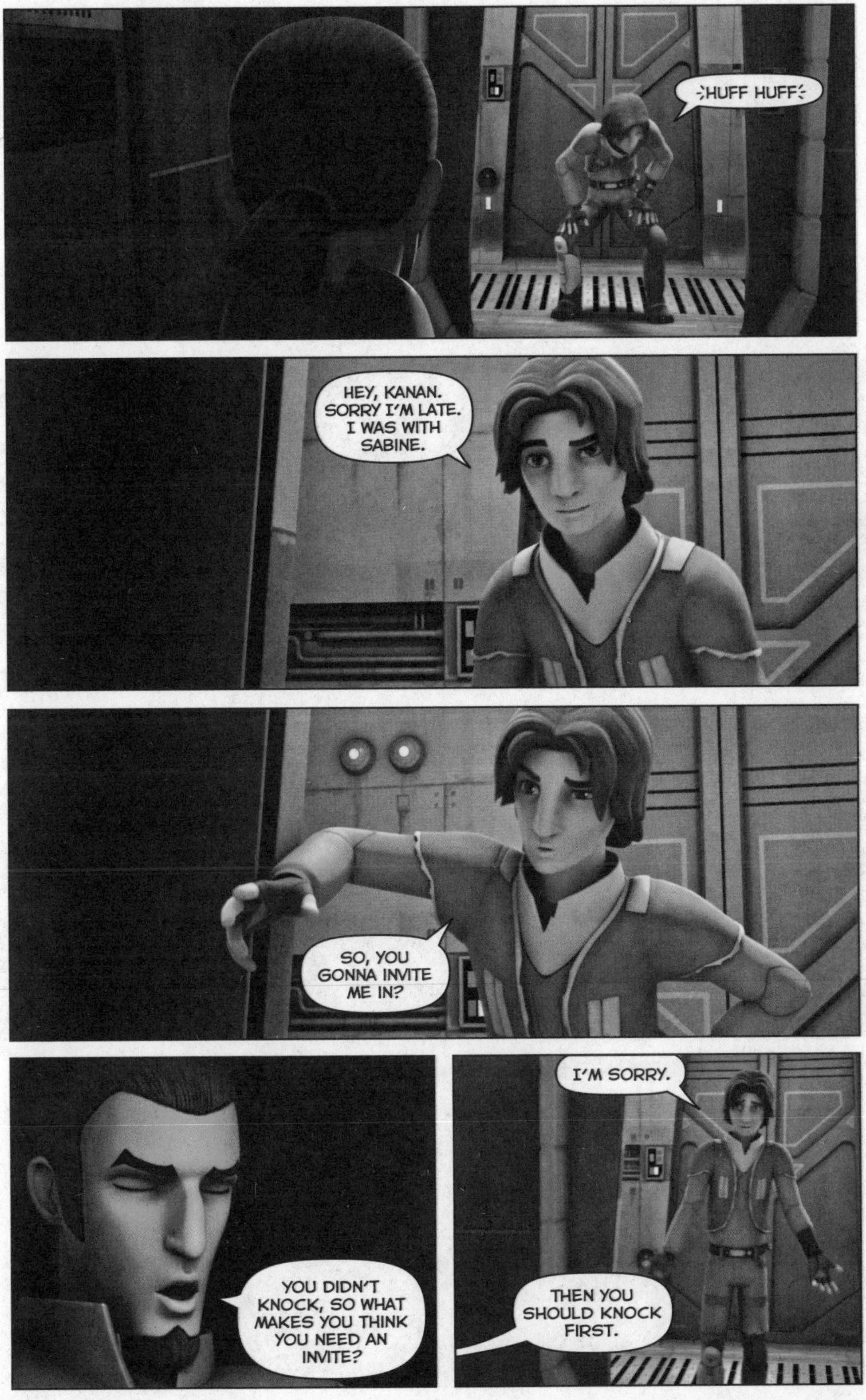
HUFF HUFF
HEY, KANAN. SORRY I'M LATE. I WAS WITH SABINE.
SO, YOU GONNA INVITE ME IN?
YOU DIDN'T KNOCK, SO WHAT MAKES YOU THINK YOU NEED AN INVITE?
I'M SORRY.
THEN YOU SHOULD KNOCK FIRST.

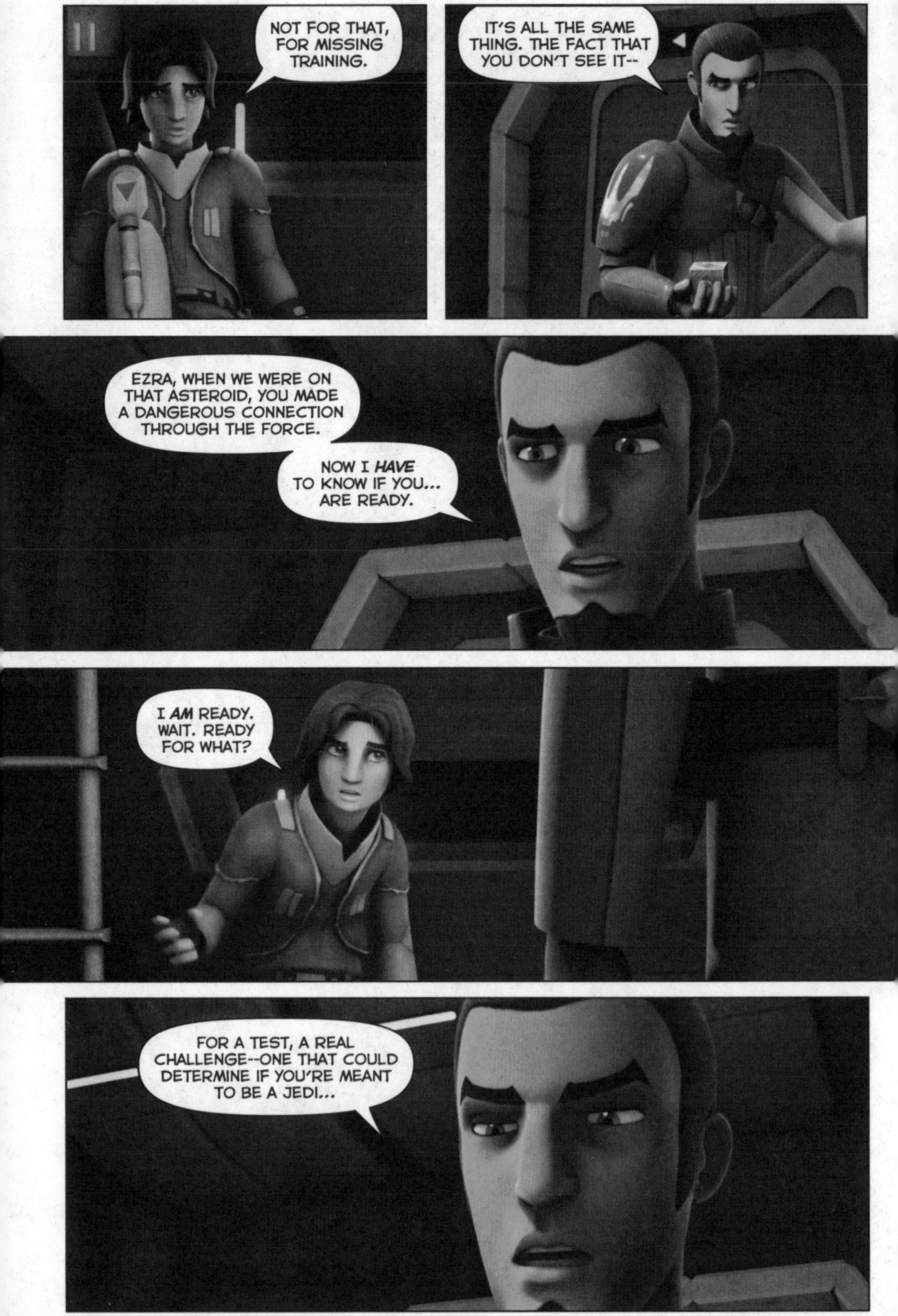
NOT FOR THAT, FOR MISSING TRAINING.
IT'S ALL THE SAME THING. THE FACT THAT YOU DON'T SEE IT--
EZRA, WHEN WE WERE ON THAT ASTEROID, YOU MADE A DANGEROUS CONNECTION THROUGH THE FORCE.
NOW I *HAVE* TO KNOW IF YOU... ARE READY.
I *AM* READY. WAIT. READY FOR WHAT?
FOR A TEST, A REAL CHALLENGE--ONE THAT COULD DETERMINE IF YOU'RE MEANT TO BE A JEDI...

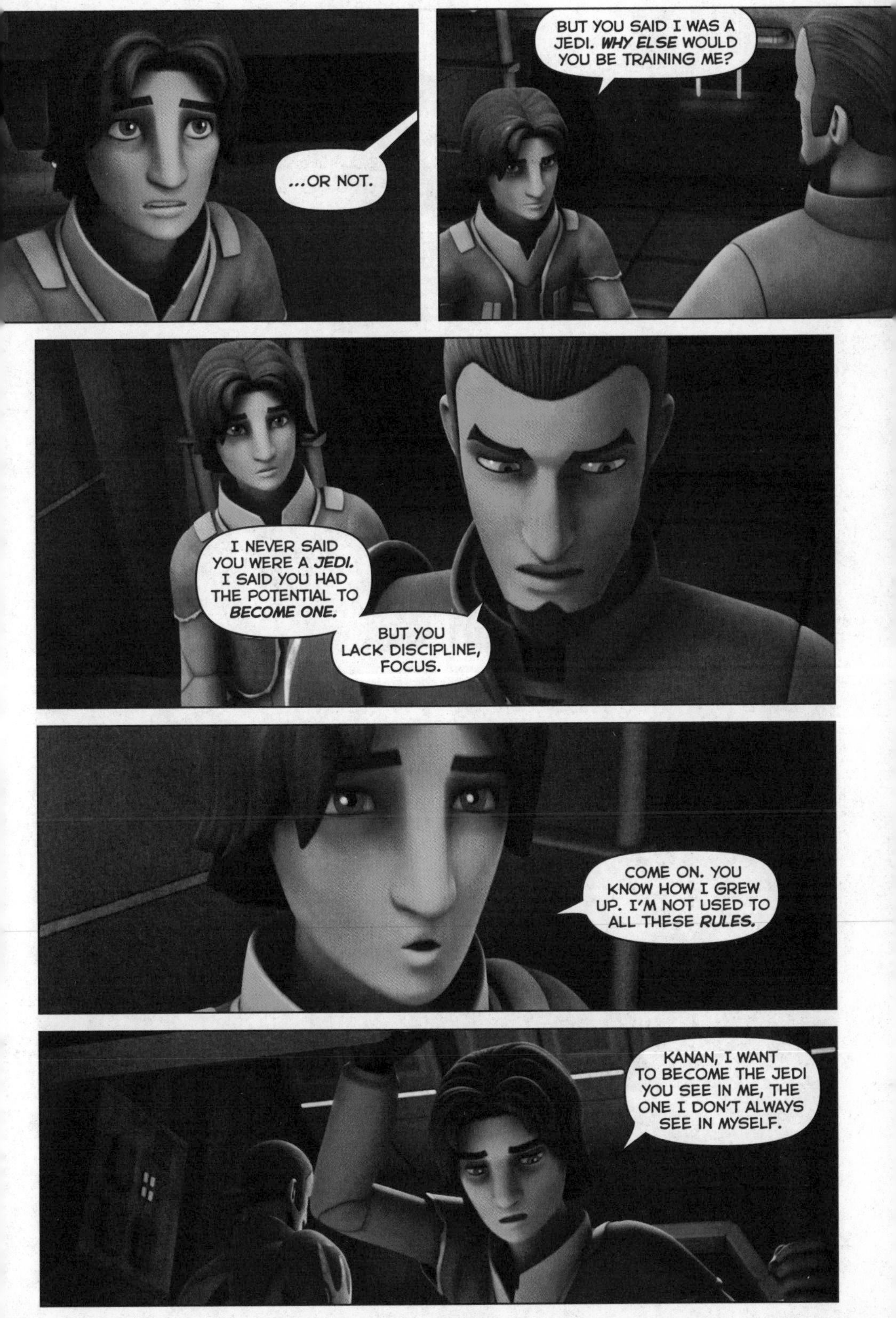
...OR NOT.
BUT YOU SAID I WAS A JEDI. WHY ELSE WOULD YOU BE TRAINING ME?
I NEVER SAID YOU WERE A JEDI. I SAID YOU HAD THE POTENTIAL TO BECOME ONE.
BUT YOU LACK DISCIPLINE, FOCUS.
COME ON. YOU KNOW HOW I GREW UP. I'M NOT USED TO ALL THESE RULES.
KANAN, I WANT TO BECOME THE JEDI YOU SEE IN ME, THE ONE I DON'T ALWAYS SEE IN MYSELF.

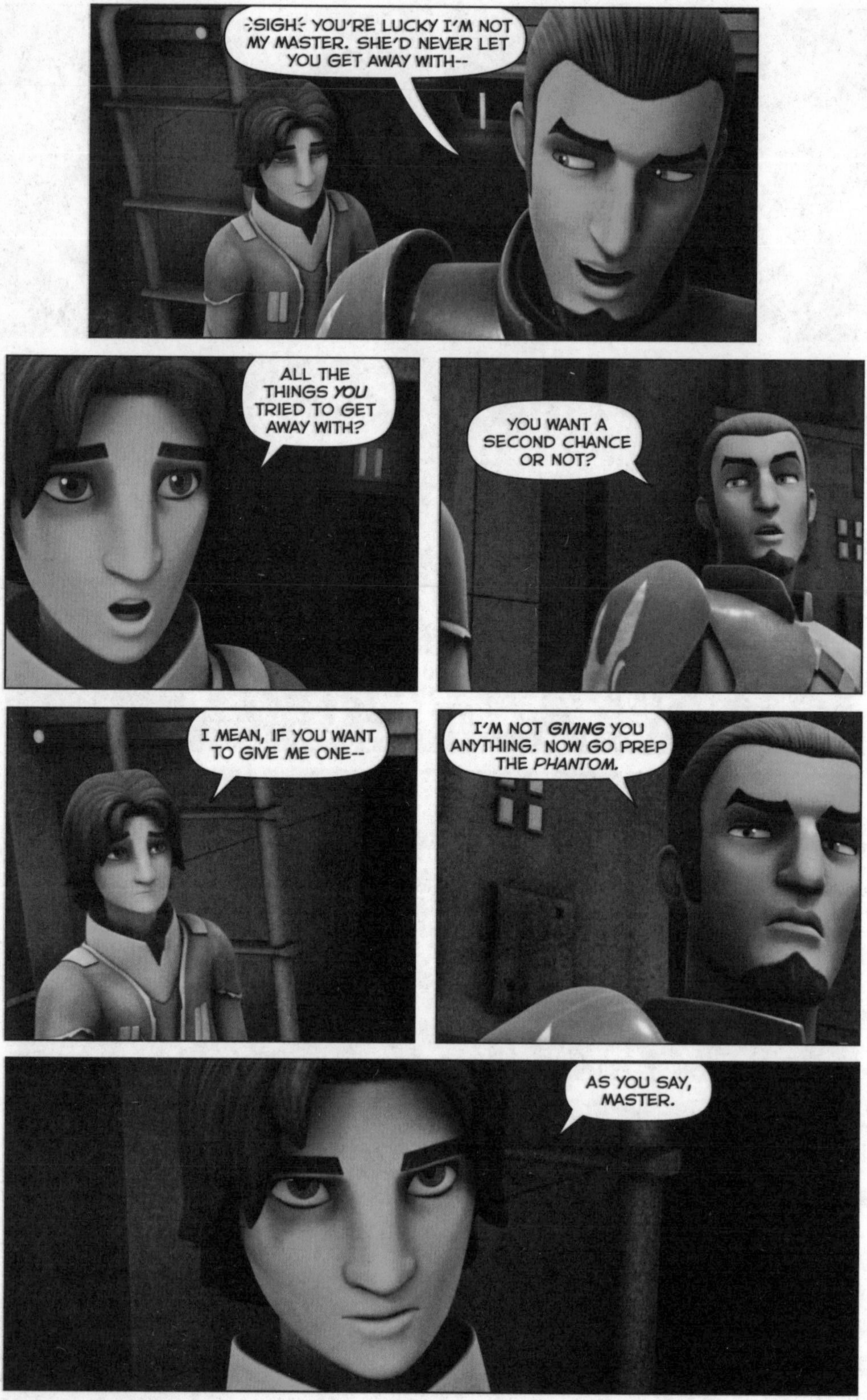
SIGH YOU'RE LUCKY I'M NOT MY MASTER. SHE'D NEVER LET YOU GET AWAY WITH--
ALL THE THINGS *YOU* TRIED TO GET AWAY WITH?
YOU WANT A SECOND CHANCE OR NOT?
I MEAN, IF YOU WANT TO GIVE ME ONE--
I'M NOT *GIVING* YOU ANYTHING. NOW GO PREP THE *PHANTOM.*
AS YOU SAY, MASTER.

AH, I MIGHT REGRET THIS.

YOU HAVE TO DO THIS, KANAN.

AFTER WHAT HAPPENED ON THE ASTEROID, YOU HAVE TO HELP HIM.

I HOPE I CAN.

I KNOW YOU CAN.

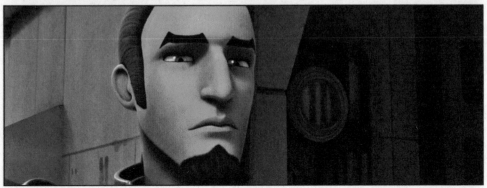

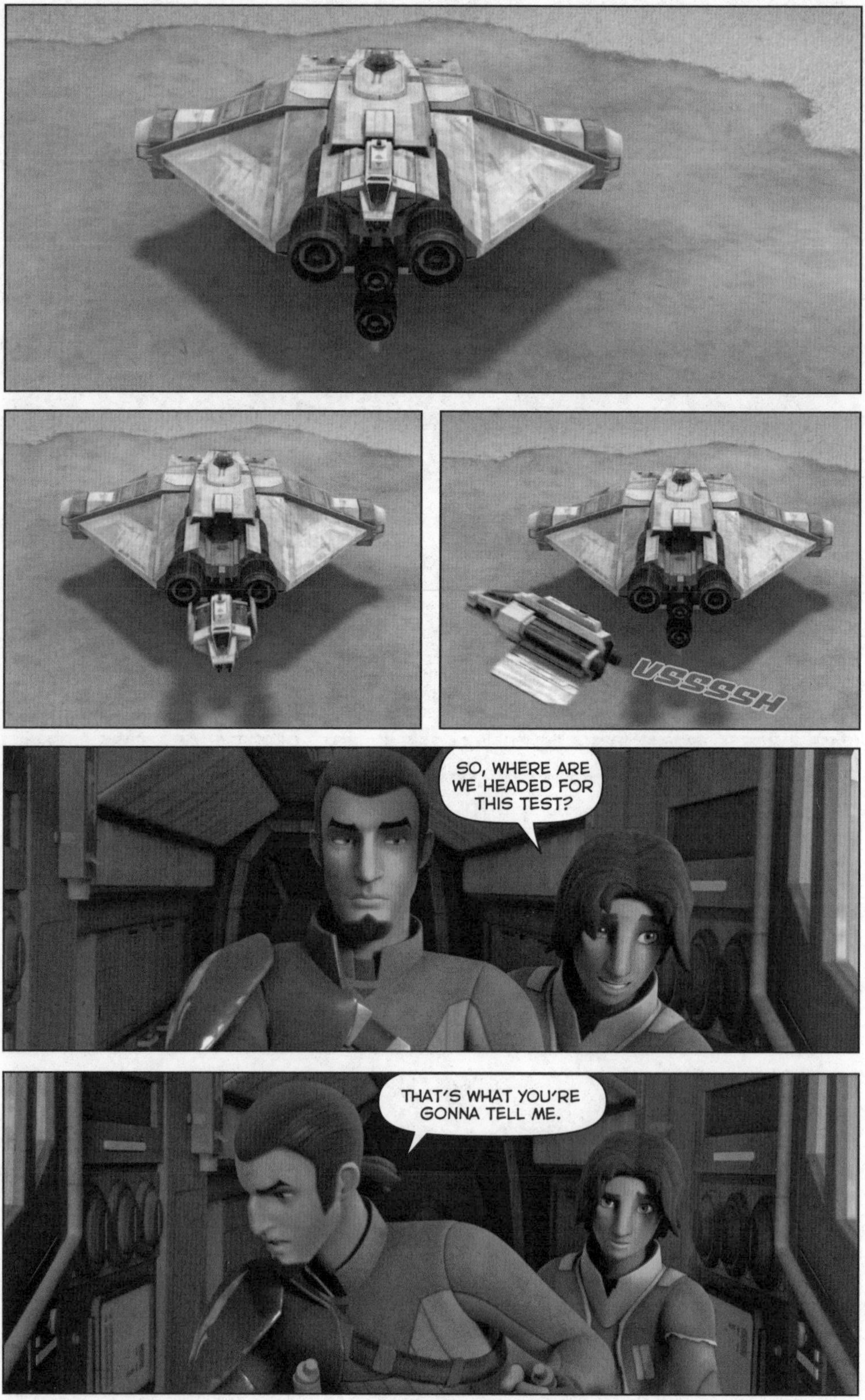
VSSSSSH
SO, WHERE ARE WE HEADED FOR THIS TEST?
THAT'S WHAT YOU'RE GONNA TELL ME.

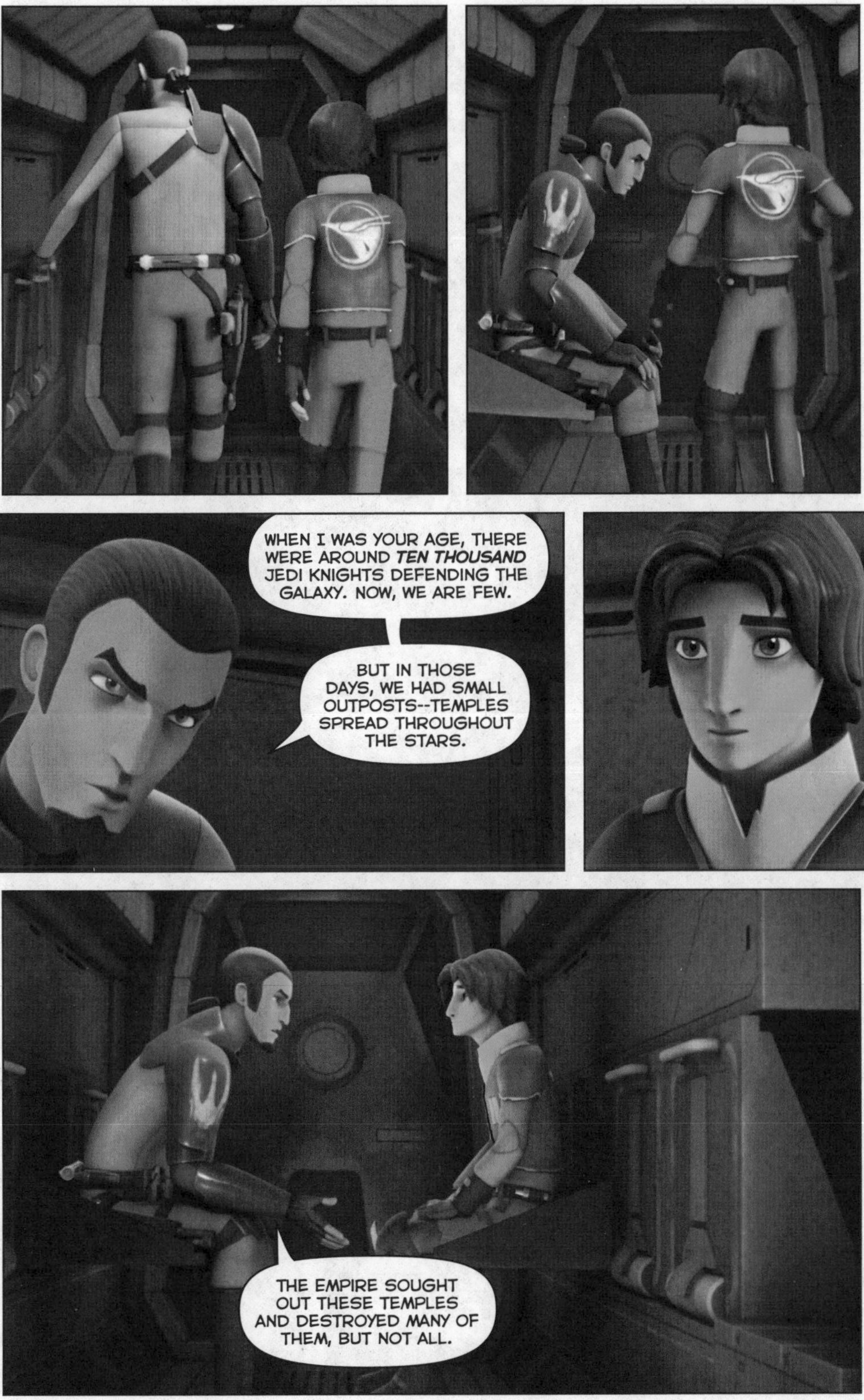
WHEN I WAS YOUR AGE, THERE WERE AROUND *TEN THOUSAND* JEDI KNIGHTS DEFENDING THE GALAXY. NOW, WE ARE FEW.
BUT IN THOSE DAYS, WE HAD SMALL OUTPOSTS--TEMPLES SPREAD THROUGHOUT THE STARS.
THE EMPIRE SOUGHT OUT THESE TEMPLES AND DESTROYED MANY OF THEM, BUT NOT ALL.

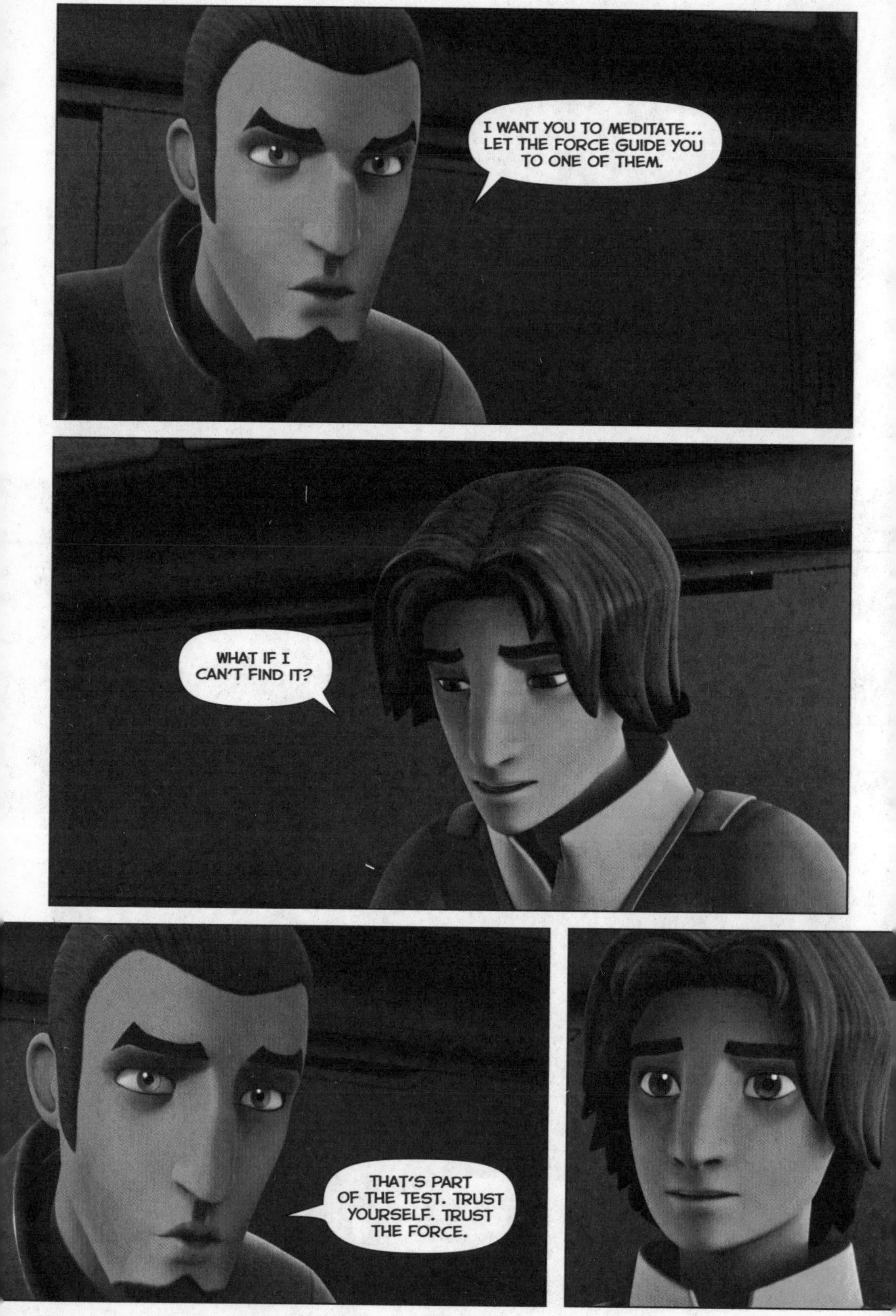
I WANT YOU TO MEDITATE... LET THE FORCE GUIDE YOU TO ONE OF THEM.
WHAT IF I CAN'T FIND IT?
THAT'S PART OF THE TEST. TRUST YOURSELF. TRUST THE FORCE.

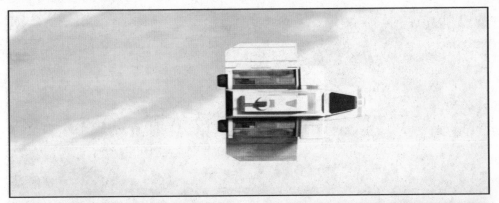

:SIGH: SO, DID YOU TAKE THIS TEST AT MY AGE?

:SIGH: IT WAS DIFFERENT FOR ME, EZRA.

EVERYTHING WAS DIFFERENT BACK THEN. ALL THAT REMAINS NOW IS THE FORCE.

AND ONLY MY CONNECTION TO THE FORCE CAN LEAD ME TO THE TEMPLE.

HAH. HE CAN BE TAUGHT.

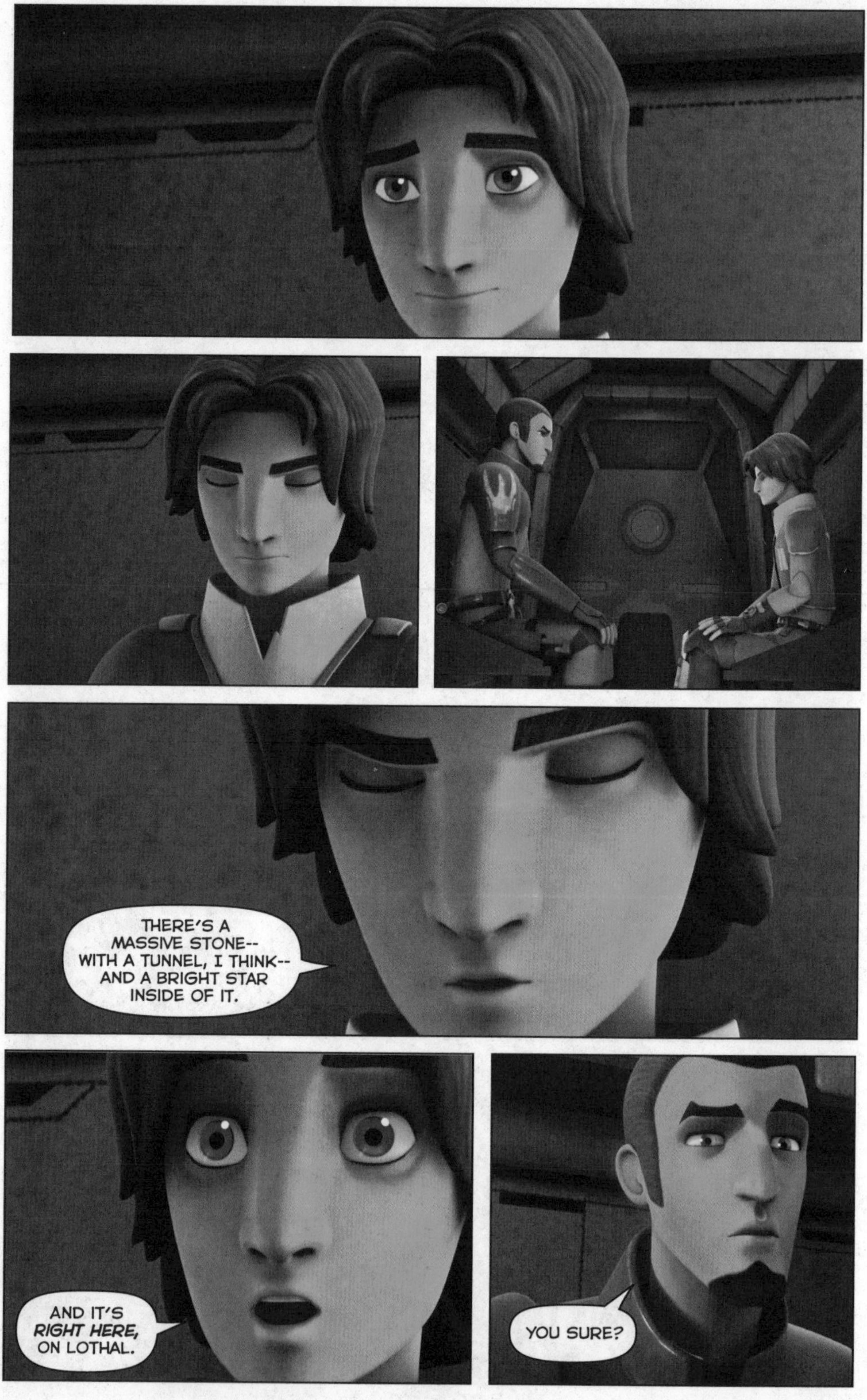
THERE'S A MASSIVE STONE-- WITH A TUNNEL, I THINK-- AND A BRIGHT STAR INSIDE OF IT.
AND IT'S *RIGHT HERE,* ON LOTHAL.
YOU SURE?

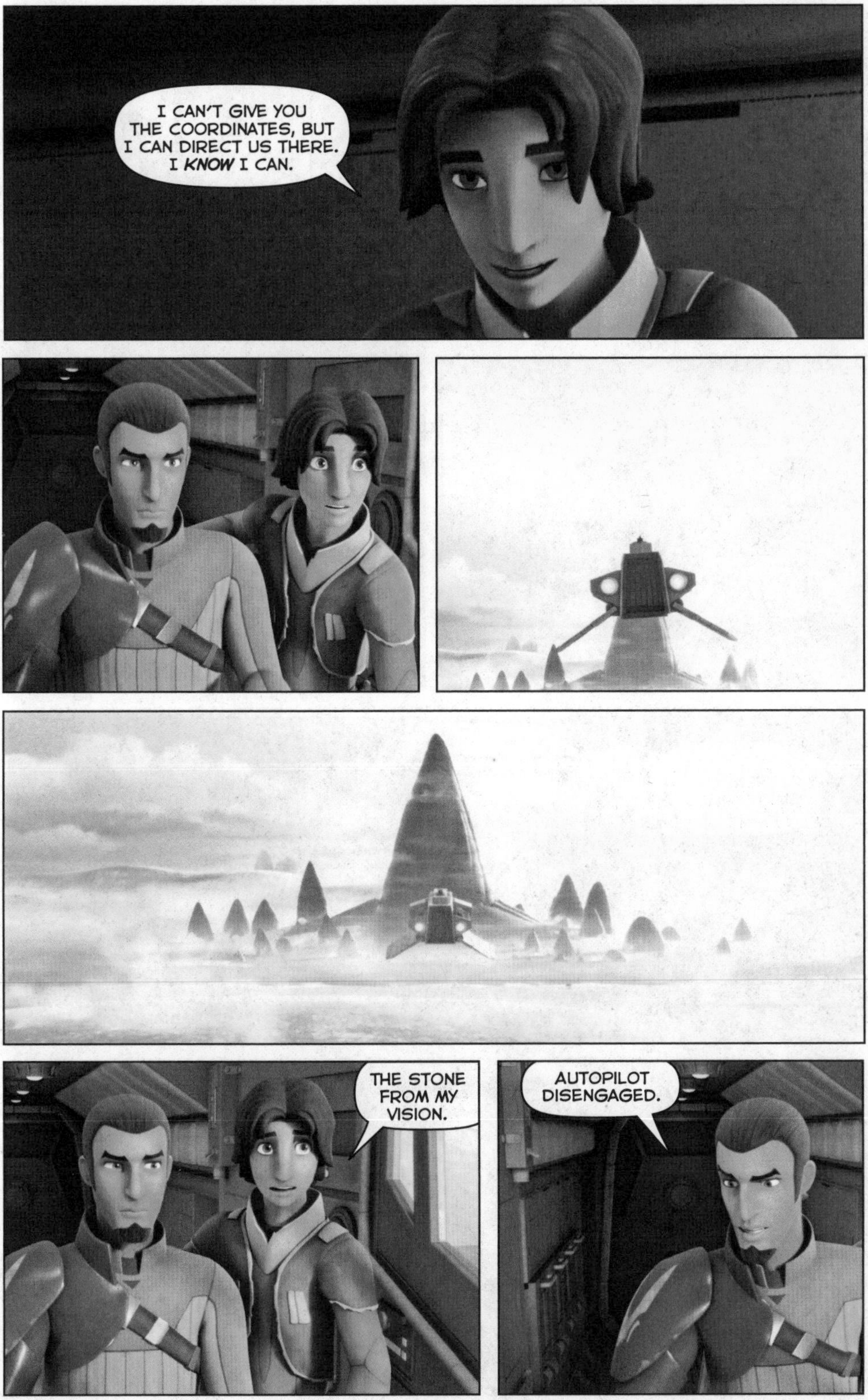
I CAN'T GIVE YOU THE COORDINATES, BUT I CAN DIRECT US THERE. I *KNOW* I CAN.
THE STONE FROM MY VISION.
AUTOPILOT DISENGAGED.

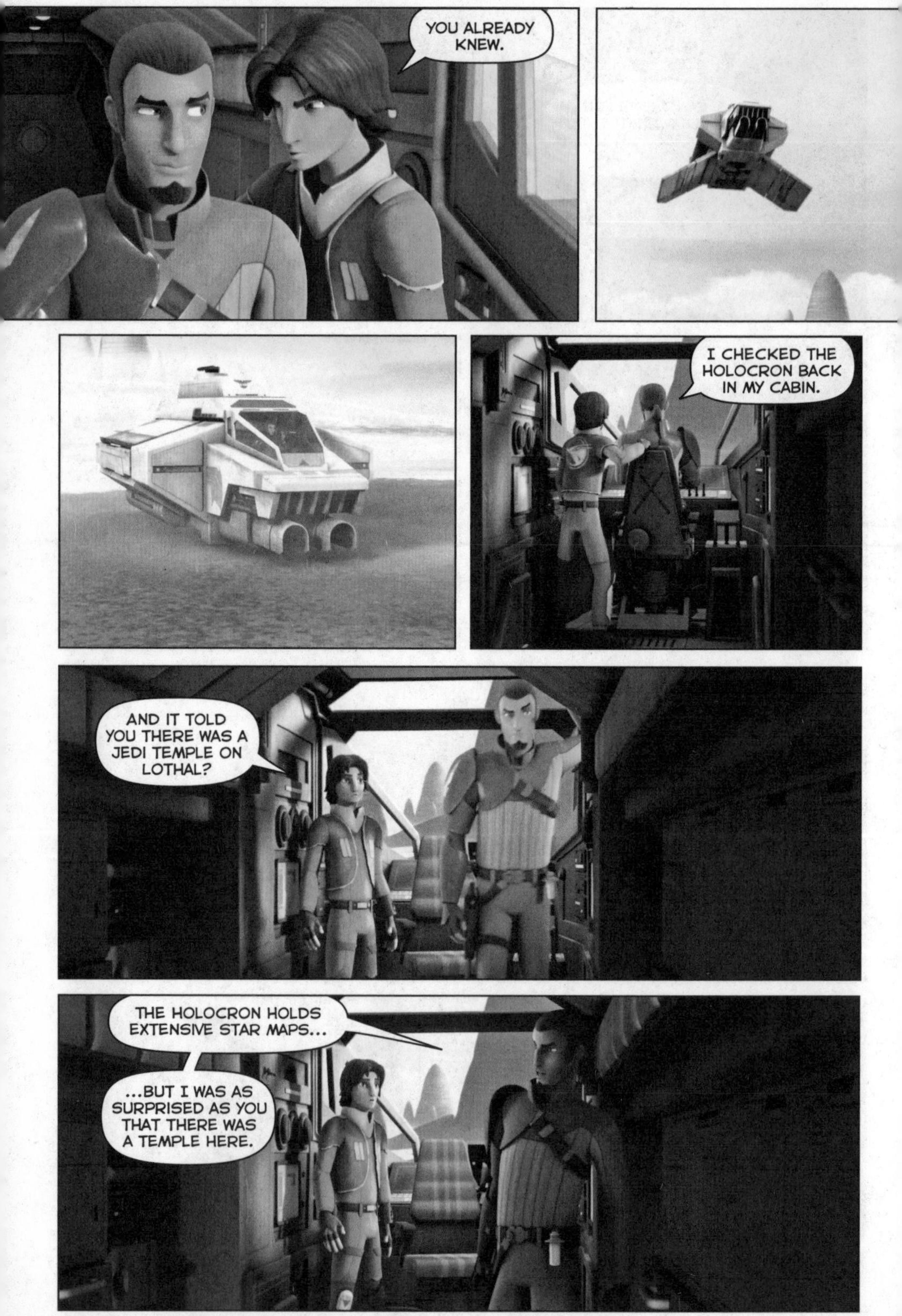
YOU ALREADY KNEW.
I CHECKED THE HOLOCRON BACK IN MY CABIN.
AND IT TOLD YOU THERE WAS A JEDI TEMPLE ON LOTHAL?
THE HOLOCRON HOLDS EXTENSIVE STAR MAPS...
...BUT I WAS AS SURPRISED AS YOU THAT THERE WAS A TEMPLE HERE.

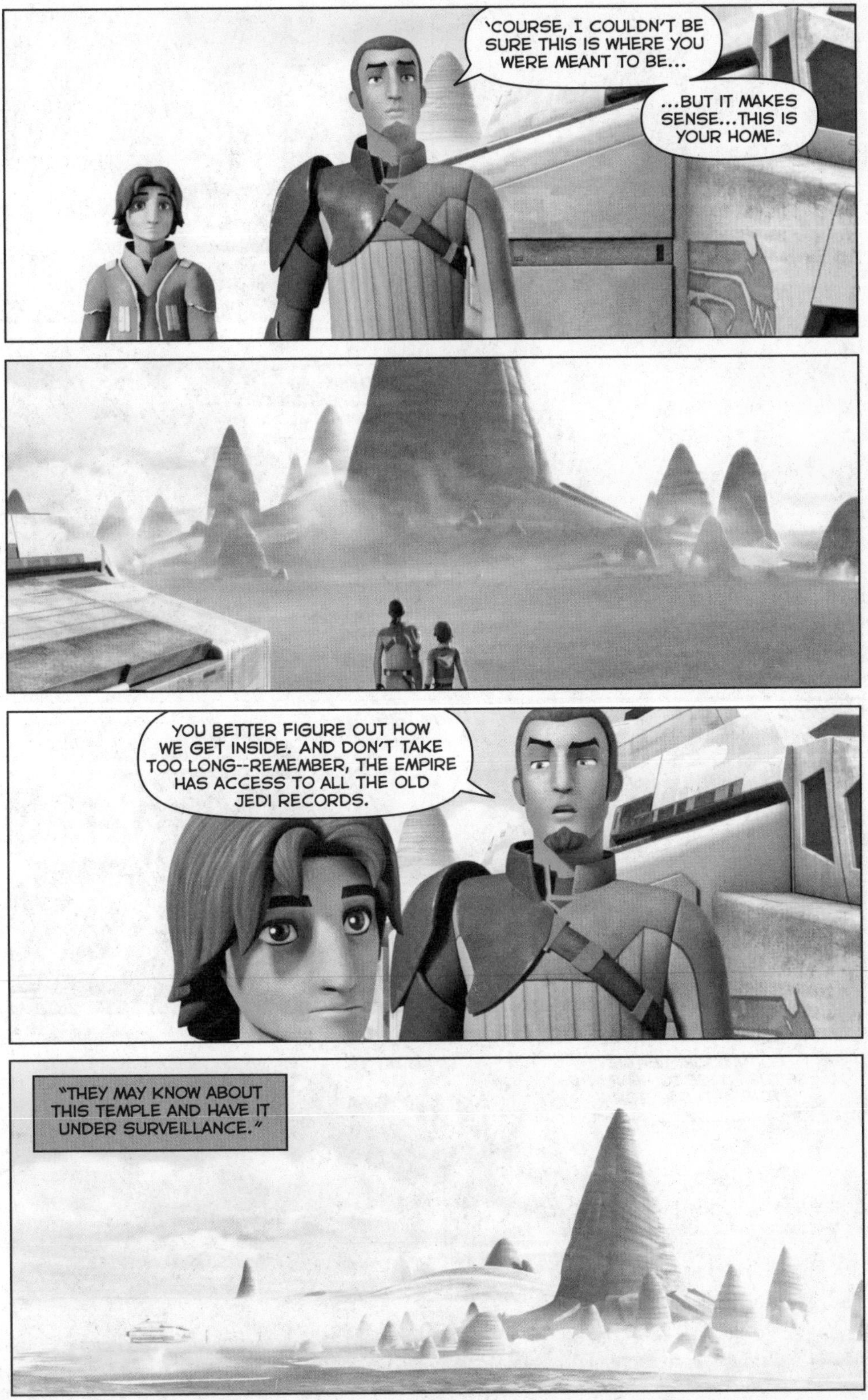
'COURSE, I COULDN'T BE SURE THIS IS WHERE YOU WERE MEANT TO BE...
...BUT IT MAKES SENSE...THIS IS YOUR HOME.
YOU BETTER FIGURE OUT HOW WE GET INSIDE. AND DON'T TAKE TOO LONG--REMEMBER, THE EMPIRE HAS ACCESS TO ALL THE OLD JEDI RECORDS.
"THEY MAY KNOW ABOUT THIS TEMPLE AND HAVE IT UNDER SURVEILLANCE."

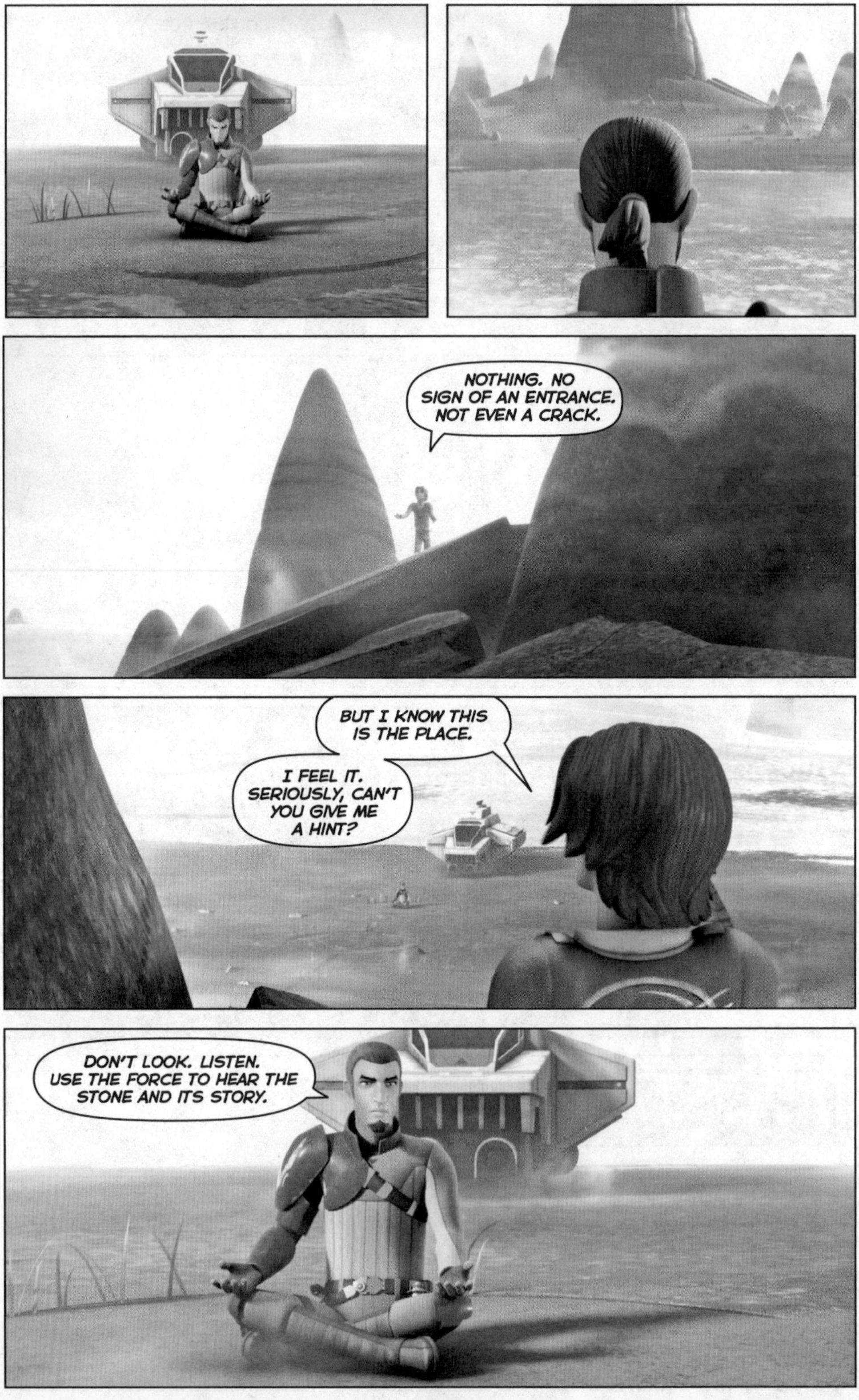
NOTHING. NO SIGN OF AN ENTRANCE. NOT EVEN A CRACK.
BUT I KNOW THIS IS THE PLACE.
I FEEL IT. SERIOUSLY, CAN'T YOU GIVE ME A HINT?
DON'T LOOK. LISTEN. USE THE FORCE TO HEAR THE STONE AND ITS STORY.

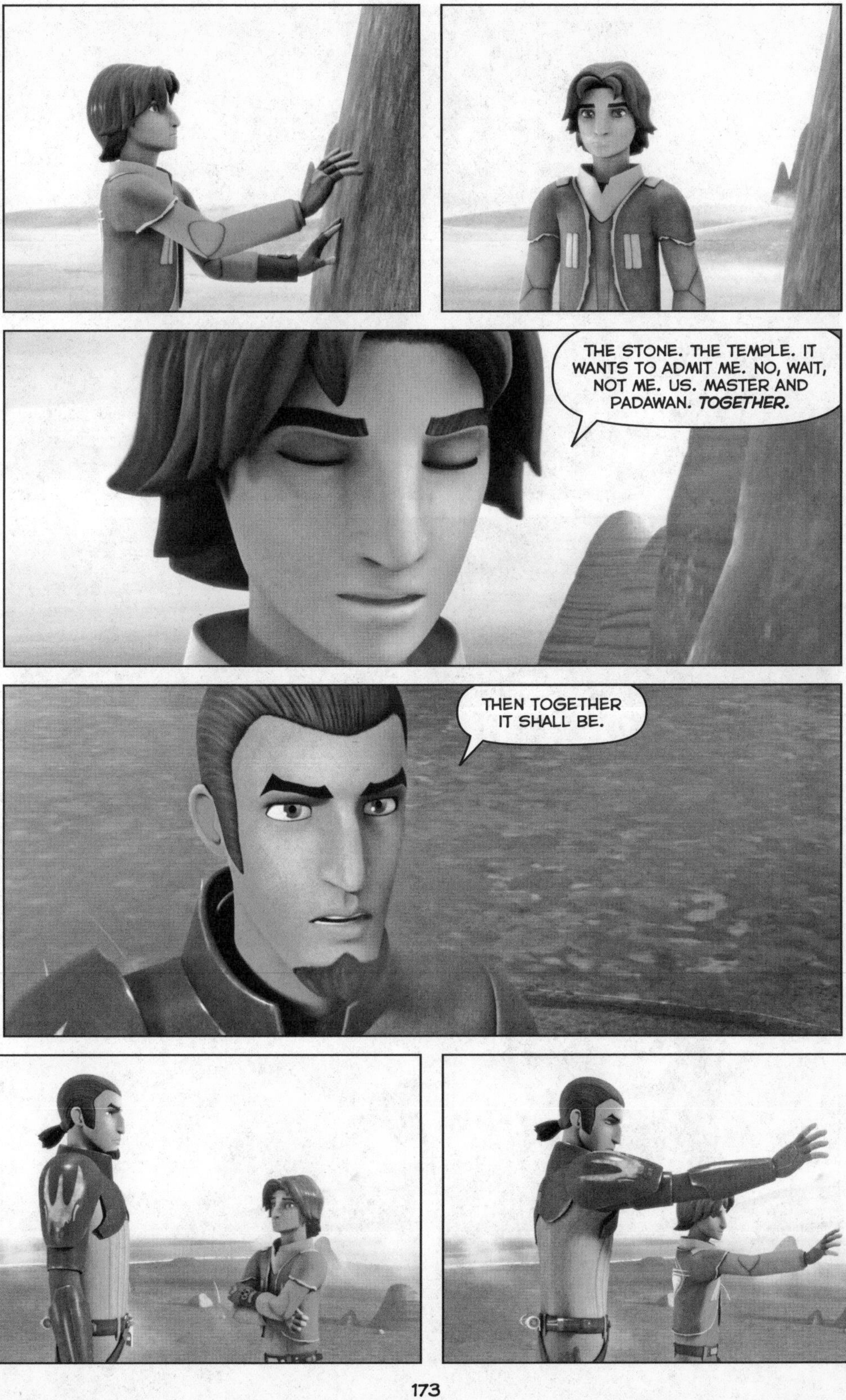
THE STONE. THE TEMPLE. IT WANTS TO ADMIT ME. NO, WAIT, NOT ME. US. MASTER AND PADAWAN. *TOGETHER.*
THEN TOGETHER IT SHALL BE.

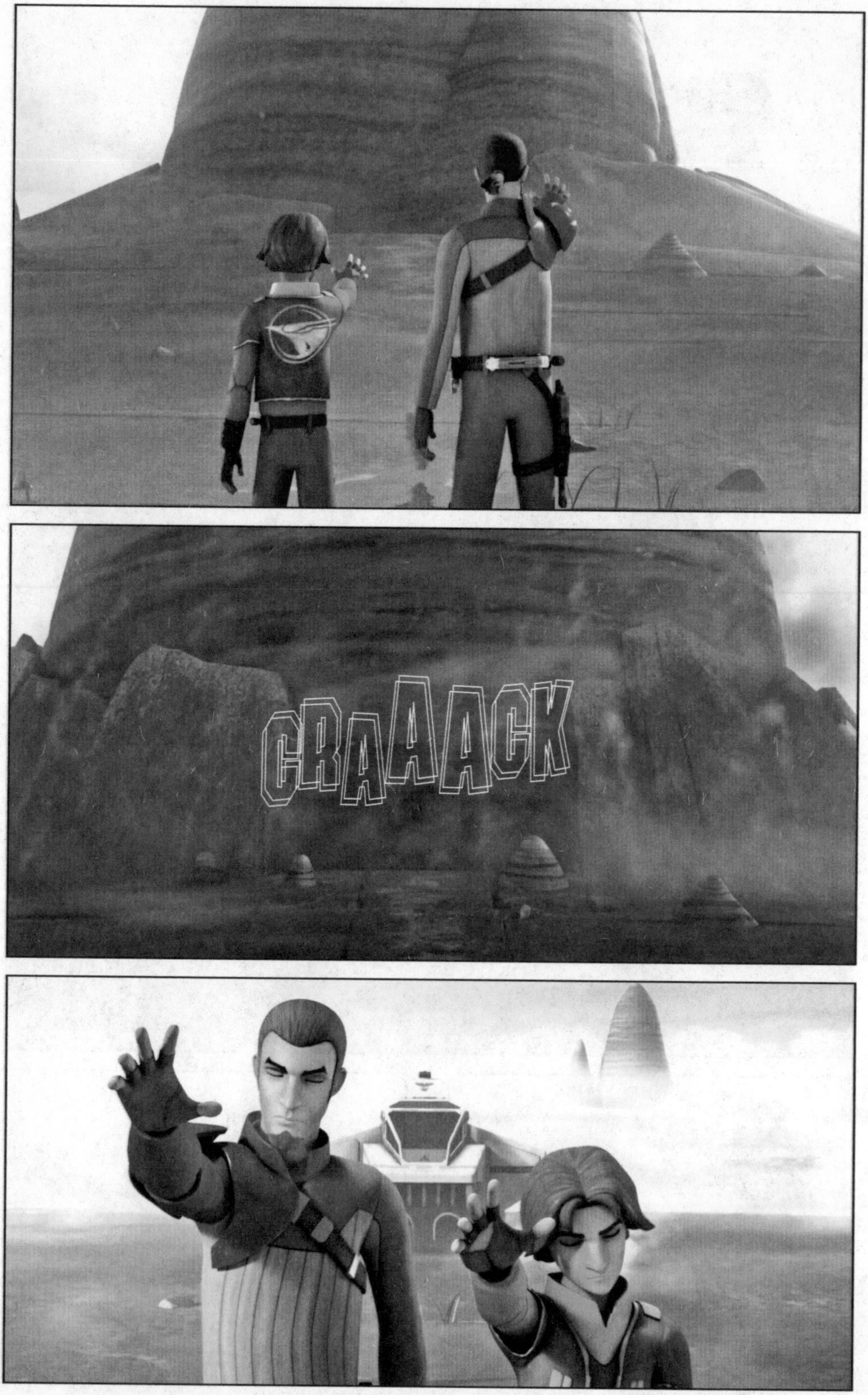
CRAAACK

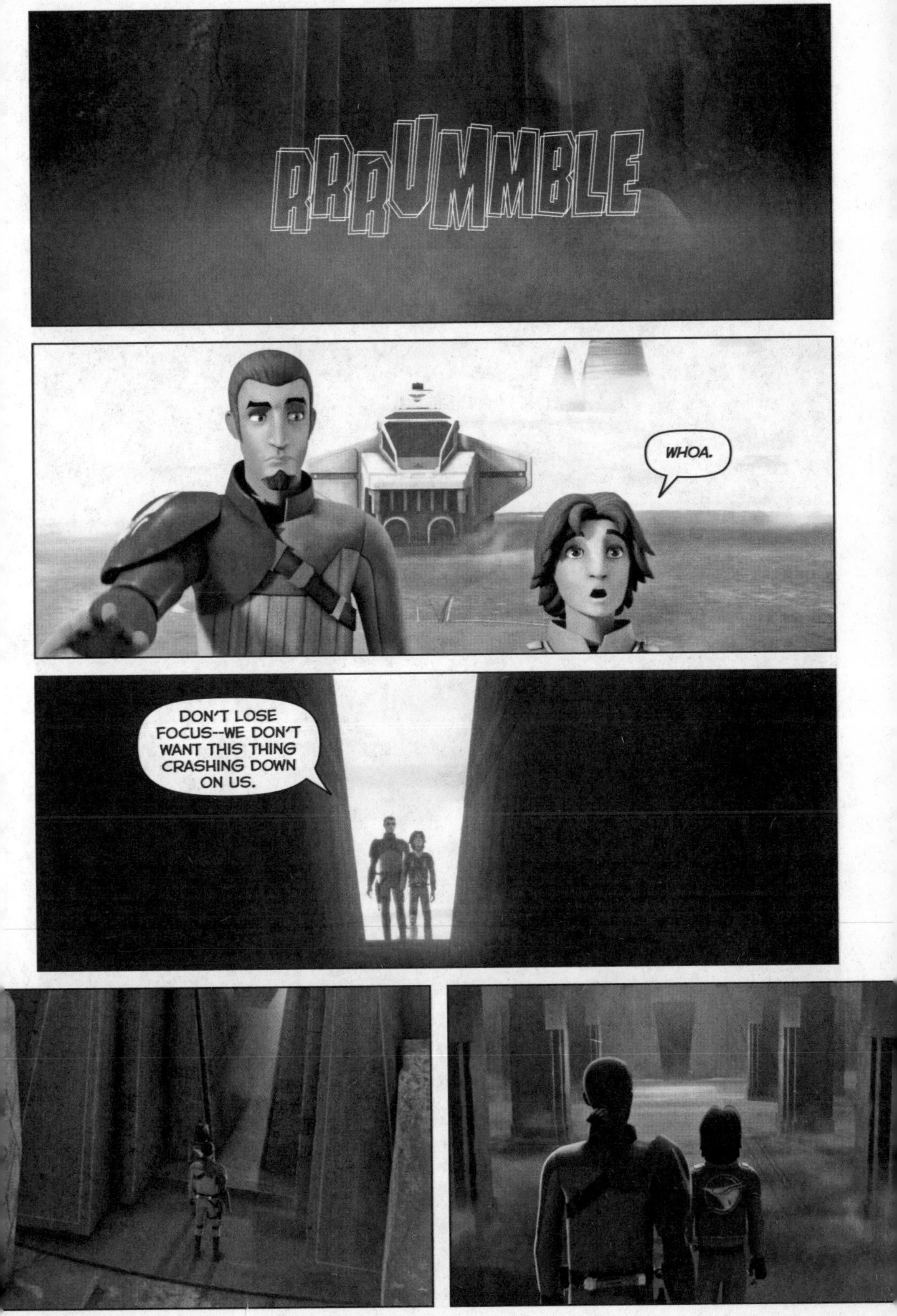
ARRUMMBLE
WHOA.
DON'T LOSE FOCUS--WE DON'T WANT THIS THING CRASHING DOWN ON US.

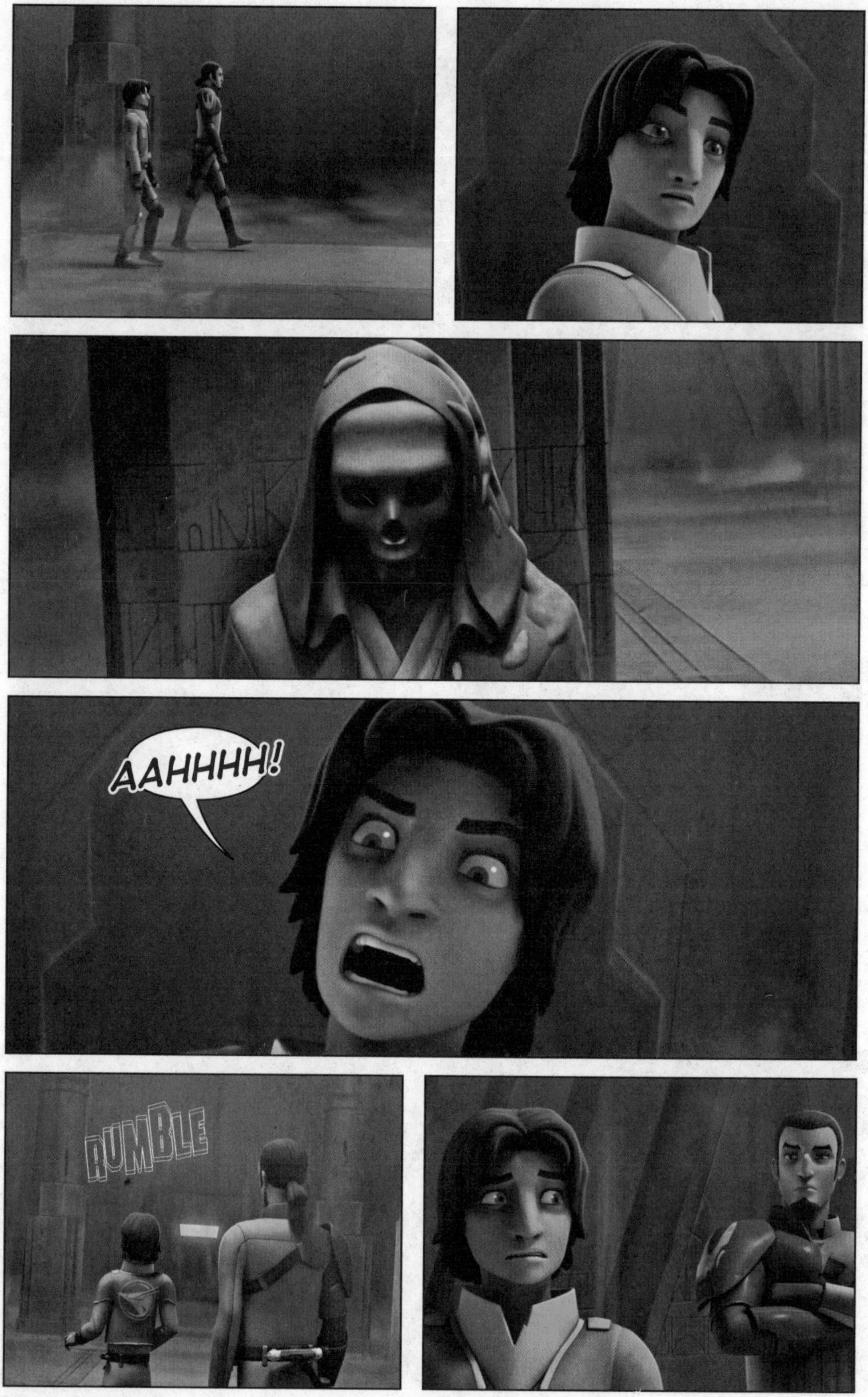
AAHHHH!
RUMBLE

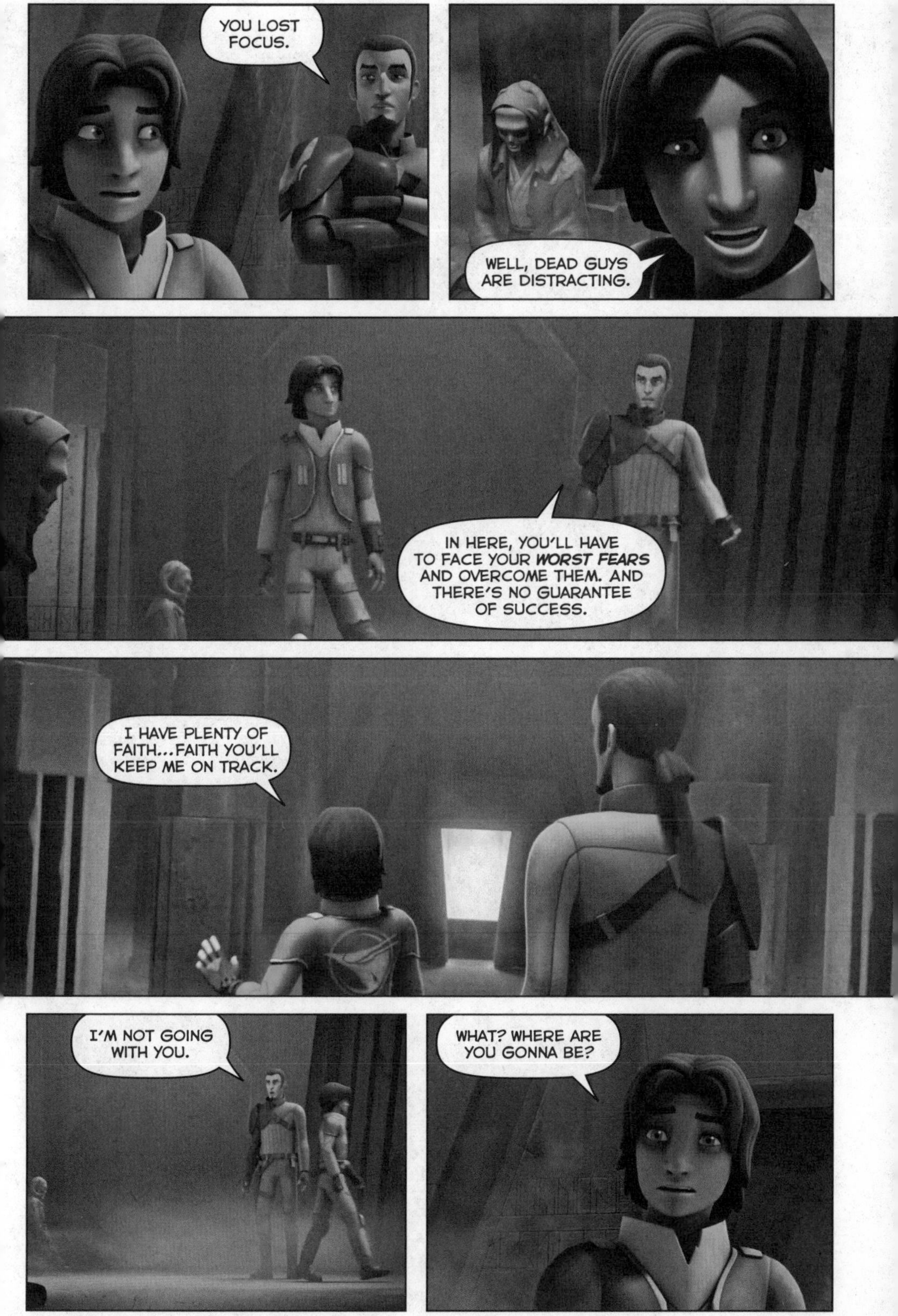
YOU LOST FOCUS.
WELL, DEAD GUYS ARE DISTRACTING.
IN HERE, YOU'LL HAVE TO FACE YOUR WORST FEARS AND OVERCOME THEM. AND THERE'S NO GUARANTEE OF SUCCESS.
I HAVE PLENTY OF FAITH...FAITH YOU'LL KEEP ME ON TRACK.
I'M NOT GOING WITH YOU.
WHAT? WHERE ARE YOU GONNA BE?

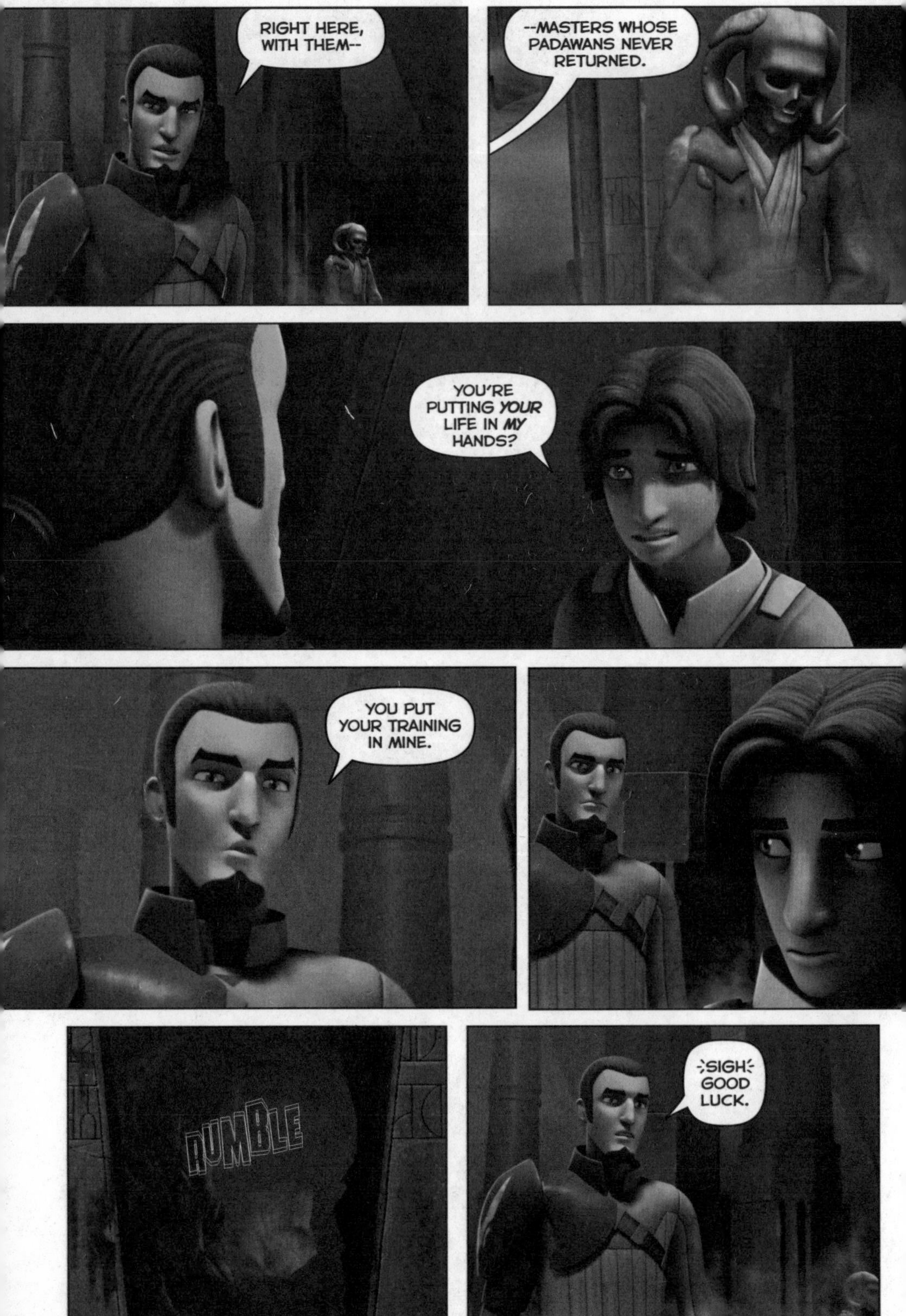
RIGHT HERE, WITH THEM--
--MASTERS WHOSE PADAWANS NEVER RETURNED.
YOU'RE PUTTING YOUR LIFE IN MY HANDS?
YOU PUT YOUR TRAINING IN MINE.
RUMBLE
SIGH
GOOD LUCK.

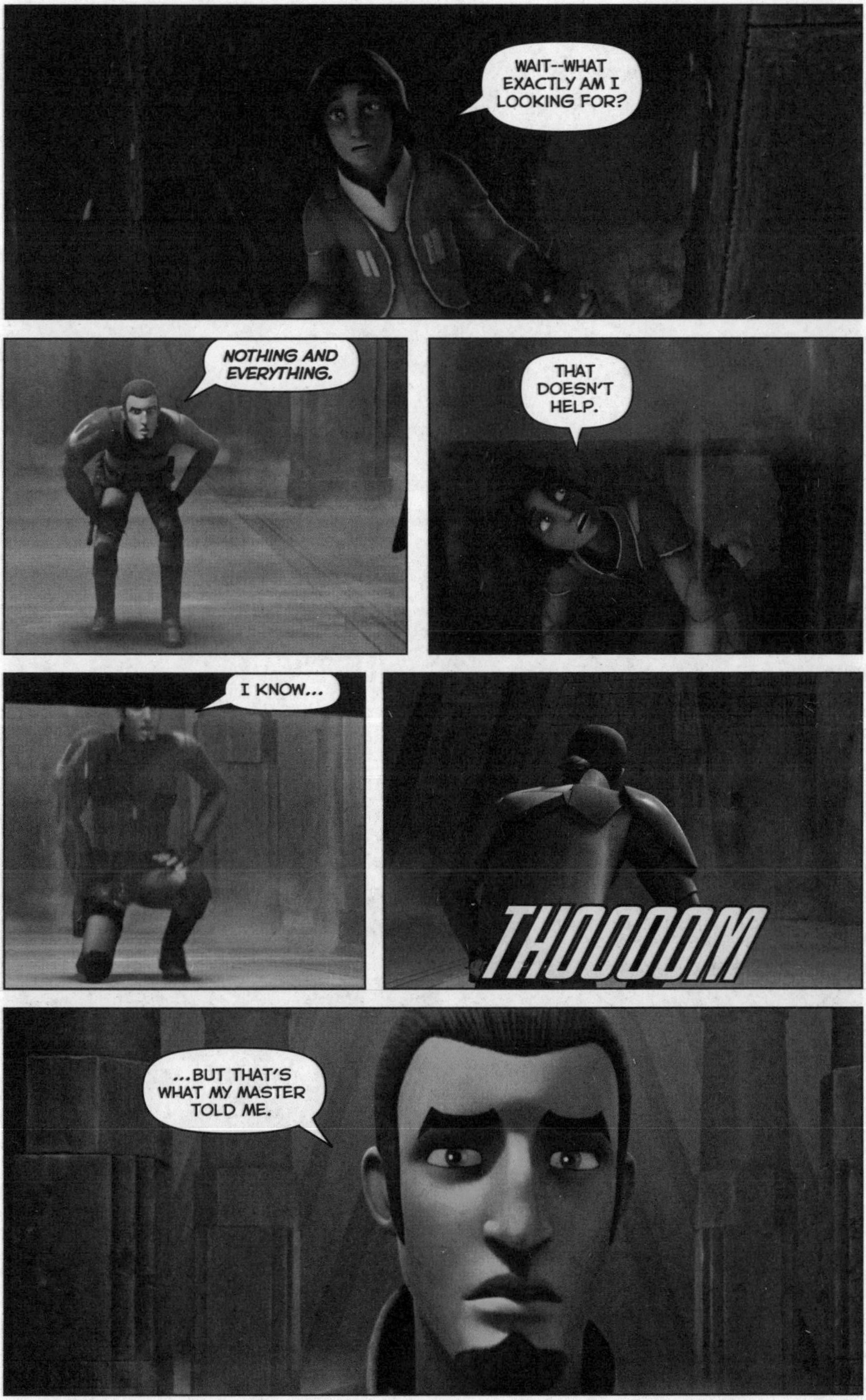
WAIT--WHAT EXACTLY AM I LOOKING FOR?
NOTHING AND EVERYTHING.
THAT DOESN'T HELP.
I KNOW...
THOOOOM
...BUT THAT'S WHAT MY MASTER TOLD ME.

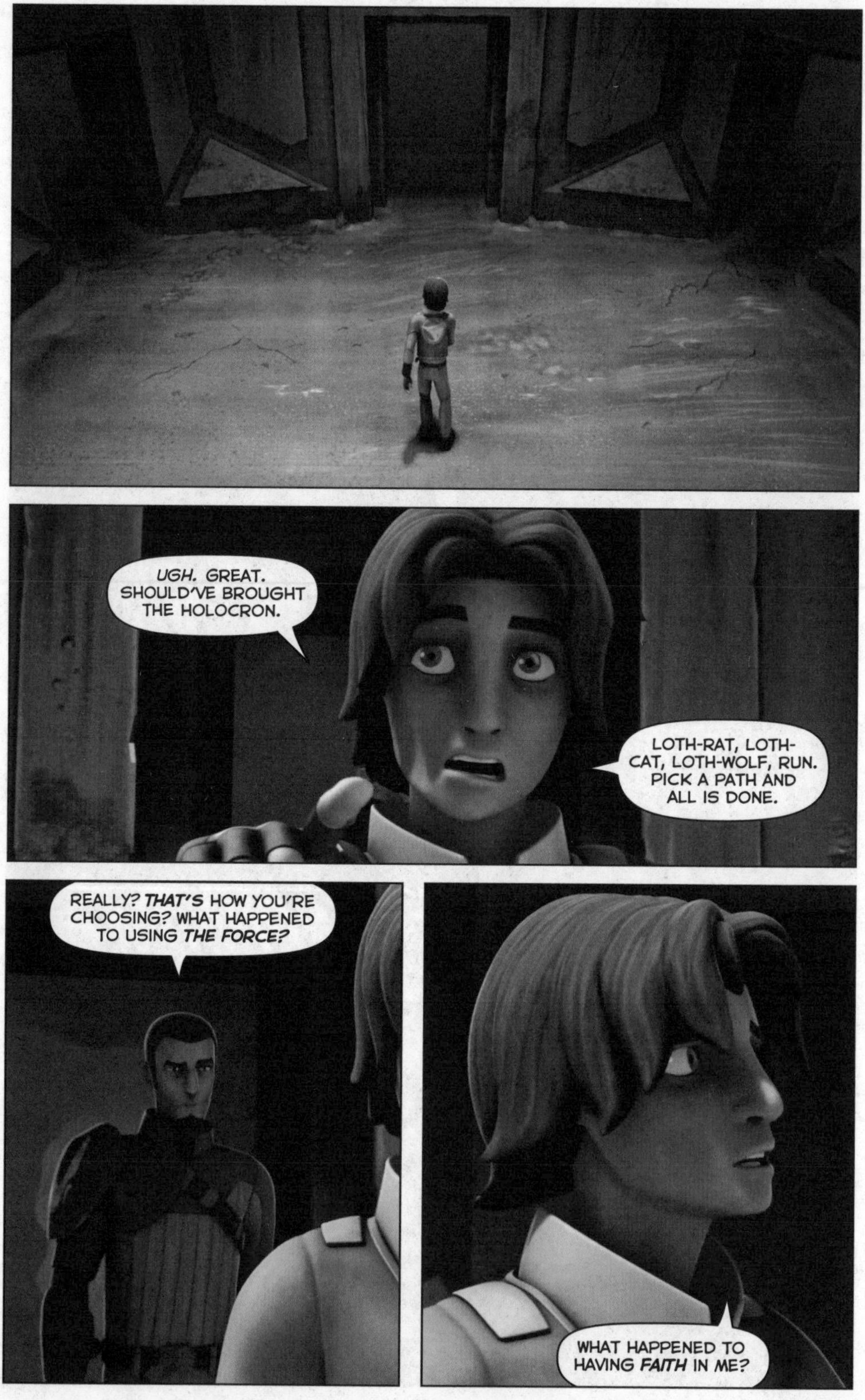
UGH. GREAT. SHOULD'VE BROUGHT THE HOLOCRON.
LOTH-RAT, LOTH-CAT, LOTH-WOLF, RUN. PICK A PATH AND ALL IS DONE.
REALLY? THAT'S HOW YOU'RE CHOOSING? WHAT HAPPENED TO USING THE FORCE?
WHAT HAPPENED TO HAVING FAITH IN ME?

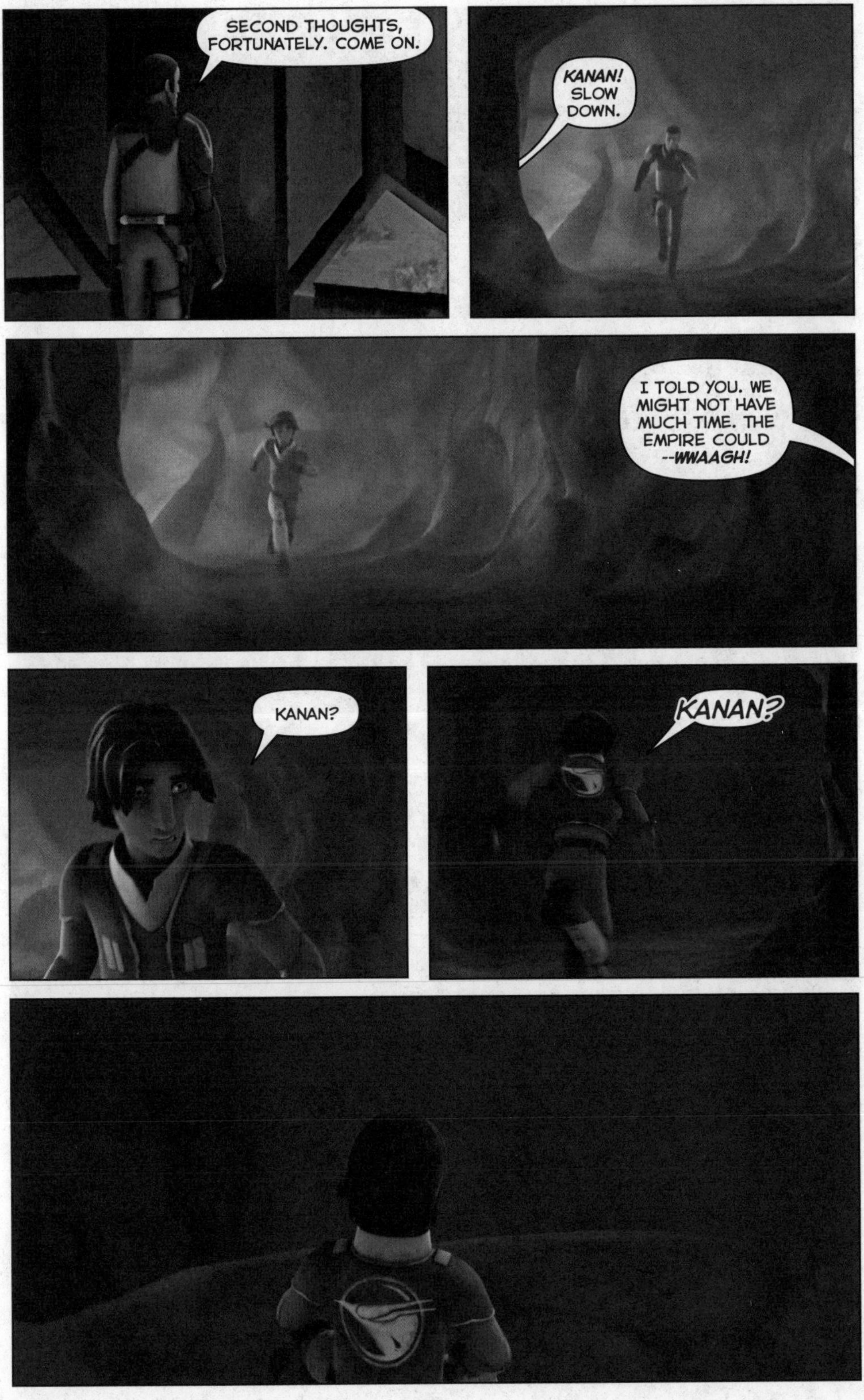
SECOND THOUGHTS, FORTUNATELY. COME ON.
KANAN! SLOW DOWN.
I TOLD YOU. WE MIGHT NOT HAVE MUCH TIME. THE EMPIRE COULD --WWAAGH!
KANAN?
KANAN?

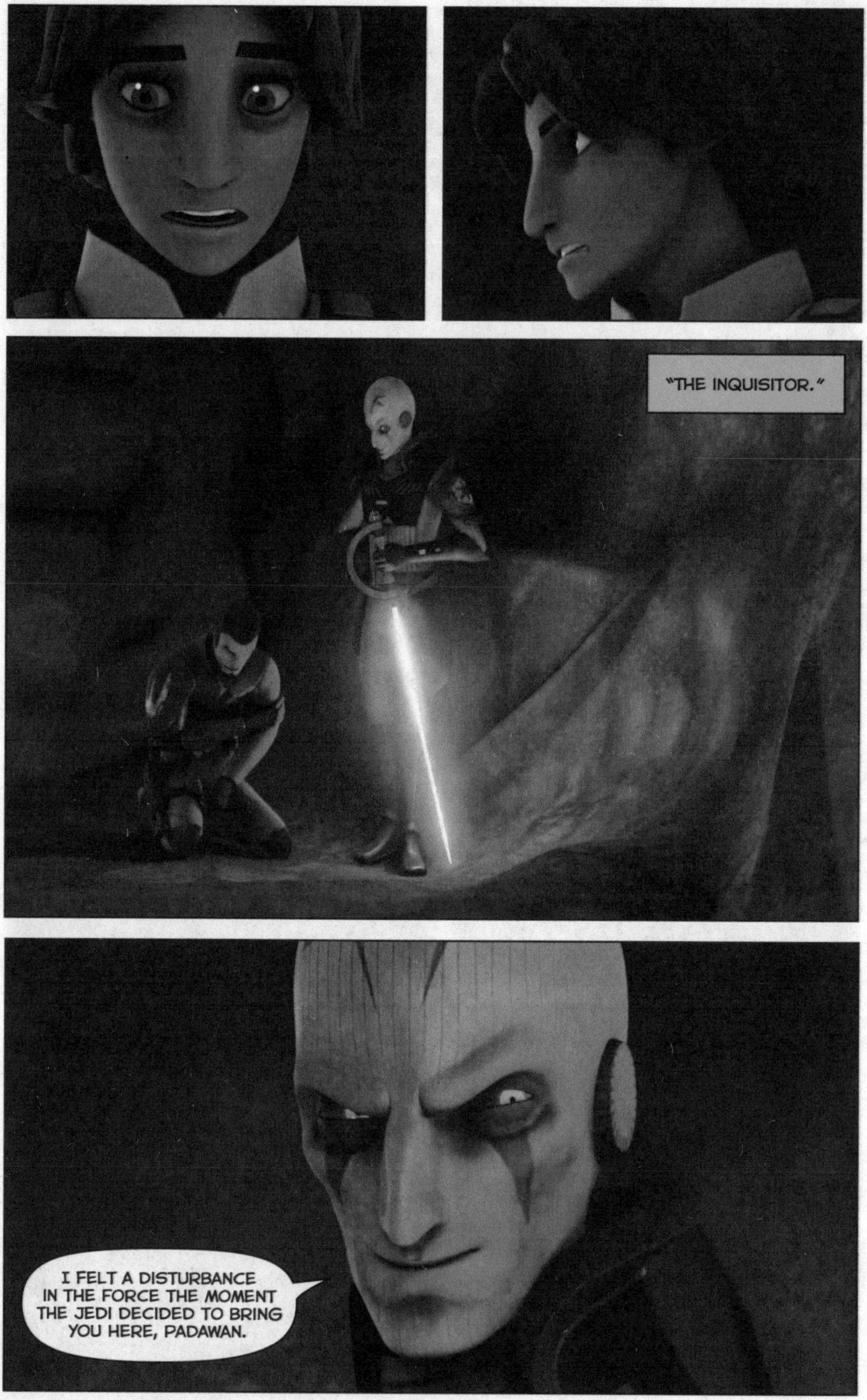
"THE INQUISITOR."
I FELT A DISTURBANCE IN THE FORCE THE MOMENT THE JEDI DECIDED TO BRING YOU HERE, PADAWAN.

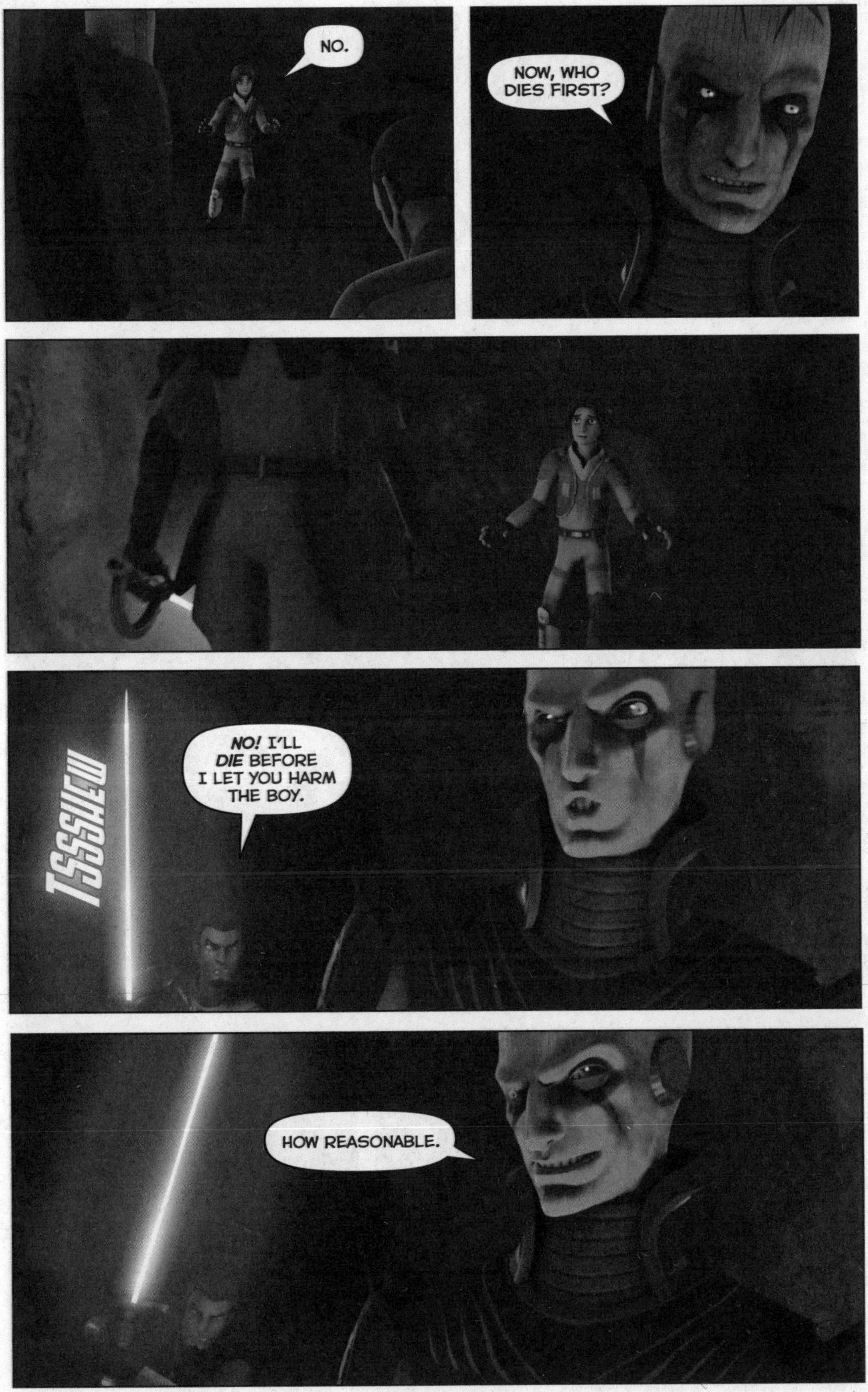
NO.
NOW, WHO DIES FIRST?
TSSSHEW
NO! I'LL DIE BEFORE I LET YOU HARM THE BOY.
HOW REASONABLE.

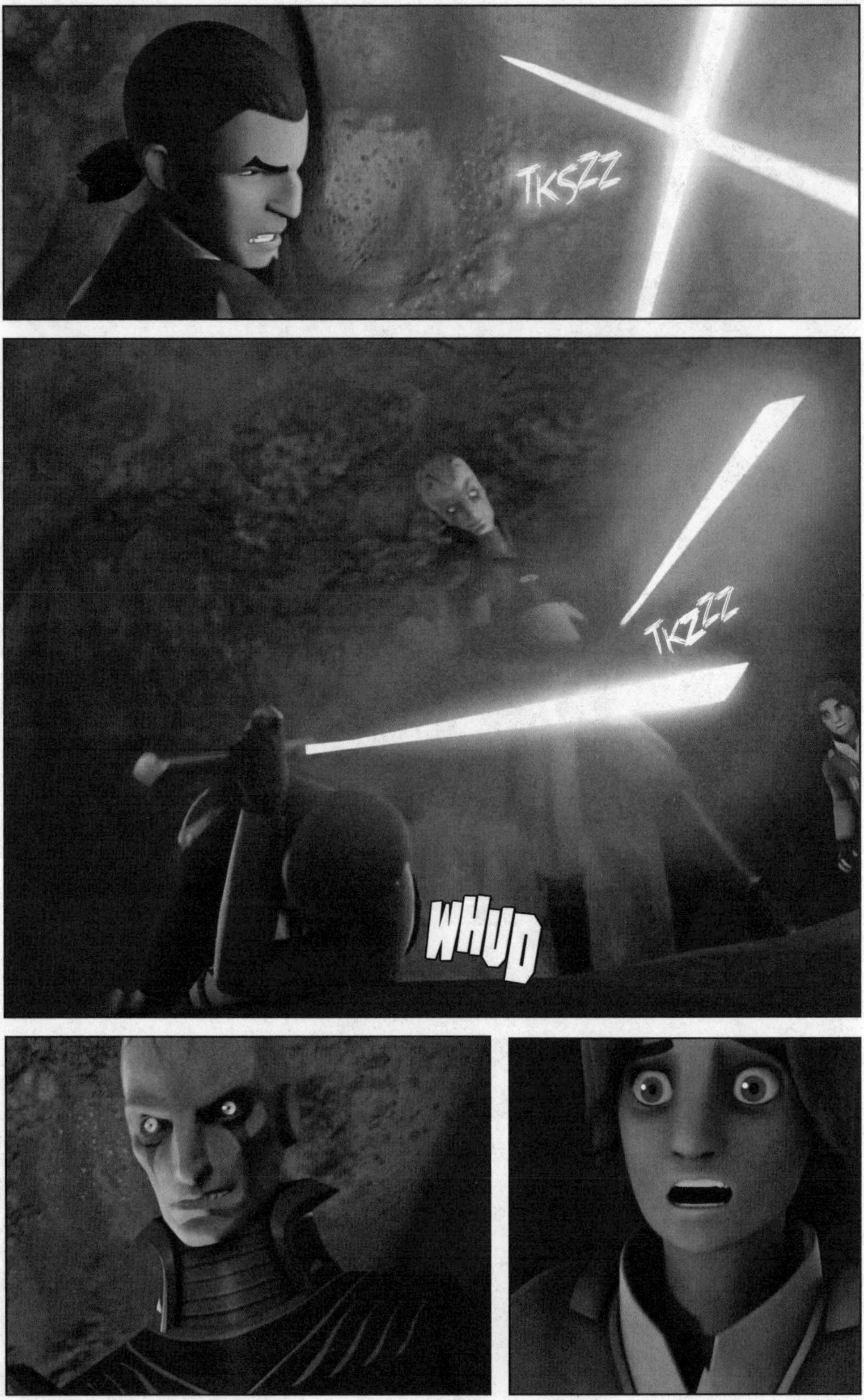
TKSZZ
TKZZZ
WHUD

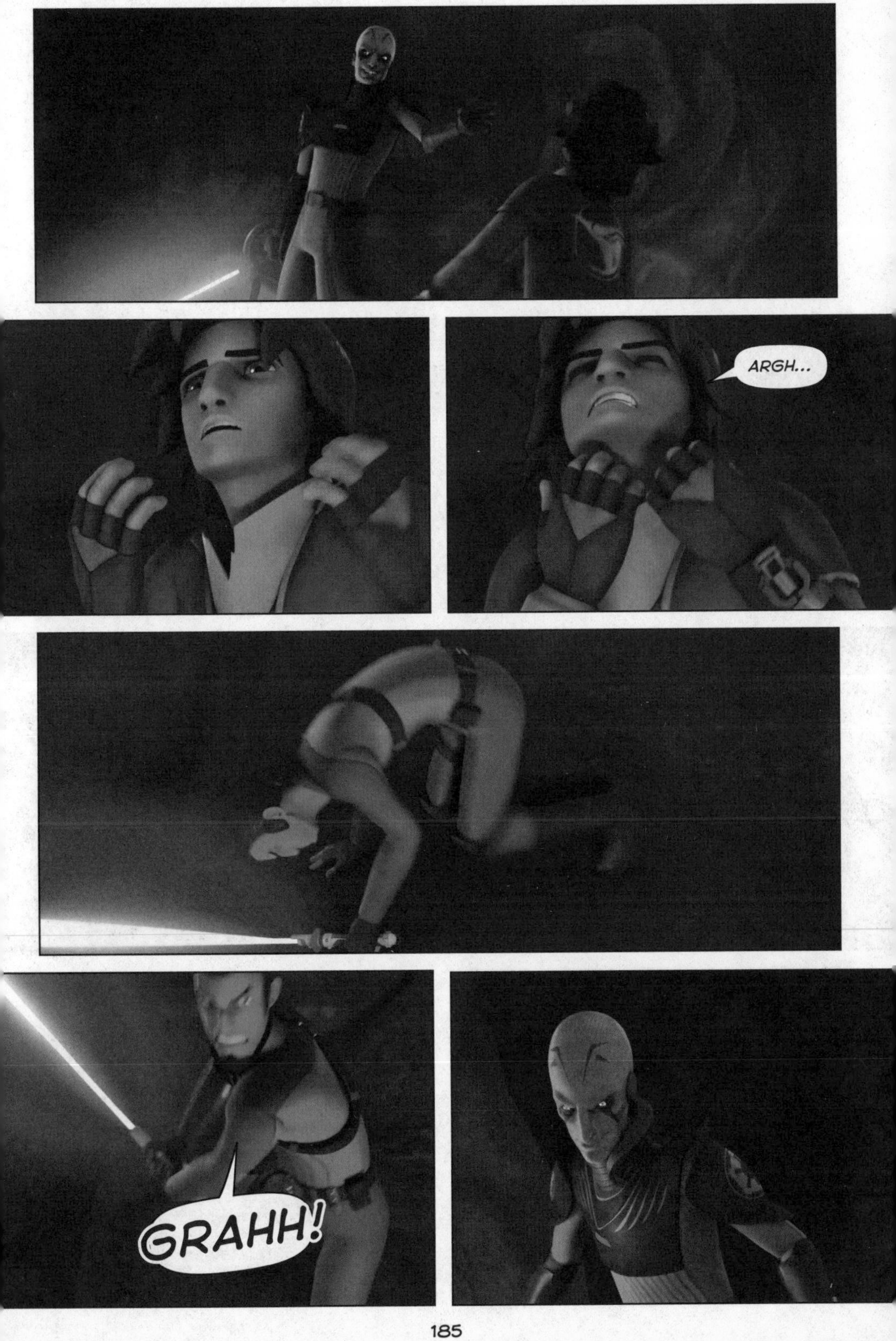
ARGH...
GRAHH!

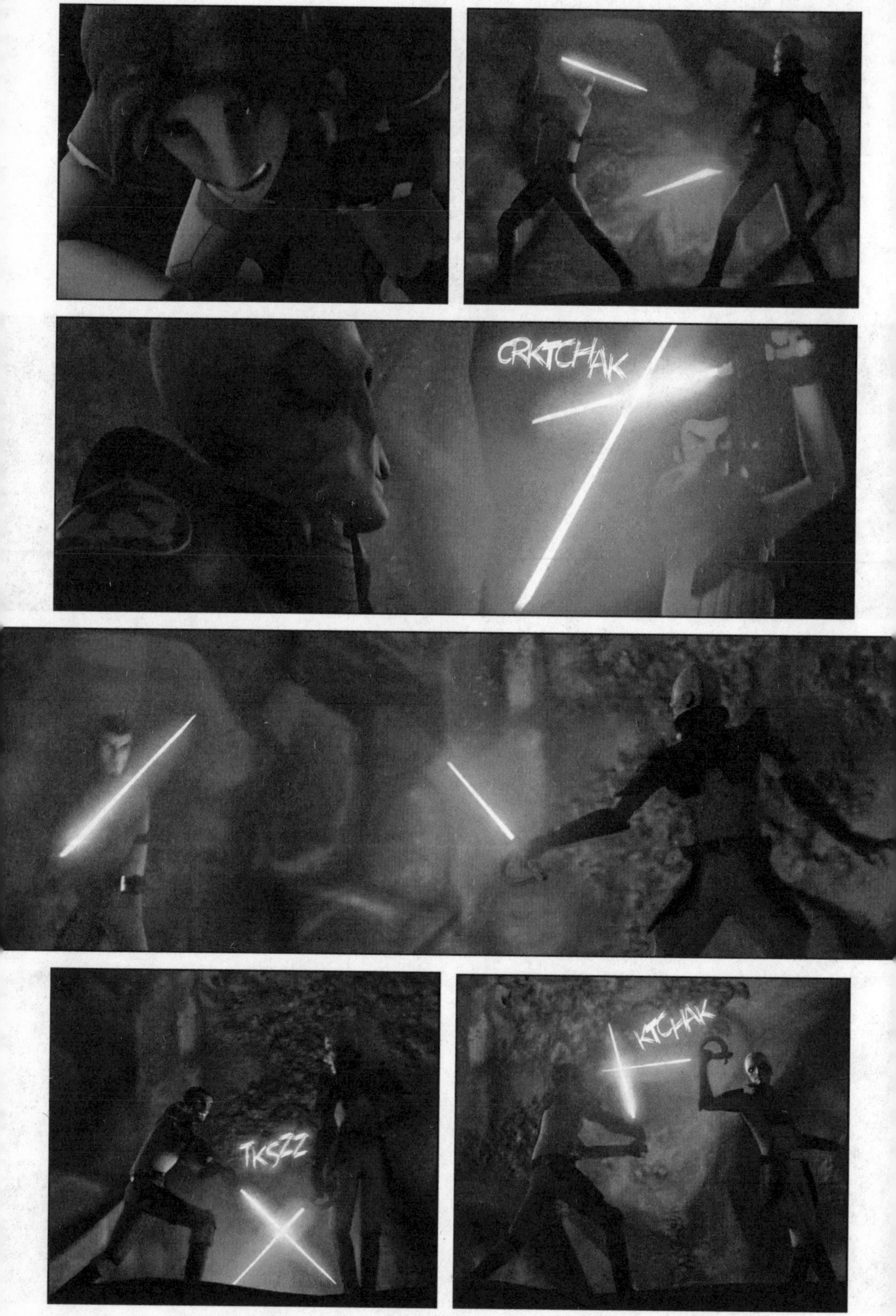
CRKTCHAK
TKSZZ
KTCHAK

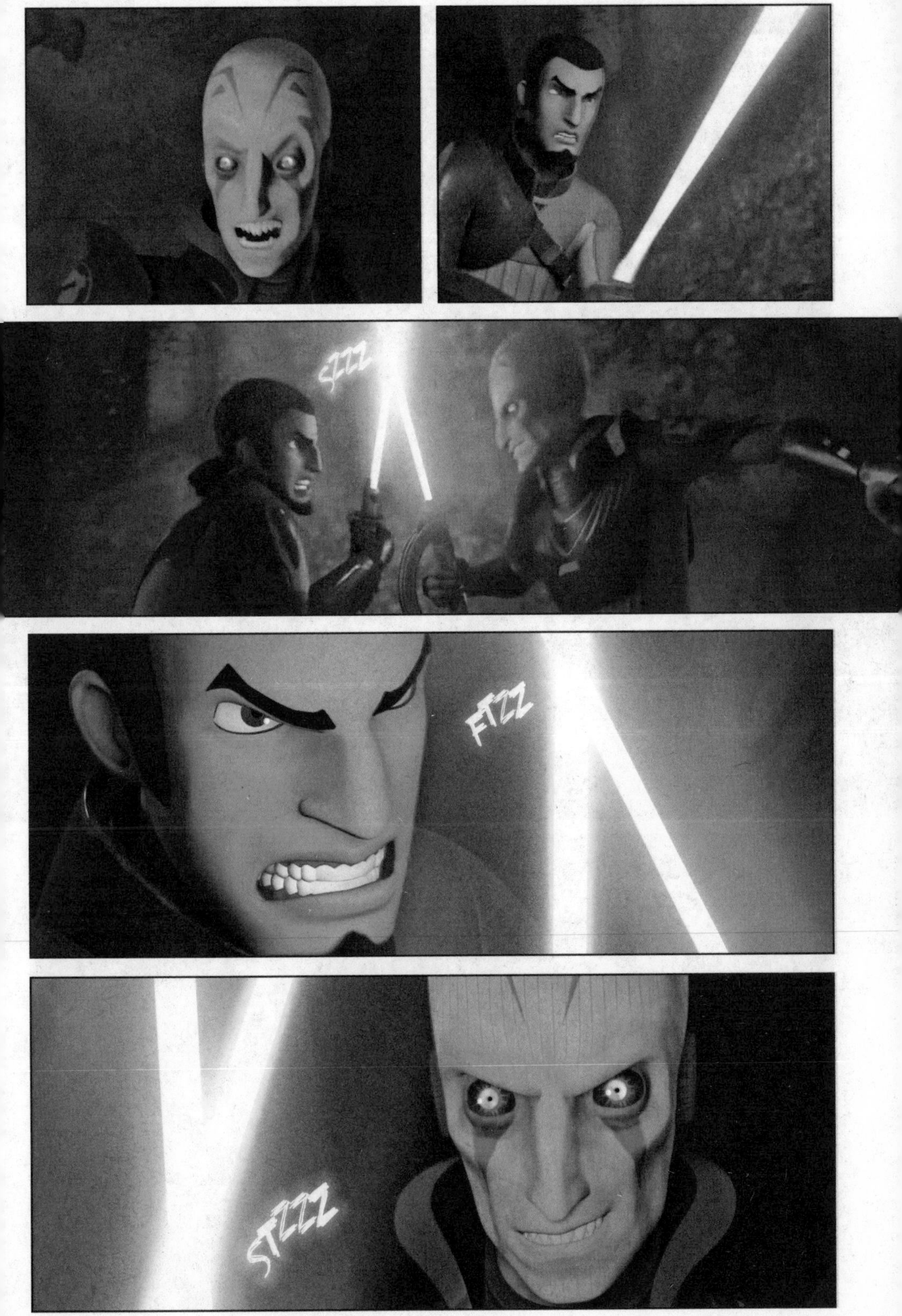
SZZZ
FTZZ
STZZZ

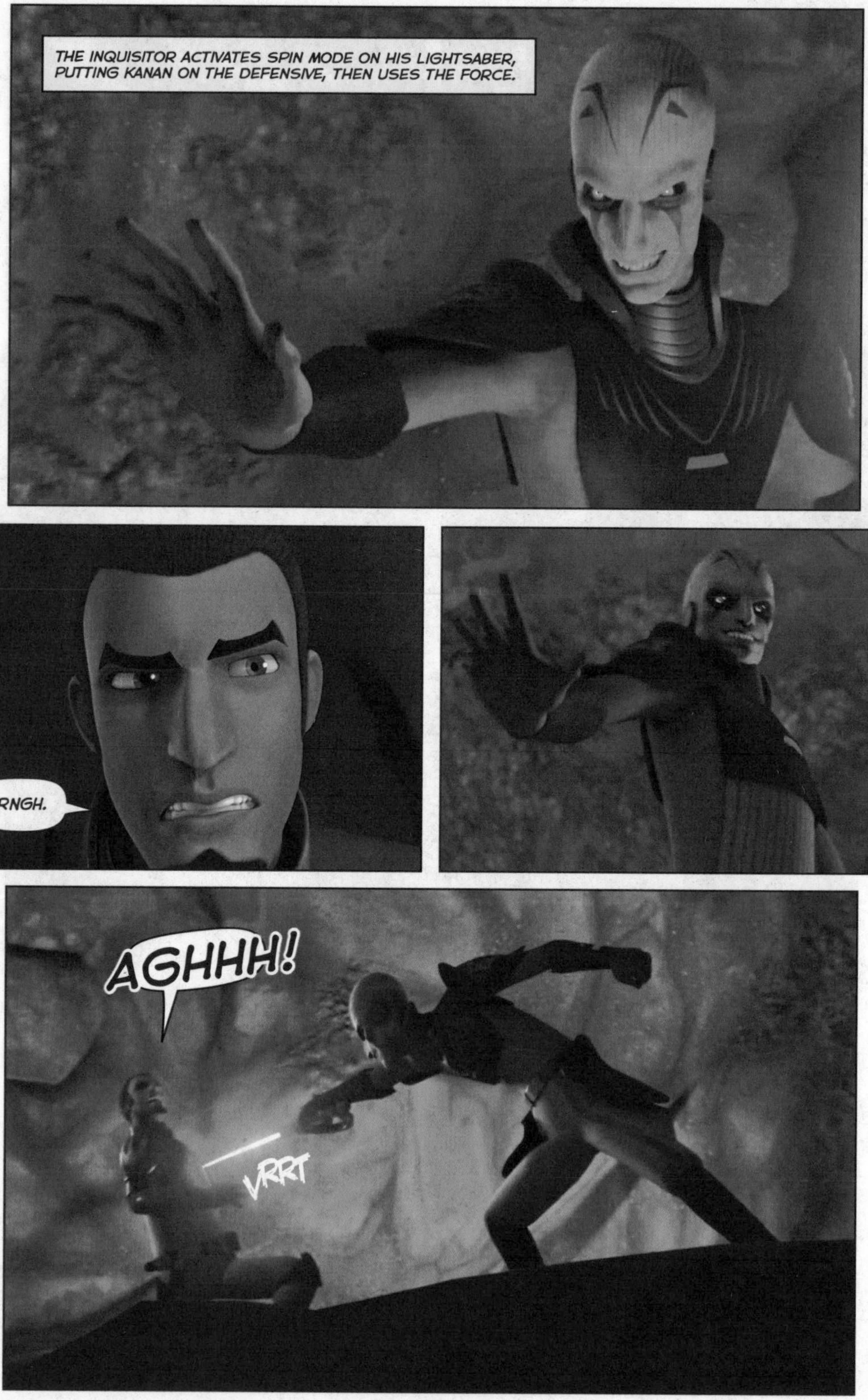

THE INQUISITOR ACTIVATES SPIN MODE ON HIS LIGHTSABER, PUTTING KANAN ON THE DEFENSIVE, THEN USES THE FORCE.
RNGH.
AGHHH!
VRRT

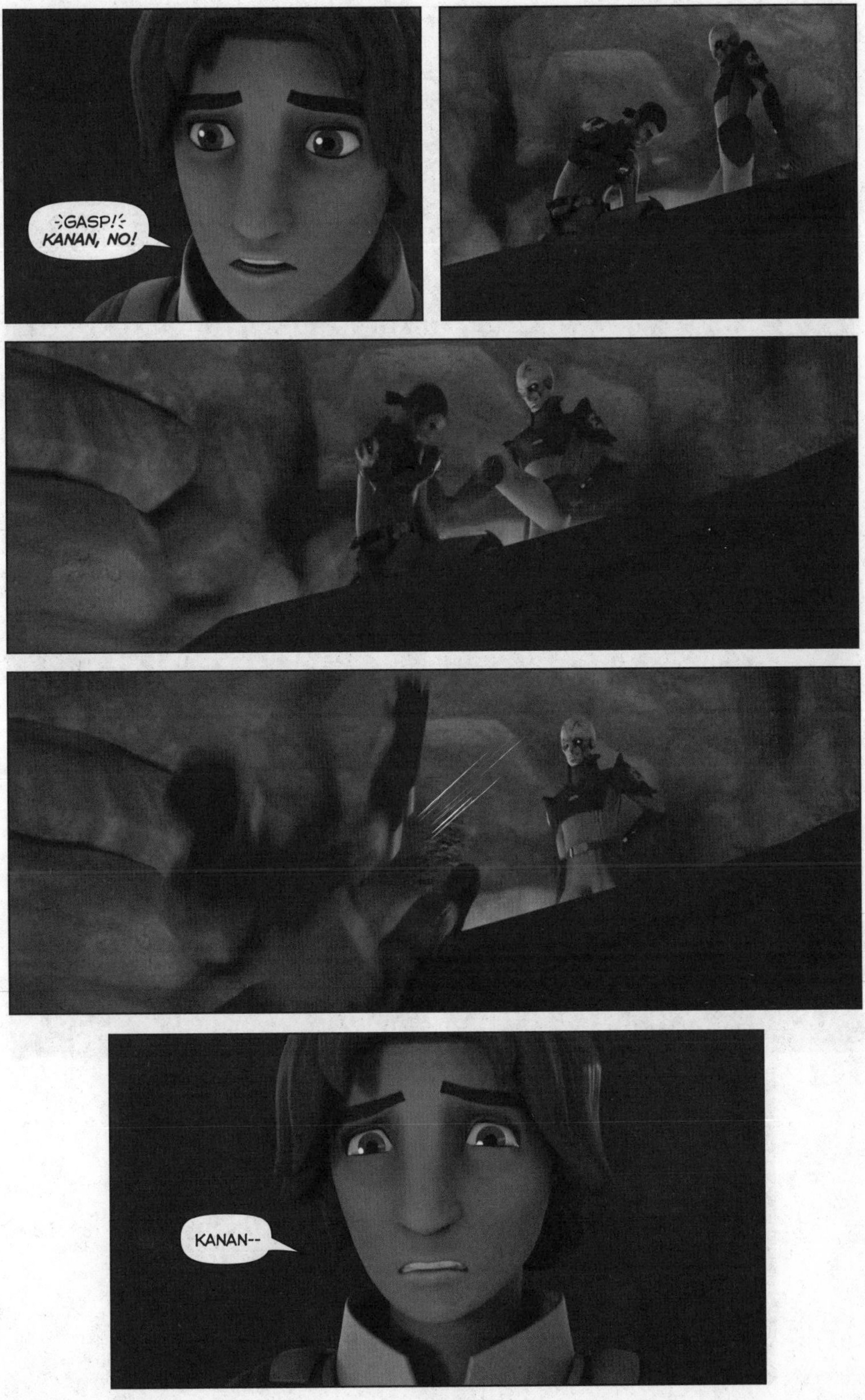
GASP!
KANAN, NO!
KANAN--

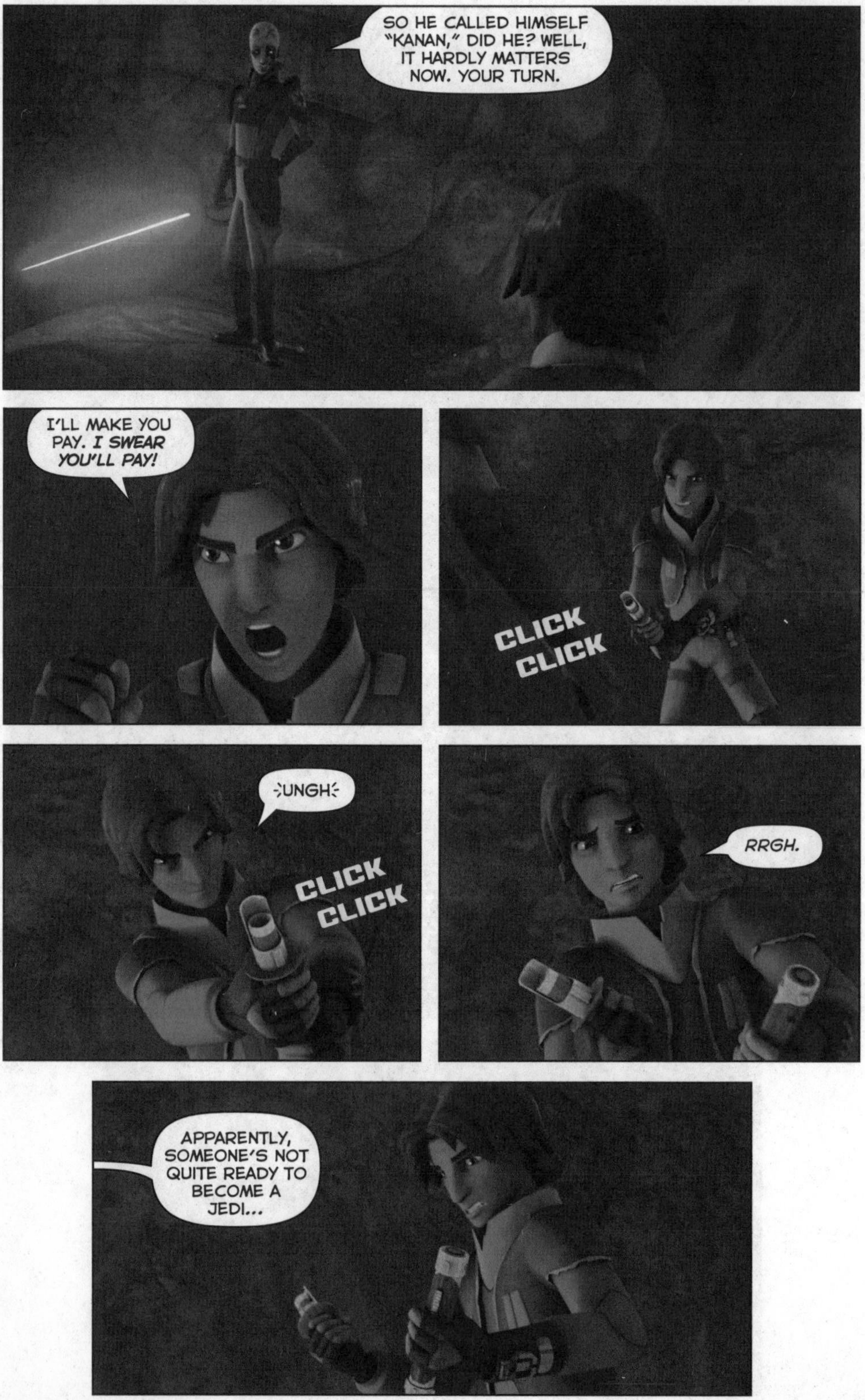
SO HE CALLED HIMSELF "KANAN," DID HE? WELL, IT HARDLY MATTERS NOW. YOUR TURN.
I'LL MAKE YOU PAY. I SWEAR YOU'LL PAY!
CLICK CLICK
UNGH
CLICK CLICK
RRGH.
APPARENTLY, SOMEONE'S NOT QUITE READY TO BECOME A JEDI...

...AND *NEVER* WILL BE.

THWACK

UNGH

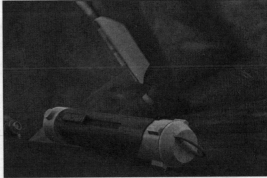

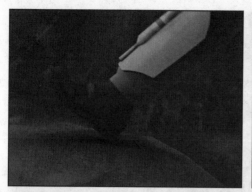

WH-WHOA!

AHHHHH!

UGH!

WHACK

?

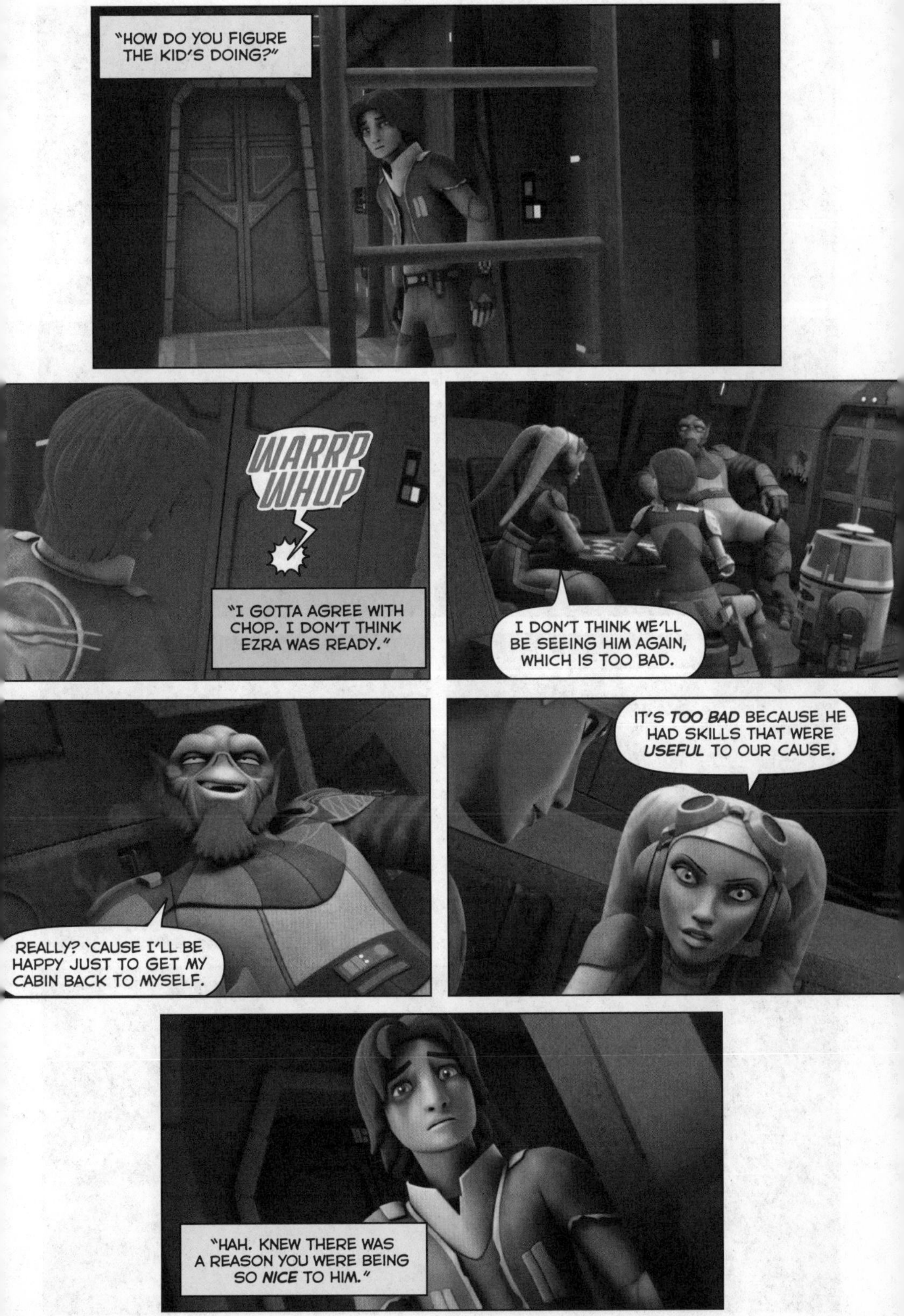
"HOW DO YOU FIGURE THE KID'S DOING?"
WARRP WHUP
"I GOTTA AGREE WITH CHOP. I DON'T THINK EZRA WAS READY."
I DON'T THINK WE'LL BE SEEING HIM AGAIN, WHICH IS TOO BAD.
REALLY? 'CAUSE I'LL BE HAPPY JUST TO GET MY CABIN BACK TO MYSELF.
IT'S *TOO BAD* BECAUSE HE HAD SKILLS THAT WERE *USEFUL* TO OUR CAUSE.
"HAH. KNEW THERE WAS A REASON YOU WERE BEING SO *NICE* TO HIM."

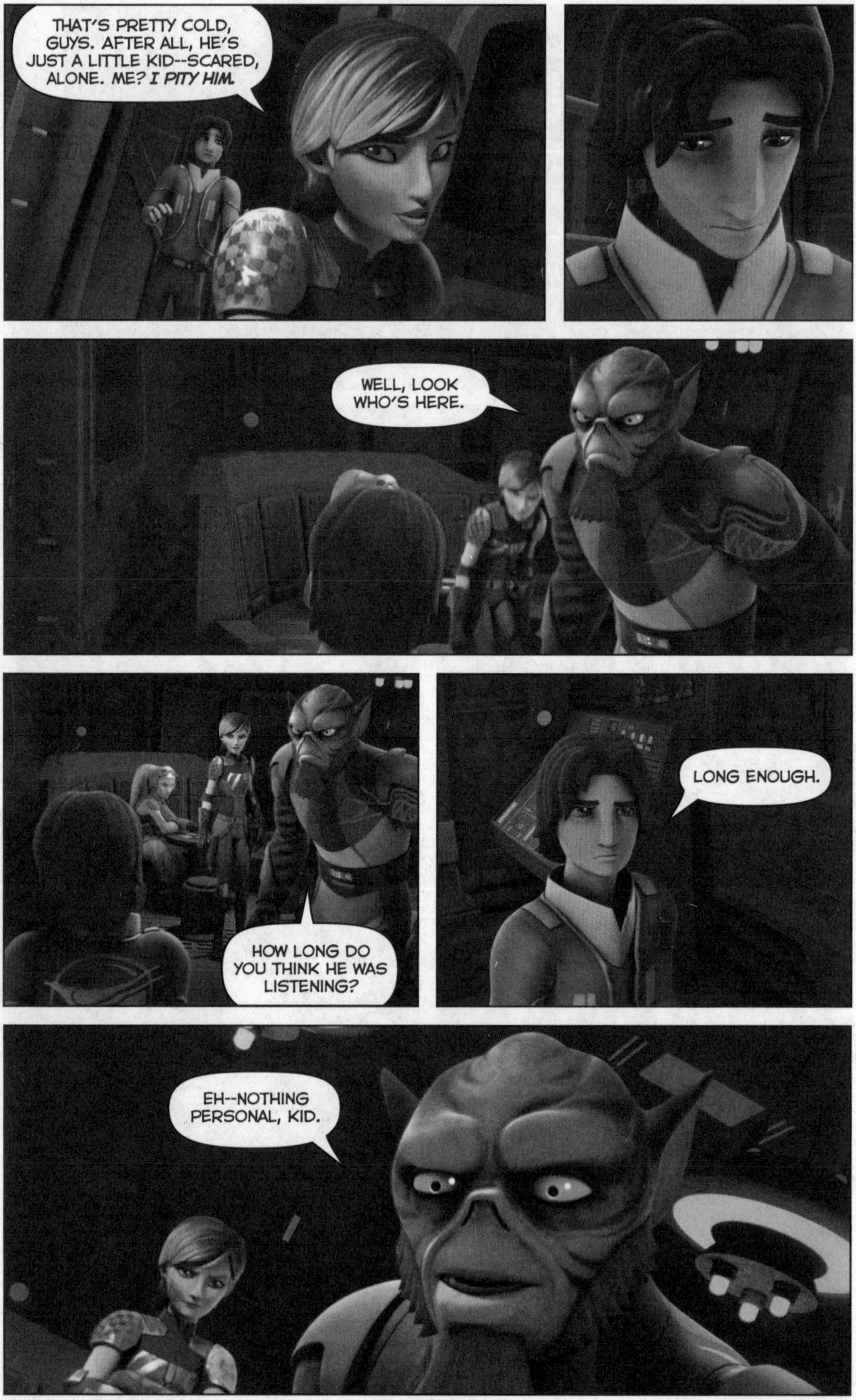
THAT'S PRETTY COLD, GUYS. AFTER ALL, HE'S JUST A LITTLE KID--SCARED, ALONE. ME? I PITY HIM.
WELL, LOOK WHO'S HERE.
HOW LONG DO YOU THINK HE WAS LISTENING?
LONG ENOUGH.
EH--NOTHING PERSONAL, KID.

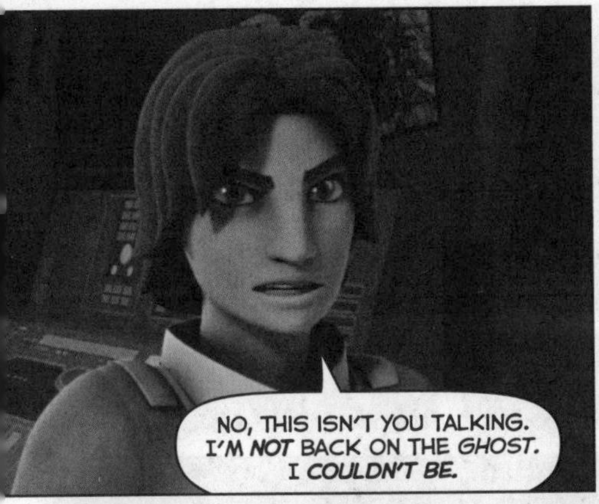
NO, THIS ISN'T YOU TALKING. I'M *NOT* BACK ON THE *GHOST*. I *COULDN'T BE.*

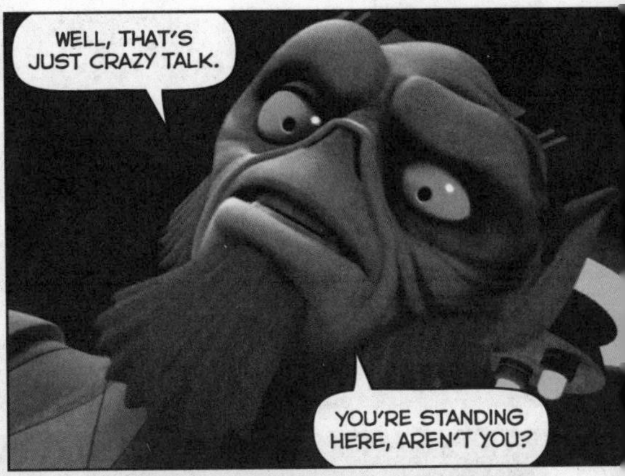
WELL, THAT'S JUST CRAZY TALK.
YOU'RE STANDING HERE, AREN'T YOU?

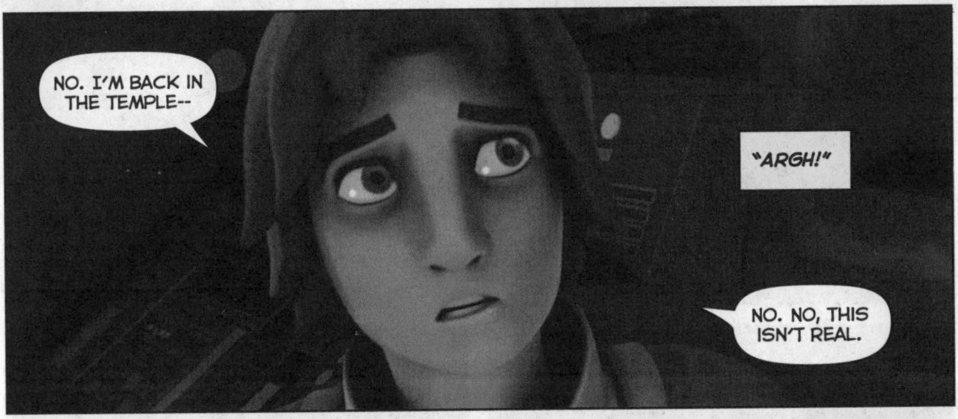
NO. I'M BACK IN THE TEMPLE--
"ARGH!"
NO. NO, THIS ISN'T REAL.

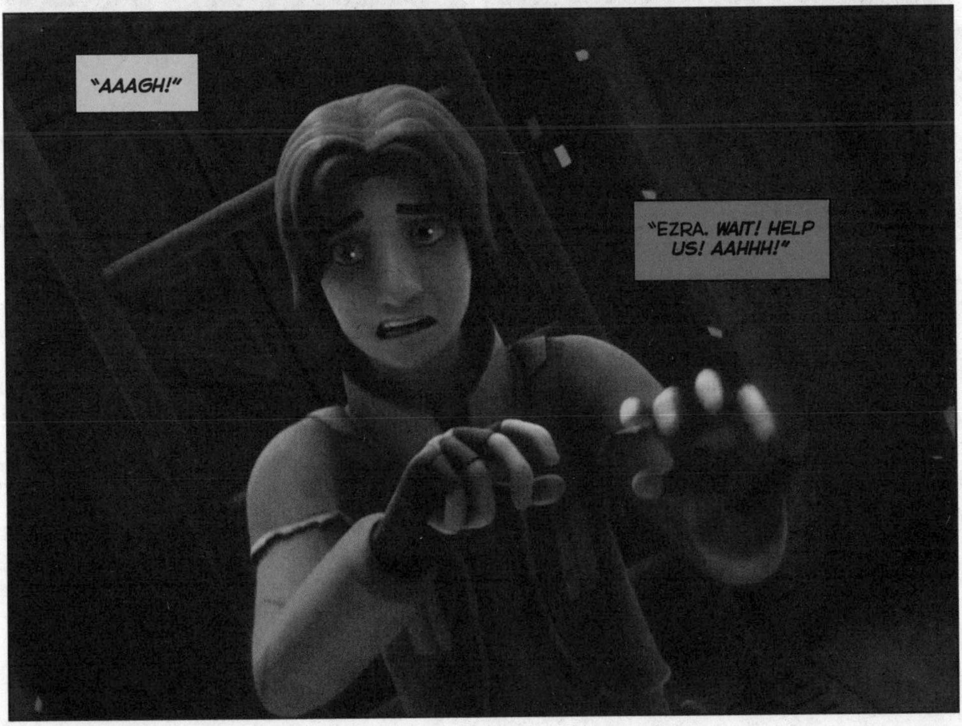
"AAAGH!"
"EZRA. WAIT! HELP US! AAHHH!"

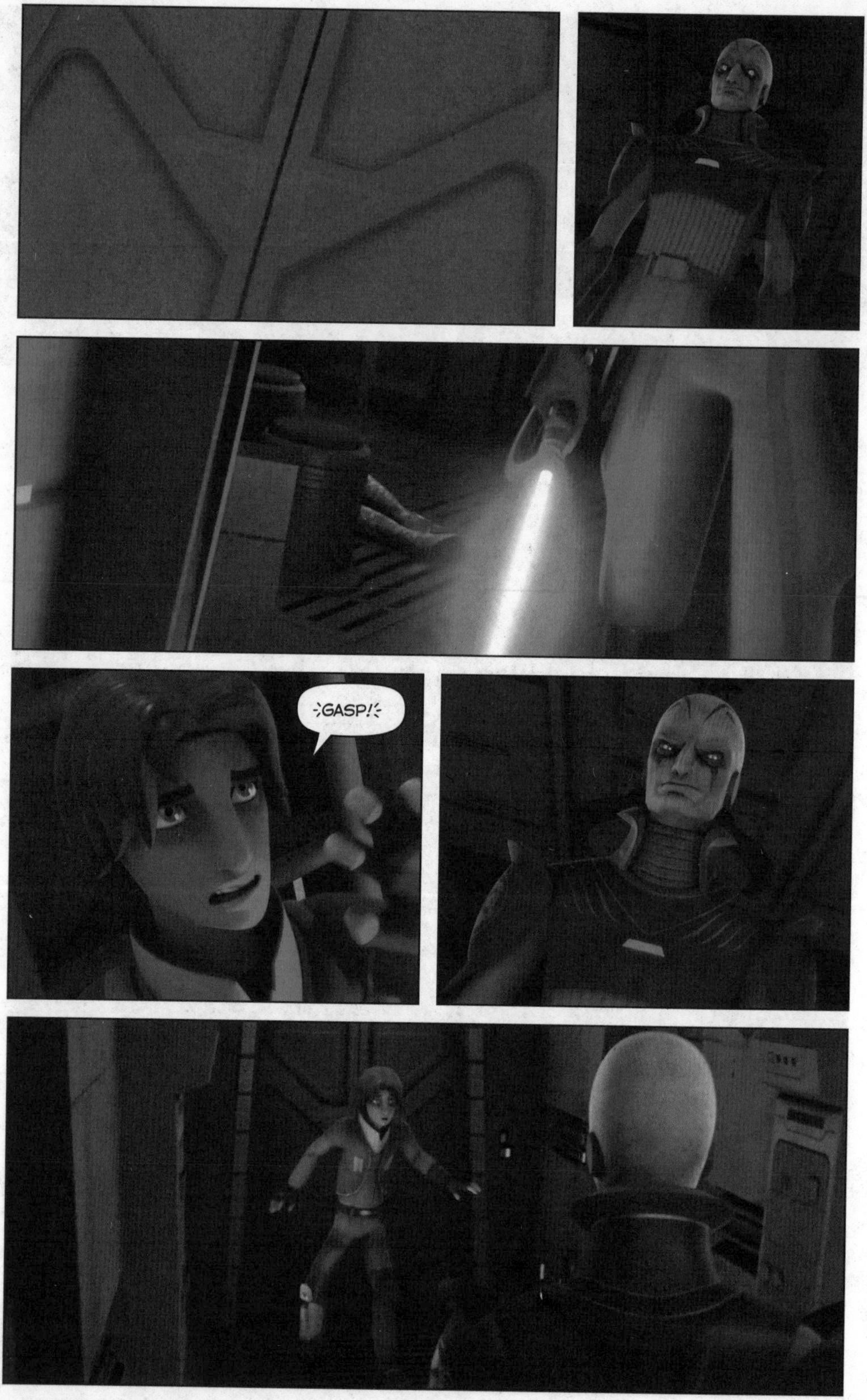
GASP!

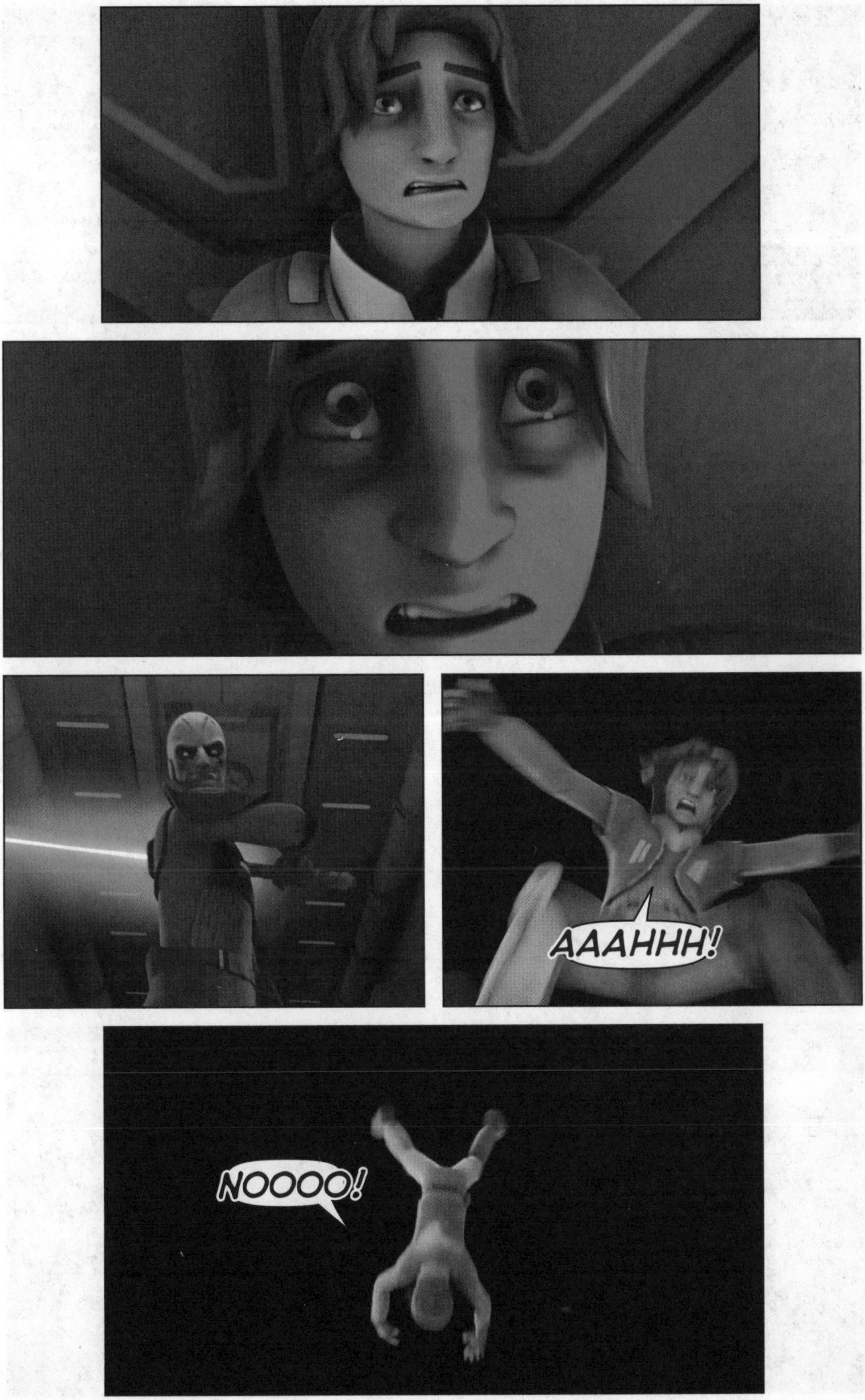
AAAHHH!
NOOOO!

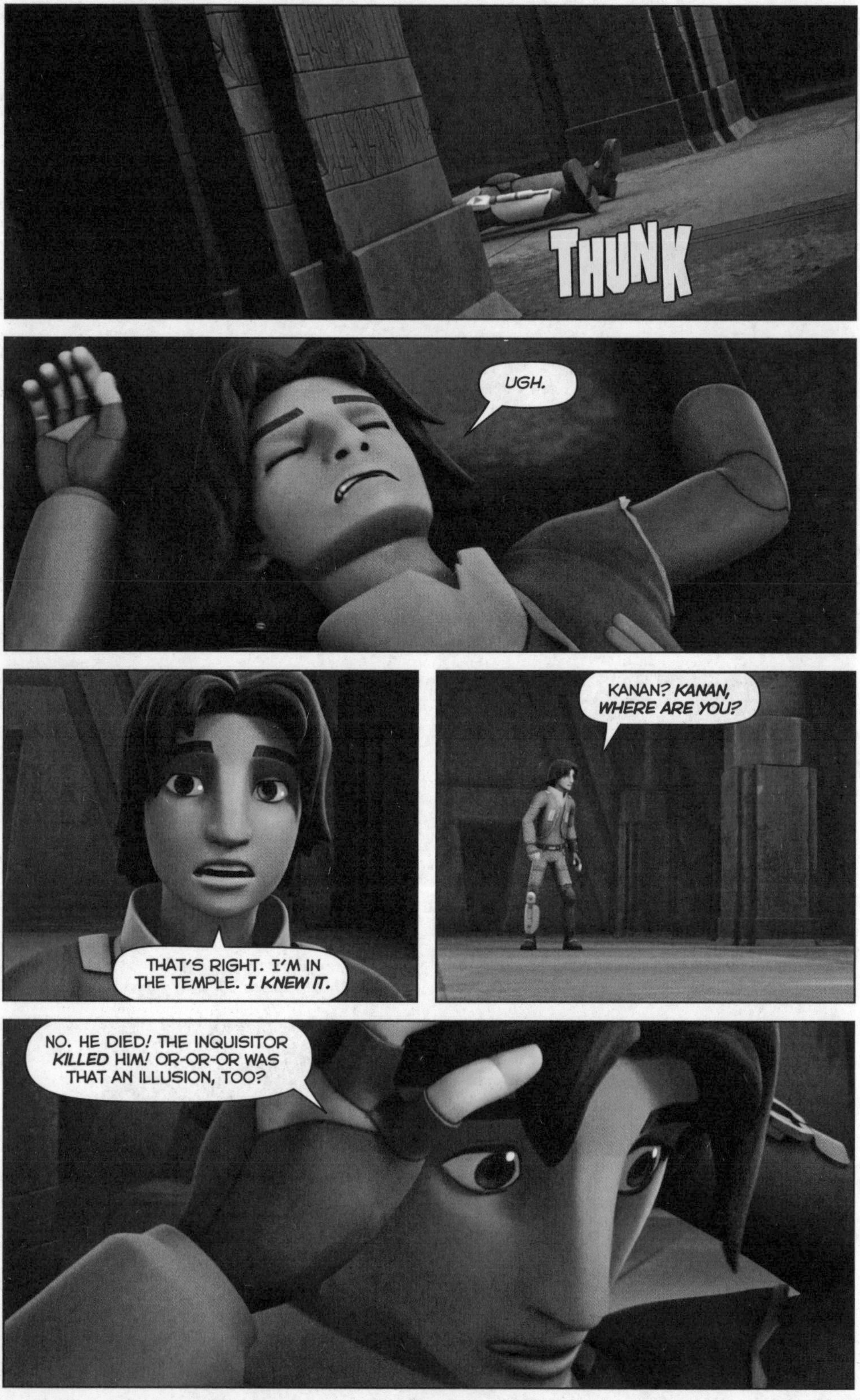
THUNK
UGH.
THAT'S RIGHT. I'M IN THE TEMPLE. *I KNEW IT.*
KANAN? *KANAN, WHERE ARE YOU?*
NO. HE DIED! THE INQUISITOR *KILLED* HIM! OR-OR-OR WAS THAT AN ILLUSION, TOO?

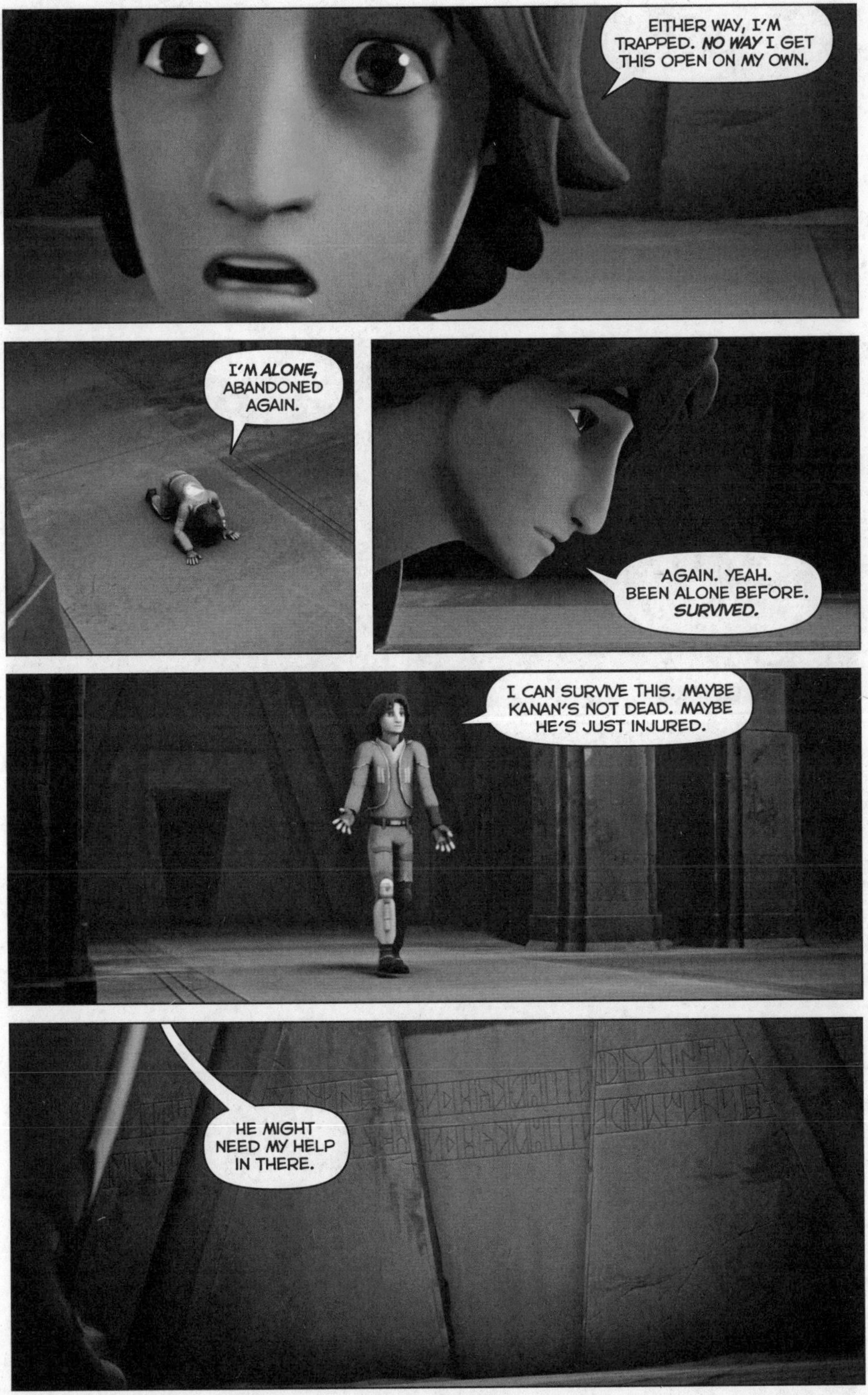
EITHER WAY, I'M TRAPPED. NO WAY I GET THIS OPEN ON MY OWN.
I'M ALONE, ABANDONED AGAIN.
AGAIN. YEAH. BEEN ALONE BEFORE. SURVIVED.
I CAN SURVIVE THIS. MAYBE KANAN'S NOT DEAD. MAYBE HE'S JUST INJURED.
HE MIGHT NEED MY HELP IN THERE.

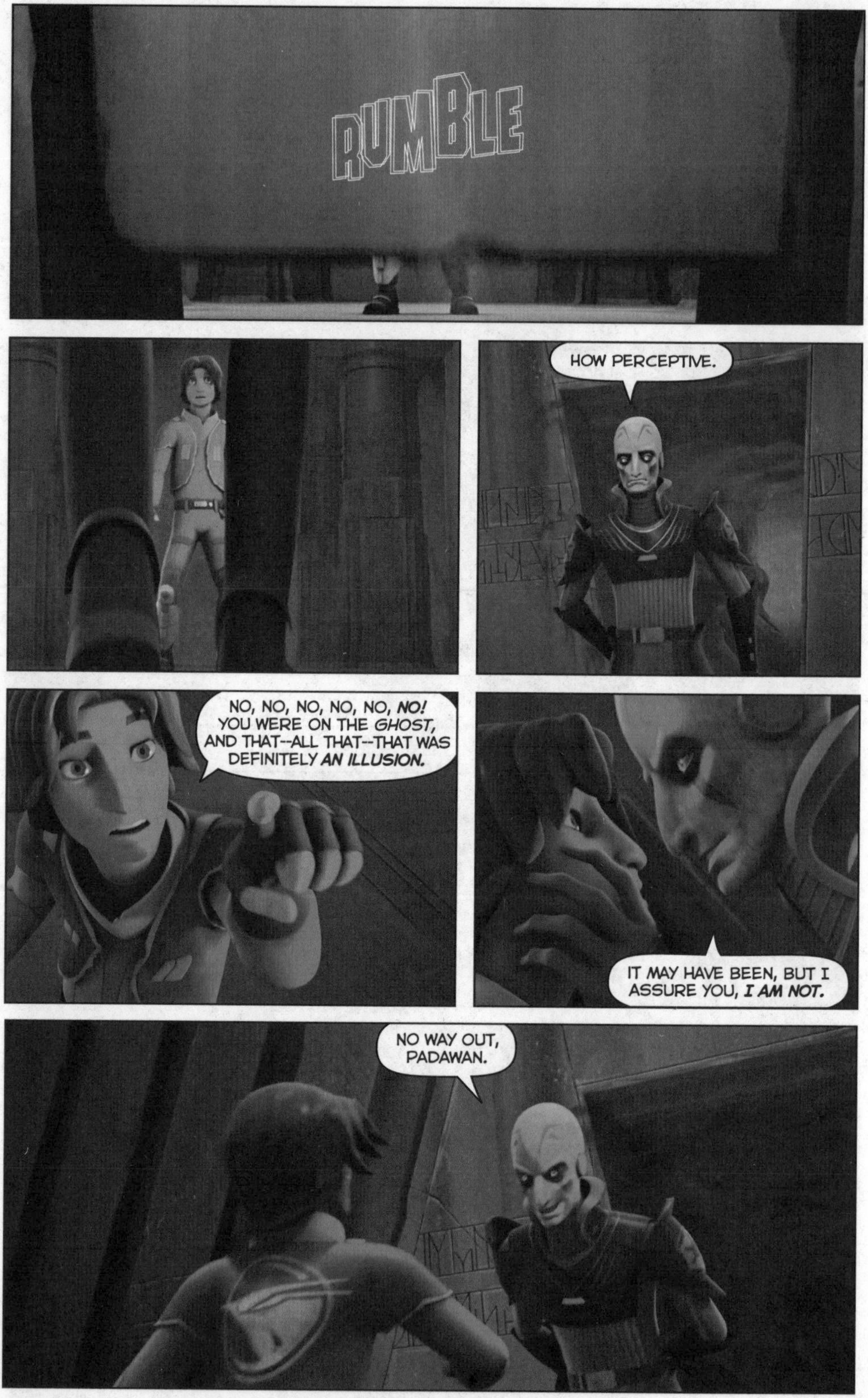
RUMBLE
HOW PERCEPTIVE.
NO, NO, NO, NO, NO, NO! YOU WERE ON THE GHOST, AND THAT--ALL THAT--THAT WAS DEFINITELY AN ILLUSION.
IT MAY HAVE BEEN, BUT I ASSURE YOU, I AM NOT.
NO WAY OUT, PADAWAN.

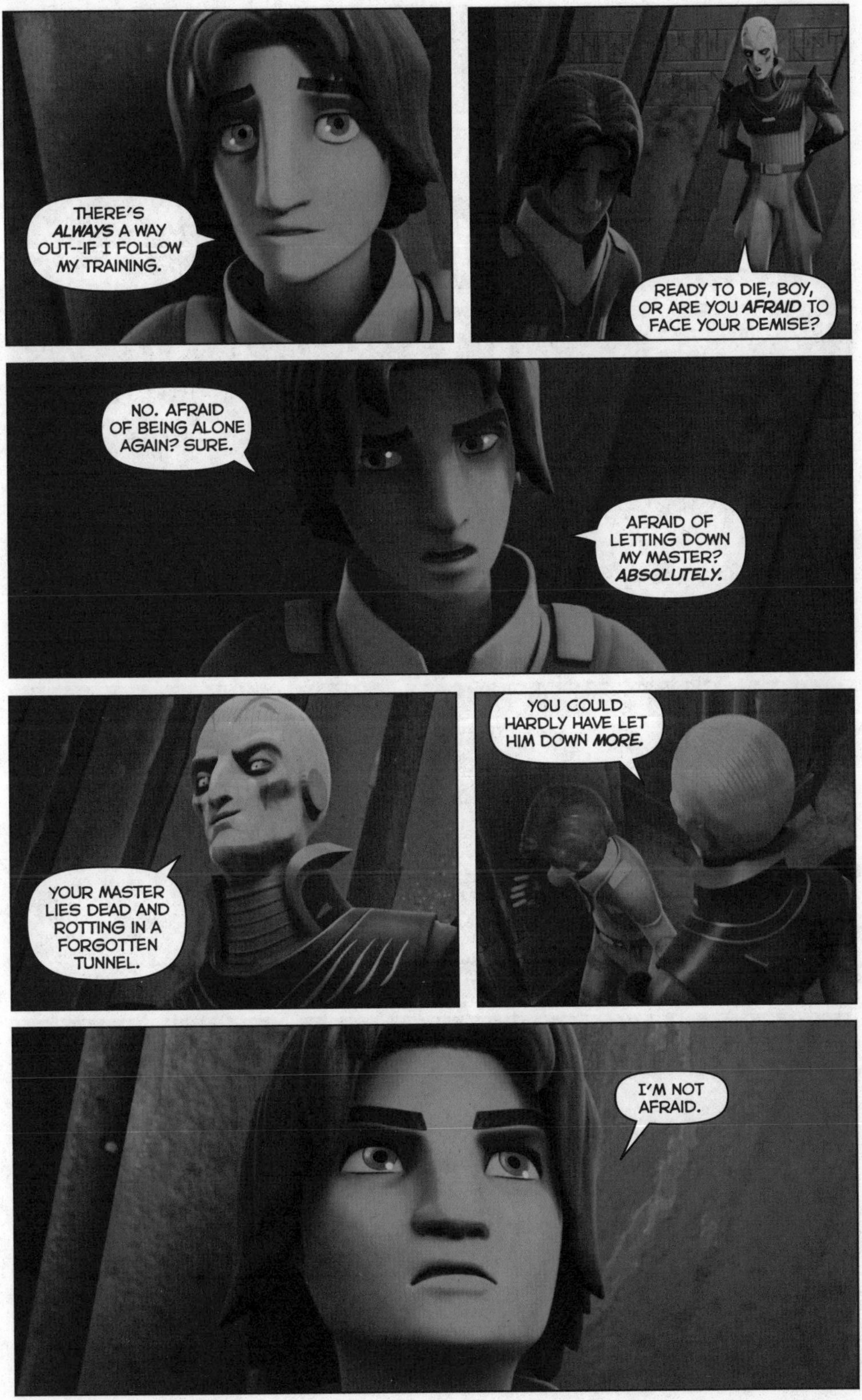
THERE'S ALWAYS A WAY OUT--IF I FOLLOW MY TRAINING.
READY TO DIE, BOY, OR ARE YOU AFRAID TO FACE YOUR DEMISE?
NO. AFRAID OF BEING ALONE AGAIN? SURE.
AFRAID OF LETTING DOWN MY MASTER? ABSOLUTELY.
YOUR MASTER LIES DEAD AND ROTTING IN A FORGOTTEN TUNNEL.
YOU COULD HARDLY HAVE LET HIM DOWN MORE.
I'M NOT AFRAID.

AARGH!
RRRAHH!

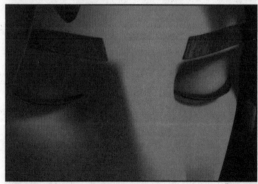

≿SIGH≿

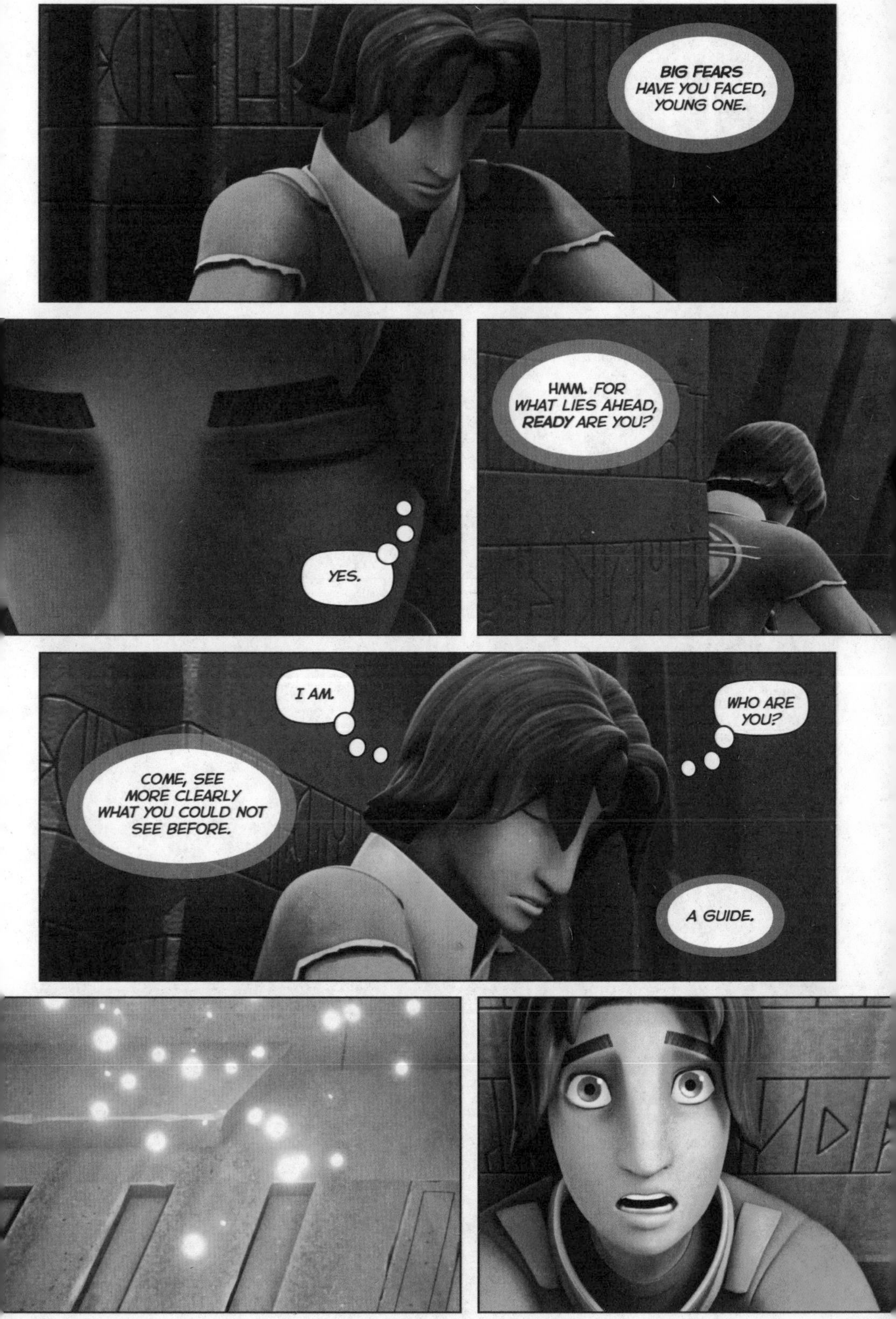
BIG FEARS HAVE YOU FACED, YOUNG ONE.
HMM. FOR WHAT LIES AHEAD, READY ARE YOU?
YES.
I AM.
WHO ARE YOU?
COME, SEE MORE CLEARLY WHAT YOU COULD NOT SEE BEFORE.
A GUIDE.

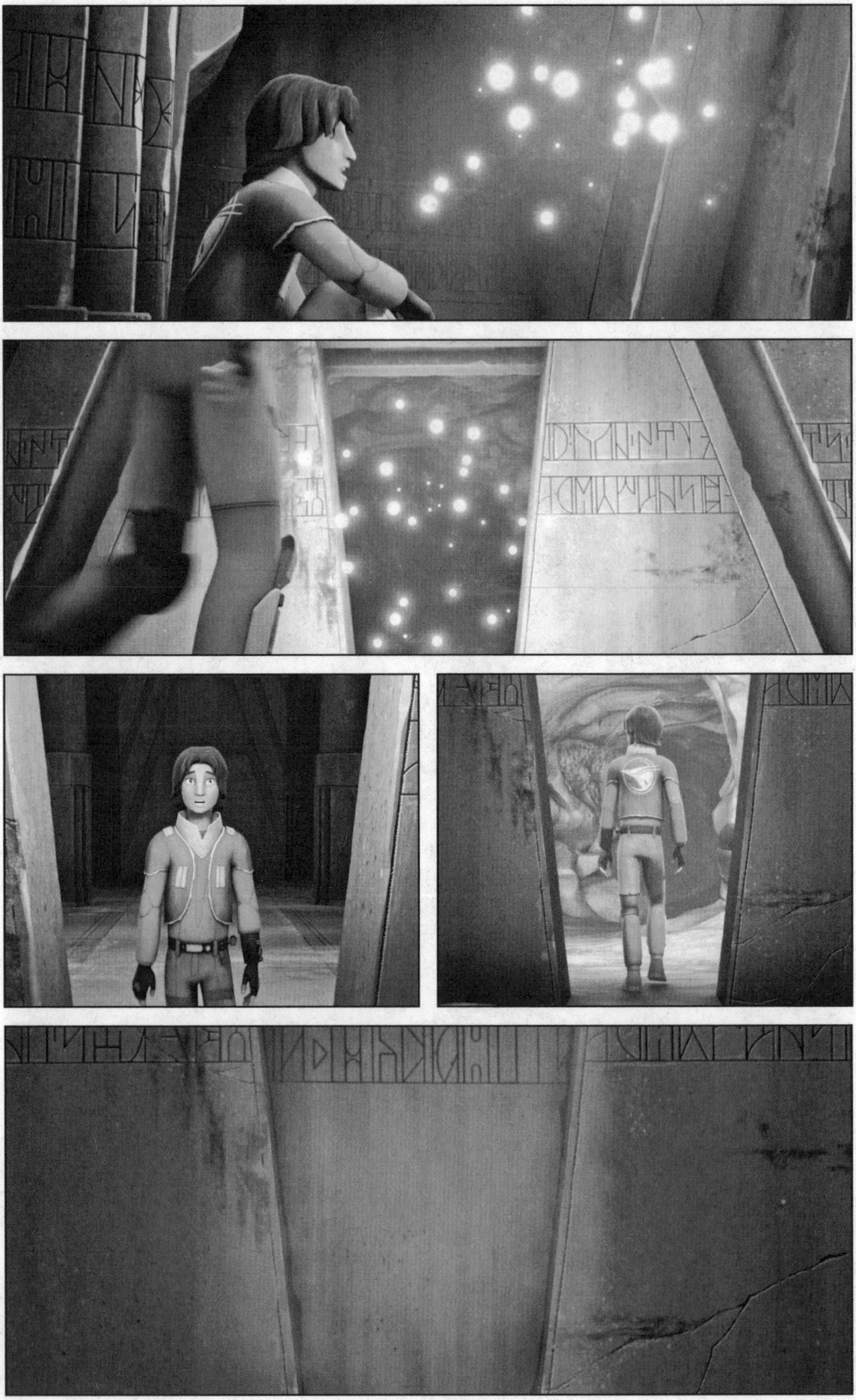

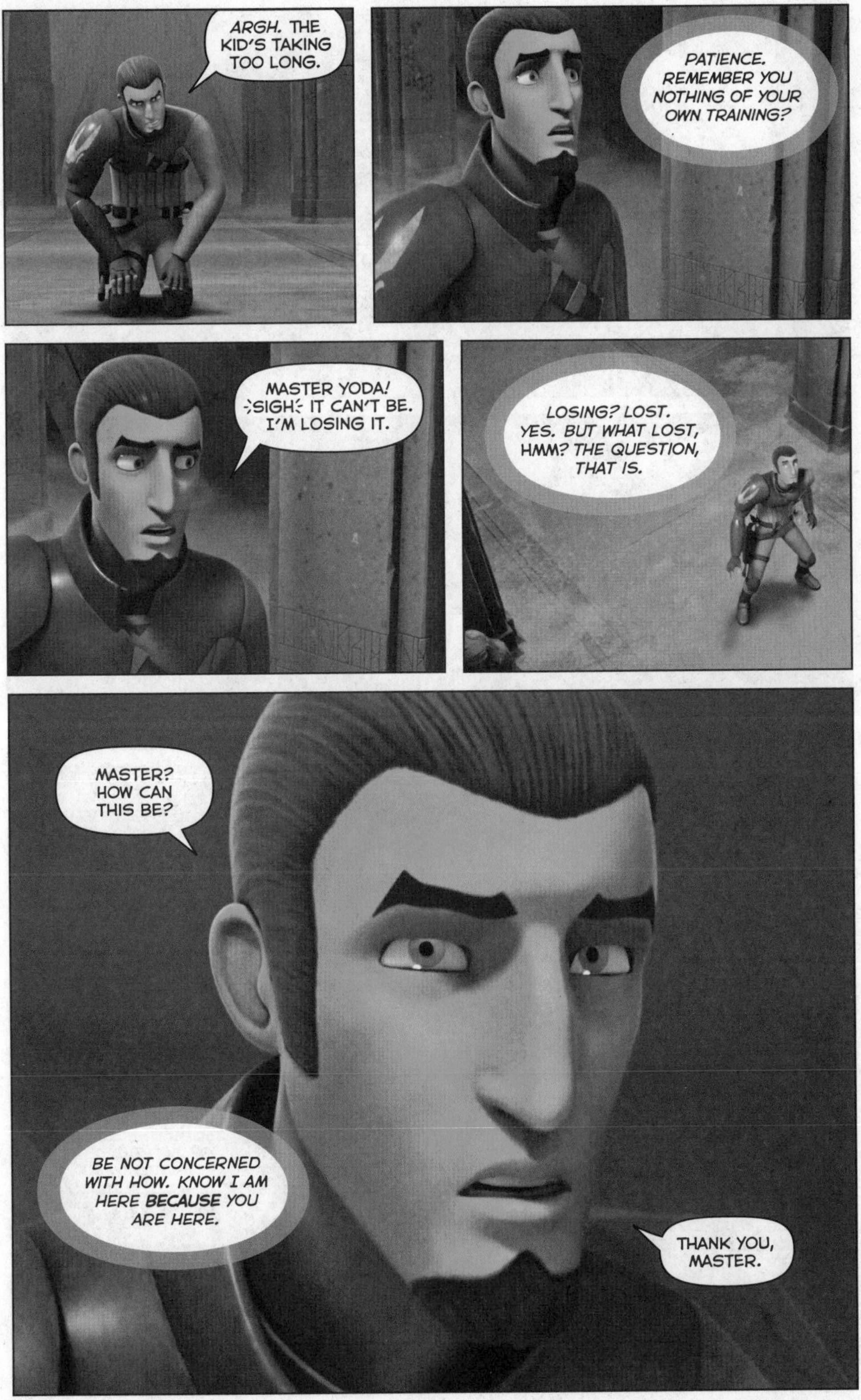
ARGH. THE KID'S TAKING TOO LONG.
PATIENCE. REMEMBER YOU NOTHING OF YOUR OWN TRAINING?
MASTER YODA! -SIGH- IT CAN'T BE. I'M LOSING IT.
LOSING? LOST. YES. BUT WHAT LOST, HMM? THE QUESTION, THAT IS.
MASTER? HOW CAN THIS BE?
BE NOT CONCERNED WITH HOW. KNOW I AM HERE BECAUSE YOU ARE HERE.
THANK YOU, MASTER.

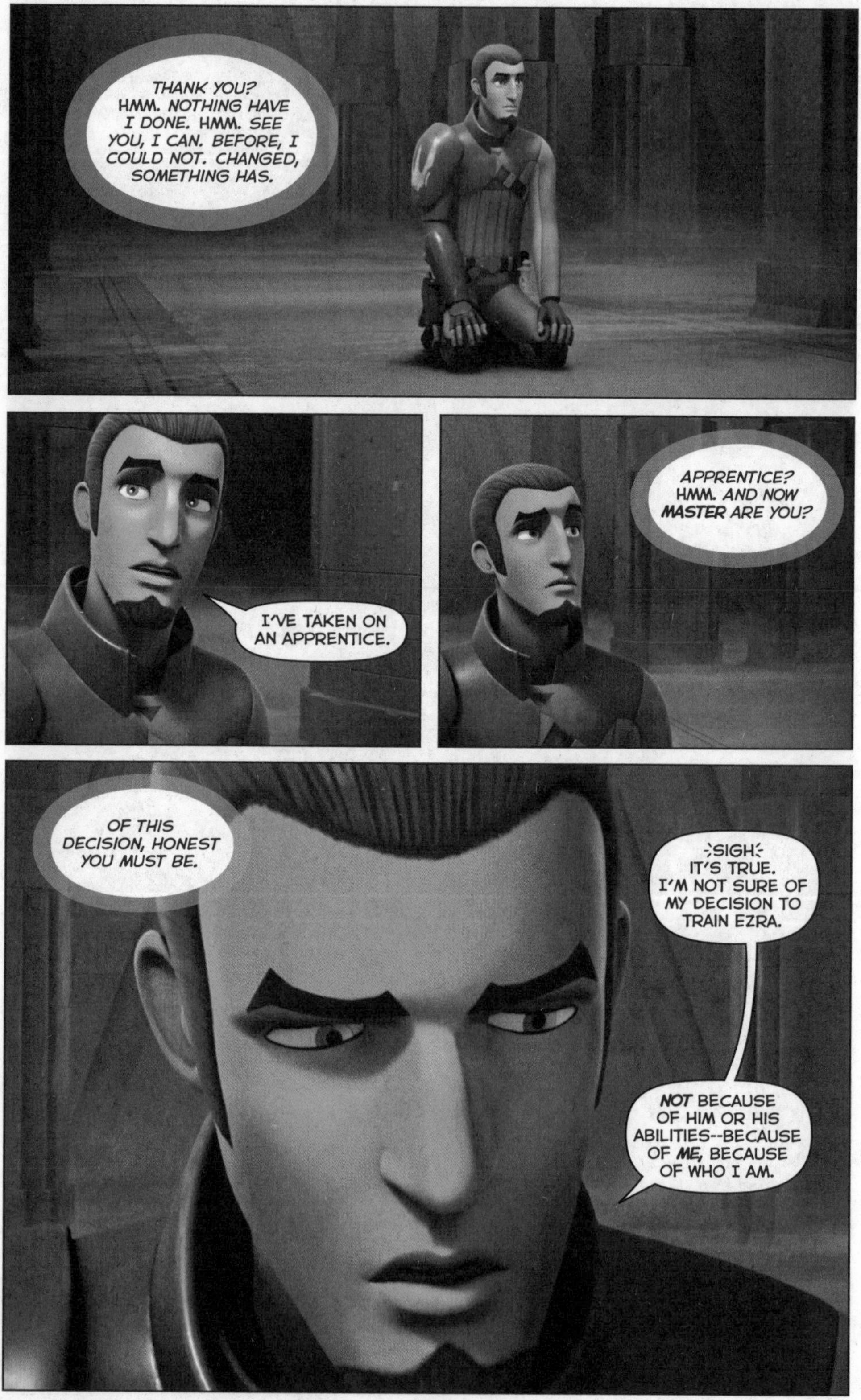
THANK YOU? HMM. NOTHING HAVE I DONE. HMM. SEE YOU, I CAN. BEFORE, I COULD NOT. CHANGED, SOMETHING HAS.
I'VE TAKEN ON AN APPRENTICE.
APPRENTICE? HMM. AND NOW MASTER ARE YOU?
OF THIS DECISION, HONEST YOU MUST BE.
SIGH IT'S TRUE. I'M NOT SURE OF MY DECISION TO TRAIN EZRA.
NOT BECAUSE OF HIM OR HIS ABILITIES--BECAUSE OF ME, BECAUSE OF WHO I AM.

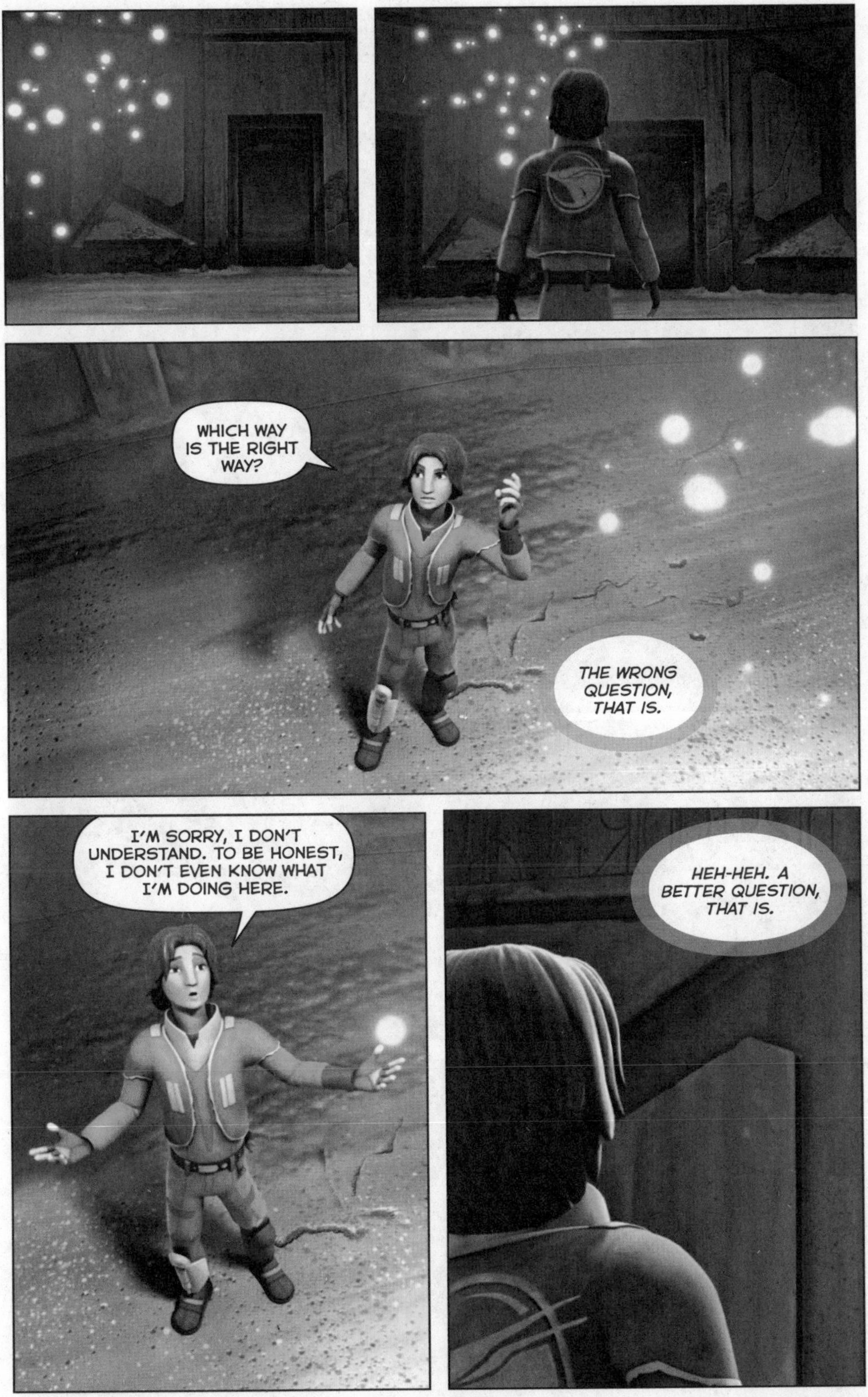
WHICH WAY IS THE RIGHT WAY?
THE WRONG QUESTION, THAT IS.
I'M SORRY, I DON'T UNDERSTAND. TO BE HONEST, I DON'T EVEN KNOW WHAT I'M DOING HERE.
HEH-HEH. A BETTER QUESTION, THAT IS.

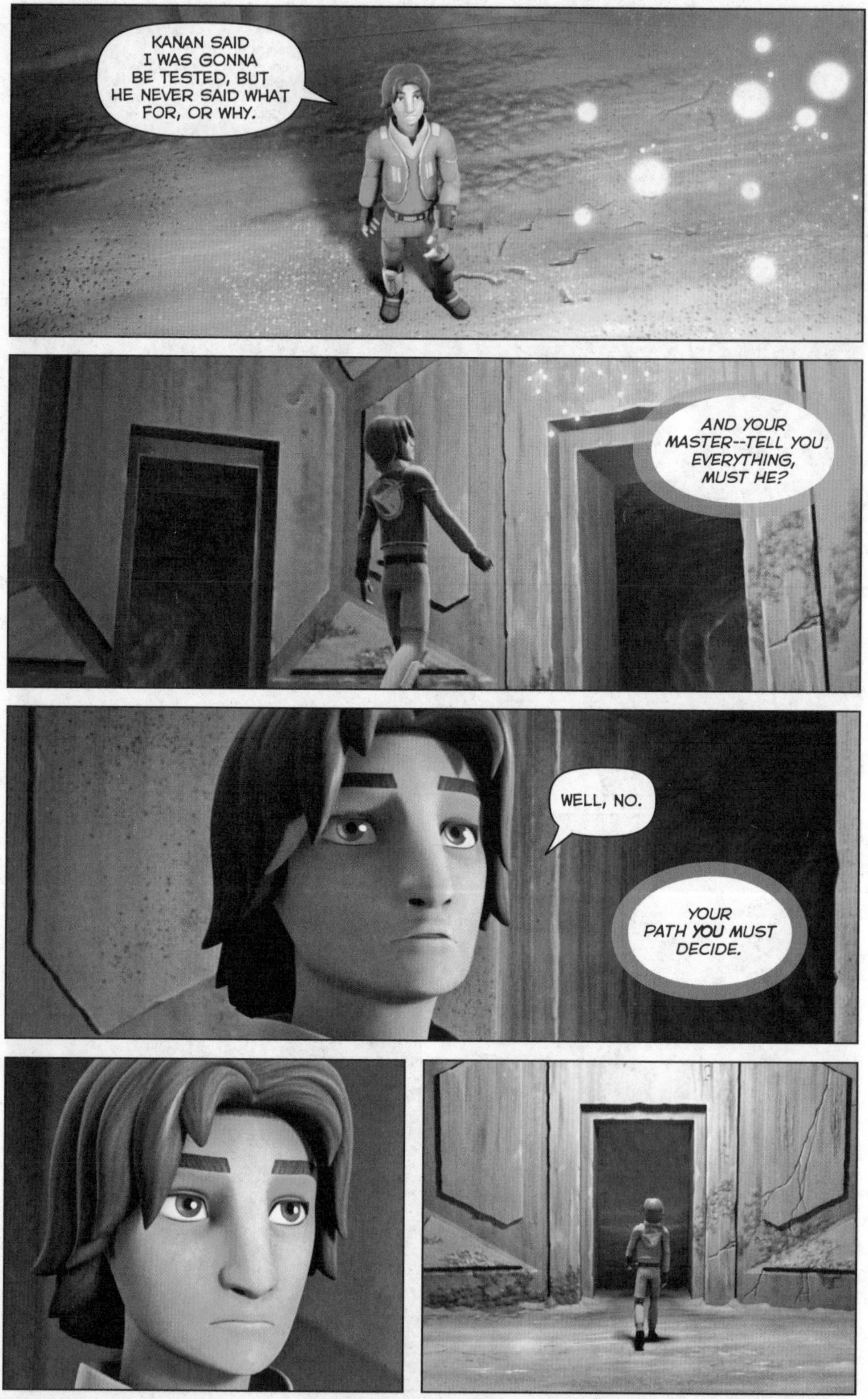
KANAN SAID I WAS GONNA BE TESTED, BUT HE NEVER SAID WHAT FOR, OR WHY.
AND YOUR MASTER--TELL YOU EVERYTHING, MUST HE?
WELL, NO.
YOUR PATH YOU MUST DECIDE.

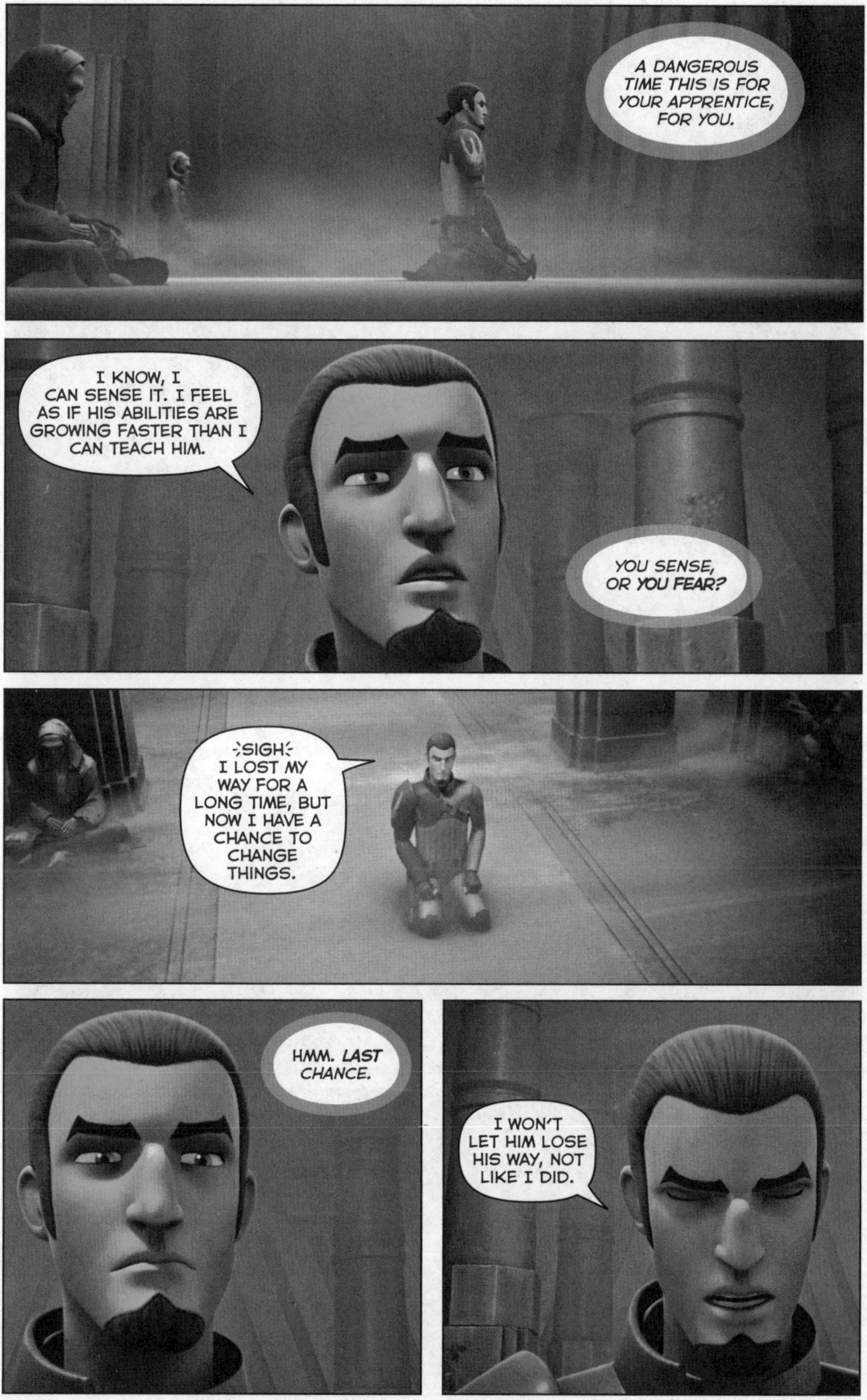
A DANGEROUS TIME THIS IS FOR YOUR APPRENTICE, FOR YOU.
I KNOW, I CAN SENSE IT. I FEEL AS IF HIS ABILITIES ARE GROWING FASTER THAN I CAN TEACH HIM.
YOU SENSE, OR YOU FEAR?
SIGH I LOST MY WAY FOR A LONG TIME, BUT NOW I HAVE A CHANCE TO CHANGE THINGS.
HMM. LAST CHANCE.
I WON'T LET HIM LOSE HIS WAY, NOT LIKE I DID.

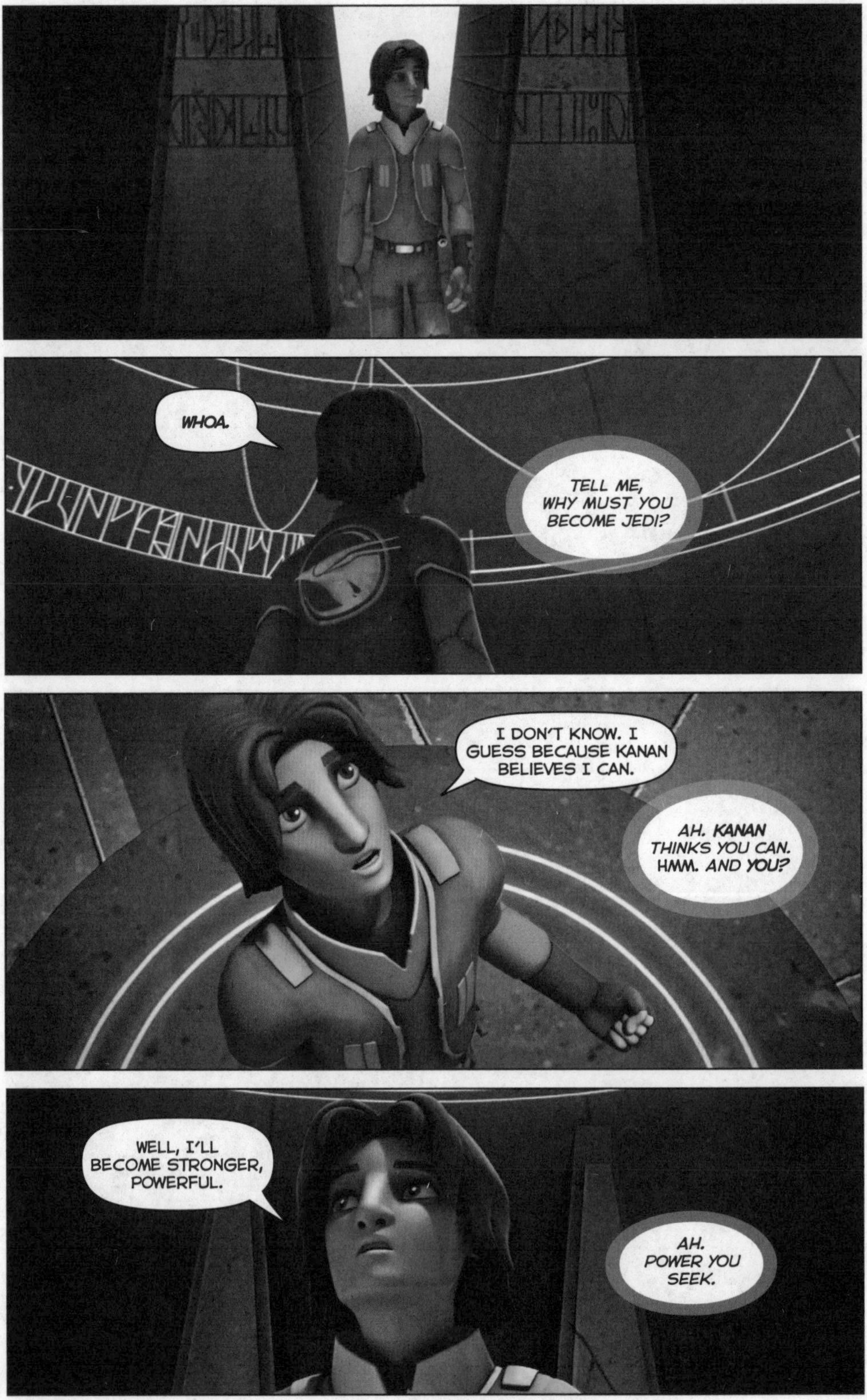
WHOA.
TELL ME, WHY MUST YOU BECOME JEDI?
I DON'T KNOW. I GUESS BECAUSE KANAN BELIEVES I CAN.
AH. KANAN THINKS YOU CAN. HMM. AND YOU?
WELL, I'LL BECOME STRONGER, POWERFUL.
AH. POWER YOU SEEK.

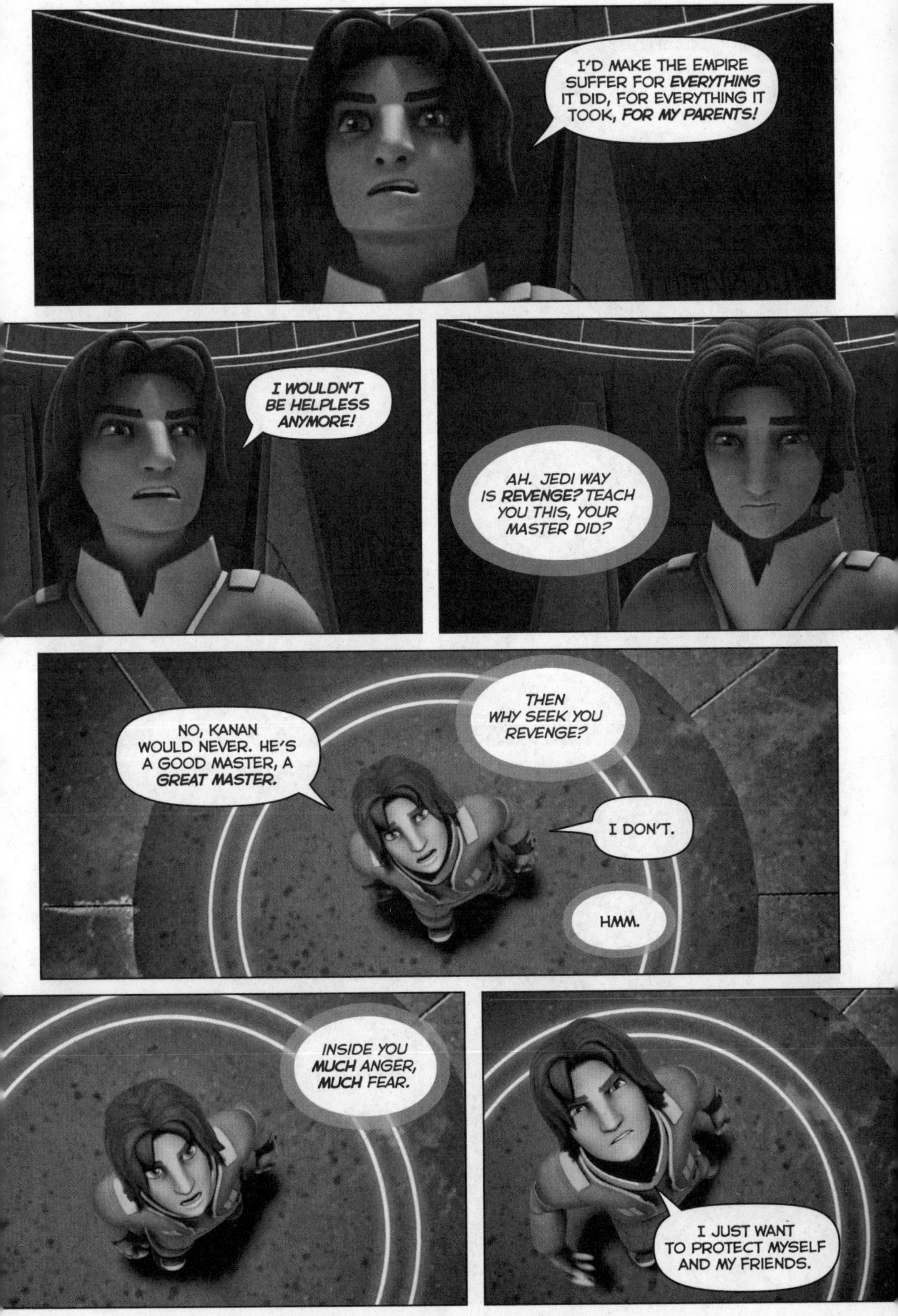
I'D MAKE THE EMPIRE SUFFER FOR EVERYTHING IT DID, FOR EVERYTHING IT TOOK, FOR MY PARENTS!
I WOULDN'T BE HELPLESS ANYMORE!
AH. JEDI WAY IS REVENGE? TEACH YOU THIS, YOUR MASTER DID?
NO, KANAN WOULD NEVER. HE'S A GOOD MASTER, A GREAT MASTER.
THEN WHY SEEK YOU REVENGE?
I DON'T.
HMM.
INSIDE YOU MUCH ANGER, MUCH FEAR.
I JUST WANT TO PROTECT MYSELF AND MY FRIENDS.

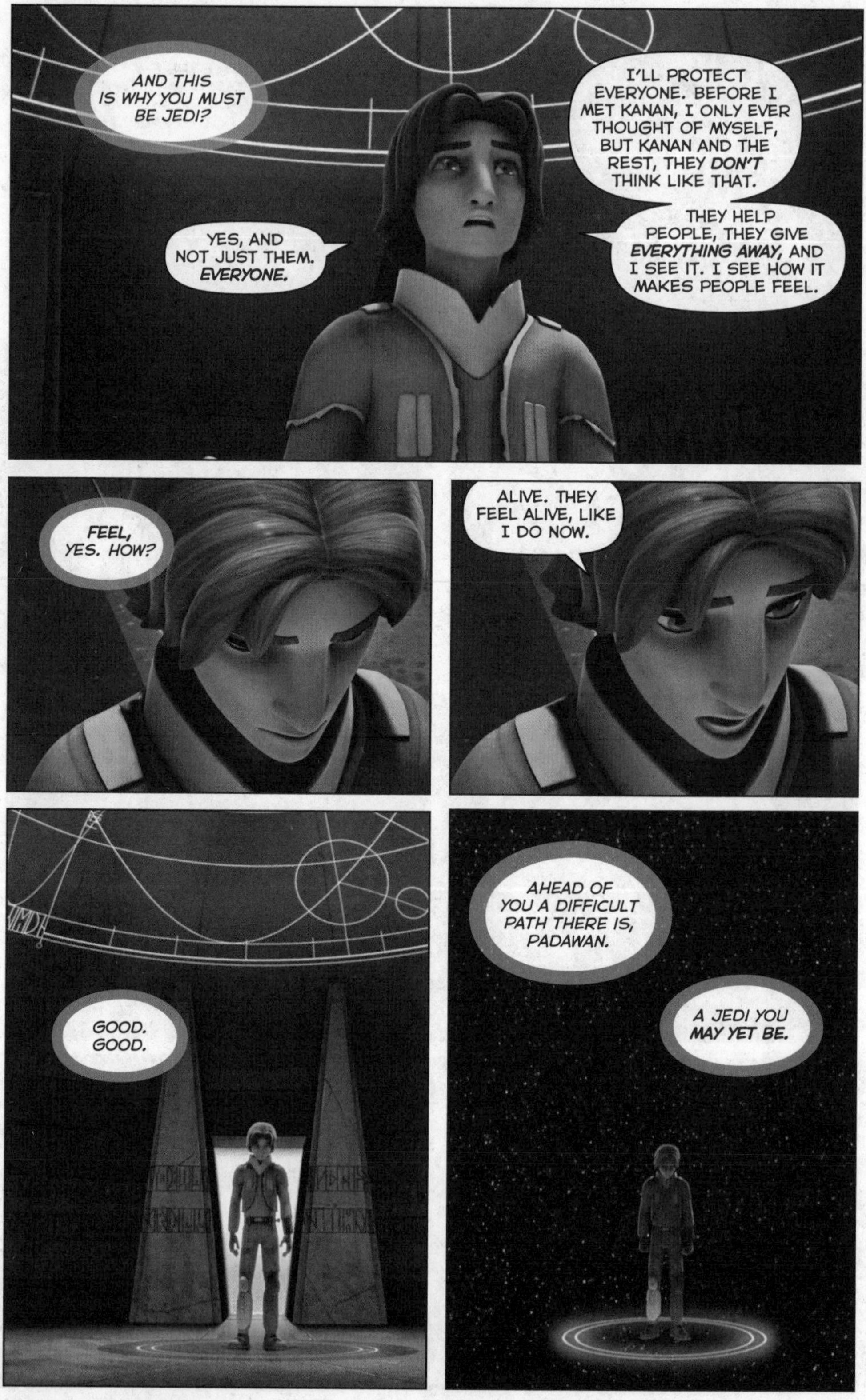
AND THIS IS WHY YOU MUST BE JEDI?
I'LL PROTECT EVERYONE. BEFORE I MET KANAN, I ONLY EVER THOUGHT OF MYSELF, BUT KANAN AND THE REST, THEY DON'T THINK LIKE THAT.
THEY HELP PEOPLE, THEY GIVE EVERYTHING AWAY, AND I SEE IT. I SEE HOW IT MAKES PEOPLE FEEL.
YES, AND NOT JUST THEM. EVERYONE.
FEEL, YES. HOW?
ALIVE. THEY FEEL ALIVE, LIKE I DO NOW.
GOOD. GOOD.
AHEAD OF YOU A DIFFICULT PATH THERE IS, PADAWAN.
A JEDI YOU MAY YET BE.

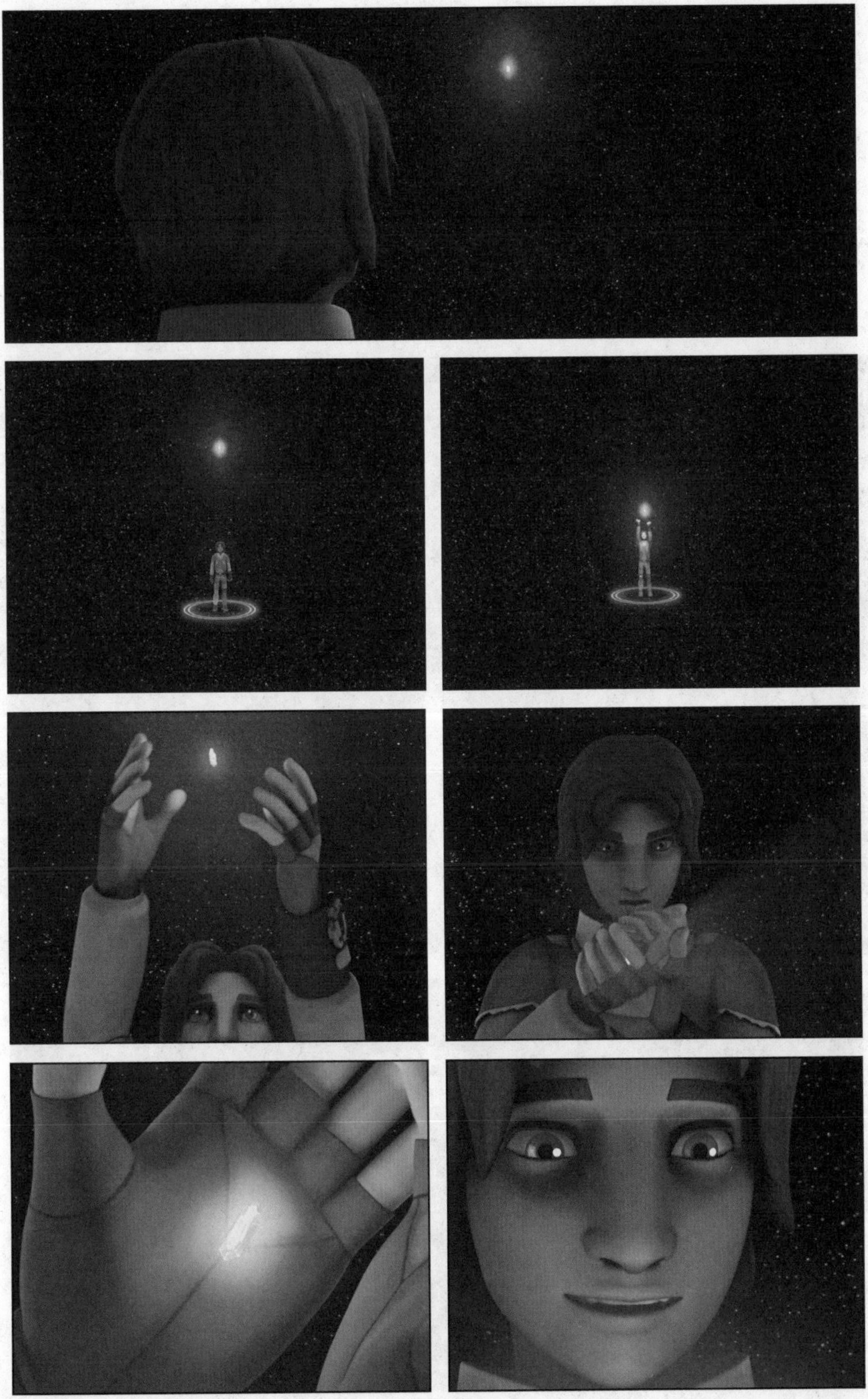

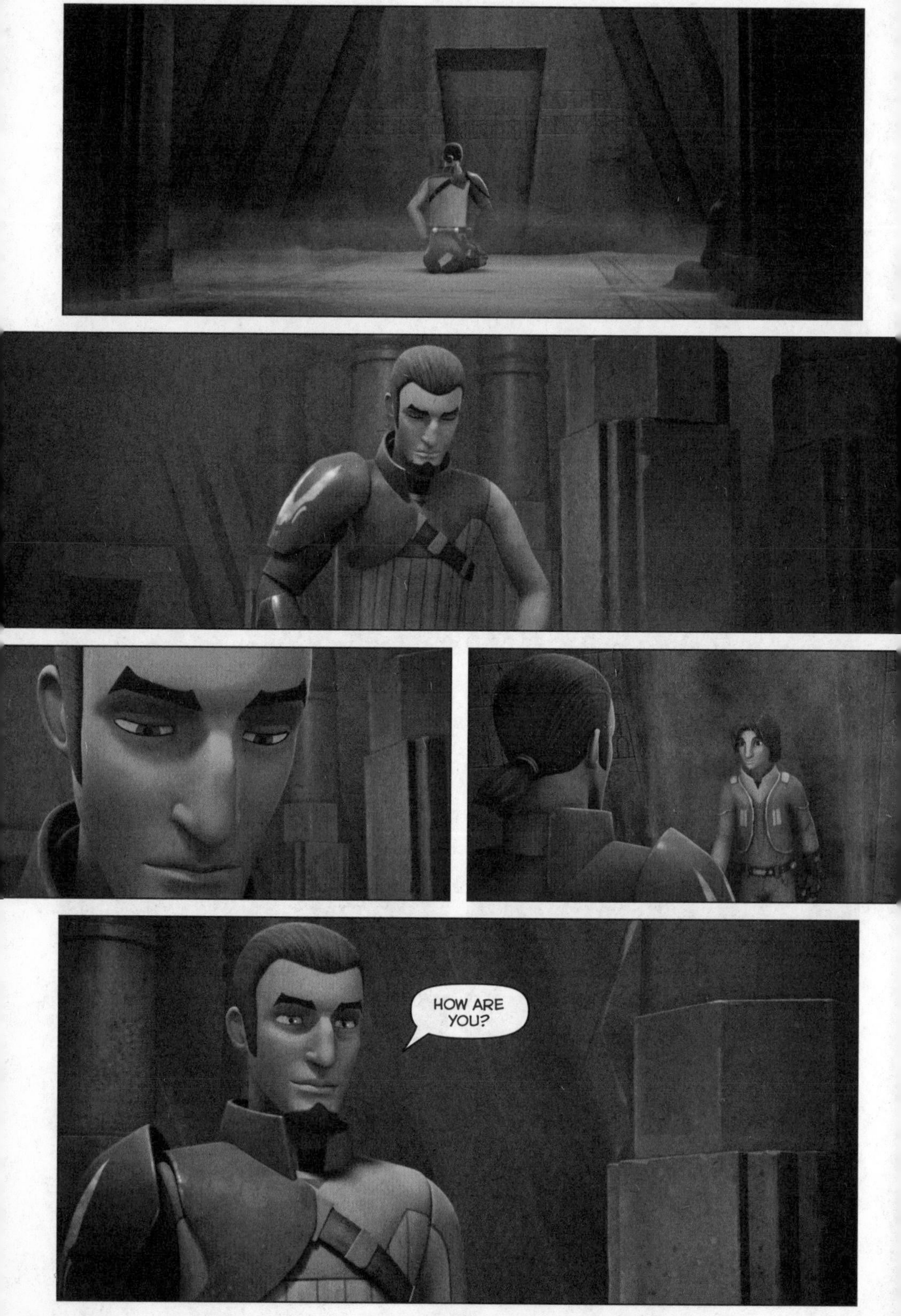
HOW ARE YOU?

DIFFERENT, BUT THE SAME.

HEH. I KNOW WHAT YOU MEAN.

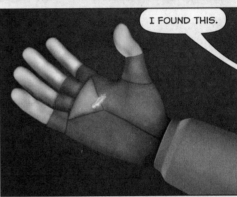

I FOUND THIS.

I DON'T BELIEVE IT.

WHAT IS IT? IT'S GOOD, RIGHT?

EZRA, THAT'S A *KAIBURR CRYSTAL!*

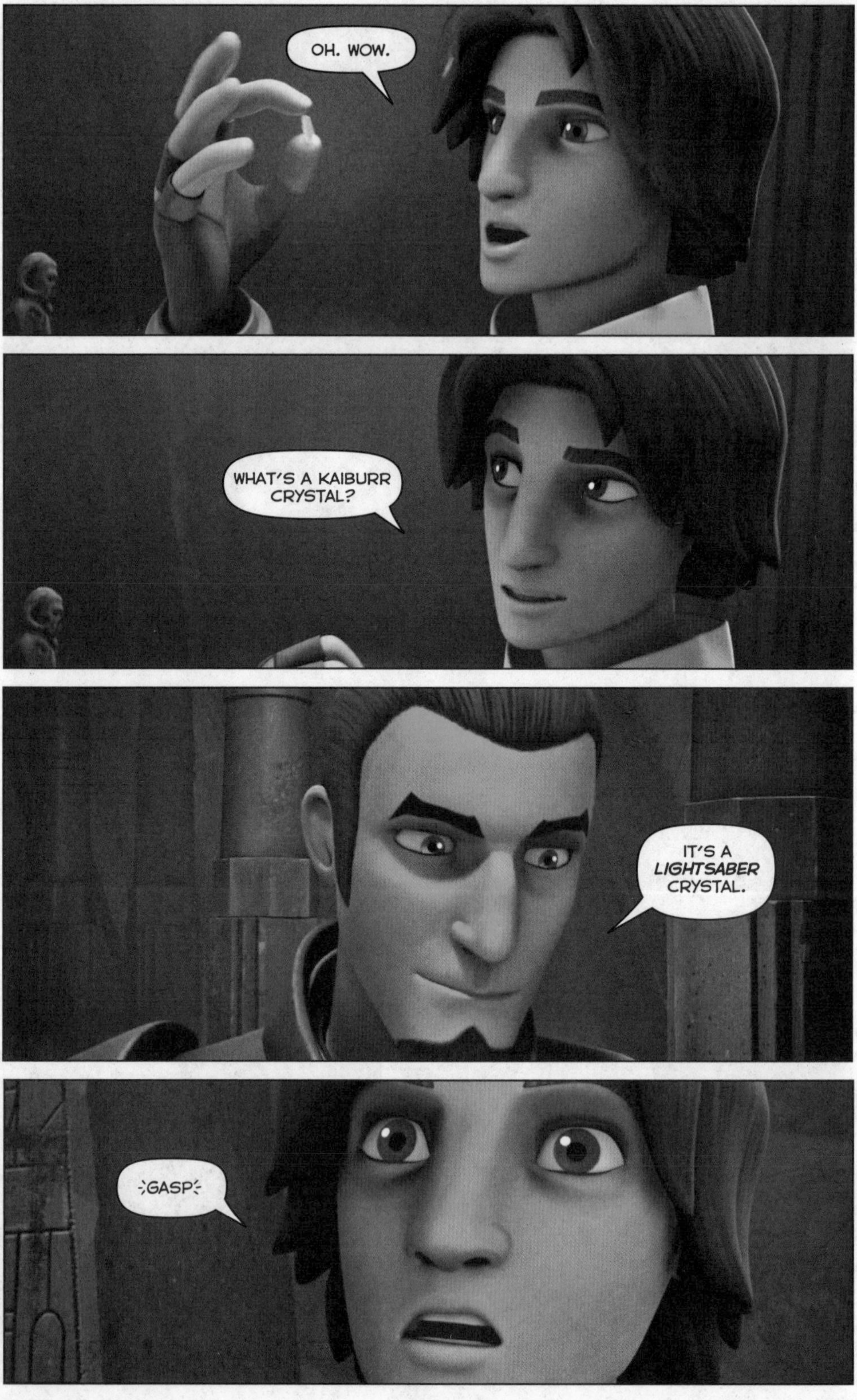
OH. WOW.
WHAT'S A KAIBURR CRYSTAL?
IT'S A *LIGHTSABER* CRYSTAL.
GASP

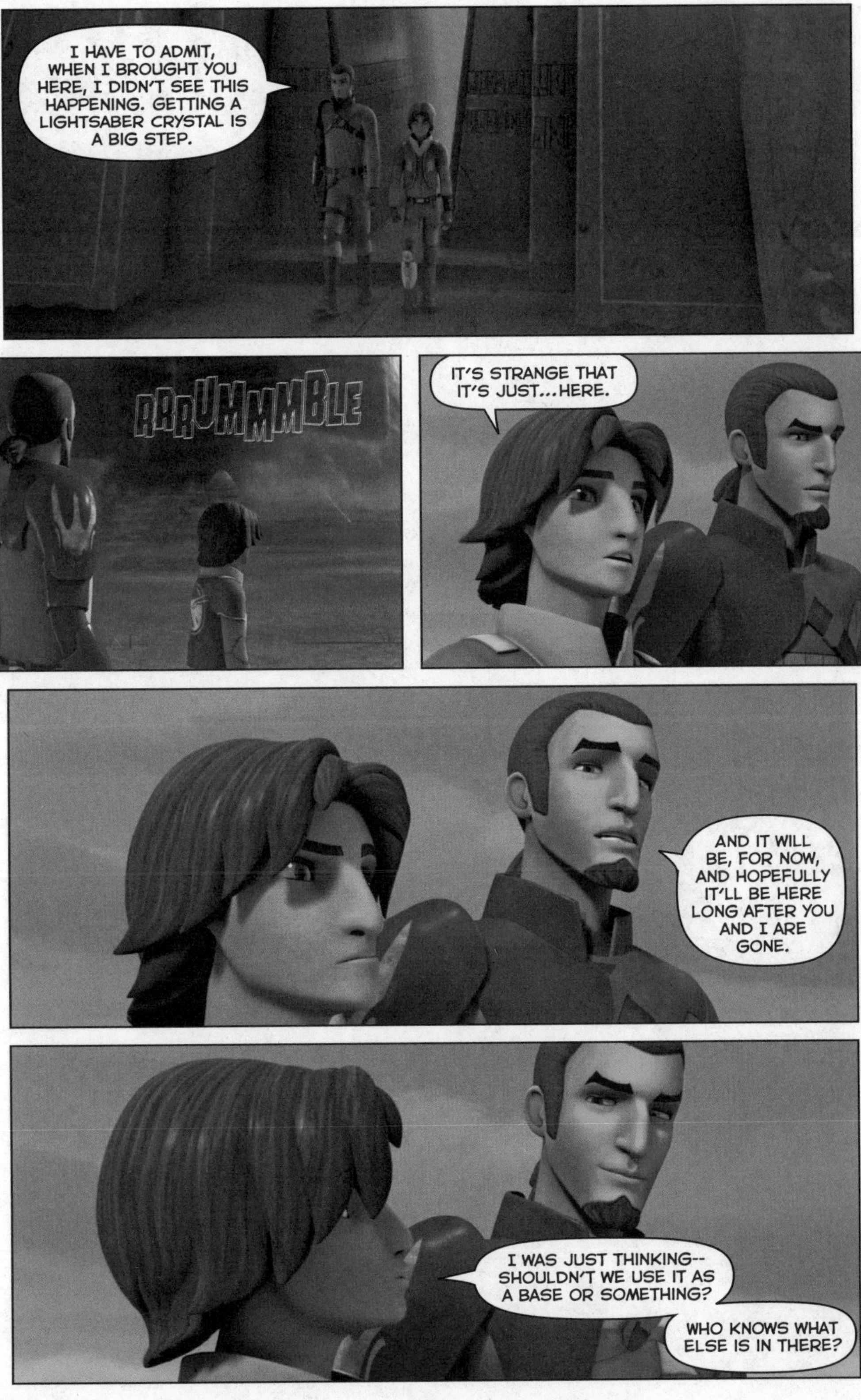
I HAVE TO ADMIT, WHEN I BROUGHT YOU HERE, I DIDN'T SEE THIS HAPPENING. GETTING A LIGHTSABER CRYSTAL IS A BIG STEP.
RRRUMMMBLE
IT'S STRANGE THAT IT'S JUST...HERE.
AND IT WILL BE, FOR NOW, AND HOPEFULLY IT'LL BE HERE LONG AFTER YOU AND I ARE GONE.
I WAS JUST THINKING-- SHOULDN'T WE USE IT AS A BASE OR SOMETHING?
WHO KNOWS WHAT ELSE IS IN THERE?

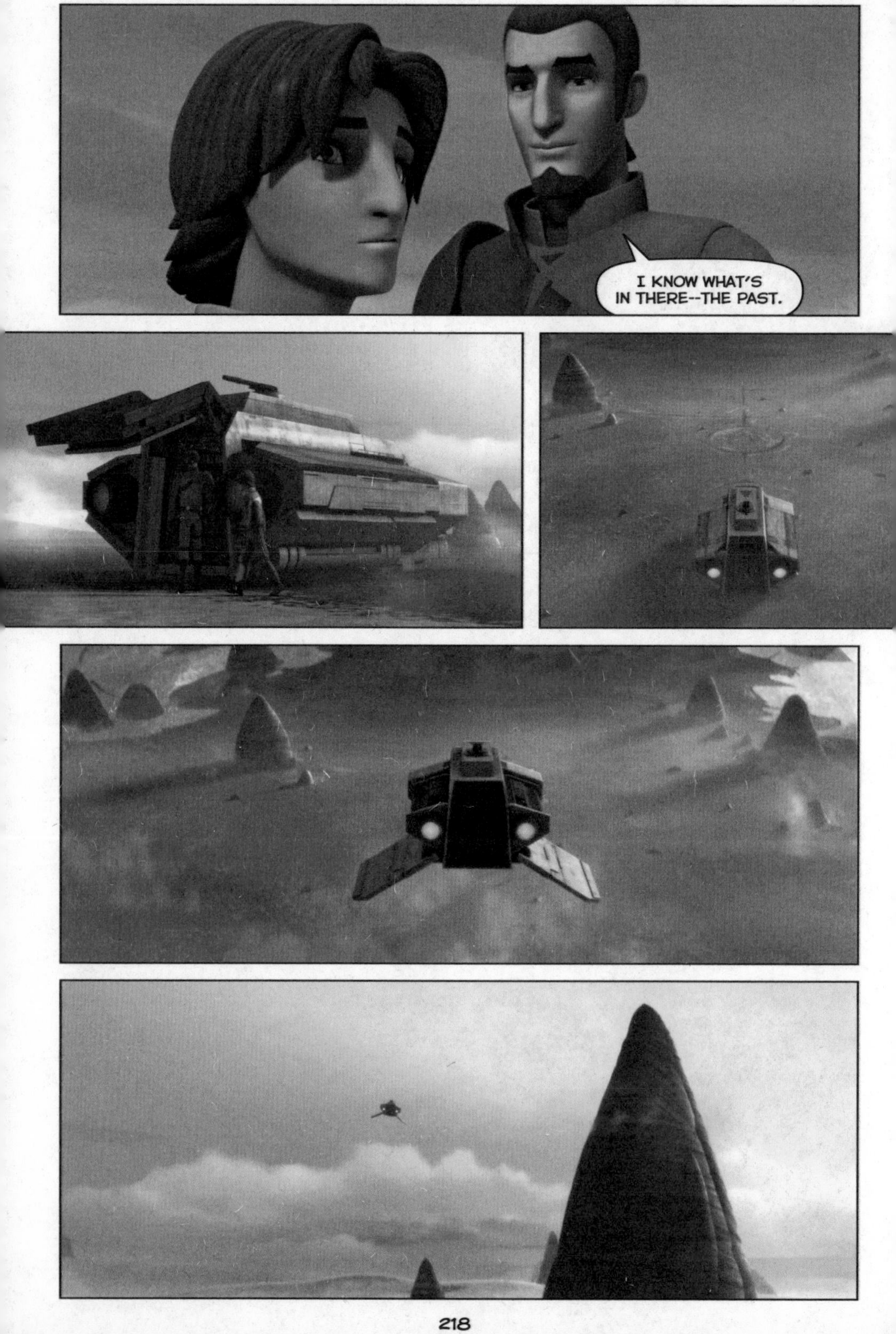
I KNOW WHAT'S IN THERE--THE PAST.

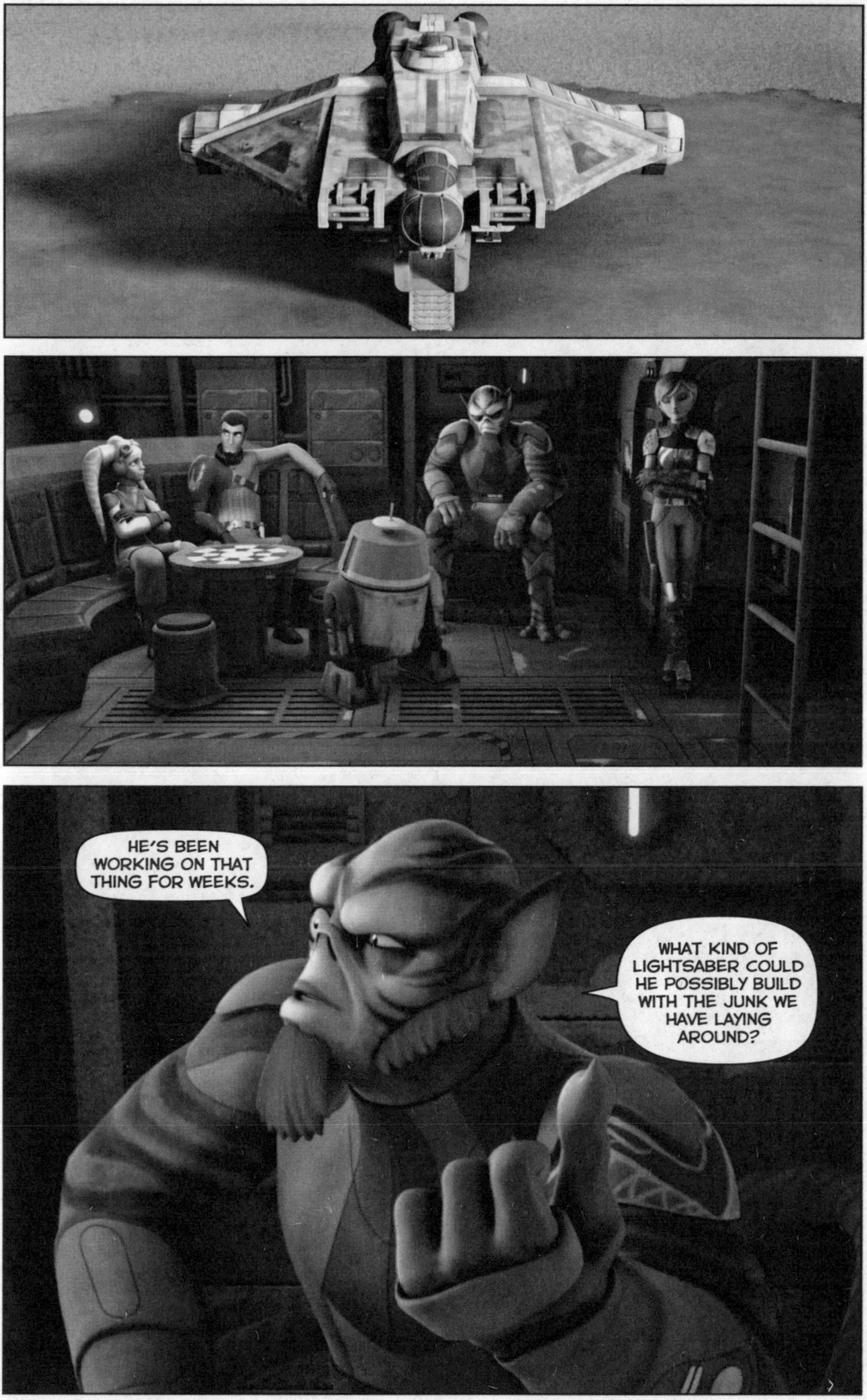
HE'S BEEN WORKING ON THAT THING FOR WEEKS.
WHAT KIND OF LIGHTSABER COULD HE POSSIBLY BUILD WITH THE JUNK WE HAVE LAYING AROUND?

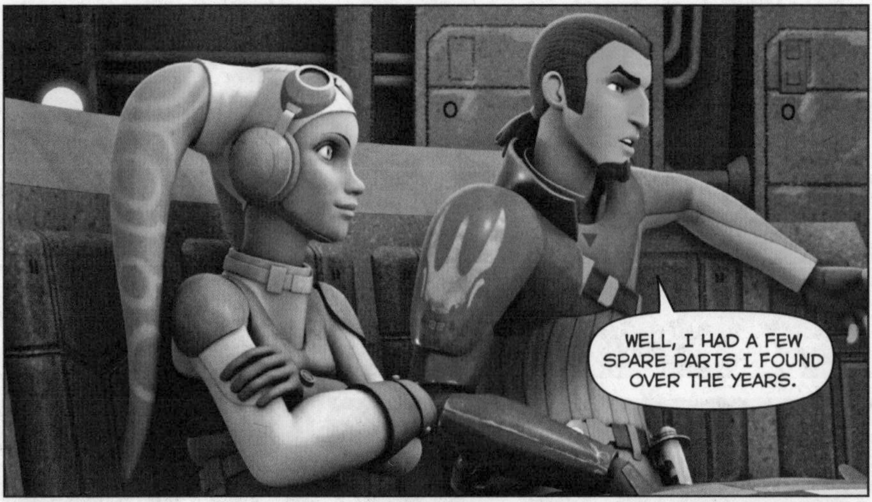
WELL, I HAD A FEW SPARE PARTS I FOUND OVER THE YEARS.

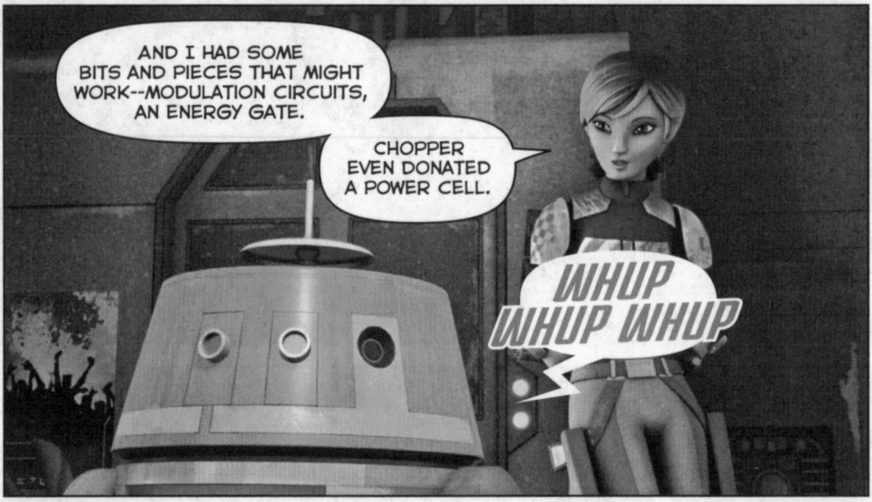
AND I HAD SOME BITS AND PIECES THAT MIGHT WORK--MODULATION CIRCUITS, AN ENERGY GATE.
CHOPPER EVEN DONATED A POWER CELL.
WHUP WHUP WHUP

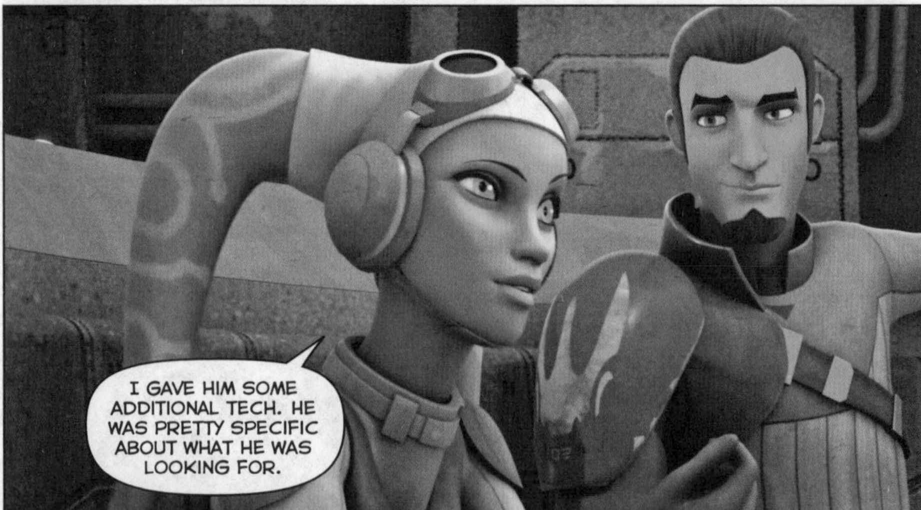
I GAVE HIM SOME ADDITIONAL TECH. HE WAS PRETTY SPECIFIC ABOUT WHAT HE WAS LOOKING FOR.

:SIGH:

:GASP!:

I THOUGHT I'D LET YOU CHECK IT OUT FIRST.

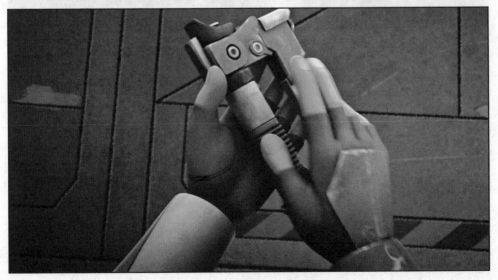

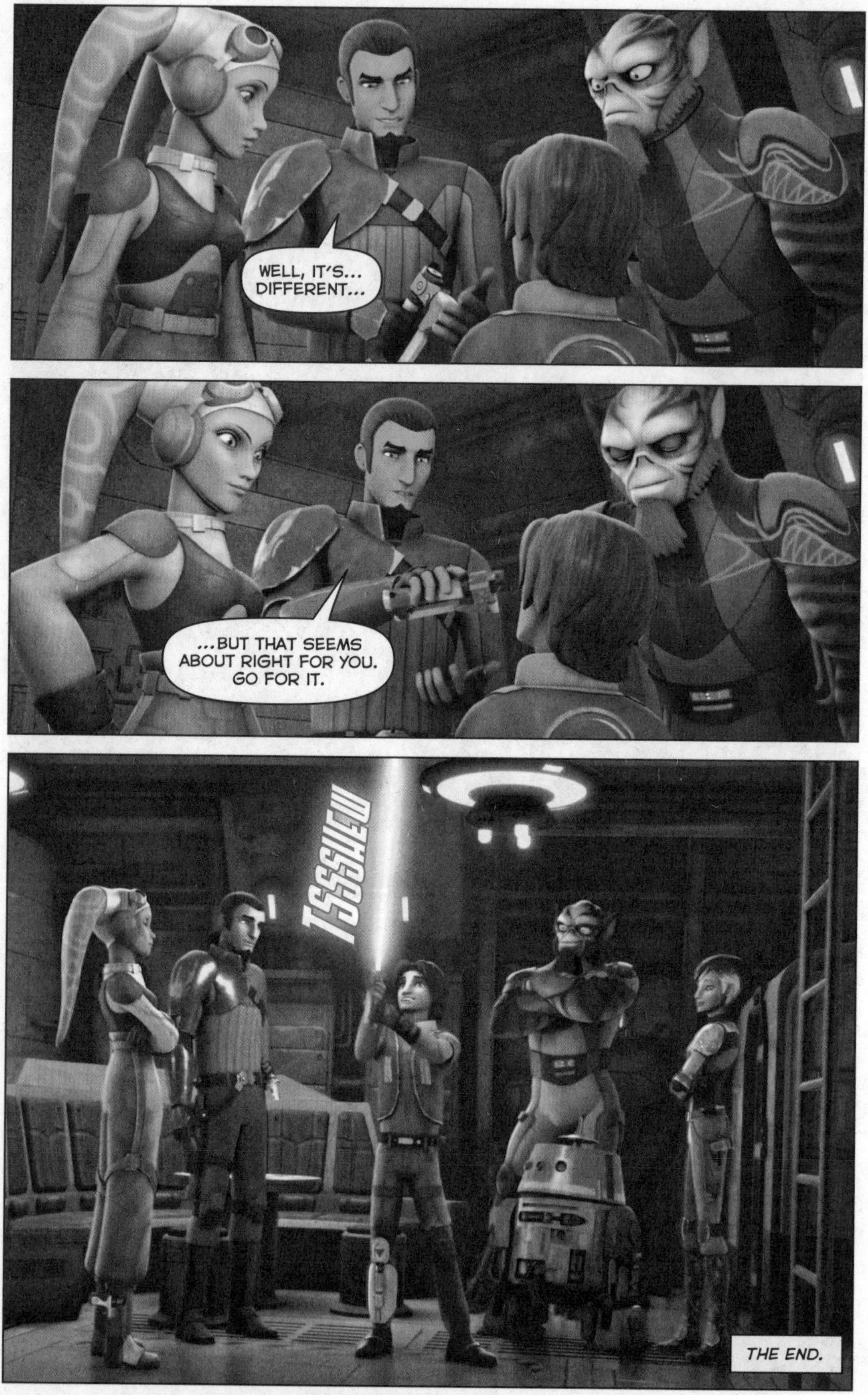
WELL, IT'S... DIFFERENT...
...BUT THAT SEEMS ABOUT RIGHT FOR YOU. GO FOR IT.
TSSSHEW
THE END.

STAR WARS REBELS™

VISION OF HOPE

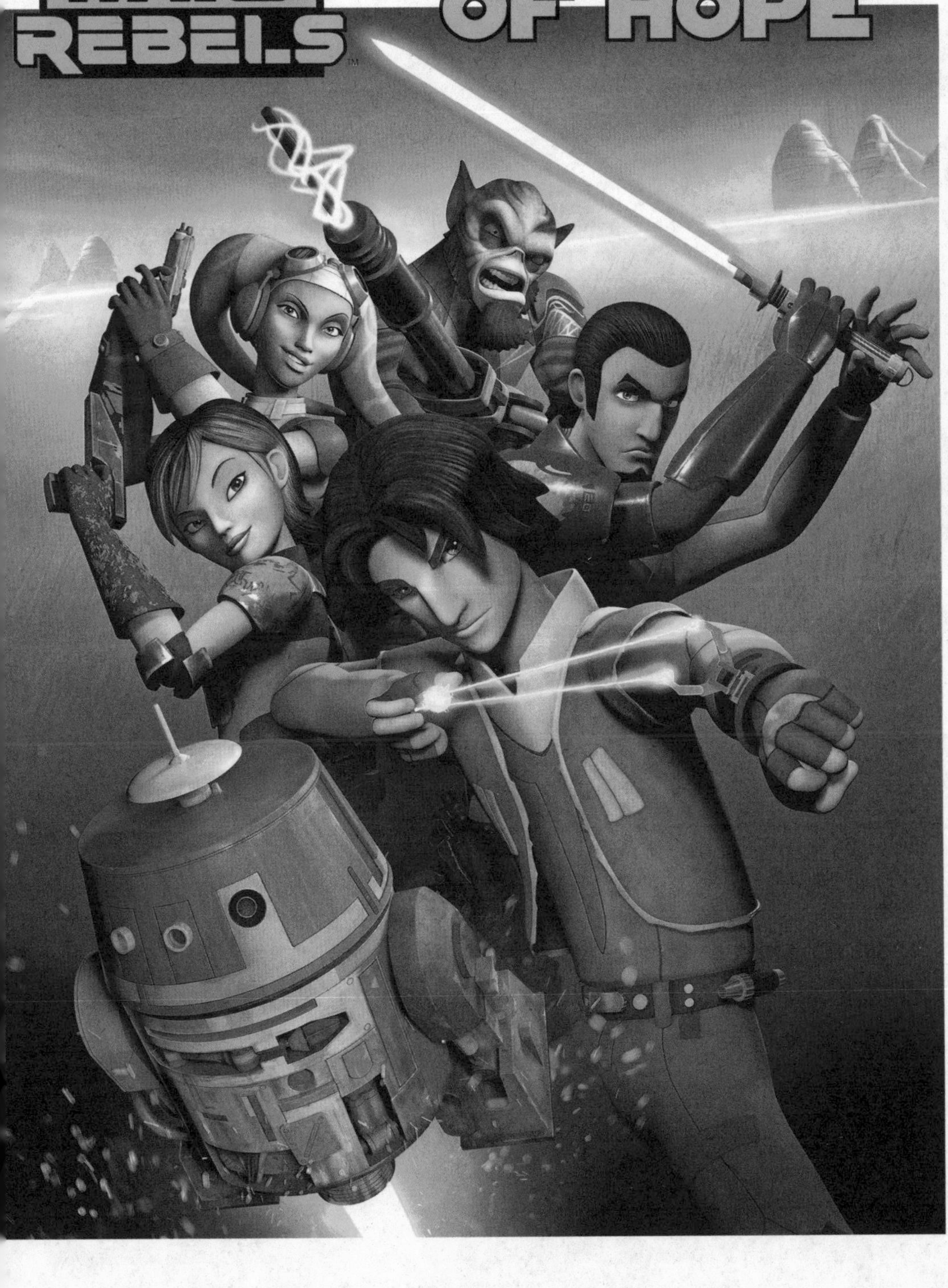

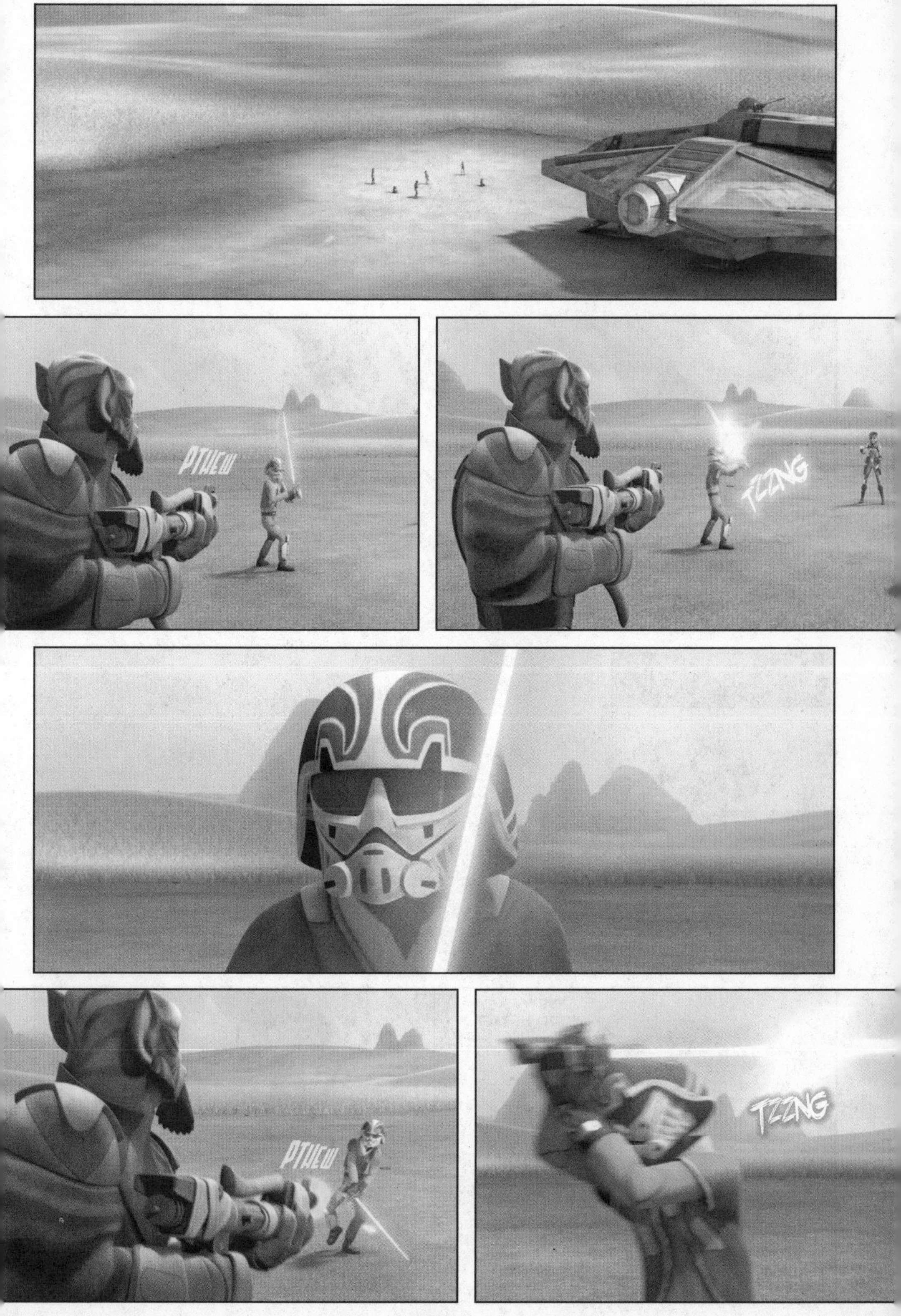
PTHEW
TZZNG
PTHEW
TZZNG

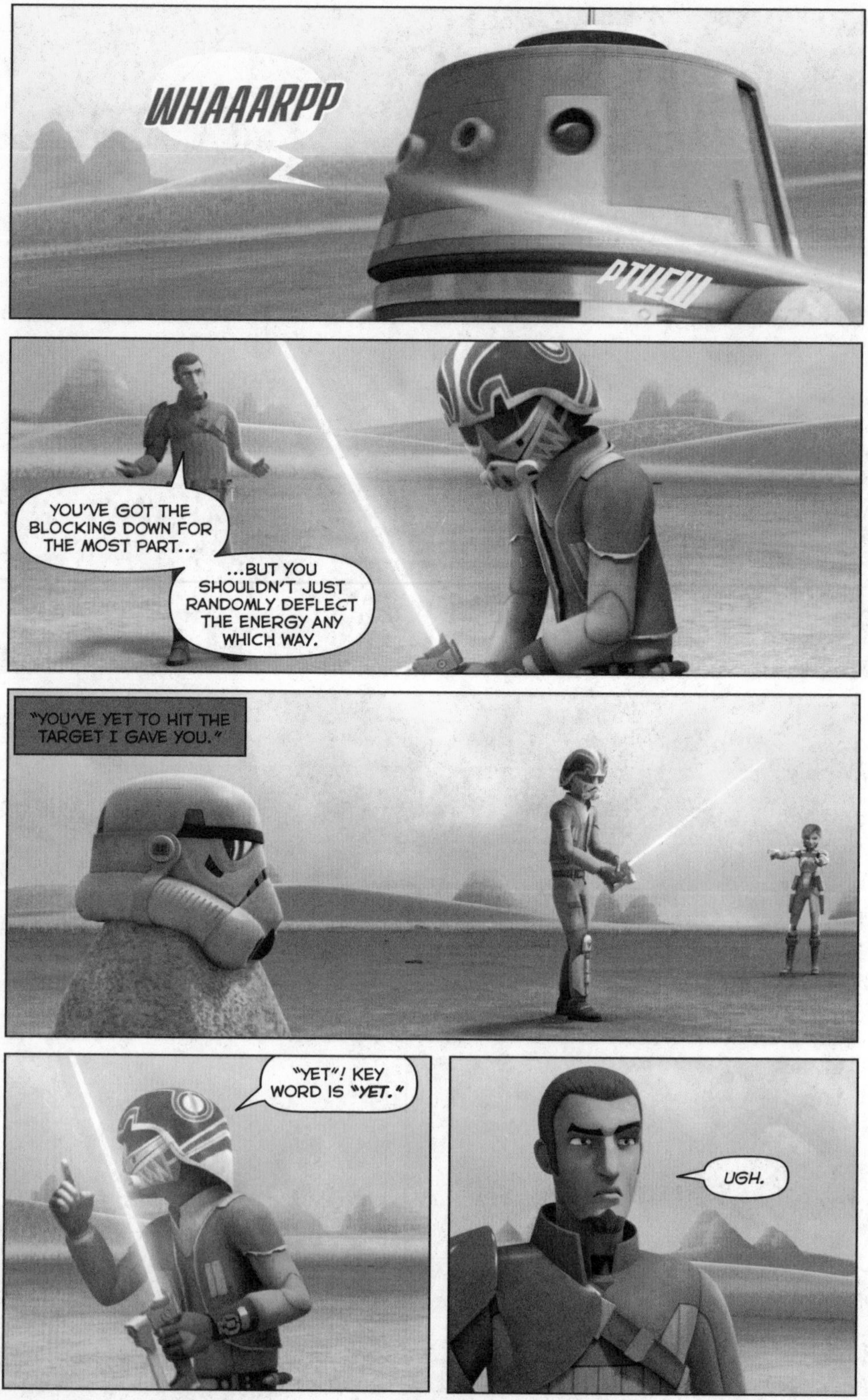
WHAAARPP
PTHEW
YOU'VE GOT THE BLOCKING DOWN FOR THE MOST PART...
...BUT YOU SHOULDN'T JUST RANDOMLY DEFLECT THE ENERGY ANY WHICH WAY.
"YOU'VE YET TO HIT THE TARGET I GAVE YOU."
"YET"! KEY WORD IS "YET."
UGH.

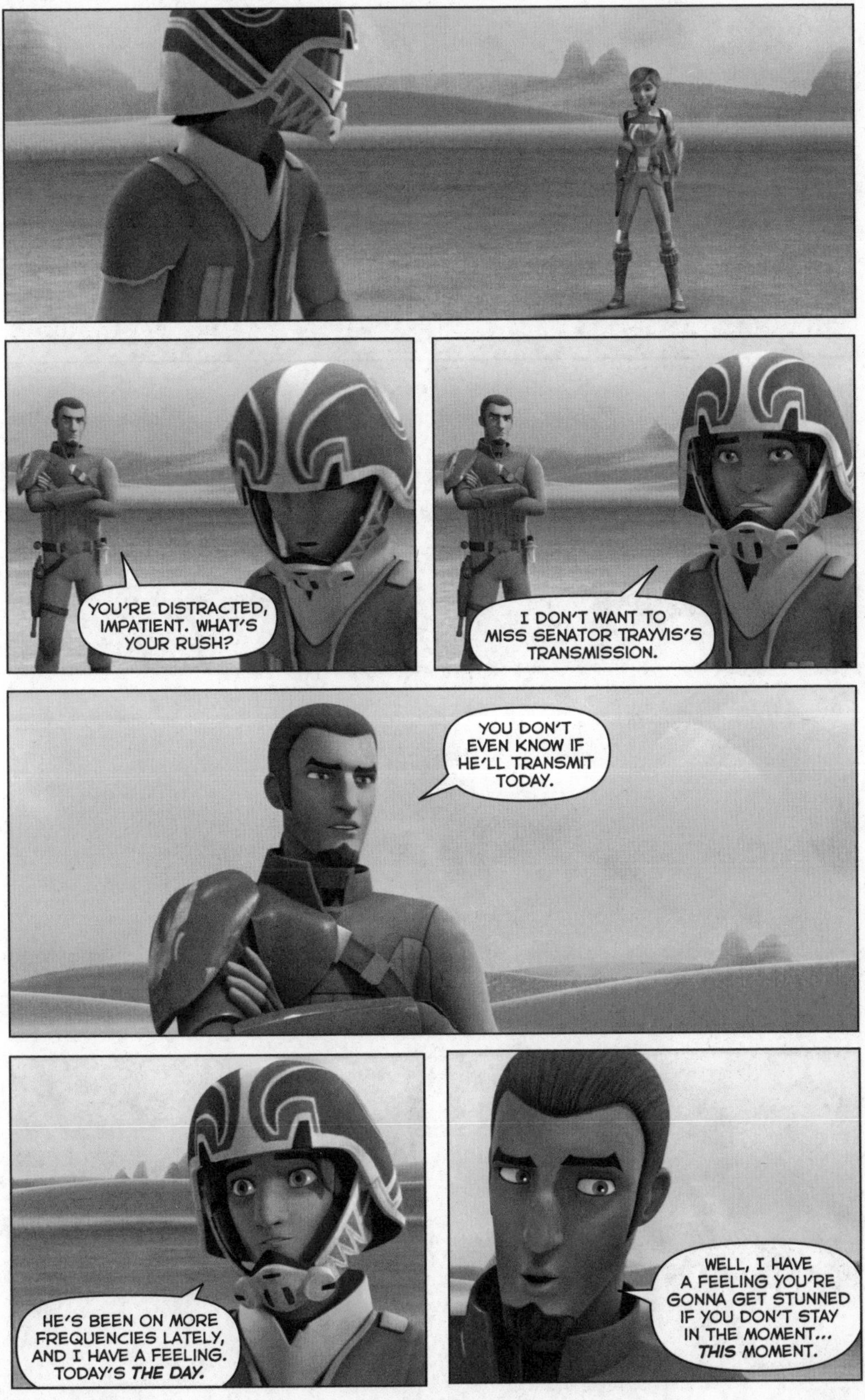
YOU'RE DISTRACTED, IMPATIENT. WHAT'S YOUR RUSH?
I DON'T WANT TO MISS SENATOR TRAYVIS'S TRANSMISSION.
YOU DON'T EVEN KNOW IF HE'LL TRANSMIT TODAY.
HE'S BEEN ON MORE FREQUENCIES LATELY, AND I HAVE A FEELING. TODAY'S *THE DAY.*
WELL, I HAVE A FEELING YOU'RE GONNA GET STUNNED IF YOU DON'T STAY IN THE MOMENT... *THIS* MOMENT.

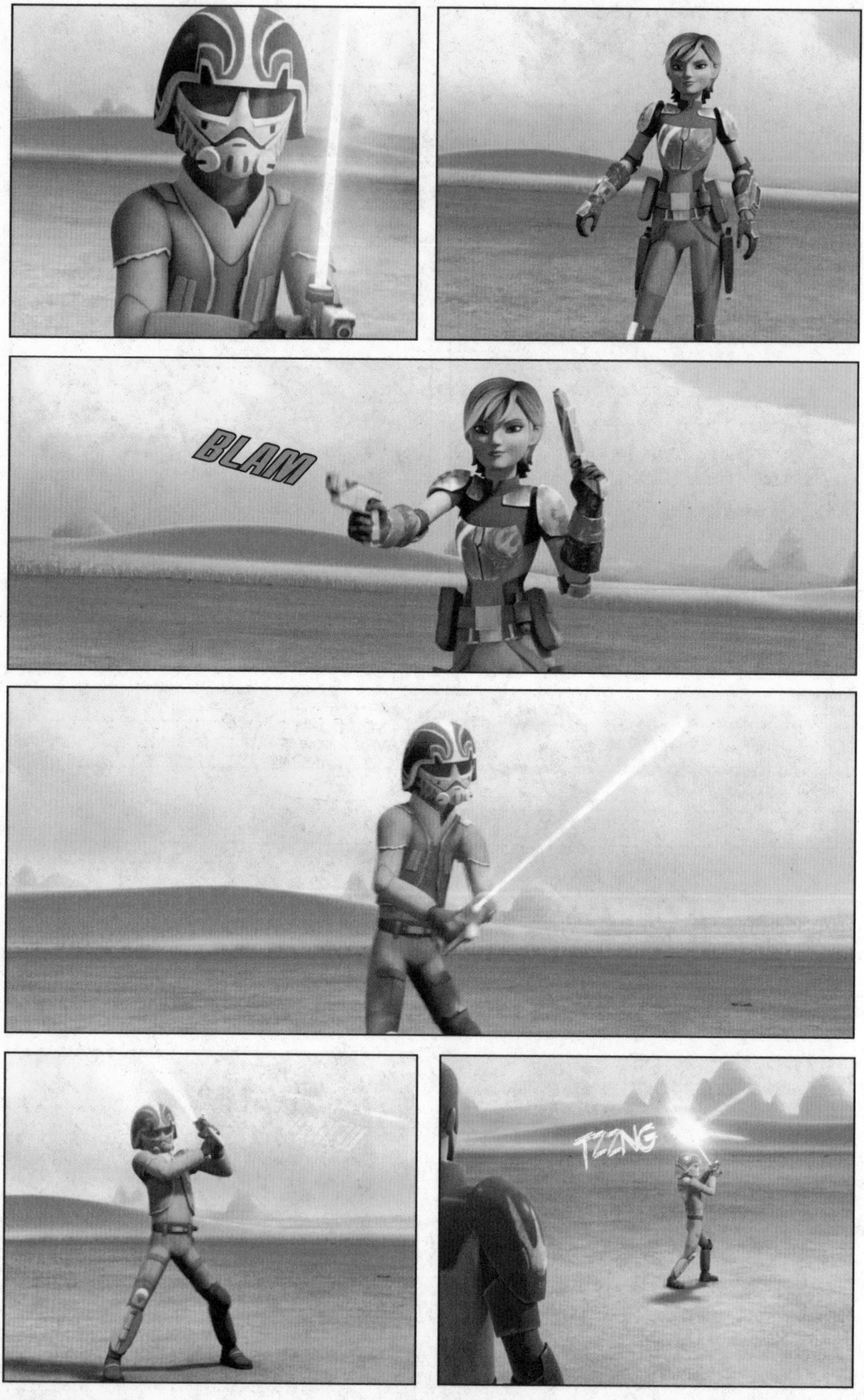
BLAM
TZZNG

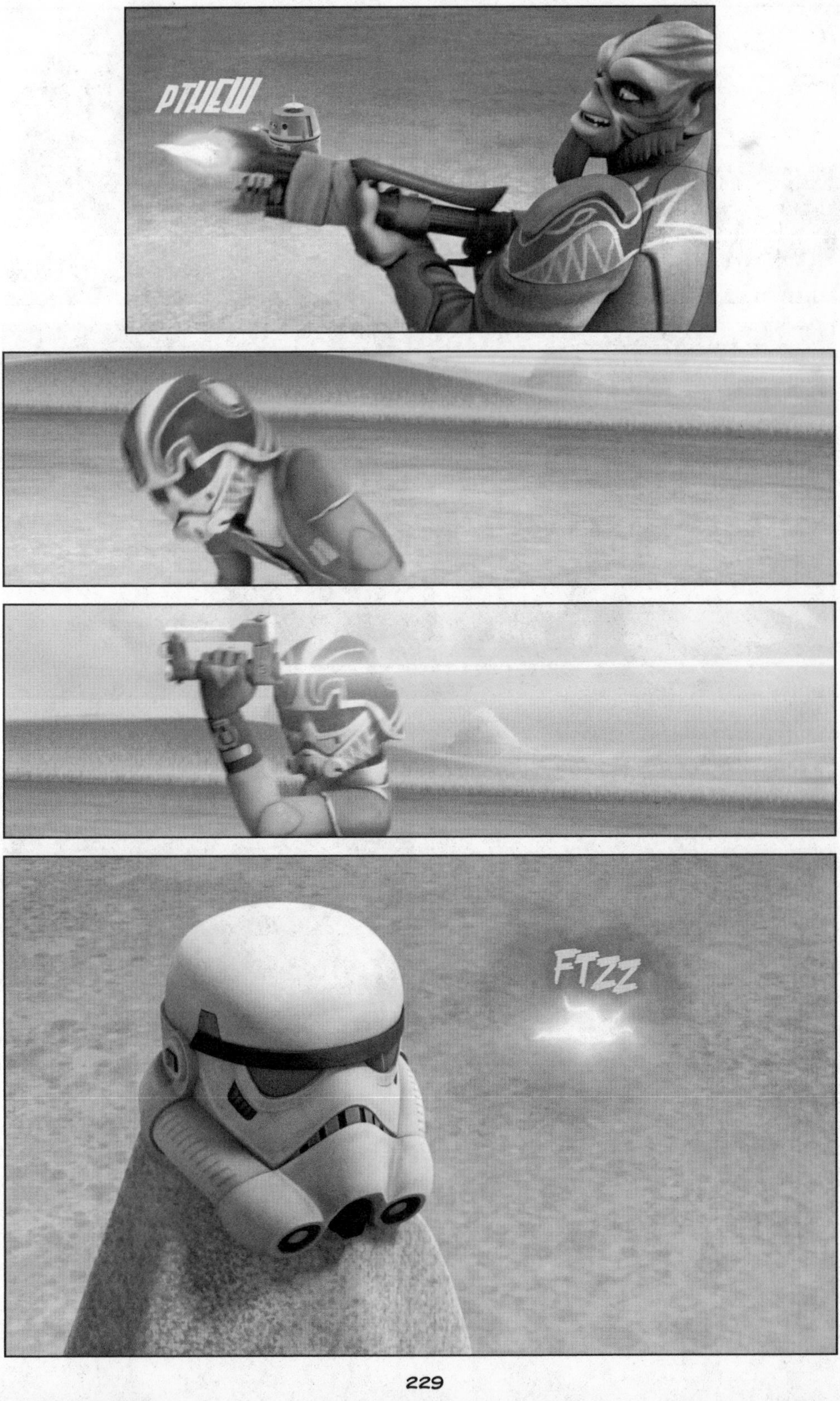
PTHEW
FTZZ

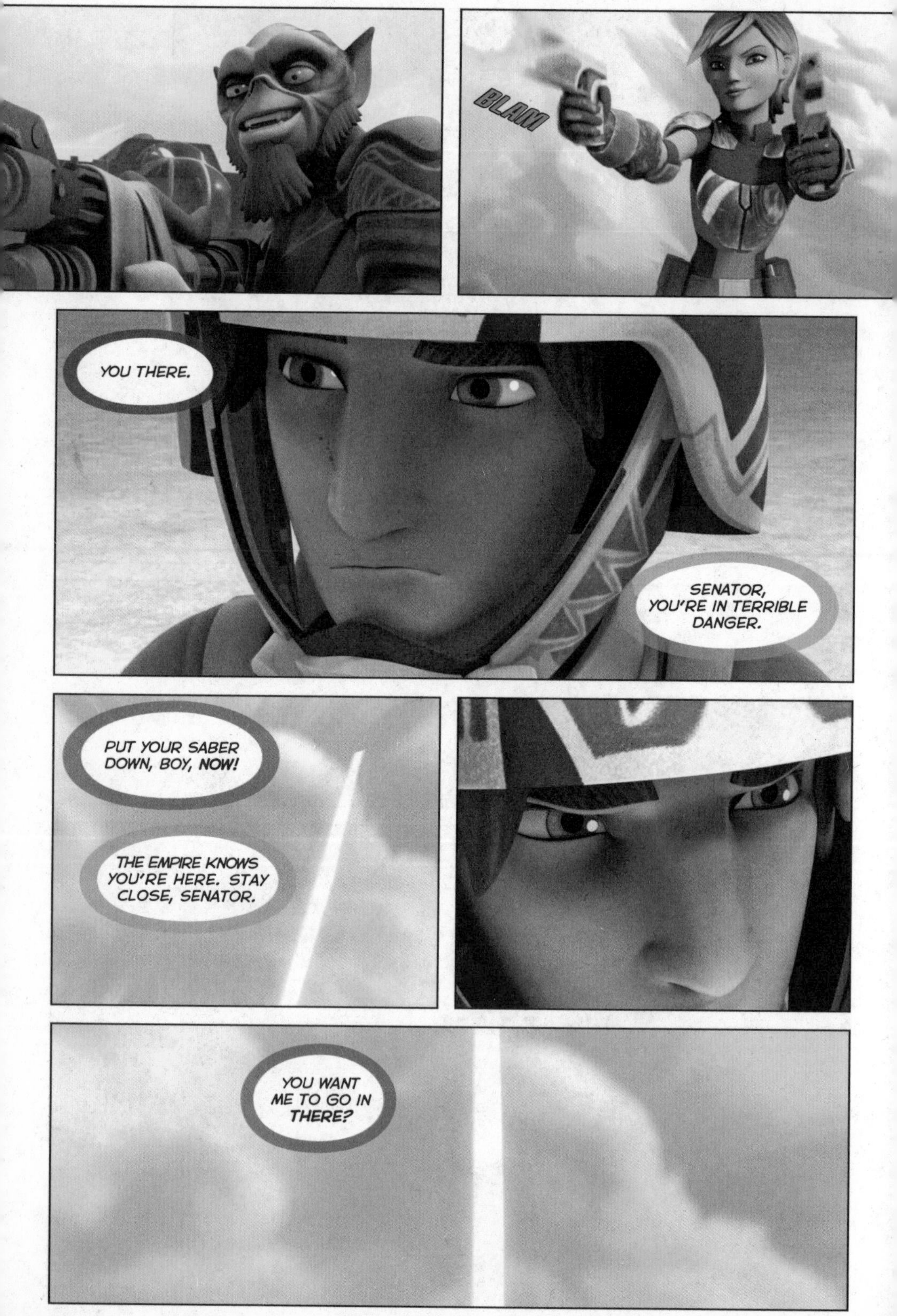
BLAM
YOU THERE.
SENATOR, YOU'RE IN TERRIBLE DANGER.
PUT YOUR SABER DOWN, BOY, NOW!
THE EMPIRE KNOWS YOU'RE HERE. STAY CLOSE, SENATOR.
YOU WANT ME TO GO IN THERE?

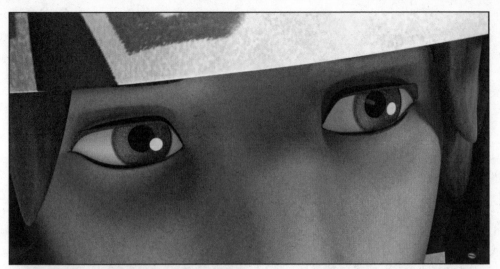

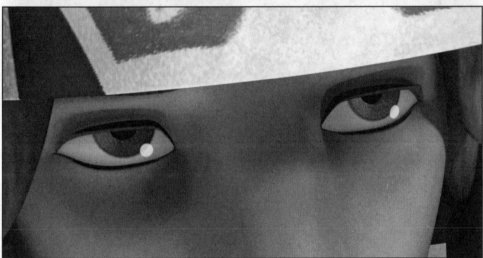

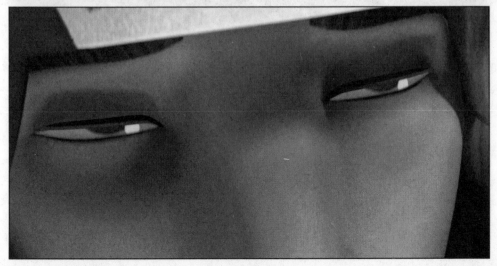

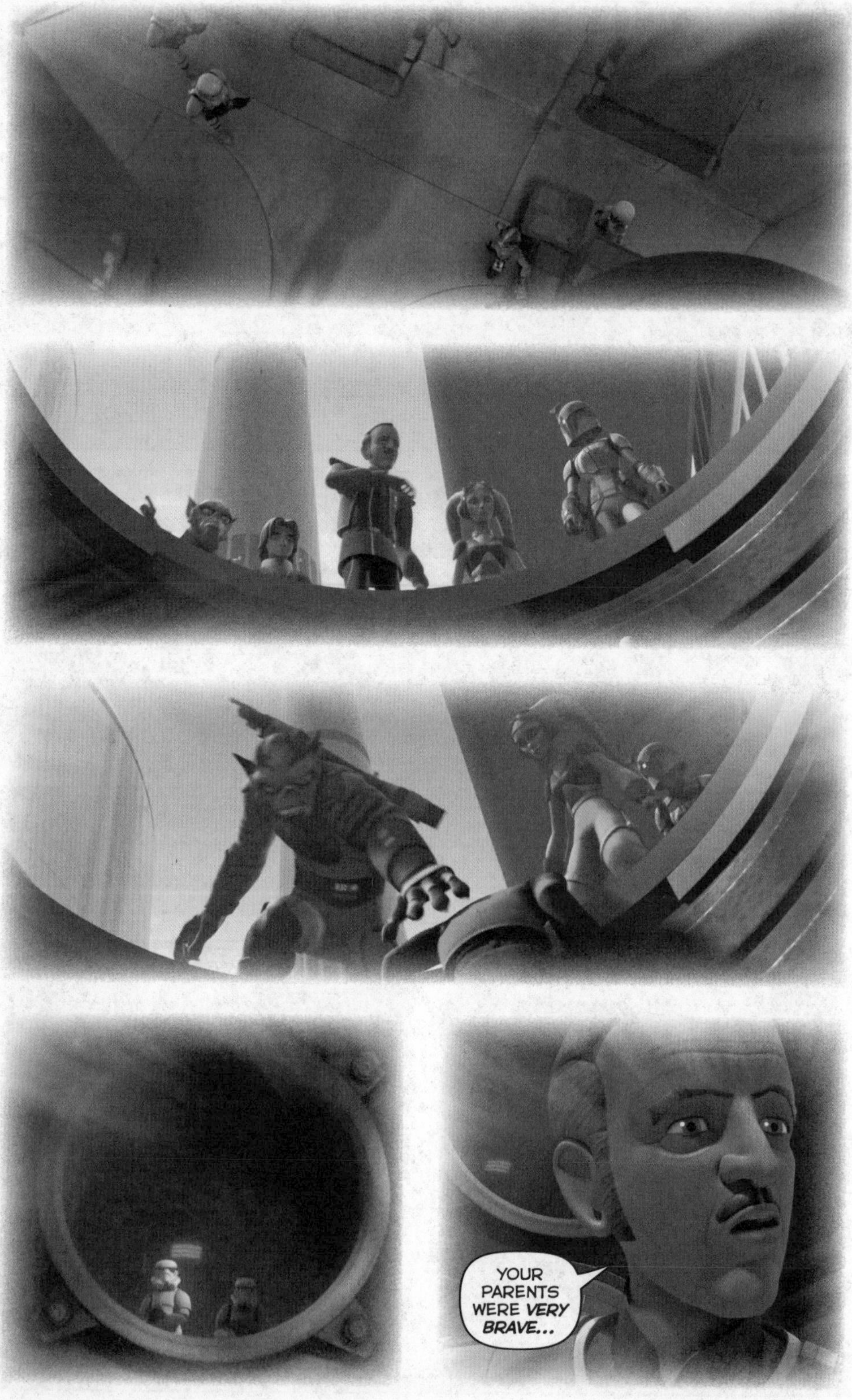
YOUR PARENTS WERE VERY BRAVE...

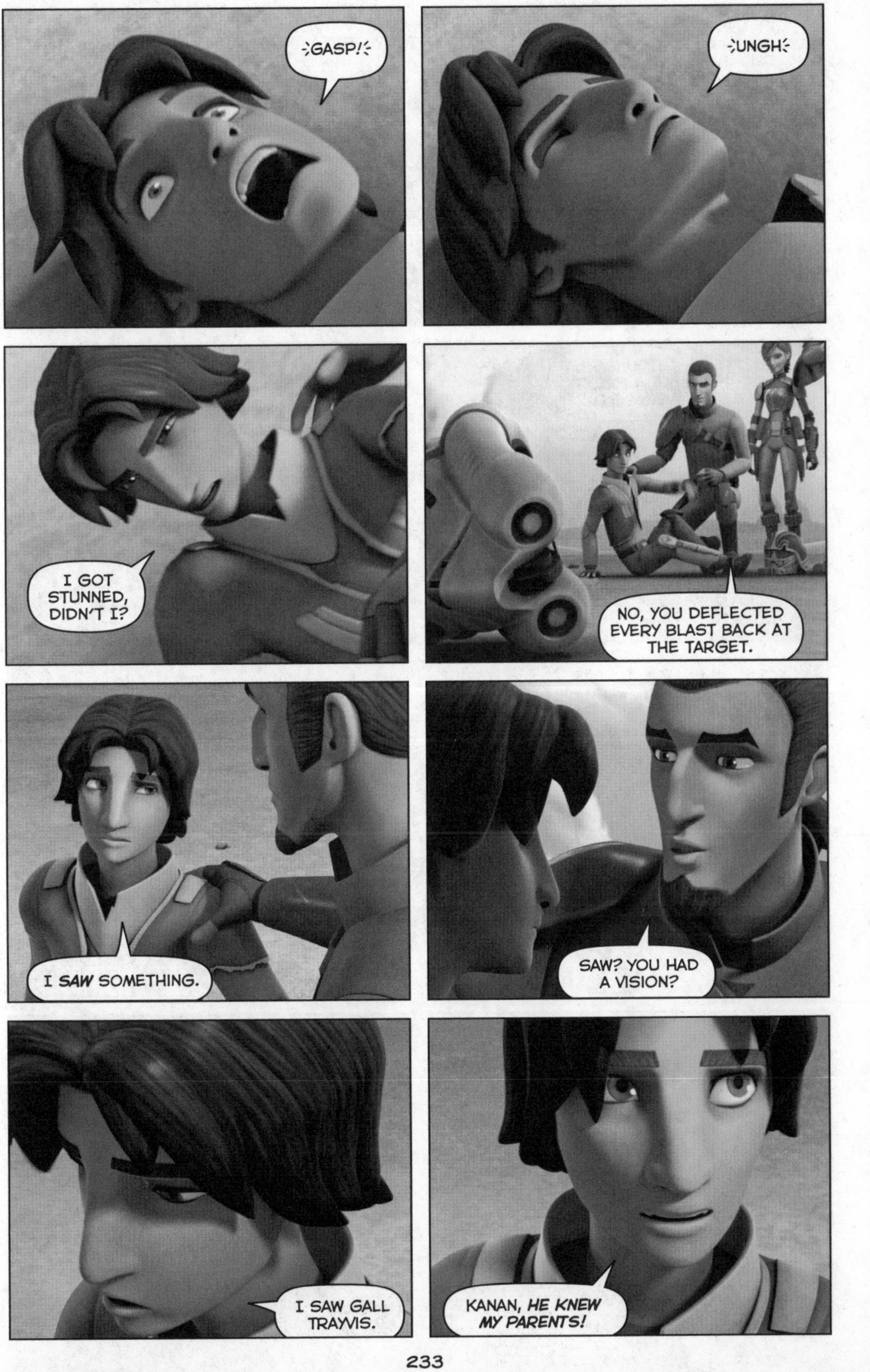

GASP!
UNGH
I GOT STUNNED, DIDN'T I?
NO, YOU DEFLECTED EVERY BLAST BACK AT THE TARGET.
I *SAW* SOMETHING.
SAW? YOU HAD A VISION?
I SAW GALL TRAYVIS.
KANAN, *HE KNEW MY PARENTS!*

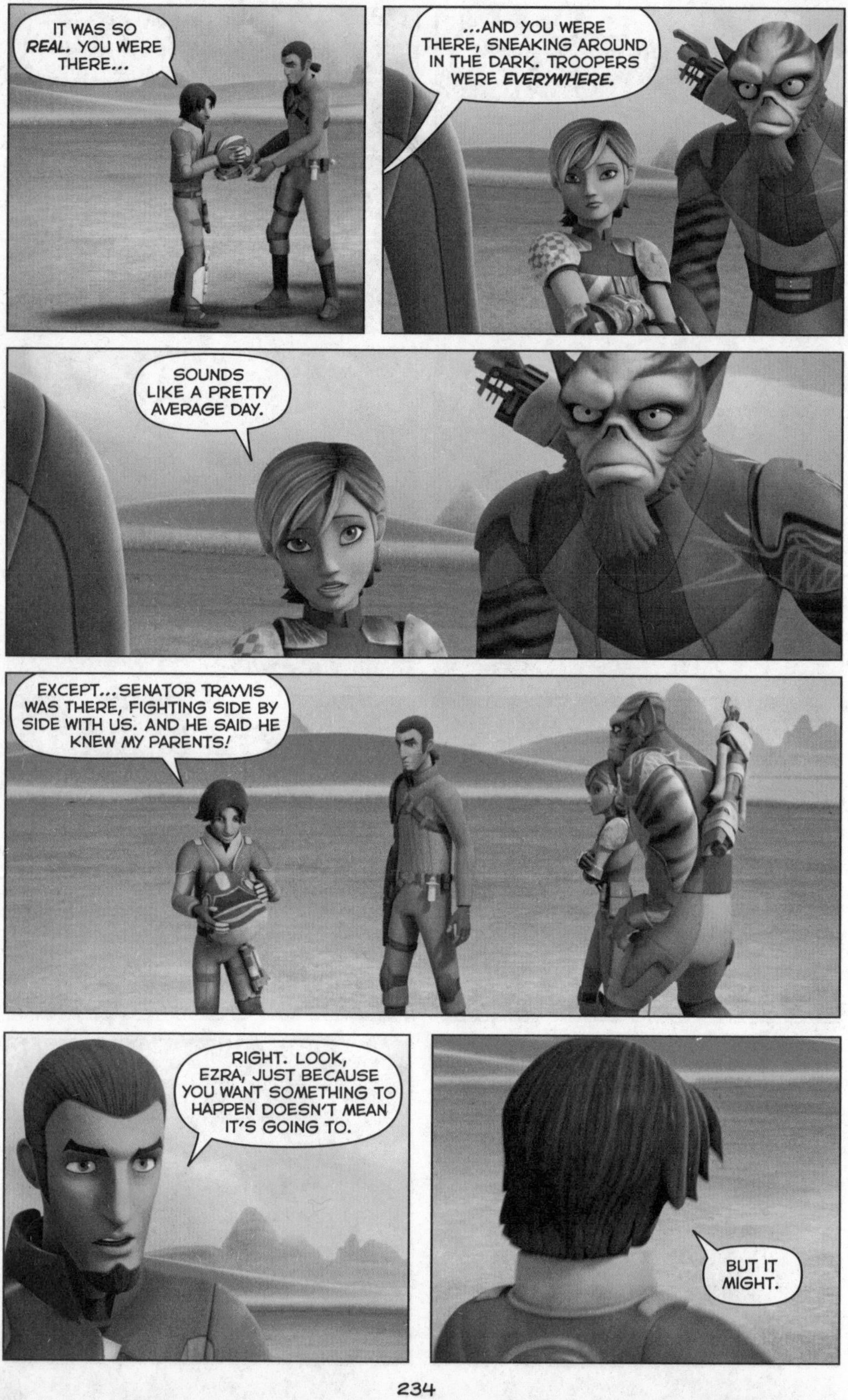
IT WAS SO REAL. YOU WERE THERE...
...AND YOU WERE THERE, SNEAKING AROUND IN THE DARK. TROOPERS WERE EVERYWHERE.
SOUNDS LIKE A PRETTY AVERAGE DAY.
EXCEPT...SENATOR TRAYVIS WAS THERE, FIGHTING SIDE BY SIDE WITH US. AND HE SAID HE KNEW MY PARENTS!
RIGHT. LOOK, EZRA, JUST BECAUSE YOU WANT SOMETHING TO HAPPEN DOESN'T MEAN IT'S GOING TO.
BUT IT MIGHT.

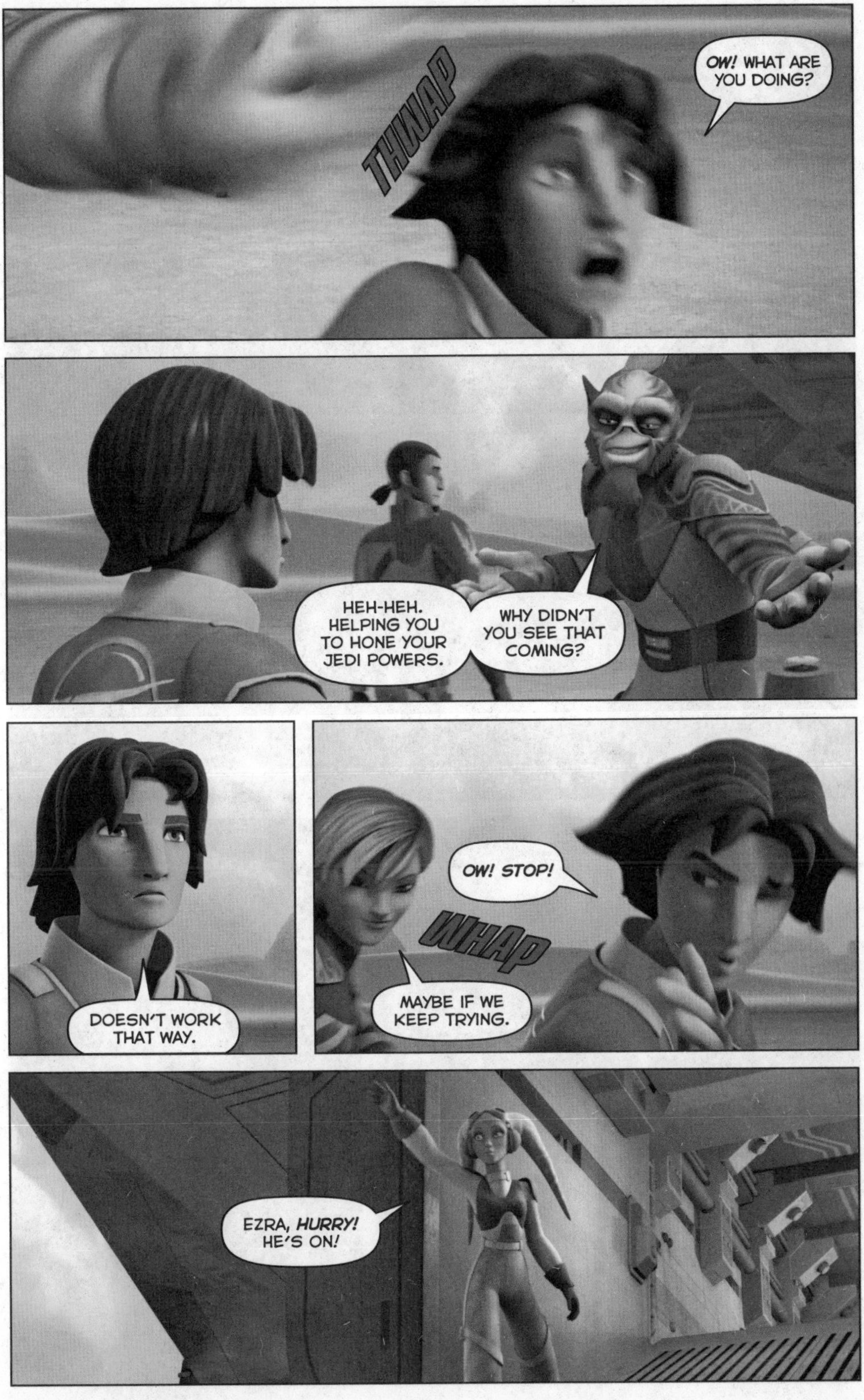
OW! WHAT ARE YOU DOING?
THWAP
HEH-HEH. HELPING YOU TO HONE YOUR JEDI POWERS.
WHY DIDN'T YOU SEE THAT COMING?
DOESN'T WORK THAT WAY.
OW! STOP!
WHAP
MAYBE IF WE KEEP TRYING.
EZRA, HURRY! HE'S ON!

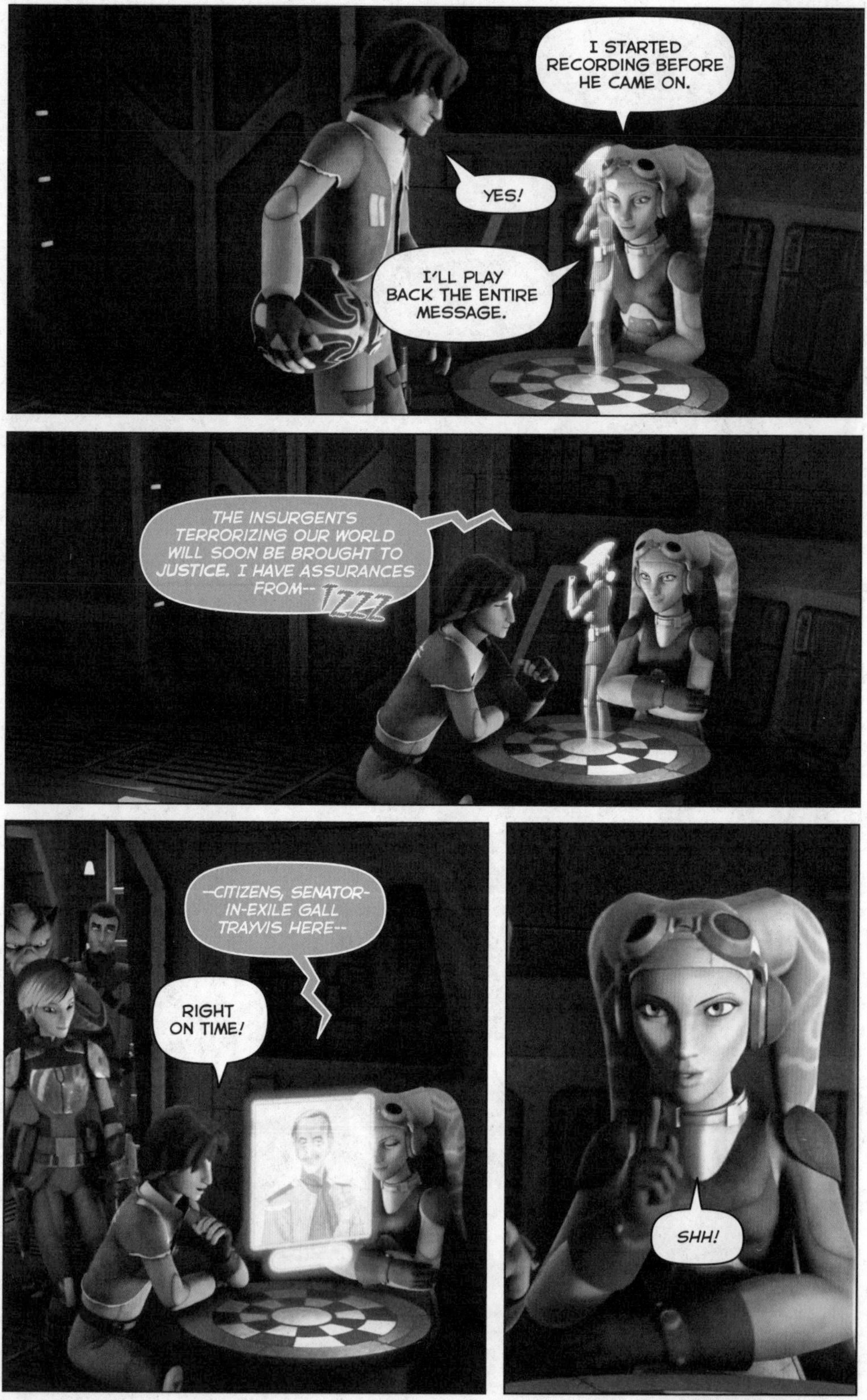
I STARTED RECORDING BEFORE HE CAME ON.
YES!
I'LL PLAY BACK THE ENTIRE MESSAGE.
THE INSURGENTS TERRORIZING OUR WORLD WILL SOON BE BROUGHT TO JUSTICE. I HAVE ASSURANCES FROM--
TZZZ
--CITIZENS, SENATOR-IN-EXILE GALL TRAYVIS HERE--
RIGHT ON TIME!
SHH!

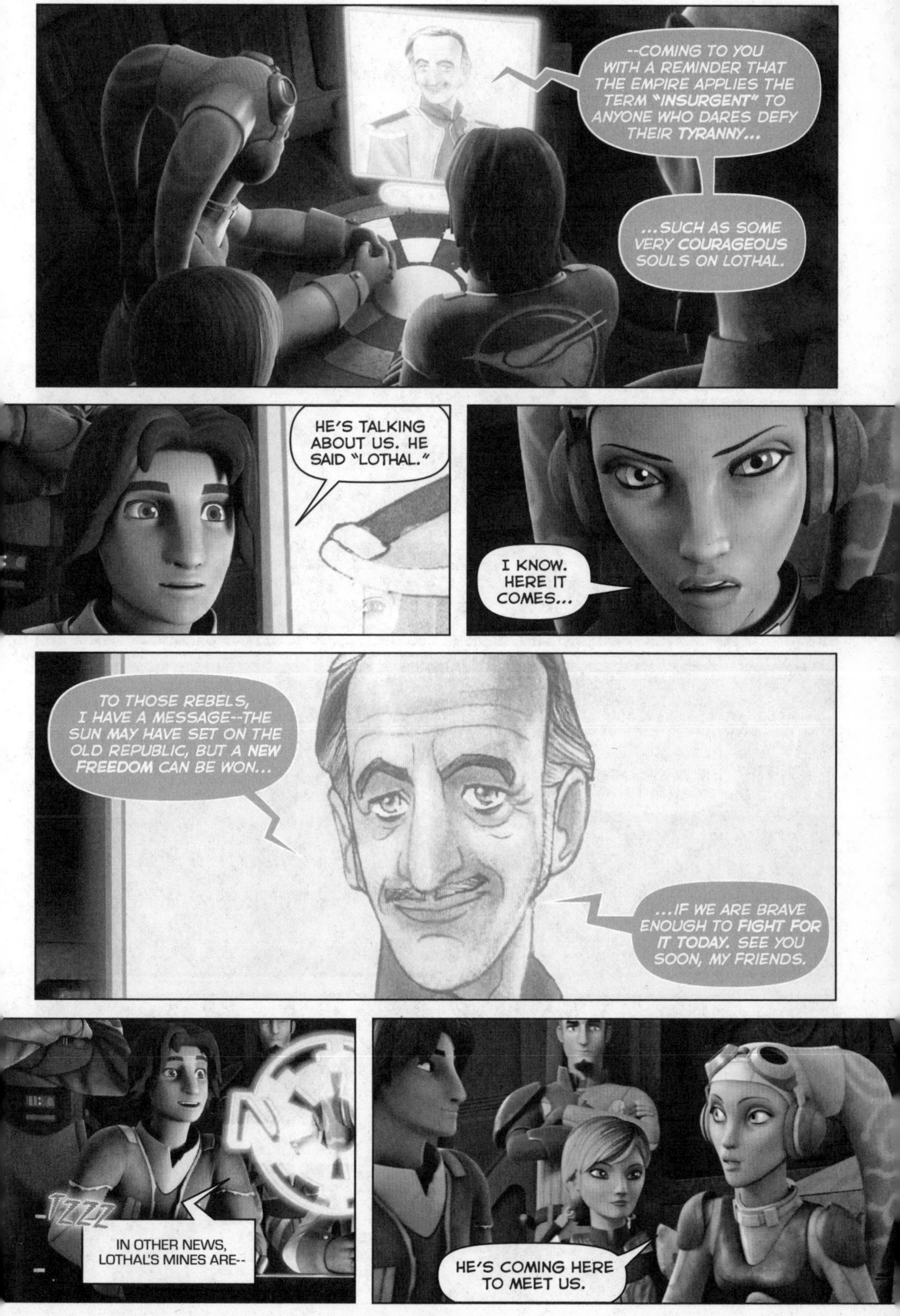
--COMING TO YOU WITH A REMINDER THAT THE EMPIRE APPLIES THE TERM "INSURGENT" TO ANYONE WHO DARES DEFY THEIR TYRANNY...
...SUCH AS SOME VERY COURAGEOUS SOULS ON LOTHAL.
HE'S TALKING ABOUT US. HE SAID "LOTHAL."
I KNOW. HERE IT COMES...
TO THOSE REBELS, I HAVE A MESSAGE--THE SUN MAY HAVE SET ON THE OLD REPUBLIC, BUT A NEW FREEDOM CAN BE WON...
...IF WE ARE BRAVE ENOUGH TO FIGHT FOR IT TODAY. SEE YOU SOON, MY FRIENDS.
TZZZ
IN OTHER NEWS, LOTHAL'S MINES ARE--
HE'S COMING HERE TO MEET US.

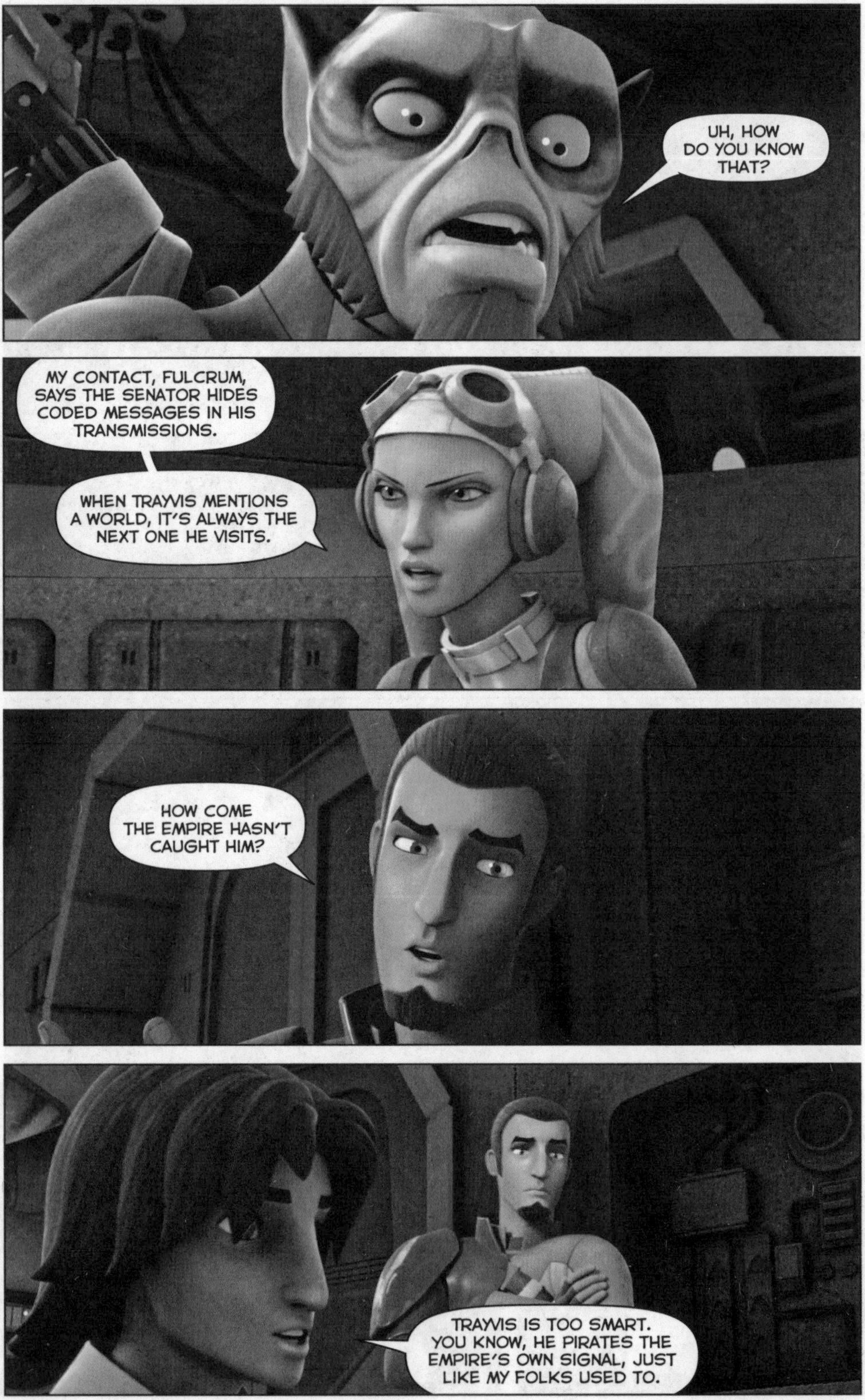
UH, HOW DO YOU KNOW THAT?
MY CONTACT, FULCRUM, SAYS THE SENATOR HIDES CODED MESSAGES IN HIS TRANSMISSIONS.
WHEN TRAYVIS MENTIONS A WORLD, IT'S ALWAYS THE NEXT ONE HE VISITS.
HOW COME THE EMPIRE HASN'T CAUGHT HIM?
TRAYVIS IS TOO SMART. YOU KNOW, HE PIRATES THE EMPIRE'S OWN SIGNAL, JUST LIKE MY FOLKS USED TO.

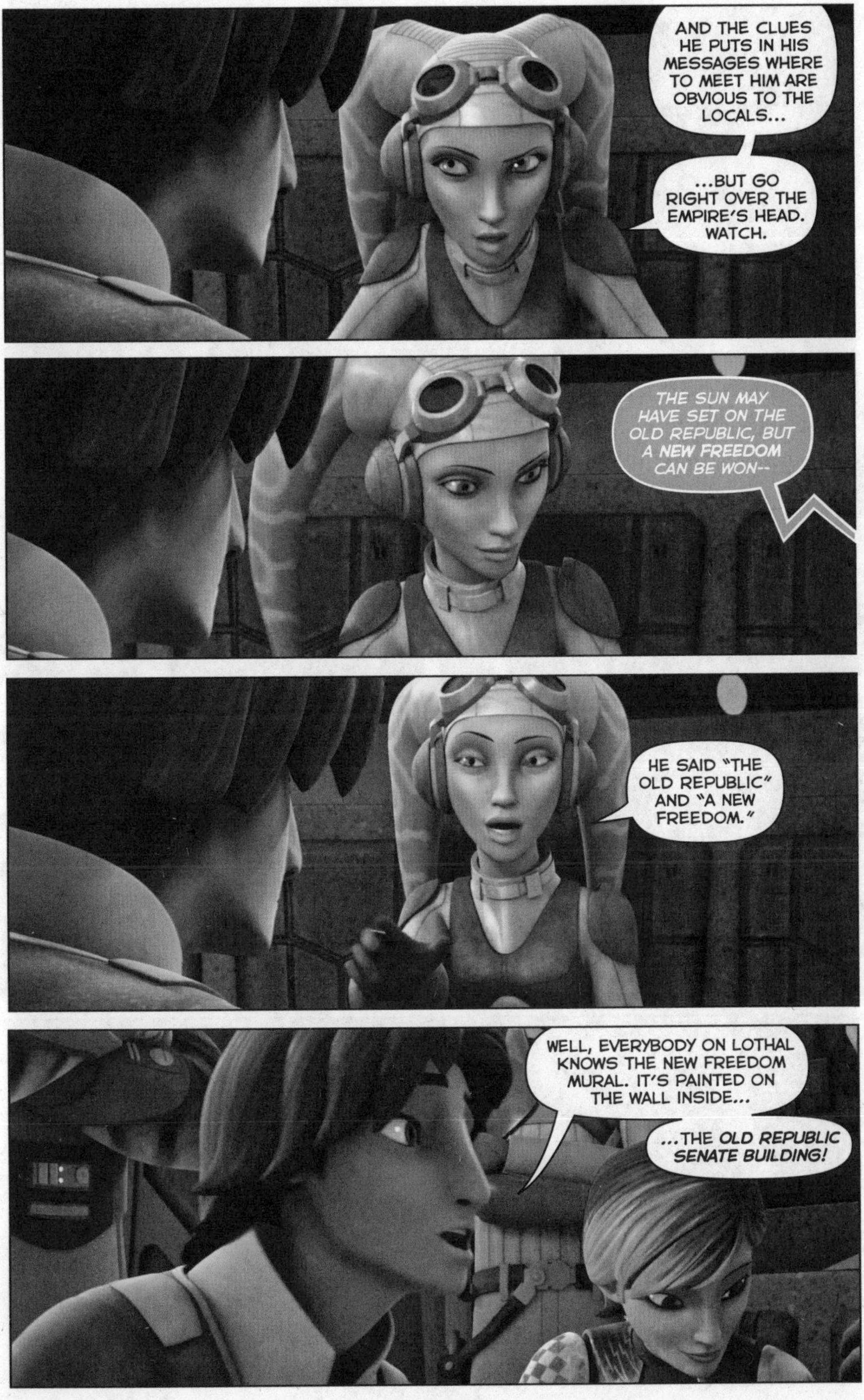
AND THE CLUES HE PUTS IN HIS MESSAGES WHERE TO MEET HIM ARE OBVIOUS TO THE LOCALS...
...BUT GO RIGHT OVER THE EMPIRE'S HEAD. WATCH.
THE SUN MAY HAVE SET ON THE OLD REPUBLIC, BUT A NEW FREEDOM CAN BE WON--
HE SAID "THE OLD REPUBLIC" AND "A NEW FREEDOM."
WELL, EVERYBODY ON LOTHAL KNOWS THE NEW FREEDOM MURAL. IT'S PAINTED ON THE WALL INSIDE...
...THE OLD REPUBLIC SENATE BUILDING!

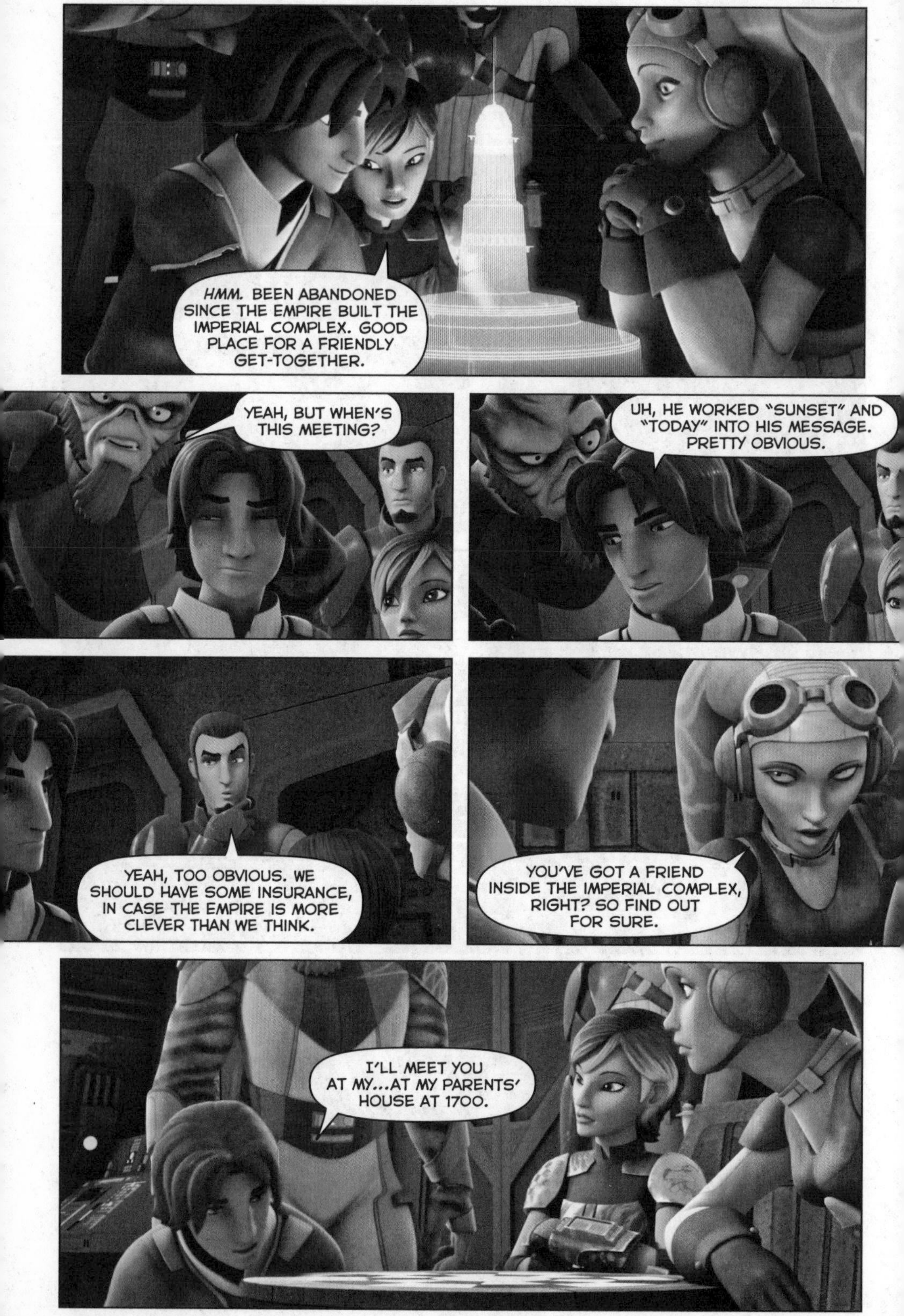
HMM. BEEN ABANDONED SINCE THE EMPIRE BUILT THE IMPERIAL COMPLEX. GOOD PLACE FOR A FRIENDLY GET-TOGETHER.
YEAH, BUT WHEN'S THIS MEETING?
UH, HE WORKED "SUNSET" AND "TODAY" INTO HIS MESSAGE. PRETTY OBVIOUS.
YEAH, TOO OBVIOUS. WE SHOULD HAVE SOME INSURANCE, IN CASE THE EMPIRE IS MORE CLEVER THAN WE THINK.
YOU'VE GOT A FRIEND INSIDE THE IMPERIAL COMPLEX, RIGHT? SO FIND OUT FOR SURE.
I'LL MEET YOU AT MY...AT MY PARENTS' HOUSE AT 1700.

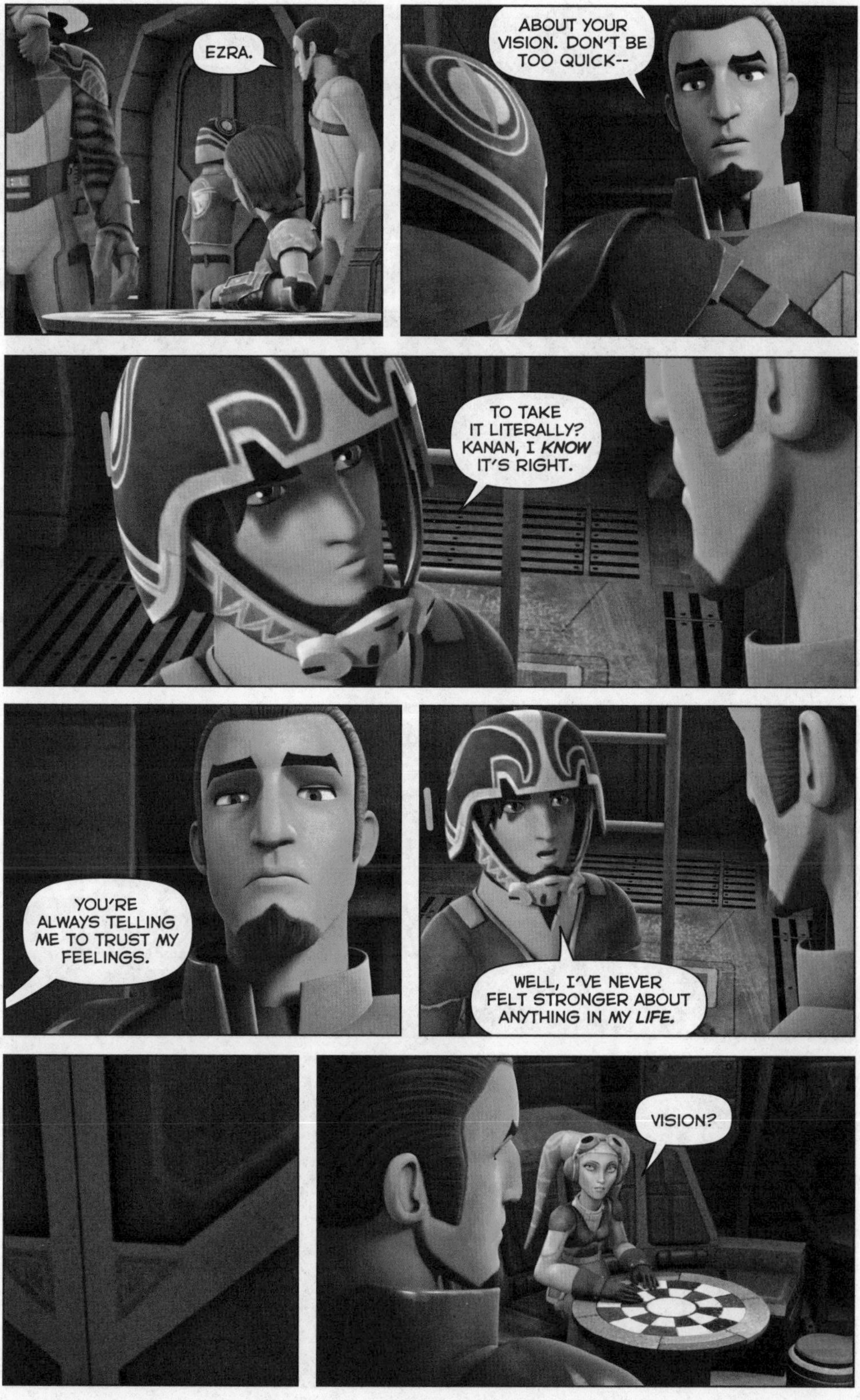
EZRA.
ABOUT YOUR VISION. DON'T BE TOO QUICK--
TO TAKE IT LITERALLY? KANAN, I *KNOW* IT'S RIGHT.
YOU'RE ALWAYS TELLING ME TO TRUST MY FEELINGS.
WELL, I'VE NEVER FELT STRONGER ABOUT ANYTHING IN *MY LIFE.*
VISION?

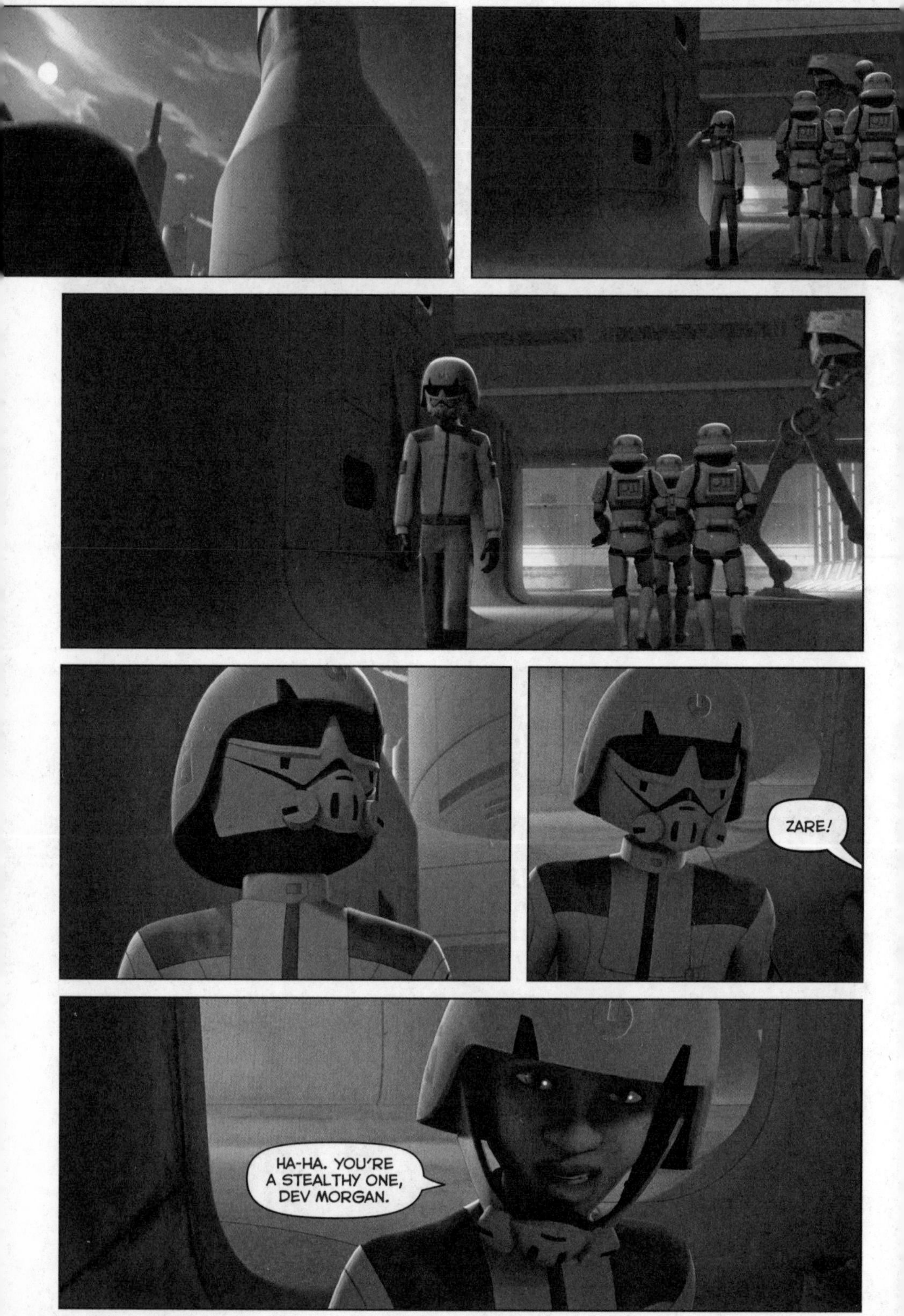
ZARE!
HA-HA. YOU'RE A STEALTHY ONE, DEV MORGAN.

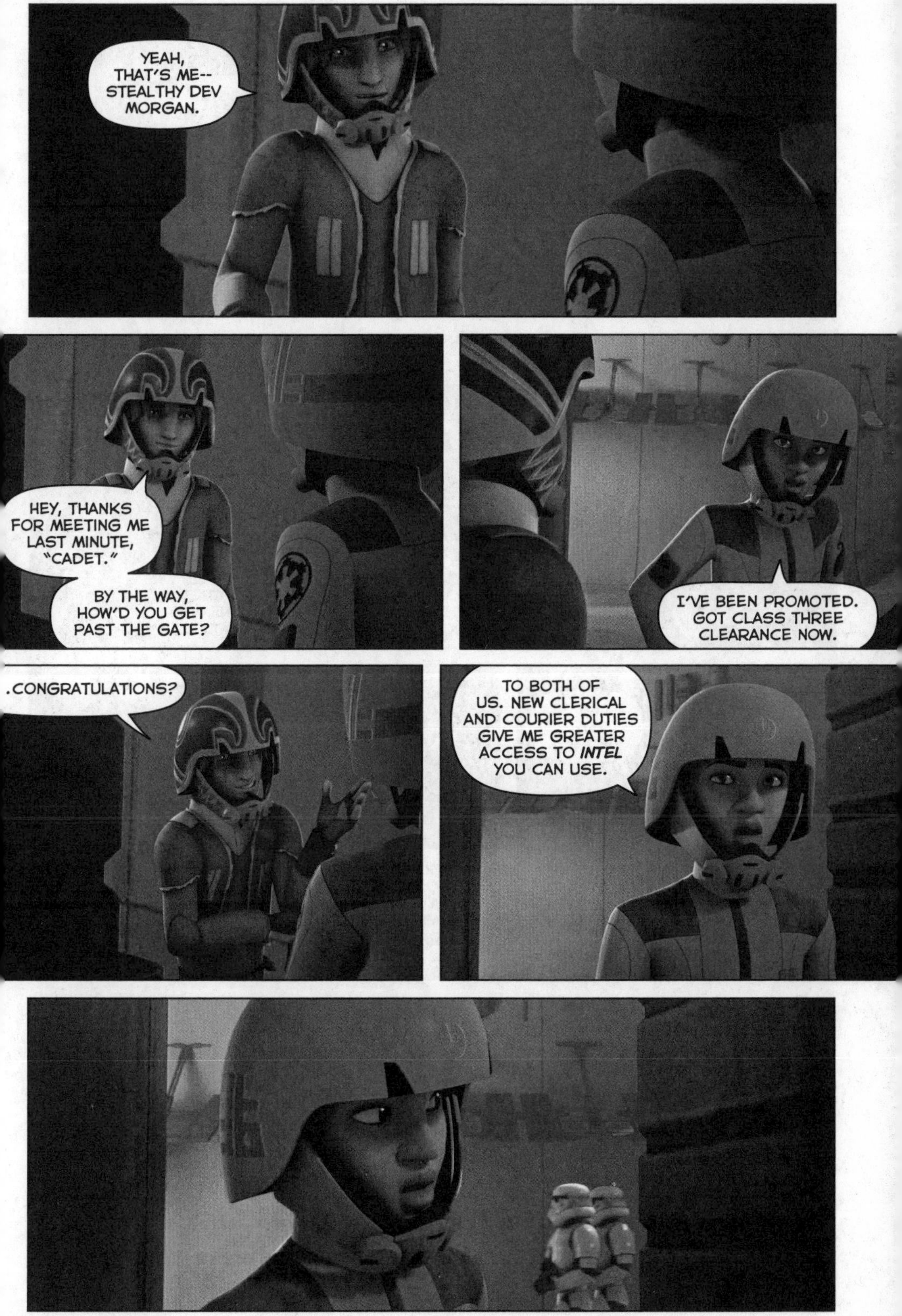
YEAH, THAT'S ME-- STEALTHY DEV MORGAN.
HEY, THANKS FOR MEETING ME LAST MINUTE, "CADET."
BY THE WAY, HOW'D YOU GET PAST THE GATE?
I'VE BEEN PROMOTED. GOT CLASS THREE CLEARANCE NOW.
.CONGRATULATIONS?
TO BOTH OF US. NEW CLERICAL AND COURIER DUTIES GIVE ME GREATER ACCESS TO *INTEL* YOU CAN USE.

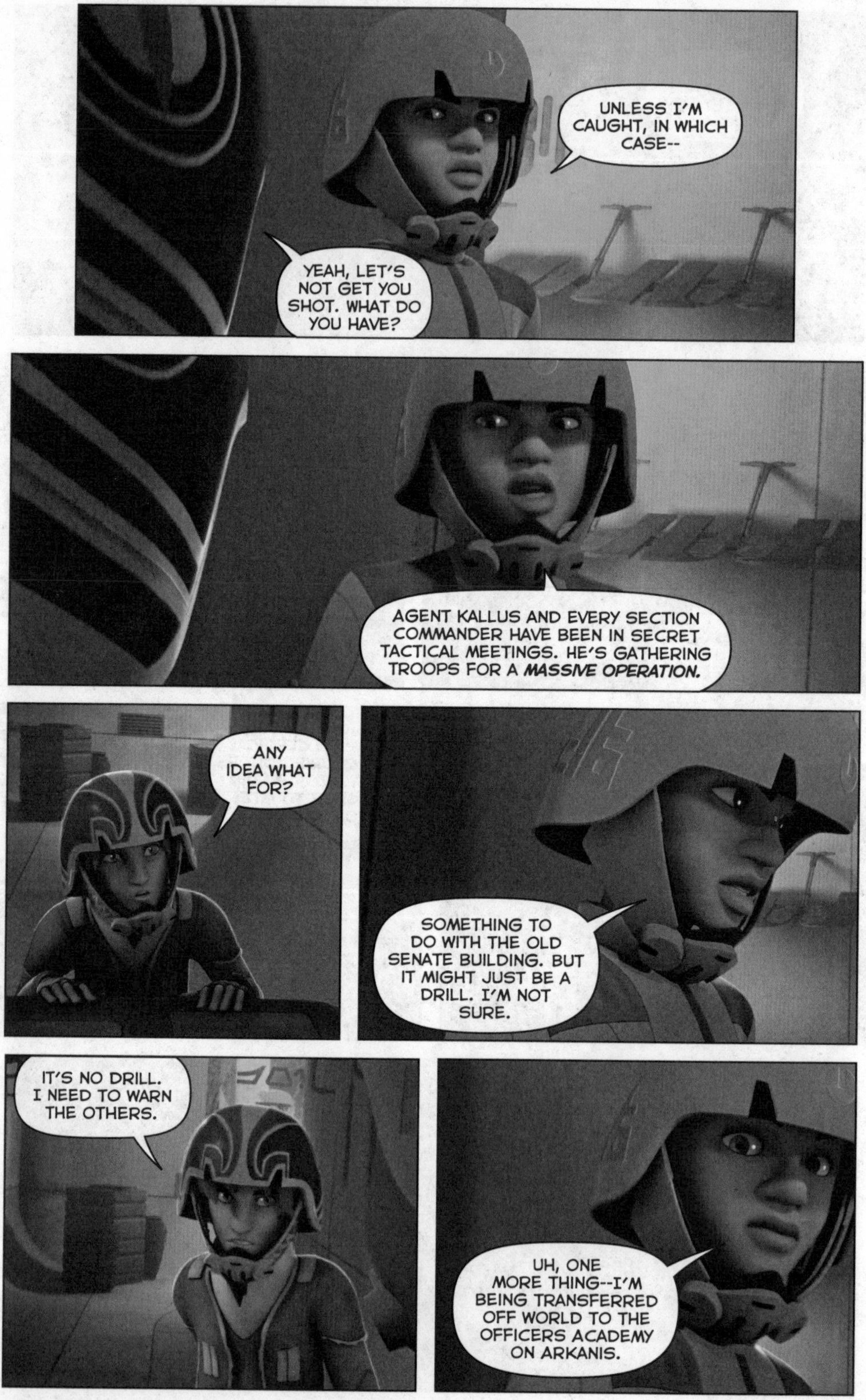
UNLESS I'M CAUGHT, IN WHICH CASE--
YEAH, LET'S NOT GET YOU SHOT. WHAT DO YOU HAVE?
AGENT KALLUS AND EVERY SECTION COMMANDER HAVE BEEN IN SECRET TACTICAL MEETINGS. HE'S GATHERING TROOPS FOR A *MASSIVE OPERATION.*
ANY IDEA WHAT FOR?
SOMETHING TO DO WITH THE OLD SENATE BUILDING. BUT IT MIGHT JUST BE A DRILL. I'M NOT SURE.
IT'S NO DRILL. I NEED TO WARN THE OTHERS.
UH, ONE MORE THING--I'M BEING TRANSFERRED OFF WORLD TO THE OFFICERS ACADEMY ON ARKANIS.

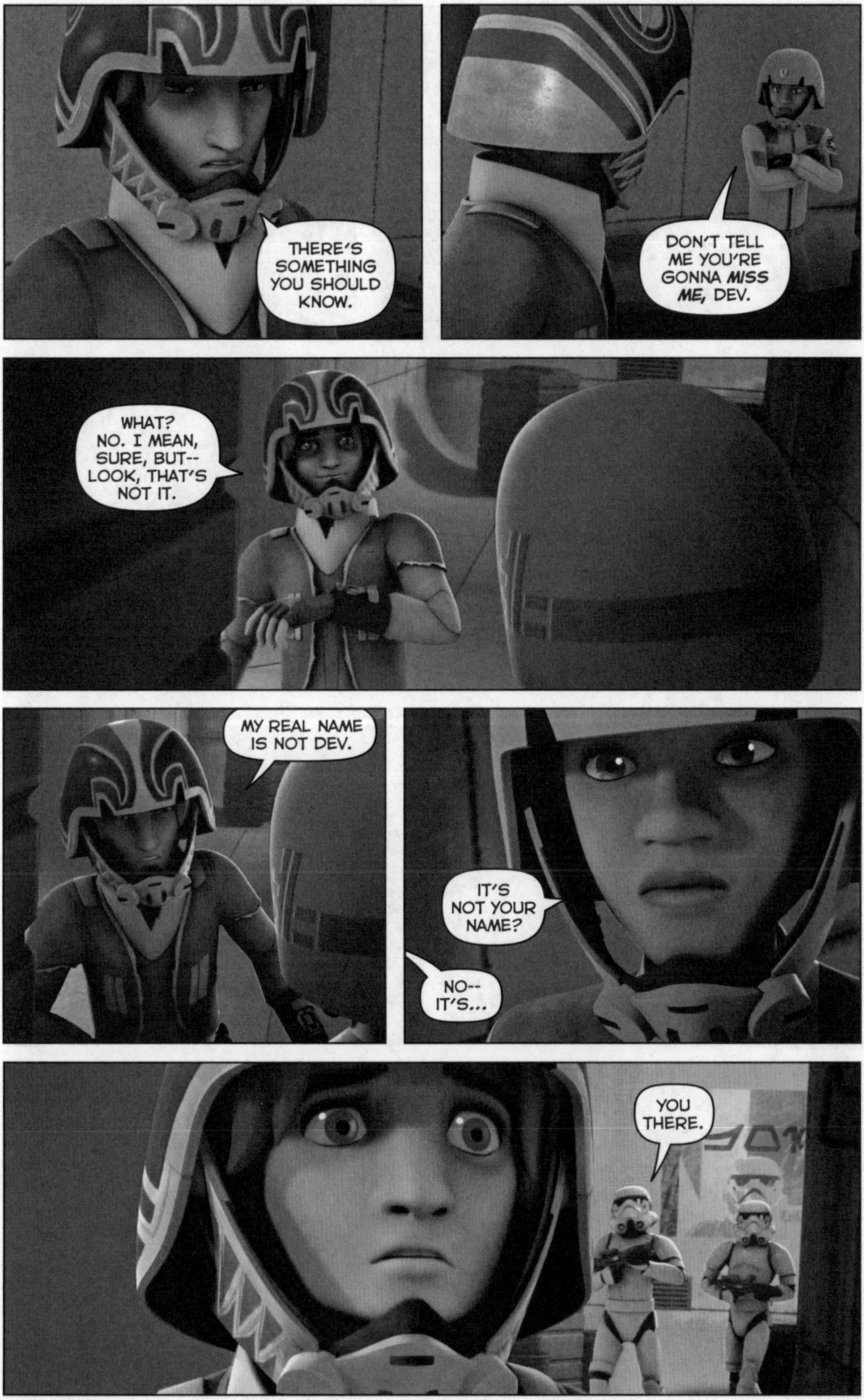
THERE'S SOMETHING YOU SHOULD KNOW.
DON'T TELL ME YOU'RE GONNA *MISS ME,* DEV.
WHAT? NO. I MEAN, SURE, BUT-- LOOK, THAT'S NOT IT.
MY REAL NAME IS NOT DEV.
IT'S NOT YOUR NAME?
NO-- IT'S...
YOU THERE.

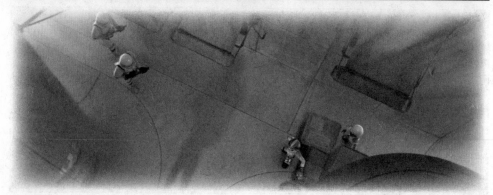

OH, NO! MY VISION!

NO TIME TO EXPLAIN.

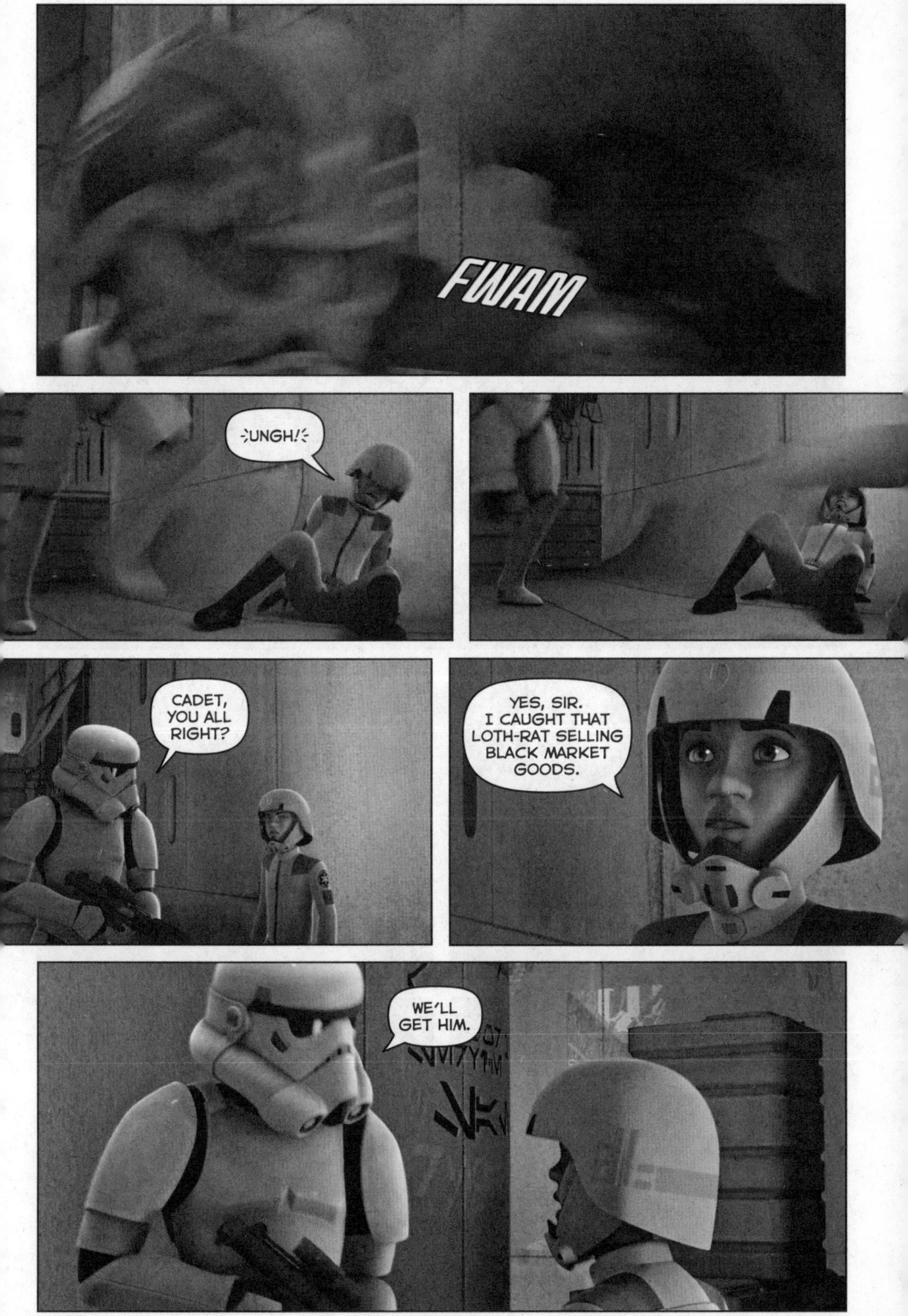
FWAM
UNGH!
CADET, YOU ALL RIGHT?
YES, SIR. I CAUGHT THAT LOTH-RAT SELLING BLACK MARKET GOODS.
WE'LL GET HIM.

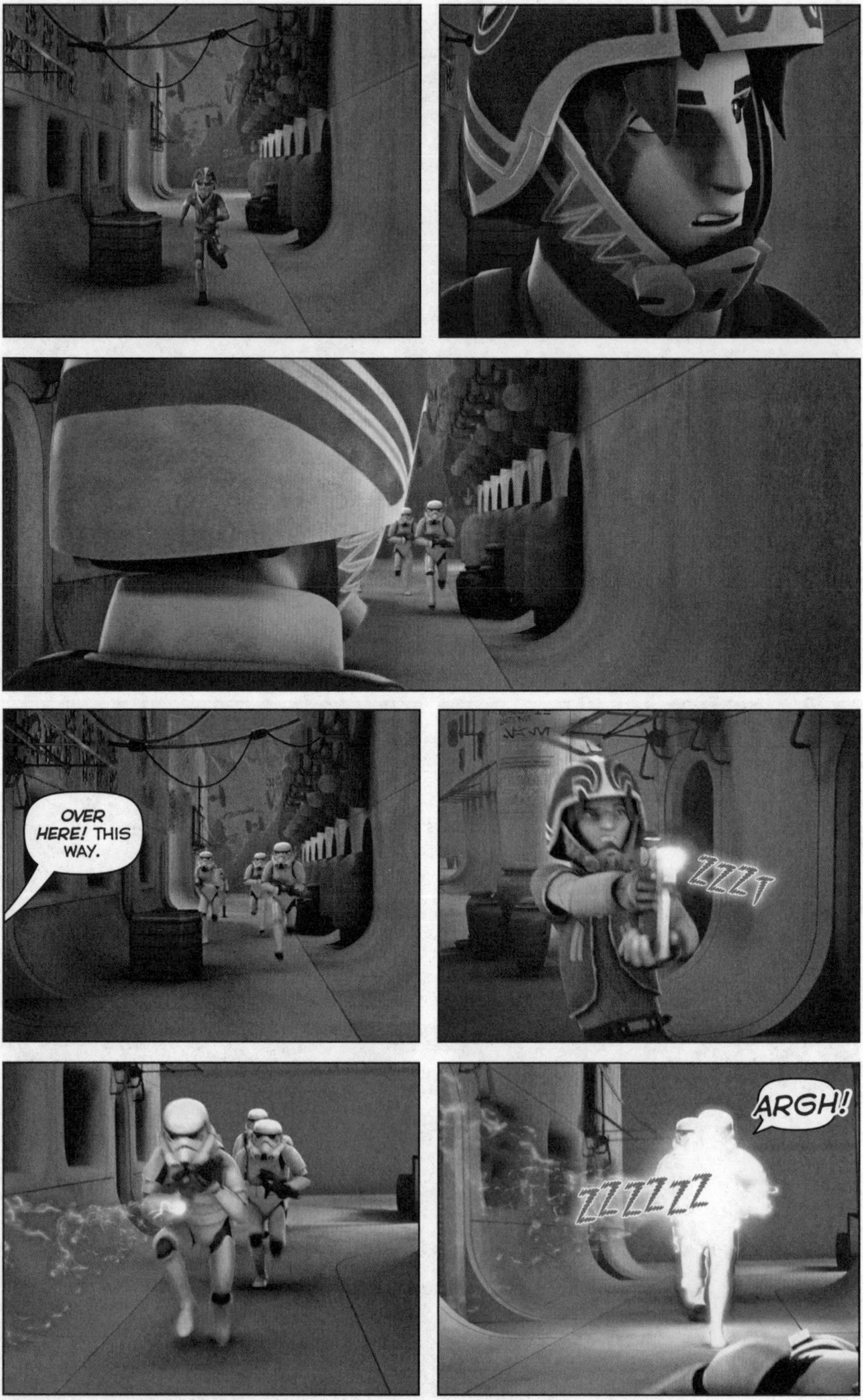
OVER HERE! THIS WAY.
ZZZT
ARGH!
ZZZZZZ

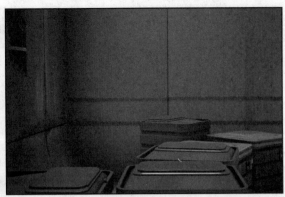

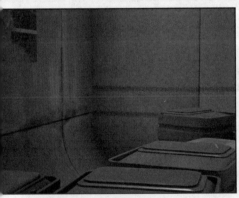

WE WERE TRACKING AN
INSURGENT, BUT THE SEARCH
WAS INCONCLUSIVE.

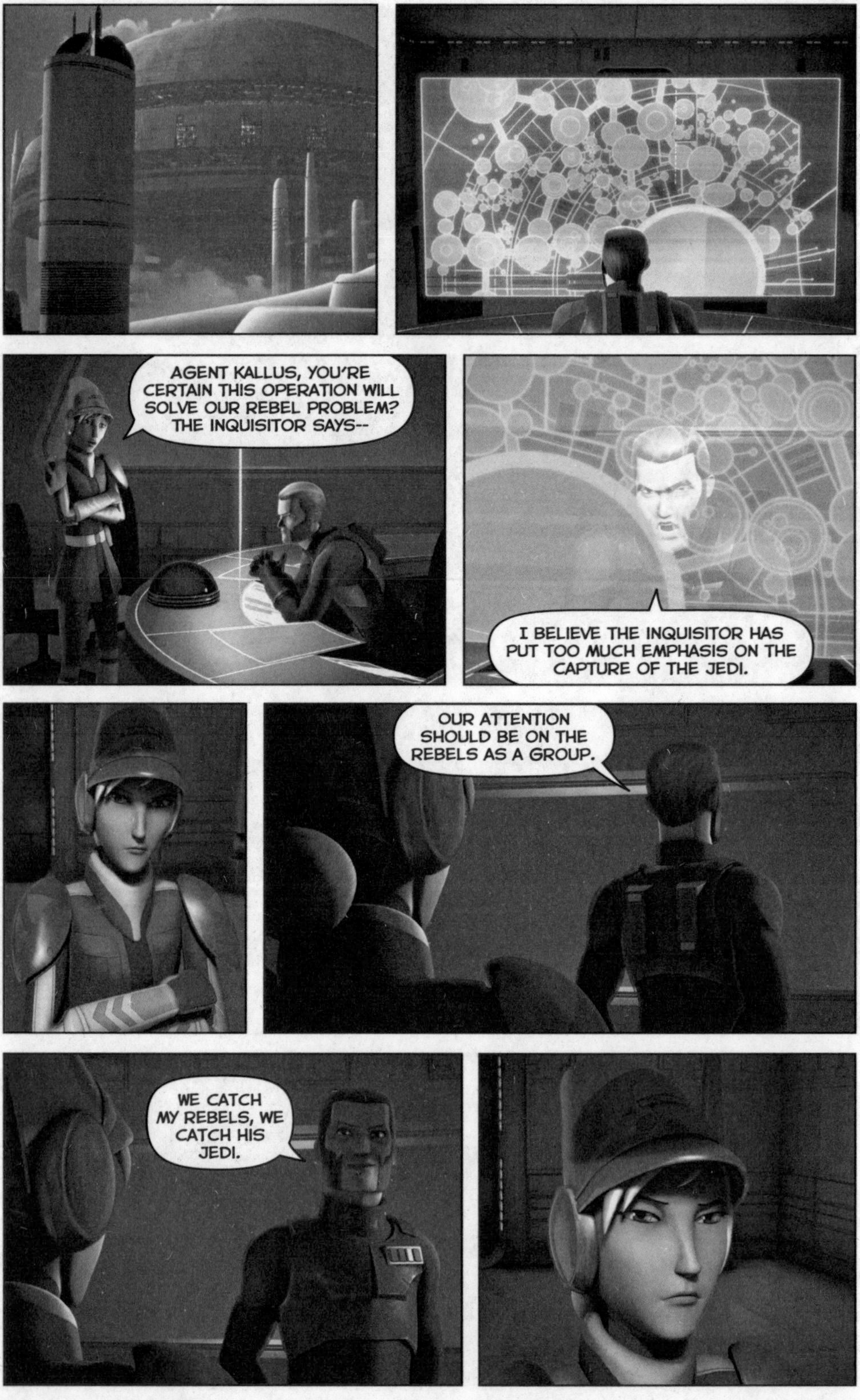
AGENT KALLUS, YOU'RE CERTAIN THIS OPERATION WILL SOLVE OUR REBEL PROBLEM? THE INQUISITOR SAYS--
I BELIEVE THE INQUISITOR HAS PUT TOO MUCH EMPHASIS ON THE CAPTURE OF THE JEDI.
OUR ATTENTION SHOULD BE ON THE REBELS AS A GROUP.
WE CATCH MY REBELS, WE CATCH HIS JEDI.

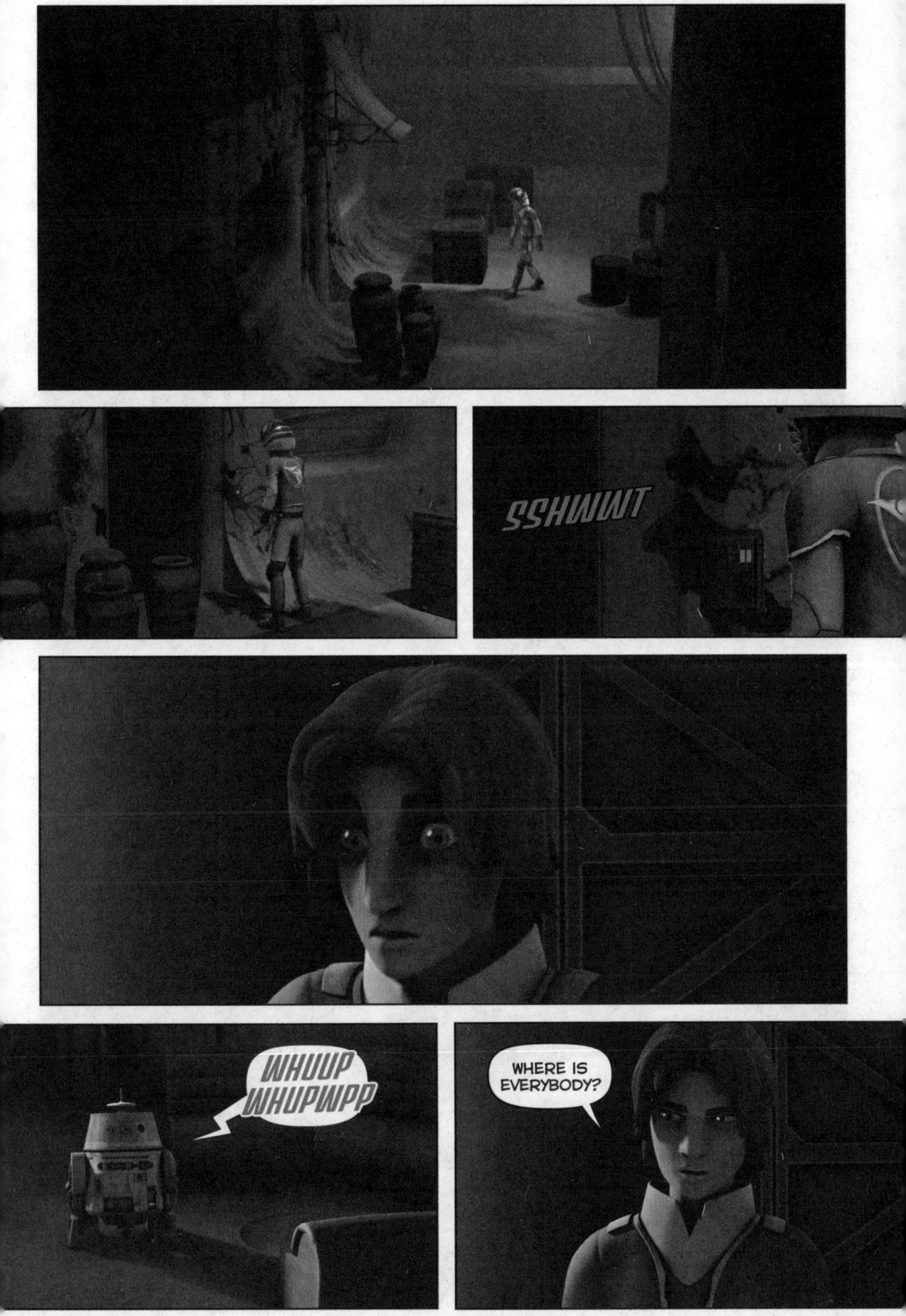
SSHWWT
WHUUP WHUPWPP
WHERE IS EVERYBODY?

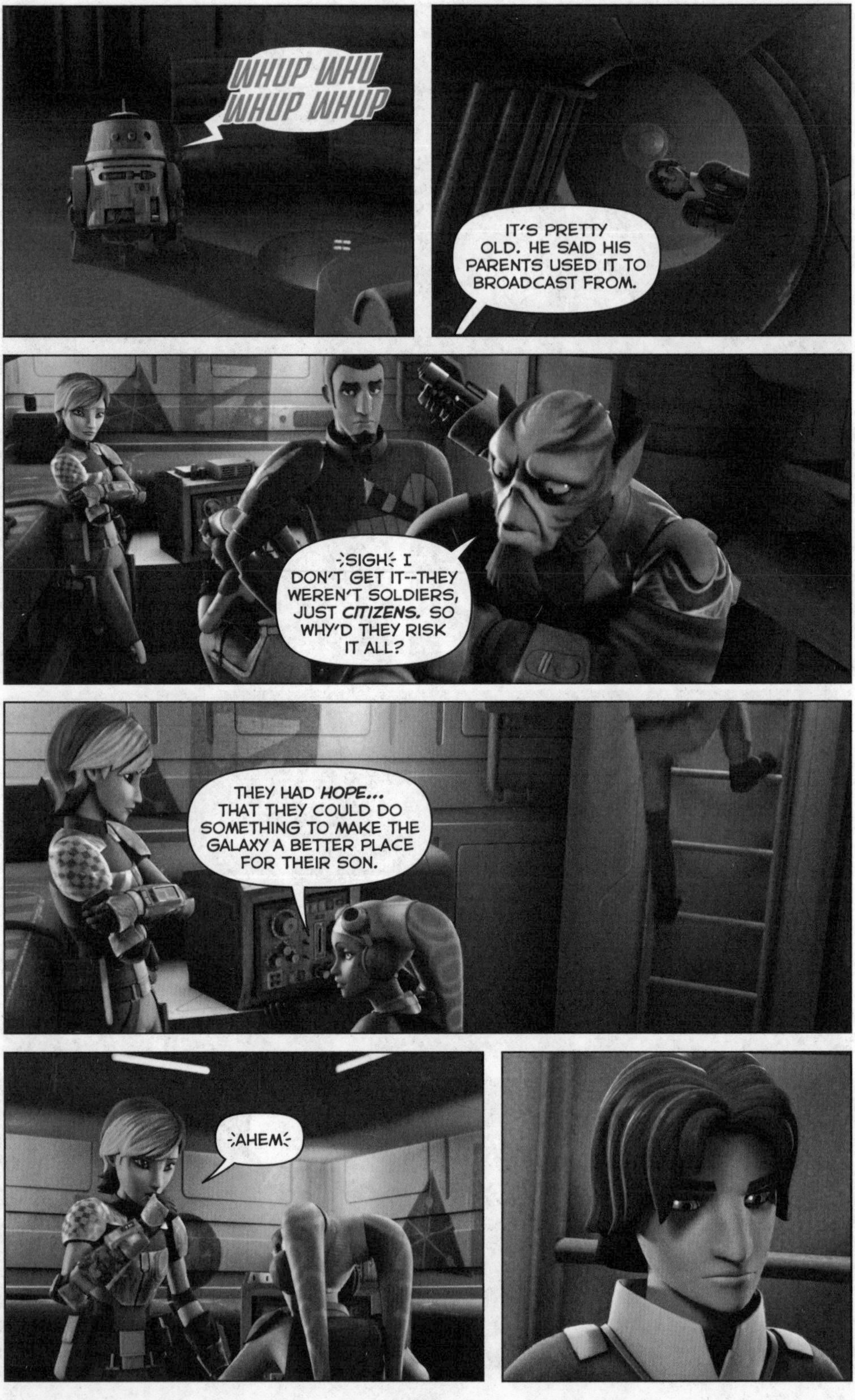
WHUP WHU WHUP WHUP
IT'S PRETTY OLD. HE SAID HIS PARENTS USED IT TO BROADCAST FROM.
SIGH I DON'T GET IT--THEY WEREN'T SOLDIERS, JUST *CITIZENS.* SO WHY'D THEY RISK IT ALL?
THEY HAD *HOPE...* THAT THEY COULD DO SOMETHING TO MAKE THE GALAXY A BETTER PLACE FOR THEIR SON.
AHEM

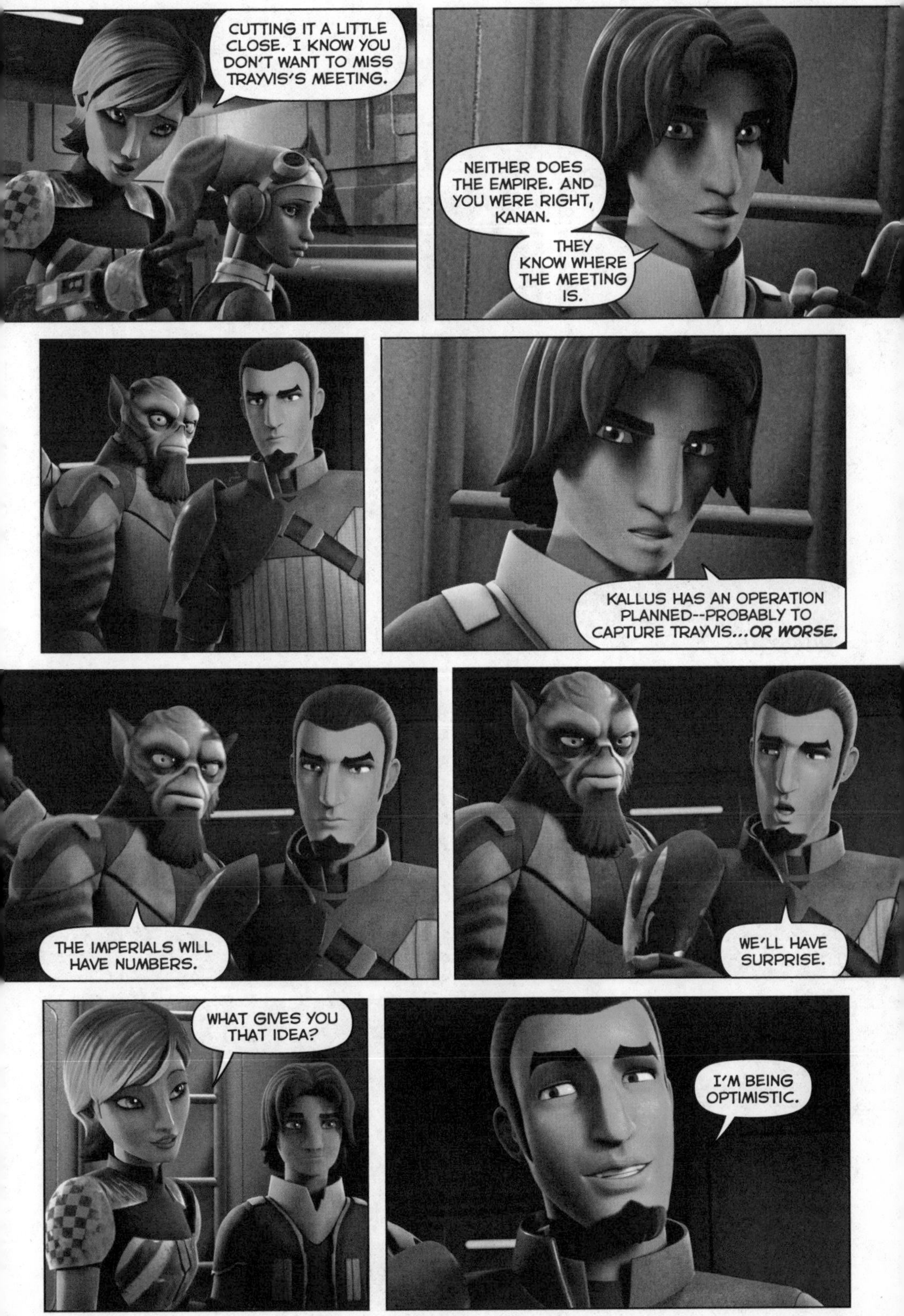
CUTTING IT A LITTLE CLOSE. I KNOW YOU DON'T WANT TO MISS TRAYVIS'S MEETING.
NEITHER DOES THE EMPIRE. AND YOU WERE RIGHT, KANAN.
THEY KNOW WHERE THE MEETING IS.
KALLUS HAS AN OPERATION PLANNED--PROBABLY TO CAPTURE TRAYVIS...OR WORSE.
THE IMPERIALS WILL HAVE NUMBERS.
WE'LL HAVE SURPRISE.
WHAT GIVES YOU THAT IDEA?
I'M BEING OPTIMISTIC.

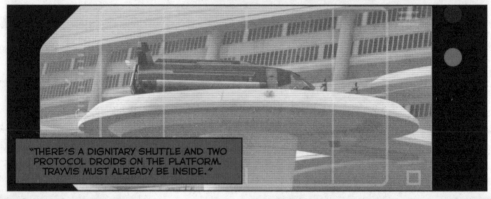

"THERE'S A DIGNITARY SHUTTLE AND TWO PROTOCOL DROIDS ON THE PLATFORM. TRAYVIS MUST ALREADY BE INSIDE."

I'M NOT SEEING ANY IMPERIAL FORCES.

"WELL, THEY GOTTA BE AROUND.

"YEAH, I FOUND THEM. LOOKS LIKE THEY HAVE THE WHOLE AREA LOCKED DOWN."

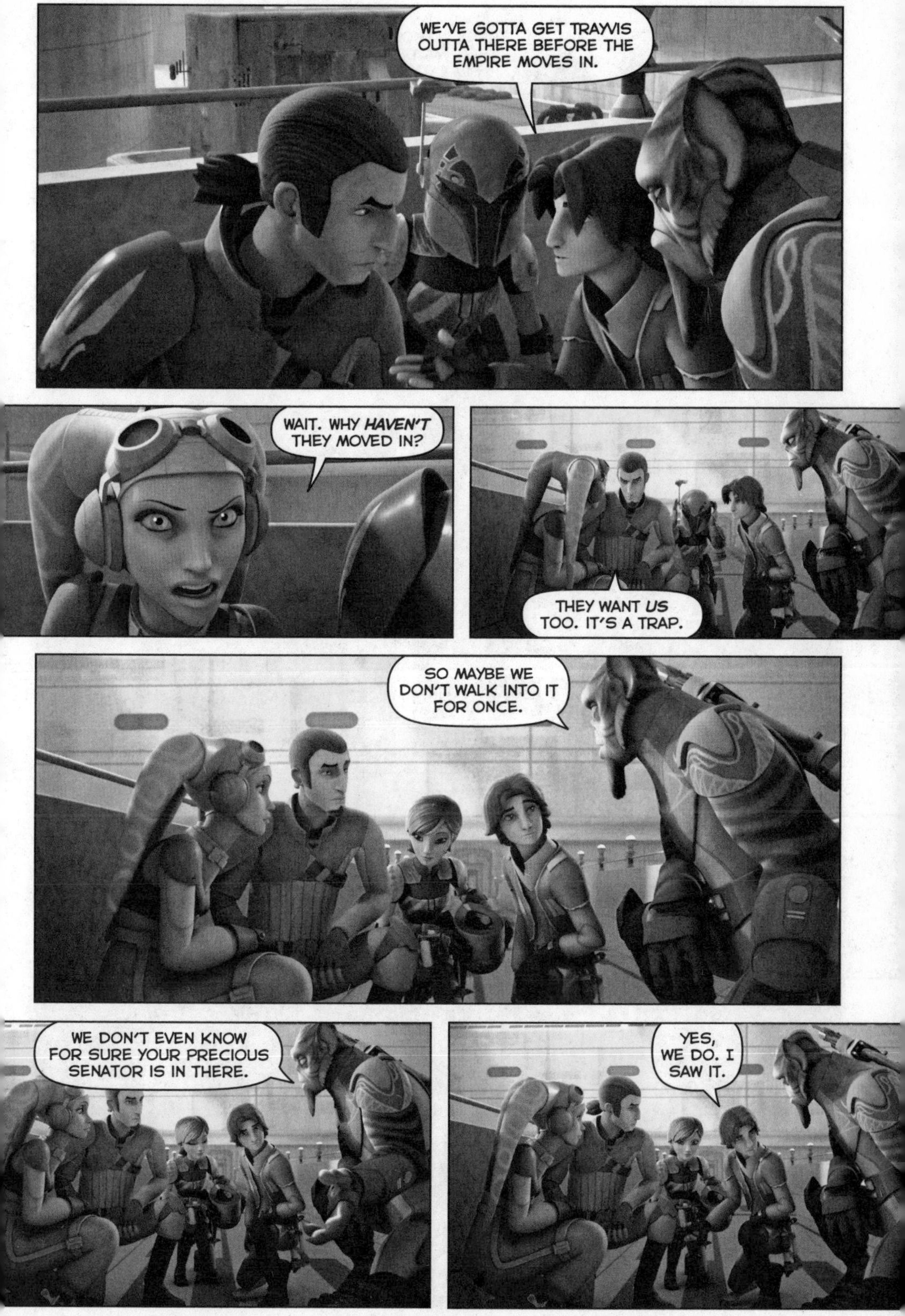
WE'VE GOTTA GET TRAYVIS OUTTA THERE BEFORE THE EMPIRE MOVES IN.
WAIT. WHY *HAVEN'T* THEY MOVED IN?
THEY WANT *US* TOO. IT'S A TRAP.
SO MAYBE WE DON'T WALK INTO IT FOR ONCE.
WE DON'T EVEN KNOW FOR SURE YOUR PRECIOUS SENATOR IS IN THERE.
YES, WE DO. I SAW IT.

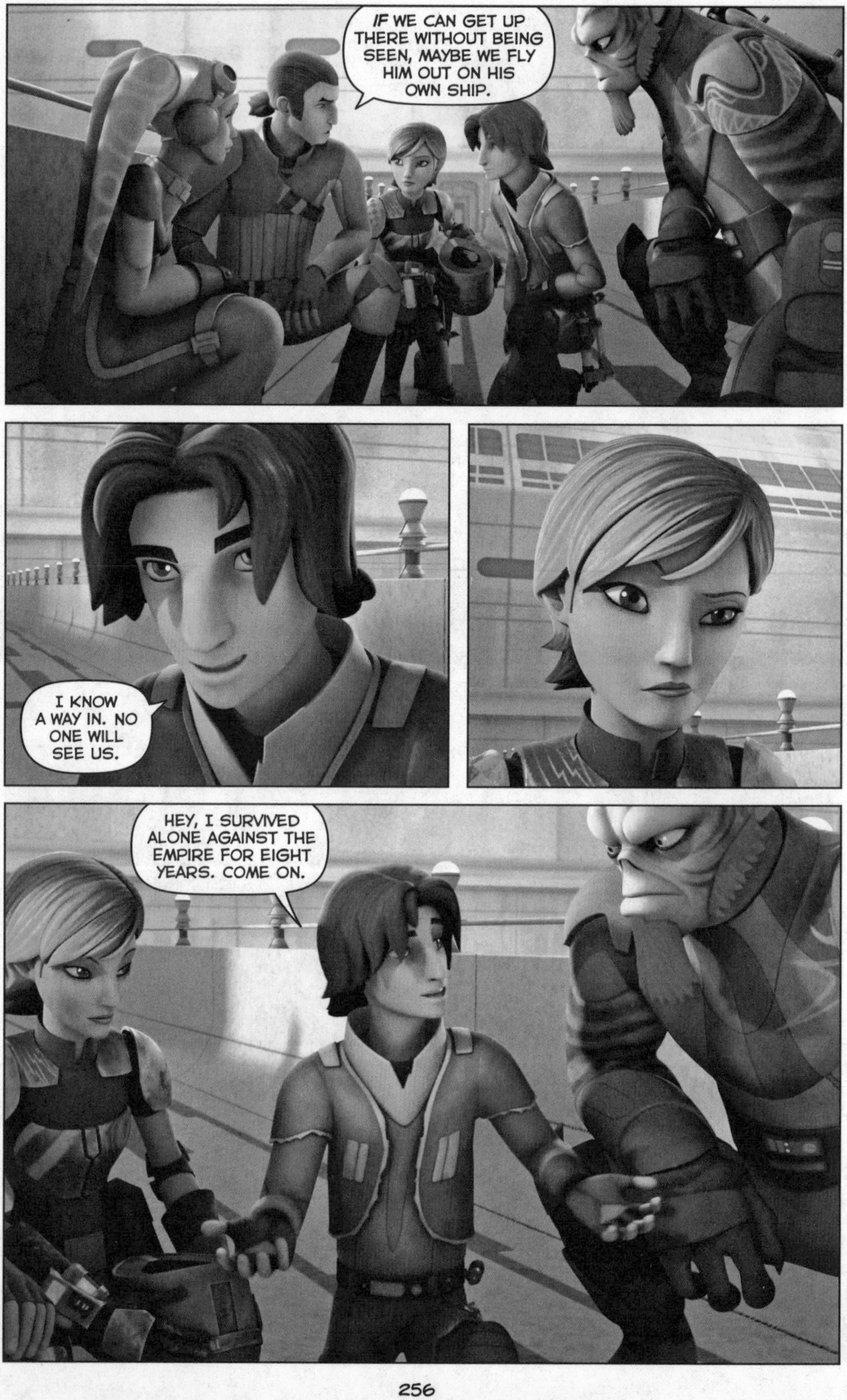
IF WE CAN GET UP THERE WITHOUT BEING SEEN, MAYBE WE FLY HIM OUT ON HIS OWN SHIP.
I KNOW A WAY IN. NO ONE WILL SEE US.
HEY, I SURVIVED ALONE AGAINST THE EMPIRE FOR EIGHT YEARS. COME ON.

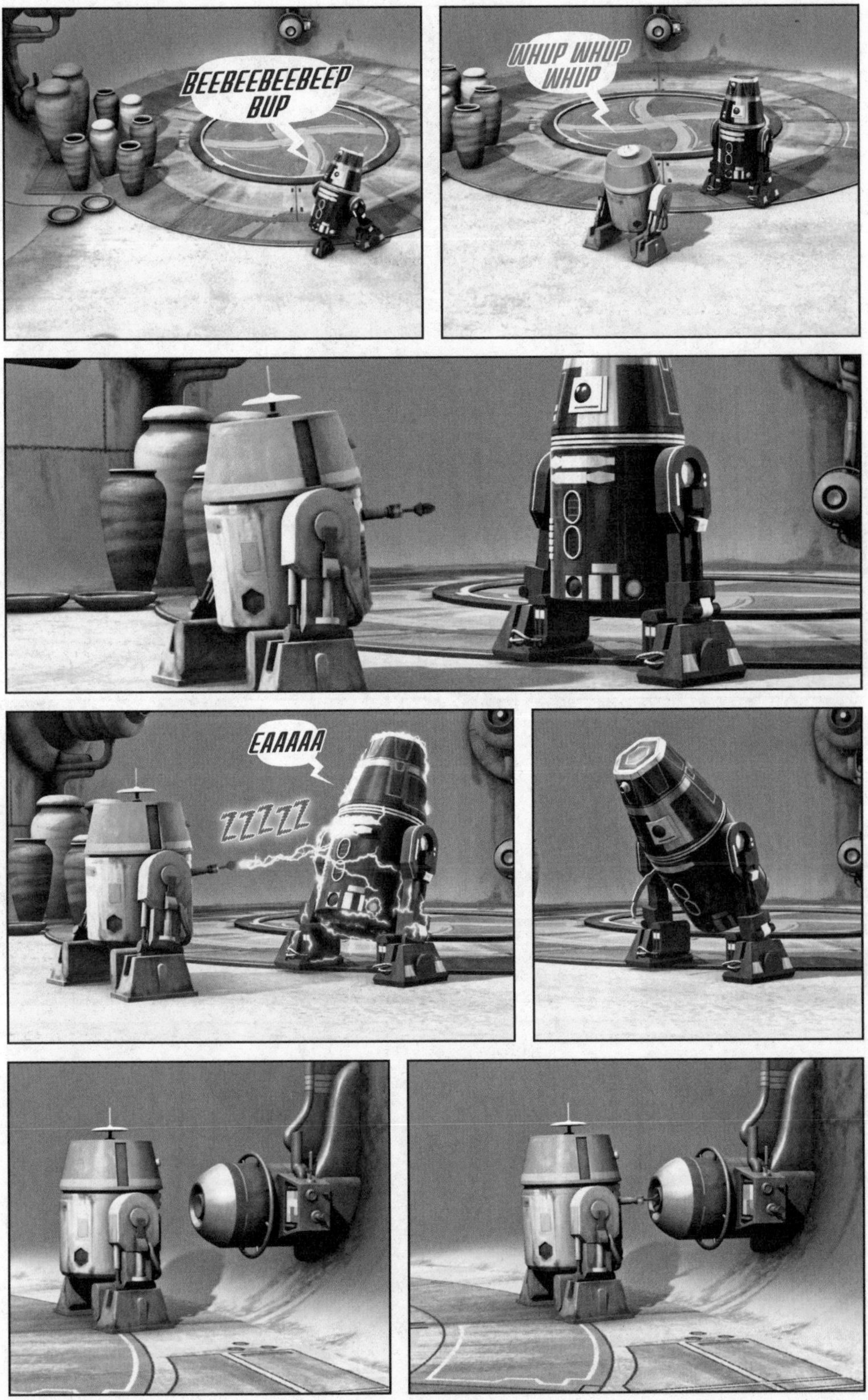
BEEBEEBEEBEEP BUP
WHUP WHUP WHUP
EAAAAA
ZZZZZ

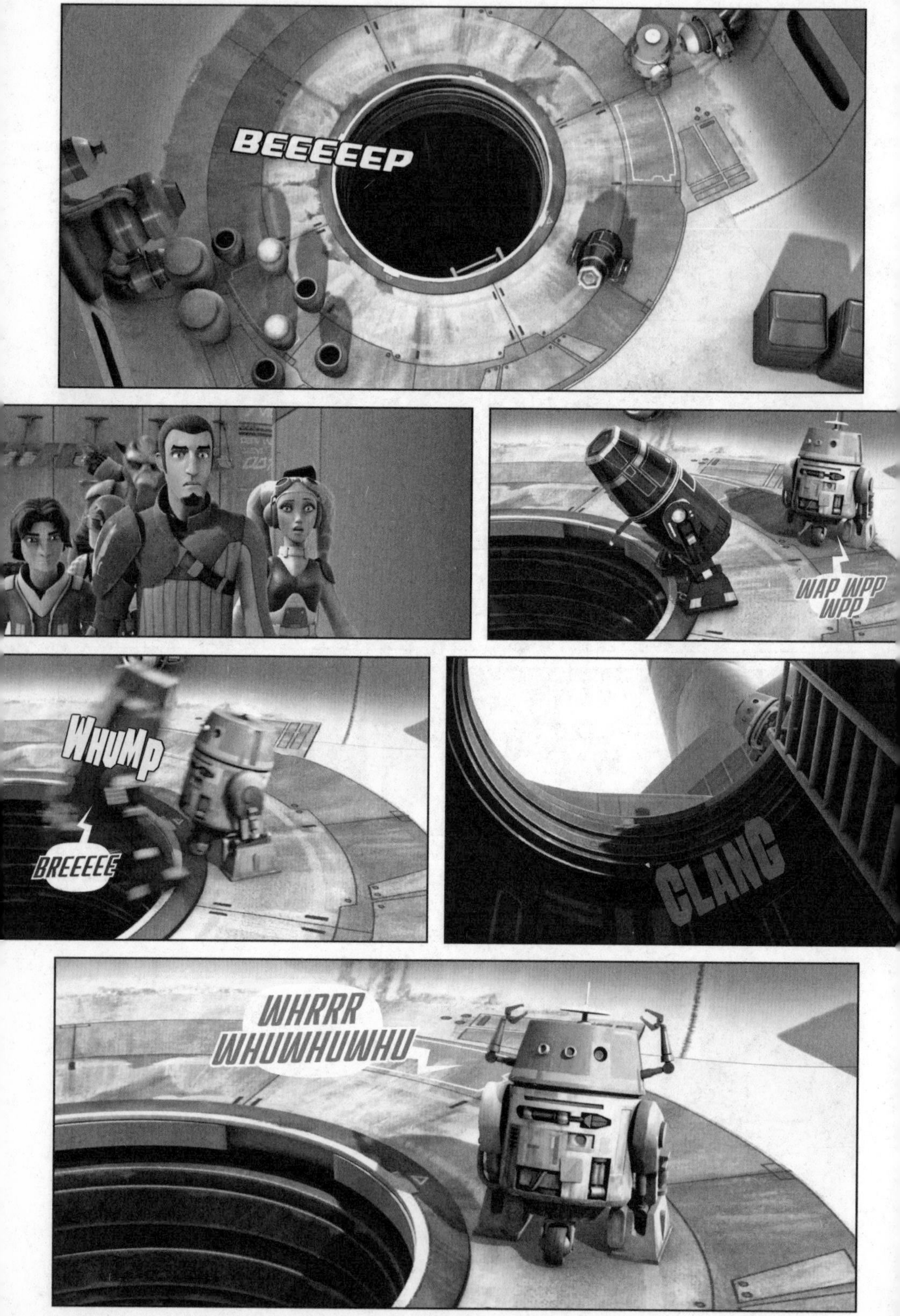
BEEEEEP
WAP WPP WPP
WHUMP
BREEEEE
CLANG
WHRRR WHUWHUWHU

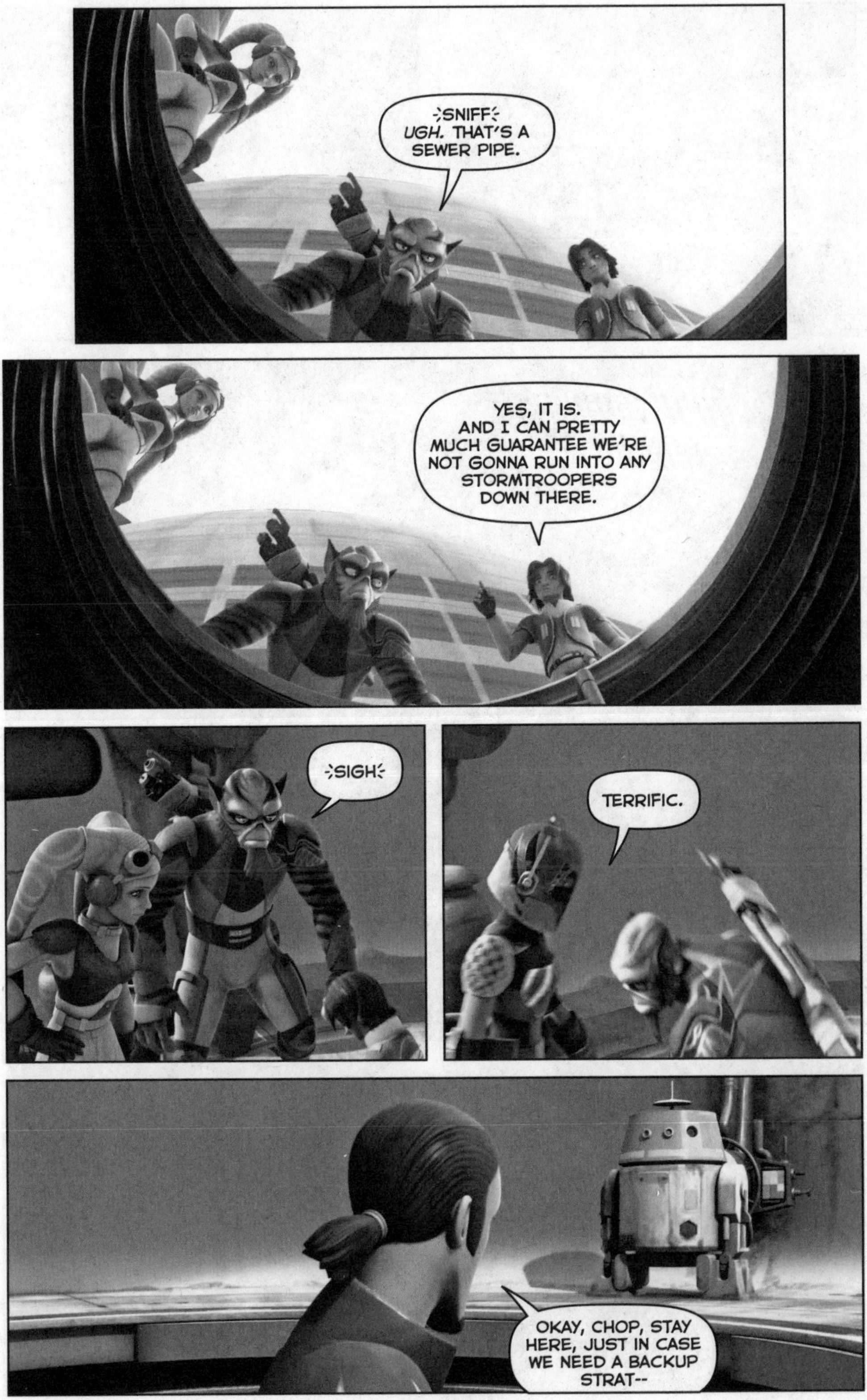
-SNIFF-
UGH. THAT'S A SEWER PIPE.
YES, IT IS. AND I CAN PRETTY MUCH GUARANTEE WE'RE NOT GONNA RUN INTO ANY STORMTROOPERS DOWN THERE.
-SIGH-
TERRIFIC.
OKAY, CHOP, STAY HERE, JUST IN CASE WE NEED A BACKUP STRAT--

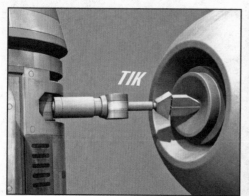

TIK

HEY!

BEEEEEP

WHUUP WHUUP WHUUP

USED TO BE TOO MUCH WATER TO WALK DOWN HERE, BUT SINCE THE EMPIRE STARTED RATIONING, PRETTY DRY.

WELL, IT HASN'T HELPED THE SMELL.

SPEAKING OF WHICH, IT DOES SMELL LIKE YOU.

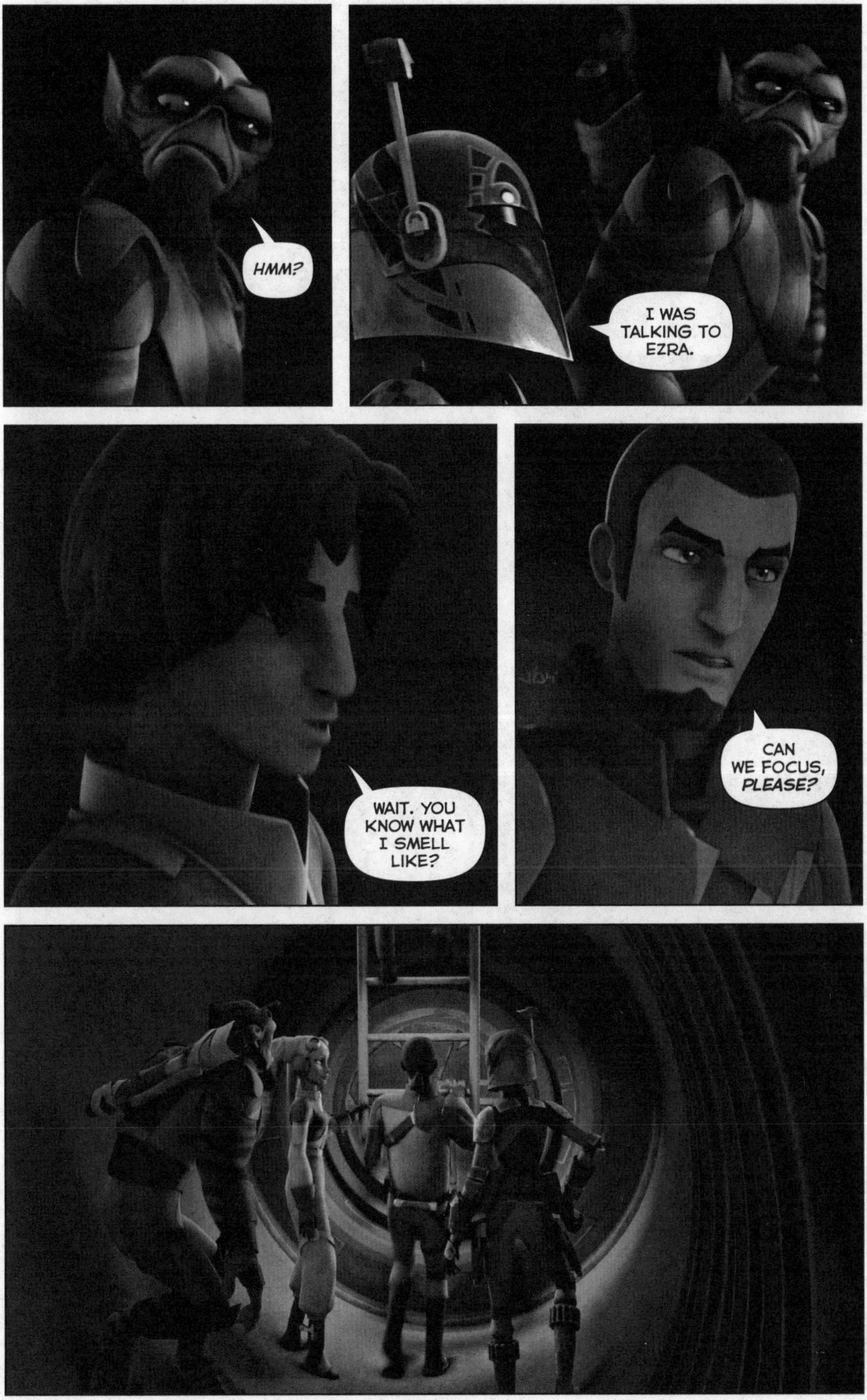
HMM?
I WAS TALKING TO EZRA.
WAIT. YOU KNOW WHAT I SMELL LIKE?
CAN WE FOCUS, *PLEASE?*

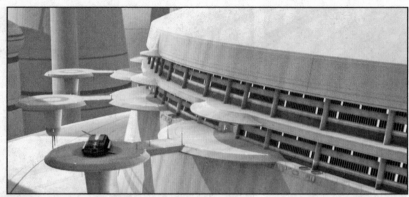

WHAT DO YOU THINK?

ARGH. BETTER SAFE THAN SORRY.

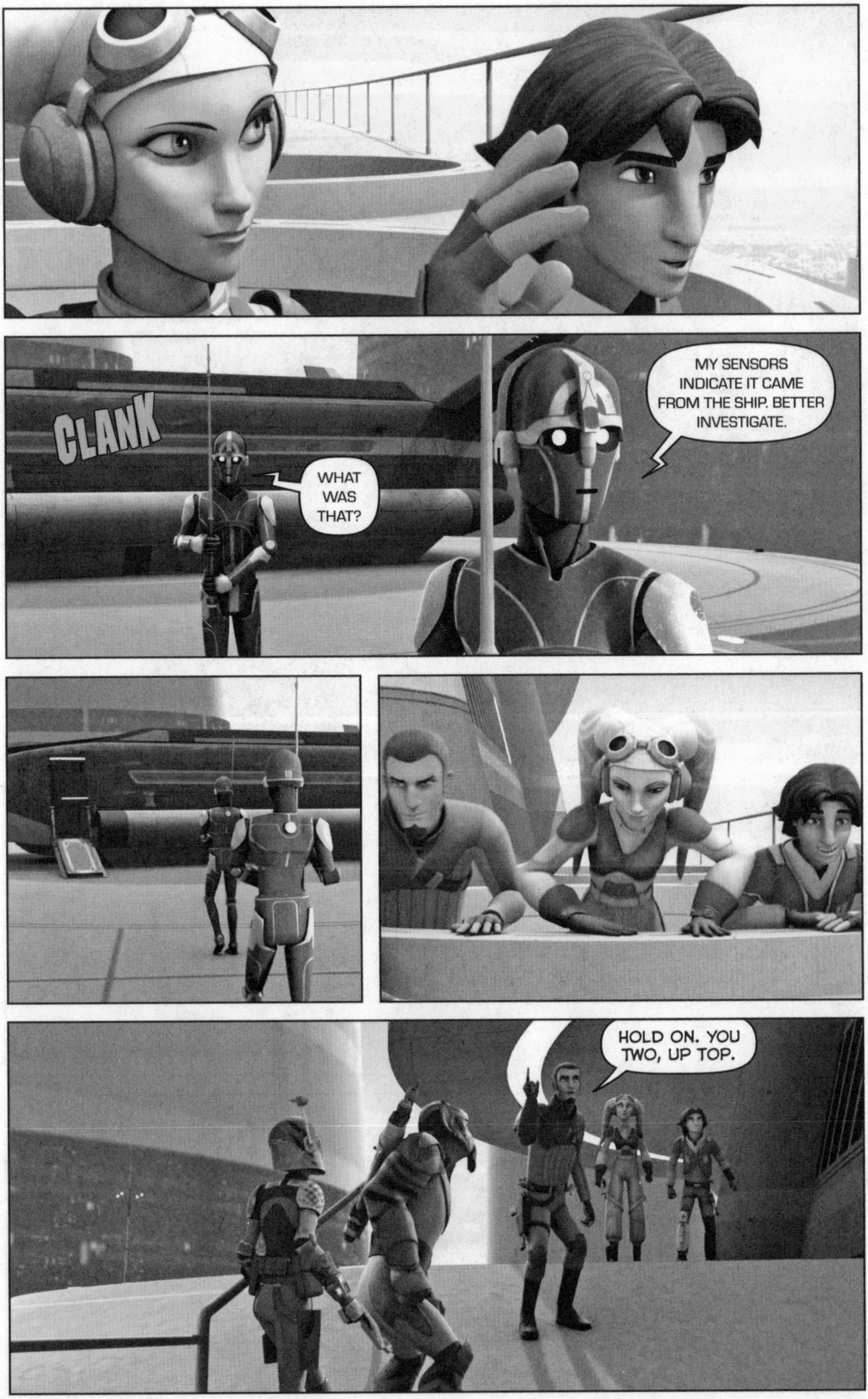
CLANK
WHAT WAS THAT?
MY SENSORS INDICATE IT CAME FROM THE SHIP. BETTER INVESTIGATE.
HOLD ON. YOU TWO, UP TOP.

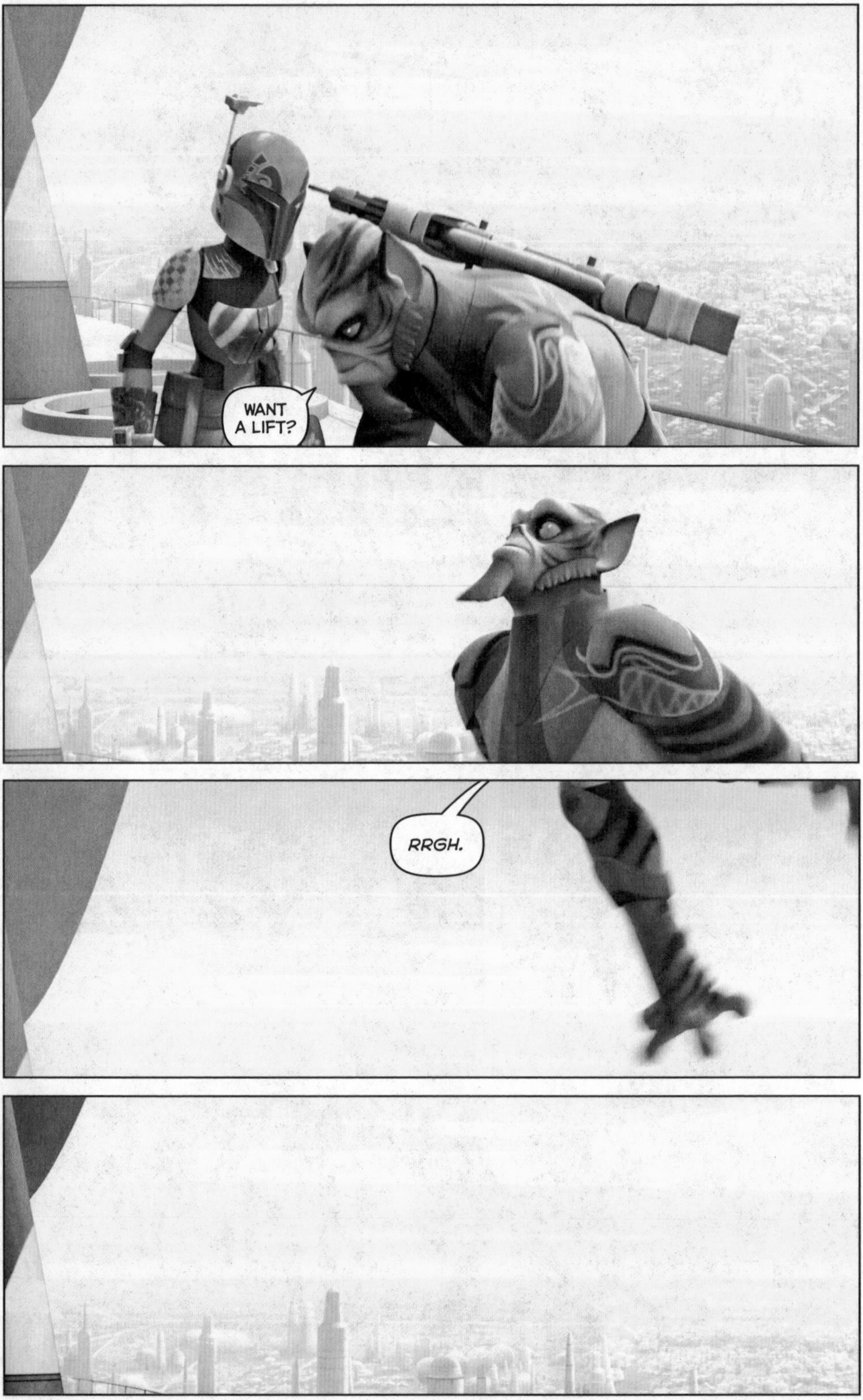
WANT A LIFT?
RRGH.

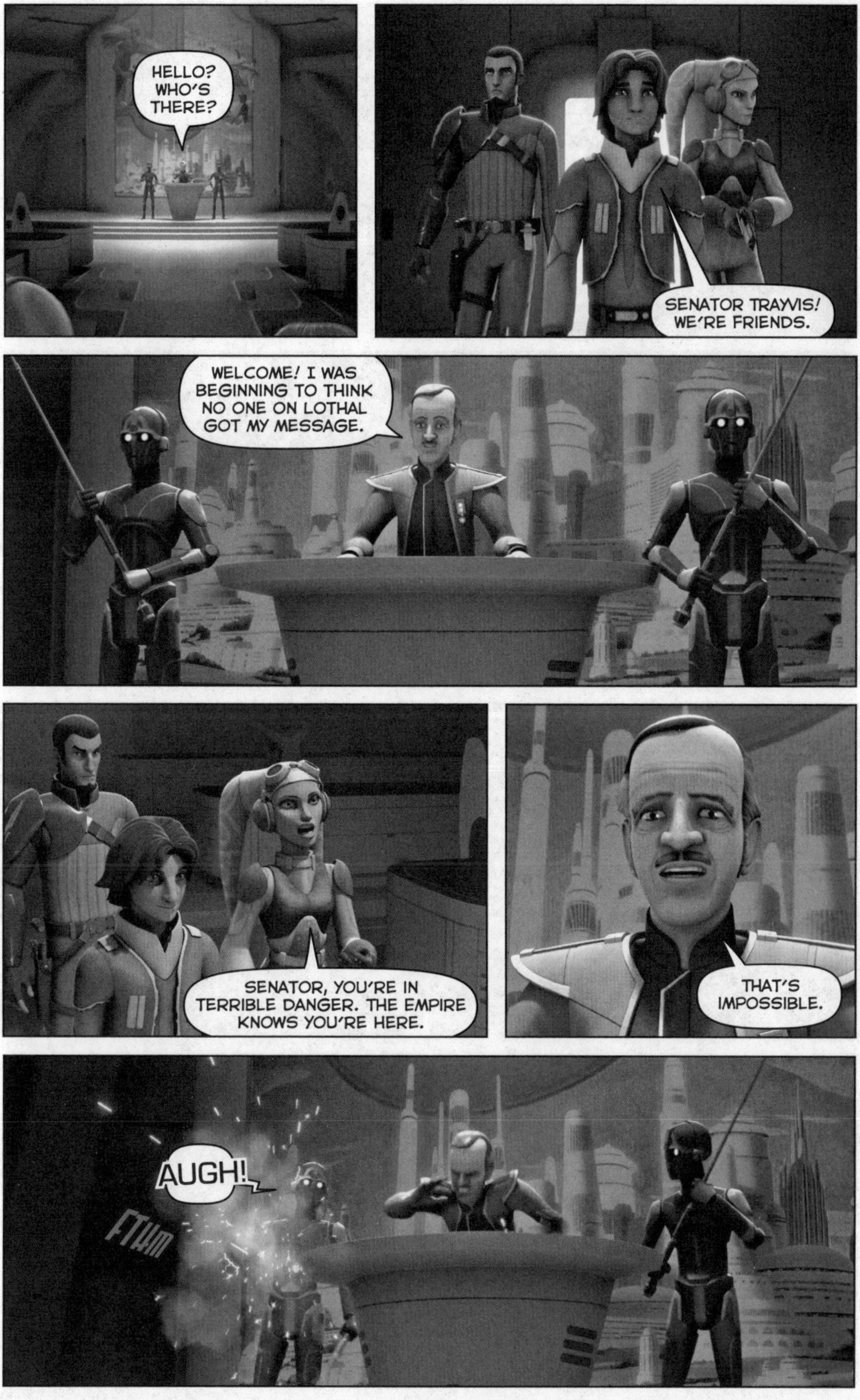
HELLO? WHO'S THERE?
SENATOR TRAYVIS! WE'RE FRIENDS.
WELCOME! I WAS BEGINNING TO THINK NO ONE ON LOTHAL GOT MY MESSAGE.
SENATOR, YOU'RE IN TERRIBLE DANGER. THE EMPIRE KNOWS YOU'RE HERE.
THAT'S IMPOSSIBLE.
AUGH!

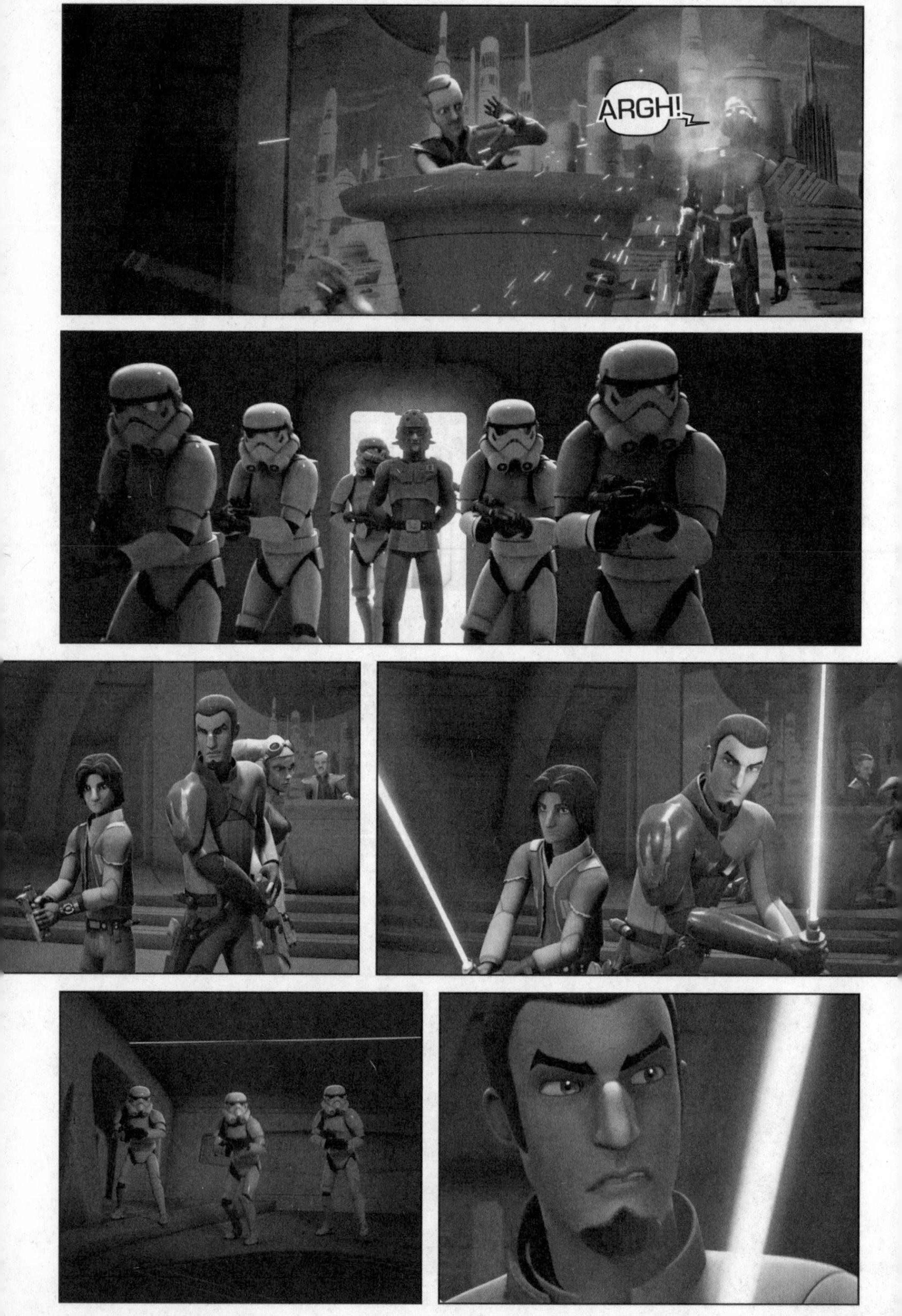
ARGH!

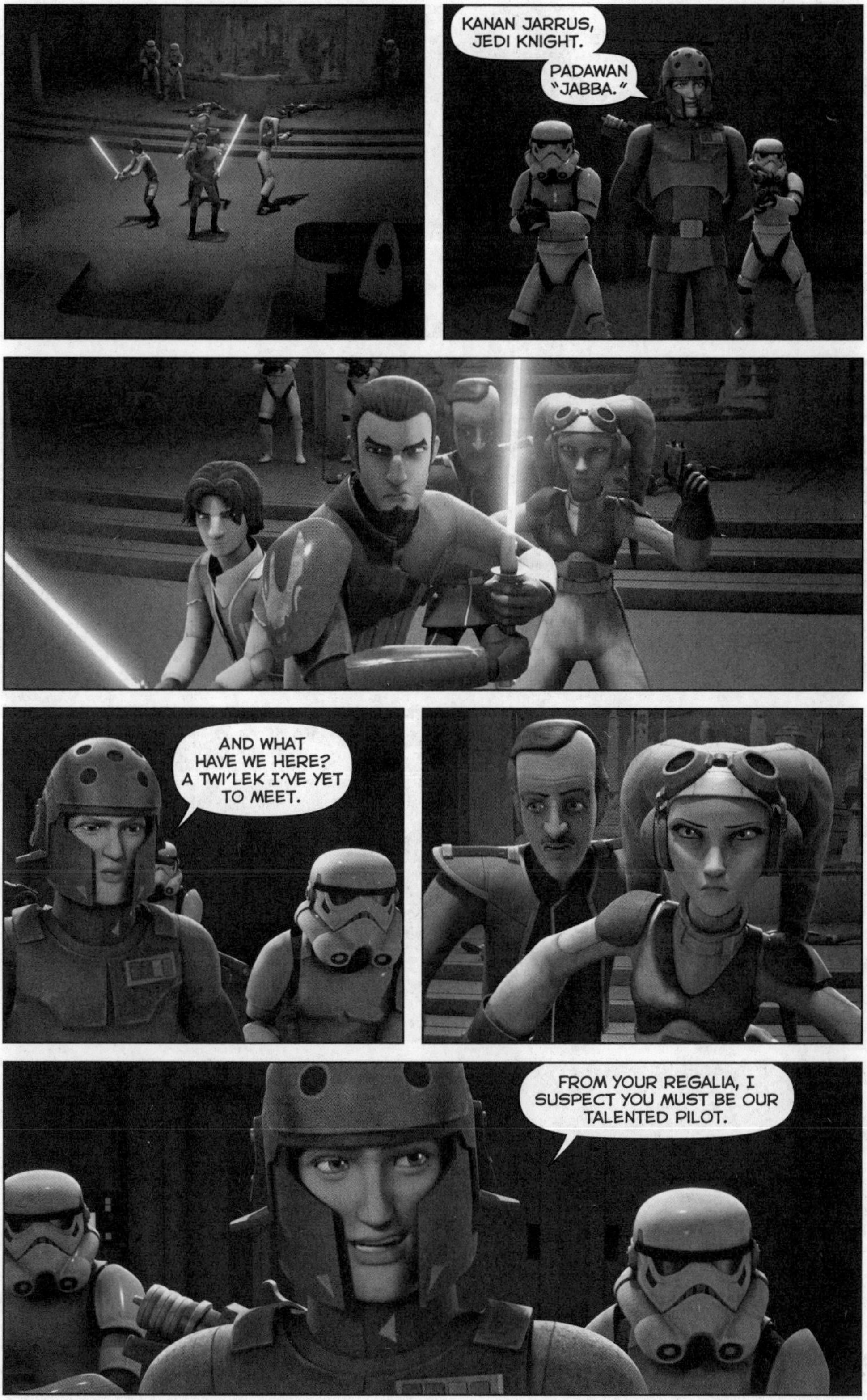
KANAN JARRUS, JEDI KNIGHT.
PADAWAN "JABBA."
AND WHAT HAVE WE HERE? A TWI'LEK I'VE YET TO MEET.
FROM YOUR REGALIA, I SUSPECT YOU MUST BE OUR TALENTED PILOT.

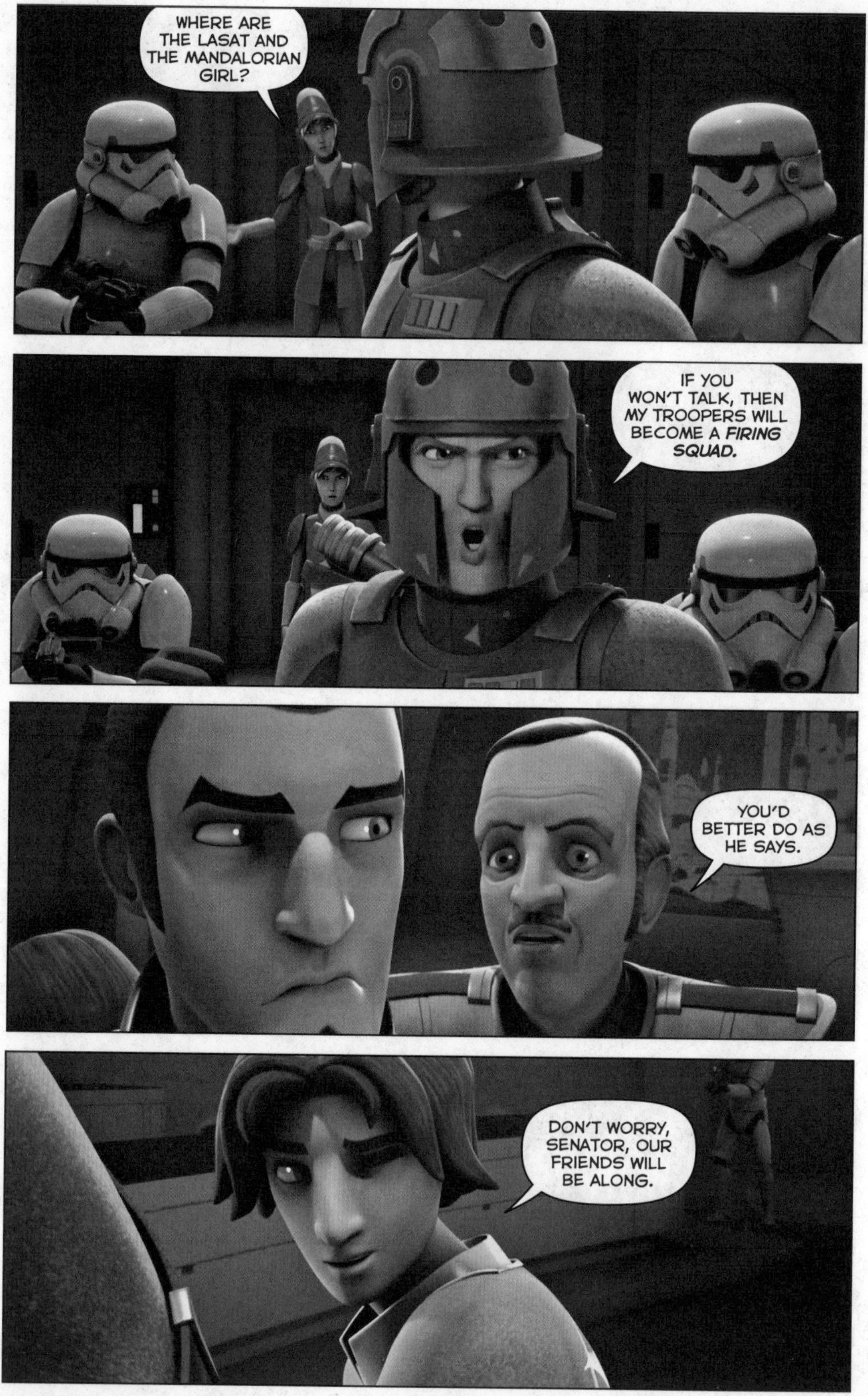
WHERE ARE THE LASAT AND THE MANDALORIAN GIRL?
IF YOU WON'T TALK, THEN MY TROOPERS WILL BECOME A *FIRING SQUAD.*
YOU'D BETTER DO AS HE SAYS.
DON'T WORRY, SENATOR, OUR FRIENDS WILL BE ALONG.

BEEP
BEEP

BEEP
BEEP

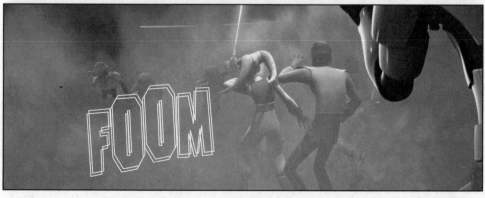

FOOM

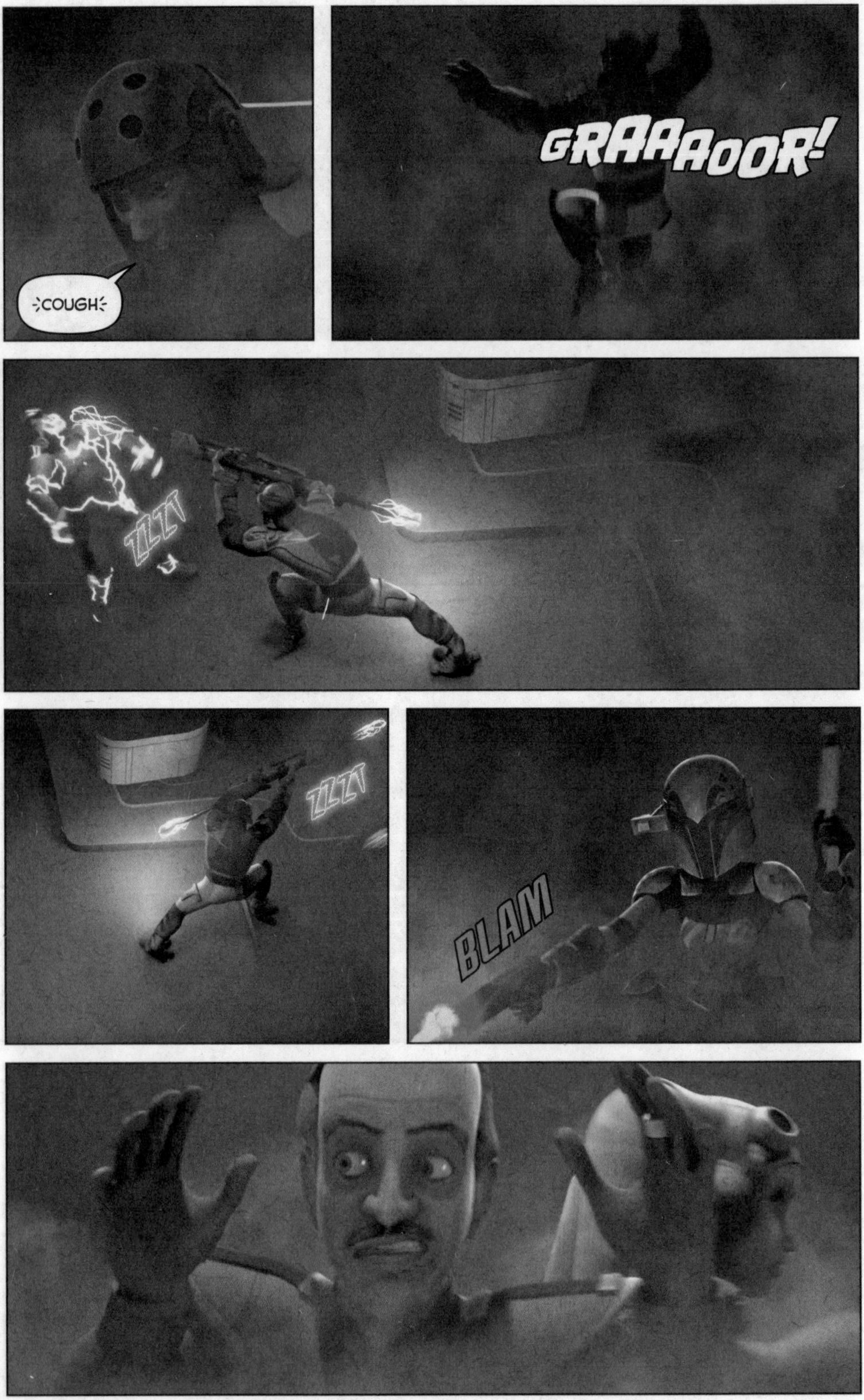
COUGH
GRAAAAOOR!
TZZZT
TZZZT
BLAM

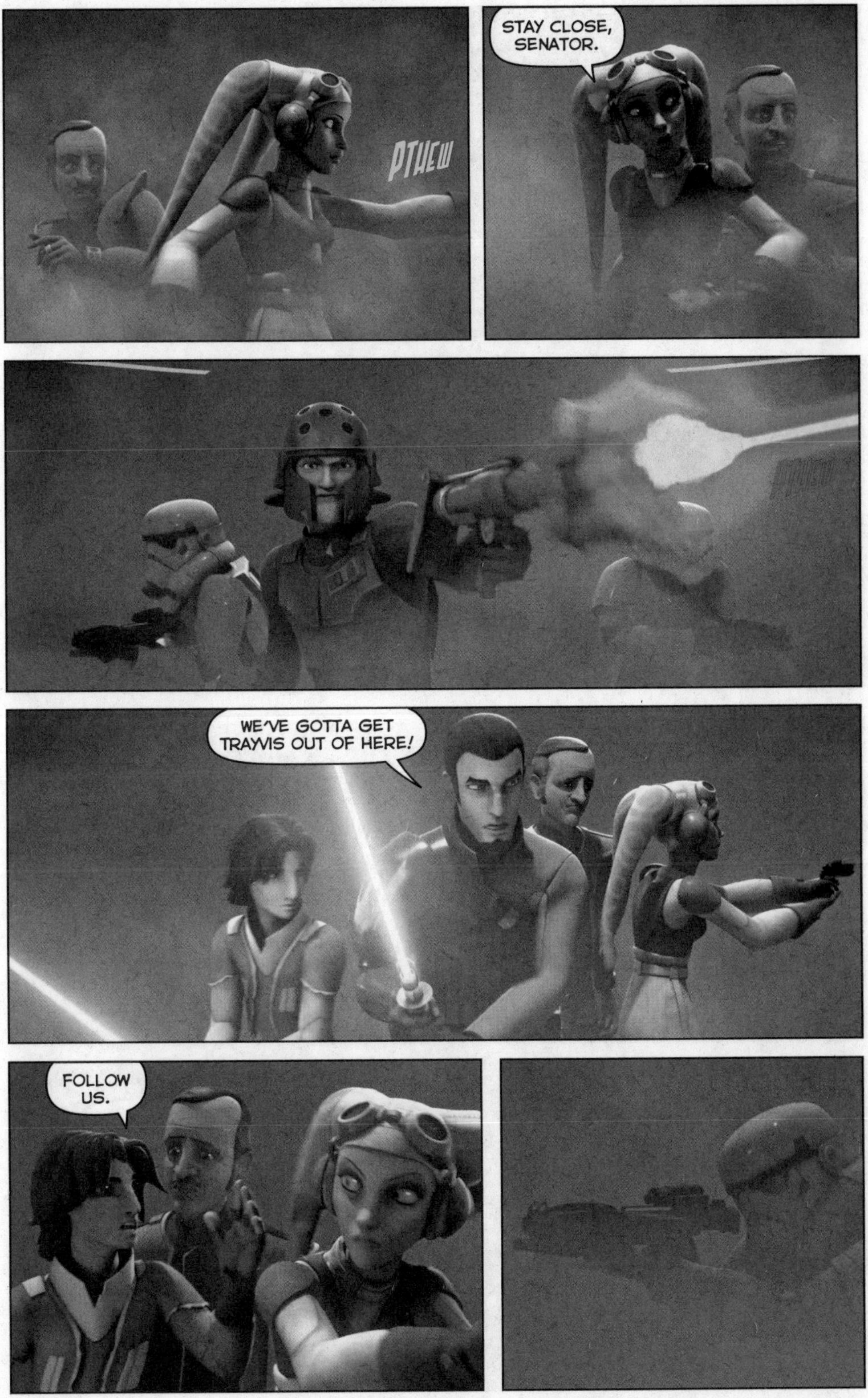
PTHEW
STAY CLOSE, SENATOR.
WE'VE GOTTA GET TRAYVIS OUT OF HERE!
FOLLOW US.

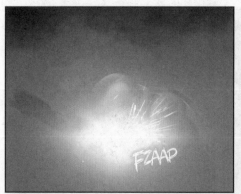

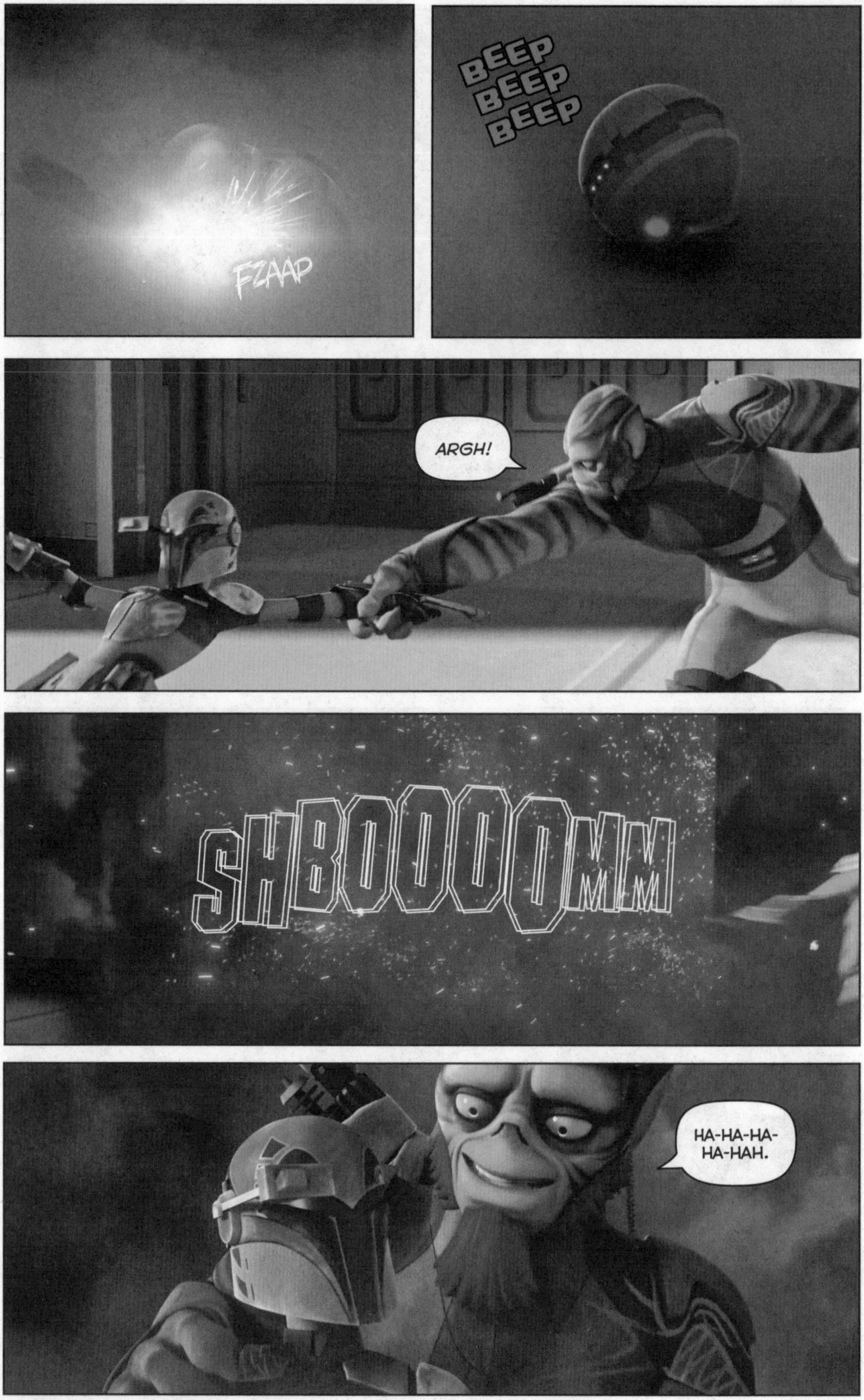
FZAAP
BEEP
BEEP
BEEP
ARGH!
SHBOOOOMM
HA-HA-HA-
HA-HAH.

WAS REALLY HOPING THAT SHUTTLE'D STILL BE HERE.

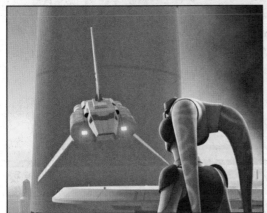

AND THAT'S NOT THE RIDE WE'RE LOOKING FOR.

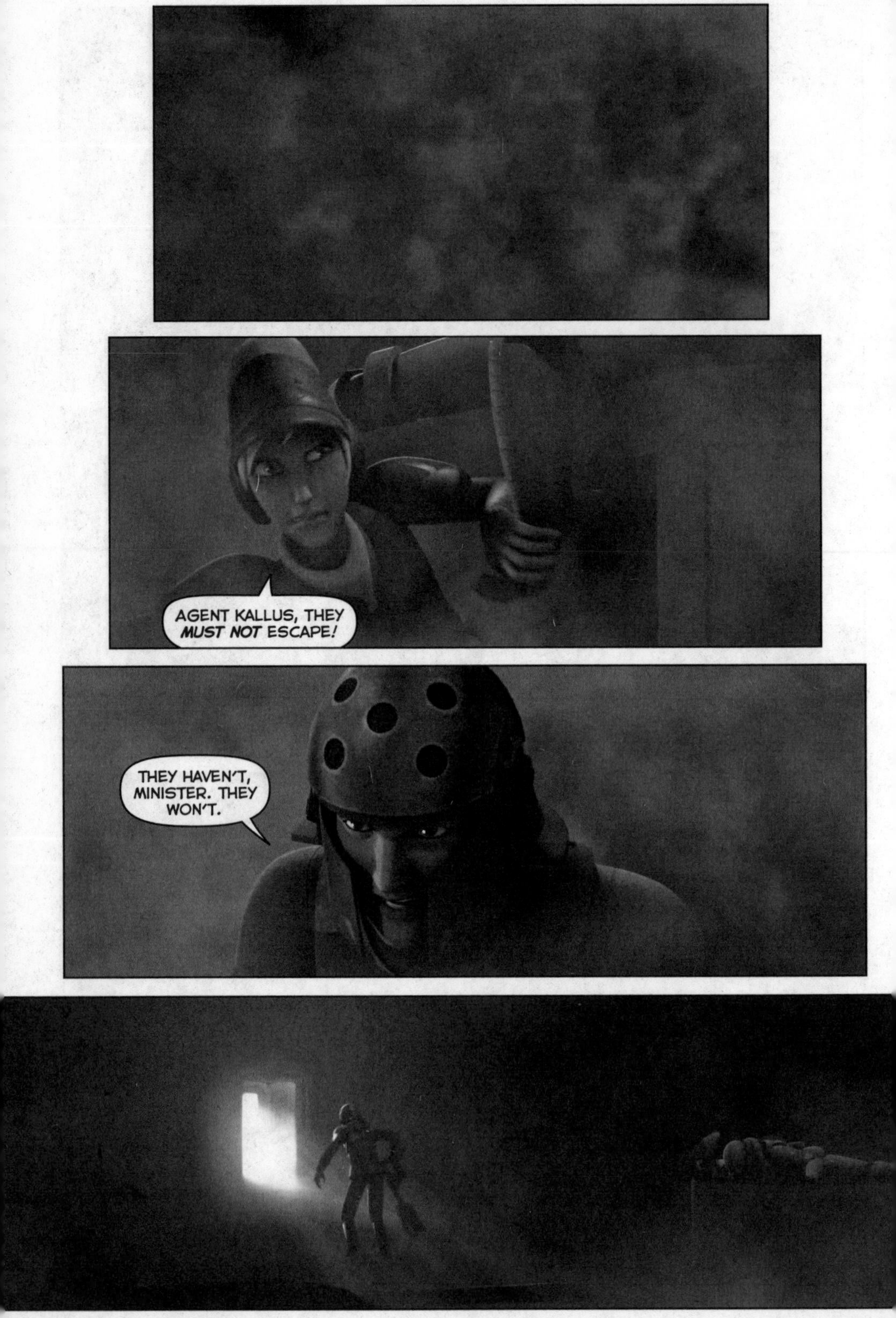
AGENT KALLUS, THEY *MUST NOT* ESCAPE!
THEY HAVEN'T, MINISTER. THEY WON'T.

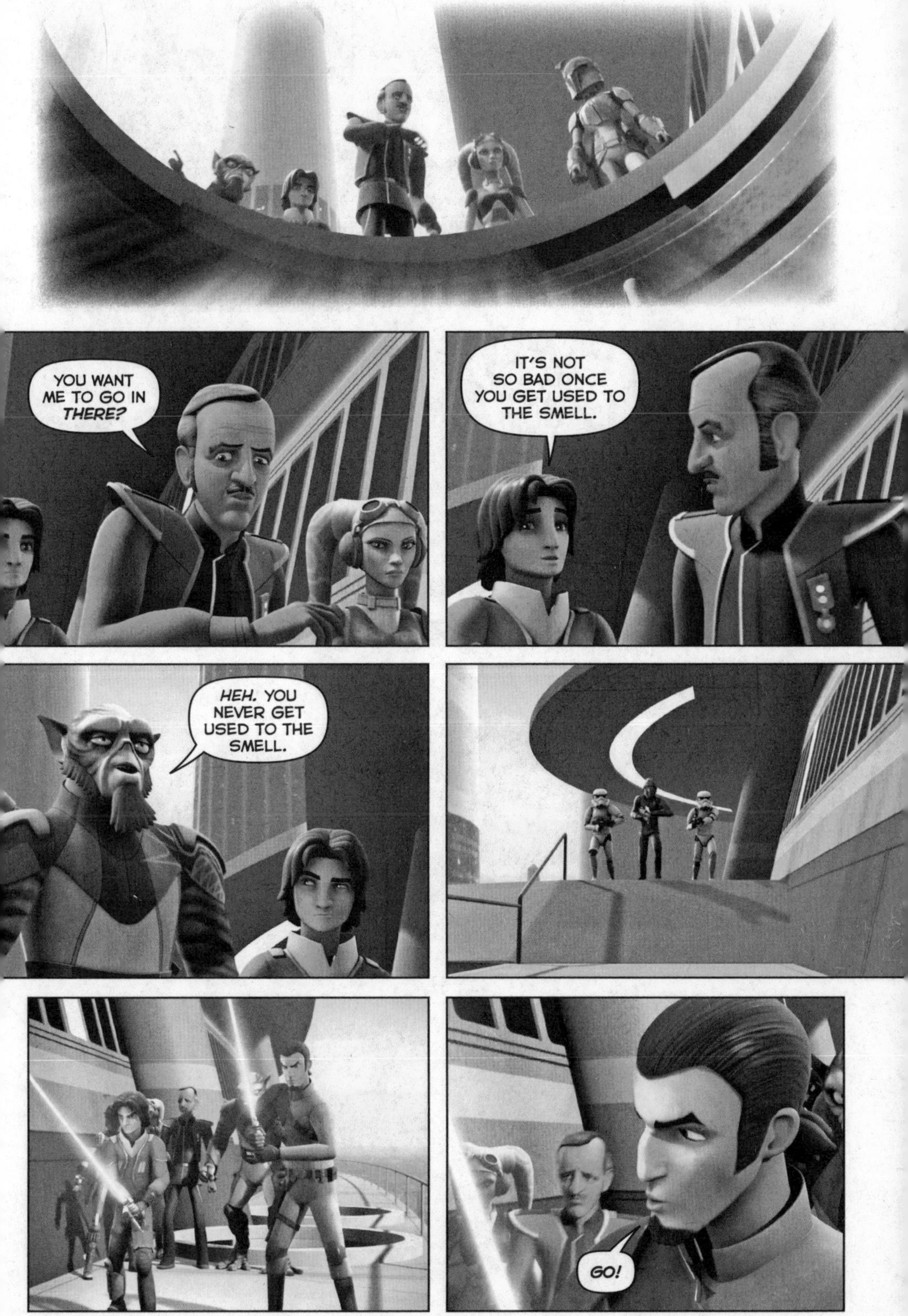
YOU WANT ME TO GO IN *THERE?*
IT'S NOT SO BAD ONCE YOU GET USED TO THE SMELL.
HEH. YOU NEVER GET USED TO THE SMELL.
GO!

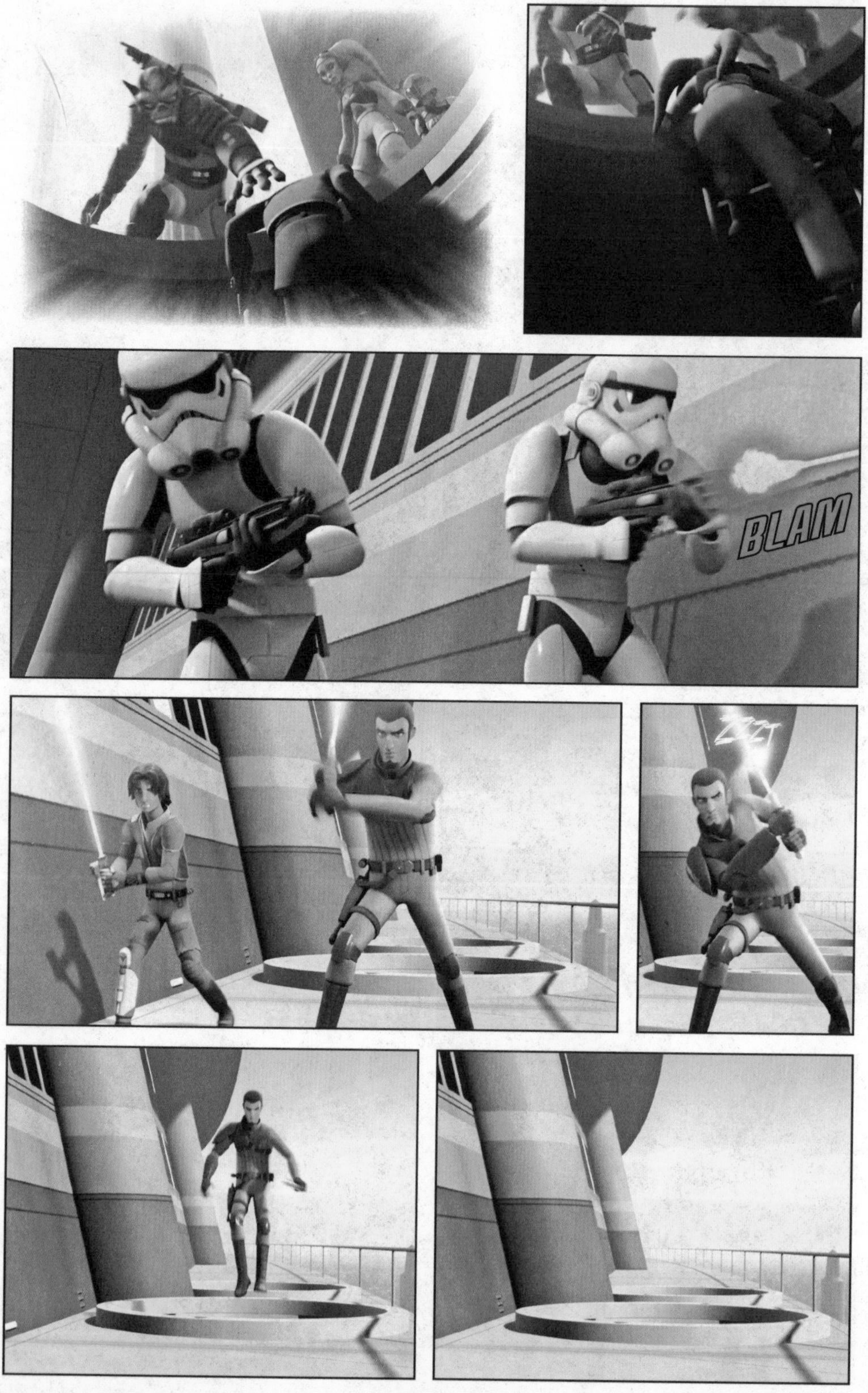
BLAM
ZZT

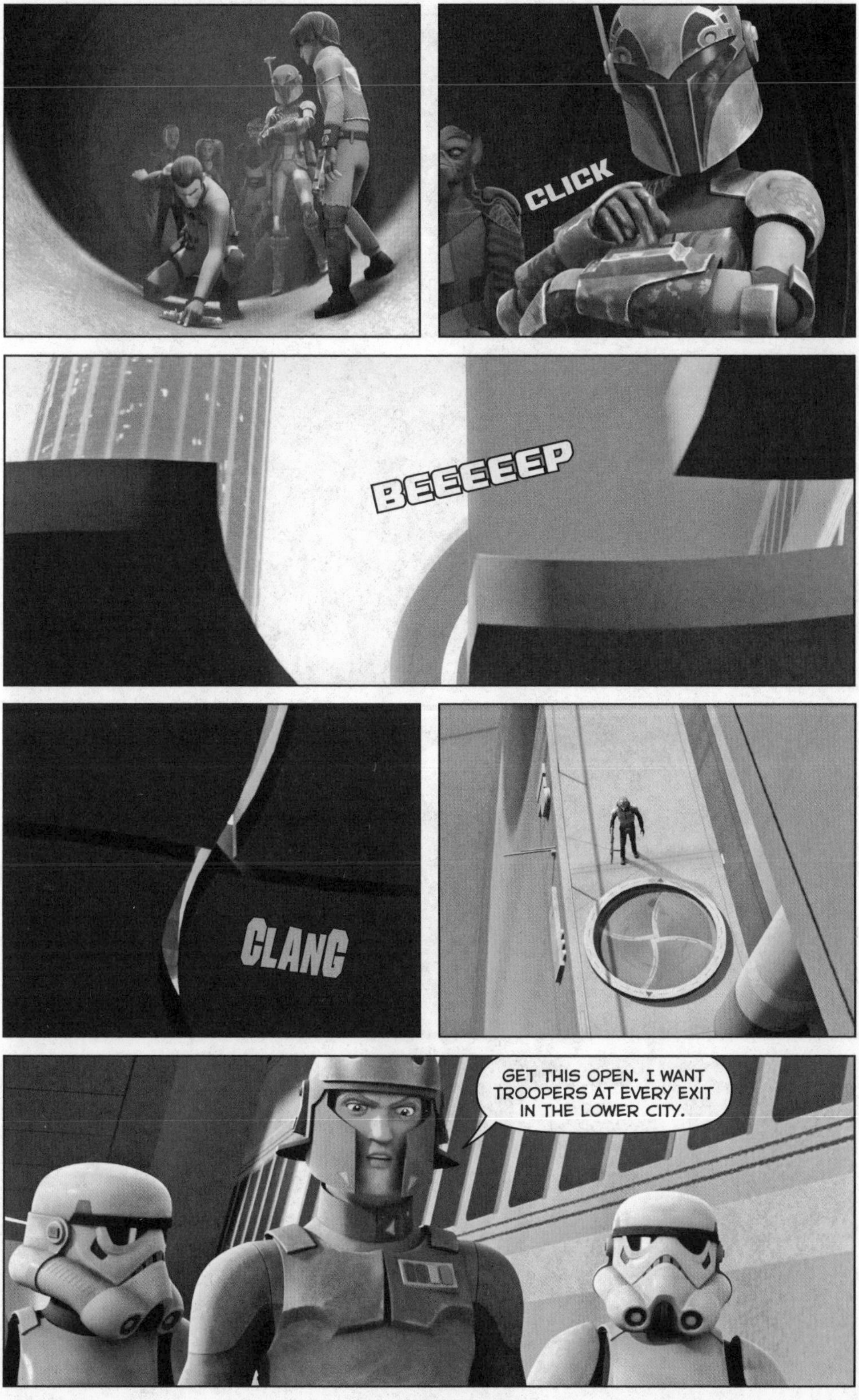
CLICK
BEEEEEEP
CLANG
GET THIS OPEN. I WANT TROOPERS AT EVERY EXIT IN THE LOWER CITY.

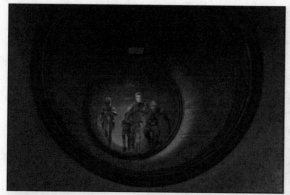

YES, I'M-I'M COMING.

EZRA, WAIT UP.

SORRY, SENATOR. WE JUST WANNA GET OUT OF HERE AS FAST AS WE CAN.

I AM THE ONE WHO SHOULD APOLOGIZE, MY YOUNG FRIEND.

I'VE BEEN PURSUED, BUT *NEVER* IN SUCH A PLACE AS THIS.

FIGURED YOU'D BE USED TO RUNNING FROM THE EMPIRE.

WELL, I-I'VE NEVER COME THIS CLOSE TO CAPTURE BEFORE.

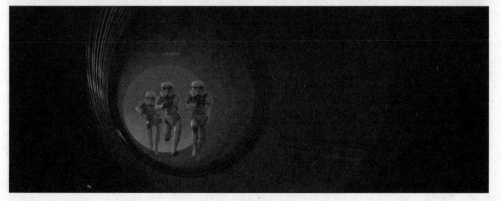

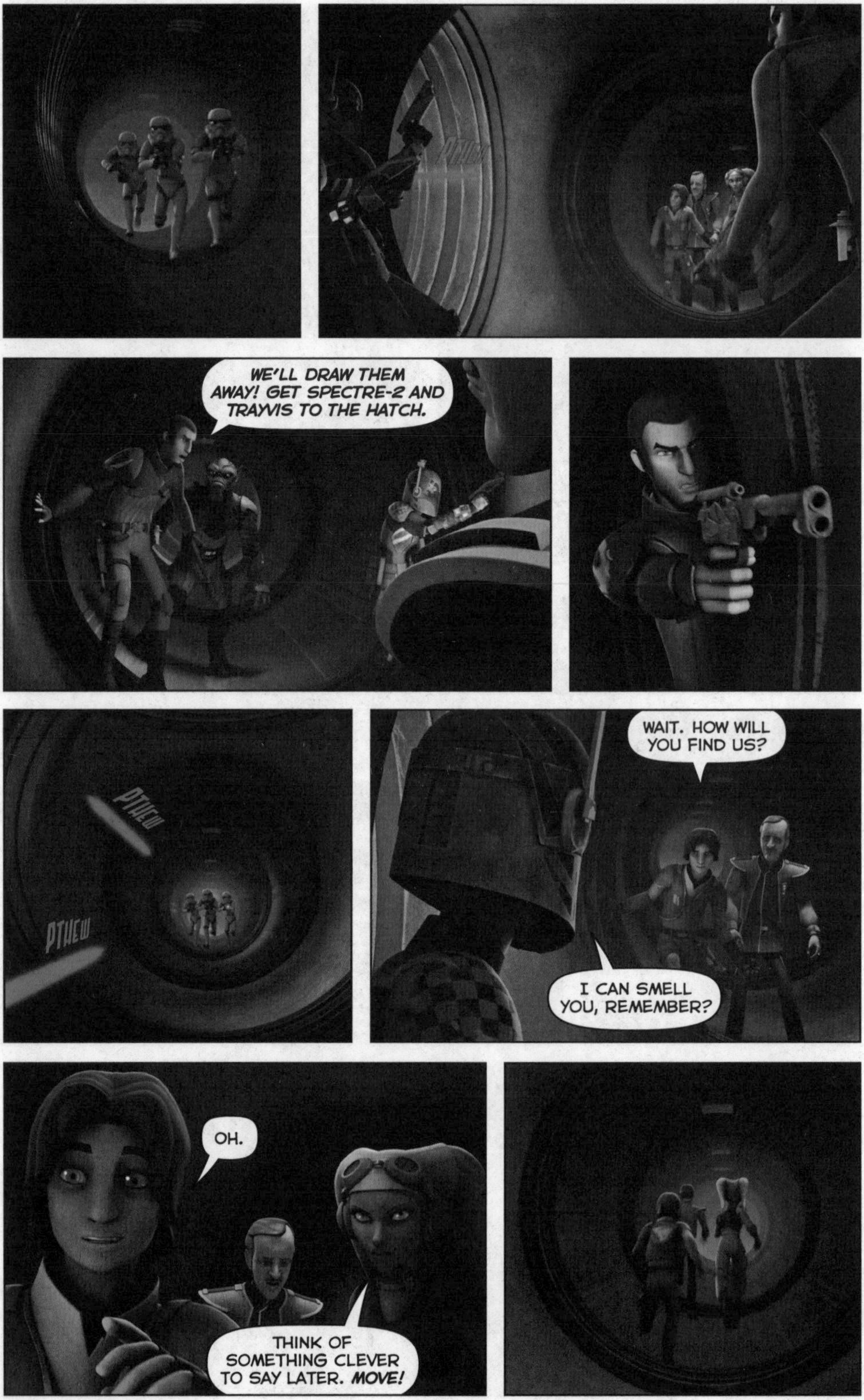
PTHEW
WE'LL DRAW THEM AWAY! GET SPECTRE-2 AND TRAYVIS TO THE HATCH.
PTHEW
PTHEW
WAIT. HOW WILL YOU FIND US?
I CAN SMELL YOU, REMEMBER?
OH.
THINK OF SOMETHING CLEVER TO SAY LATER. *MOVE!*

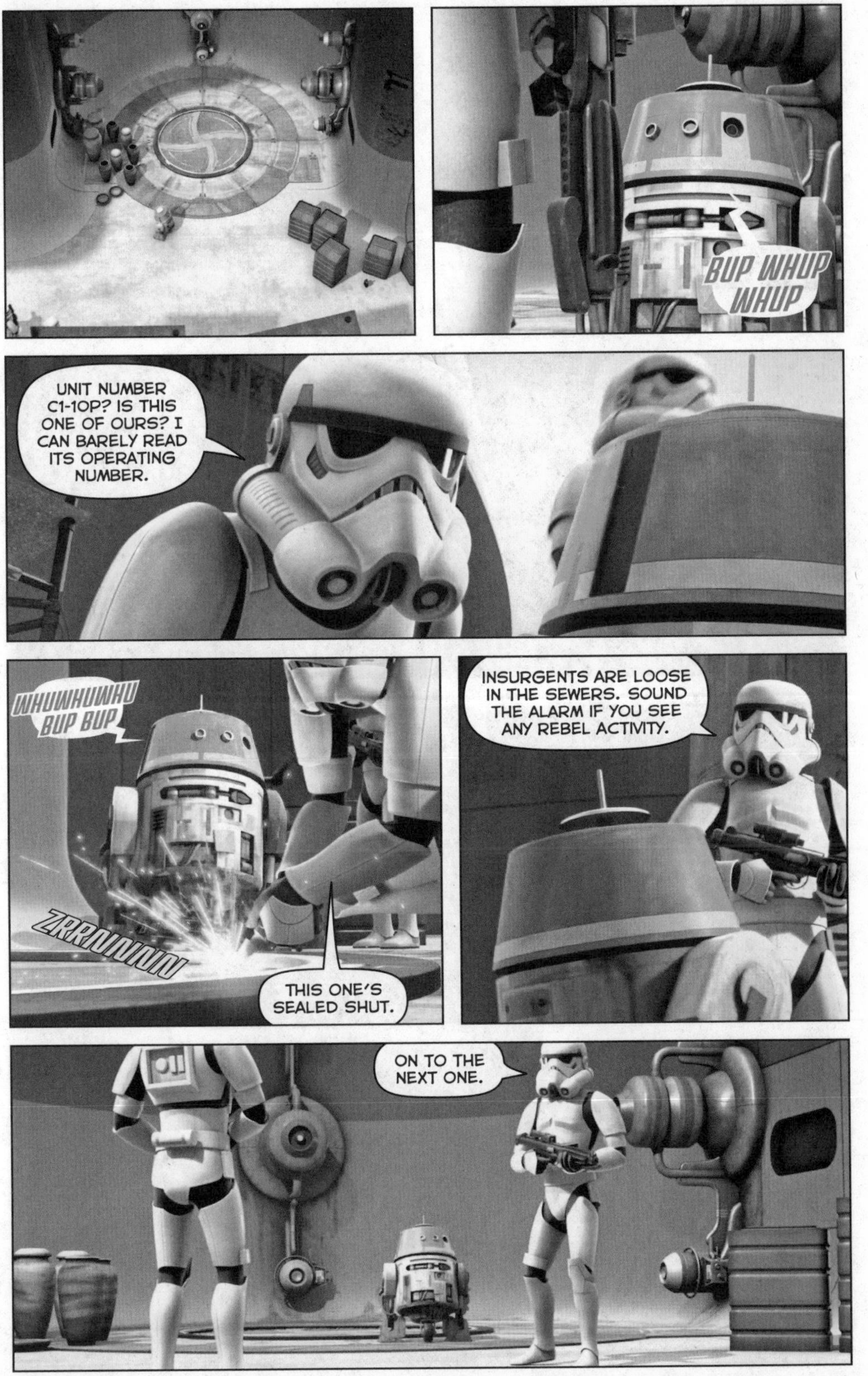
BUP WHUP WHUP
UNIT NUMBER C1-10P? IS THIS ONE OF OURS? I CAN BARELY READ ITS OPERATING NUMBER.
WHUWHUWHU BUP BUP
ZRRRNNNN
THIS ONE'S SEALED SHUT.
INSURGENTS ARE LOOSE IN THE SEWERS. SOUND THE ALARM IF YOU SEE ANY REBEL ACTIVITY.
ON TO THE NEXT ONE.

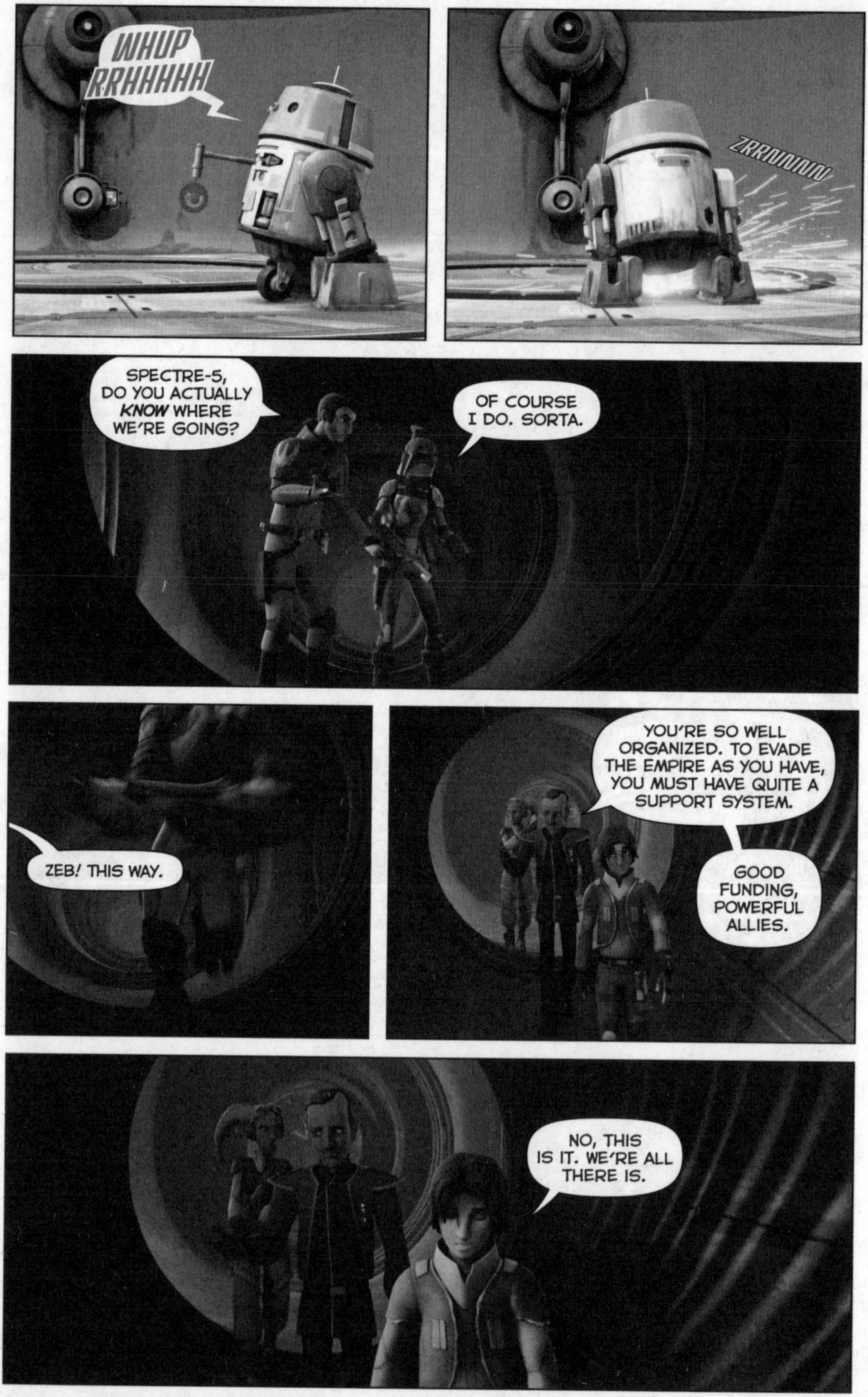
WHUP RRHHHHH
ZRRNNNNN
SPECTRE-5, DO YOU ACTUALLY KNOW WHERE WE'RE GOING?
OF COURSE I DO. SORTA.
ZEB! THIS WAY.
YOU'RE SO WELL ORGANIZED. TO EVADE THE EMPIRE AS YOU HAVE, YOU MUST HAVE QUITE A SUPPORT SYSTEM.
GOOD FUNDING, POWERFUL ALLIES.
NO, THIS IS IT. WE'RE ALL THERE IS.

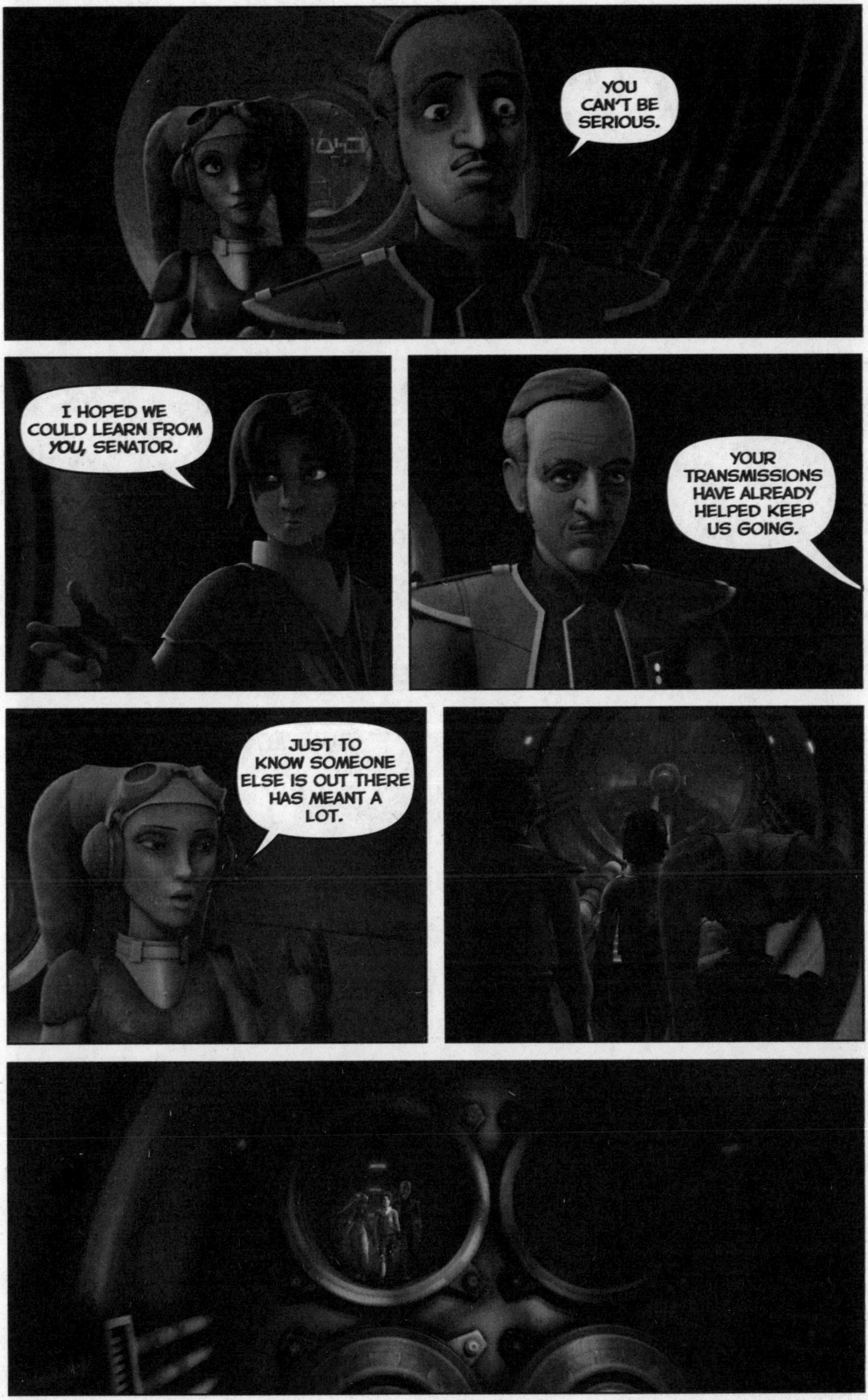
YOU CAN'T BE SERIOUS.
I HOPED WE COULD LEARN FROM *YOU*, SENATOR.
YOUR TRANSMISSIONS HAVE ALREADY HELPED KEEP US GOING.
JUST TO KNOW SOMEONE ELSE IS OUT THERE HAS MEANT A LOT.

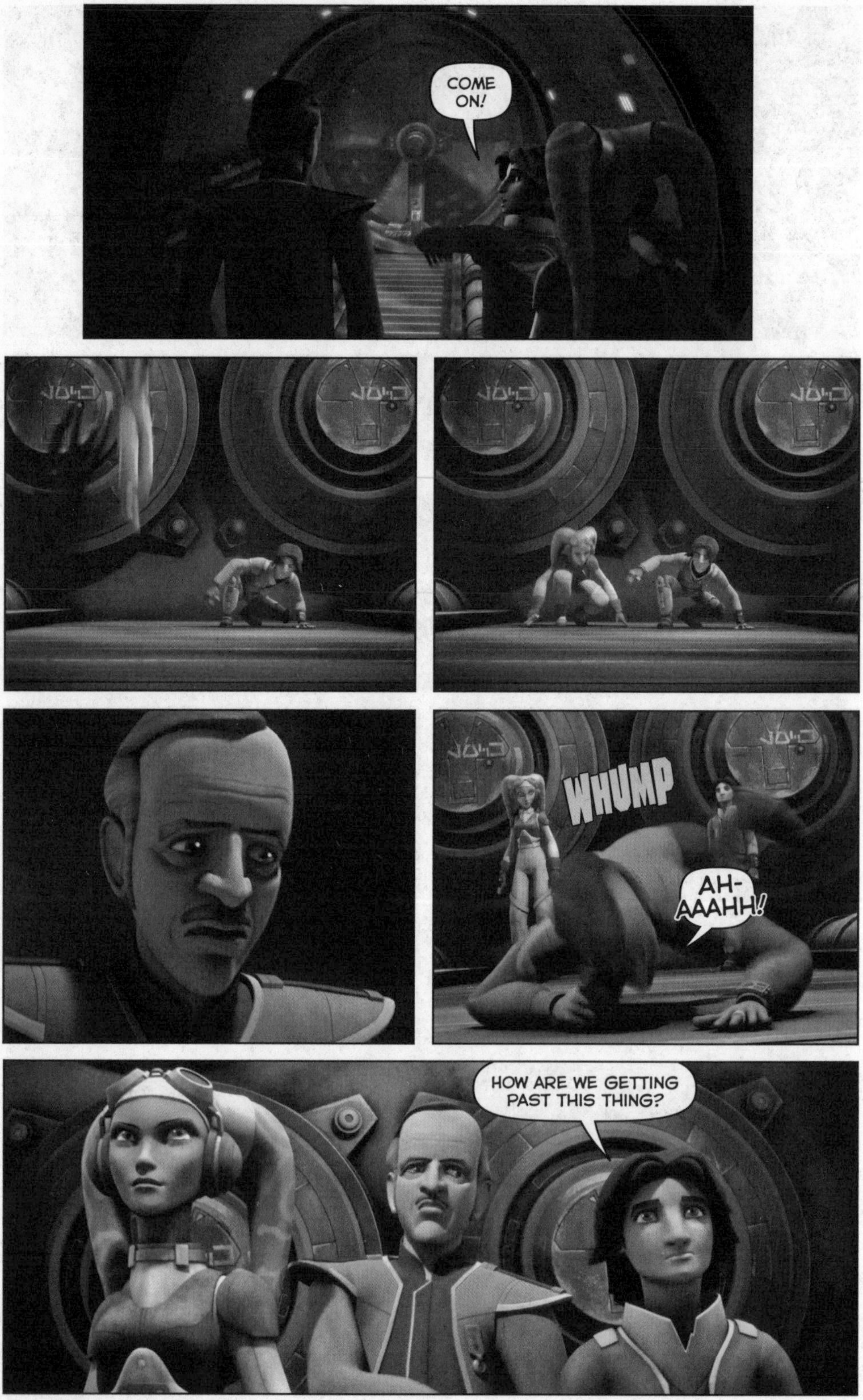
COME ON!
WHUMP
AH-AAAHH!
HOW ARE WE GETTING PAST THIS THING?

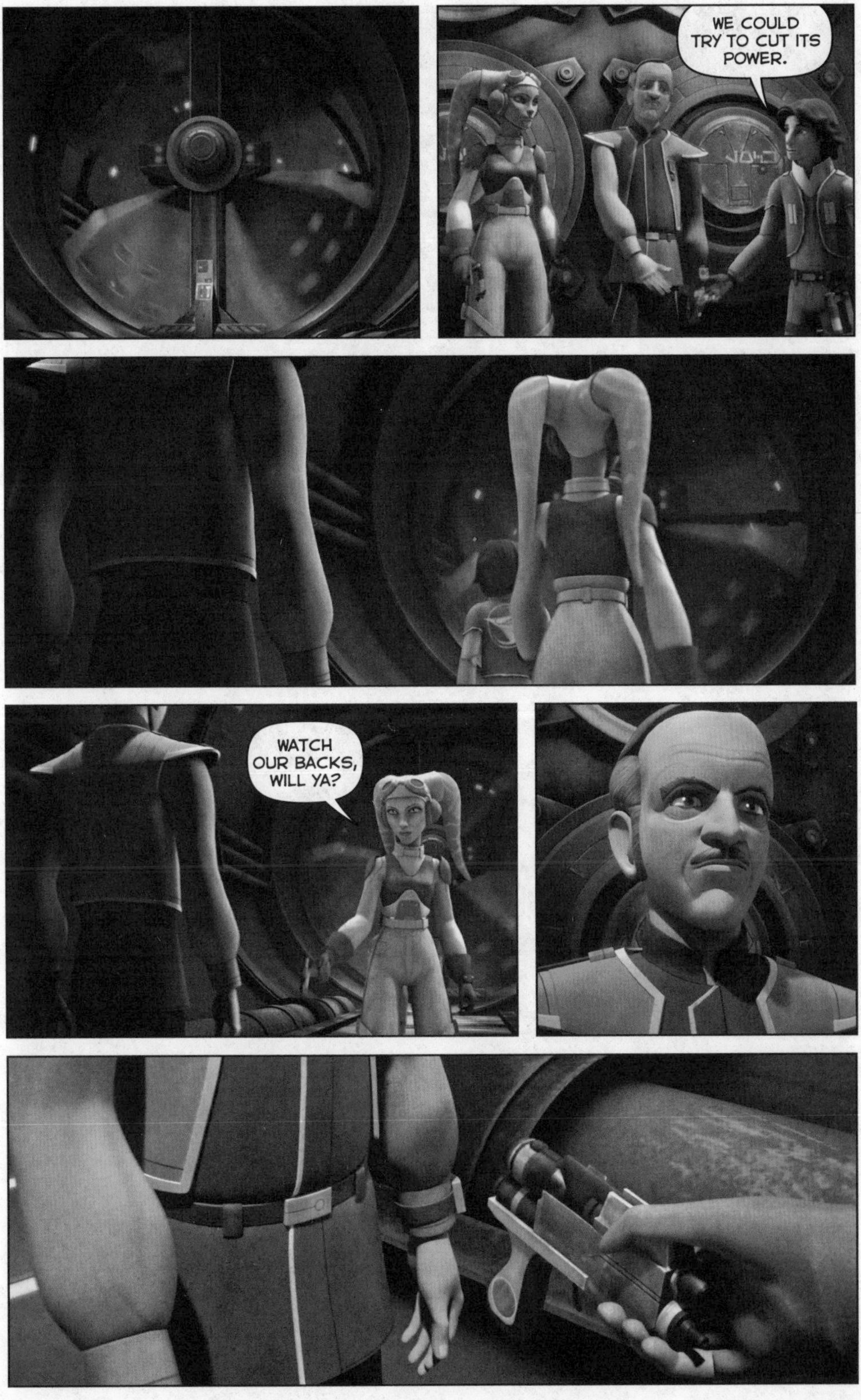
WE COULD TRY TO CUT ITS POWER.
WATCH OUR BACKS, WILL YA?

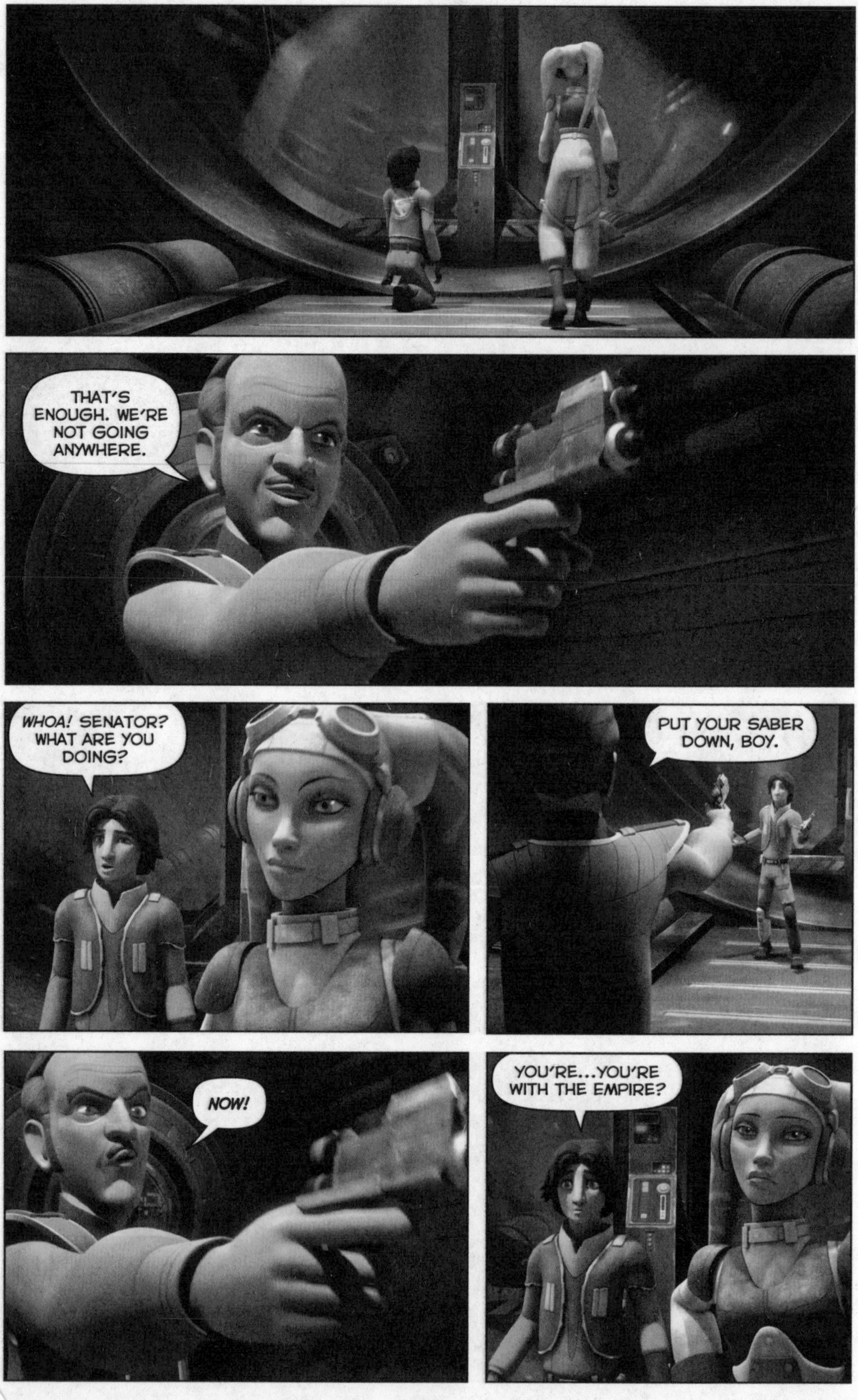
THAT'S ENOUGH. WE'RE NOT GOING ANYWHERE.
WHOA! SENATOR? WHAT ARE YOU DOING?
PUT YOUR SABER DOWN, BOY.
NOW!
YOU'RE...YOU'RE WITH THE EMPIRE?

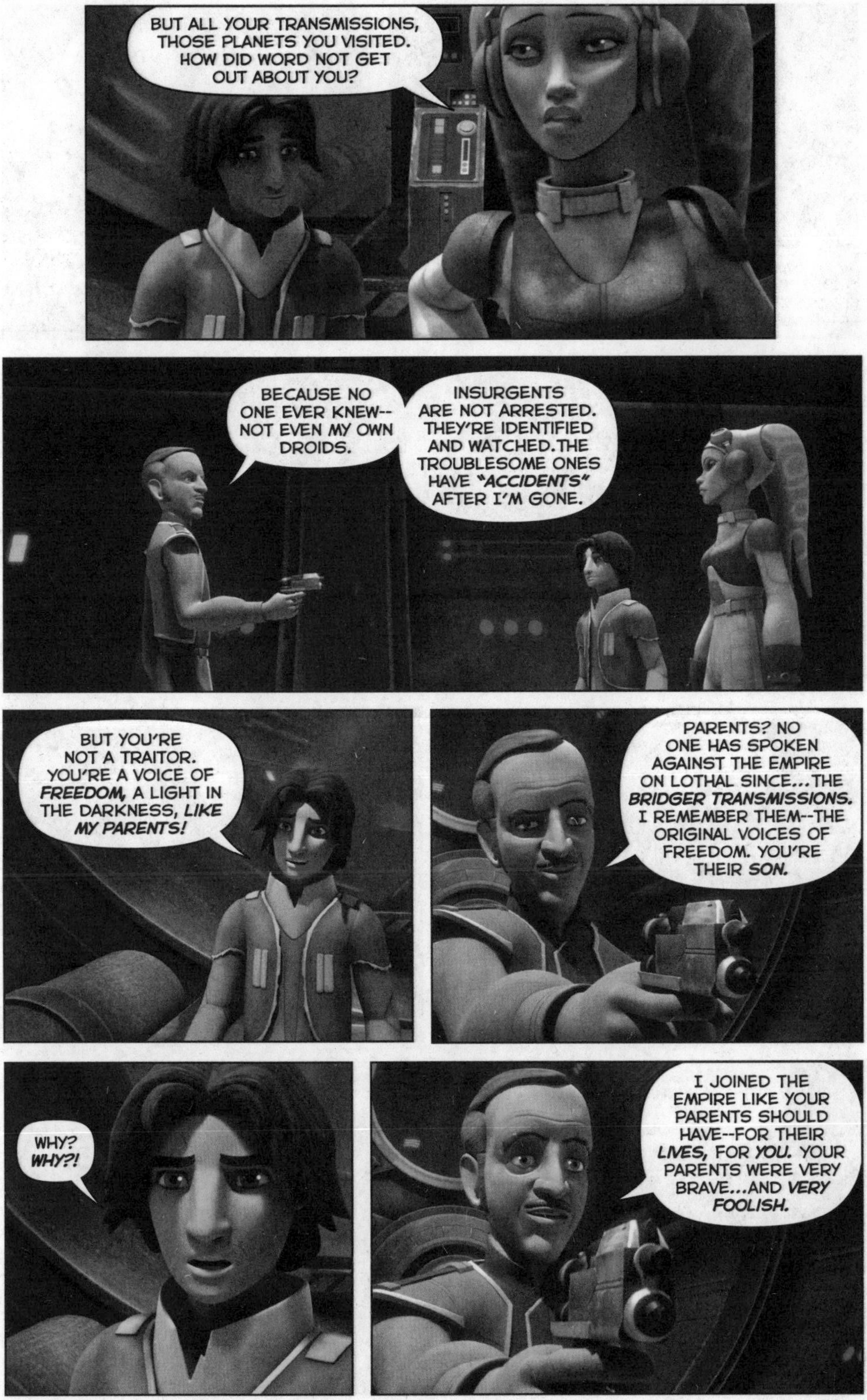
BUT ALL YOUR TRANSMISSIONS, THOSE PLANETS YOU VISITED. HOW DID WORD NOT GET OUT ABOUT YOU?
BECAUSE NO ONE EVER KNEW-- NOT EVEN MY OWN DROIDS.
INSURGENTS ARE NOT ARRESTED. THEY'RE IDENTIFIED AND WATCHED.THE TROUBLESOME ONES HAVE *"ACCIDENTS"* AFTER I'M GONE.
BUT YOU'RE NOT A TRAITOR. YOU'RE A VOICE OF *FREEDOM,* A LIGHT IN THE DARKNESS, *LIKE MY PARENTS!*
PARENTS? NO ONE HAS SPOKEN AGAINST THE EMPIRE ON LOTHAL SINCE...THE *BRIDGER TRANSMISSIONS.* I REMEMBER THEM--THE ORIGINAL VOICES OF FREEDOM. YOU'RE THEIR *SON.*
WHY? *WHY?!*
I JOINED THE EMPIRE LIKE YOUR PARENTS SHOULD HAVE--FOR THEIR *LIVES,* FOR *YOU.* YOUR PARENTS WERE VERY BRAVE...AND *VERY FOOLISH.*

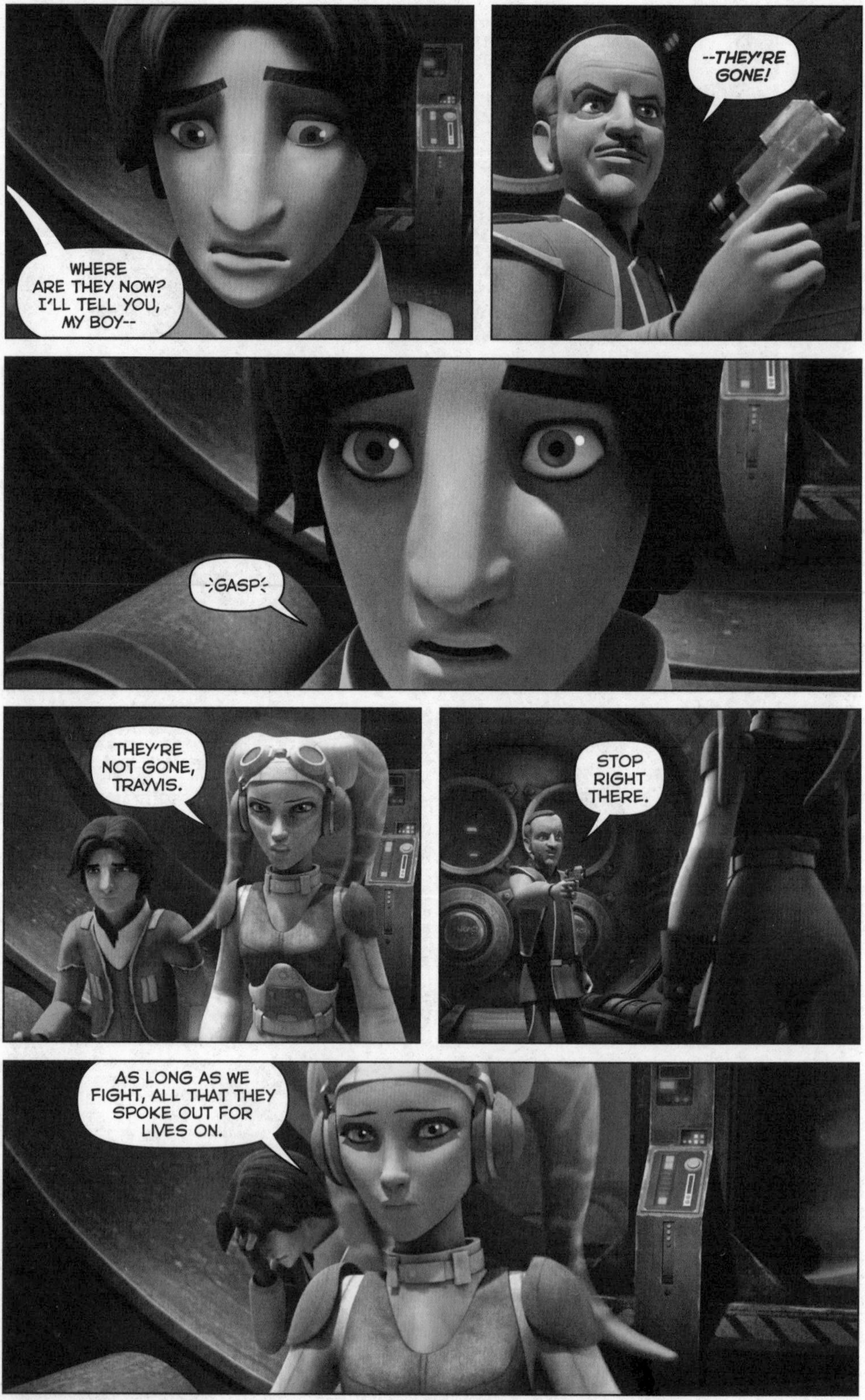
WHERE ARE THEY NOW? I'LL TELL YOU, MY BOY--
--THEY'RE GONE!
GASP
THEY'RE NOT GONE, TRAYVIS.
STOP RIGHT THERE.
AS LONG AS WE FIGHT, ALL THAT THEY SPOKE OUT FOR LIVES ON.

I SAID STOP!

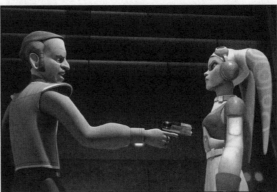

CLICK
CLICK

WHAT? NO!

FWACK

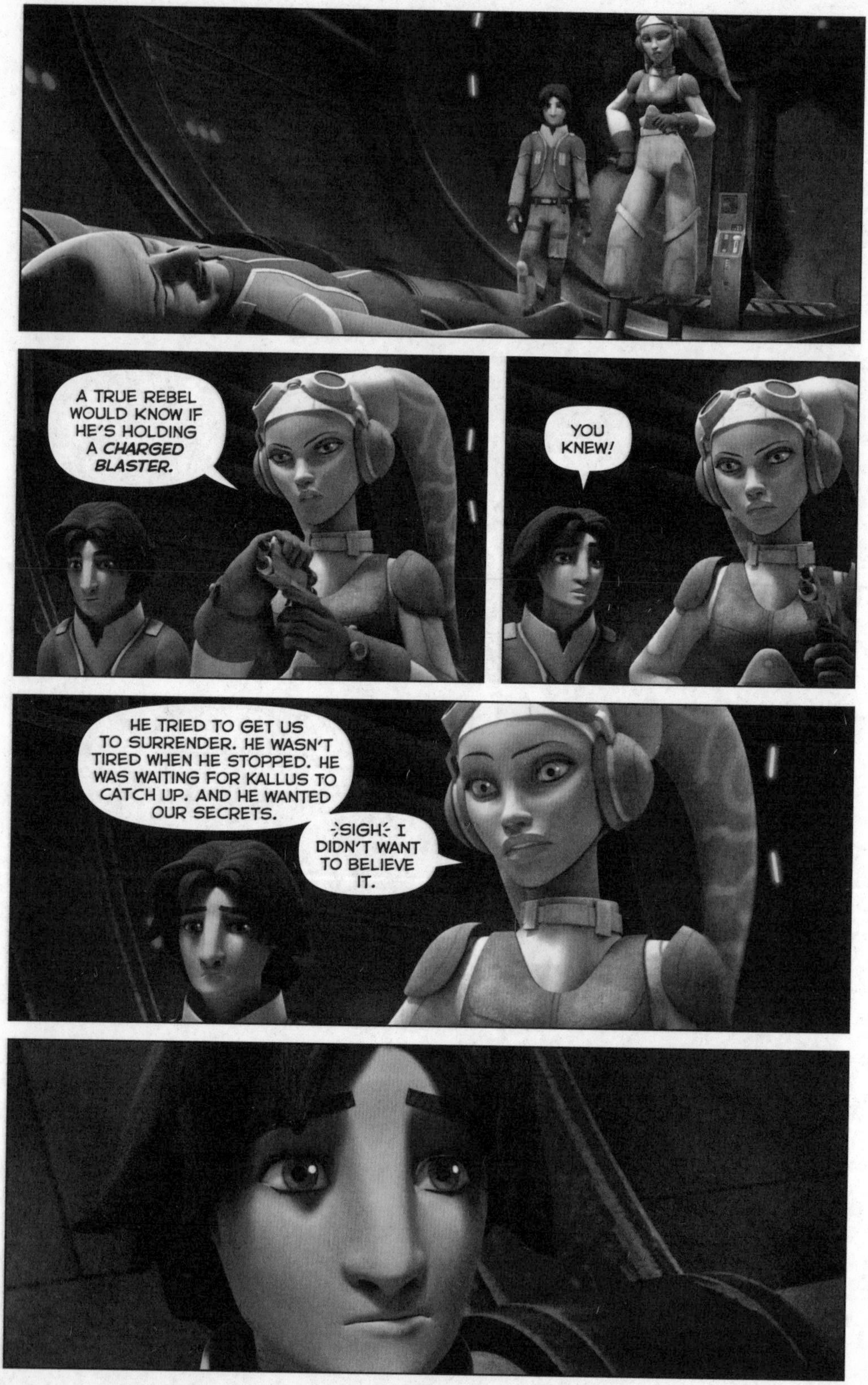
A TRUE REBEL WOULD KNOW IF HE'S HOLDING A *CHARGED BLASTER.*
YOU KNEW!
HE TRIED TO GET US TO SURRENDER. HE WASN'T TIRED WHEN HE STOPPED. HE WAS WAITING FOR KALLUS TO CATCH UP. AND HE WANTED OUR SECRETS.
-SIGH- I DIDN'T WANT TO BELIEVE IT.

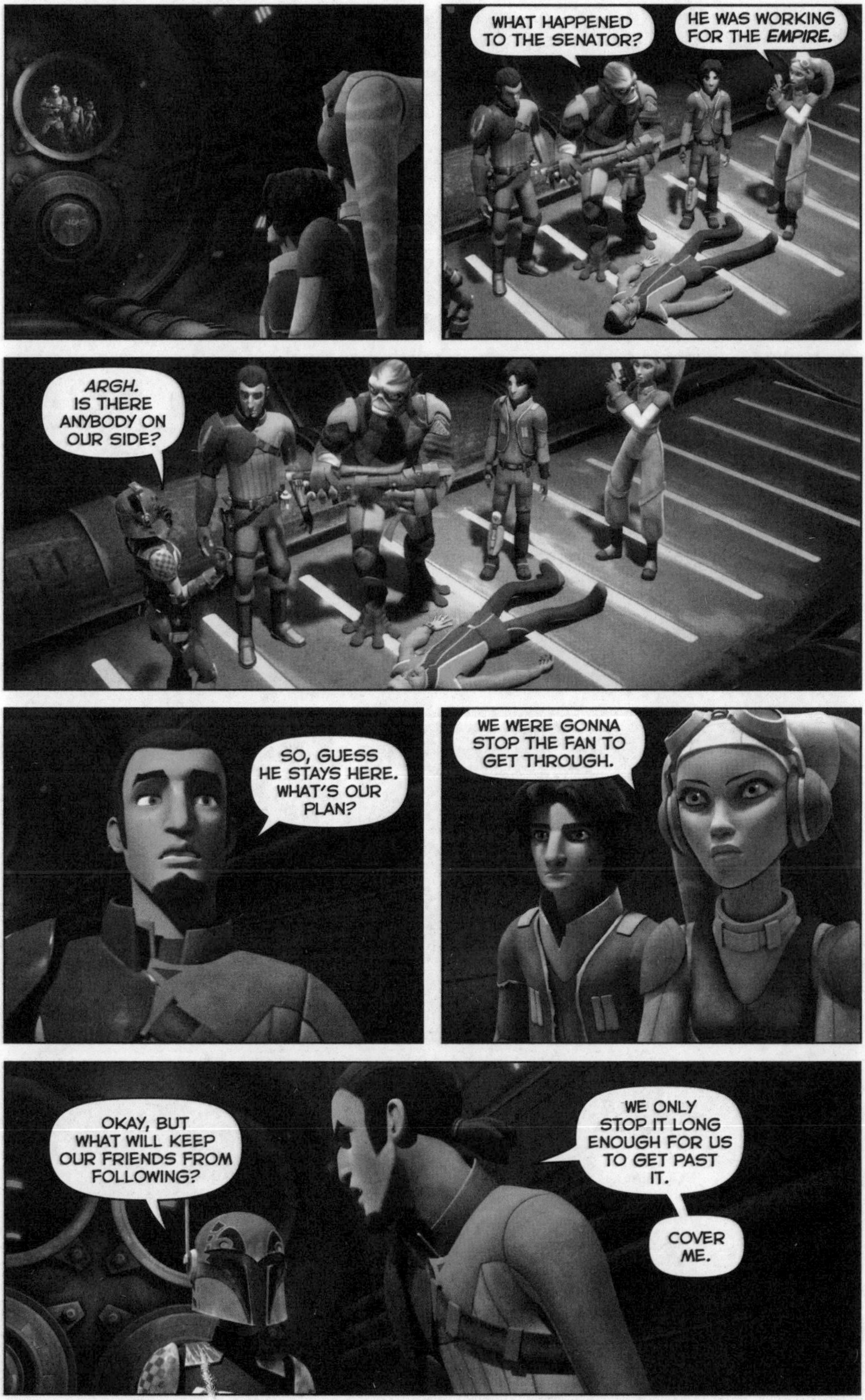
WHAT HAPPENED TO THE SENATOR?
HE WAS WORKING FOR THE *EMPIRE.*
ARGH. IS THERE ANYBODY ON OUR SIDE?
SO, GUESS HE STAYS HERE. WHAT'S OUR PLAN?
WE WERE GONNA STOP THE FAN TO GET THROUGH.
OKAY, BUT WHAT WILL KEEP OUR FRIENDS FROM FOLLOWING?
WE ONLY STOP IT LONG ENOUGH FOR US TO GET PAST IT.
COVER ME.

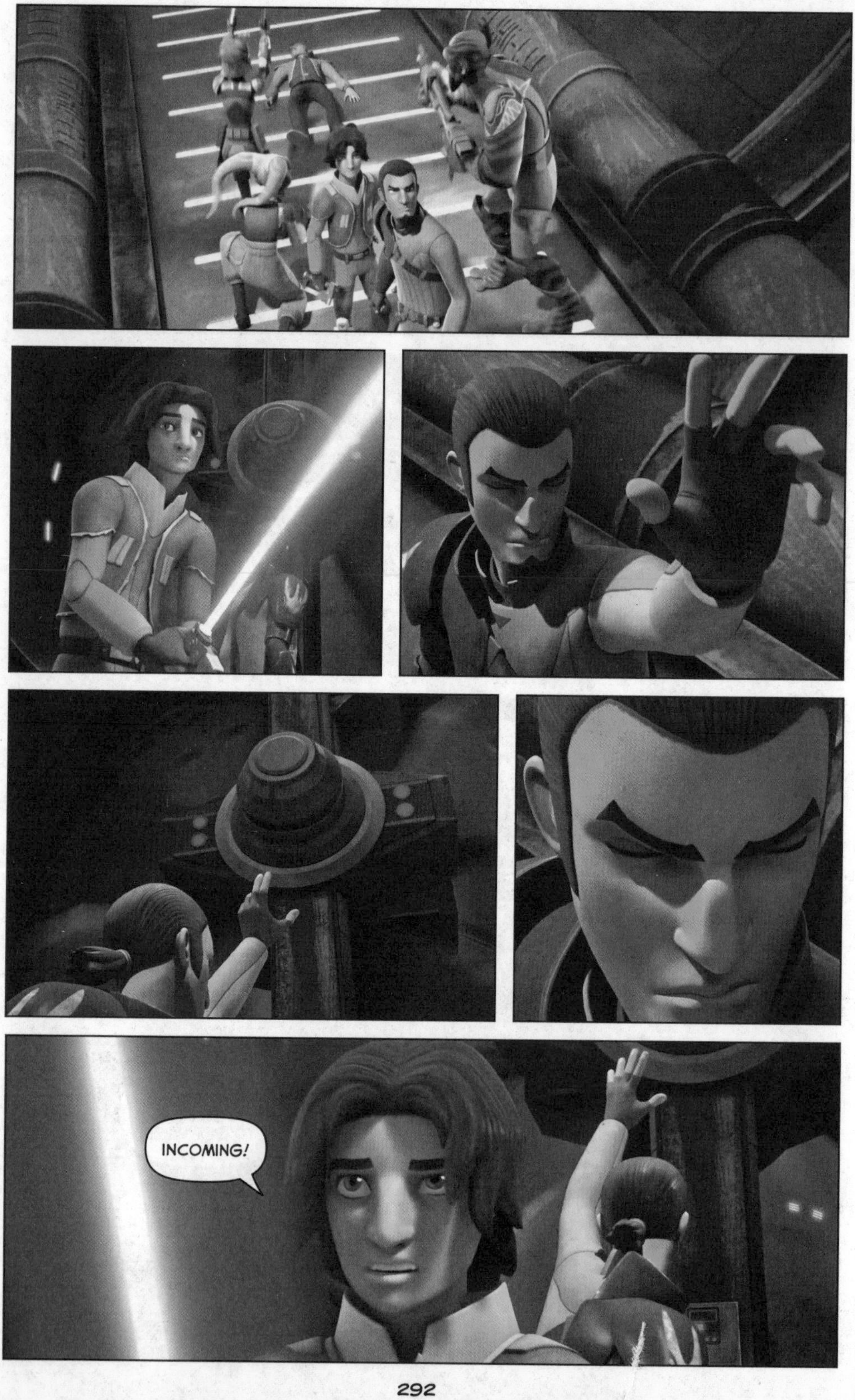
INCOMING!

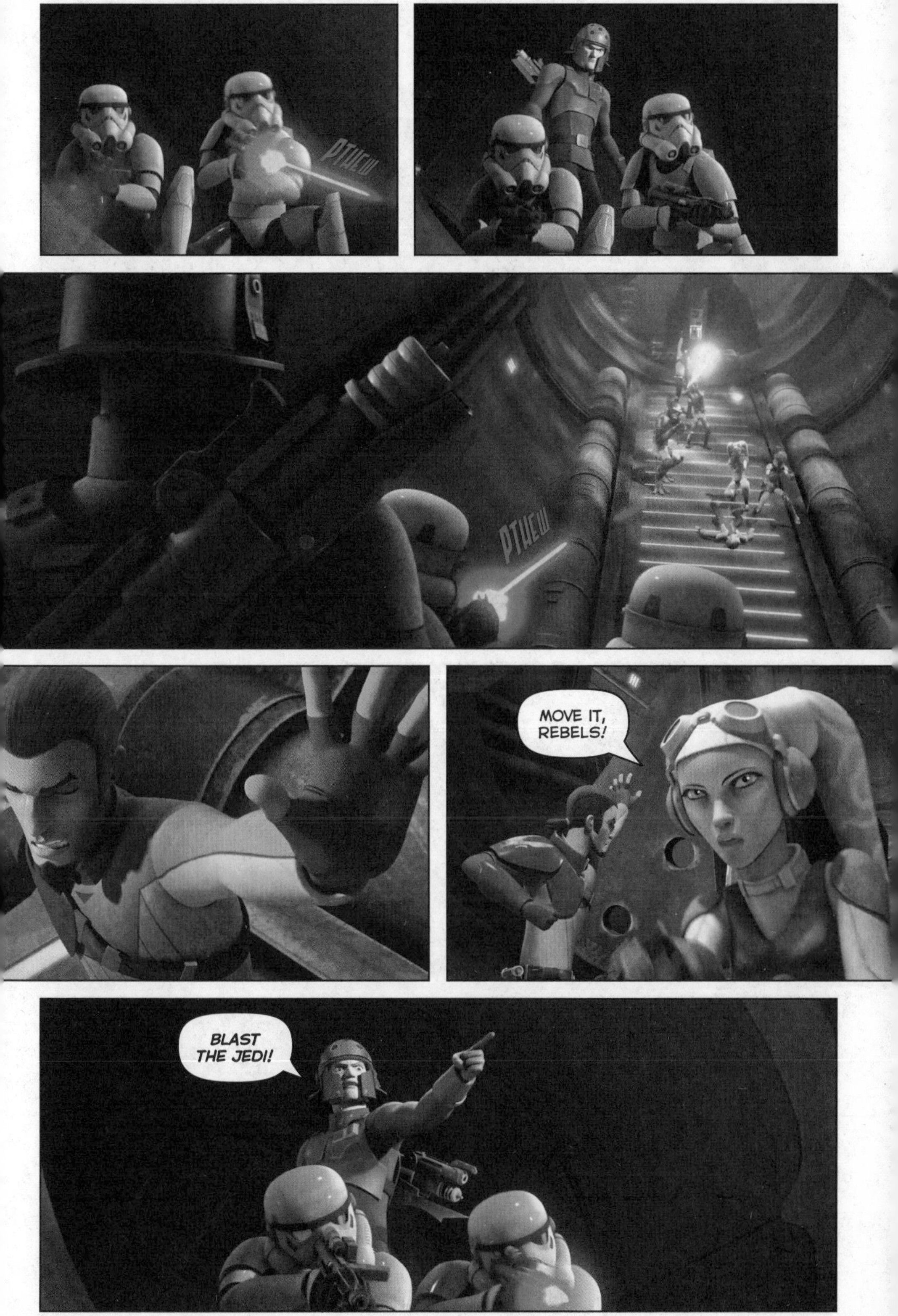
PTHEW
PTHEW
MOVE IT, REBELS!
BLAST THE JEDI!

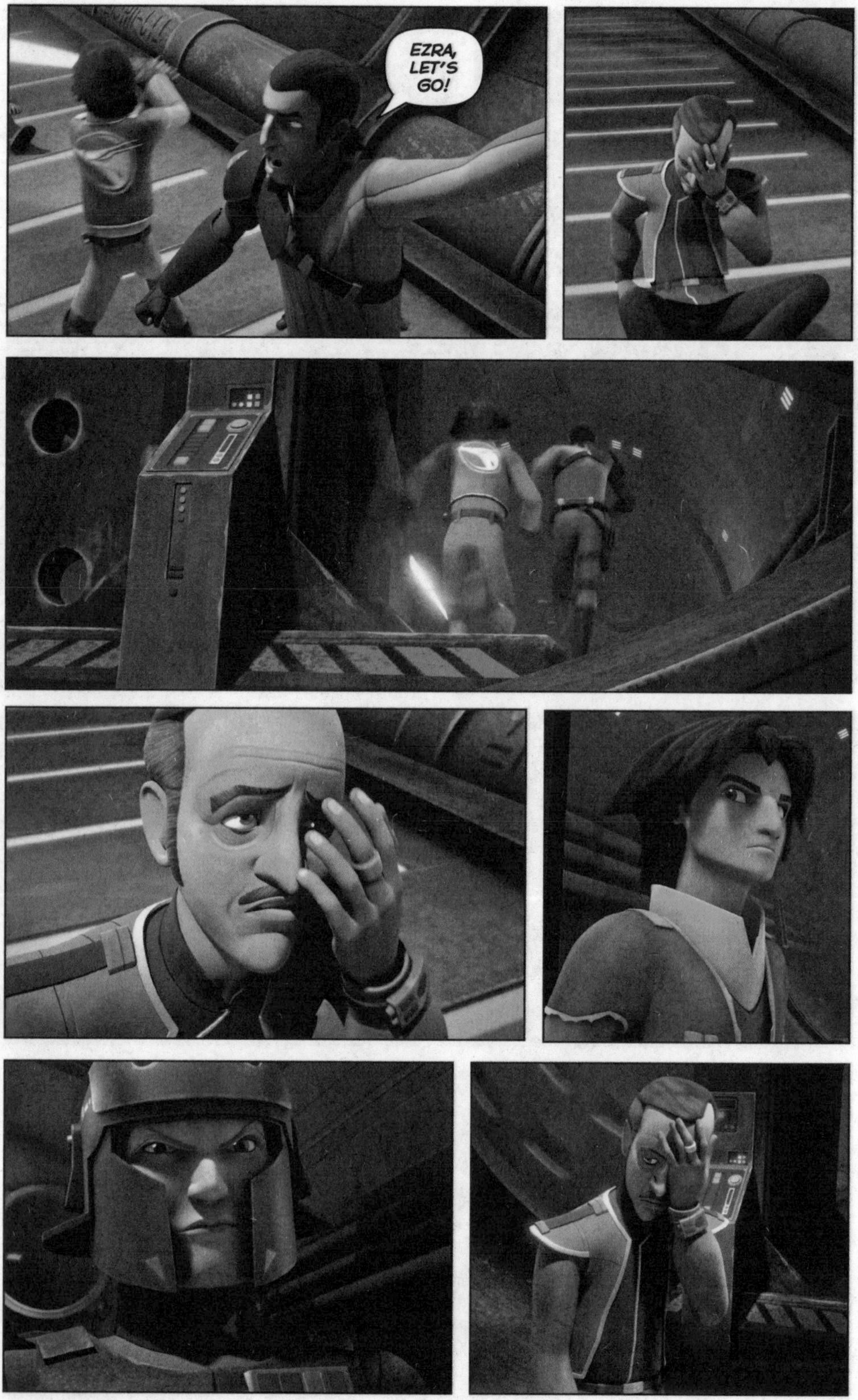
EZRA, LET'S GO!

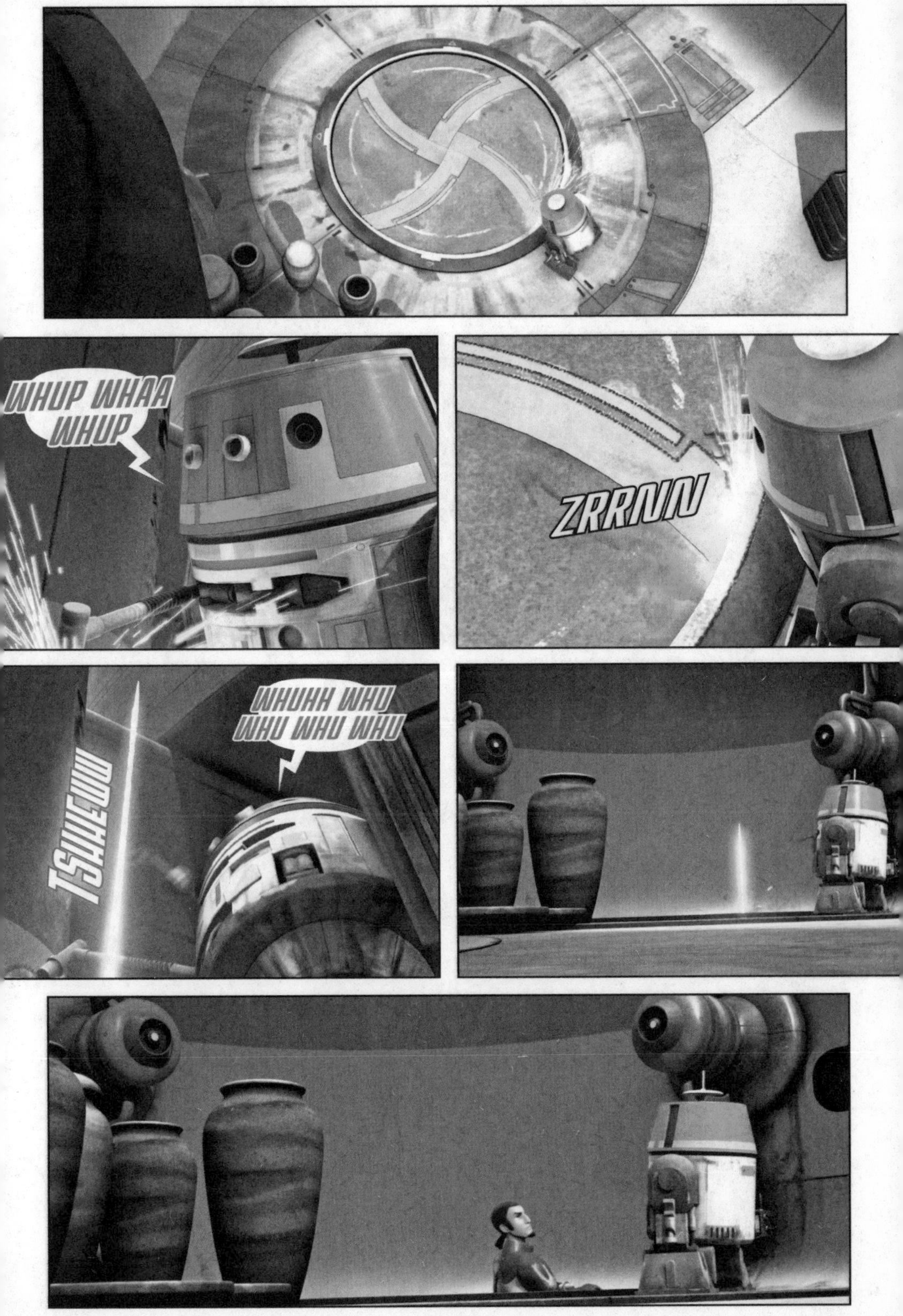
WHUP WHAA WHUP
ZRRNN
TSHHEWM
WHUHH WHU WHU WHU WHU

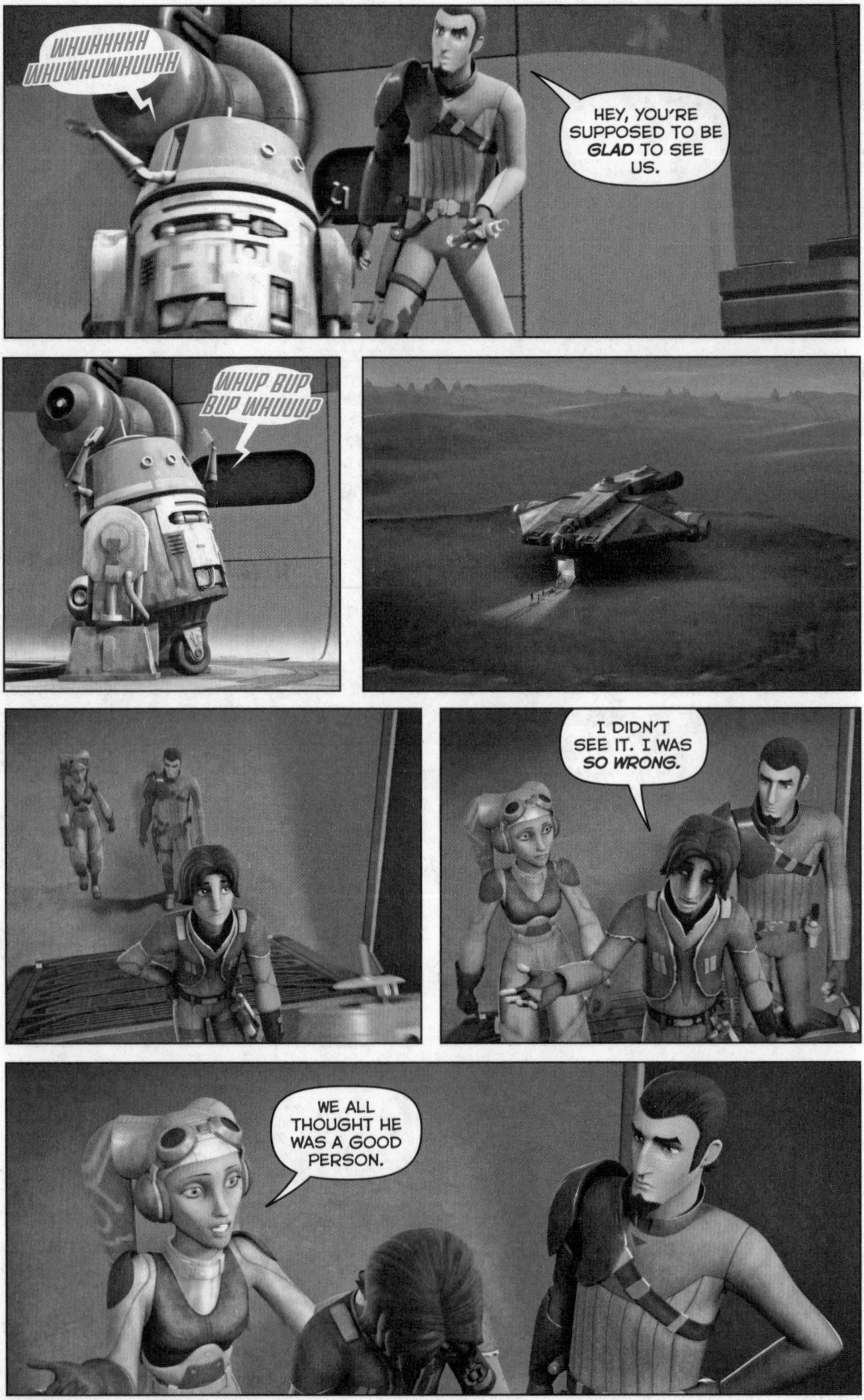
WHUHHHHH WHUWHUWHUUHH
HEY, YOU'RE SUPPOSED TO BE ***GLAD*** TO SEE US.
WHUP BUP BUP WHUUUP
I DIDN'T SEE IT. I WAS ***SO WRONG.***
WE ALL THOUGHT HE WAS A GOOD PERSON.

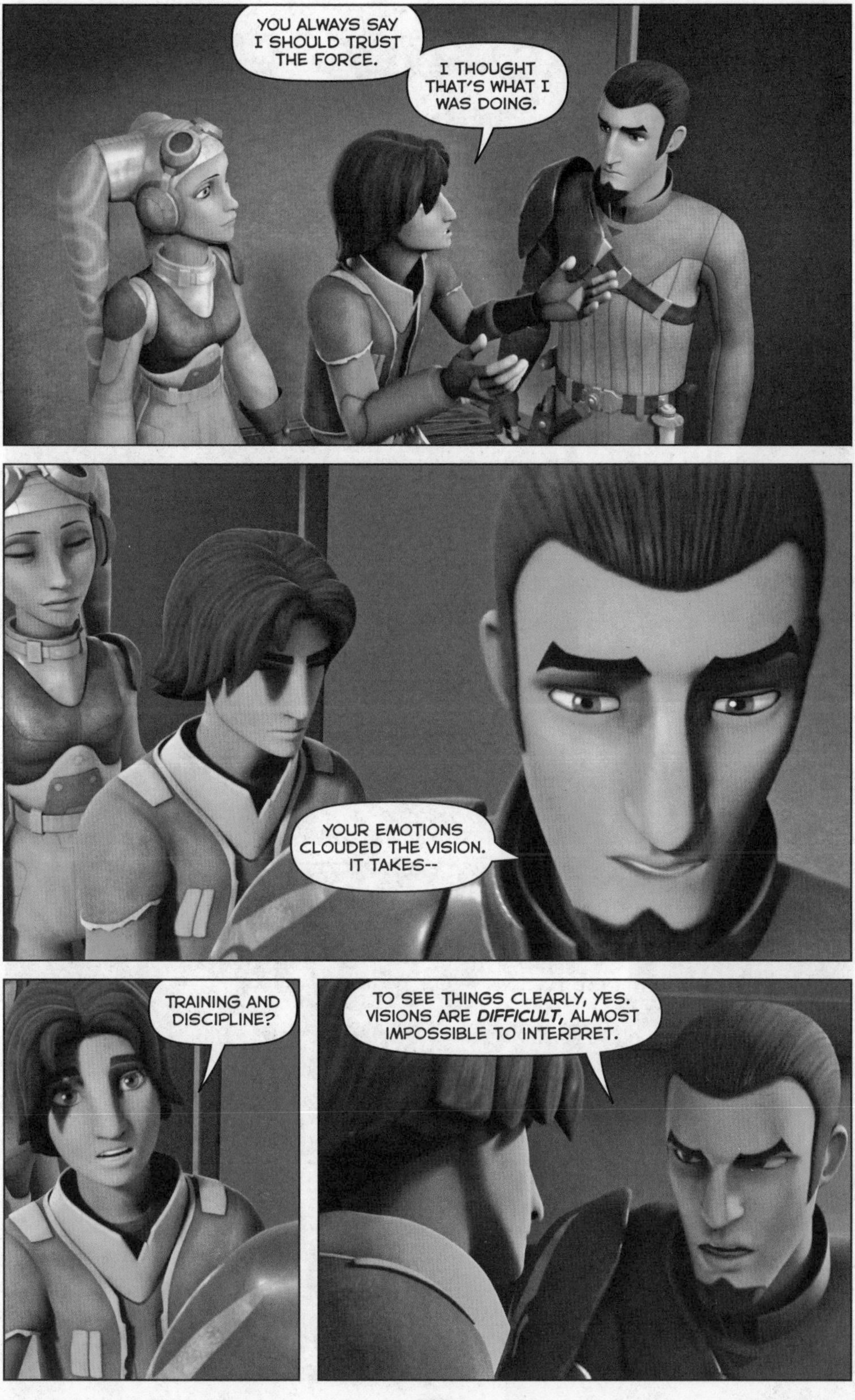
YOU ALWAYS SAY I SHOULD TRUST THE FORCE.
I THOUGHT THAT'S WHAT I WAS DOING.
YOUR EMOTIONS CLOUDED THE VISION. IT TAKES--
TRAINING AND DISCIPLINE?
TO SEE THINGS CLEARLY, YES. VISIONS ARE ***DIFFICULT,*** ALMOST IMPOSSIBLE TO INTERPRET.

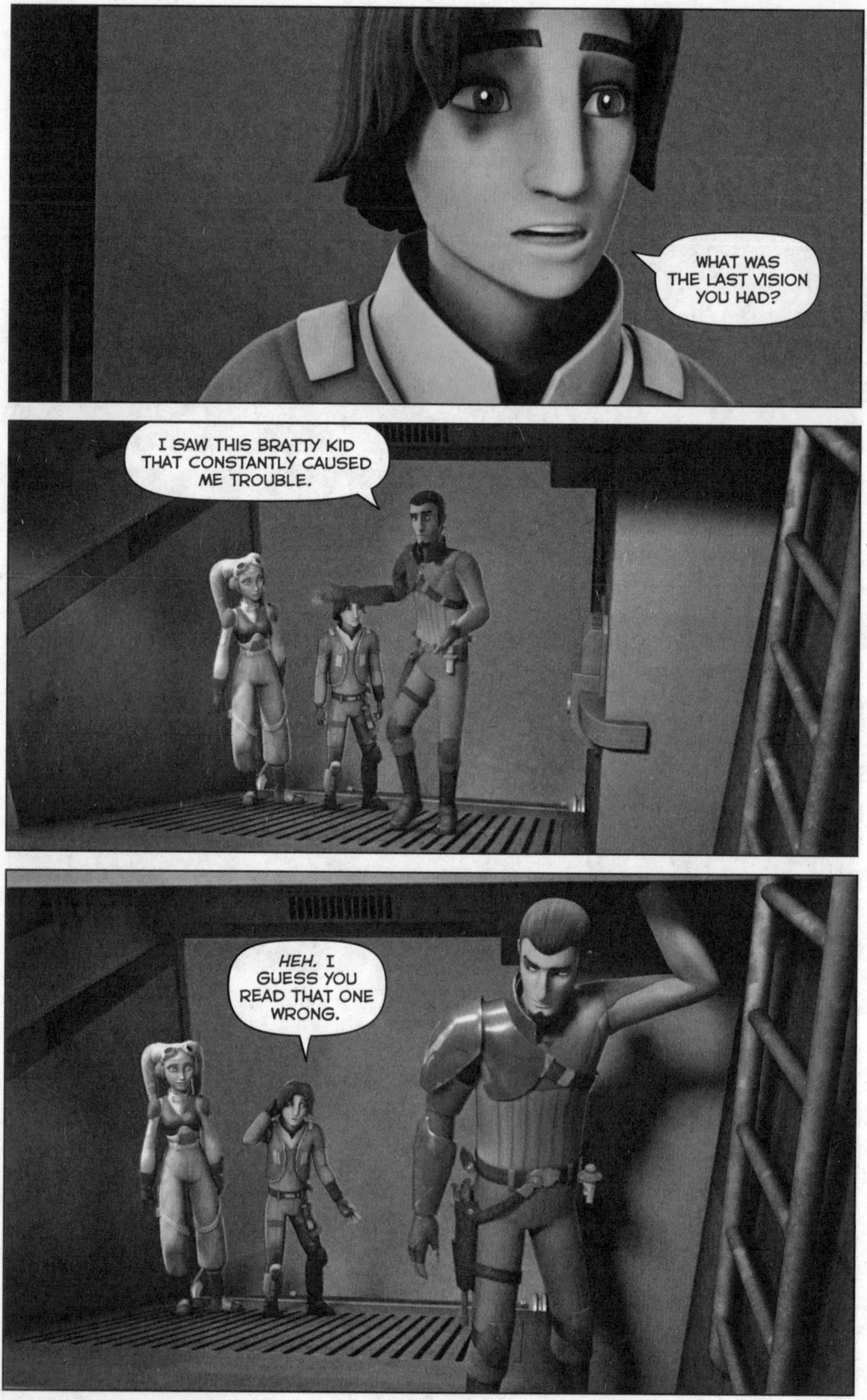
WHAT WAS THE LAST VISION YOU HAD?
I SAW THIS BRATTY KID THAT CONSTANTLY CAUSED ME TROUBLE.
HEH. I GUESS YOU READ THAT ONE WRONG.

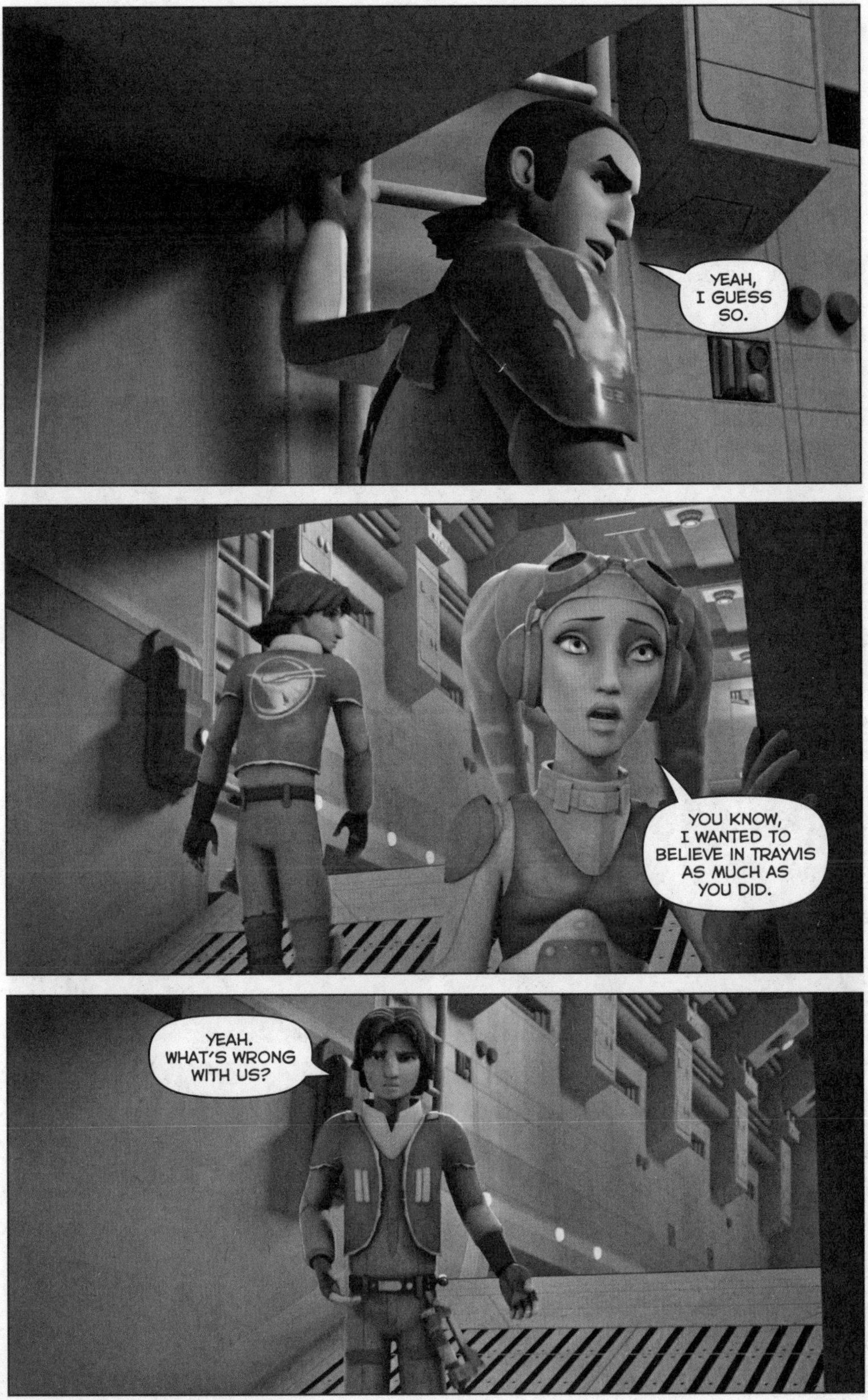
YEAH, I GUESS SO.
YOU KNOW, I WANTED TO BELIEVE IN TRAYVIS AS MUCH AS YOU DID.
YEAH. WHAT'S WRONG WITH US?

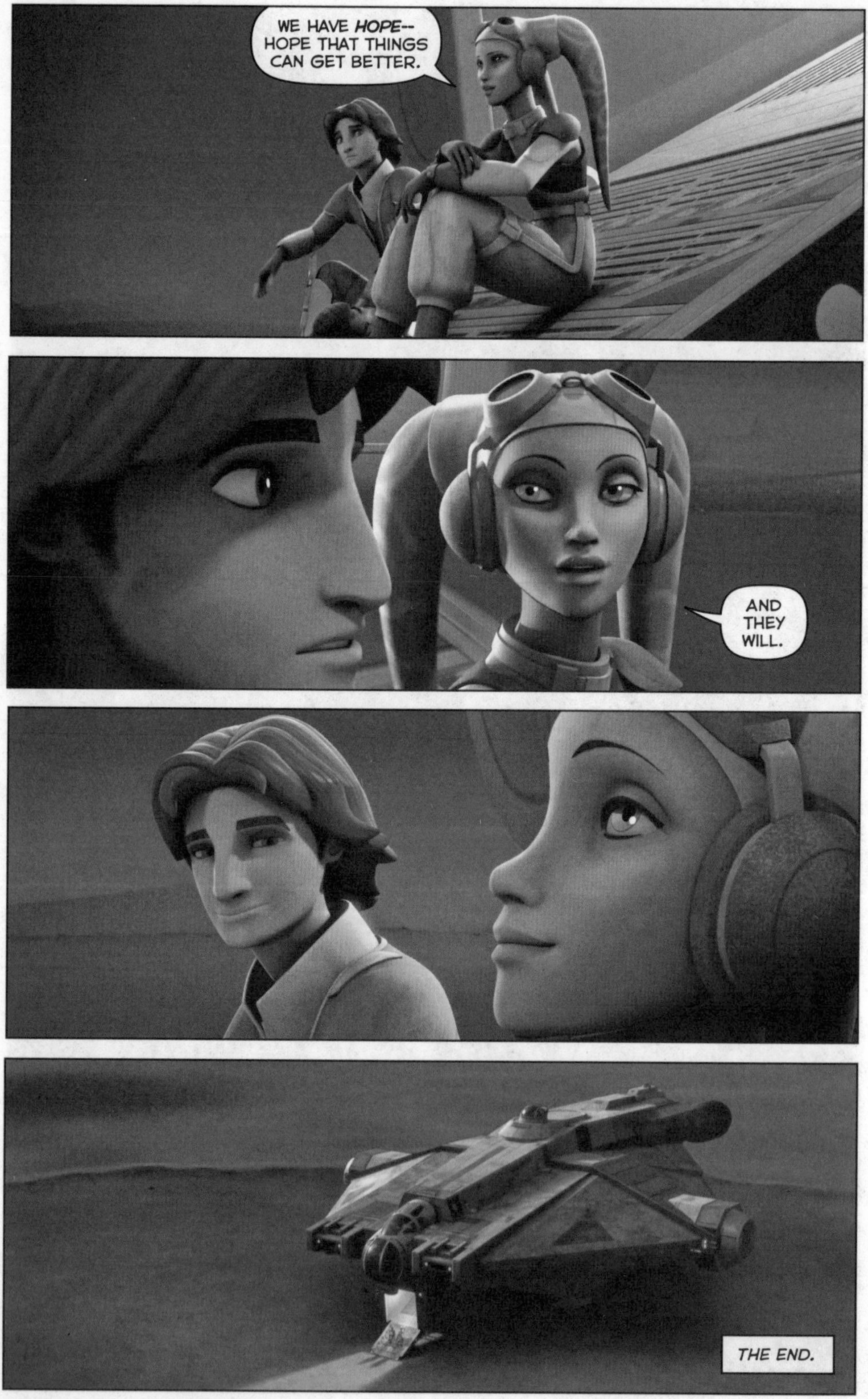
WE HAVE *HOPE*--
HOPE THAT THINGS
CAN GET BETTER.
AND
THEY
WILL.
THE END.

STAR WARS REBELS™

CALL TO ACTION

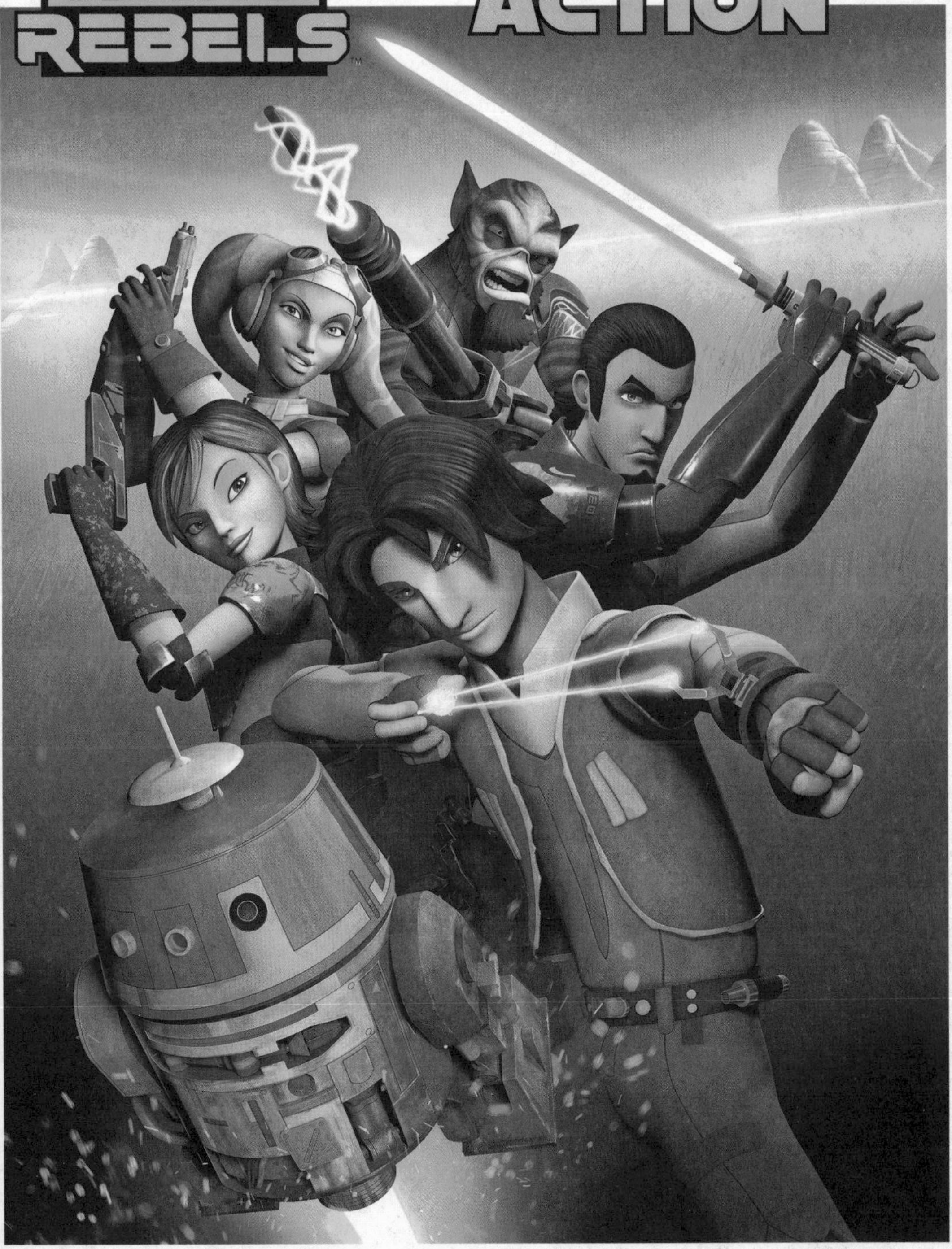

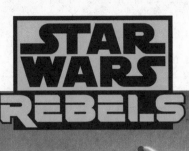

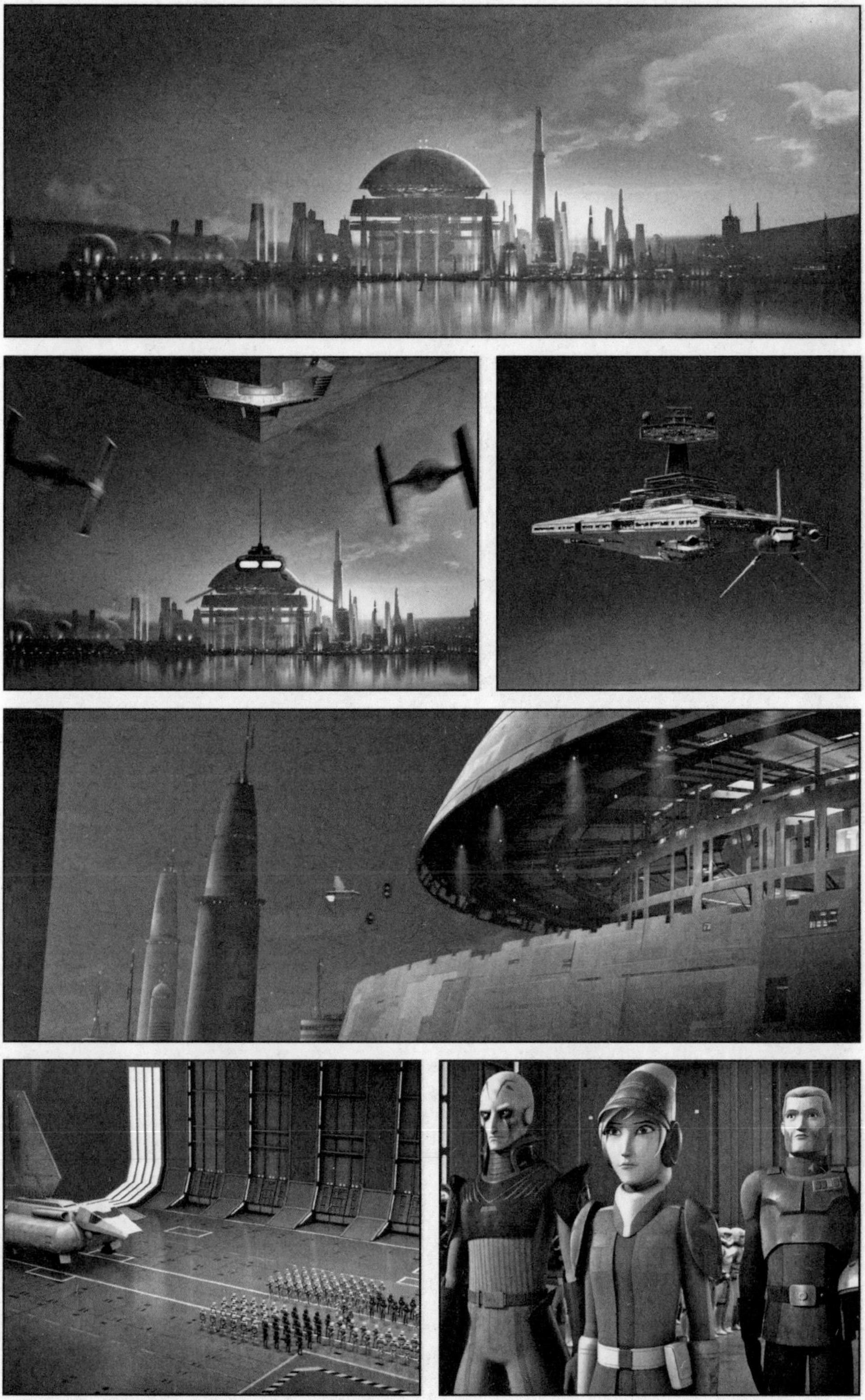

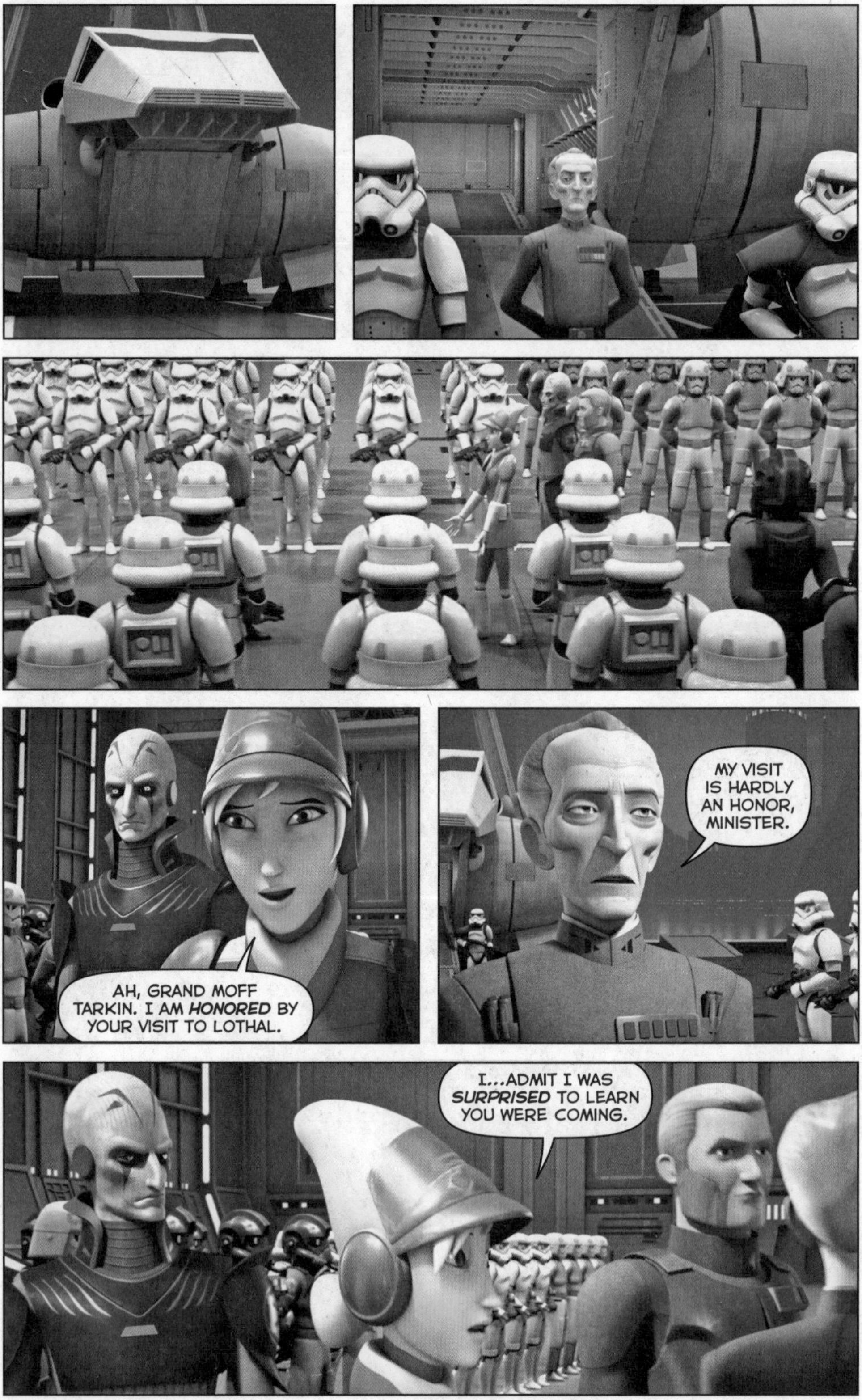
AH, GRAND MOFF TARKIN. I AM *HONORED* BY YOUR VISIT TO LOTHAL.
MY VISIT IS HARDLY AN HONOR, MINISTER.
I...ADMIT I WAS *SURPRISED* TO LEARN YOU WERE COMING.

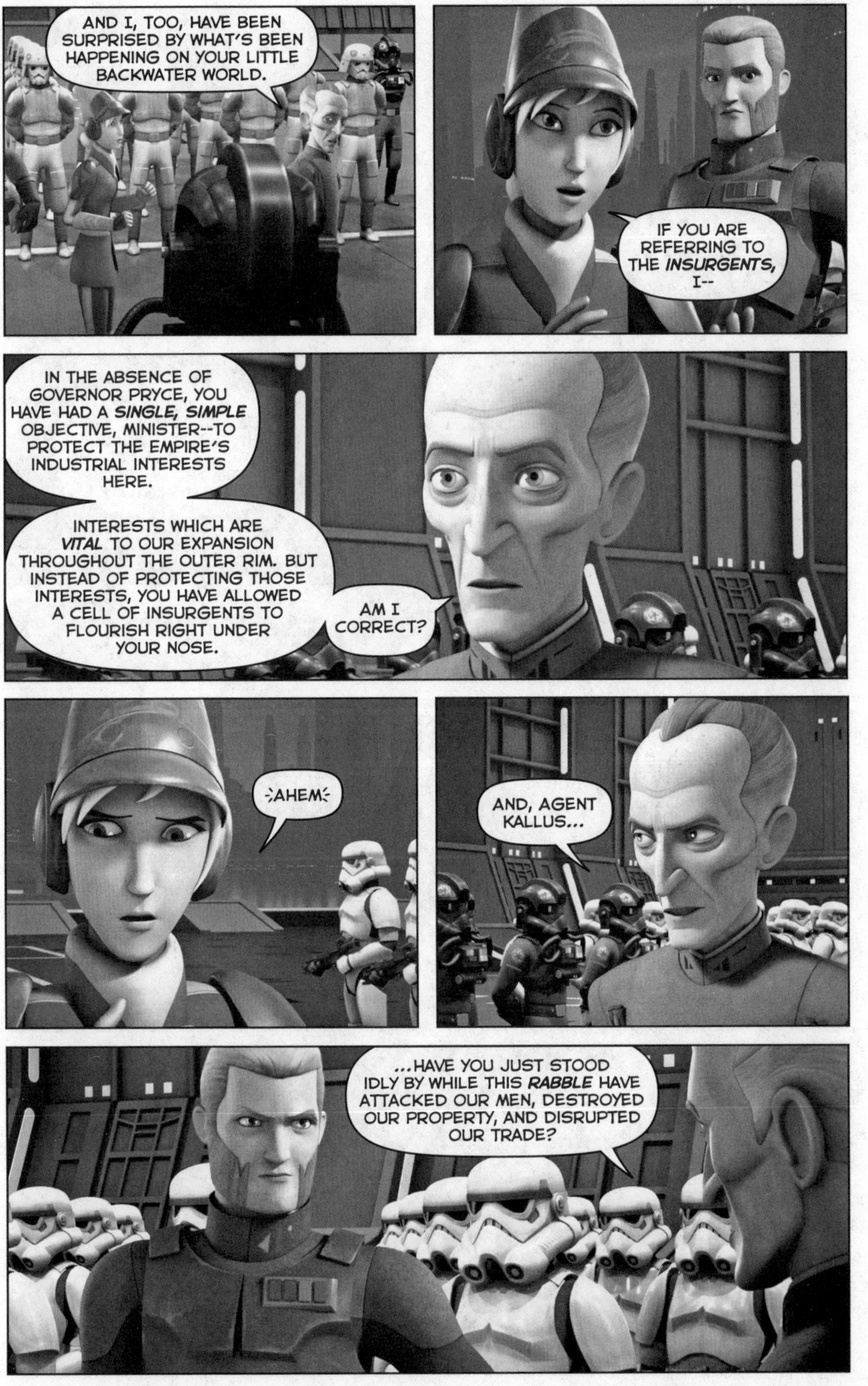

AND I, TOO, HAVE BEEN SURPRISED BY WHAT'S BEEN HAPPENING ON YOUR LITTLE BACKWATER WORLD.
IF YOU ARE REFERRING TO THE *INSURGENTS*, I--
IN THE ABSENCE OF GOVERNOR PRYCE, YOU HAVE HAD A *SINGLE, SIMPLE* OBJECTIVE, MINISTER--TO PROTECT THE EMPIRE'S INDUSTRIAL INTERESTS HERE.
INTERESTS WHICH ARE *VITAL* TO OUR EXPANSION THROUGHOUT THE OUTER RIM. BUT INSTEAD OF PROTECTING THOSE INTERESTS, YOU HAVE ALLOWED A CELL OF INSURGENTS TO FLOURISH RIGHT UNDER YOUR NOSE.
AM I CORRECT?
AHEM
AND, AGENT KALLUS...
...HAVE YOU JUST STOOD IDLY BY WHILE THIS *RABBLE* HAVE ATTACKED OUR MEN, DESTROYED OUR PROPERTY, AND DISRUPTED OUR TRADE?

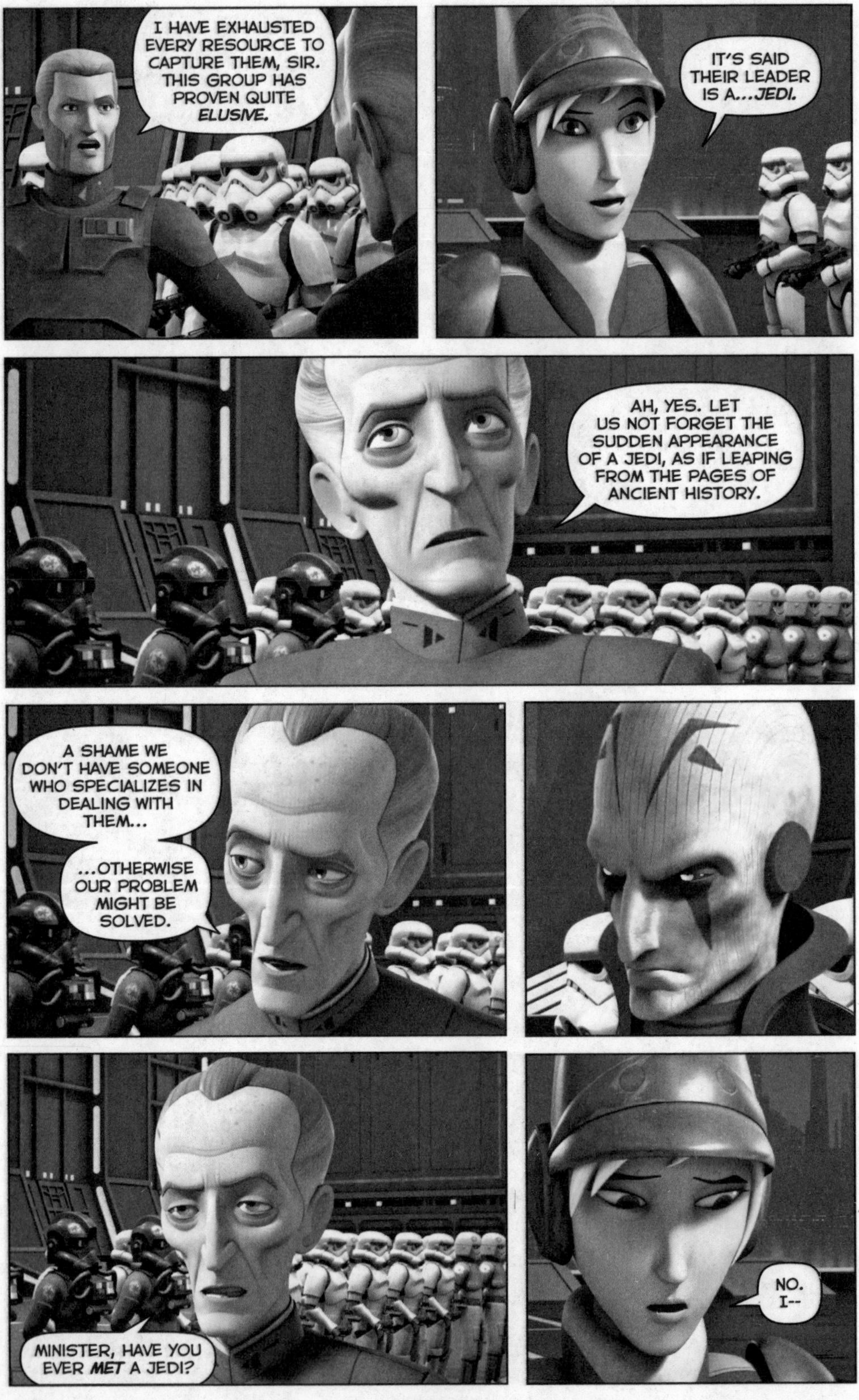
I HAVE EXHAUSTED EVERY RESOURCE TO CAPTURE THEM, SIR. THIS GROUP HAS PROVEN QUITE *ELUSIVE.*
IT'S SAID THEIR LEADER IS A...*JEDI.*
AH, YES. LET US NOT FORGET THE SUDDEN APPEARANCE OF A JEDI, AS IF LEAPING FROM THE PAGES OF ANCIENT HISTORY.
A SHAME WE DON'T HAVE SOMEONE WHO SPECIALIZES IN DEALING WITH THEM...
...OTHERWISE OUR PROBLEM MIGHT BE SOLVED.
MINISTER, HAVE YOU EVER *MET* A JEDI?
NO. I--

I ACTUALLY KNEW THE JEDI--NOT FROM THE PAGES OF FOLKLORE OR CHILDREN'S TALES, BUT AS FLESH AND BLOOD. AND DO YOU KNOW WHAT HAPPENED TO THEM?

WELL, THERE WERE RUMORS...

THEY DIED. EVERY LAST ONE OF THEM.

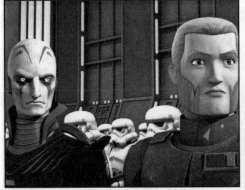

SO YOU SEE, THIS CRIMINAL CANNOT BE WHAT HE CLAIMS TO BE...

...AND I SHALL PROVE IT.

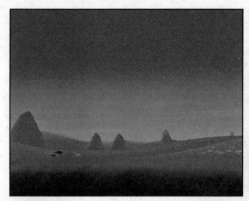

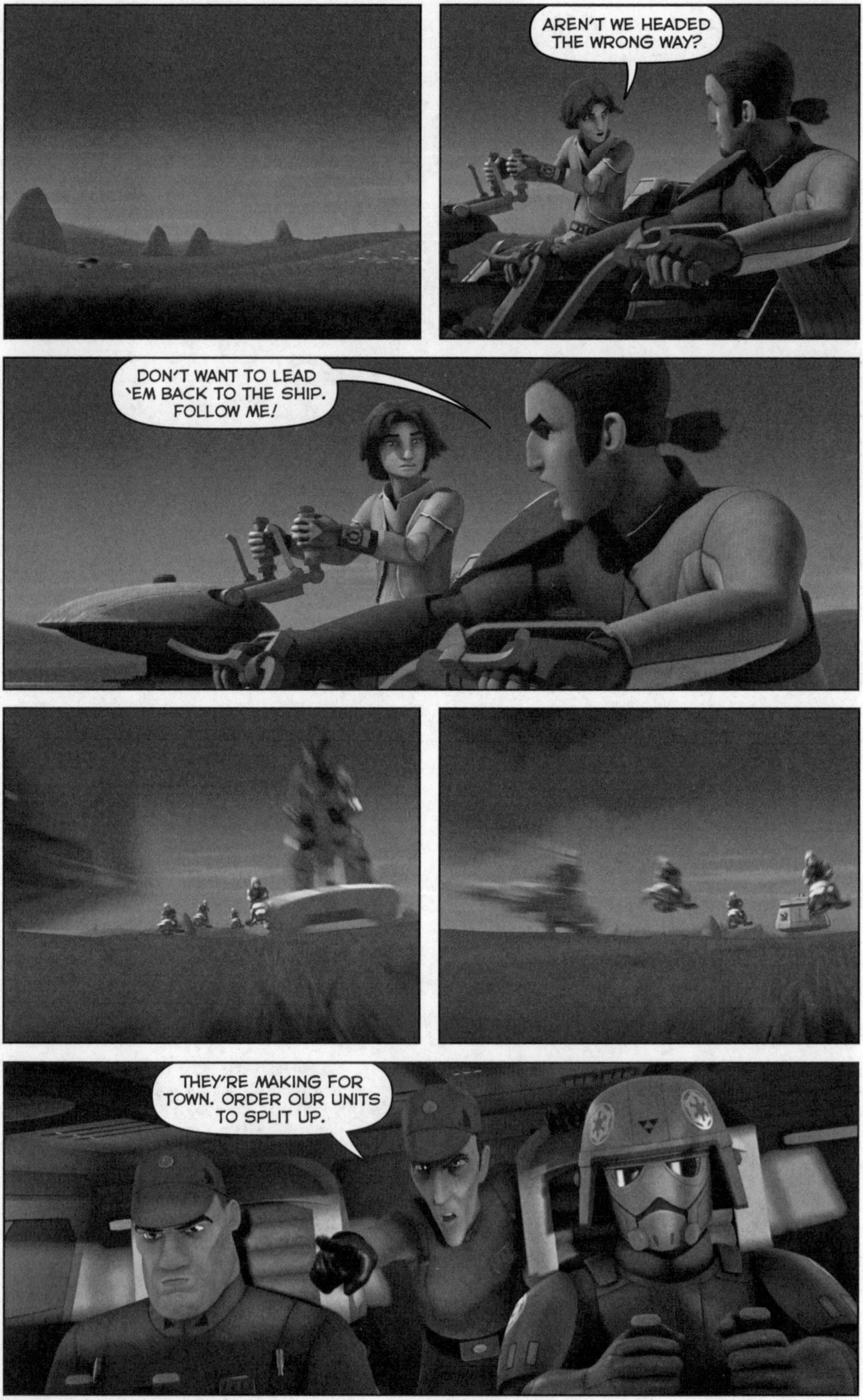
AREN'T WE HEADED THE WRONG WAY?
DON'T WANT TO LEAD 'EM BACK TO THE SHIP. FOLLOW ME!
THEY'RE MAKING FOR TOWN. ORDER OUR UNITS TO SPLIT UP.

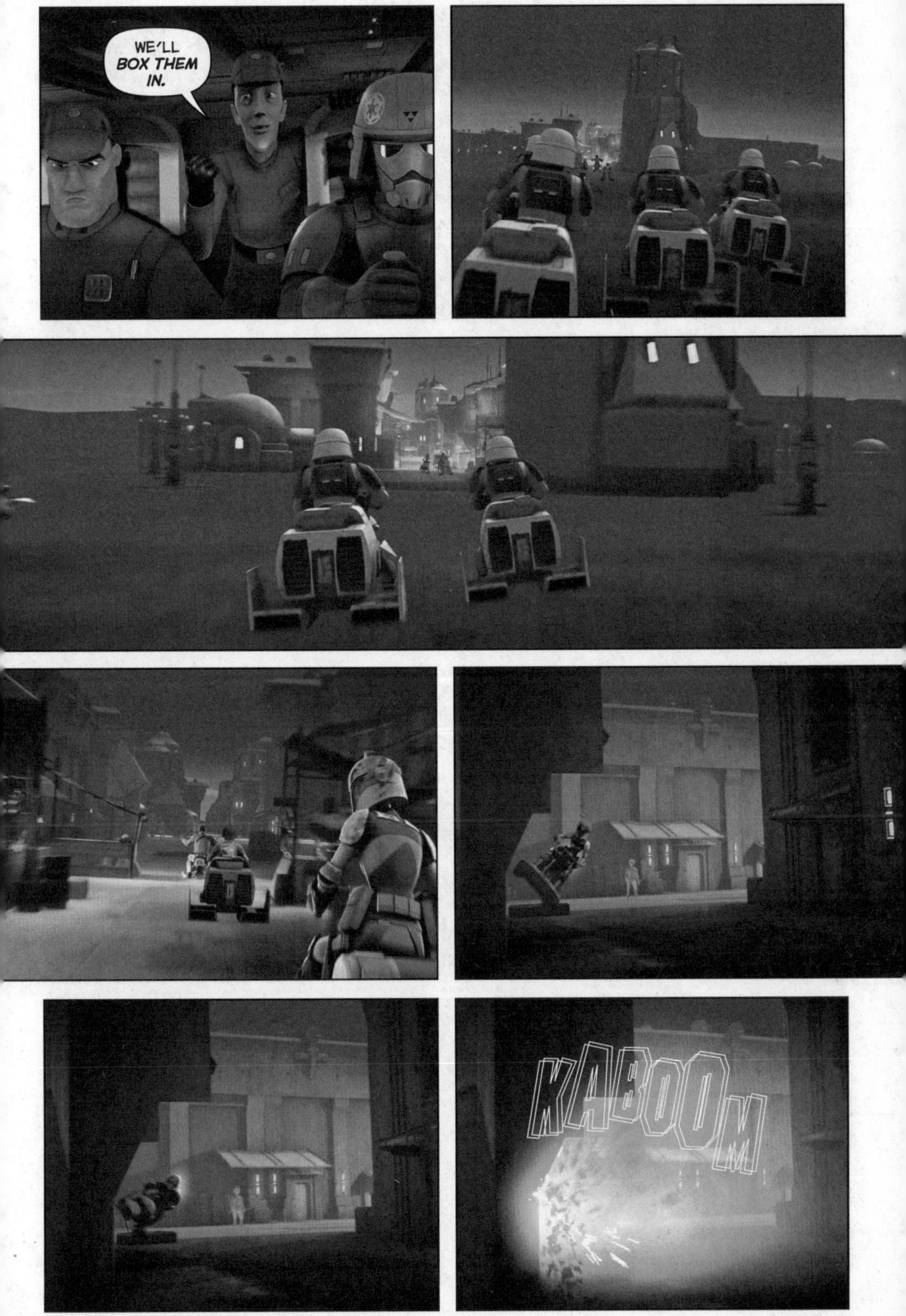
WE'LL BOX THEM IN.
KABOOM

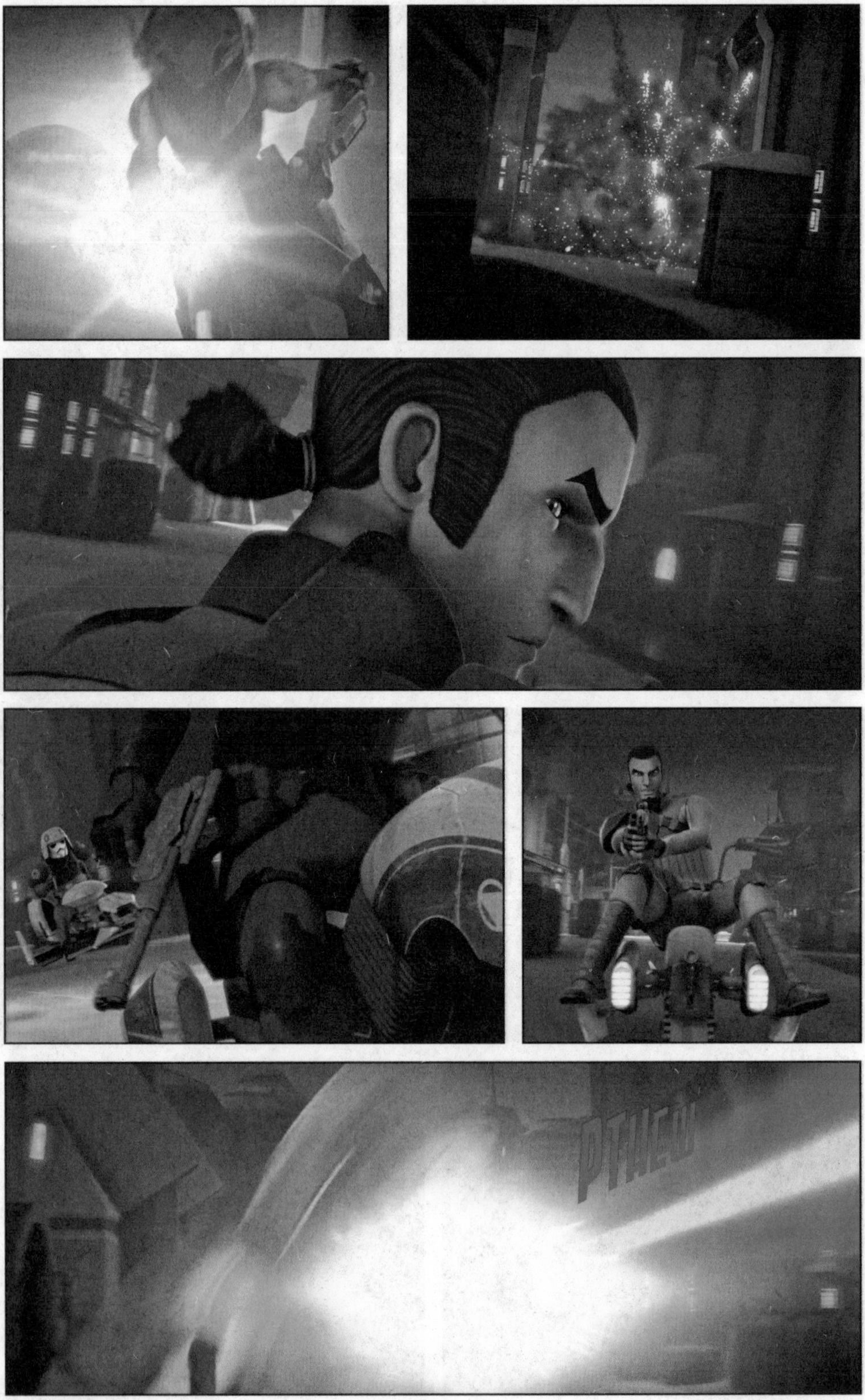
PTHEW

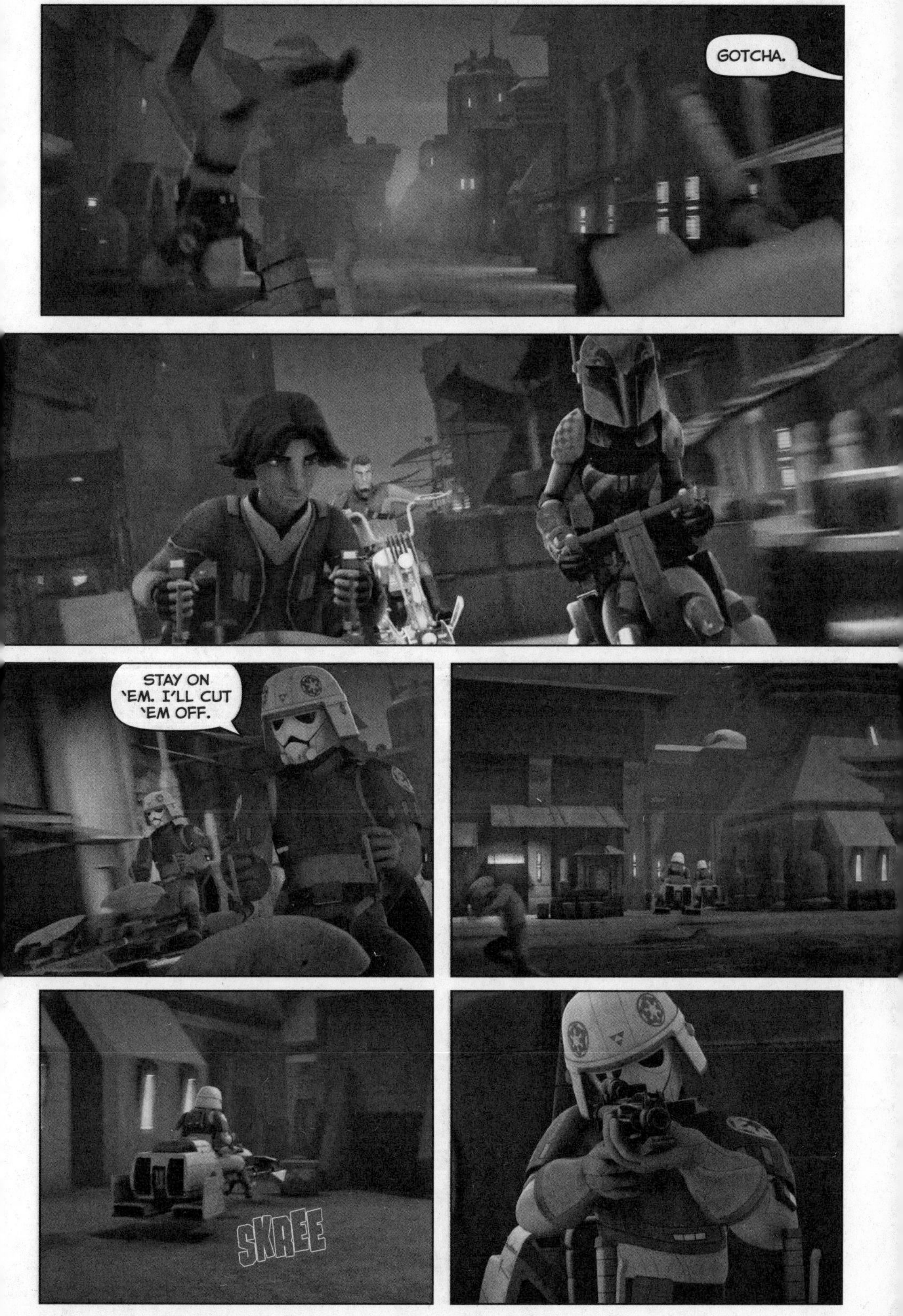
GOTCHA.
STAY ON 'EM. I'LL CUT 'EM OFF.
SKREE

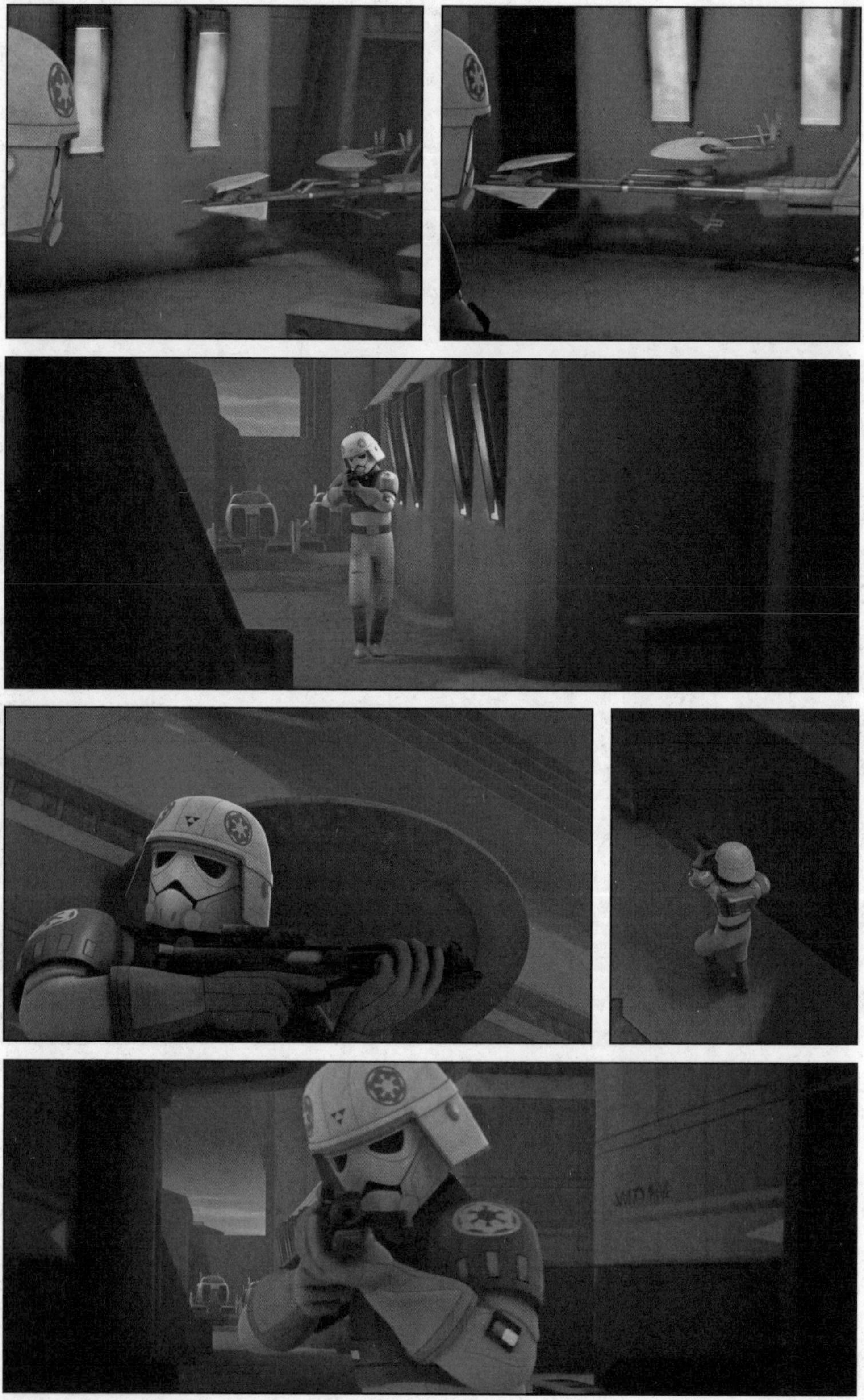

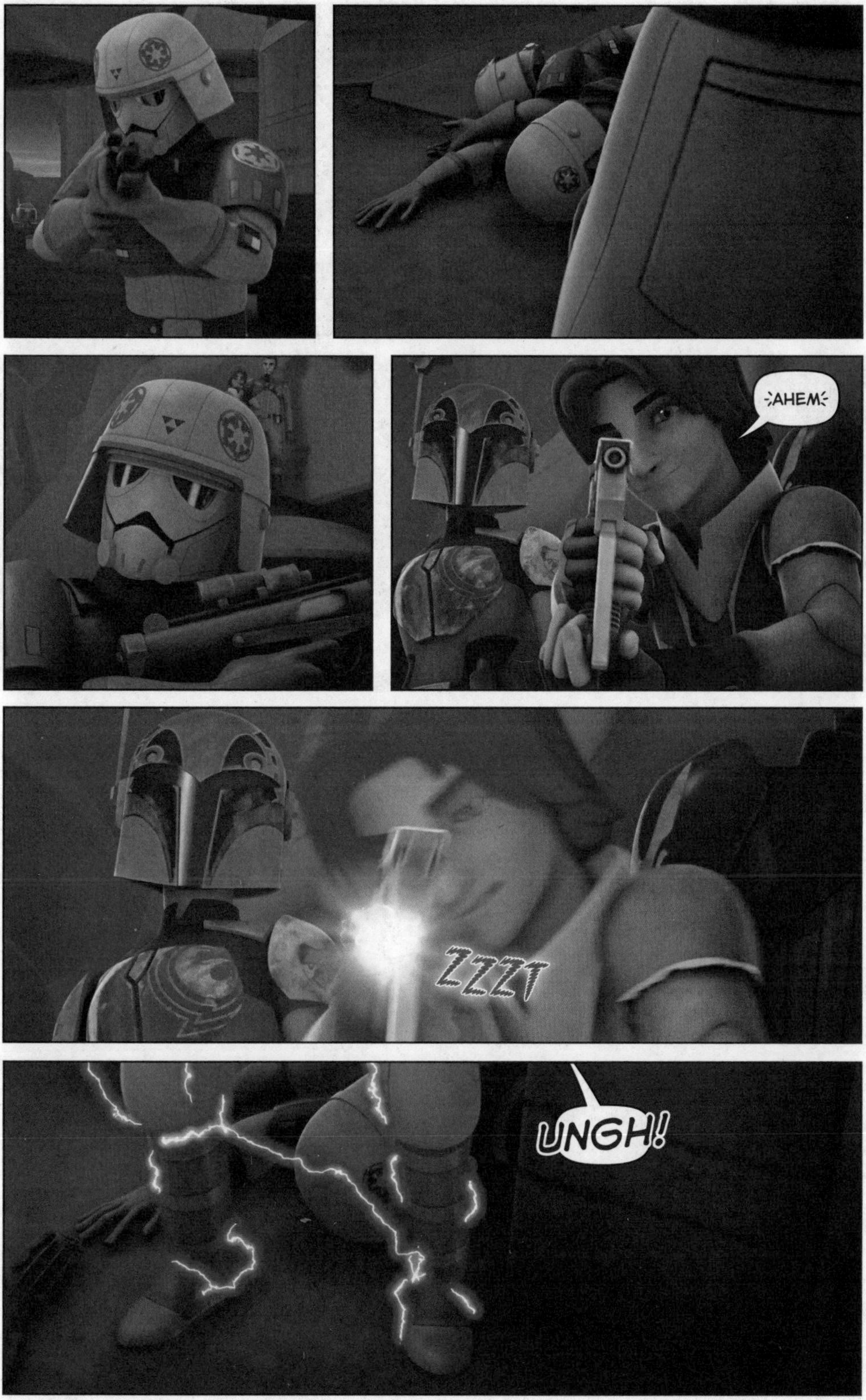
AHEM
ZZZT
UNGH!

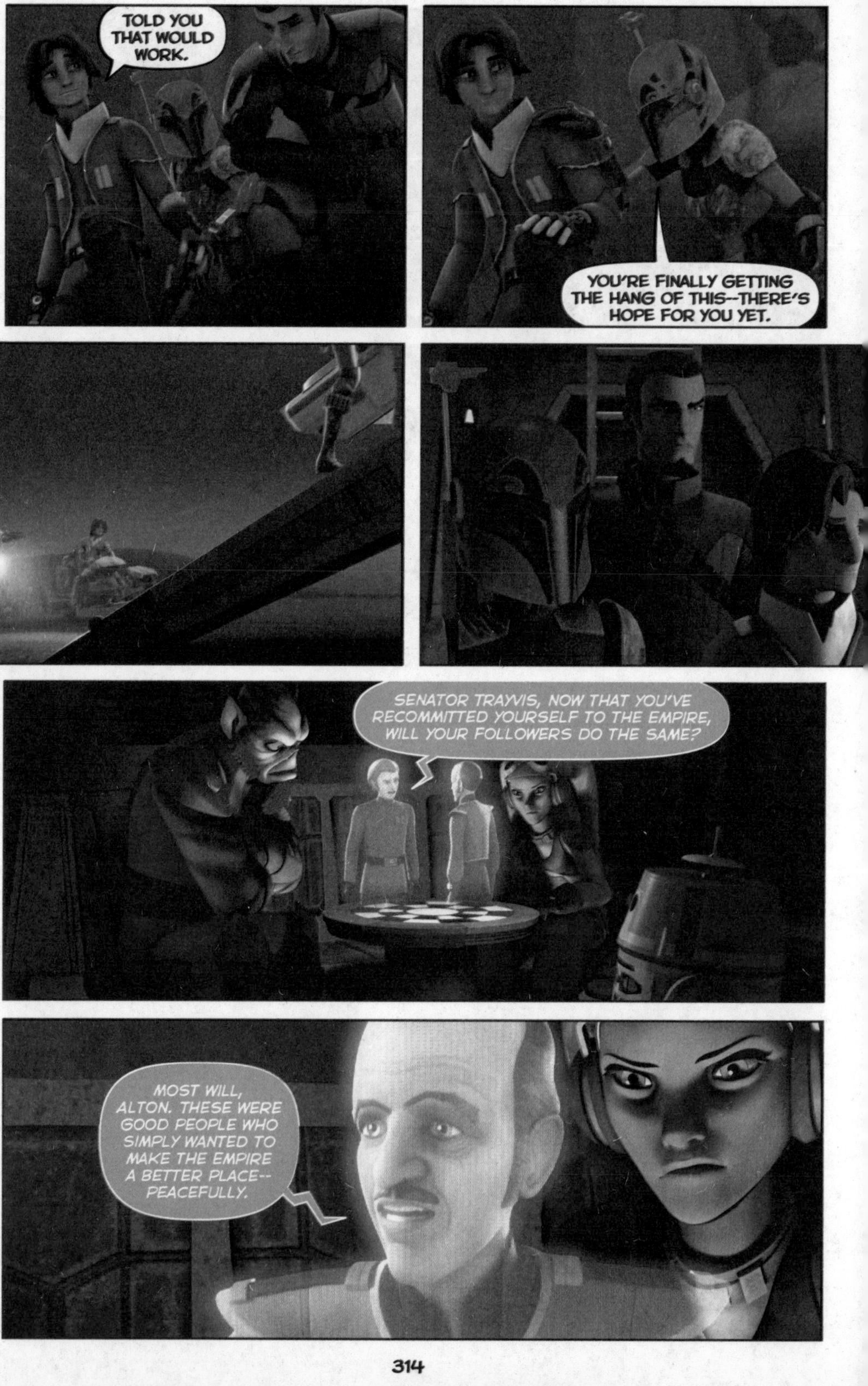
TOLD YOU THAT WOULD WORK.
YOU'RE FINALLY GETTING THE HANG OF THIS--THERE'S HOPE FOR YOU YET.
SENATOR TRAYVIS, NOW THAT YOU'VE RECOMMITTED YOURSELF TO THE EMPIRE, WILL YOUR FOLLOWERS DO THE SAME?
MOST WILL, ALTON. THESE WERE GOOD PEOPLE WHO SIMPLY WANTED TO MAKE THE EMPIRE A BETTER PLACE--PEACEFULLY.

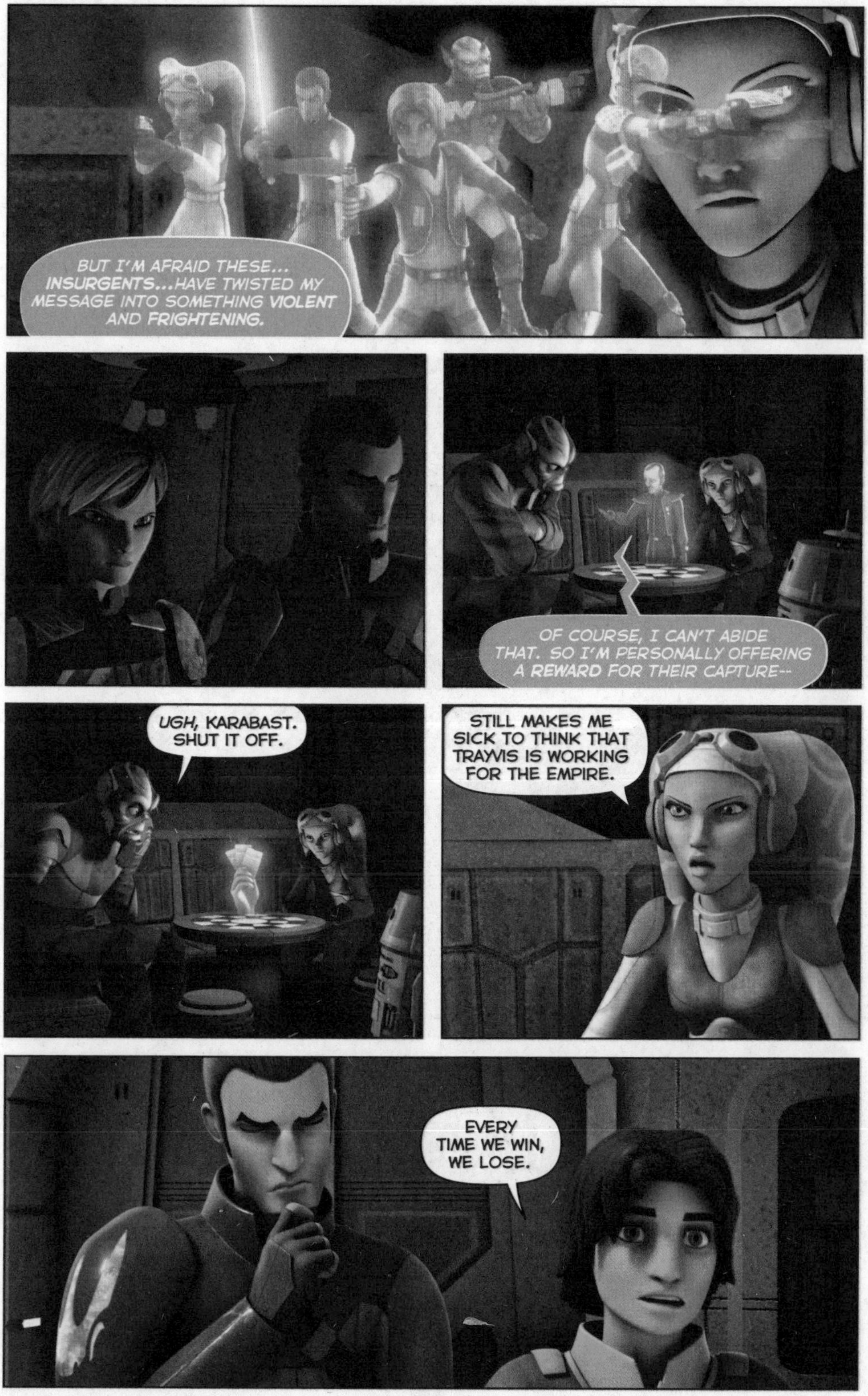
BUT I'M AFRAID THESE... INSURGENTS...HAVE TWISTED MY MESSAGE INTO SOMETHING VIOLENT AND FRIGHTENING.
OF COURSE, I CAN'T ABIDE THAT. SO I'M PERSONALLY OFFERING A REWARD FOR THEIR CAPTURE--
UGH, KARABAST. SHUT IT OFF.
STILL MAKES ME SICK TO THINK THAT TRAYVIS IS WORKING FOR THE EMPIRE.
EVERY TIME WE WIN, WE LOSE.

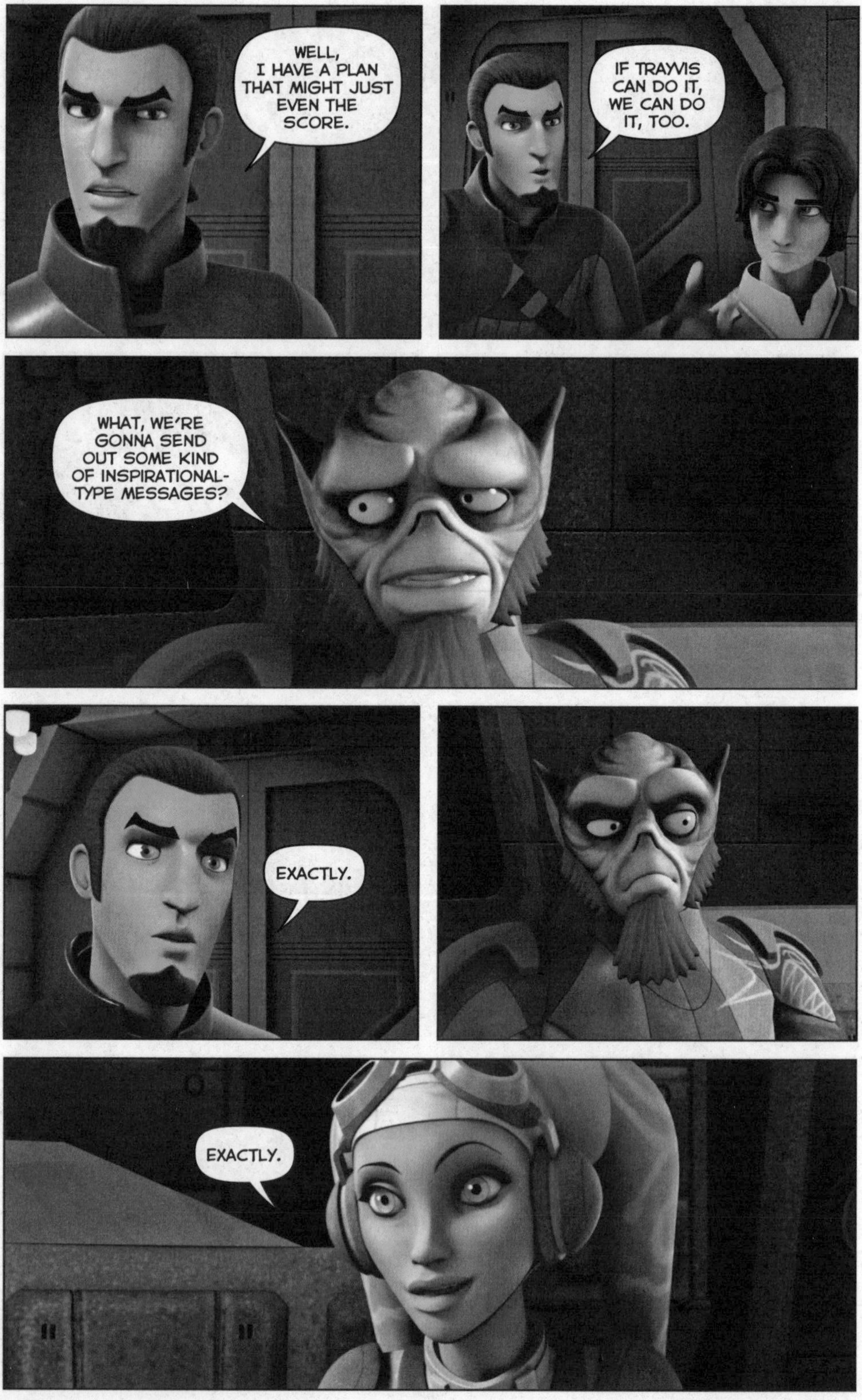
WELL, I HAVE A PLAN THAT MIGHT JUST EVEN THE SCORE.
IF TRAYVIS CAN DO IT, WE CAN DO IT, TOO.
WHAT, WE'RE GONNA SEND OUT SOME KIND OF INSPIRATIONAL-TYPE MESSAGES?
EXACTLY.
EXACTLY.

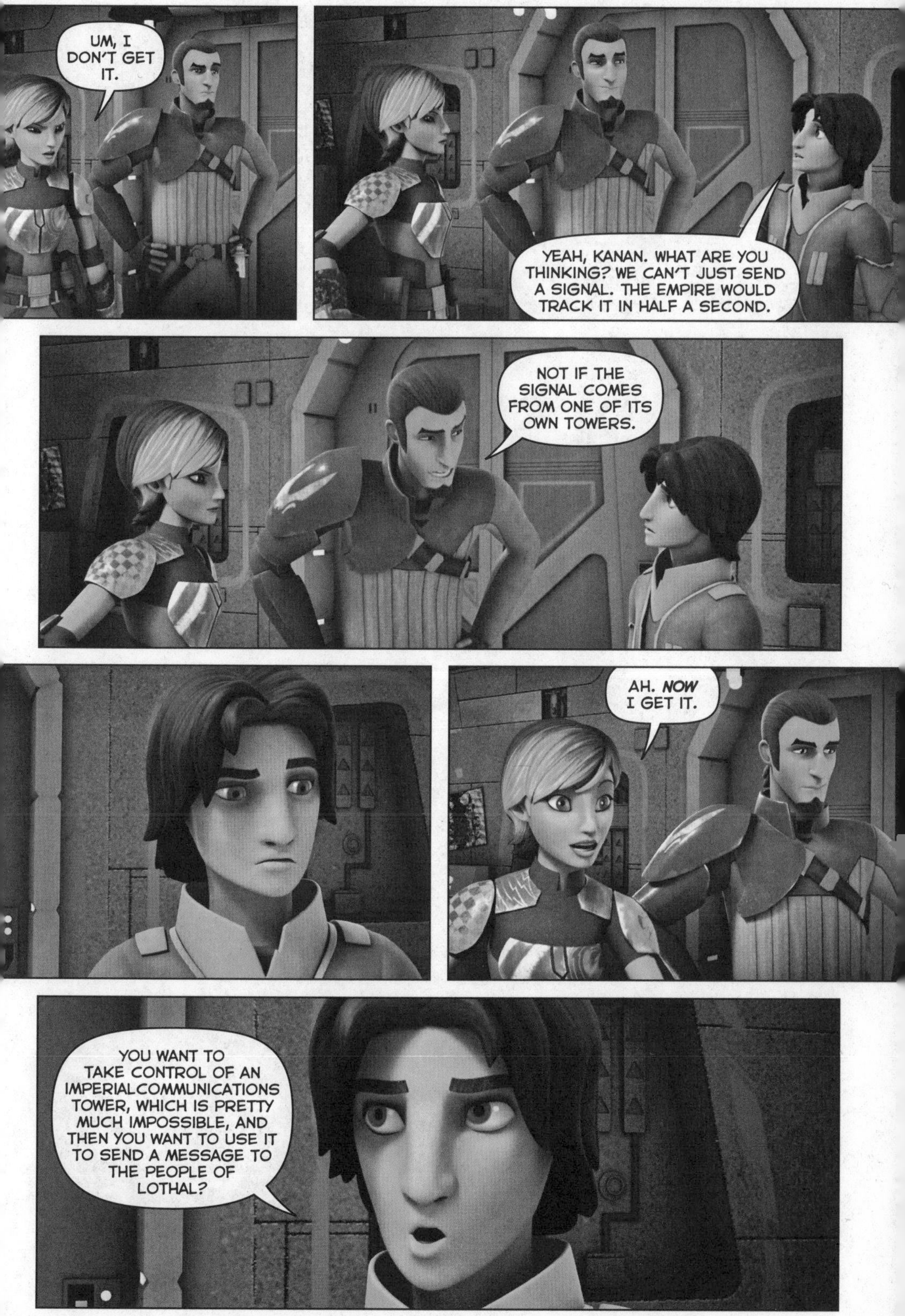
UM, I DON'T GET IT.
YEAH, KANAN. WHAT ARE YOU THINKING? WE CAN'T JUST SEND A SIGNAL. THE EMPIRE WOULD TRACK IT IN HALF A SECOND.
NOT IF THE SIGNAL COMES FROM ONE OF ITS OWN TOWERS.
AH. *NOW* I GET IT.
YOU WANT TO TAKE CONTROL OF AN IMPERIALCOMMUNICATIONS TOWER, WHICH IS PRETTY MUCH IMPOSSIBLE, AND THEN YOU WANT TO USE IT TO SEND A MESSAGE TO THE PEOPLE OF LOTHAL?

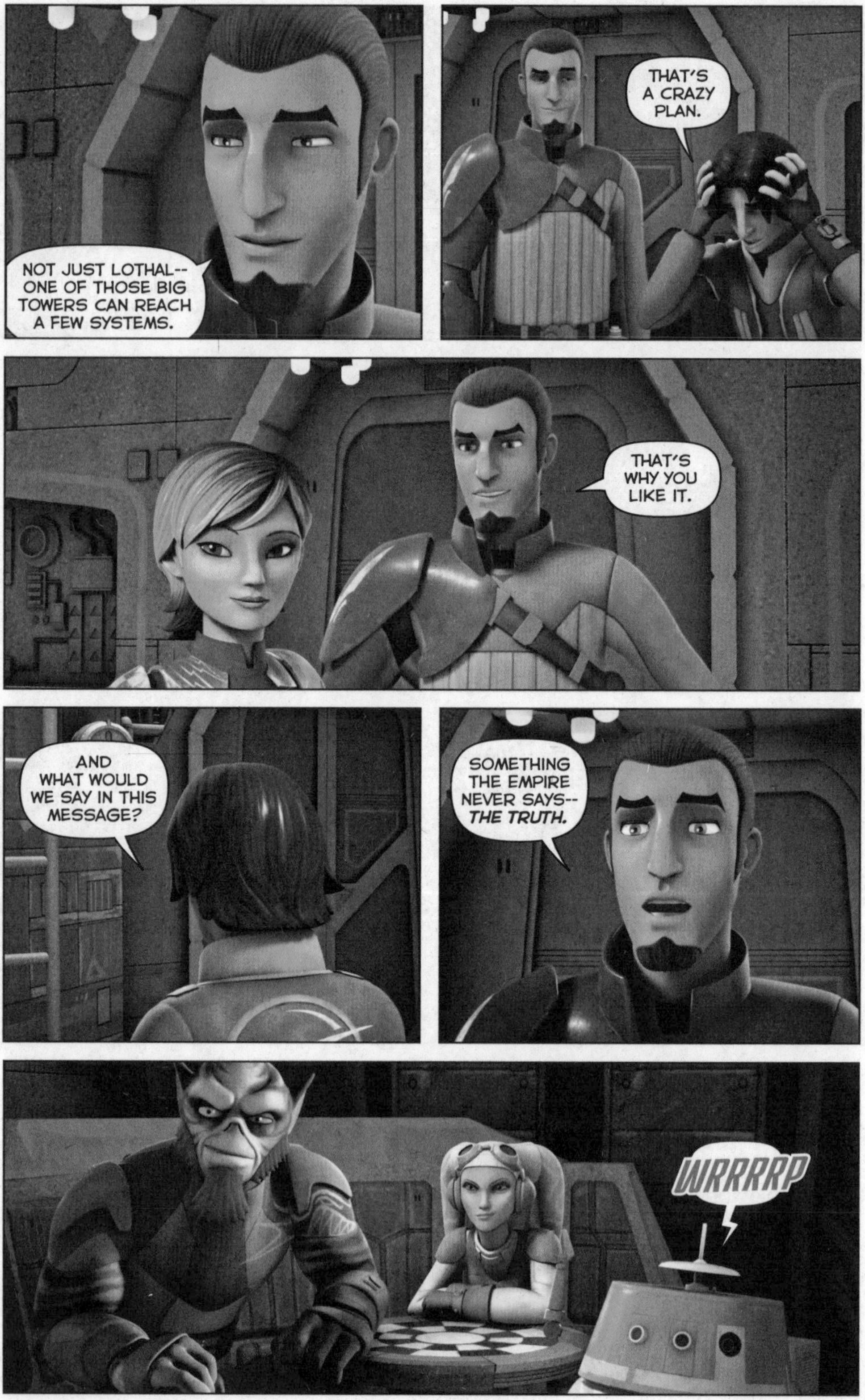
NOT JUST LOTHAL-- ONE OF THOSE BIG TOWERS CAN REACH A FEW SYSTEMS.
THAT'S A CRAZY PLAN.
THAT'S WHY YOU LIKE IT.
AND WHAT WOULD WE SAY IN THIS MESSAGE?
SOMETHING THE EMPIRE NEVER SAYS-- *THE TRUTH.*
WRRRRP

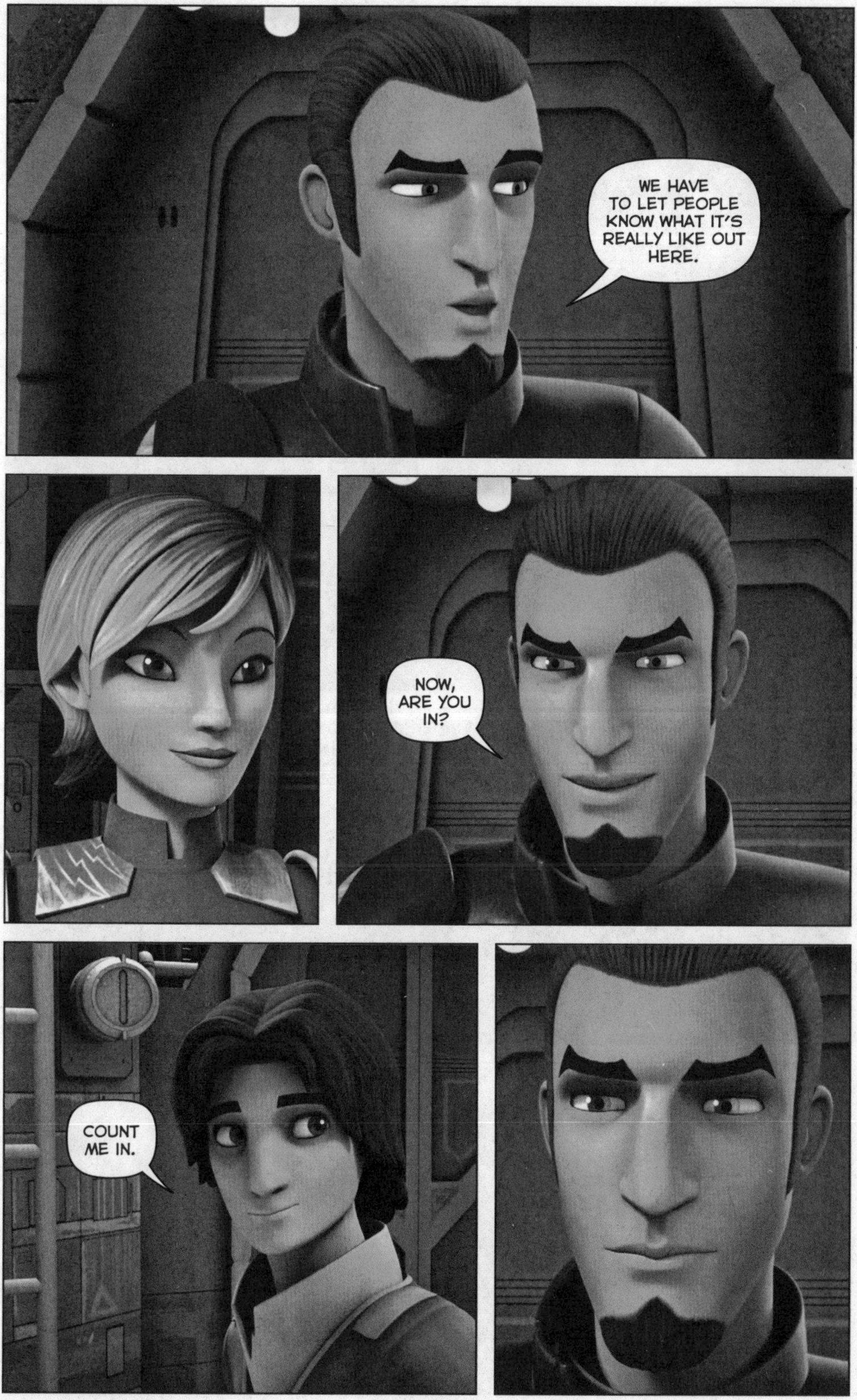
WE HAVE TO LET PEOPLE KNOW WHAT IT'S REALLY LIKE OUT HERE.
NOW, ARE YOU IN?
COUNT ME IN.

COMMANDANT CUMBERLAYNE ARESKO AND TASKMASTER MYLES GRINT REPORTING.

GENTLEMEN, SIT.

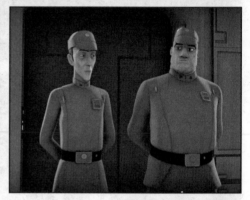

I UNDERSTAND YOU HAVE EXPERIENCE DEALING WITH THESE INSURGENTS.

OH, YES, SIR.

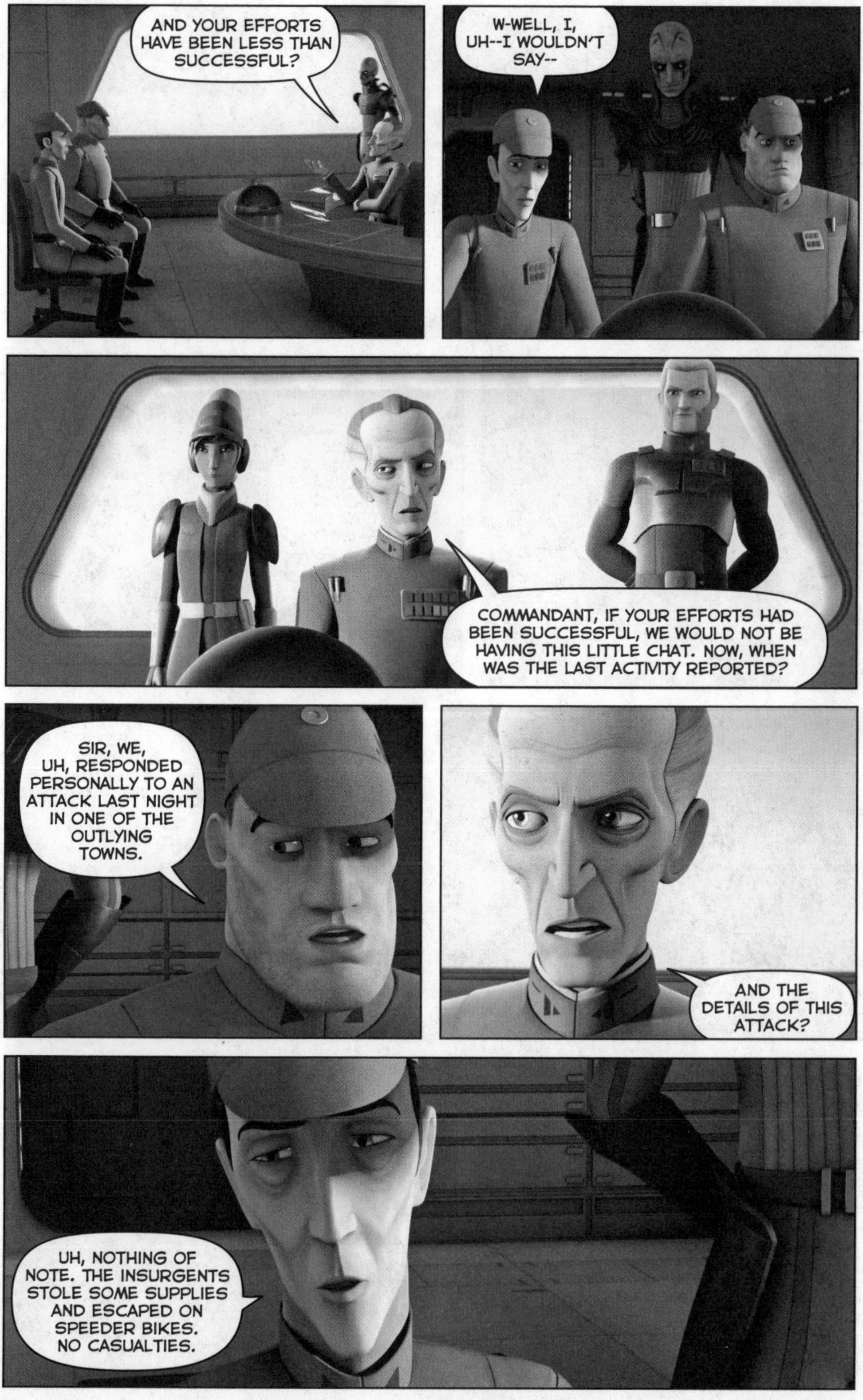
AND YOUR EFFORTS HAVE BEEN LESS THAN SUCCESSFUL?
W-WELL, I, UH--I WOULDN'T SAY--
COMMANDANT, IF YOUR EFFORTS HAD BEEN SUCCESSFUL, WE WOULD NOT BE HAVING THIS LITTLE CHAT. NOW, WHEN WAS THE LAST ACTIVITY REPORTED?
SIR, WE, UH, RESPONDED PERSONALLY TO AN ATTACK LAST NIGHT IN ONE OF THE OUTLYING TOWNS.
AND THE DETAILS OF THIS ATTACK?
UH, NOTHING OF NOTE. THE INSURGENTS STOLE SOME SUPPLIES AND ESCAPED ON SPEEDER BIKES. NO CASUALTIES.

AH, BUT YOU SEE, COMMANDANT, THERE IS SOMETHING OF NOTE IN THAT REPORT--"NO CASUALTIES." YOUR REBEL CELL IS MORE PRINCIPLED THAN OTHERS.

OTHERS, SIR? YOU MEAN THERE ARE OTHER CELLS?

CELLS, FACTIONS, TRIBES--CALL THEM WHAT YOU WILL.

THEY LACK THE ONE THING THAT WOULD MAKE THEM A CREDIBLE THREAT TO THE EMPIRE--*UNITY*.

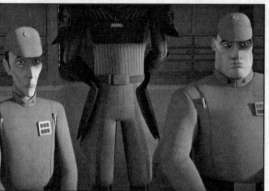

WHILE YOUR CELL SEEMS UNINTERESTED IN VIOLENCE, IT DOES PRESENT A SPECIFIC THREAT--THE *JEDI*.

WE HAVE ENCOUNTERED HIM, SIR, AND HE LIVES UP TO THEIR REPUTATION.

OH, I DOUBT THAT VERY MUCH. BUT I AM NOT CONCERNED WITH HIS SKILLS AS A WARRIOR.

I AM CONCERNED WITH WHAT HE REPRESENTS. OR PERHAPS I SHOULD SAY, I AM CONCERNED BY WHAT YOU *ALLOW HIM* TO REPRESENT BY FAILING TO STOP HIM--*HOPE.*

THERE ARE WHISPERS OF THIS ALLEGED JEDI IN THE STREETS.

IN TIME, SUCH WHISPERS MIGHT SPARK BELIEF IN SOMETHING OTHER THAN THE STRENGTH AND SECURITY OF THE EMPIRE. AND THAT, GENTLEMEN...

...IS SOMETHING I CANNOT HAVE.

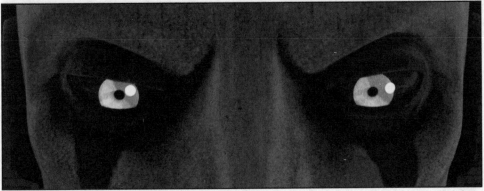

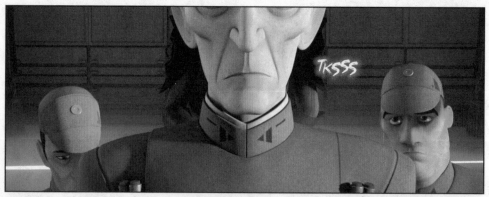

MAKE NO MISTAKE--FROM NOW ON, FAILURE WILL HAVE *CONSEQUENCES.*

AGENT KALLUS, YOU WILL DISPATCH PROBE DROIDS TO EVERY KNOWN LOCATION OF INSURGENT ACTIVITY ON LOTHAL.

WE WILL DISCOVER THE WHEREABOUTS OF THESE CRIMINALS AND WE WILL *MAKE EXAMPLES* OF THEM.

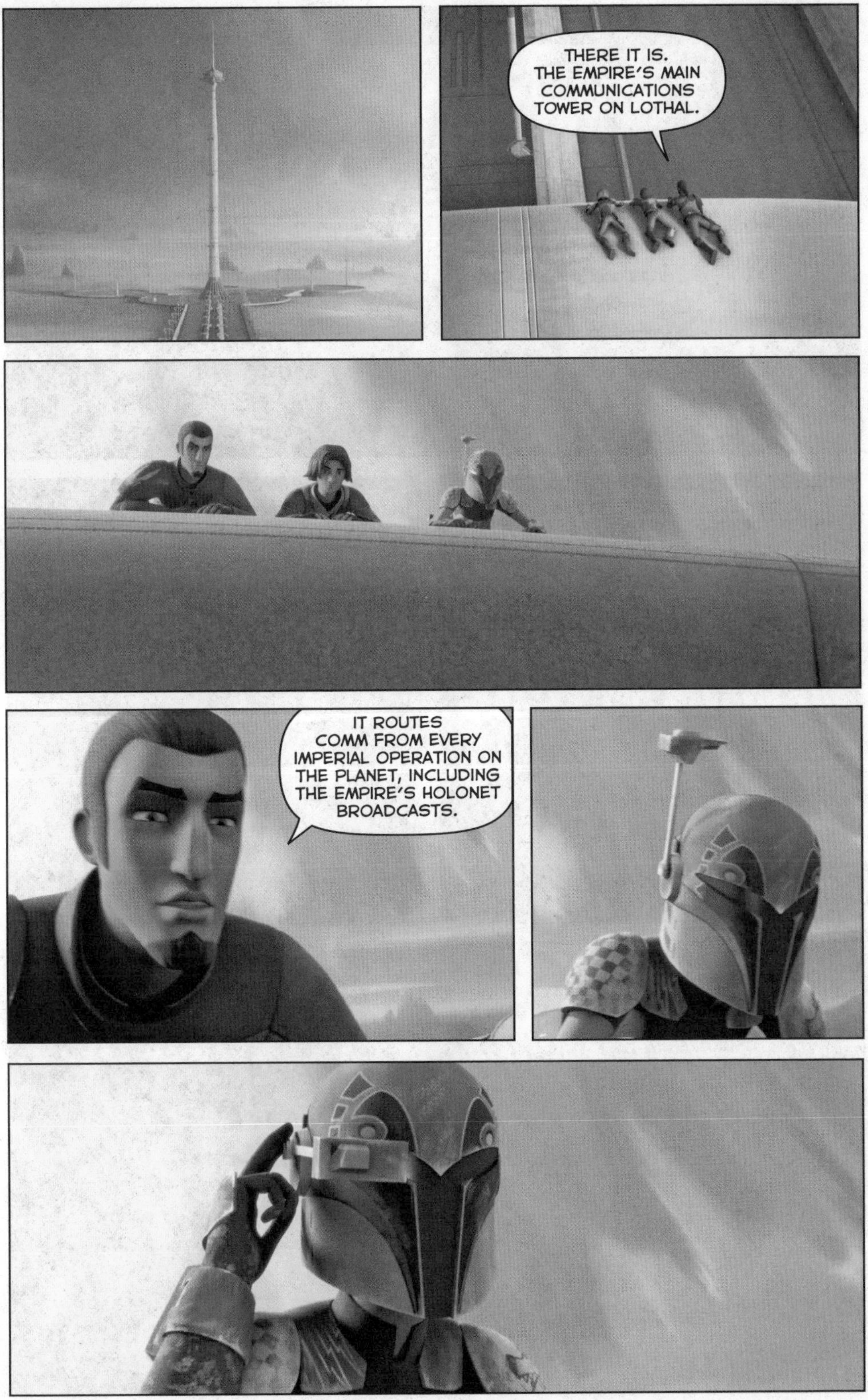
THERE IT IS. THE EMPIRE'S MAIN COMMUNICATIONS TOWER ON LOTHAL.
IT ROUTES COMM FROM EVERY IMPERIAL OPERATION ON THE PLANET, INCLUDING THE EMPIRE'S HOLONET BROADCASTS.

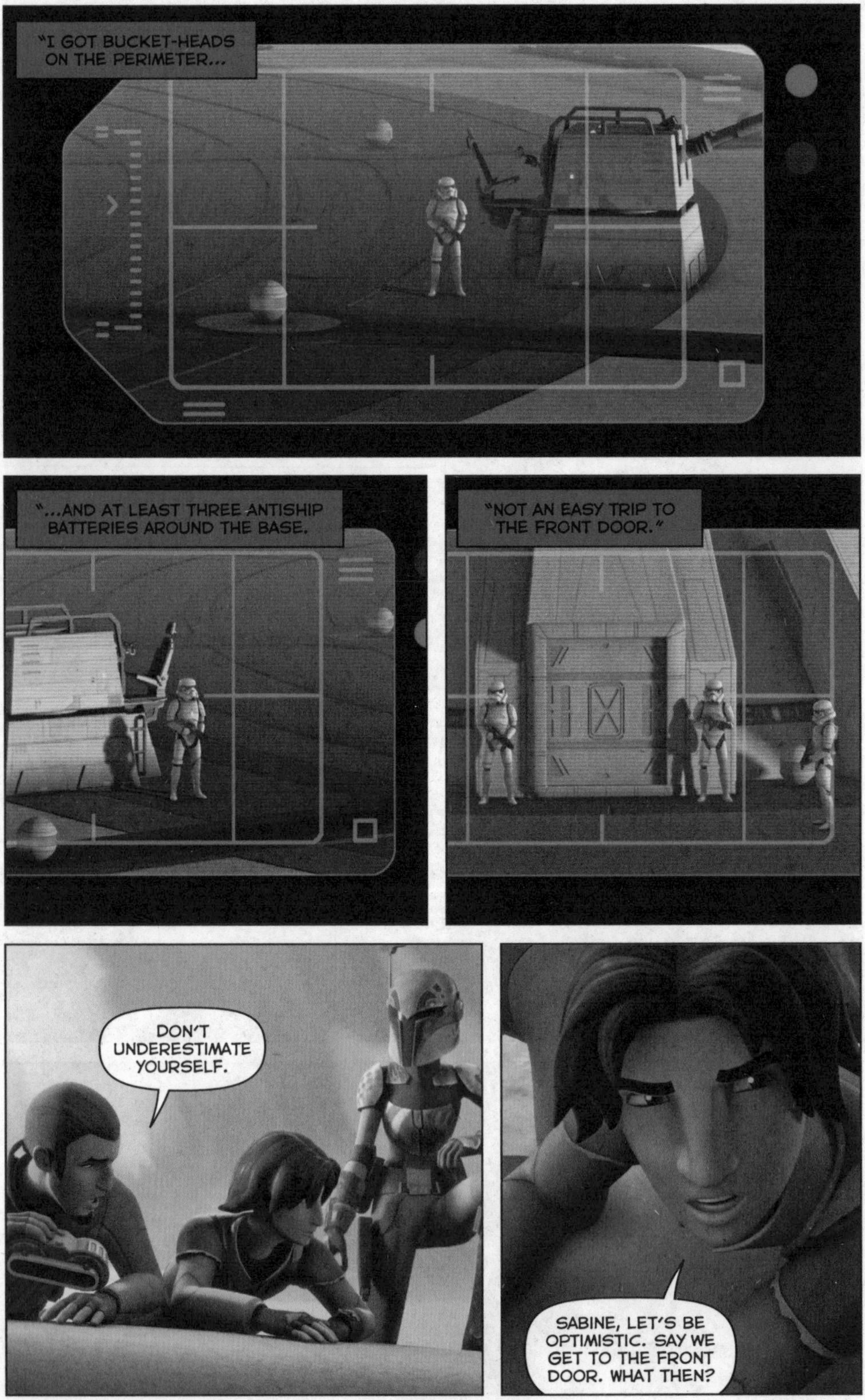
"I GOT BUCKET-HEADS ON THE PERIMETER...
"...AND AT LEAST THREE ANTISHIP BATTERIES AROUND THE BASE.
"NOT AN EASY TRIP TO THE FRONT DOOR."
DON'T UNDERESTIMATE YOURSELF.
SABINE, LET'S BE OPTIMISTIC. SAY WE GET TO THE FRONT DOOR. WHAT THEN?

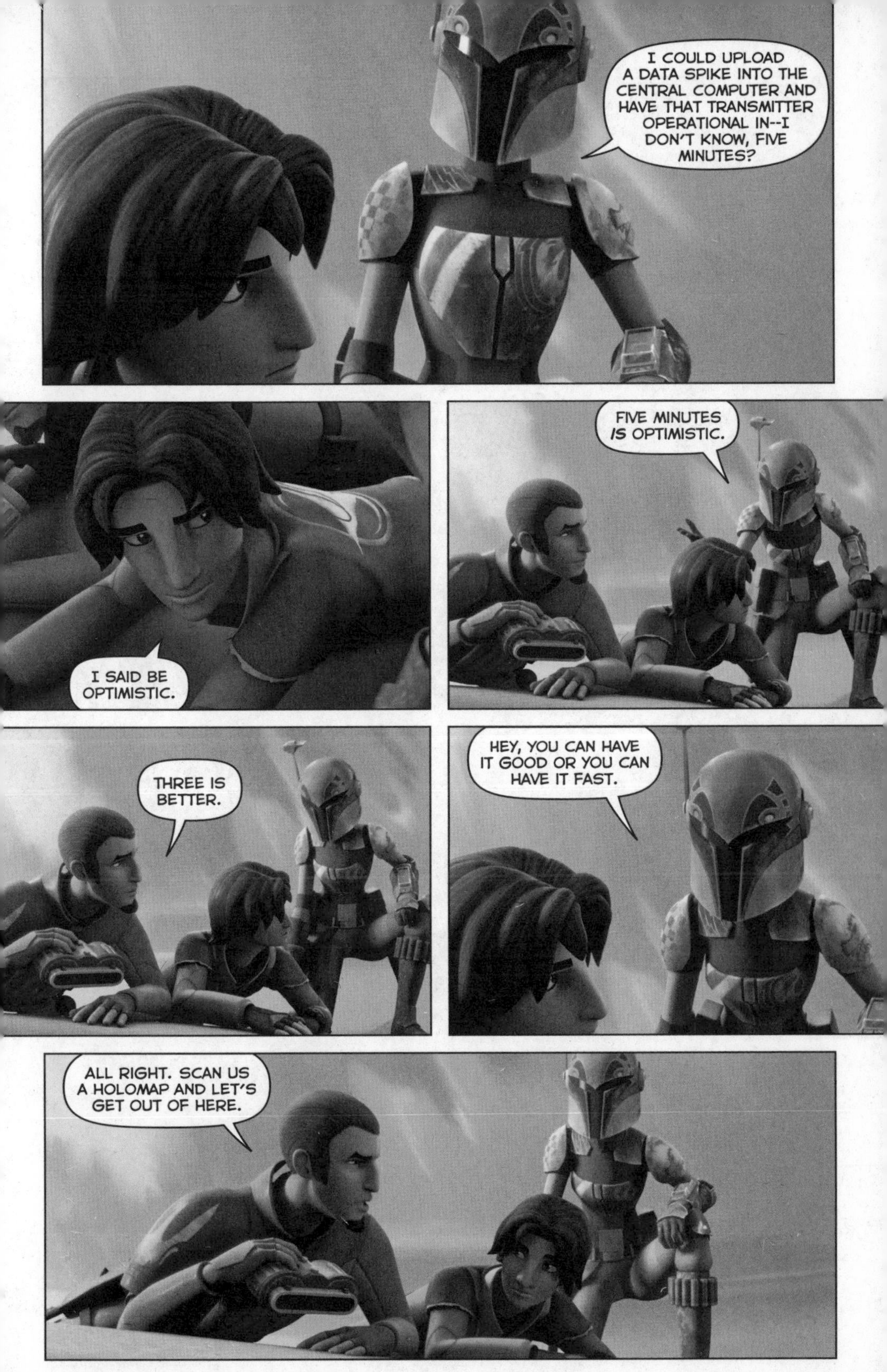
I COULD UPLOAD A DATA SPIKE INTO THE CENTRAL COMPUTER AND HAVE THAT TRANSMITTER OPERATIONAL IN--I DON'T KNOW, FIVE MINUTES?
I SAID BE OPTIMISTIC.
FIVE MINUTES IS OPTIMISTIC.
THREE IS BETTER.
HEY, YOU CAN HAVE IT GOOD OR YOU CAN HAVE IT FAST.
ALL RIGHT. SCAN US A HOLOMAP AND LET'S GET OUT OF HERE.

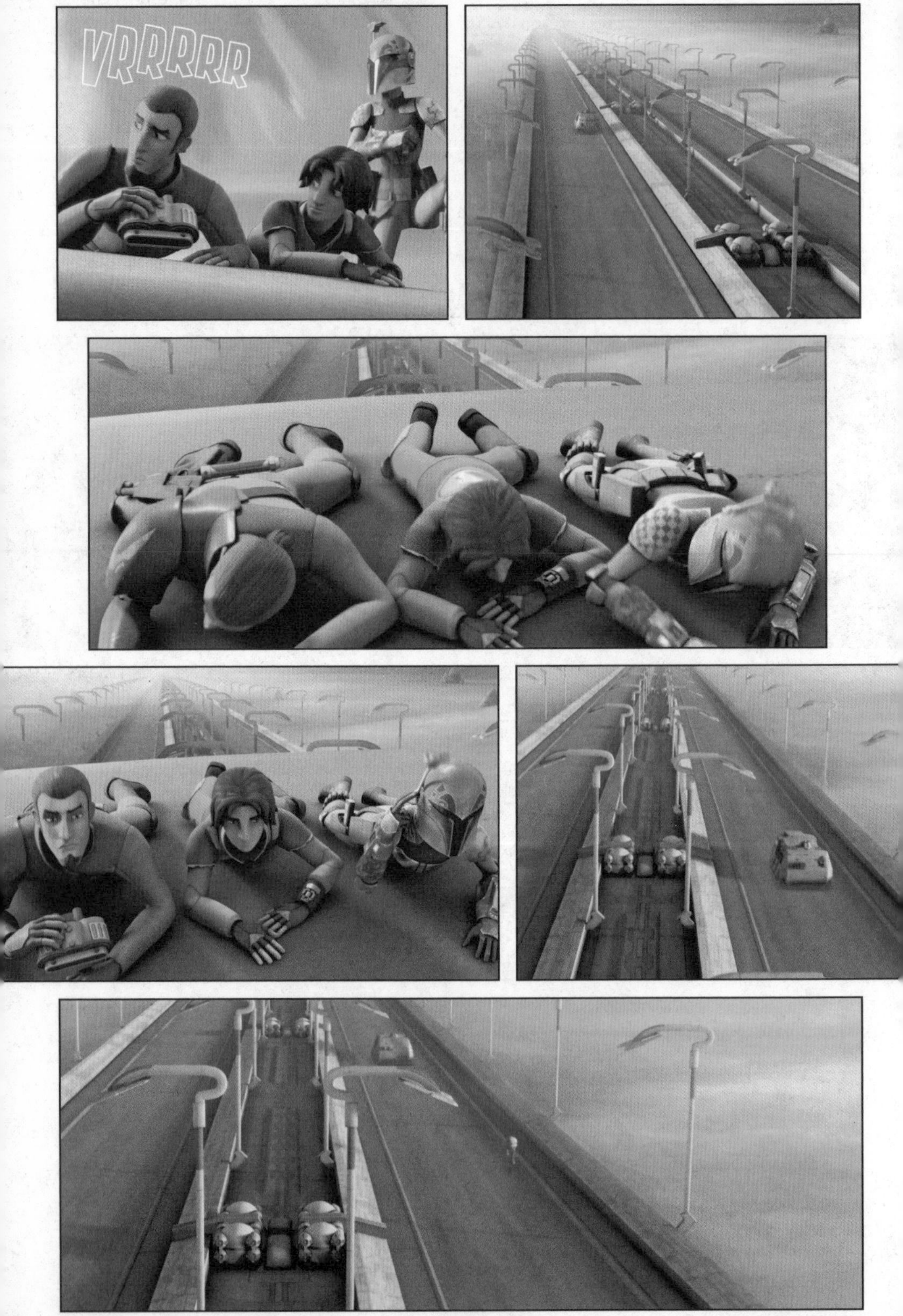
VRRRRR

I DON'T LIKE THE LOOK OF THAT THING.

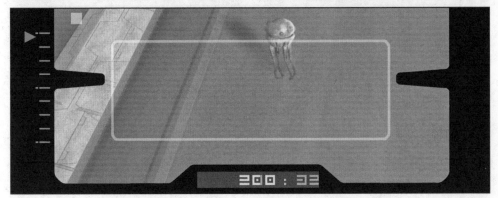

200 : 32

IMPERIAL PROBE DROID.

DOES IT SEE US?

NOT YET.

HOW CAN YOU TELL?

BECAUSE WE'RE NOT DEAD.

ZWRRRP

WE NEED TO MOVE.

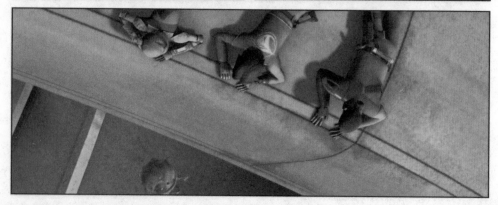

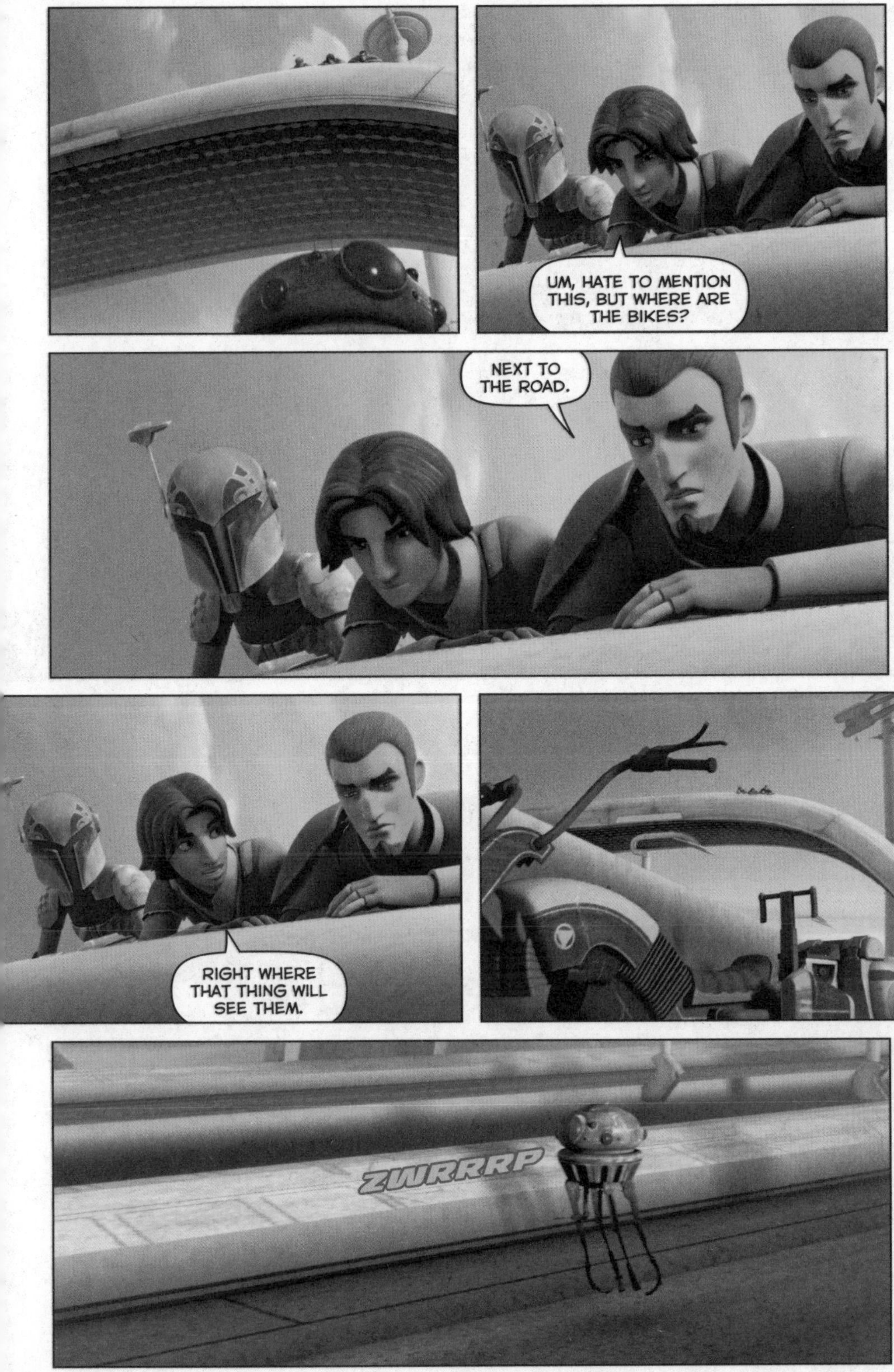
UM, HATE TO MENTION THIS, BUT WHERE ARE THE BIKES?
NEXT TO THE ROAD.
RIGHT WHERE THAT THING WILL SEE THEM.
ZWRRRP

HOPE SOMEBODY'S GOT AN IDEA, OR THIS WHOLE PLAN IS *SHOT.*

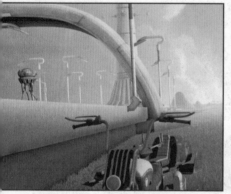

GRR

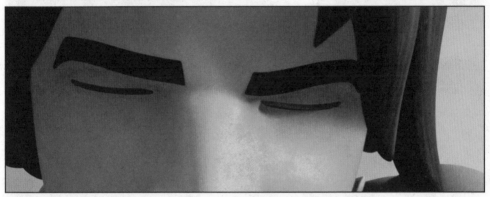

HISS!

RRRARR

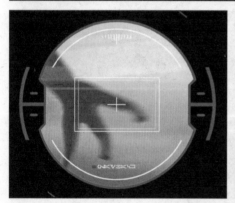

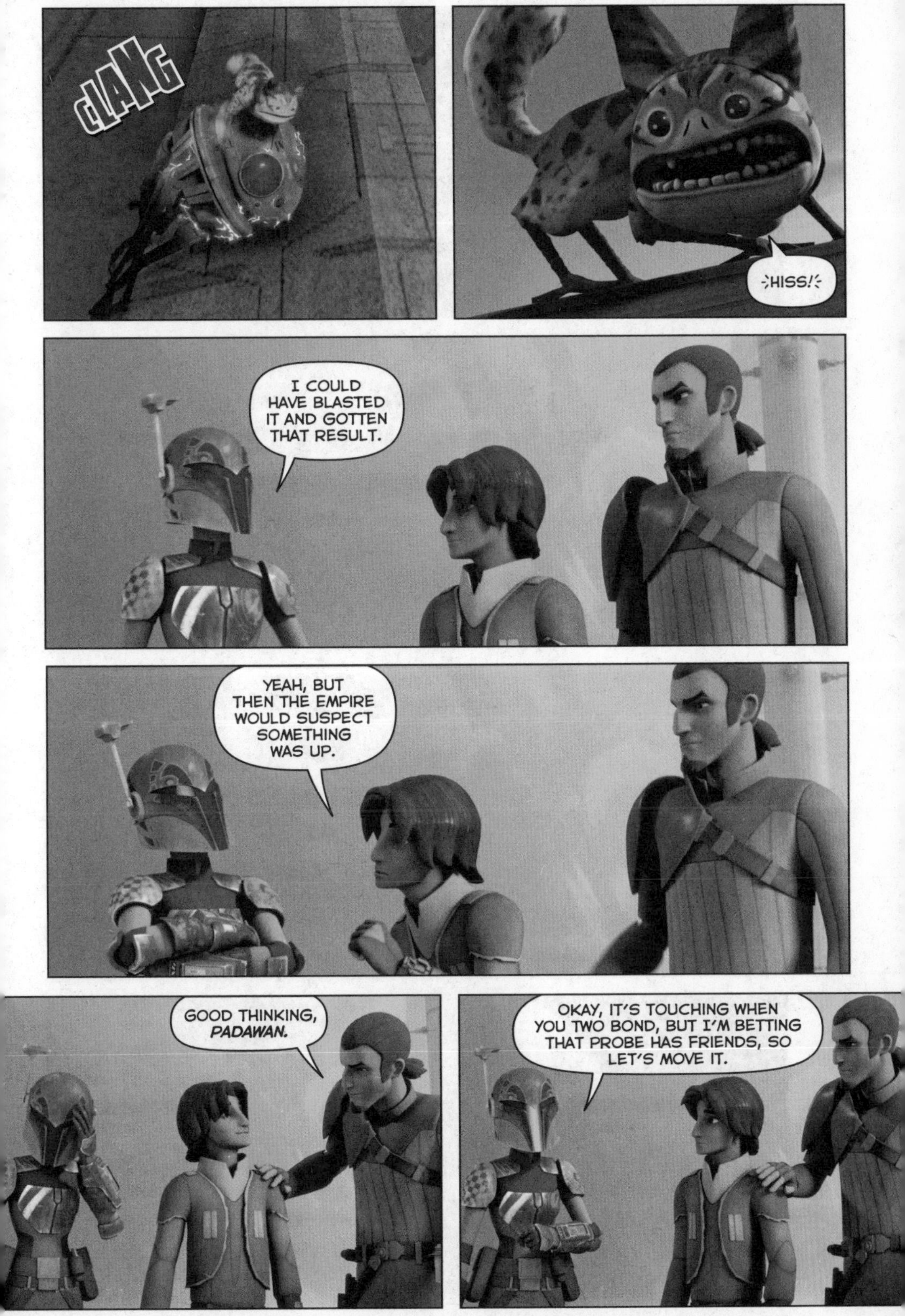
CLANG
HISS!
I COULD HAVE BLASTED IT AND GOTTEN THAT RESULT.
YEAH, BUT THEN THE EMPIRE WOULD SUSPECT SOMETHING WAS UP.
GOOD THINKING, PADAWAN.
OKAY, IT'S TOUCHING WHEN YOU TWO BOND, BUT I'M BETTING THAT PROBE HAS FRIENDS, SO LET'S MOVE IT.

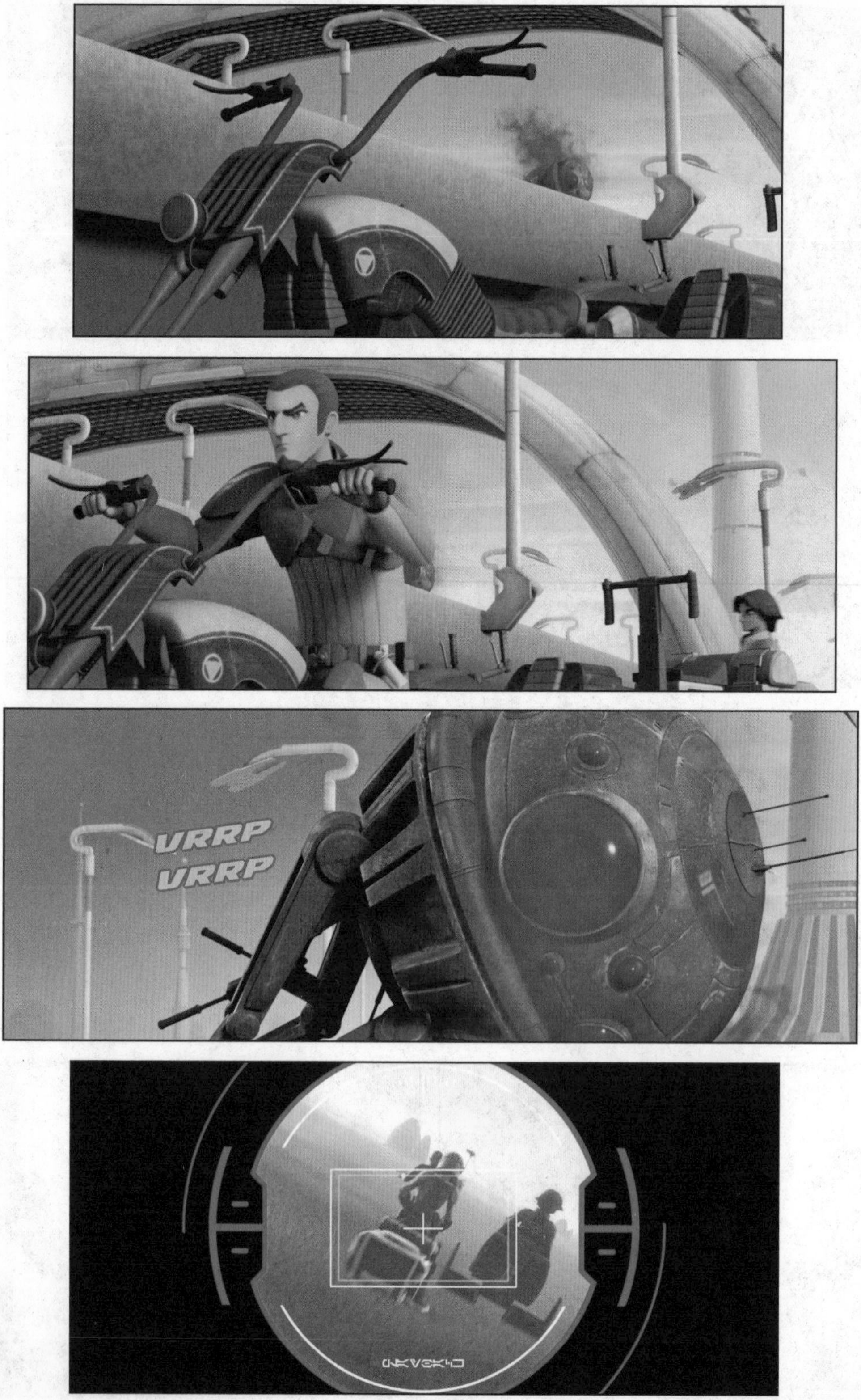
URRP
URRP

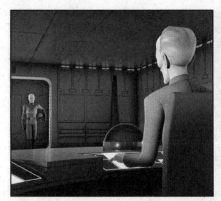

GOVERNOR, ONE OF OUR PROBES SEEMS TO HAVE FOUND SOMETHING.

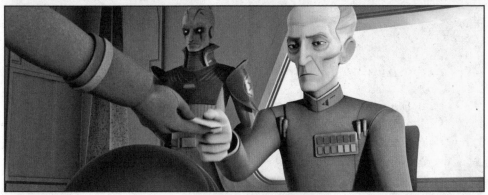

WE BELIEVE THESE ARE THE SPEEDER BIKES RESPONSIBLE FOR THE REBEL ACTIVITY NEAR JALATH.

WHERE WAS THIS FOOTAGE TAKEN?

OUTSIDE THE MAIN COMMUNICATIONS TOWER.

A PERFECT TARGET FOR THESE CRIMINALS.

WE CAN'T RISK LOSING THE TOWER. WE SHOULD REINFORCE SECURITY--

NO. LET THEM BELIEVE THEY STILL POSSESS THE ELEMENT OF SURPRISE. LURE THEM IN, AND WE SHALL BE WAITING.

AS YOU WISH.

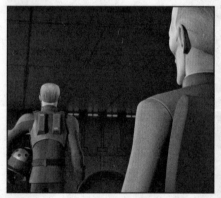

INQUISITOR, I AM GIVING YOU THE OPPORTUNITY TO REDEEM YOURSELF. *DO NOT* DISAPPOINT ME.

AND REMEMBER, I WANT THIS JEDI *ALIVE*.

YOUR FAITH WILL BE REWARDED.

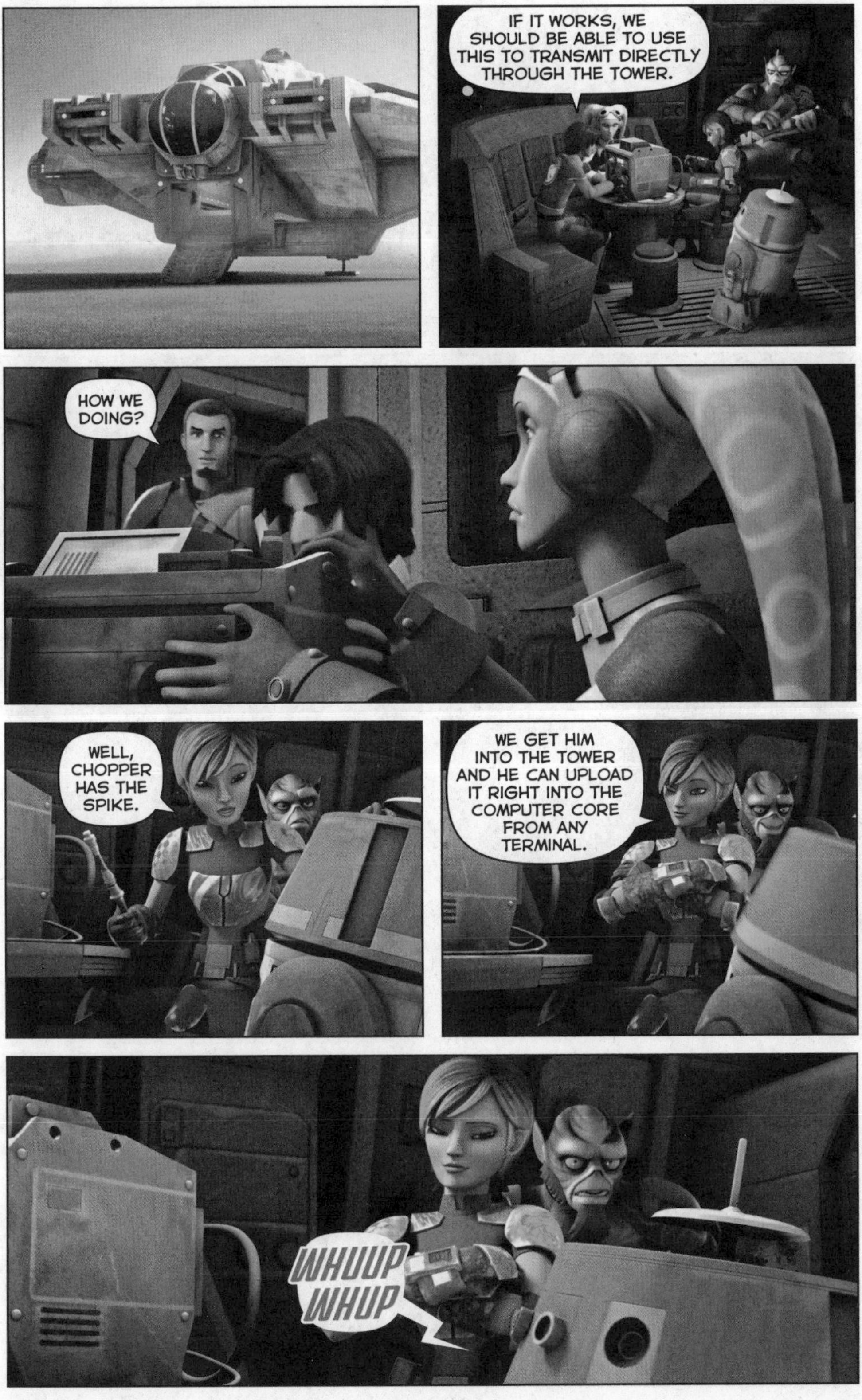
IF IT WORKS, WE SHOULD BE ABLE TO USE THIS TO TRANSMIT DIRECTLY THROUGH THE TOWER.
HOW WE DOING?
WELL, CHOPPER HAS THE SPIKE.
WE GET HIM INTO THE TOWER AND HE CAN UPLOAD IT RIGHT INTO THE COMPUTER CORE FROM ANY TERMINAL.
WHUUP WHUP

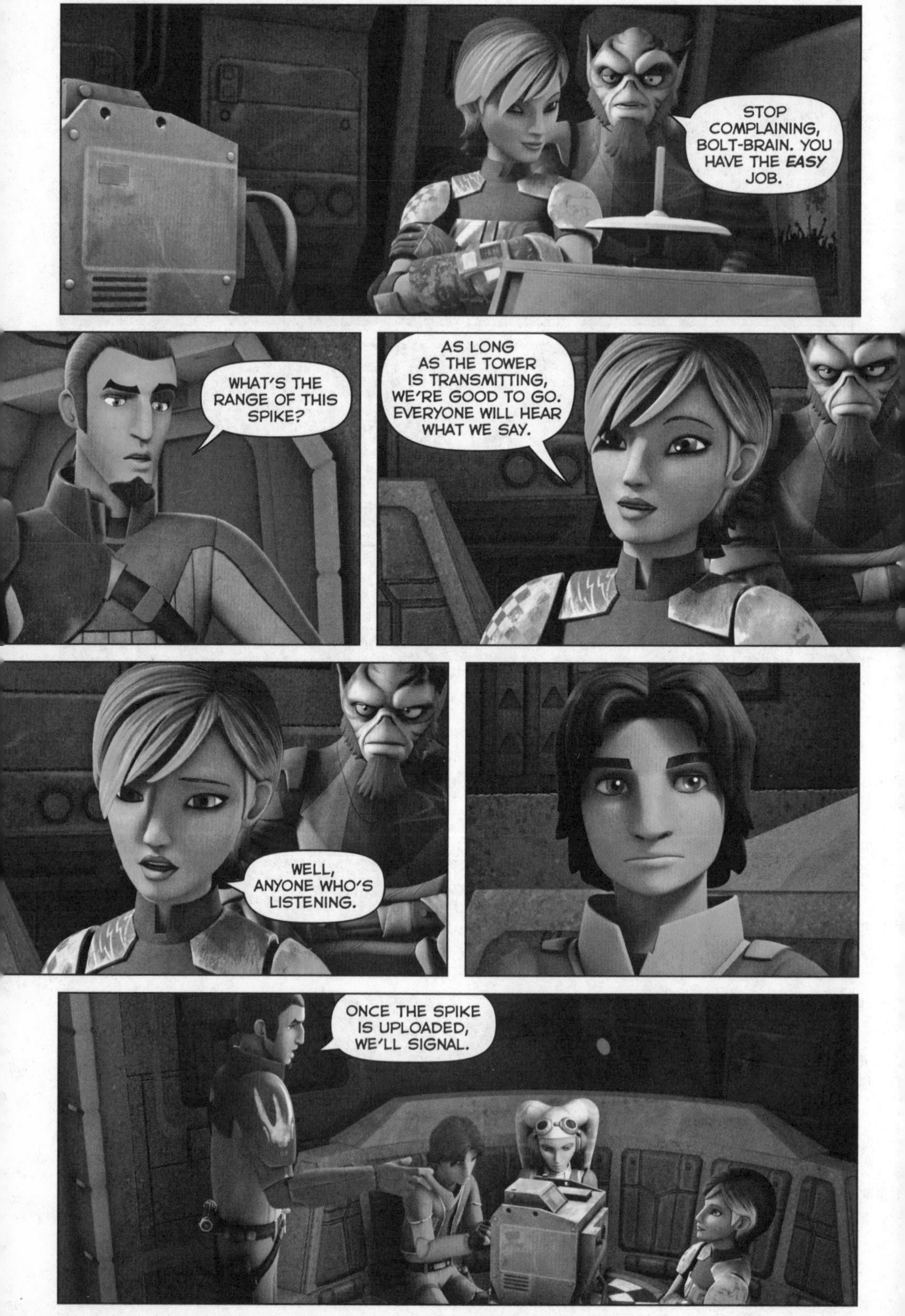
STOP COMPLAINING, BOLT-BRAIN. YOU HAVE THE *EASY* JOB.
WHAT'S THE RANGE OF THIS SPIKE?
AS LONG AS THE TOWER IS TRANSMITTING, WE'RE GOOD TO GO. EVERYONE WILL HEAR WHAT WE SAY.
WELL, ANYONE WHO'S LISTENING.
ONCE THE SPIKE IS UPLOADED, WE'LL SIGNAL.

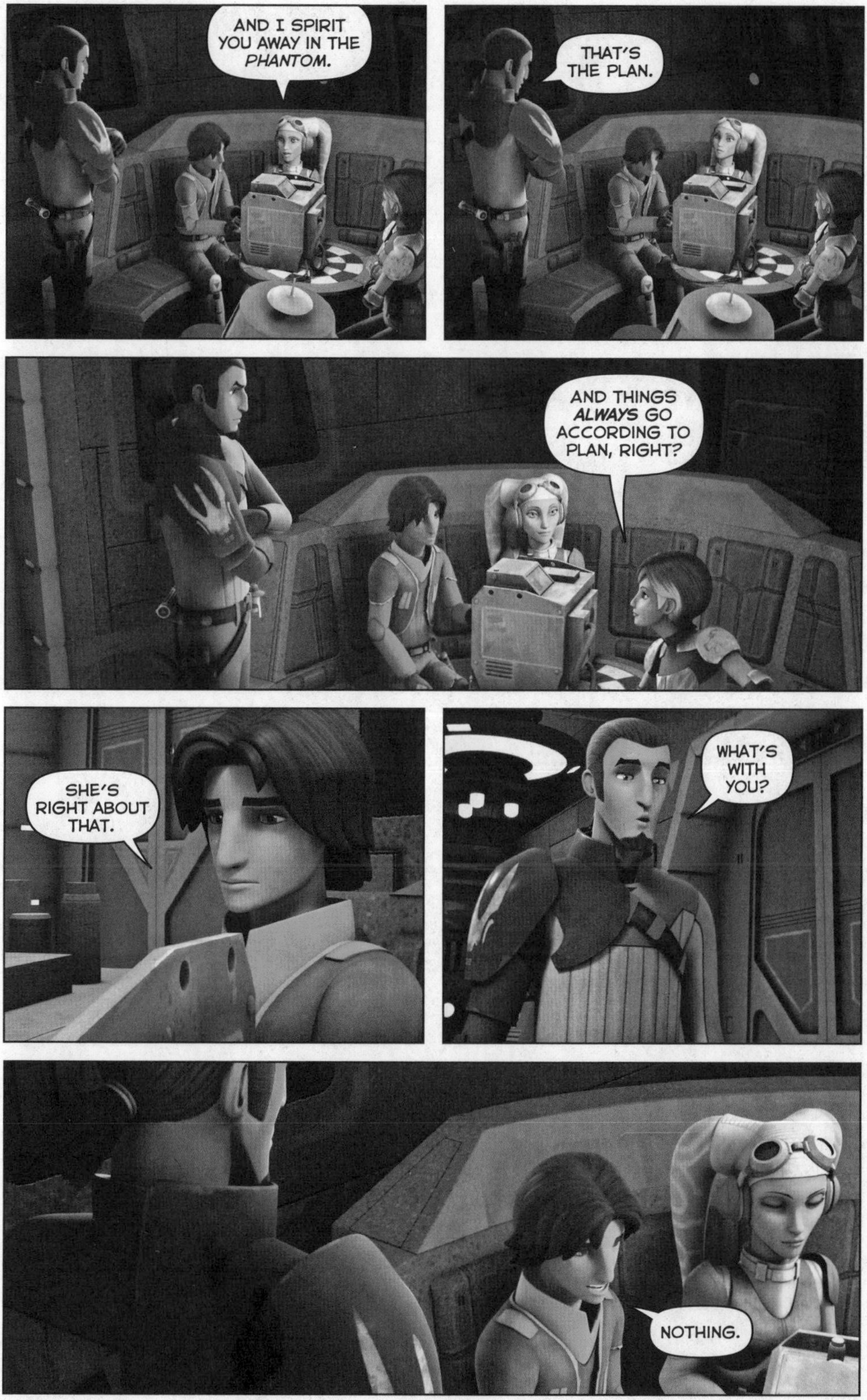
AND I SPIRIT YOU AWAY IN THE *PHANTOM*.
THAT'S THE PLAN.
AND THINGS *ALWAYS* GO ACCORDING TO PLAN, RIGHT?
SHE'S RIGHT ABOUT THAT.
WHAT'S WITH YOU?
NOTHING.

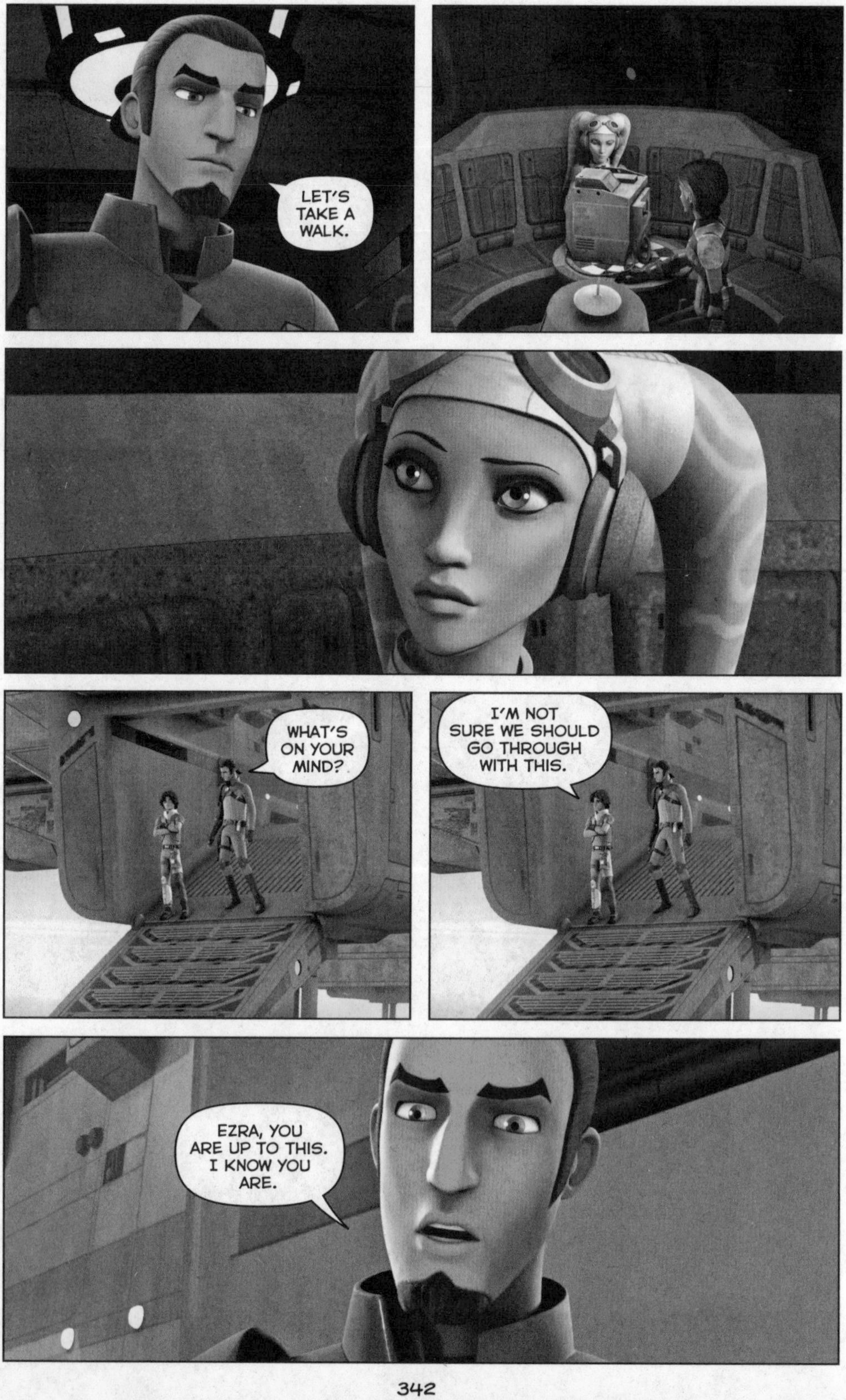
LET'S TAKE A WALK.
WHAT'S ON YOUR MIND?
I'M NOT SURE WE SHOULD GO THROUGH WITH THIS.
EZRA, YOU ARE UP TO THIS. I KNOW YOU ARE.

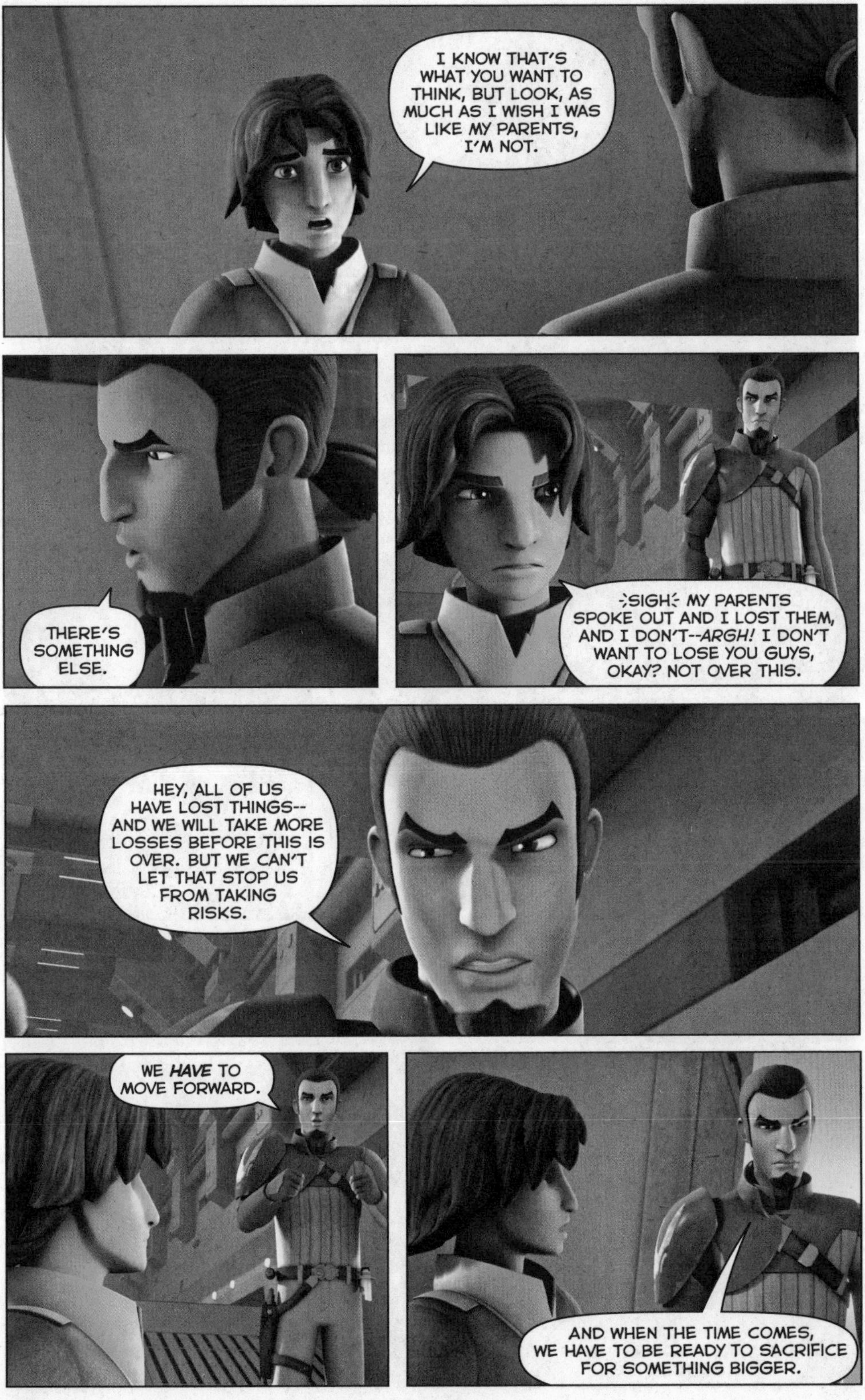
I KNOW THAT'S WHAT YOU WANT TO THINK, BUT LOOK, AS MUCH AS I WISH I WAS LIKE MY PARENTS, I'M NOT.
THERE'S SOMETHING ELSE.
-SIGH- MY PARENTS SPOKE OUT AND I LOST THEM, AND I DON'T--*ARGH!* I DON'T WANT TO LOSE YOU GUYS, OKAY? NOT OVER THIS.
HEY, ALL OF US HAVE LOST THINGS-- AND WE WILL TAKE MORE LOSSES BEFORE THIS IS OVER. BUT WE CAN'T LET THAT STOP US FROM TAKING RISKS.
WE ***HAVE*** TO MOVE FORWARD.
AND WHEN THE TIME COMES, WE HAVE TO BE READY TO SACRIFICE FOR SOMETHING BIGGER.

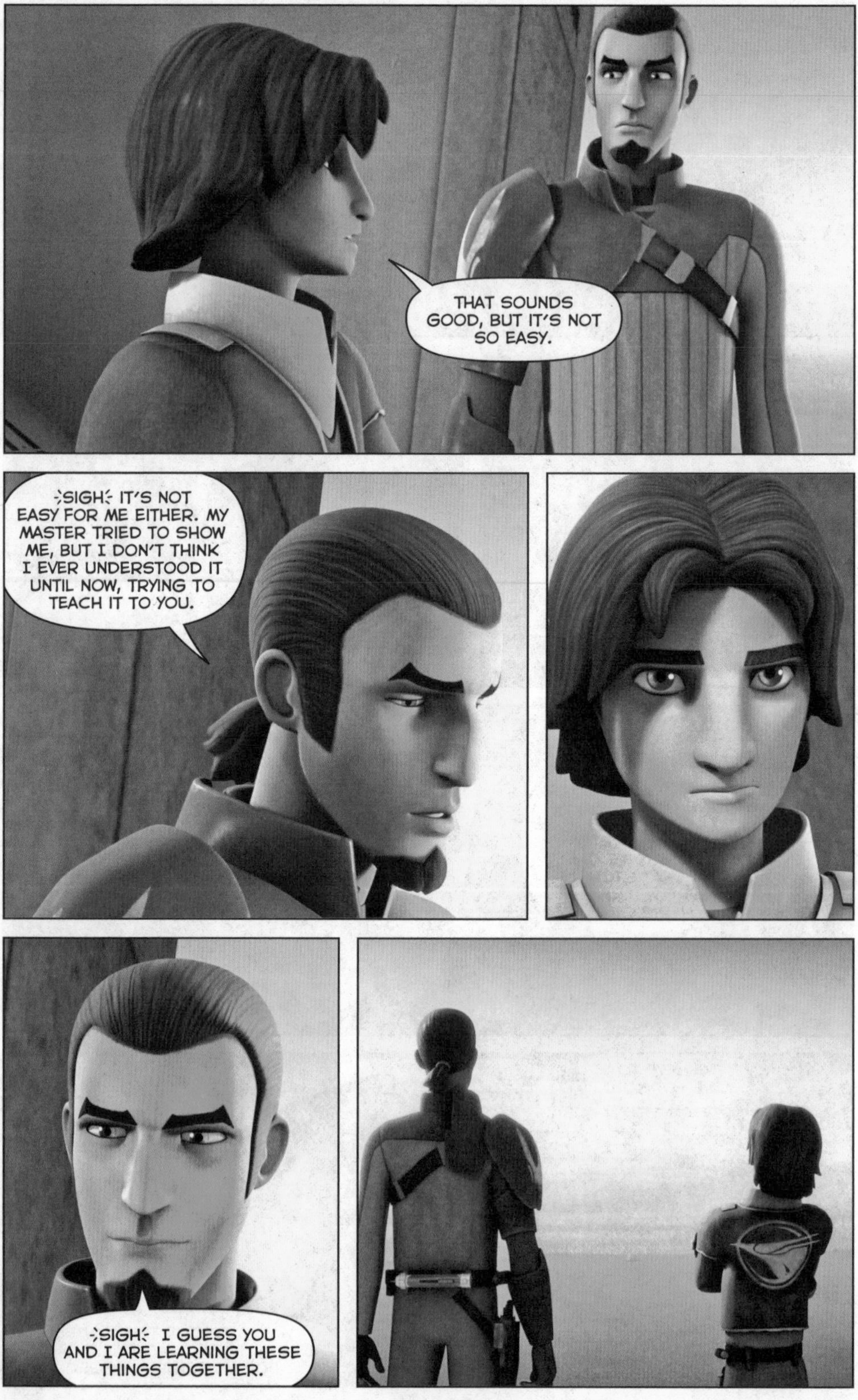
THAT SOUNDS GOOD, BUT IT'S NOT SO EASY.
⁖SIGH⁖ IT'S NOT EASY FOR ME EITHER. MY MASTER TRIED TO SHOW ME, BUT I DON'T THINK I EVER UNDERSTOOD IT UNTIL NOW, TRYING TO TEACH IT TO YOU.
⁖SIGH⁖ I GUESS YOU AND I ARE LEARNING THESE THINGS TOGETHER.

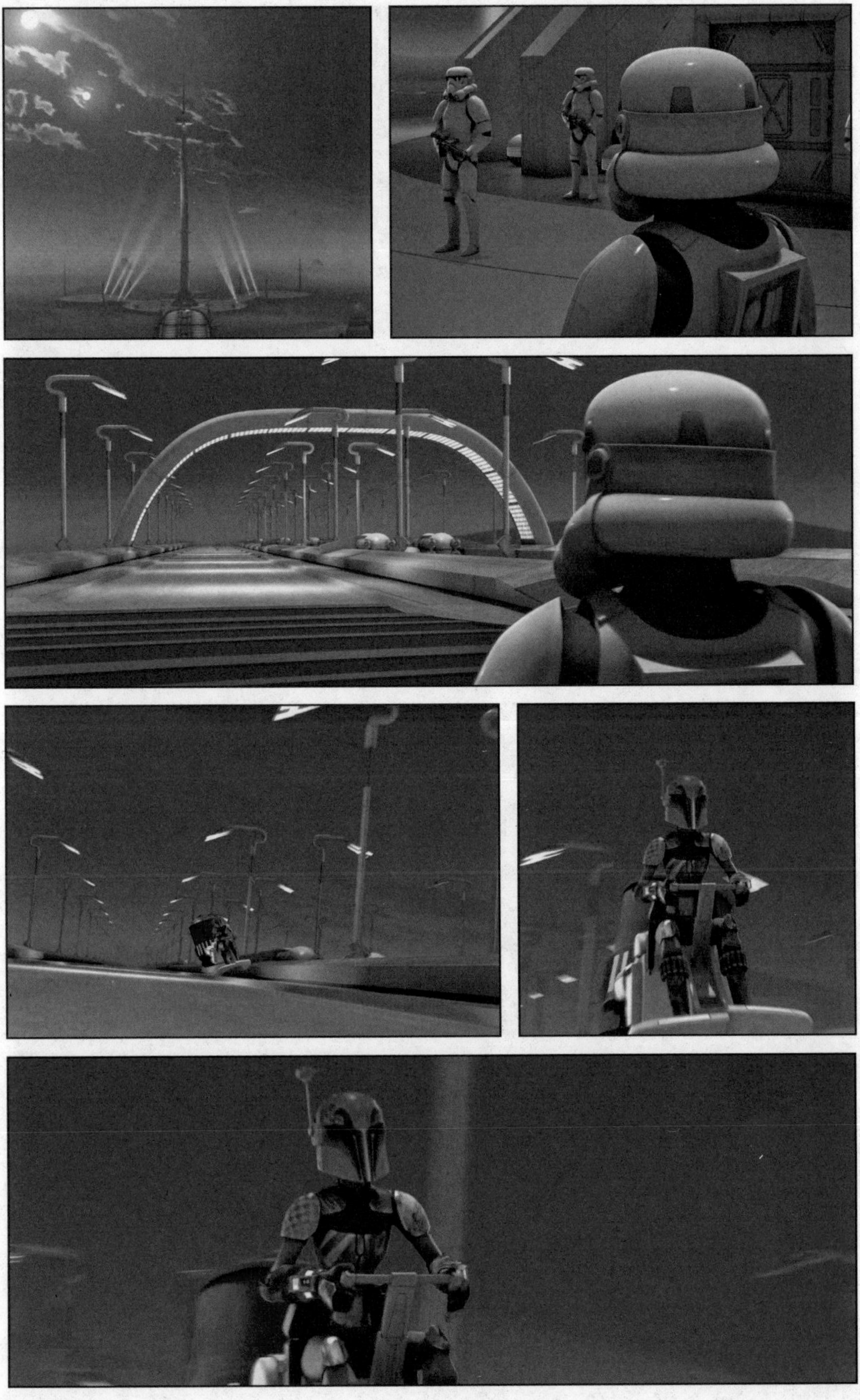

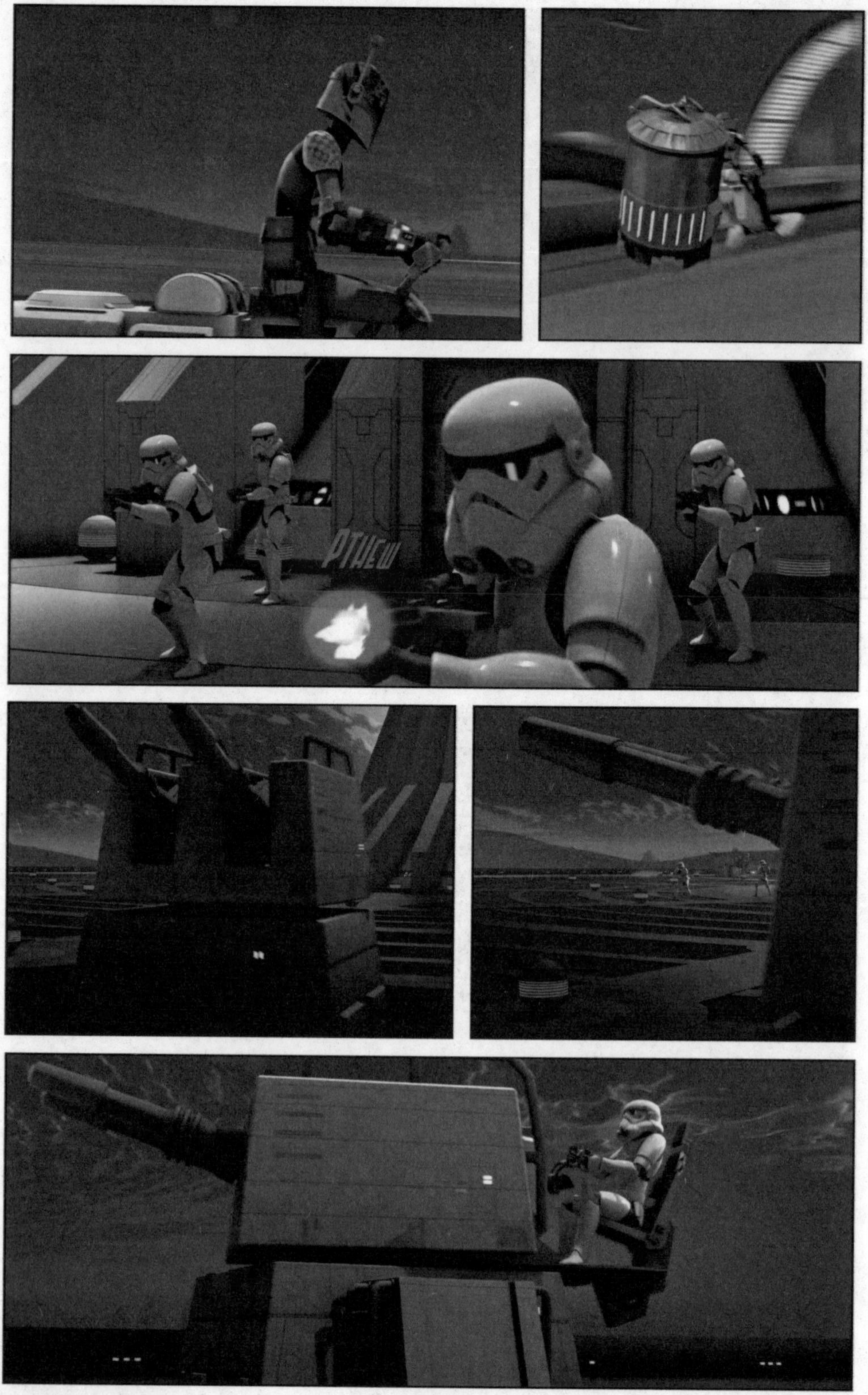
PTHEW

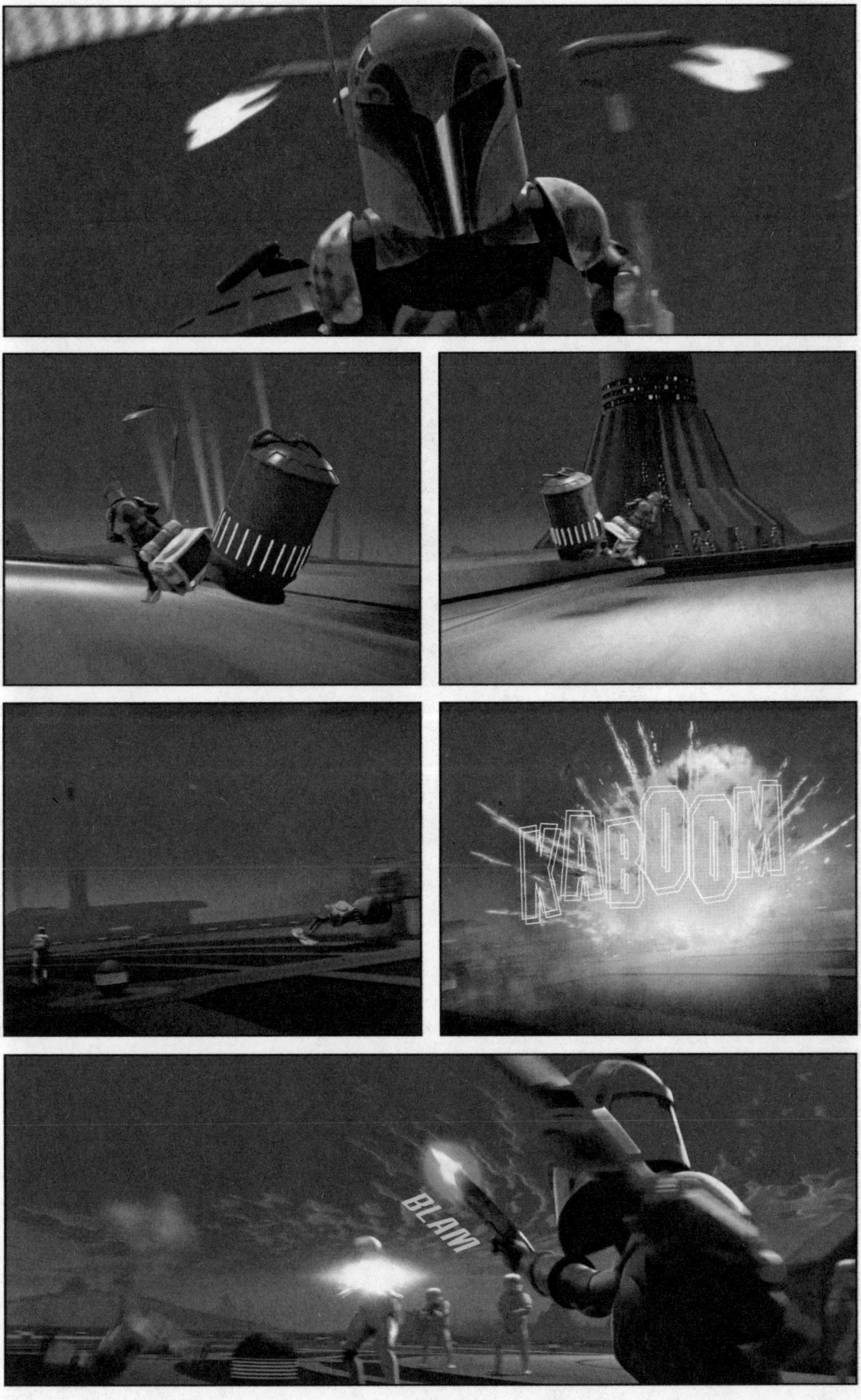
KABOOM
BLAM

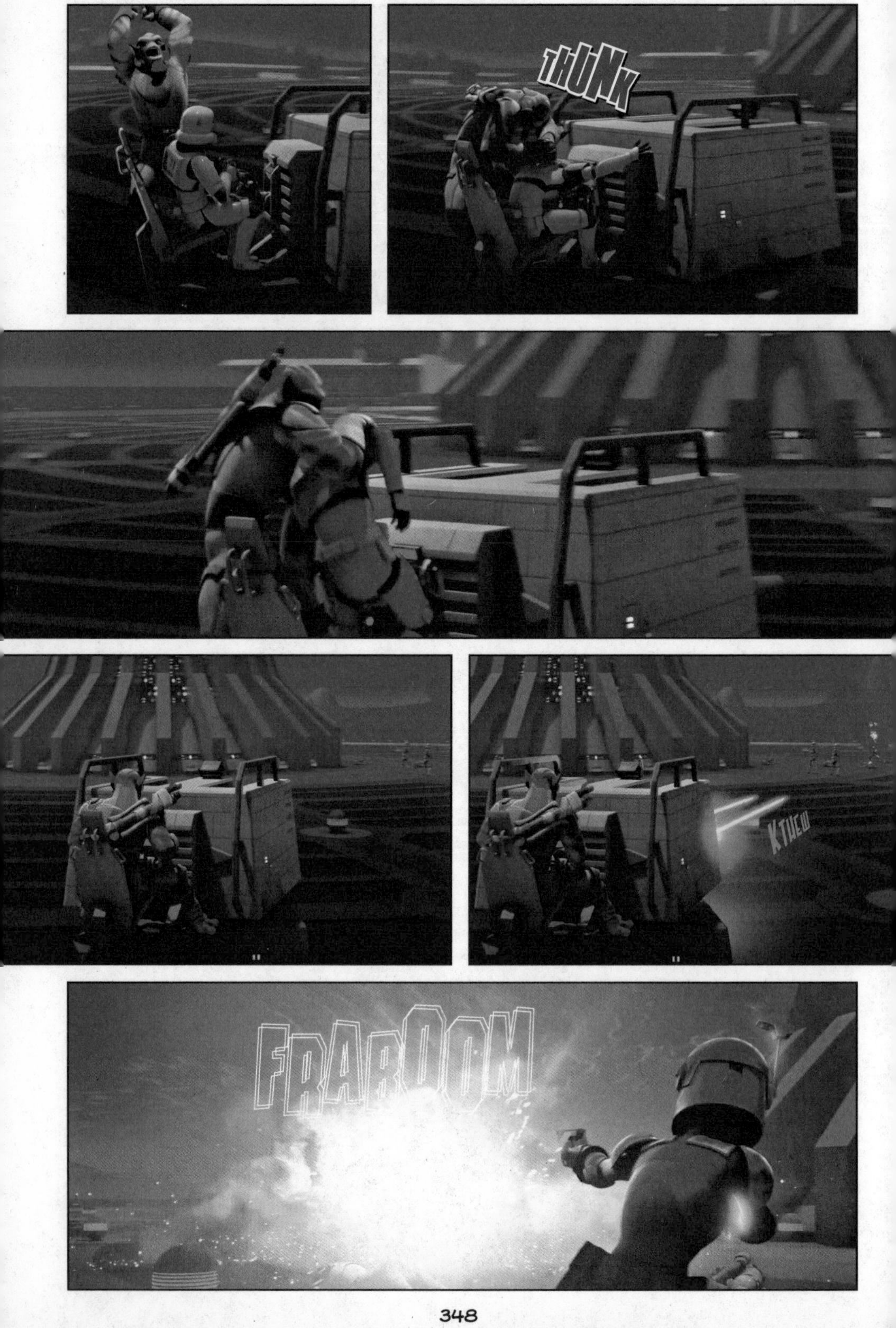
THUNK
KTHEW
FRAROOM

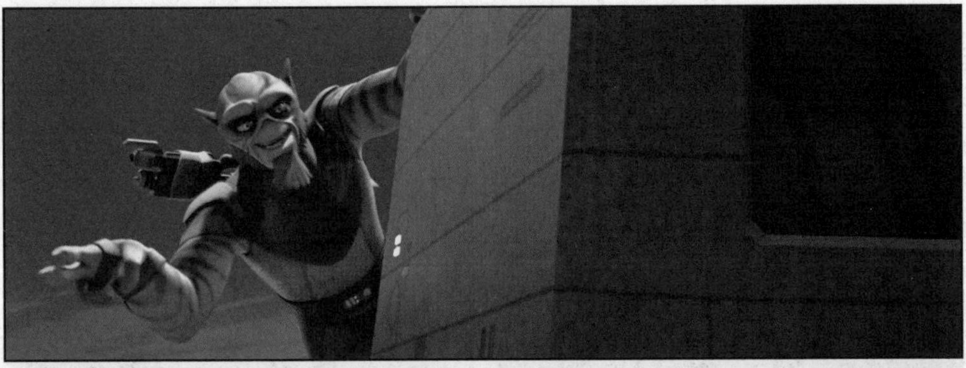

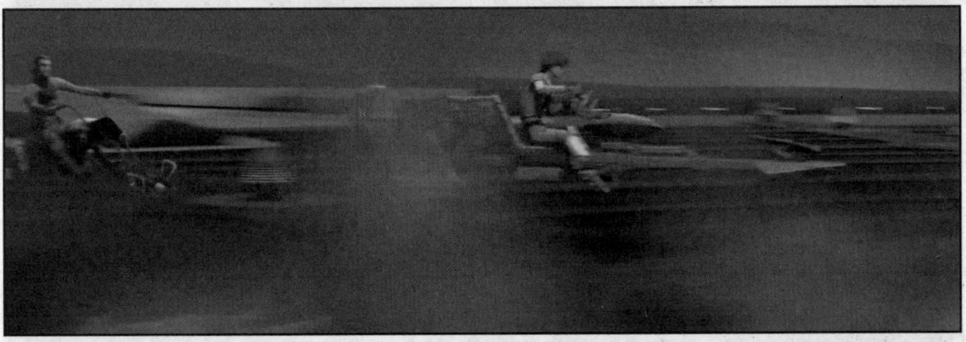

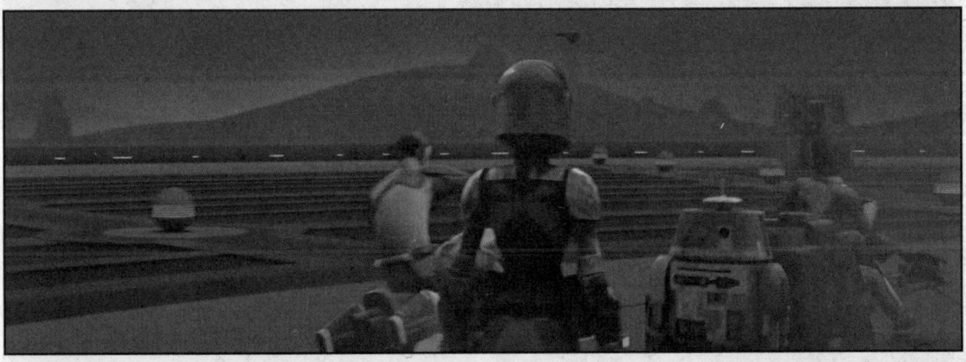

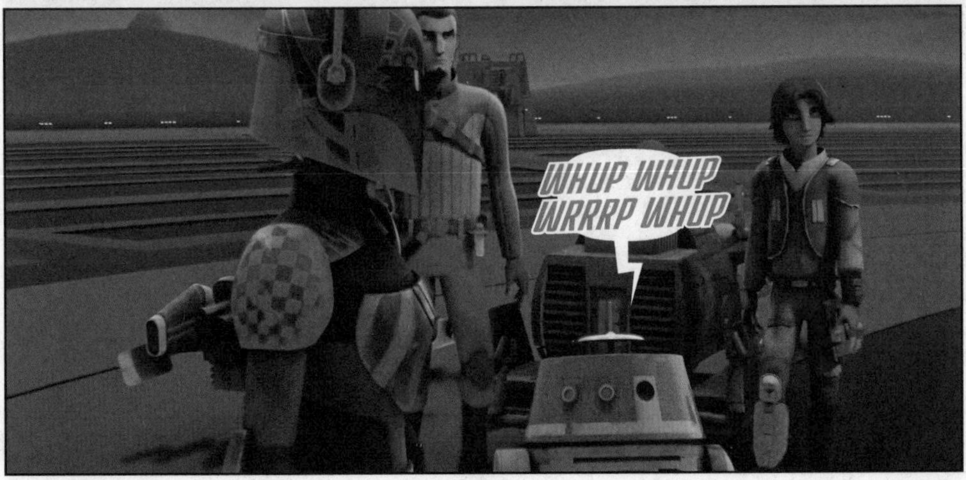
WHUP WHUP WRRRP WHUP

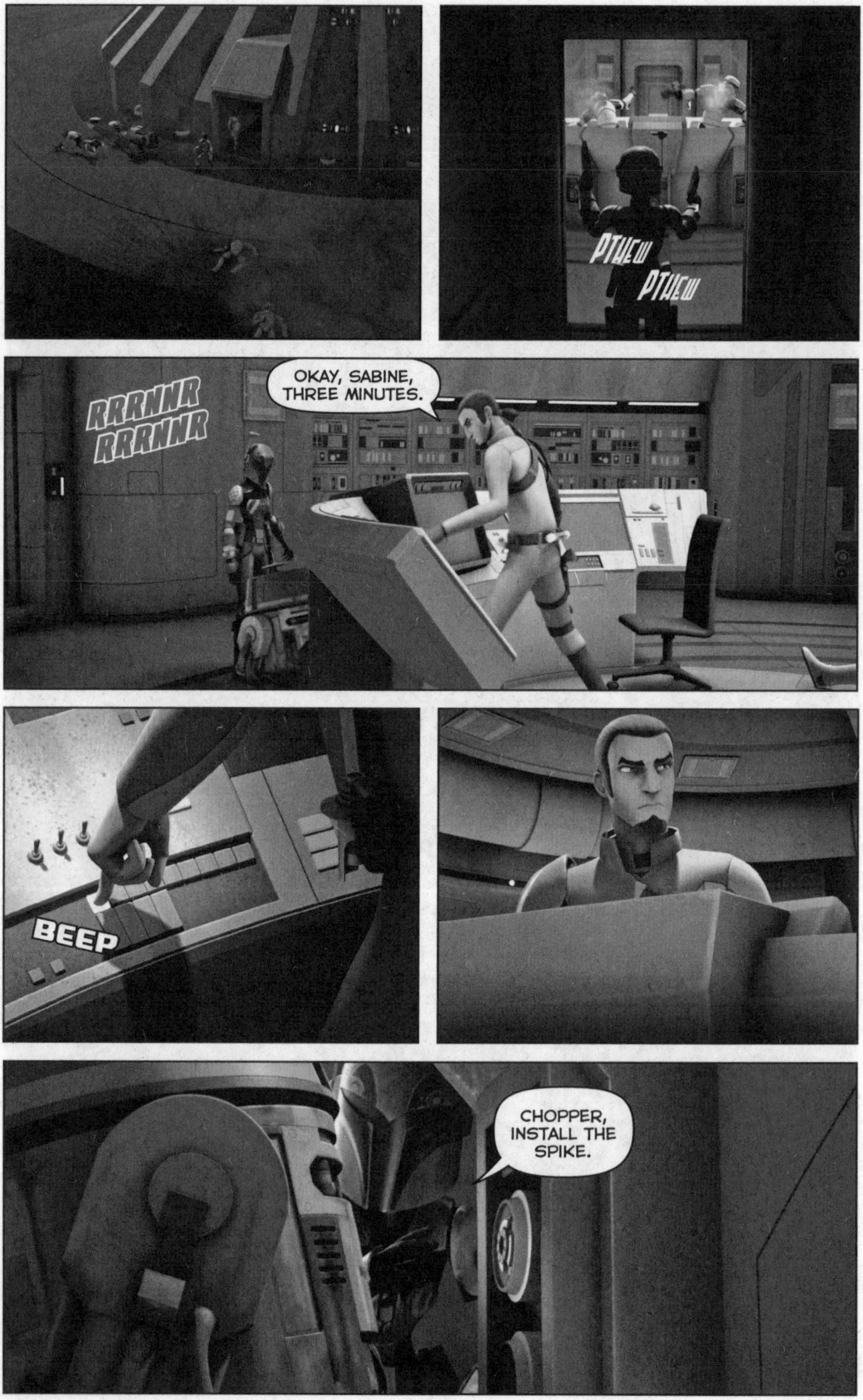
PTHEW
PTHEW
RRRNNR
RRRNNR
OKAY, SABINE, THREE MINUTES.
BEEP
CHOPPER, INSTALL THE SPIKE.

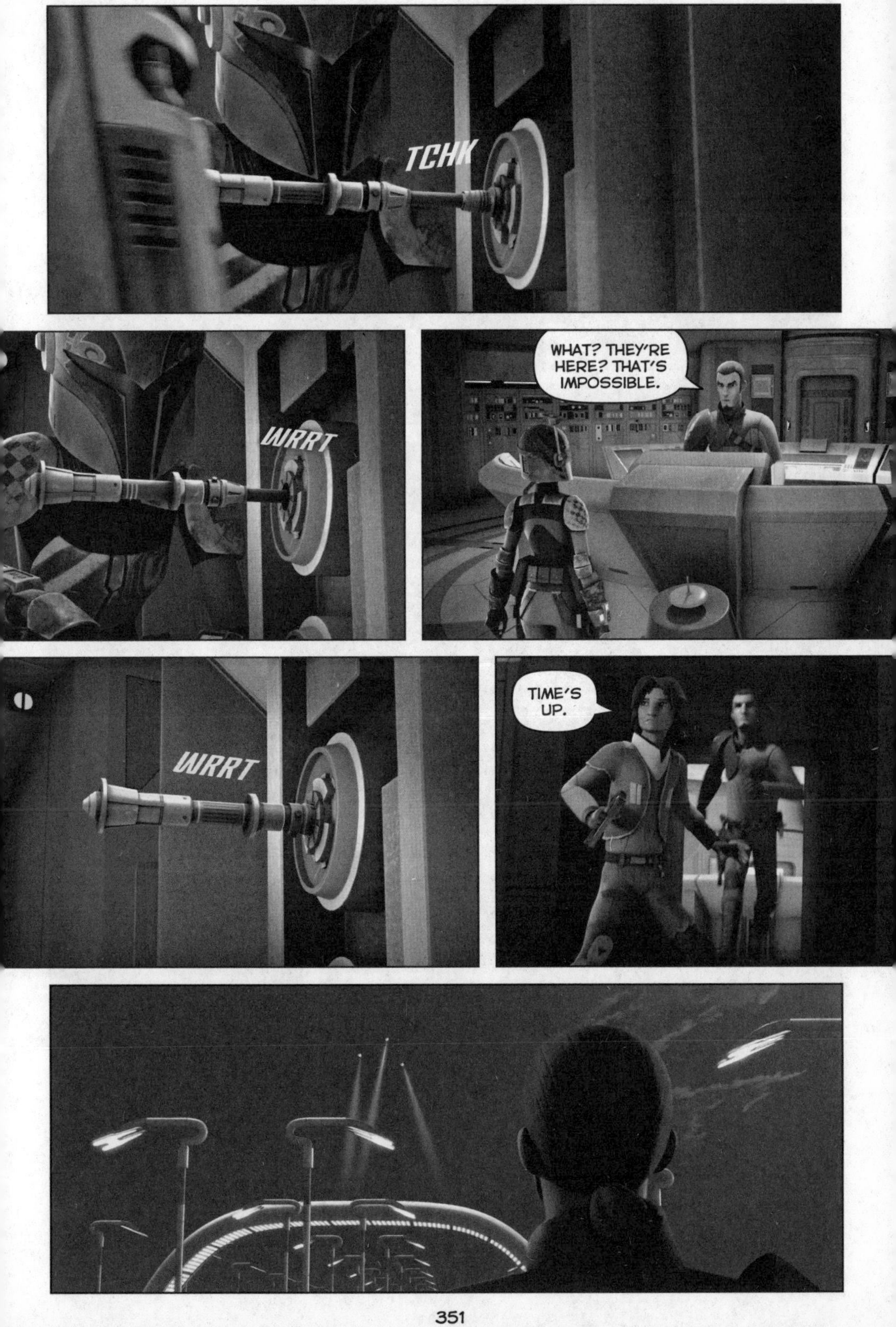
TCHK
WRRT
WHAT? THEY'RE HERE? THAT'S IMPOSSIBLE.
WRRT
TIME'S UP.

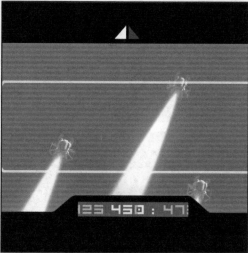

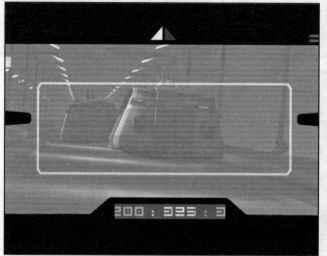

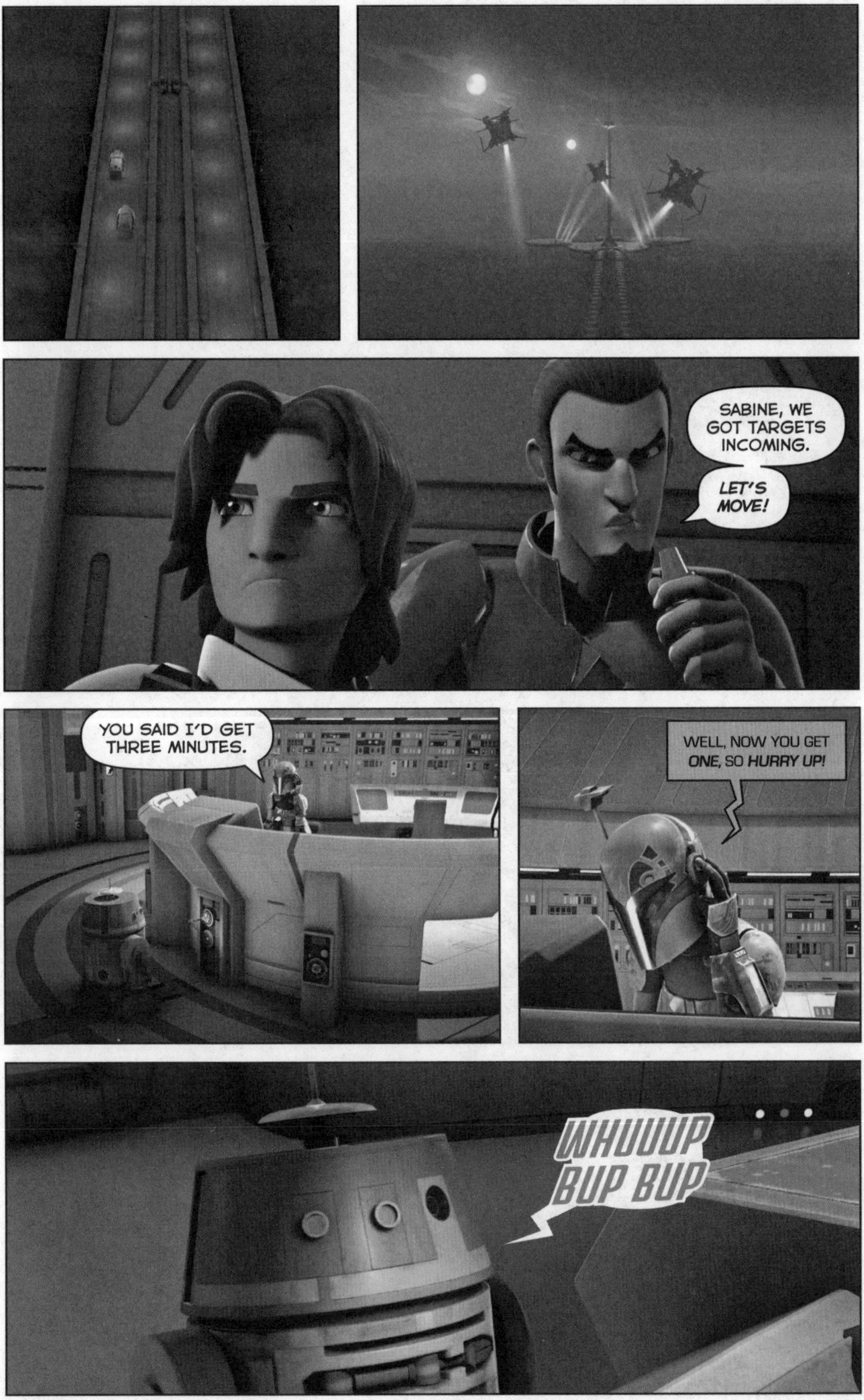
SABINE, WE GOT TARGETS INCOMING.
LET'S MOVE!
YOU SAID I'D GET THREE MINUTES.
WELL, NOW YOU GET ONE, SO HURRY UP!
WHUUUP BUP BUP

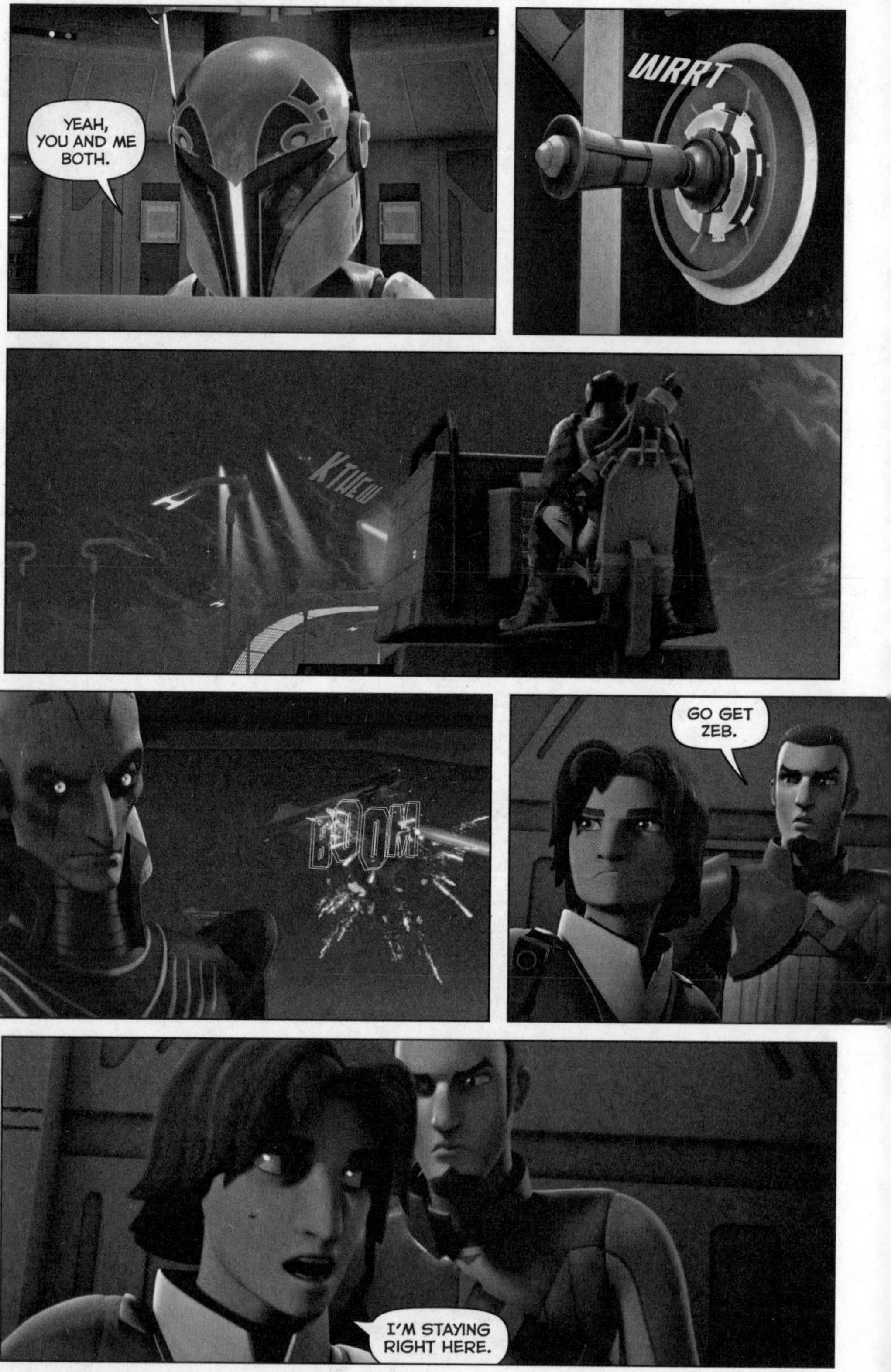
YEAH, YOU AND ME BOTH.
WRRT
KTHEW
BOOM
GO GET ZEB.
I'M STAYING RIGHT HERE.

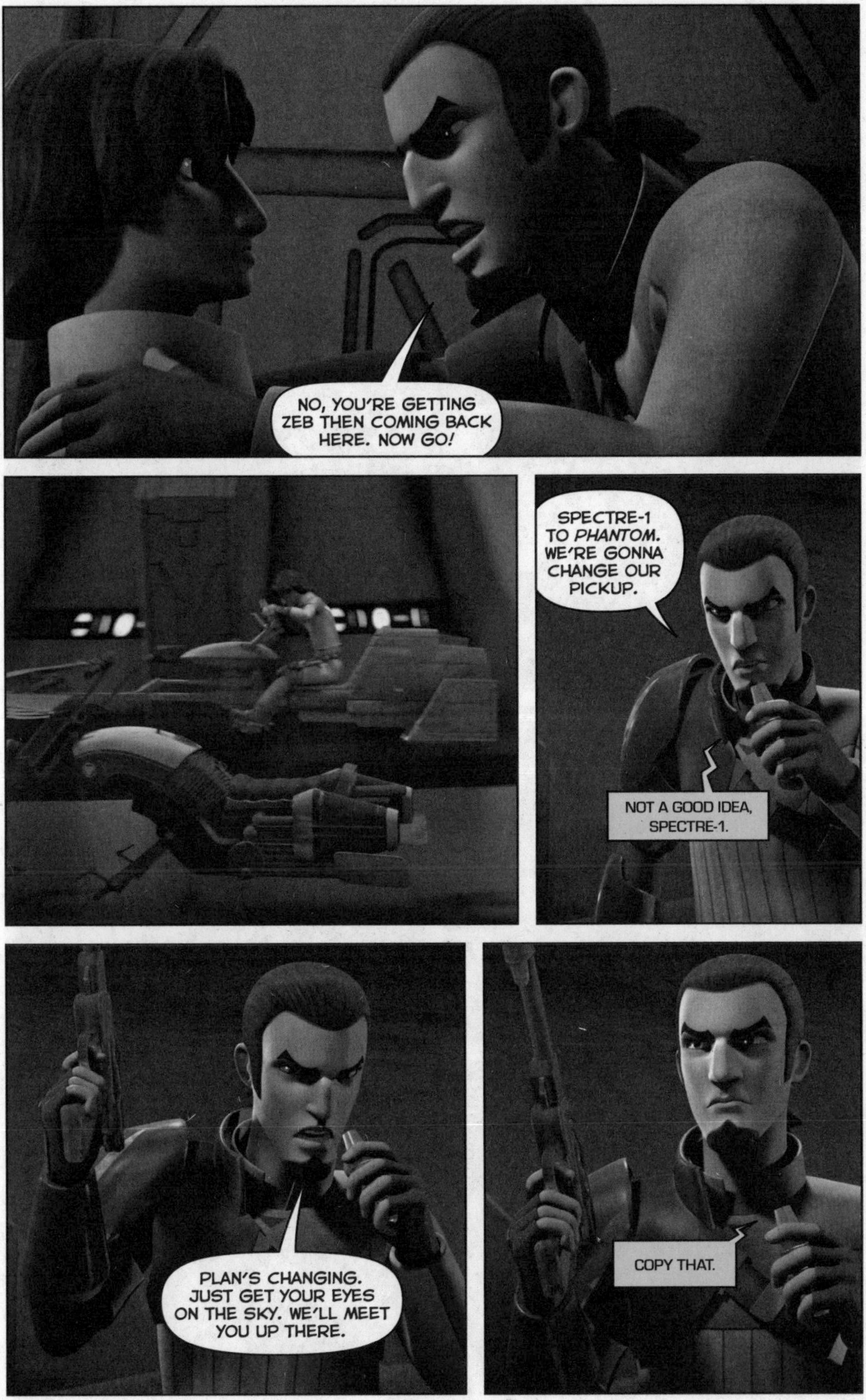
NO, YOU'RE GETTING ZEB THEN COMING BACK HERE. NOW GO!
SPECTRE-1 TO *PHANTOM*. WE'RE GONNA CHANGE OUR PICKUP.
NOT A GOOD IDEA, SPECTRE-1.
PLAN'S CHANGING. JUST GET YOUR EYES ON THE SKY. WE'LL MEET YOU UP THERE.
COPY THAT.

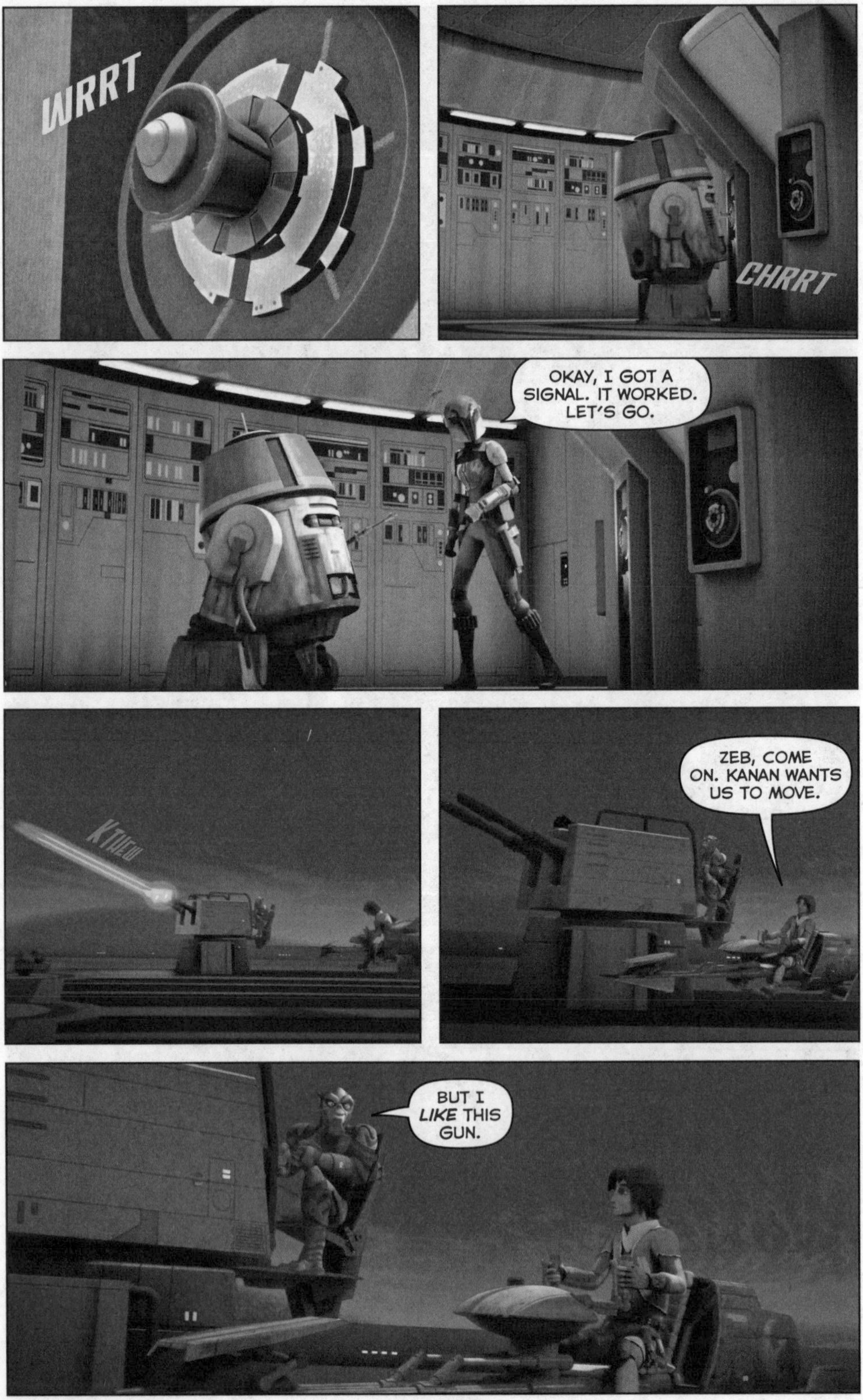
WRRT
CHRRT
OKAY, I GOT A SIGNAL. IT WORKED. LET'S GO.
KTHEW
ZEB, COME ON. KANAN WANTS US TO MOVE.
BUT I *LIKE* THIS GUN.

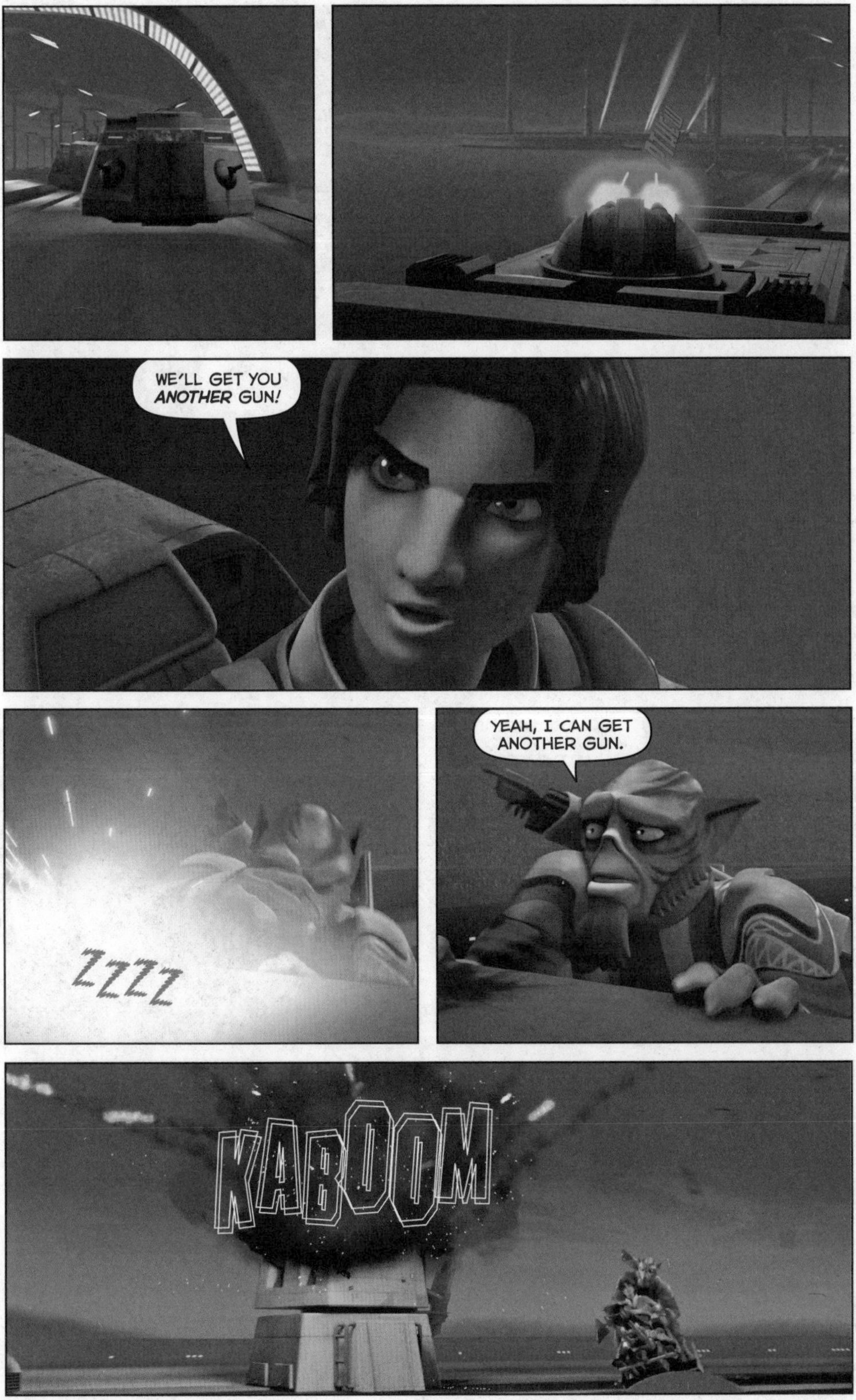
WE'LL GET YOU *ANOTHER* GUN!
ZZZZ
YEAH, I CAN GET ANOTHER GUN.
KABOOM

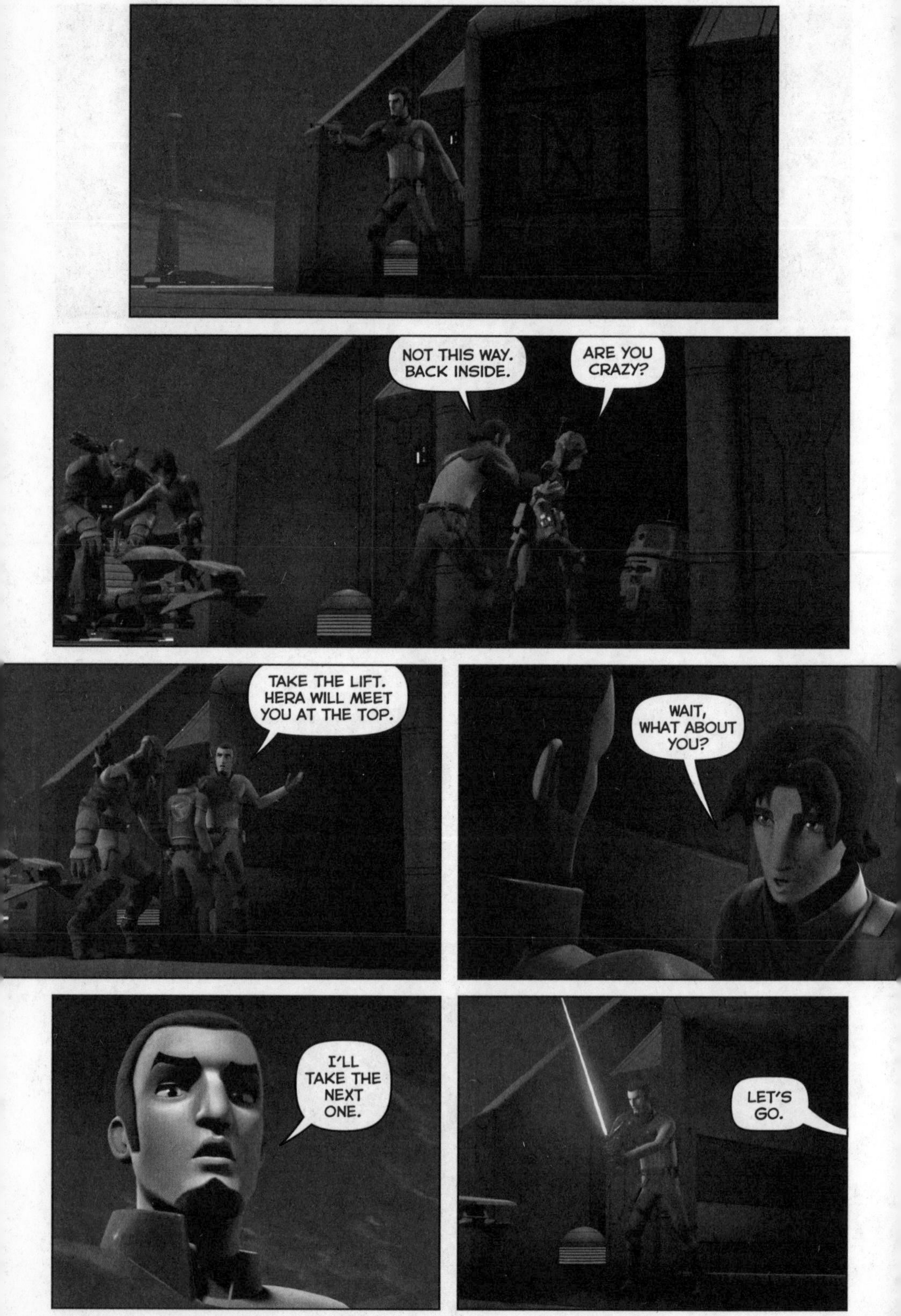
NOT THIS WAY. BACK INSIDE.
ARE YOU CRAZY?
TAKE THE LIFT. HERA WILL MEET YOU AT THE TOP.
WAIT, WHAT ABOUT YOU?
I'LL TAKE THE NEXT ONE.
LET'S GO.

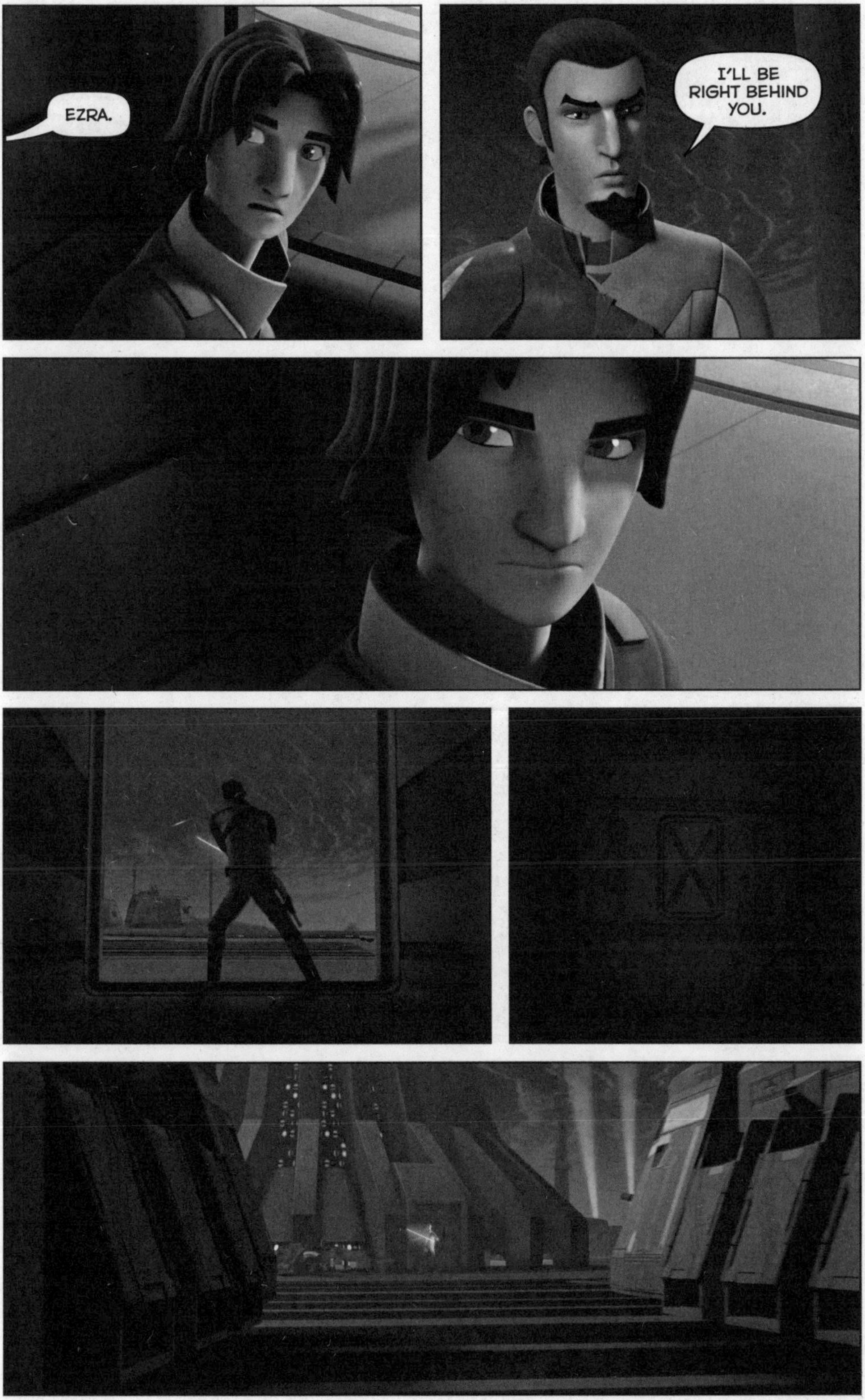
EZRA.
I'LL BE RIGHT BEHIND YOU.

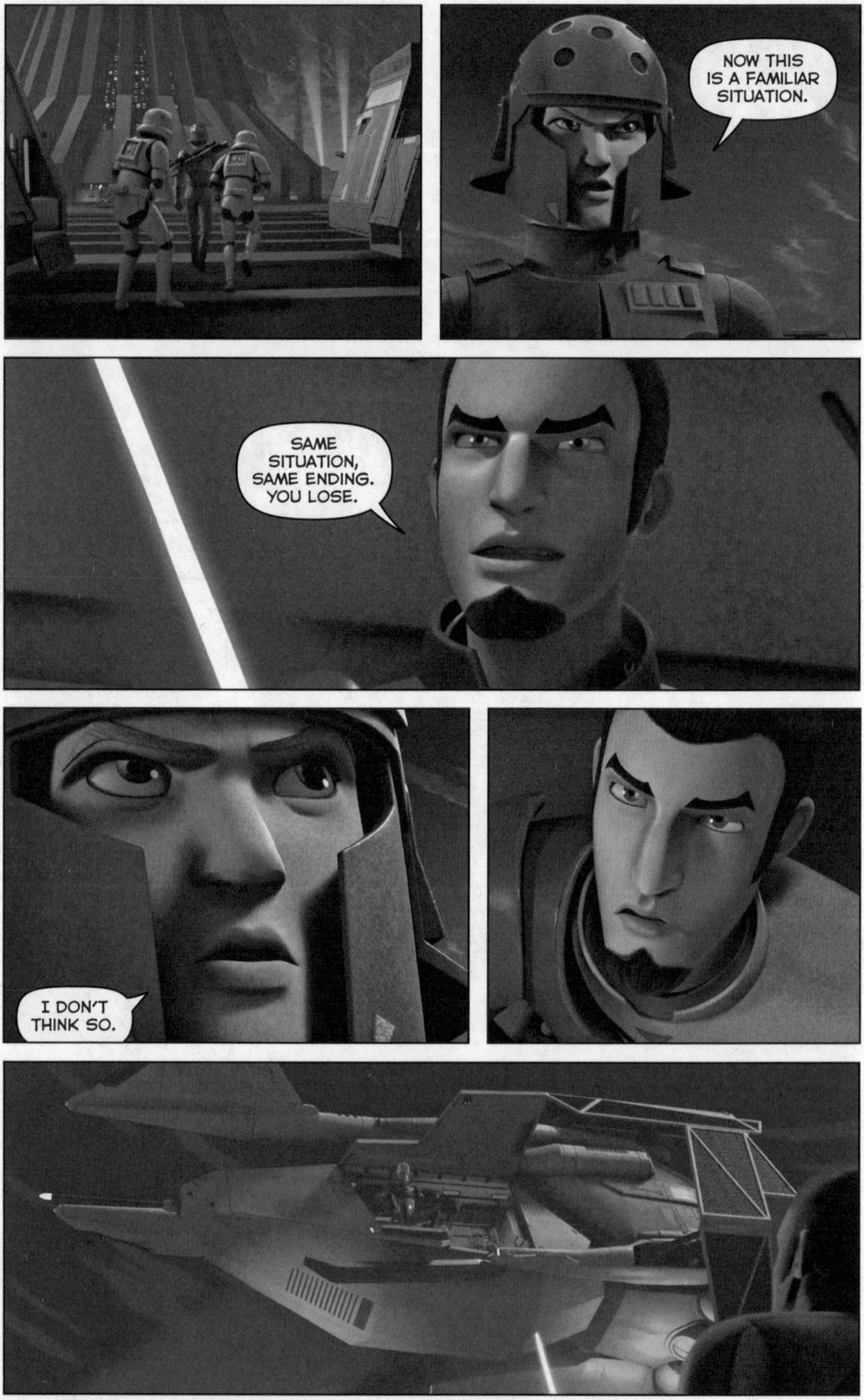
NOW THIS IS A FAMILIAR SITUATION.
SAME SITUATION, SAME ENDING. YOU LOSE.
I DON'T THINK SO.

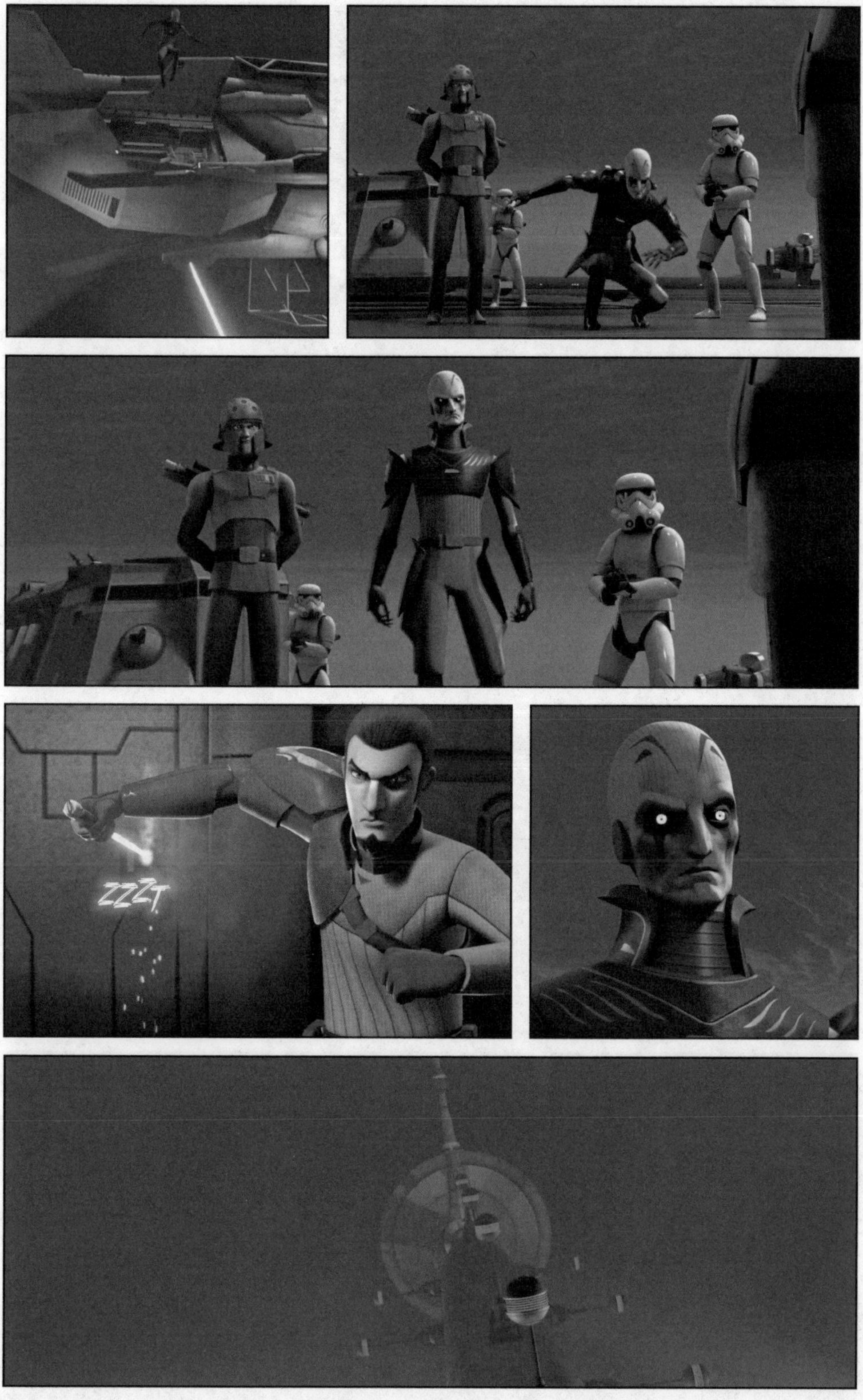
ZZZT

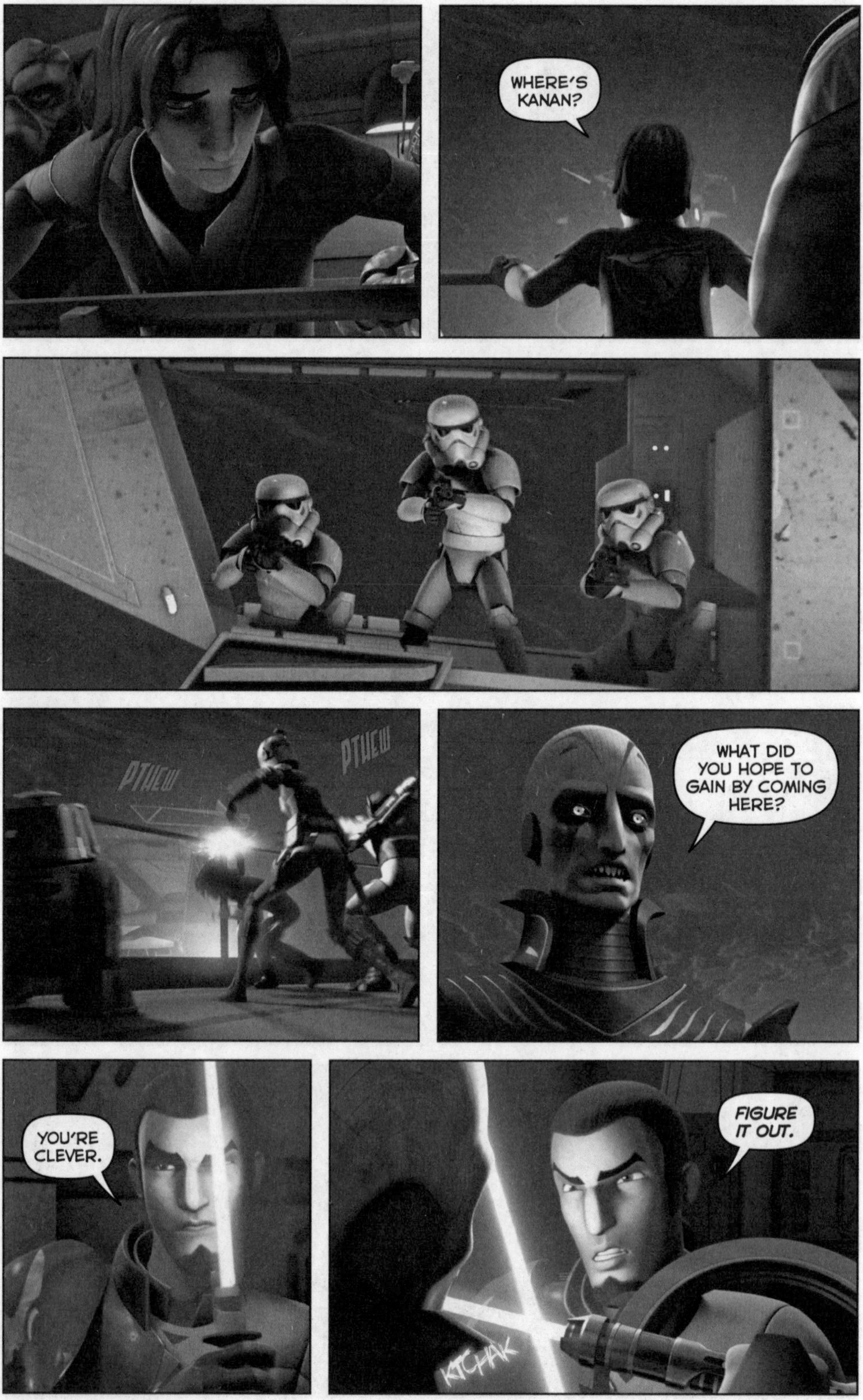
WHERE'S KANAN?
PTHEW
PTHEW
WHAT DID YOU HOPE TO GAIN BY COMING HERE?
YOU'RE CLEVER.
FIGURE IT OUT.
KTCHAK

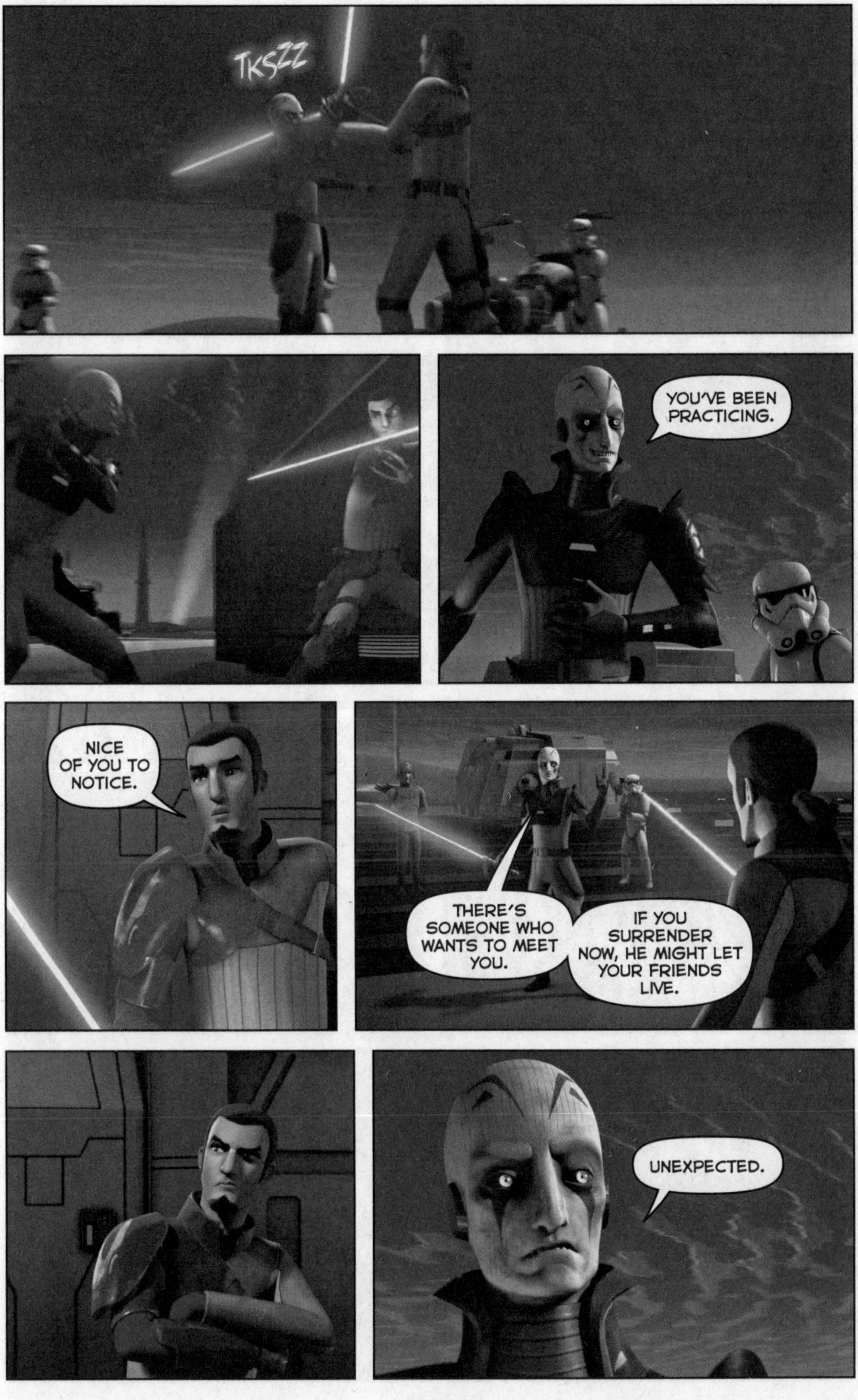
TKSZZ
YOU'VE BEEN PRACTICING.
NICE OF YOU TO NOTICE.
THERE'S SOMEONE WHO WANTS TO MEET YOU.
IF YOU SURRENDER NOW, HE MIGHT LET YOUR FRIENDS LIVE.
UNEXPECTED.

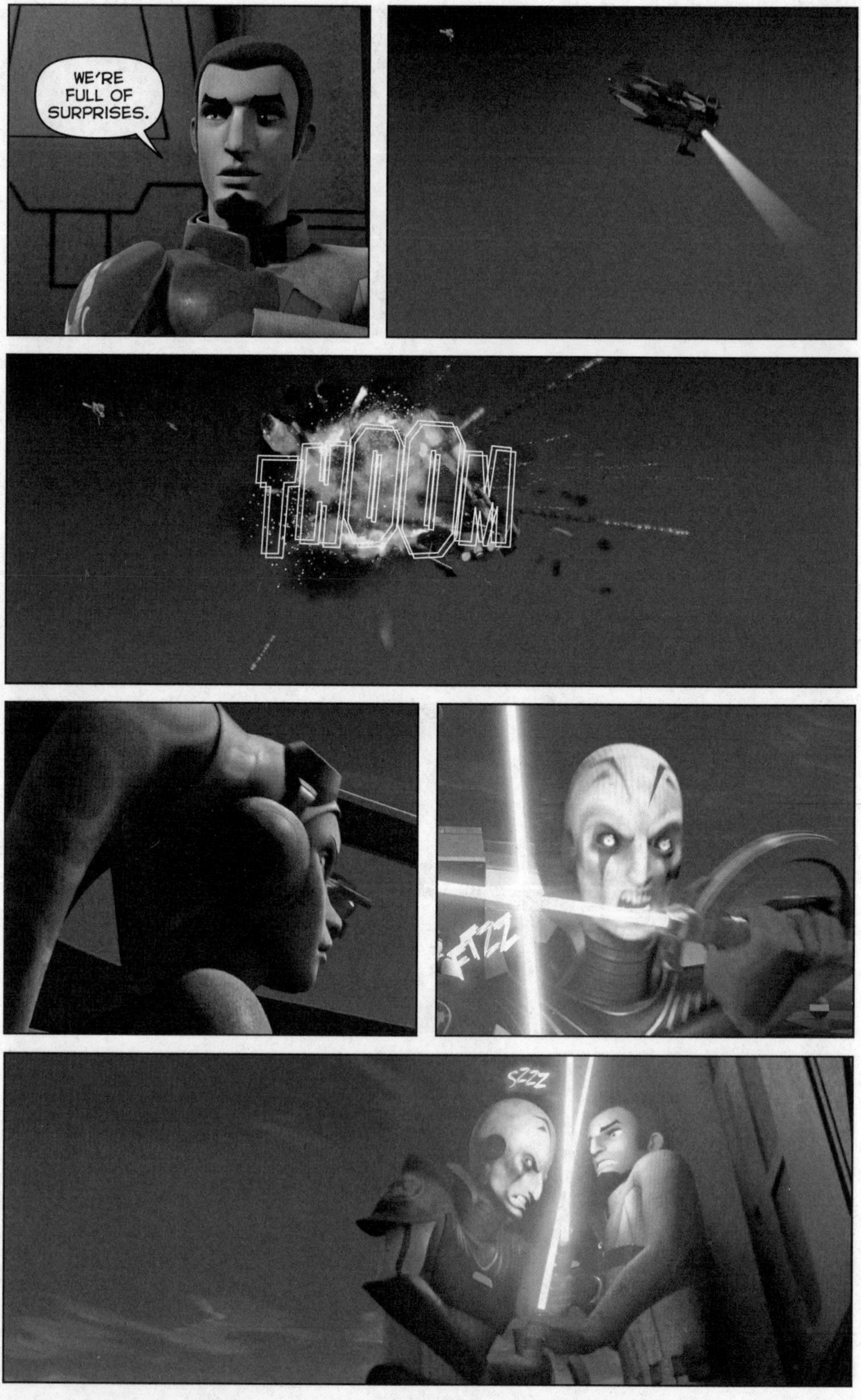
WE'RE FULL OF SURPRISES.
THOOM
FTZZ
SZZZ

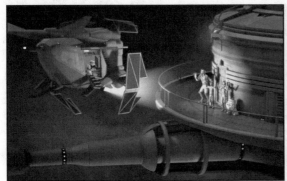

BEEP
BEEP BEEP
BEEP BEEP

KABLAM

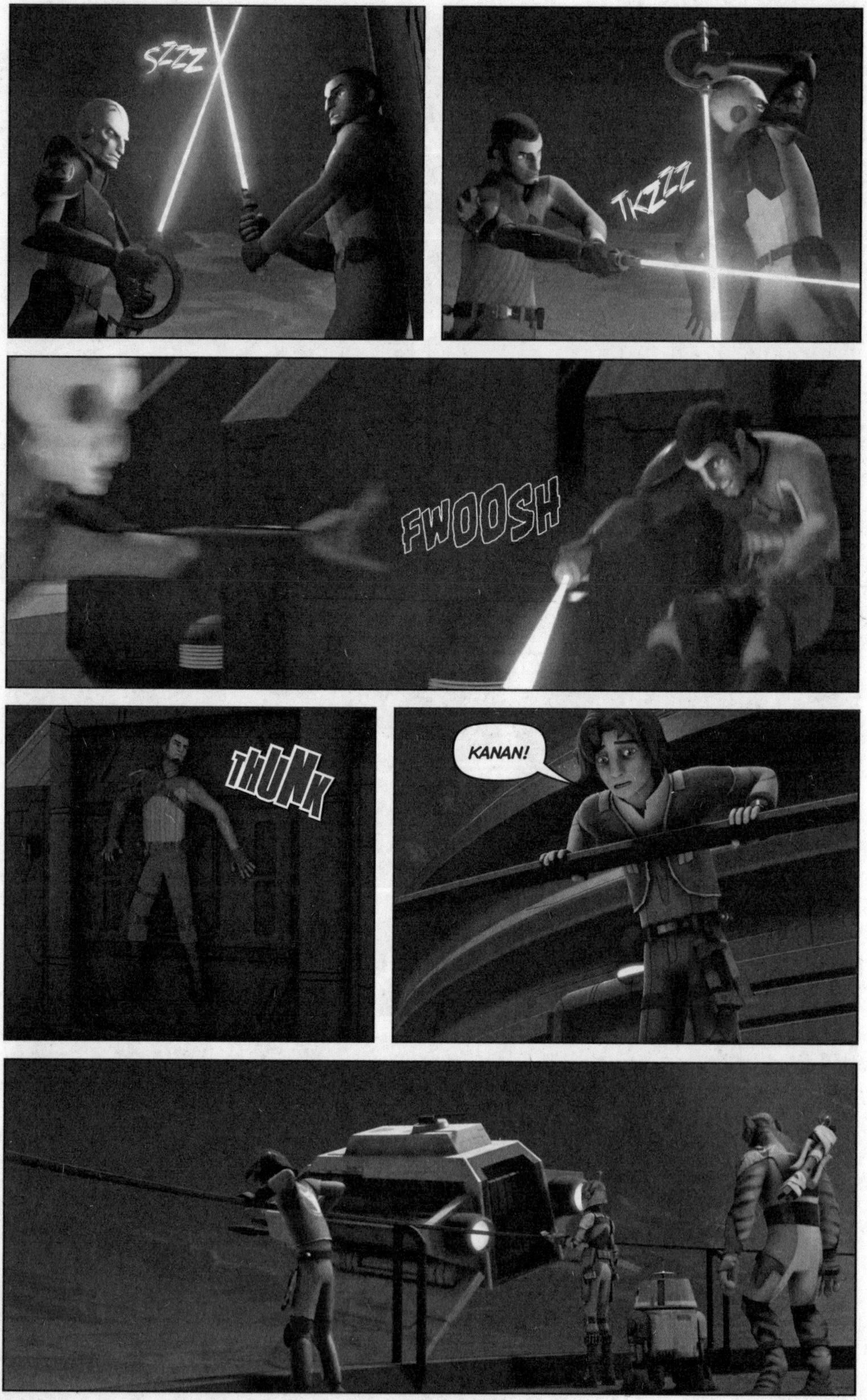
SZZZ
TKZZZ
FWOOSH
THUNK
KANAN!

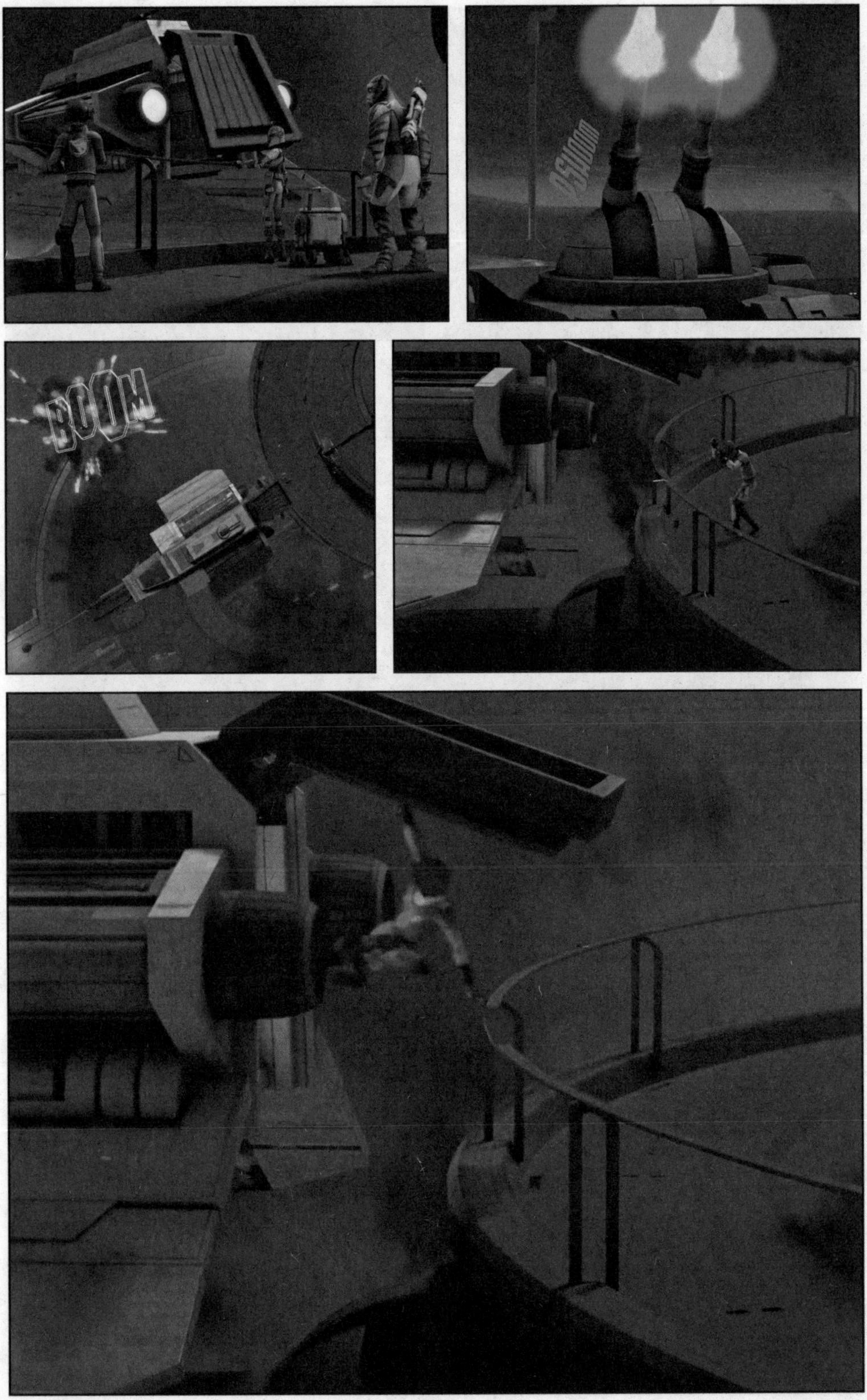
WOOOSH
BOOM

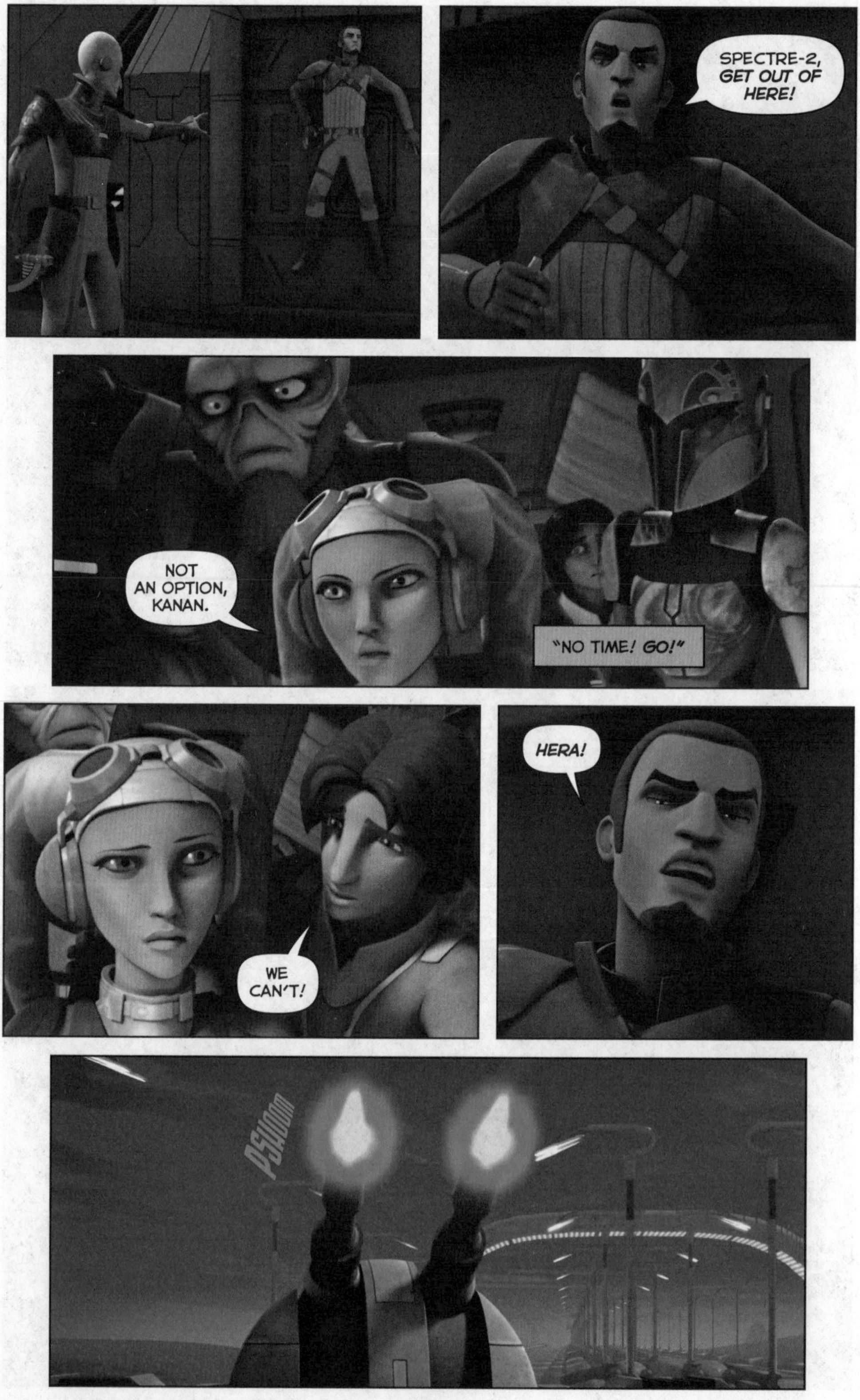
SPECTRE-2, GET OUT OF HERE!
NOT AN OPTION, KANAN.
"NO TIME! GO!"
WE CAN'T!
HERA!
PSUOOM

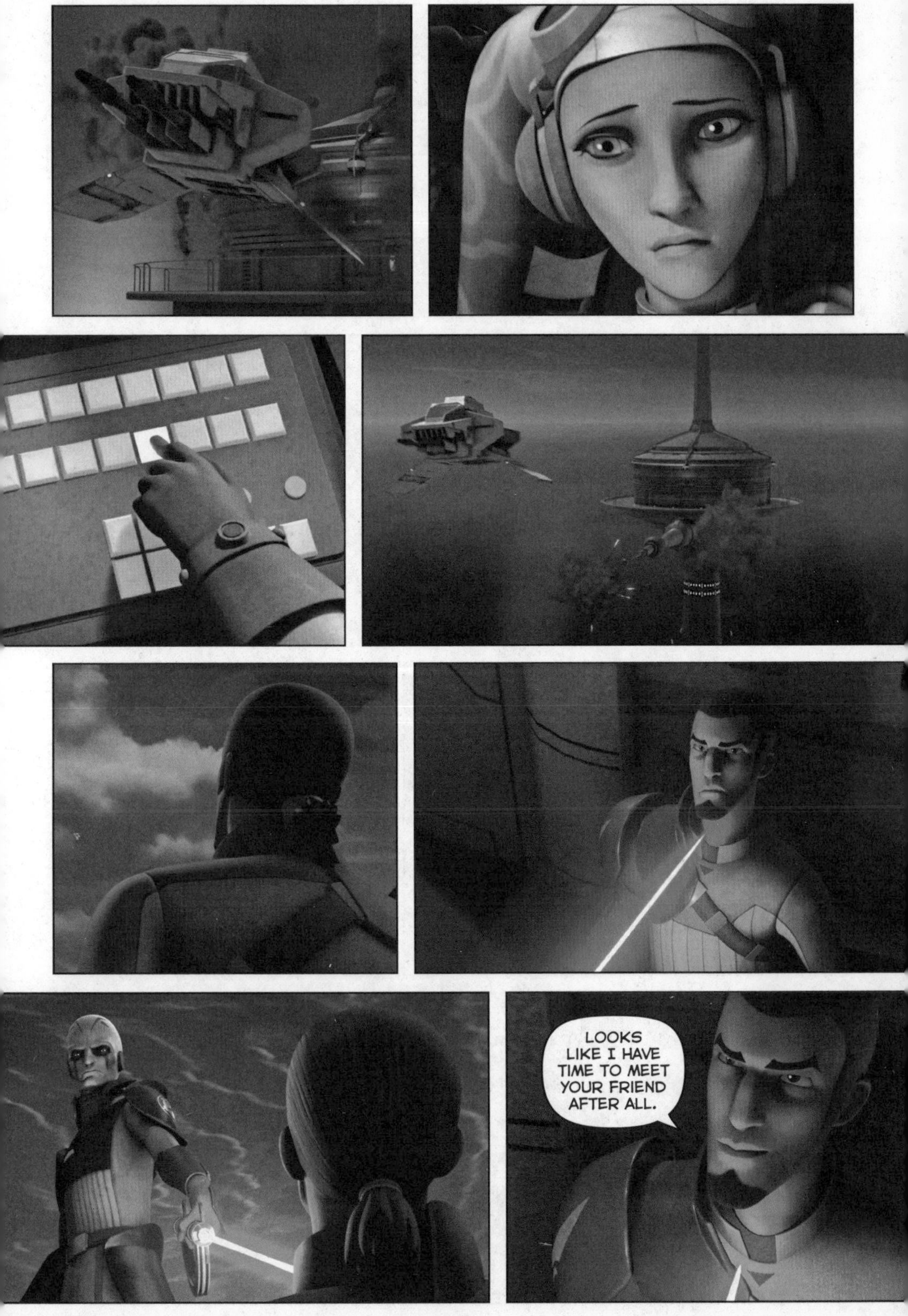
LOOKS LIKE I HAVE TIME TO MEET YOUR FRIEND AFTER ALL.

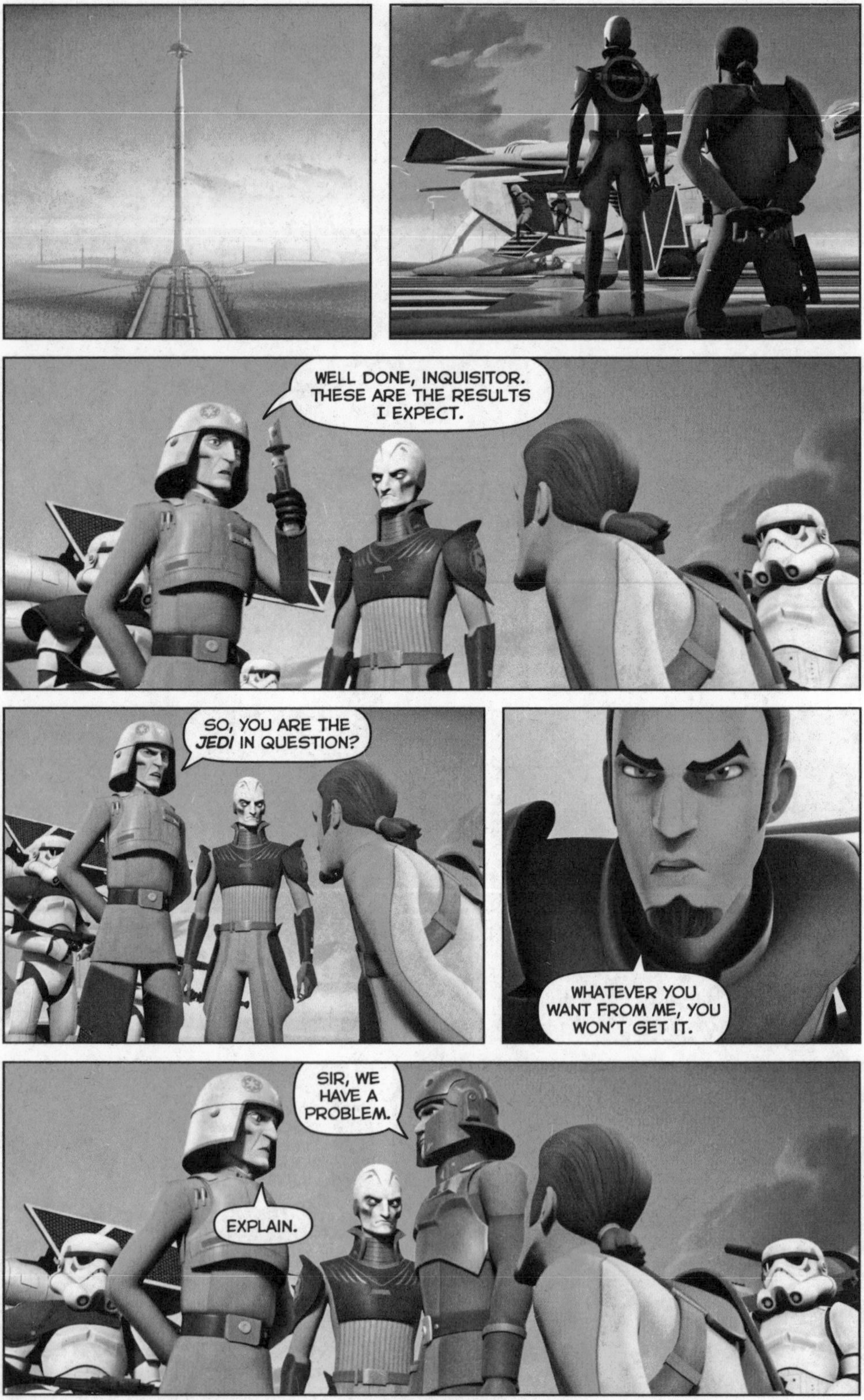
WELL DONE, INQUISITOR. THESE ARE THE RESULTS I EXPECT.
SO, YOU ARE THE *JEDI* IN QUESTION?
WHATEVER YOU WANT FROM ME, YOU WON'T GET IT.
SIR, WE HAVE A PROBLEM.
EXPLAIN.

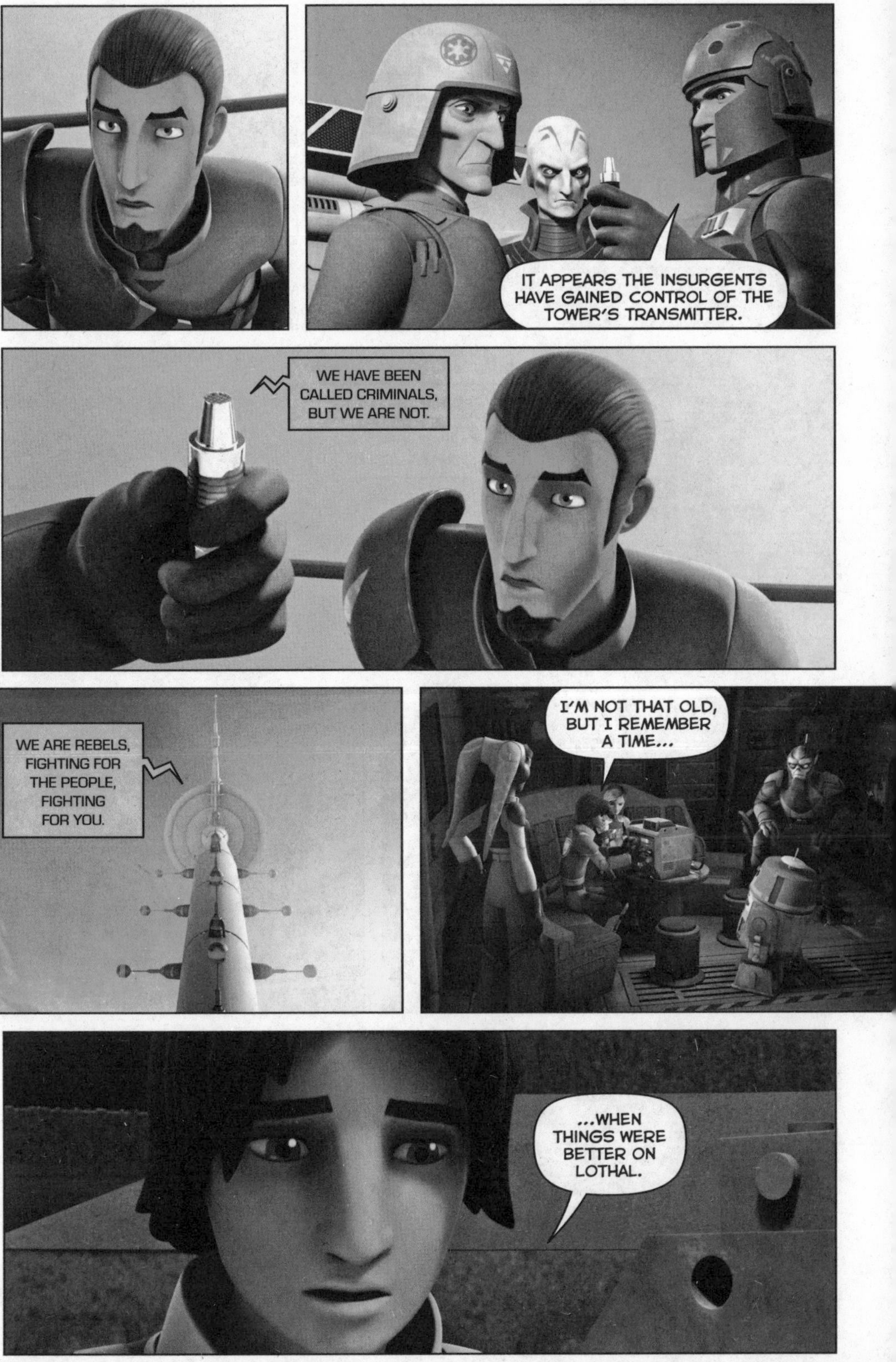
IT APPEARS THE INSURGENTS HAVE GAINED CONTROL OF THE TOWER'S TRANSMITTER.
WE HAVE BEEN CALLED CRIMINALS, BUT WE ARE NOT.
WE ARE REBELS, FIGHTING FOR THE PEOPLE, FIGHTING FOR YOU.
I'M NOT THAT OLD, BUT I REMEMBER A TIME...
...WHEN THINGS WERE BETTER ON LOTHAL.

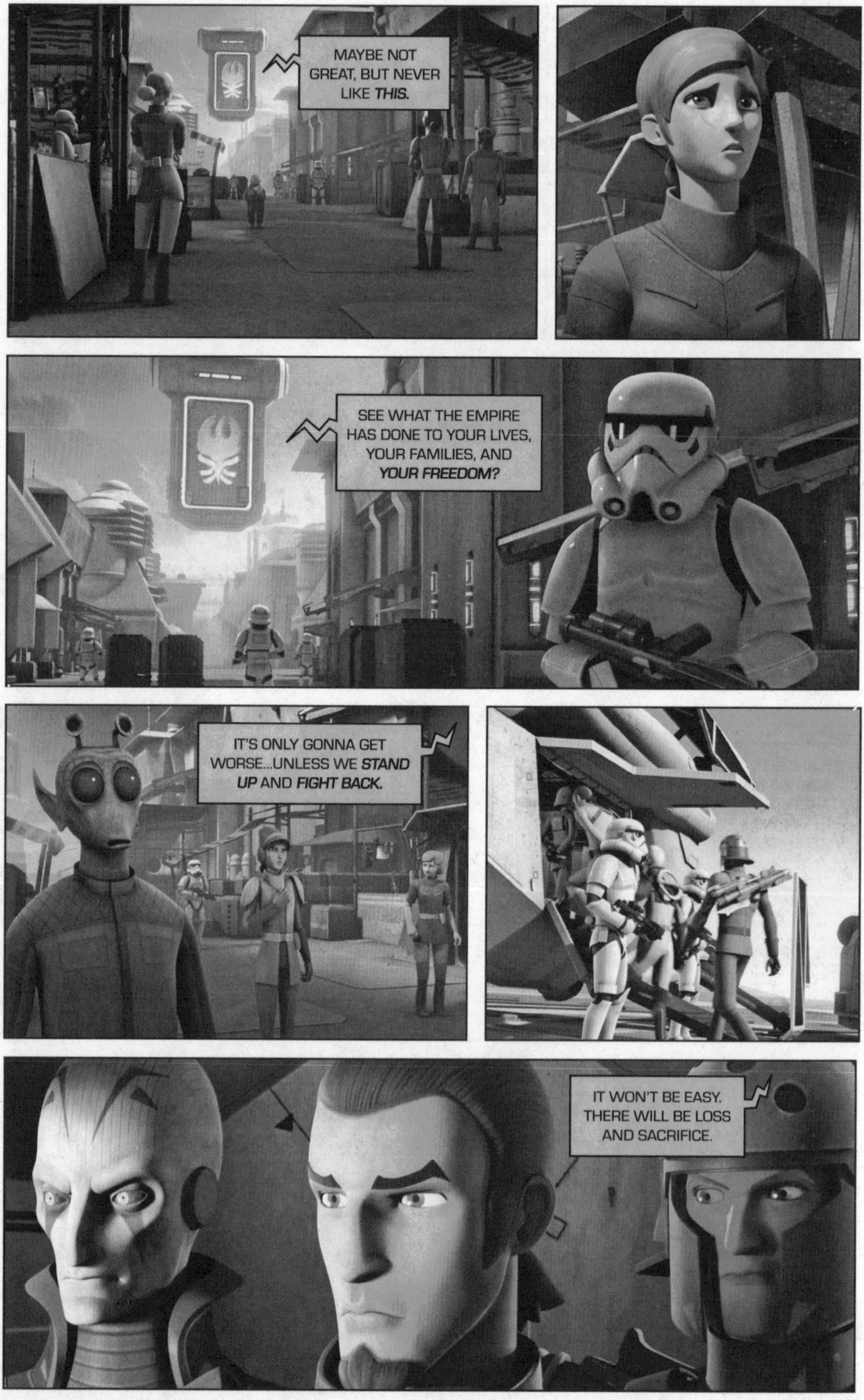
MAYBE NOT GREAT, BUT NEVER LIKE THIS.
SEE WHAT THE EMPIRE HAS DONE TO YOUR LIVES, YOUR FAMILIES, AND YOUR FREEDOM?
IT'S ONLY GONNA GET WORSE...UNLESS WE STAND UP AND FIGHT BACK.
IT WON'T BE EASY. THERE WILL BE LOSS AND SACRIFICE.

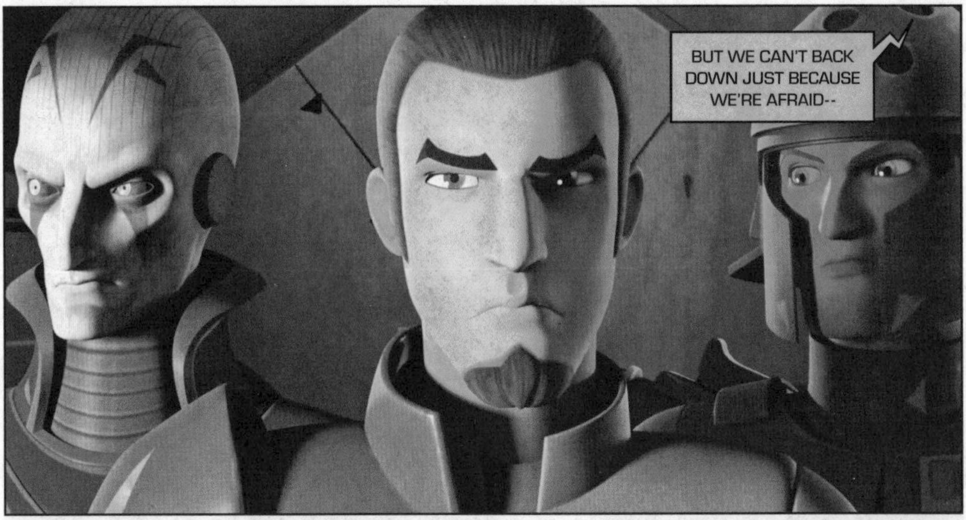
BUT WE CAN'T BACK DOWN JUST BECAUSE WE'RE AFRAID--
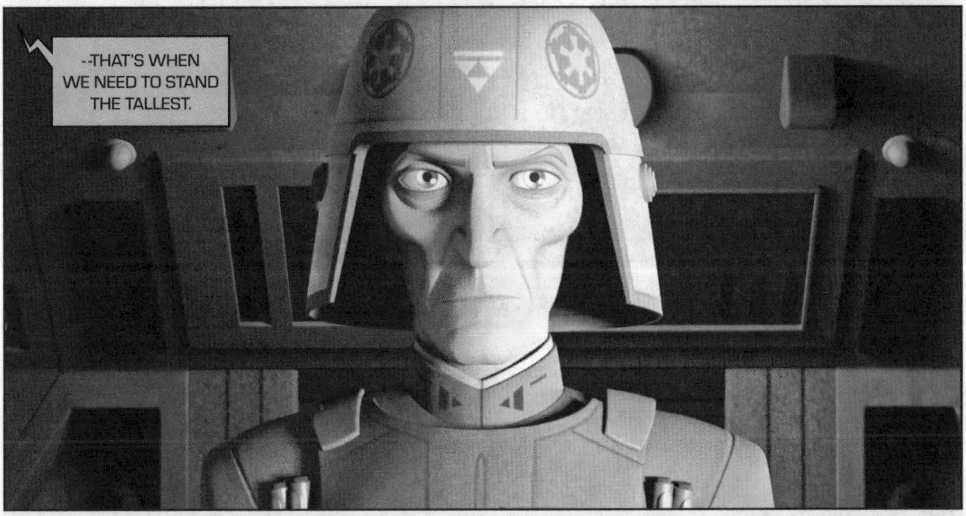
--THAT'S WHEN WE NEED TO STAND THE TALLEST.
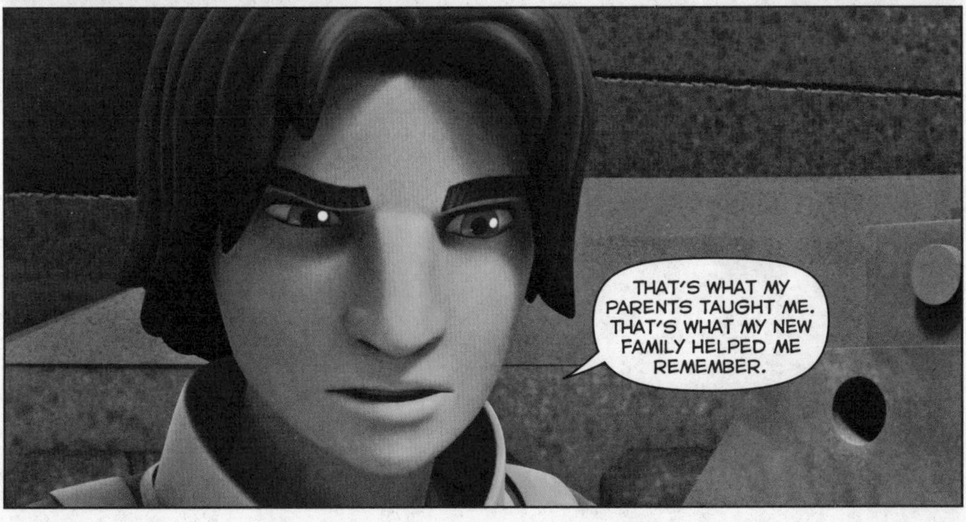
THAT'S WHAT MY PARENTS TAUGHT ME. THAT'S WHAT MY NEW FAMILY HELPED ME REMEMBER.

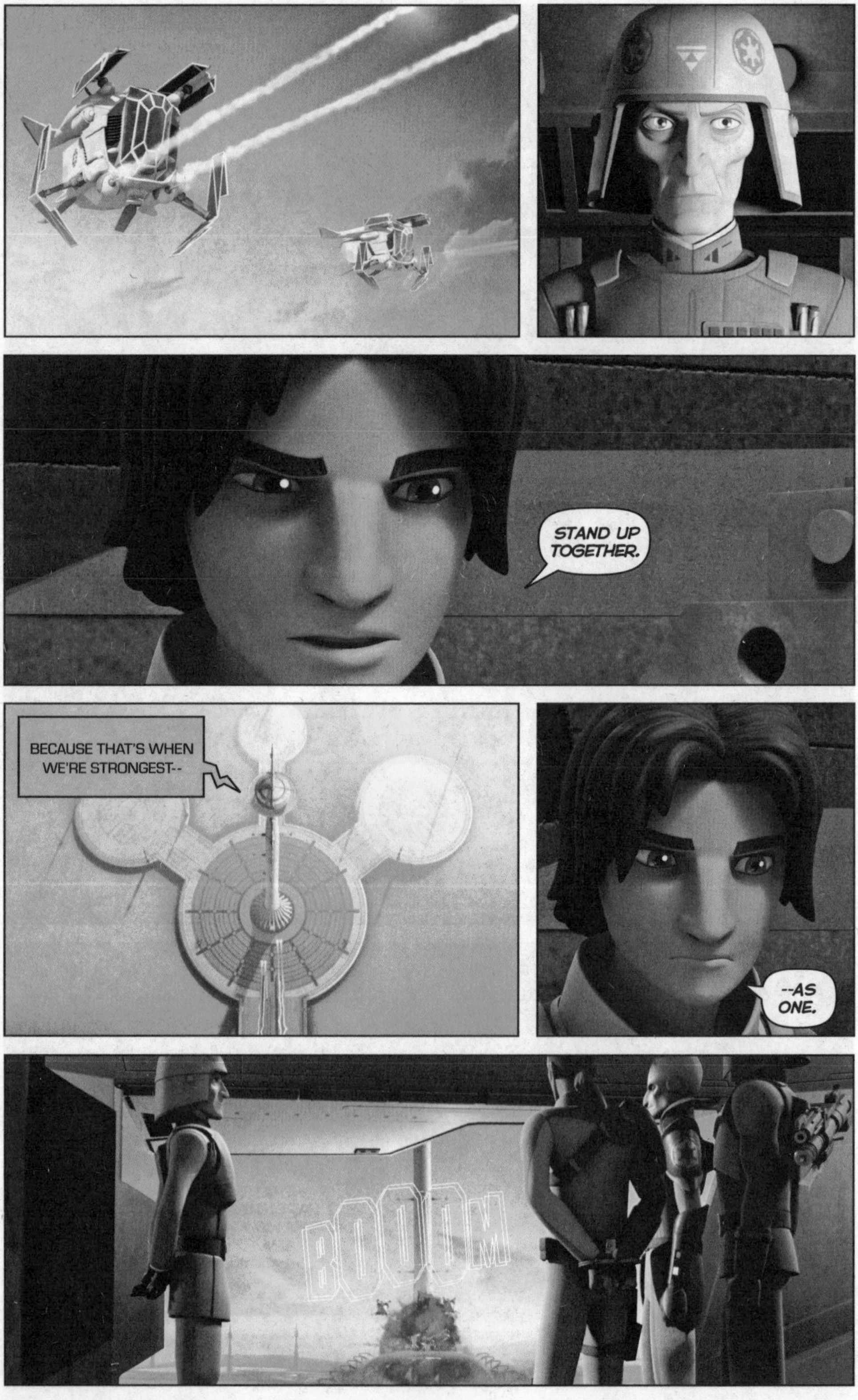
STAND UP TOGETHER.
BECAUSE THAT'S WHEN WE'RE STRONGEST--
--AS ONE.
BOOOM

YOU DO NOT KNOW WHAT IT TAKES TO WIN A WAR.

BUT *I DO.*

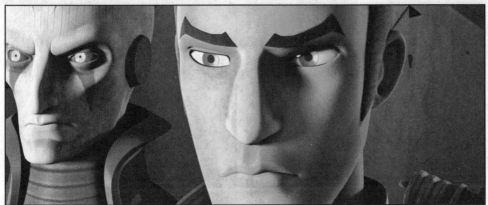

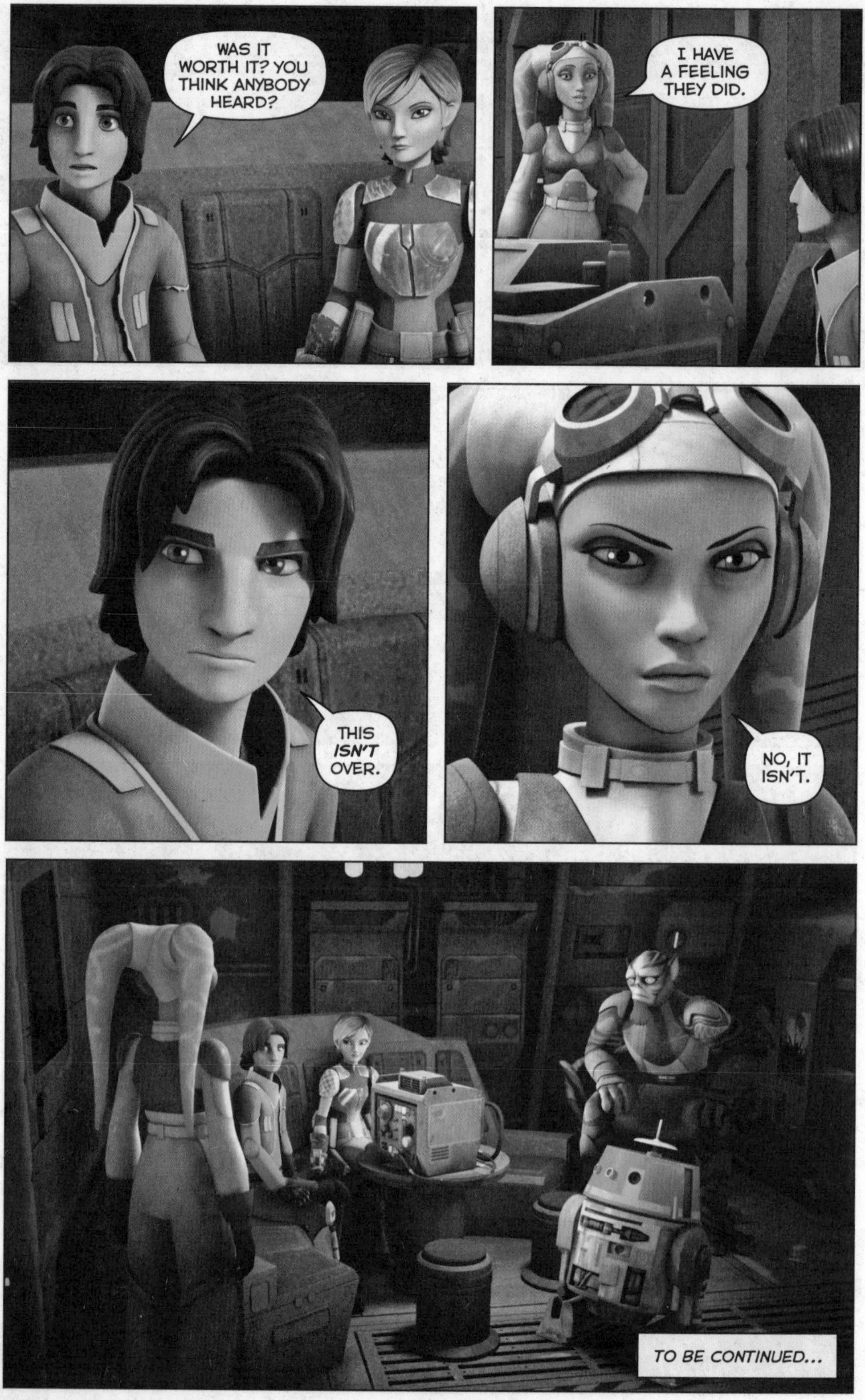
WAS IT WORTH IT? YOU THINK ANYBODY HEARD?
I HAVE A FEELING THEY DID.
THIS *ISN'T* OVER.
NO, IT ISN'T.
TO BE CONTINUED...